GOD'S Children

Stephen F. Freind

BⓉB
BEECH TREE BOOKS
WILLIAM MORROW
New York

Grateful acknowledgment is made for permission to re-
print from the following:
TWILIGHT TIME
Lyric by Buck Ram
Music by Morty Nevins and Al Nevins
TRO—© Copyright 1944 and renewed 1972 Devon
  Music, Inc., New York, N.Y.
Used by permission

Library of Congress Cataloging-in-Publication Data

Freind, Stephen F.
  God's children.

  I. Title.
PS3556.R3938G6   1987   813'.54   86-28830
ISBN 0-688-06691-7

Printed in the United States of America

First Edition

1 2 3 4 5 6 7 8 9 10

BOOK DESIGN BY RHEA BRAUNSTEIN

BTB

The word "book" is said to derive from boka, or beech.
The beech tree has been the patron tree of writers since ancient times and
represents the flowering of literature and knowledge.

To Judy, the best of the best.
To Bill, who always knew I could.
And to all God's children, particularly those yet to be born.

ACKNOWLEDGMENTS

There is, in my opinion, nothing more arduous than writing a novel. In addition to being incredibly difficult, it is an inherently lonely task— a struggle between the writer and the blank paper which seems to mock him.

Yet no writer can do it by himself. There must be others to inspire, to assist, and, at times, to console him.

Such is the case with this book. As the dedication implies, I owe a tremendous debt to my wife, Judy, for her love, her patience, and—sometimes inadvertently—her challenging me to complete this work.

My single greatest source of encouragement has been my brother, Bill. Without his unselfish support and pep talks when I was down, I seriously doubt that this book would have become a reality.

Special thanks go to my friends and co-workers Mary Ann Del Pizzo and Maria Cahill, for their many hours of assistance in typing, correcting, and collating the manuscript.

I am deeply grateful to my agent, Al Hart, of Fox Chase Agency, for taking a chance on a first novel.

To a great extent, a writer is only as good as his editor, and I consider myself fortunate to have one of the very best in Jim Landis. He knew when to demand and when to soothe, and he made the task of cutting and revising almost enjoyable. My thanks also go to Jim's assistant, Jane Meara, an accomplished author in her own right (*Growing Up Catholic*), for her help, her friendship, and her jokes.

Finally, my deepest thanks go to the real heroes of the pro-life movement: the thousands of ordinary men and women who so generously give of themselves to defend and speak on behalf of those who have no voice. They, more than anyone, were the inspiration for this book.

Prologue

THE parking lot was a sea of caps and gowns as Villanova's Class of 1963 assembled for its final march.

To the considerable relief of both his parents and the ruling Augustinians, Kevin Murray was one of the graduates. After grinding a cigarette into the asphalt, he approached two of his classmates. "Step into my office."

They walked across the lot to an alcove by one of the dorms.

"One last plot against the Auggies?" asked Vince Grosso.

"The hell with them. They're history. The only thing that matters is the three of us." Reaching under his gown, Kevin took out a flask and three plastic glasses.

"Kevin, you're unbelievable," said Pat Carney. "Trying one last time to get expelled."

"Life's no fun if it's dull." He filled each glass. "Let's drink to our futures." He pointed to Pat. "A pope." Then to himself. "A president." And then to Vince. "And the next Al Capone."

"No chance," Vince said. "He wasn't Sicilian."

Their laughter was forced. It was hard to say good-bye.

Kevin sighed. "Four years."

"Four great years," Pat said.

"Yeah. The battles with the Auggies, the horror shows, the friends we've made. But when you boil it all down, it gets down to us. That's the way it's always been. No matter what happens, let's keep it that way." Kevin lifted his glass. "Always together."

"Always together," they answered.

BOOK
One

1981

One

THE pitcher was definitely in a jam: winning run on third and big trouble at the plate. He stared at the batter with challenging eyes.

"Don't try digging in on me, big time," he said. "I just may plant one in your ear."

The batter was unimpressed. "You're so silly, Daddy," she giggled.

"We'll see who's silly," he answered, gently lobbing the Wiffle ball to the waiting five-year-old. She swung violently and missed.

"You're trying to kill it, Connie!" screamed the base runner. "Just try to meet it!"

"You be quiet, Anthony. I know what I'm doing."

The pitcher turned to his defense. "On your toes, gang. This is it."

Michael, playing shallow center, was in a semi-crouch, the killer waiting for his prey. *Just like his old man,* the pitcher thought. *He has to win everything.* It was a thought that both pleased and unnerved him. He turned to the first baseman, who was trying to catch the first lightning bug of the evening.

"Ay, Lucia Maria Grosso," he said. "What's the matter f'you? You no care if your team win disa game?"

The runner on third was getting edgy. "Come on, Dad, throw the ball."

"Okay, *impaziente.* Okay." He stepped closer to the plate and lobbed it in. This time the batter made contact, a slow roller

[13]

down the first baseline. The pitcher fielded it, lunged at the runner, and missed her by inches.

"We win!" Anthony screamed as he crossed the plate. "Twenty-four to twenty-three."

The pitcher rose slowly, shaking his head. "The old man gave it everything he had, sports fans. But in the end the big bat of Concetta Grosso was just too much."

Michael had reached him now, fury etched on his face. "That's not fair, Dad! You let 'em win. You coulda had her by a mile!"

"No way, *michelaccio*. She was just too quick for me."

His oldest son was now in tears. "That's why I hate playing with you. You always let them win just because they're little!"

"Come on, Mike," his father said, now serious. "Don't be so uptight all the time. It was just a fun game. Tell the truth now. You had fun, didn't you?"

"Yeah, but—"

"No buts, biggest. Now if you wanta get serious, I'll give you something to get serious about." He grabbed his son in a headlock and wrestled him to the ground.

"Get Daddy!" Connie screamed, and for the next five minutes they tried to pin their father to the lawn. The match was ended by their mother's voice.

"Children, it's time to come in," she called from the patio.

"Aw, Mom, can't we stay out a little longer?" Anthony pleaded.

"No. It's past eight-thirty. Girls, Therese is waiting upstairs for you. After your bath you can have a snack. Michael and Anthony, put away your bikes and toys; then get your showers. And don't forget to shampoo your hair."

With relatively few complaints the children did as commanded. She then turned to her husband, who had been staring at her.

"You've got that dirty grin, Vincent. I know what you're thinking."

"You're right. I'm thinking how lucky I am to be married to such a luscious piece. Especially when her body is so tan and she's wearing a sexy summer dress." He put his arms around Lena's waist, pulling her into a tight embrace.

Her reaction was predictable. "Vincent!" she said, trying to break free. "Stop it. What if the children see you?"

[14]

"Who cares? Does them good to see that their old man still gets turned on by their mother."

"You're impossible."

"And you love it. Beneath that dignified exterior is one hot-blooded guinea. I have it on the best authority."

They sat on the steps leading to the lawn. "The kids are growing up real nice, Lena. Because of you."

"Because of us. You're a good father to them."

"I try. You know, I can't believe how big they're getting. Michael starting high school in September and Anthony right behind. Where the hell do the years go?"

"You sound like an old man. Forty's not exactly antique, you know."

"I know, but it's not really young anymore, either."

"What's the matter, Vincent? This doesn't sound like the eternal kid. Is something bothering you?"

He kissed her, briefly and gently. "No, really. Everything's fine. It's just that I love you and the kids so much. I don't know what I'd do without you."

She rose. "Well, you're stuck with us. I'd better go up and see how Therese is doing with the girls. How about fixing us a drink?"

"Okay. In a few more minutes."

He liked to be alone at times, particularly in the evening, when the sounds of the woods blended with those of his family upstairs.

Slowly he walked across the lawn, surveying with satisfaction the manicured perfection that only professional gardeners can provide. He stopped at the edge of the woods—his woods—and listened to the music of the stream in the valley below. Then he turned and took in what was his. The house—twenty-two rooms, five baths, and servants' quarters—had been built before the Revolution and was certified as an historic site. Slightly to the rear was the recreation area: swimming pool, shuffleboard, basketball, and tennis. The "play building" housed a racquetball court, a bowling alley, and, as a reluctant concession to the kids, a dozen of the most modern electronic games. Though two centuries newer than the house, it had been built with history in mind and matched its counterpart admirably. Beyond, down the path through the orchard, were the stables and training area.

It was a long way from South Philly, where kids played stickball in the streets and splashed under fire hydrants. He had it all now—family, wealth, a Main Line showplace.

Yet there were still worries. Like tonight.

It took all his willpower to shake himself free from the fear. Fear accomplished nothing, and it was a sign of weakness. And weakness, when sensed by others, became a danger. You did your best, you made your plans, then you held the line.

The logic was comforting, and he strolled back to the house. He made the drinks—Ambassador on the rocks for him, amaretto for Lena—then walked to the patio.

"Kids done their baths, Therese?"

"Yes, Mr. Grosso," the young woman answered. "They're getting their snacks."

Her resemblance to his wife still amazed him. She could be her younger sister. Lena's complexion was a shade darker, her face slightly more angular. But the chestnut hair, the aquiline eyes, slightly slanted, the slender, muscled bodies were almost frightening in their similarity.

In the nine months that she had been with them, Vince had come to regard her as family. At least that's what he told himself.

"Hey, Therese," he said, trying to sound casual, "I know you're underage, but what the hell, you go to Villanova. And I know it hasn't changed all that much since my days. Would you like a drink?"

"No, thank you, Mr. Grosso. I don't think Mrs. Grosso would like that."

"Like what?" Lena said, walking onto the patio and taking her drink.

Vince smiled. "I was trying to corrupt the young coed. I offered her a drink."

"The last time I checked, the drinking age in Pennsylvania was twenty-one. Therese has three years to go."

Shrugging his shoulders, Vince turned to the younger woman. "I tried, Therese. But I'm married to a prude. That's my cross to bear in life."

"You don't seem to mind," his wife said.

Lena was right. He didn't mind. Their fifteen years together had been good ones. She was a steady and faithful partner. And no one in the world was a better mother.

[16]

True, Vince could never quite shake the feeling that he didn't really know her, know what went on inside her. She was always too much in control, as if she were guarding something that was forbidden even to her husband.

But nothing was perfect. Not marriage, not life. And he could have done a lot worse than Lena.

When their drinks were done, the children were gathered for the evening ritual.

"Time for the rosary," Lena said.

"Aw, Mom, do we have to?" Michael protested. "*Dallas* is coming on."

"I've told you before, Michael," his mother answered softly, "you are entirely too young for that show."

"Too young! I'm fourteen."

"That's enough, Mike. Do as your mother says."

Lena took her rosary from the pouch, kissed the crucifix, and crossed herself. "It's Friday, so it's the Sorrowful Mysteries. Michael, you may begin."

"Okay." He sighed. "The Apostles' Creed. I believe in God the Father Almighty, Creator of heaven and earth . . ."

Although he would be the last to know, Angie Lucido was about to die.

A month ago, at the instant the decision was made, he had become a dead man. True, he continued to breathe and to eat and, on occasions that were increasingly less frequent, to copulate. But his death had been irrevocably ordained, a monument carved in granite. Only its circumstances were flexible, and now even those had been meticulously arranged.

Dominic Barrone knew this, and it caused him pain. As he sat across from his friend, whom he matched in girth, if not height, he thought of their years together. A lifetime. Big Ox and Little Ox. They both were from Cinisi, arriving in America in the same year. Their careers had begun during Prohibition, hauling Canadian whiskey from Atlantic City. They had made their bones in the same assignment, a short but bloody encounter in a South Philadelphia garage. As a result, they had been accepted into the family on the same day.

Together they had prospered. Like good soldiers, they each

married Sicilian girls. Like good Sicilian girls, their wives had quickly given them children. Each had stood as godfather for his friend's firstborn.

Though they craved advancement within the family, they never looked upon each other as rivals. And as it turned out— until now—they never were. In time each had become a *capo*, enjoying the confidence of the boss.

Now it was ending. But while Barrone permitted himself grief, he never wavered in his duty. Orders were orders. The boss was the boss. It was as simple as that.

Lucido finished his wine with a belch. "Y'know, whenever I eat here, I think of the old days. Y'know what I mean, Little Ox?"

Barrone smiled. "I hear you, Angie."

"Lotta years. Lotta years. And still going strong. Right?"

"Right."

"Everything changes, but not us. You and me. We'll always be here. We'll piss on the graves of the world."

"Angie, like I've always said, you're a goddamn poet."

Lucido's face clouded. Lately he was always close to anger, which was the problem.

"Yeah, you and me," he said. "We have it all. We built this family. Built it! Made it what it is! So what happens? Some goddamn snotnose comes along, not old enough to wipe his own ass, and starts giving orders!" He slammed his fist on the table, knocking two glasses to the floor. "Well, fuck him! No *gioventù* is telling Angie Lucido what to do!"

Barrone kept his smile. "Easy, Oxie. Doesn't do you any good to get bent out of shape. Besides, things ain't that bad."

They had been over this before, and it was always the same.

"Not so bad?" Lucido bellowed. "Just what the hell would you call it? I give my life to the outfit, work my way up according to the rules, and what happens? I tell ya what happens. I get my balls cut off! Put on a friggin' allowance, like a school kid!"

"C'mon, Angie, it's not that bad. We all got to tighten our belts. The boss wants us to consolidate till we get strong."

"Consolidate! Christ, you sound just like him. Words like that don't mean shit in the street. And who says we're not strong?"

"New York says. That's why they been shittin' on us for years. The boss wants to change that."

"Ha! With what, a friggin' college textbook?"

Barrone looked at his watch. Timing was important. "Hey, *amico mio,* it's getting late. Rose will be worried. Go home to her."

"She can wait."

"Count your blessings," Barrone said soberly. "You still have someone you can go home to."

The bigger man softened and crossed himself. "Gloria, God rest her soul. How long has it been, Dominic?"

"Three years this September." He rose and placed his arm around his friend. "Go home, my brother. Enjoy what you have."

When his friend had departed, Barrone was alone in his world, the back room of a restaurant. Being alone, he allowed himself a luxury. Placing his head in his hands, Dominic "Little Ox" Barrone began to cry.

As Lucido stepped into the July night, he carried with him the experience of almost seventy years of survival. The problem with experience, though, is that too much of it tends to make you careless. Shortcuts are learned, corners are cut, and confidence gives way to arrogance.

There was a time that Lucido would never have moved without bodyguards, but now he was alone. Once he had known that the most certain way to invite a hit was to fall into a pattern. But for the last two years he had eaten at the same restaurant every Wednesday night, parking in the same lot, walking the same two blocks, and, most significantly, crossing the same alley.

As he approached the alley, he failed to notice that the streetlight was out, the same way he missed the sedan that had been idling a half block behind and now was upon him.

Two men stepped from the alley. Each took one of his arms and thrust him into the sedan's back seat.

"On the floor, Mr. Lucido," one of them said. "And don't be no hero."

"What the hell's goin' on? Where you takin' me?" He felt his heart hammer in his chest, more from shock than fear.

"We go for a ride. Face to the floor."

Lucido's four captors were all young Sicilians who had illegally entered the States. They worked in a chain of Bucks County pizza parlors, where they would remain until they proved themselves. If they did, the proper arrangements would be made with the immigration authorities. If they failed, they would find themselves

[19]

either dead or deported. Their loyalty to the family was thus assured.

The car they used was a brown '81 Fairmont, one of the most common and nondescript on the road. Still, there was always the danger of a witness, a problem that had been solved shortly after the young boss had taken control. A Harrisburg contact in Motor Vehicles had been carefully cultivated. Whenever necessary, duplicate tags and registration were provided.

If tonight someone noted the plate, Horace Busby, RD 1, Pleasant Unity, owner of a brown '81 Fairmont, father of four and president of the local Kiwanis, would be interviewed by the FBI. It would probably be the highlight of his life.

The execution mirrored the style of the new boss: swift and surgical, nothing left to chance—and nothing left behind, not even a body.

The ride took exactly ten minutes. The destination was a recent acquisition of the family, a twenty-acre lot strewn with cars whose lives, like Lucido's, were ending. In its center stood a large crane-like device, attached to massive pincers. It had been built in the early sixties, when the nation began to realize that its supply of metal was not endless.

The operation was relatively simple. The pincers crushed and scooped a jawful of cars, then swung them into a huge receptacle. Seconds later tiny chunks of metal were spewed into waiting railroad cars. The next stop was Detroit, where the load would be reincarnated. By this process a Chevy could graduate to a Cadillac. Only in America.

As planned, the night shift was on break. The car weaved among the wreckage, stopping at the target area for the next sweep of the pincers.

One of the Sicilians in the back seat broke the silence, if briefly. "*Ciao,* Mr. Lucido," he said, firing one shot into his head. Equipped with a silencer, the gun made only a soft, spitting sound. The license plate, which the driver had removed, and the gun were left with the corpse.

The second car was on schedule. They drove to a rise, a half mile away, where the driver could train his infrared binoculars. Within ten minutes the shift returned and the pincers swung to life. The Fairmont shuddered, then was lifted into the air. Seconds later it was gone.

[20]

"Well, that's it," the driver said. "Happy motoring, Angie."

He took out a cigar, biting off the end, and spit it out the window. "Y'know, for his sake I hope to Christ he doesn't end up as one of those friggin' compacts. That'd really frost his ass."

He swung onto the highway and stopped at a pay phone a short distance ahead. Only after inserting his dime did he notice the wire had been cut.

"Fuckin' niggers!" he exploded. "No goddamn respect for property."

He settled for a gas station. "Dominic, it's me."

"Go."

"Handled."

"You certain?"

"Positive."

"Good." Barrone pressed down the receiver. His grief was gone, and once again he was all business. He began to dial. The boss would want to know.

The house was quiet now. Therese and Lena had gone to a movie, one of those British comedies at the Bryn Mawr that Vince hated. He had started to watch the Phillies, then got bored. Baseball wasn't made for television. You had to be there.

He decided to check the children. The boys were fine. His big, strong boys. They were getting to be his friends as well as his sons. As usual, Connie was upside down, her head on the afghan that Lena had knitted, while her feet rested on the pillows.

Gently he rearranged her. "Good night, my precious one," he said, kissing her forehead. "Your daddy loves you."

Before he could check Lucy, the phone rang, and his stomach tightened. He lifted the receiver.

"Yes?"

"Boss, that case we talked about has just been settled."

"A final settlement?"

"Absolutely final."

"Grazie!"

"Prego, Don Vincenzo," Dominic Barrone answered.

CHAPTER
Two

IF it were true that a neat office was the sign of a sick mind, then the sanity of Kevin Murray was completely assured.

Files, letters, and assorted other documents oozed over his desk, competing for space with two ashtrays, both loaded with discarded Winstons, and a coffee mug, half full. Other papers were strewn over the floor and stacked on both chairs.

Although the coffee had been cold for hours, Kevin alternated short sips with drags from his cigarette and the instructions he snapped into the dictating machine.

"Okay, Janet, next thing I want you to do is get envelopes ready for a mailing to our senior citizens. We'll enclose the outline of the increased rebate benefits, so run off enough copies, will ya? Also, we'll do a mailing to the people on our education list, as soon as the budget's passed. Oh yeah, get envelopes ready for the Manoa Road drainage project, too, will ya? I wanna get an update out on that."

He picked up the next letter, read it, and grinned. It was one of the better ones:

Dear Representative Murray:

What right do you have to tell women what to do with their bodies? Abortion is a personal matter between a woman and her doctor, and no man has any right at all getting involved in it. Until you grow a uterus, keep out of my business.

I saw you on television last Sunday, and I wanted to punch you in the mouth. You make me sick! I will do everything in my power to drive you out of office.

Ruth B. Telford

Kevin pressed the record button. "Time for some fun, Janet. Letter to Ruth B. Telford, address is on the letter." He dictated:

Dear Mrs. Telford:

Thank you for your warm and gracious letter of June 30.

Although I may not be the most perceptive person in the world, it strikes me that you are not in complete agreement with my position on abortion. I guess I'm one of those old-fashioned people who still object to the killing of innocent, unborn children.

As far as your threat to defeat me is concerned, I invite you to take your very best shot. If you are successful, several results will follow. First, I will at least be satisfied knowing that I went down for something worthwhile. Secondly, my wife will be delighted that I am finally out of politics. Thirdly, I will make considerably more money. And finally, the people of the 166th District will have lost one hell of a good legislator.

Despite your feelings, you are stuck with me, at least for the time being, as your legislator. Accordingly, I hope that you will continue to feel free to contact me at any time if I can be of assistance to you in any way. I must draw the line, however, at allowing you to punch me in the mouth. Besides, my wife handles that task nicely.

Sincerely,
Kevin A. Murray

P.S. As far as my growing a uterus is concerned, I have a difficult enough time with hair.

"Am I disturbing anything important?" came a voice from the door.

It was Jim Wilson, legislative liaison for the county's Intermediate Unit.

"I never do anything important. I'm a legislator. Come on in. If you've been inoculated, that is."

Wilson stepped into the room, then hesitated.

"Sit down," Kevin said.

[23]

"Uh, where?"

"Either chair. Just throw that shit on the floor."

Happy for the break, Kevin leaned back, propped his feet on the desk, and lit another cigarette. "You been over the Senate?"

"Yeah. They called a conference committee meeting for one."

"Good. That means they won't get started till about two." He pointed to the squawk box on the wall, which was broadcasting the House debate. "Fat Boy's probably the last speaker. We should vote around midnight."

"Will it pass this time?"

"No. We're still at least six or seven short. After the vote we'll caucus till maybe three. When we break, work on Jackie and Fred."

"What about Lorenzo?"

"I'll handle him. Besides, if Fred goes, so will Lorenzo. Dante says that if we can increase nonpublic subsidies, he can deliver us at least three Philly Ds."

"Do you think he really can?"

"Tenaglia will do everything he can to block it, but Dante knows his people. If he says he can deliver, he will."

The phone rang. "Five-O. McGarrett," Kevin answered.

It was the whip, calling from the floor. As usual, he was nervous. "Kevin, we're getting ready to vote."

"Didn't you hear, Rod? I resigned about ten minutes ago. I'm cleaning out my expense account and taking off for Tahiti. Or maybe Camden."

"C'mon, Kevin, cut me a break, will you? We need everybody on the floor."

"Take a couple of Maalox, Rod, and relax. I'll be there."

He hung up the phone and turned back to Wilson. "You know, breaking Rod's stones is one of the great pleasures of my life."

"You're rotten."

"You're right." He glanced at the clock. "Almost midnight. If things go right, we could have it wrapped up by dawn. Hell of a way to make a living, isn't it?"

"It sure is," Wilson answered. "Listen, Kevin, no matter how things go, I want you to know how much we appreciate everything you've done. You've always been there when we need you. The amount of hours you put into this budget fight has been fantastic."

[24]

"Number of hours, stupid shit. Not amount. But what the hell can you expect from a St. Joe's grad?"

"You bastard"—Wilson grinned—"you never let up."

"You'd be disappointed if I did." He rose. "Okay, old buddy, Tenaglia sounds like he's wrapping up, so I'm going onto the floor. After the vote I'll be in the Speaker's office. Remember, key in on Jackie and Fred."

The most important vote for any legislative body is the adoption of its annual budget. The General Assembly of Pennsylvania was no exception. Pennsylvania's fiscal year begins on July 1. If no budget is passed by then, the machinery of the entire commonwealth grinds to a halt. No pay for state employees. No welfare checks. No funds for mental health, education, and a hundred other programs.

One of the few hard-and-fast rules in passing a budget is that a crisis never occurs in an even-numbered year. A budget vote is difficult only when it requires a tax increase. And since even years are election years, with the entire House and half the Senate running and avoiding a tax vote like the plague, the real struggles are reserved for the off-season.

Harrisburg had seen some classic budget brawls. One of the bloodiest had been 1977, when the problem wasn't resolved until August 20. Week after week the pressure and the emotion mounted. Legislators had their homes picketed, with some of them even receiving death threats. Welfare rights activists camped in the rotunda. State employees struck, and the Capitol was under round-the-clock state police guard. The crowning blow, presented live and in color by public television, was a fistfight on the floor of the House. Not surprisingly, it occurred between two Democrats. When it came to real down-home entertainment, the GOP always ran a poor second.

Unlike the federal government, Pennsylvania is constitutionally mandated to have a balanced budget. The Washington luxury of eternally deferring judgment day by going deeper into the bucket is forbidden in Harrisburg. And unlike Congress, Pennsylvania is bound by a constitutional requirement that all bills receive an absolute majority for passage. Regardless of attendance, more than half the elected membership of each house must approve a bill before sending it to the governor. The full complement of the Pennsylvania House is 203; the Senate, 50. Un-

[25]

less a bill generates at least 102 House and 26 Senate votes, it dies.

The resolution of a budget struggle usually occurs through a sugar-acid approach. Recalcitrant legislators are enticed with goodies for their districts: a new bridge, a state job for a local ward leader, or maybe a promise from leadership to move a pet bill. At the same time a conscious effort is made to reduce the members to such a state of physical and mental exhaustion that they finally cave in, if for no reason other than survival.

The 1977 battle had tested the limits of even the toughest. John Tenaglia had been majority leader, and befitting his personality, he used a bludgeon. The House was scheduled to begin its session at ten each morning. At five minutes to ten the squawk box announced that the session was delayed until noon. Then two, then four, and on and on. Finally, at three or four in the morning, the House convened. After a few hours of debate the vote was taken, fell short of 102, and the entire process began again. Seven days a week for almost the entire summer. Vacations were ruined, anniversaries and birthdays were missed, and three members required hospitalization. But in the end John Tenaglia got his way. Taxes were increased, the budget was passed, and the Commonwealth of Pennsylvania again moved, presumably forward.

Carrying his dictating machine and an expansion folder full of correspondence, Kevin swung through the brass gate at the rear of the chamber. As he did, he was again struck by the contrast. The House chamber was magnificent. Almost twice the size of its counterpart in Washington, it was constructed of marble imported from the Pyrenees. Solid bronze chandeliers, each weighing four tons, hung from a domed ceiling. Under that dome Edwin Austin Abbey had lain for almost five years to complete the fresco which adorned it, a depiction of the twenty-four hours of the day.

The room was actually an amphitheater, its carpeted floor sloped so that each row of mahogany desks rested on a different level and provided an unobstructed view of the Speaker's platform. The entire wall behind that platform contained another Abbey, this one featuring more than thirty figures whose lives had affected the history of Pennsylvania.

Although there were windows on the side walls, they were completely draped, making it impossible to judge either the time or

[26]

the weather in the world beyond. Spectators observing the House in session did so from a balcony in the rear, separated from the legislators by a barrier of bulletproof glass, installed in the mid-seventies. Left unclear was whether it had been designed to protect legislators from the public or vice versa.

John Tenaglia, all 340 pounds, was at the minority rostrum, voice booming and fist pounding. He always put on a great show. A few members were actually listening, and that was unusual. The others were asleep, reading the newspaper, or gathered in small clusters in conversation throughout the chamber. Except, of course, for the half dozen or so who were manning the perpetual poker game in the members' lounge.

"Happy Fourth of July, Lorenzo," Kevin said as he slumped into his seat. "Ain't democracy great?"

"Jesus." Although the same age as Kevin, Lorenzo Gambesi had just begun his first term.

"And you know what makes the sin mortal, old buddy? We actually run for this job. Bust our balls to get it. How's your wife holding up?"

"Not too good, Kevin. She's really pissed. We were supposed to go to a family picnic. Does it get any easier?"

"No. Actually it gets worse. I called Karen an hour ago, and she hung up on me. She hates this job. And I think she's getting to hate me because of it." Kevin nodded toward Tenaglia. "The Fat Boy's still going strong, huh?"

John Tenaglia was definitely still going strong. It was his chance to even a few scores, if only for the record.

"Our Republican colleagues call themselves fiscal conservatives. That's fashionable these days. And yet, Mr. Speaker, who is it who wants to rape our citizens by adding to their tax burden. The Democrats, the so-called big spenders? No! We're being asked to follow our governor, our Republican governor, a self-avowed disciple of Reaganomics, who now finds it necessary to rip off the poor and the middle class to offset the unbelievable generosity he has shown to his party's ancient constituency—big business, the rich, and the privileged!"

"Why don't we just break for the night?" Lorenzo moaned.
"We can't. Tonight's the night."

[27]

"How can you be sure?"

"I can't. It's just a feeling. Mike feels it, too, and he's been around a lot longer than I have. There's a point in every budget when you just know it's time. And when that happens, you have to get the job done. We're close. The worst thing we could do is break and let everybody scatter for the weekend. Back in their districts they'll be bombarded from both sides. We'd have to start from scratch next week. Trust me, baby, tonight's the night."

> "But the worst thing about this sordid scenario is the way it's being jammed down our throats. Again. For the third year in a row the Republican leadership has trampled on the work of the Appropriations Committee. They've emasculated each one of us, on both sides of the aisle, by denying us our mandated legislative prerogative. Once again they've taken the entire budget and placed it into a totally unrelated conference report, requiring us to vote merely yes or no. Is there any opportunity to offer amendments, to provide input? No! Mr. Speaker, I say with complete conviction that if this charade succeeds again, the biggest loser of all will be the democratic process that we all cherish!"

"You have to admit he's right about that," Lorenzo said.

"Philosophically, yes. From a practical standpoint, it's pure bullshit."

"Whaddya mean?"

"Lorenzo, if we opened the bill up for amendments, everybody and his brother would be offering them. It's a great way to whore it up for the folks back home. And voting against some of them would be like coming out against motherhood. So the bill gets Christmas-treed with goodies, which is fine except we don't have the money and everybody knows it. So in the end the bill goes to a conference committee anyway. We're just shortcutting the process a little, that's all. You get my drift, *paisan?*"

It took a lot to convince Lorenzo. He was a worrier. "Yeah, but won't we get killed in the press for pulling this shit?"

"Hell, no. We've done it for the last three years, and the only thing they've said is, 'Congratulations for passing the budget on time.' Liberal as those turkeys are, they understand practical politics. Nobody cares about the process, baby, just the result."

[28]

"For too long this commonwealth has suffered under the tyranny of the rich. The poor and the handicapped remain prisoners of the privileged. And there is no one to speak for them but us. Though we may be temporarily in the minority, Mr. Speaker, we do not hesitate to take up the gauntlet, for we are, and always have been, the bastions of freedom. And so, Mr. Speaker, I again urge my colleagues to keep faith with the people and vote no!"

On cue the Democrats roared their approval as Tenaglia took his seat.

"I gotta have some fun," Kevin said. He rose and walked to the nearest mike.

Rod Coyne was immediately on his feet. "You're not going to debate this, are you, Kevin? I mean, we have to caucus, and then—"

"Relax, Rod. I just want to tweak Fat Boy a little." Kevin pressed the button, and a green light came on, indicating that his mike was now live.

"The chair recognizes the gentleman from Delaware, Mr. Murray."

"Thank you, Mr. Speaker. Would the minority whip stand for a brief interrogation?"

All three of Tenaglia's chins nodded yes, and he lumbered back to the rostrum.

"The minority whip indicates that he will stand for interrogation," the Speaker said. "The gentleman Mr. Murray may proceed."

"Thank you, Mr. Speaker," Kevin said, a small grin appearing on his face. He turned to Tenaglia. Although protocol dictated that all remarks be directed through the Speaker, he was now talking to the minority whip. For once the chamber fell silent. Everyone, with the possible exception of Tenaglia himself, knew that Kevin was setting him up. "Mr. Speaker, like all my colleagues, I was absolutely enthralled by your soliloquy, if for no other reason than your endurance."

"I try, Mr. Speaker," Tenaglia cut in.

"Yes, Mr. Speaker," Kevin snapped back, "and someday you may even succeed. At any rate, toward the end of your speech, you referred to yourself and your Democratic colleagues as the something or other of freedom. I think it was *bas* something or other."

"Bastions, Mr. Speaker," Tenaglia answered. "The bastions of freedom."

"Oh. Bas-*tions*, was it?" Kevin said innocently. "I thought you said something else, and for once I was about to agree with you."

The chamber went wild. Even the Dems broke up. Tenaglia's face went scarlet. He started to reply, thought better of it, and walked away. The reporters in the press box all were scribbling. Tomorrow the exchange would be the subject of sidebar stories throughout the state. .

As the laughter subsided, the Speaker banged his gavel. It was time for the vote. "The question is, Will the House adopt the conference report to Senate Bill Seven-four-one? The ayes and nays will be taken. The members will proceed to vote."

Legislators ran for their seats to pull their switches, green for yes, red for no. All eyes turned to the electronic tally boards on the two side walls. The boards listed the name of each member, with the color beside the name indicating his or her decision. At the top of the board a running total of the vote count was kept.

Tenaglia was at the rostrum again. "Mr. Speaker," he boomed.

"Nothing is in order but the taking of the vote."

"I'm aware of that, Mr. Speaker. I'd just appreciate your giving us a nice slow count so I can make sure that everyone's in their seats."

"The chair has every intention of keeping the board open for the full ten minutes—if need be."

Since few issues went straight down party lines, it was rare that votes were challenged. The constitutional requirement that a member be present and in his seat to vote was trampled upon regularly. It was an unwritten rule that you hit the switch of a temporarily absent colleague. Usually the absence was for a good reason, such as attending a committee meeting, greeting a group of constituents, or, less lofty but more necessary, answering a call of nature. It was true that some members, particularly in the Philadelphia delegation, were guilty of flagrant abuse, voting colleagues who were still back home. Ghost voting, the press called it, and now and then exposés were published. The reaction was predictable. For a few days the public was outraged and the legislature was penitent. Then things got back to normal.

Kevin pulled his green switch, but Lorenzo hesitated. "What'll I do, Kevin?" He agonized. "I gotta vote no."

[30]

"No problem. Vote no. Just get on the board. You look like a whore if you hang out."

House rules permitted the board to stay open for a maximum of ten minutes. During that time a legislator could switch his vote. The Speaker had sole discretion in calling for the vote to be recorded, which command electronically froze the switches and the tally on the board. In a close vote the Speaker's timing had to be perfect.

All the members of the Delaware County delegation were Republican. Except for the Speaker, they sat together in two rows near the front of the chamber. When Lorenzo hit his red switch, it was the delegation's third no vote.

It was late. The Republicans were tired and testy. Since they were in the majority, it was their job to get the budget passed. So far they had failed, and no one knew whether a 1977 was to recur. When three members from the Speaker's own county went off the reservation, the hostility spilled out.

"You fuckin' heroes from Delaware County are gonna keep us here all summer," bellowed Ken Hecht. He was Pennsylvania Dutch with a short fuse.

Next to the Speaker, Kevin was the senior member of the delegation. He felt obliged to defend his people, particularly new ones like Lorenzo. The best way to do it was with humor.

"Stay cool, shit kicker," he said, grinning. "We'll have you out of here in time to slop the hogs. Hey, is it true that on dull nights you guys hump the sheep?"

Hecht had to laugh. "Yeah, Kevin, but only the cute ones."

The affirmative vote total was jumping between 92 and 99. When the count got close to 102, Lorenzo tensed, hoping to be taken off the hook. "We might get it, Kevin," he said.

"No way. Some of the Ds are pulling our chain. In the end they'll go back to red."

The whip approached, his forehead glistening with sweat. "How 'bout it, Lorenzo? Can't you, Fred, and Jackie give us a vote? I mean, it's really embarrassing to Mike, having his delegation screw him."

Lorenzo always found it difficult to say no. "I know, Rod. Jesus, I want to help, but—oh, Christ, I don't know."

"C'mon, Lorenzo, we really need you. If you go green, Jackie and Fred will, too. Whaddya say?"

"I'm gonna be diplomatic, Rod," Kevin said. "Fuck off. Even if they switch, we're still short."

"Yeah, Kevin, but—"

"Look, Rod, we got public TV covering this whole damn mess, and it doesn't do any of us any good having one of our new members worked over by leadership. In living color, no less. I'll make you a promise, okay? After the vote goes down and we break, things are gonna come together. Before we leave for home tonight, we'll have a budget. Guaranteed. The problem will be solved and in such a way that everybody in the delegation will be voting yes. Trust me."

Coyne shook his head and forced a smile. "Okay, Kevin. Your word's always been good."

"Thanks, Kevin," Lorenzo said after the whip had gone. "But are you sure? I mean, about its passing tonight."

"Hell no, but it sounded good, didn't it?"

"Mr. Speaker," said a voice over the mike, a voice so shrill that it could belong to only one person: Carmella Melchiore. Senior female member and the House scold. She was holding up the alarm clock that she always kept in her desk.

"The chair bows to the inevitable and recognizes the lady from Somerset, Miss Melchiore."

"Just a time check, Mr. Speaker. You have five minutes and twenty seconds left."

"The chair thanks the lady." Still keeping a straight face, the Speaker continued. "Say, Carmella, isn't that the same clock that woke us up this morning?"

Carmella didn't flinch. When the laughter died down, she got in the last line, as she always did. "Certainly, Mr. Speaker. Just one more example of how we're always getting screwed by leadership."

Despite Carmella's gem, Lorenzo remained a basket case. "Jesus, ten minutes is forever."

"Count your blessings that it's not like the old days."

"Whaddya mean?"

"There wasn't any time limit for the board. In 'seventy-one, when they were trying to pass the income tax, they left the board open for three *days*. The guys who were around then said it was the worst pressure they've ever seen. You name it. Threats, blackmail, outright bribes. But they got their income tax."

"Jesus."

They were joined by Craig Harrington. Unlike Kevin, who was always in shirt sleeves, with his collar open and tie pulled down, Harrington looked precisely as he had when the session had begun fourteen hours earlier: three-piece suit perfectly creased; shirt buttoned, collar starched; shoes gleaming; not a hair out of place.

He frowned at Kevin's lit cigarette. "Say, Kevin, someone wants to see you at the rear of the hall."

"Fine, tell him I'll be there as soon as I'm done with this cigarette."

"You realize you're violating a House rule, don't you?"

"Absolutely. Along with about fifty others. Makes it taste better. You know, forbidden fruit."

"I have to save you from yourself. Do you realize your life is shortened with each cigarette."

"If the alternative is to be like you, eating that goddamned disgusting health food, running five miles a day, never touching booze, and making a complete pain in the ass of yourself by lecturing anyone you can corner on the evils of smoke, drink, and junk food, I think I'd rather die."

Harrington shook his head. "You're hopeless."

"And you're a jerkoff. But to business. As soon as the budget is done, we gotta get cracking. I want the bill introduced before the recess so the committee can get the hearings out of the way during the summer."

"I hear you."

"Yeah, well, do more than hear. Monday morning. I'll be here by nine. Let's get moving. And for once in your life, try to be on time. Okay?"

"Okay. And so the shit starts all over again."

"You got it. We're gonna kick ass and take names."

"But no prisoners."

The Speaker's voice came over the mike. "Have all the members voted?" The vote was about to be recorded, causing a number of last-minute changes. "The clerk will record the vote."

It was 95 to 102. Two were absent, and four had taken a walk.

"The ayes are ninety-five; the nays a hundred and two. Less than a majority having voted in the affirmative, the conference report on Senate Bill Seven-four-one is not adopted."

[33]

A scattering of applause came from the Democratic side. Even Tenaglia smiled. When you were in the minority, you savored every victory even if it was only temporary.

The whip walked up the aisle, making sure the troops were in line. "Two procedural votes before we break. Everybody stays on the reservation."

"*Two* votes?" Lorenzo asked. "Reconsideration and what else?"

"Suspending the rules," Kevin answered. "You can reconsider a vote only once. When a bill goes down the second time, you have to suspend the rules before reconsideration. You're yes on both votes. You know that, don't you?"

"I know. I may be new, but I know that."

An inviolate rule of any caucus was that you supported your party on all procedural votes. Break it, and you instantly became a pariah.

With a minimum of debate the rules were suspended, reconsideration was approved, and the budget bill was alive again. As they broke for caucus, the Speaker summoned Kevin to the platform. Michael Patrick Callaghan looked exhausted, but the twinkle was still there. "Doesn't time fly when you're having fun?"

"Absolutely," Kevin said. "I haven't enjoyed myself this much since my first communion."

"Look, I have to make an appearance in caucus. About ten minutes. Let's meet in my office after that."

"Yassah, boss."

Kevin had ten minutes to kill, and since he was in no mood to dictate any more constituent letters, he decided to do something unusual and attend caucus.

There were some members who attended regularly. That amazed him. For one thing, he never had the time. If he wasn't working on his own legislation, he was trying to put a dent in his constituent backlog.

More important, he considered caucus a colossal waste of time. Rarely was anything accomplished. True, the bills on the House calendar were discussed, but you got the same information from a ten-minute review of the calendar summary. More often than not, caucus was a time when the same members got up and said the same things. Maybe the breast-beating away from the public and the press served as a catharsis for some. Kevin figured that since he had confession, he didn't need it.

[34]

He slumped into a chair beside Pete Swift, also from Delaware County.

"Oh, Jesus," Swift said, "now I know we're in trouble. Murray's coming to caucus."

"I figured I needed a little comic relief."

"That's about all you'll get. Don't you love the irony, Kevin? The heroes are gonna get up and bitch about disloyalty, but they're talking to the wrong audience. Everybody here is already a yes. I don't think any of our people who are off the reservation will show up. It doesn't make sense."

"Pete, you're doing it again. Trying to be logical. How many times have I told you that any connection between logic and government is purely accidental?"

"I'm sorry. I keep forgetting."

The show got started with the same old script. After about twenty minutes the Speaker nodded to the caucus chairman, who immediately recognized him.

"As much as I'd like to stay and listen to all this good stuff, I've got to try to put the pieces together. We've got a problem. We all know that. And it's got to be solved. Tonight. Not next week or the week after. Tonight. We're close. A lot closer than the last vote showed."

He turned to Kevin. "Our ambassador to the Holy See here may have the answer. He figures once we pass the budget, we can get on to something less controversial, like abortion." He became serious again. "I know you're tired. So am I. But once we solve the problem, you have a whole summer to rest. One thing. I heard somebody suggest stopgaps. That's out. The stopgap route is no answer. It's a goddamn cop-out. Every time the feds do it, it turns my stomach. It's an admission that they don't have the brains or the balls—excuse me, ladies—to get the job done. We do. And we will. Tonight. Any questions?"

"Yeah, Mike," Ken Hecht said. "Where's our fearless governor? We haven't heard word one from him."

"The governor has assured us that he's there if we need him. Right now we don't. And you said it right, Ken. He's *our* governor."

The Speaker's office complex adjoined the caucus room. Despite the hour, his entire staff was still there.

[35]

"Greetings, ladies," Kevin said. "I thought I'd brighten your life a little with my boyish good looks and Irish charm."

The mood of the office brightened noticeably. Kevin was a favorite of the House staff. Once he had been one of them, and nothing had changed after his election. Unlike many of the members, he insisted on a first-name basis.

"How 'bout some coffee, Kevin?" asked Joyce Swenson.

"Best offer I've had since I was propositioned on State Street."

"Kevin, you'll never change, thank God. Incidentally, a friend of yours is in Mike's office."

"Impossible. I don't have any. Who?"

"Your state senator."

"Great. I really need her right now."

State Senator Hope Riley Pendleton was agitated. It was hardly surprising. Convinced that she possessed a divine right to lead the GOP, both within and beyond Delaware County, she was never pleased when her party faltered. In her Republican mind the recent budget vote was pure heresy.

Kevin was barely inside the door when she opened up. "Kevin, that vote was an unmitigated disgrace. An outrage! I can't believe that three of our own members would embarrass Michael and our entire county that way."

Kevin returned the Speaker's smile, lit a cigarette, and chose the sofa on the far end of the room. "You know, Hope, this may come as a surprise to you, but in the Western world we normally begin a conversation with some sort of greeting. Something like hello, hi, how's it hanging? Hello, Hope."

Her smile was perfunctory. "Hello, Kevin. I apologize, but I'm quite upset."

"Gee, Hope, that's not like you. You're normally so very calm and self-controlled."

"I don't think sarcasm will solve anything, Kevin."

"Probably not. But neither will a lot of sermonizing bullshit."

"Isn't it great when good friends get together?" the Speaker said, propping his feet on the desk. For once he was enjoying the luxury of being a spectator.

Hope continued. "You've never understood, have you, Kevin? A party doesn't survive very long without discipline."

"The old discipline speech. Page eighteen, paragraph six. Christ, Hope, you really should get some new material."

[36]

"Make your snide remarks, if you like, but the fact remains that we'll stay in power only if we're strong. And that takes work—hard, unpleasant work. But you wouldn't know about that. The gut work of keeping a party strong has always been beneath you. Kevin Murray's too good for things like fund-raising and patronage. I'll give you credit, Kevin: You're a great legislator. No one is more brilliant, and no one works harder at his job. But it's not enough."

Kevin let out a sigh. "Look, Hope, it's almost one o'clock in the morning. None of this has a damn thing to do with passing a budget."

"It has *everything* to do with the budget. Three of our own are off the reservation. It has to be made unmistakably clear to them that they get back in line or suffer the consequences."

"Such as?" Kevin asked. His eyebrows arched, a sign of anger.

Hope disregarded the unspoken warning. "Fred Malatesta's son-in-law works for Revenue. Jackie Daniels's father is a state store manager. Two of Lorenzo Gambesi's cousins have courthouse jobs. And each of them has a district aide on the House payroll."

Kevin clenched his fists, his knuckles white. "Why don't you be like Tenaglia and go the whole route? Cut off their phones. Take away their desks."

"John Tenaglia may be personally repulsive, but he understands practical politics."

"He doesn't understand shit—and neither do you. When are you gonna learn, Hope? It's not what you do that counts; it's how you do it. You're dealing with human beings, for Christ's sake."

"I'm well aware of that."

"The hell you are. Every day you make more enemies with your goddamn Boss Tweed attitude."

"And you don't?"

"Sure, I make enemies. A lot of them. But on the issues. If someone wants to hate me because of the abortion thing or because I stick it to the teachers, I can't help that. With you it's different. Anyone you can't control becomes the enemy."

Kevin shook his head slowly. The anger was gone, replaced with disgust. "I feel sorry for you, Hope, honest to God I do. You're building your whole career on threats. And when the

[37]

crunch comes, that's never enough. Maybe someday you'll learn that the only supporters worth having are the ones who are with you because they want to be, not because they have to."

Hope rose from her chair. "This is leading nowhere." She started for the door, then turned back. "Kevin, I love you dearly, but you don't live in the real world."

"Maybe you're right, Hope, but it's the only one I want to live in."

"Well," Callaghan said when they were alone, "I'm glad to see you're becoming more diplomatic."

"Just trying to polish the rough edges."

The door opened, and Jerry Strock, the speaker's administrative assistant, entered, notepad in hand.

"Where the hell have you been?" Callaghan asked.

"When Kevin Murray and Hope Pendleton are in the same room, I stay clear."

"You'll go far, my lad," Callaghan said. "Okay, let's get on with it. Here's where we stand. We got eight off the reservation and one absent."

Kevin nodded. "Abe Forsythe. He's in Bermuda, isn't he?"

"Was," Callaghan said. "We're flying him up by private plane. Which, I might add, is costing us an arm and a leg. Jerry, what's the latest word?"

"He should be here within an hour, Mike."

"Good. That'll bring us up to ninety-six. I figure three of the eight are hopeless."

"Which ones?" Kevin asked.

"Turek, for one, that goddamn whore. After all we've done for that son of a bitch. I personally raised ten thousand dollars for his last election. And every time there's been a tough vote, we've had to buy him. We got him a bridge, a railroad spur, and about a dozen other things. No more. I refuse to deal with him. If we buy him off again, we'll have a mutiny. Then there's Hopkins. In sixteen years that bastard has never given us a tax vote. It's pretty bad when one of your own committee chairmen screws you."

"Yeah," Kevin said. "That's a sore spot for a lot of the troops."

"Don't I know it. Look, Kevin, if we're at a hundred eight or a hundred nine, I wouldn't think twice about stripping him. But a hundred and four I can't take that chance. His district's two to one Democratic. If he takes a walk across the aisle, we're two votes

[38]

away from losing control. And the new kid from Erie, Rankin. He got himself boxed in during the campaign and promised to vote against any tax increase. Now he figures he can't break his word. Who's left, Jerry, besides our three from the county?"

"Criswell and Blake."

"Oh, yeah, our Montgomery County flakes. Criswell's nuts. You never know where the hell he's coming from. And Blake's miffed because he didn't get tapped for Congress last time. Why he's taking it out on us is beyond me, but that's Blake."

"Any problem holding on to our yes votes?" Kevin asked.

"Sure. There're always problems. Carmella's on me to increase the truck weight limit; Bellotti wants studded tires extended until May; about ten of them want a new gym for Penn State. And on and on. But for all their bitching, I don't think we'll lose any. What do you got?"

"Senate Bill Four-two-one. It's in conference. They're meeting at one. School discipline bill. Doesn't really do much, but the teachers want it. It's a School Code bill, so it's a perfect vehicle. We lift the aid ratio from point-one-five to point-two. You follow me?"

Callaghan shook his head. "You know I don't understand that education crap. That's why you're on the Education Committee. What's the bottom line?" Mike Callaghan never troubled himself with the details of legislation. That was for others. He believed strongly in nothing except getting the job done. And that job was to protect the caucus and the party. In short, he was a perfect speaker.

"Simple. Fifteen school districts, mostly suburban, that are getting screwed by the subsidy formula will benefit. Our people represent fourteen of them. Harding's the only donkey who gets helped. We also sweeten the pot by increasing funding for non-public textbooks and transportation."

Callaghan smiled. "You always gotta help us papes, don't you?"

"Shit, yeah. I want to be able to receive communion on Sunday."

"Purely out of curiosity, what's the tab?"

"Only thirteen million. Four for the subsidy, three for the textbooks, and six for transportation."

"*Only* thirteen million. You're getting to sound like a Demo-

[39]

crat." He looked at Jerry, who was scribbling computations. "Can we afford it?"

Strock gave a tentative nod. "Yeah. It's tight, but figuring on lapses from other departments, we can do it."

"Okay," Callaghan said. "Assuming we've got the money, what's it get us?"

"For openers, it gets us Fred, Lorenzo, and Jackie."

"For sure?"

"Yeah. I'll nail it down when we're done. But bet on it."

"Okay, that takes us to ninety-nine."

"Dante can deliver us at least three Ds. Some of their districts are so Catholic they've got no choice."

"Not good enough. We need at least one more of our own. There's no way any donkeys come over until we put up a hundred."

"I figured as much. So we have to get either Criswell or Blake. I'll take Criswell. We have a common bond—namely, nailing the teachers. Why don't you get McFarland to stroke Blake? They're from the same county."

"Sold," Callaghan said. "How long do you need to get the language drafted?"

"Already handled. Should be down from Legislative Reference any minute. Just make sure our people on the conference committee are solid."

"Don't sweat that. They wanta get out of here as much as anybody. I better fill our charming majority leader in or he'll pout. Jerry, ask Seth if he can meet with me in five minutes."

Strock left, and the Speaker turned back to Kevin. "You do nice work."

"Like Hope says, all for the good of the party."

"About Hope, Kevin. Go a little easy. You don't need her for an enemy, and as irritating as she can be, she holds the party together more than anyone."

"I'm not about to kiss her ass, Mike."

"I'm not asking you to. Just bend a little now and then. Let her think you're a team player."

"Anything else?"

"Nope. The mass has ended. Go in peace, to love and serve the caucus."

"Deo gratias."

Despite the hour, the hallway outside the caucus room was jammed with lobbyists. Labor unions, contractors, universities, public utilities, physicians, even undertakers—all were represented by professionals who specialized in developing a rapport with the members. Whenever the legislature was in session, regardless of the hour, they were there.

When the legislature was in recess, Harrisburg went quietly about its business, not unlike a shore resort town in the off-season. On session days, however, it was filled to the breaking point with transients who wanted to be where the action was.

Kevin fought his way through the crowd, stopping now and then to answer a question, then extricate himself as quickly as possible.

Just ahead Jim Wilson was huddled with Dante Inverso, lobbyist for the Philadelphia School District. Before he could reach them, he was cornered by Al Hollis of the *Delaware County Daily Times*. "I know you were in with the Speaker, Kevin. What's happening?"

"It's in the bag, Al."

"No kidding?" the reporter asked, sensing an exclusive.

"Yep. Cooler heads prevailed, and we reached a compromise. Our pay's been increased to a hundred thou, abortion's a capital offense and Philly secedes from the commonwealth. Not a bad night's work."

"Damn it, Kevin, I thought I had something."

"You do. Seriously, I think we're gonna work it out and there's a good local angle. I'll talk to you when we're back on the floor. About an hour, two at the most."

His conversation with Wilson and Inverso was brief. Things were coming together. At least four Philly Democrats would come if the Republicans got close. Mike was right. They probably needed a hundred of their own. Wilson had spoken with Fred and Jackie. Both had been noncommittal. He would accompany Kevin to confront them again while Inverso made certain the conference committee was greased.

It was convenient that the three dissidents were in Lorenzo's office. They all could be handled together.

"What the hell is this, a siege?" Kevin asked.

[41]

"God, it's nice to see a friendly face for a change," Jackie said. "You wouldn't believe the crap we've been getting from our so-called friends."

"Cheer up. I bring you a solution. You can now support the budget and still come off as heroes back home."

"This oughta be good," Malatesta said.

"As a matter of fact, it is, Fred. The best we can get. SB Four-two-one's in conference. We're gonna use it to lift the aid-ratio floor to point-two. We're also jacking up nonpublic transportation and textbooks. Comments?"

"Yeah. What's it mean?" Lorenzo asked. "I don't understand the aid-ratio part."

"Okay," Kevin said. "Here's how it works. Our public school districts are funded in two ways: by the local property tax and by state subsidy. Keep in mind that the subsidy money isn't made in Harrisburg. It doesn't come from God either. *We* send it to Harrisburg, mostly by the income tax and the sales tax. Remember, almost half the state budget goes for education. You with me so far?"

Lorenzo nodded.

"Okay. The problem with the subsidy money is the formula that distributes it to the five hundred and one school districts. It's complicated as hell. In fact, if you put it on a blackboard, it'd look like the formula for the atomic bomb. But the bottom line is that city districts, like Philly and Pittsburgh, do okay, rural districts make out like bandits, and suburban districts, like ours, get absolutely screwed. Roughly speaking, the aid ratio means the percentage of the expenses of the school districts that the state assumes. If a district has a ratio of point-three-eight, the state is picking up the tab for about thirty-eight percent of that district's costs. The richer a district is, at least as reflected in the formula, the lower its aid ratio. Up until 'seventy-nine even the richest districts had to have a point-one ratio. In other words, the minimum assistance from the state would be ten percent. In 'seventy-nine we raised the minimum to point-fifteen."

"Didn't you engineer that, too, Kevin?" Jackie asked.

"I thought you'd never ask. Yeah. The same way as now. During a budget fight at four in the morning. The more things change, the more they remain the same. Anyway, let's talk numbers. Jackie, under this plan your district gets three hundred fourteen thousand dollars. Lorenzo, yours gets two hundred ninety-five thousand, and Fred's gets three hundred thirty-nine thousand dollars. So you don't think I'm hiding anything, my district's the biggest winner in the county with four hundred sixty-two thousand dollars."

Malatesta wasn't sold. "You're still asking us to support a tax increase. How do we handle that?"

"Number one, you and I both know that nobody ever lost an election because of a tax vote. The election's almost a year and a half away, and the memory span of the average voter is three weeks. Number two, the amount we're gaining is more than we're giving up by the tax hike. The PR on this is a piece of cake. We'll look like heroes."

Kevin turned to Wilson. "Jim, fill them in on what the IU is doing."

"We've contacted the superintendents of all our local districts," Wilson said. "Naturally they love it. Each of them has promised to send out a newsletter praising you guys and explaining how the subsidy change will help hold the line on the property tax. They'll also appear at the news conference."

"What news conference?" Lorenzo asked.

"Day after tomorrow," Kevin answered. "In time for the deadline of our weeklies. We'll hold it at the courthouse and milk it for all it's worth. And don't forget the nonpublics. I'll make sure our pastors get the word out. So whaddya say, gang? Is it a go?"

The next ten minutes was hand-holding time for Kevin, easing their fears, countering their arguments and making certain he didn't oversell. They trusted him; that made him effective. He wasn't leadership; he was one of them. And above all, he always told it straight.

It wasn't surprising that the last holdout was Jackie. She, more than the others, felt a need to be stroked. She knew that Kevin was right, that the subsidy change more than compensated for the tax vote, but she needed a little more, something to reassure her that she was special and, more important, that she was noticed.

"Look, guys," she said, "my district's a lot more blue-collar than yours. Labor still has some clout. I take it the teachers support the budget and the subsidy change, right?"

"Right," Kevin answered. "The more money to the school districts, the more they can demand at budget time. Why?"

[43]

"Because I don't trust the bastards. I went with you in the 'seventy-nine subsidy change and guess what? PSEA still endorsed my opponent. Why should I stick my neck out again when I know they're just dying to cut it off?"

Kevin tried to mask his impatience. "You're a tough broad, sweetheart. Sit tight for a few minutes. I'll be back."

"Where are you going?"

"To get you a present."

He plunged back into the hallway and quickly found his target: George Sawyer, executive director of the most powerful organization in the state.

The Pennsylvania State Education Association exceeded even the AFL-CIO and the Teamsters in political clout. It had the largest campaign war chest and the most troops to send into any campaign. It also had developed one of the most sophisticated computer operations in the state. The PSEA knew that it had muscle and never hesitated to flex it.

"Kevin," Sawyer said brightly. "How's my favorite reactionary?"

"Couldn't be better, George. And do I have a deal for you. The opportunity for us to work together—for the good of education, of course."

"I always work for the good of education. Nothing's more important than the children."

"Sure, George. Except maybe a no-layoff clause, twenty sick days, five personal days, a guaranteed hour of prep time, and whatever other bullshit you can dream up."

"All components of a quality education. Anyway, what's up?"

"Have you gotten the word on how we're trying to solve the problem?"

"Sure. SB Four-two-one. It has the fine hand of Kevin Murray all over it. How can I help?"

"Jackie Daniels. As usual, she needs to be stroked a little bit. Look, this budget means a lot to you, right?"

"Absolutely. It's the first time in years basic ed gets any kind of increase."

"Then how about an agreement that if Jackie goes along, you guys stay neutral in her race next time?"

Sawyer thought for a moment. "That's not unreasonable, Kevin. Jackie's not a red flag to our people, like you. But I don't control endorsements. The board decides on that. The best I can do is promise you that I'll strongly recommend we stay out of Jackie's election. How's that?"

"Good enough," said Kevin, extending his hand. "You know, we work pretty well together. Maybe someday you turkeys will even endorse me."

"Kevin," Sawyer answered with a smile, "the odds on hell's freezing over are considerably better."

"How did I know you were gonna say that?"

"I'll level with you. We always endorse your opponent because our membership wouldn't stand for anything less. To them, you're public enemy number one. But we're always pleased when you win."

"You gotta be kidding."

"Not at all. You're against us on most of the issues; but your door's always open, and we always know where you stand. And on the really important votes, like tonight, you're the guy who makes things happen."

"Christ, I wish I had a tape of this conversation."

"I don't. I'd be impeached."

"We can't have that. You might end up back in a classroom. And like you, I care about the children."

"Screw you. And good luck."

Kevin took the agreement back to Jackie. They both knew that the board would reject Sawyer's recommendation and endorse her opponent and that she would still win. None of that was important. The important thing was that the game had been played.

"Kevin, you're the only one who could bring all this together," she said. "And you're the only one I trust. Why the hell aren't you in leadership?"

"No, thanks, sweetheart. I want my freedom."

The last stop was Joe Criswell. With him Kevin used a slightly different approach.

"Criswell, you're a pimple on the ass of progress, but I need your vote. You got me, shithead?"

Criswell's response was equally low-key. "Balls, Kevin! This budget's a fuckin' disgrace, and you know it. We call ourselves conservatives, and what do we do? Increase the goddamn dole to the lazy sons of bitches who won't work. What we should be doing instead of raising taxes is taking an ax to the whole thing. Ten

[45]

percent cut, across the board. No exceptions. Fuck all of 'em. And the teachers! Those pricks! I can't believe that you'd support a budget that gives them more money. All those worthless bastards are good for is slitting tires on the picket line. You want me to support the budget? Put a line item in it to buy all the mothball ships down the navy yard."

"What for?"

"To ship all the teachers and the niggers halfway to Africa. I just can't believe that when we finally get a real honest-to-Christ conservative in the White House, we're willing to turn around and pass a budget that even Tip O'Neill would be proud of. And I'm disappointed as shit, Kevin, that you're a part of it."

Kevin grinned and shook his head. "You are really a piece of work. How the hell does your wife put up with you?"

"She's got no goddamn choice. There's none of this women's lib shit in my house. I call the shots, and if she doesn't like it, she can waltz her ass out the door."

"I'm sure she knows what a good thing she has. I mean, she could've married Hitler or even Jack the Ripper." Kevin lit another cigarette. "Okay, are you done with the bullshit rhetoric now?"

Criswell's face relaxed. It was hard to tell how much he meant, how much was act, and how much was caused by insanity. "Yeah, I guess," he said.

"Good. Let's get to the facts. First, you know goddamn well this is no giveaway budget. Less than a six percent increase in spending, way below the inflation rate. Secondly, the increase in public assistance benefits is the lowest in ten years. Thirdly, there's no money for teachers. We're hiking the basic ed subsidy less than ten percent, and that money goes to the school districts, not the teachers."

"What about the tax increase?"

"A perfectly acceptable outgrowth of Reaganomics. The whole thrust of the federal cutbacks has been to give the states more power. If there has to be a tax increase, wouldn't you rather see it at the state level? It's our own money going for our own programs, not to the goddamn Sun Belt states, and with no federal strings attached. And we're turning around and dumping more money and control back to the counties with block grants. That's conser-

[46]

vative. But there is one important point I think you're forgetting, Joe."

"What's that?"

"We're Republicans and we're in the majority. Our job is to govern, and a big part of that job is to pass a budget on time. If we fail, we're gonna find ourselves back in the minority. I've been there, Joe. I know what it's like. And I think you'll agree that the state is in much better shape when we're in control and not the Ds."

Criswell rose and started to pace. "Dammit, Kevin, I know a lot of what you're saying is true. But Jesus, I hate to give in all the time. Especially when I get nothing in return. And I mean nothing. How many bills have we introduced to repeal Act One-nine-five? Not one of them has been considered in committee. Orders from leadership. Too controversial. So the goddamn teacher strikes continue. Our own goddamn leadership, and we can't even get a shot. And then they turn around and want my vote on the budget."

"We're gonna get our shot, Joe. This fall. With or without leadership."

"How?"

"After we recess, the Education Committee will be considering a lot of Senate bills. There'll be a heavy calendar in September. We'll pick off a Senate education bill and run an amendment to outlaw teacher strikes. What do you think?"

"I love it! Is the shit ever gonna hit the fan! The whores are finally gonna have to take a stand! We're gonna stick it right up their ass!"

"Crassly put, but quite correct. Okay, jerkoff, are you with us, or are you gonna make that fat pig Tenaglia happy by seeing us go down again?"

"Okay, Kevin. I'm in. But for you, not for the rest of those gutless bastards."

It was go. There would still be a few last-minute problems and another protracted floor debate, but this time it would fly. First the tax vote, then the budget, and finally, as a reward, the goodies in SB 421.

After calling the Speaker to give him the word, Kevin found himself with a half hour or so to kill. It would take at least that

[47]

long to round up the troops and herd them onto the floor, in much the same way that a teacher attempts to usher her third-grade charges back to class after a recess. Except, of course, that unlike their younger counterparts, a number of reps would reassemble in a less than sober state to continue the democratic process.

In no mood for more constituent letters, Kevin started to walk, with no particular destination. His pace quickened. The challenge. That was what it was all about. Dealing, sometimes literally, with other humans to put together something workable. An hour ago there had been only ashes. Now victory was near.

He entered the rotunda, taking the marble staircase to the second floor. Only then did he pause. Never had he taken this for granted: the waxed perfection of the cobblestone floor, the brilliance of the marble, and, five stories above, the splendor of the dome. And entwined through it all, the human drama that gave it life.

It was his world, his life, and he loved it. But because there was love, there was also agony. Even now, in a moment of triumph, the doubts flooded back to assail him.

You're a goddamned idiot, Kevin. If you had any brains, you'd get the hell out. It's tearing you up inside, costing you a fortune, and destroying your marriage. And for what? A few headlines, forgotten before the ink's dry? The applause of the masses? Horseshit. Drop dead tomorrow, and in two weeks it'll be Kevin who? Go ahead, moron, smoke your two packs a day. Bite your fingernails to the skin. Keep trying to be in three places at once performing the great Kevin Murray juggling act. One day the whole thing is gonna come crashing down on your head.

As usual, Kevin was torn. He reacted in his usual manner. Lighting another cigarette, he turned and headed into the House chamber.

CHAPTER
Three

WITH a look of grim resolve the Right Reverend Monsignor Patrick Gerard Carney tossed the horseshoe, making certain that it landed a yard past the stake.

"Two red!" the little girl exclaimed, dancing about the yard. "I win again, Father Pat!"

"You're just too tough for me, Megan," the priest answered, shaking his head.

The victor swooped down on her father, throwing her arms around his neck. "Did you see me, Daddy? I won three straight!"

"I sure did, sweetheart," Kevin answered. "You're dynamite. And you know what else?"

"What?"

"You're my favorite daughter."

"And you're my favorite daddy."

And then she was off, to announce her triumph to her brothers.

"She's a doll, Kevin," Pat said, stooping to take a beer from the cooler, then dropping into a lawn chair. "Absolutely beautiful and so sweet."

"Yeah, she sure is. They're all super."

The priest affected an Irish brogue. "But methinks that the wee lassie is the apple of her daddo's eye."

Kevin grinned. "I don't have a favorite. I love all five the same. But there's something special about a daughter. You know, whenever Karen's been pregnant, I never cared what the baby would be. Oh, I thought it would be nice if the first were a boy,

[49]

just so there would be an older brother. But it didn't really matter as long as Karen and the baby were okay. And when the first three were boys, I was thrilled. Then Megan came along. I swear, Pat, from the time she's born a little girl has a way of wrapping her daddy around her little finger. When I come home and she runs to me and throws her arms around me—God, it's just super."

Peter ran to them, his golden curls dancing in the evening breeze. He pulled on his father's leg, pointing excitedly to the sky. The nonstop torrent that poured from his mouth was in an unknown language.

Kevin lifted the baby onto his lap, kissing his blond head. "Peewee, I wonder if you'll talk by high school graduation."

"Is there a . . . problem?" Pat asked cautiously.

"There sure is," Kevin said as the baby broke free and scampered away. "It's called being the youngest of five and spoiled rotten. He doesn't have to talk. All he does is point to something and the kids get it for him. But that's gonna change pretty soon."

"You mean—"

"Yep. Number six. In February. And don't ask me how. We're still looking for the star in the east."

"God! I mean, congratulations—I guess."

"You know, you priests really crack me up. You're against birth control, you push the procreation bit, then you give a wiseass crack like that. You guys better decide which way you want it."

"C'mon, Kevin. You know I'm thrilled for you. How's Karen taking it?"

"Ask her yourself," Kevin said as his wife approached, carrying a tablecloth and a tray of utensils. She always seemed to be working.

"Ask me what?" Karen said. She saw Kevin's grin, and the question left her eyes, replaced by an accusing stare.

"You told him, didn't you, big mouth?" she said. "And they say women can't keep a secret."

"Aw, c'mon, hon," Kevin said, trying to hug her but thwarted by the utensil tray. "You know how excited I am. Besides, it's not gonna be a secret much longer."

"Congratulations," Pat said, rising and kissing her cheek. "How do you feel?"

[50]

"Well, I've pretty much recovered from the shock, Pat. It should make life interesting, to say the least."

"Don't worry, baby. I'll be there to help," Kevin said.

"That's a riot," his wife answered. "Like this morning, getting home at seven?"

"But we passed the budget, didn't we? We're almost done for the summer."

Karen's voice was cold. "Please don't, Kevin. We both know that if it's not the budget, it'll be something else. So don't make promises you won't be able to keep. Besides, Pat's here, and I'm sure he's not the slightest bit interested in this conversation."

Kevin decided to let things ride. He was grateful for Pat's presence, which required Karen to treat him at least civilly. "Why don't you two chat for a while without the world's biggest S.O.B. around? It's time for me to challenge the turkeys."

He walked across the yard to the new basketball court. It was something they couldn't really afford, which was par for the course, but it had been an investment for the kids.

"Okay, sports fans, the big guy is ready to take you on. Murray's the name, jump-shooting's the game. How 'bout a quickie to ten?"

"Fifteen," countered Kevin, Jr., his oldest.

"Okay, faggimundo, fifteen it is."

"We take it in," said Sean, his number two son.

"Fine with me. Just don't miss, because I won't."

"Big man!"

"Not big, just tough. Where I come from, the kids get tougher as you go down the street—"

"I know. And you live in the last house."

"You got it. Now let's play basketball."

While Kevin was rolling to a 15–8 win, Karen was taking a few rare moments to relax with Pat.

"Karen, you look better than you did in college. No lie."

"Kevin says the same thing. I think all men must be blind. Blue veins all over my legs, hips that won't stop spreading. C'mon, Pat. If I'd looked like this at Villanova, I would've gone into the convent." She paused, a sad smile crossing her face. "Maybe that's what I should have done."

"But then five great kids—soon six—wouldn't be on this earth."

[51]

She smiled again, this time with the same mischief Pat remembered. "You never know, Monsignor. The church is changing all the time. In fact, I hear nuns are allowed to date now."

The priest sat upright. "Absolutely not! Where did you hear something like that?"

"It's true. As long as they wear No Nonsense panty hose and a Cross My Heart bra."

Pat leaned his head back and roared. "God, that's great, Karen. I'll have to remember that one the next time I speak at Immaculata."

"I'd think that one over, Pat. The IHMs were never known for their sense of humor."

Pat looked at the mother of five. She *was* still lovely. "You know, Karen, when you laugh like that, it reminds me of the old days. You and Kevin cutting each other up at the parties. They were great times, weren't they?"

"Yes, they sure were."

"You thought Kevin was the funniest guy alive." He hesitated. "Do you still laugh at him?"

"Not too much." It was her turn to pause. "There never seems to be any time."

"He's on the go a lot, huh?"

"What do you think? The most active legislator in the state. The leader of the pro-life movement. And now they want him to run for Congress."

"I saw that in the papers. Will he?"

Karen shrugged. "Who knows?"

"Allworth will be tough to unseat."

"I know. But Kevin really wants him. Allworth's against everything Kevin stands for, particularly on abortion. Besides, you know it's in his blood. Since he was fifteen, he's wanted to be president."

"He'd make a good one. We're really proud of him, you know. The Church couldn't ask for a better spokesman."

"I know. It's just tough sometimes. Sometimes it seems he belongs to everyone except me. Don't get me wrong. He tries. He takes the train home from Harrisburg every night. He never misses the children's activities. But it seems like we're constantly in a relay, and I never get the baton."

[52]

She reached for a cigarette, one of three she allowed herself every day. Pat lit it, and she inhaled deeply, letting the smoke slowly escape. "But enough of me. The word is that you're our next auxiliary bishop. How do you plead?"

"Nolo contendere," he laughed. "That's up to the boss, and you never know what's going on in his mind."

"What's he like, Pat? Really?"

His words were deliberate. "The cardinal is one of the most brilliant men I've ever known. He's also one of the toughest. He even had me working this morning. On the Fourth of July."

The note delivered to his desk the evening before was to the point: "Please see me at eight tomorrow morning."

It was unsigned, but the scrawl of the boss was unmistakable. Pat was just turning into the driveway of the mansion when KYW beeped eight. Late again. But even though he felt like a truant schoolboy, he was again amused by the location of the cardinal's residence. Right beside St. Joseph's College. Hawk Hill. Mortal enemy of Villanova. He had to give the Jesuits credit. They always did know how to position themselves.

The nun who answered the door did nothing to boost his confidence. Her eyes pierced right through him, and suddenly he was back in fourth grade. "His Eminence is on the back lawn," she said coldly. "He's been expecting you."

Stephen Cardinal Pulski's mood was less than jovial, but not for the reason Pat expected. Dressed in light blue slacks and a white Izod, His Eminence was being tortured by his two wood. Plastic golf balls were strewn about the lawn, most within ten feet of the man with the club.

"I don't understand it, Patrick," he said without looking up. "My game off the tee is gone. Vanished overnight. A week ago I was getting two hundred plus every drive. Straight down the middle. Now look at me. Yesterday at Overbrook was an embarrassment."

Pat couldn't resist. "Have you tried prayer, Eminence?"

"I'm in no mood for your misplaced humor. You're looking at a desperate man." A slight smile creased the corner of his mouth. "Three rosaries, if you must know. Didn't help."

It was no accident that Pat held a four handicap. Like any

[53]

other rising executive, a young priest could use it to his advantage.

"Hit a few more," he suggested. "Maybe I can spot something."

The cardinal complied, slicing two and topping the third. "Well?" he asked impatiently.

"The mortal sin of golf. You're not keeping your head down."

"That's all?"

"And you're not throwing it out the window."

"What?"

"Address the ball," Pat said, enjoying the chance to order around a prince of the church. "I want you to imagine there's a window, about three feet off the ground and a foot to the right of the ball. On your downswing, try to put the club through the window."

"I don't know, Patrick. I—"

"Trust me. And keep your head down."

Again the cardinal obeyed. He made perfect contact, and the ball almost cleared the far wall.

"Unbelievable!" he roared.

"Told you," Pat said nonchalantly. "Aim for the window, and centrifugal force does the rest."

The cardinal hit a dozen more balls. All straight, all long.

"I'm in your debt, Patrick," he said, beaming.

"Always glad to help, Eminence." Feeling very pleased with himself, Pat was doing his best to mask it. His leader helped.

"Good," the cardinal shot back, all business again. "You can start by being on time for meetings."

By an unspoken command, Pat was led to the wrought-iron table on the patio. The cardinal lifted the coffee carafe and poured. "If I remember correctly, you take cream and one sugar."

Pat could only nod. Fifty meetings a week, a budget of more than a hundred million dollars, and this seventy-year-old man could still remember every detail.

"Our Lady of Knock," the cardinal said abruptly when they were seated. "Ring a bell?"

Desperately Pat's mind raced back to the seminary. Apparitions. Guadalupe, Mexico. Lourdes, France. Fatima, Portugal. Knock. "It was an apparition last century. Germany?"

The cardinal's look of disdain was unmistakable. "Ireland," he said icily. "August twenty-first, 1879. How could you possibly say Germany?"

"I was kind of guessing. You know, knockwurst." Deeper and deeper, Pat thought.

"Unlike other apparitions, Our Lady never spoke at Knock." The cardinal allowed himself a slight smile. "Legend has it that since she was among the Irish, she couldn't get a word in edgewise."

Pat briefly considered a crack about Poles, then wisely rejected the thought.

"As sophisticated as Irish-Americans pretend to be, they still retain a great devotion to Our Lady of Knock." He reached into the briefcase beside his chair and handed a file to Pat. It was stamped "Confidential."

"Several months ago, February third, to be exact, a certain Liam Flaherty arrived in the States."

"Is he a priest?" Pat asked.

Again a twinkle. "No, he's a Jesuit. At any rate, Father Flaherty's mission was to establish a shrine to Our Lady of Knock in the Philadelphia area. He chose Chester County and, with his undisputable Irish charm, quickly managed to have ten acres near Exton donated to him by one of the flock." He paused to pour his own coffee.

"Go on," Pat said, immediately regretting the words.

"I intend to, *Father* Carney." Pulski let the words sink in, then pressed on. "Flushed with his initial success, the good reverend then got down to some very serious and quite effective fundraising. To date, he has raised in excess of one million dollars, presently earning a shade under thirteen percent in the Delaware Cash Reserve. For the reasons detailed in that file, we believe that Father Flaherty has no intention of using that money for a shrine."

"For what then?"

"At present, God only knows. But *you* will, Patrick—and soon."

"Our Lady of Czestochowa all over again," Pat whispered softly.

"It'd better not be. You are to take personal charge of this matter immediately. No one, I repeat, no one is to know of this. You will report directly, and exclusively, to me. Understood?"

[55]

"Yes, Your Eminence."

"Good. And, Patrick, I'm depending on you to handle this discreetly. I will not tolerate another Doylestown."

Pat enjoyed his visits with the Murrays, but the aftermath was always the same. He felt lonely, aware of how much he had missed. There was also a feeling of guilt. It was the latter emotion that caused him to reject Megan's plea that he accompany them to the fireworks. Instead, he drove to West Philadelphia and the old neighborhood.

Could it really be six months since he had seen his father? He tried to tell himself that it had been unintentional, a necessary result of his schedule, but he knew the truth. Only a few miles apart, they now lived in different worlds.

The neighborhood had changed. It was dusk, but the streets were already deserted. Once they had teemed with vitality. Children played stickball or kick the can. Teenagers held hands as they walked to the corner drugstore to share a milk shake. Adults sat on their front steps drinking beer as they listened to the Phillies or talked with their neighbors. The bell of the ice cream truck would set off a litany of little voices, begging their parents for a dime.

Pat remembered it all as he drove past the aging façade of Most Blessed Sacrament. Once the largest Catholic grade school in the country, with more than thirty-two hundred students, today it had fewer than four hundred, and there were rumblings that it was on the cardinal's hit list of parishes to be closed.

The little boy squeezed his mother's hand as they entered the school. His heart thumped wildly as a nun approached, a giant in black and white.

"I'll take him now, Mrs. Carney. He'll be fine."

He refused to let go. "Please, Mommy, don't leave me."

Her voice was reassuring. The little boy had no idea that she, too, was fighting back tears.

"It's okay, Patty. You're a big boy now."

Sometimes Pat found it impossible to remember her. It had been so long. He had pictures, but they were different. The woman in the photographs was seen through the eyes of an adult.

Even now he would lie in bed and try to recall her as she was when she was the center of a seven-year-old's life.

"Slumming it tonight, Chuck?"

There were three of them, all wearing colors. This was Rover turf. The youngest, no more than fourteen, carried the box. Out of it spewed heavy metal.

Pat grinned nervously, thankful that the light had turned green. It was so different now. Location was defined by gang turf. Once it had been by parish. If someone asked you where you were from, you never gave your street. You replied MBS or De Sales or Transfiguration, and immediately you were understood. The church had been the center of life, with Sunday mass and the walk home the fulcrum on which the rest of the week was balanced.

It was gone now. The West Philly Pat had known was scattered to the winds, a Catholic diaspora. Its people had fled to the suburbs. Instead of West Catholic, their children attended Monsignor Bonnor or Cardinal O'Hara. Row homes were replaced by singles—with lawns no less. It was a good life, but somehow it just wasn't the same.

There were still a handful like George Carney who refused to yield, a white island in a sea of black. He had been born at MBS, and he would die there, in the home where he had raised his family.

Pat's pulse quickened as he approached the house. Its exterior mirrored the man who lived within. Once it had sparkled with pride, the class of the block, and everyone marveled at how George could do it. The pride was gone now, and like a derelict broken by the world, it had yielded to the ravages of time.

There was no answer. That came as no surprise. Pat knew where his father would be. Still, he had hoped.

He retraced his steps and walked the block and a half to Finnegan's. It, too, had seen better days.

The bartender eyed him suspiciously. It'd be just like those creeps in the LCB to pull a raid on the Fourth of July.

"Yeah?"

"I'm looking for George Carney."

"He in trouble?"

Pat smiled. "No. No trouble. Honest."

[57]

"Over there," the bartender said, nodding to the far end of the room. "And if he's a friend of yours, maybe you'd like to do something about his tab."

"How much?"

The bartender pulled a slip from the register. "Thirty-five."

Pat handed him two twenties. "Keep it," he said.

For the first time the bartender smiled. "Thanks, pal. Hey, I didn't mean to be no heavy. I mean, I like old George. He's harmless. I don't even bitch when he brings in his own pint. But I'm running a business, you know what I mean?"

"Sure."

There were about a dozen people in the bar, probably half of the neighborhood's white population, and they all were watching him.

His father sat alone. His eyes were closed, and every few seconds his head would start to drop. Without opening his eyes, he would catch hold, shake himself upright, and start the process again.

Gently Pat touched his shoulder. "Are you asleep, Dad?"

He was exhausted from a day at the plant. Dinner was over, but there was still so much to be done. Dishes to be washed and dried. Homework to be checked. Lunches to be made for school tomorrow. Baths for the little ones. Just a few minutes' rest, before he got on with it.

It frightened the little boy when his father closed his eyes. Only when he was awake could he protect him.

"Daddy, are you asleep?"

"Not on your life, Patty boy. I'm just resting my eyes."

The old man nodded and a smile formed. His words were slurred, as much by the years as the alcohol. "Not on your life, Patty boy. I'm just resting my eyes."

"C'mon, Dad. Let's go home."

"It's my son," George called as they shuffled toward the door. The pride was evident even through the booze. "*Monsignor* Patrick Carney it is, so you'd better be on your good behavior."

Pat was embarrassed as they rose to greet him. They were old Irish, forever in awe of the collar, even when it wasn't worn.

"I didn't recognize ya, Patty, I mean, Father," one of them said, timidly extending his hand. "It's been so long. Leo Moran. Fifty-third and Greenway."

"Sure, Mr. Moran, how've you been? How're Tommy and the girls?"

"The girls are fine," he said, beaming. "Sally's over in Cherry Hill. Three children. Peggy's out in Goshen. She's expecting her second next month. Her husband's got a great job. He's in computers with Burroughs. And Missy, she's up in New York. In advertising. She's the women's libber of the family. Married to her career."

"And Tom?" Pat saw the man's eyes and knew he shouldn't have asked.

"Tommy's—he's gone, Father. He died a few years back." He paused again, then poured out the rest, as if he were in confession, fearing the sacrilege of omission more than the wrath of the priest. "Drugs, Father. He was never the same after Vietnam."

"I'm very sorry, Mr. Moran. I really am," Pat said, edging his father to the door. "I'll remember Tommy in my prayers."

Outside Pat took his father's arm. "I really blew that one," he muttered to himself. Or so he thought.

"You did that, Patty boy. If he'd wanted you to know about Tommy, he would have told you."

"Yeah, you're right. As usual." Pat sighed. "But I didn't mean any harm."

"Not good enough, Patty boy." The old man grinned and squeezed his son's hand. "Especially for a bishop."

He held his father's hand as they walked down the corridor. It was his first time in a hospital, and he was frightened. Especially by the smell. Everything smelled—so sick.

His father looked handsome in his suit, bought new for the occasion. The little boy's suit was also new, white gabardine, to welcome his Little White Guest. He clutched his boutonniere, a red rose, in his other hand, a present for his mother.

"Are you sure it's okay, Daddy?" he whispered again.

"Of course it is, Patty boy. I told you, no one is about to stop a young man on the most important day of his life from visiting his mother. And his baby sister."

The nurse rose from the desk when they approached. Her face was stern. "Mr. Carney, you can't go in there."

"Sure we can, Nurse. Just for a few minutes. His mother wants to see him on his first communion day."

[59]

"Mr. Carney, please." The nurse seemed ready to cry. She led his father to a small room a few feet away. The little boy was only able to hear parts of what they said.

"Hemorrhage . . . everything possible . . . tried to call . . ."

His father's voice sounded strange, as if he, too, were going to cry. Only his father never cried. He was a man.

They didn't speak until they were almost home, but the little boy knew something was wrong. They had taken a cab instead of the 26 trolley.

"I want to talk to you, Patty boy," his father finally said. "The twins won't understand what I'm going to tell you."

"It's about Mommy, isn't it?" His heart pounded, just as it had on that first day of school.

"Yes, son, it is. Mommy won't be coming home anymore. She went to God today. I want you to remember this, Patty boy. You're special. Jesus loves you so much that He took your mommy to heaven on the same day you received Him."

He pulled his son to him, holding him tightly. "Go ahead, Patty boy, let it out. It's okay to cry."

His world so abruptly destroyed, the little boy sobbed in his father's arms. His hand still clutched the rose.

Pat helped his father onto the sofa, then untied his shoes. Just like the old days.

"How about some coffee, Dad?"

"Good idea, Patty boy." He took out a cigarette, "I'll just rest my eyes while you're making it."

Pat walked to the kitchen. It seemed that whenever he thought of his family, they were in the kitchen. Doing homework. Dyeing Easter eggs. Wrapping Christmas presents. How many years had he sat at that table? At the end opposite his father, helping the twins cut their meat while his father fed Kristy.

The kettle whistled, and he poured two cups, black for his father. He needn't have bothered. When he returned to the living room, George Carney was fast asleep. The lit cigarette was still in his hand. Gently Pat removed it and stubbed it out in the ashtray.

The little boy huddled under the covers. The November wind rattled the window. For the first time this year the radiator hissed, a sure sign that Christmas was coming. Only this time it would be different.

So much had happened today. His mother had been buried. He had sat with his father in the limousine as the procession wound its way from MBS to Holy Cross Cemetery. Some of the neighbors said it was the largest procession they could remember. That made him feel a little better.

Afterward, when everyone had gone back to the house, he went with his father to the hospital to bring his baby sister home.

"She's a princess, Patty boy," his father said as he took the little bundle from the nurse. "Her first ride, and it's in a limousine."

All the women cried when they brought her in, the baby who would never know her mother. Even some of the men were blowing their noses.

Pat stayed by his father that whole day, never allowing him out of his sight. His father was so strong. It was he who comforted the rest of the people, telling them not to cry, that his Alice was in heaven and everything would be all right. When Pat grew up, he would be just like his father.

It seemed he always had to go to the bathroom when the weather changed. He got out of bed and walked into the hall. A sound was coming from his father's room. Even though his mommy had told him never to eavesdrop, he crept closer to the door. It was open a crack, and he peeked inside. He couldn't believe it. His father was lying on the bed, his arm over his eyes, crying.

"Alice, my Alice," he sobbed. "I need you so. What am I going to do?"

The little boy entered the room and took his father's hand. "Don't worry, Daddy. I'll take care of you."

From the day George buried his wife, his life had but one goal: to raise his children the way Alice would have wanted. Nothing else mattered.

For twenty-two years he was both father and mother. He ironed, he scrubbed, he cooked, and through it all he kept the charm, the Irish grace of being, that had attracted a beautiful young woman to him long ago.

Pat remembered as special their Friday nights. Meat was forbidden, so dinner was generally grilled cheese sandwiches and tomato soup. When the dishes were done, the children would gather in the kitchen to watch their father make popcorn. Then the Monopoly board was spread on the table, and the battle began, with George serving as both banker and referee.

As a special badge of his age Pat was permitted to stay up later than the others. He would sit on the rocker as his father brought out the ironing board. Then the two of them would watch the Friday night fights on the *Gillette Cavalcade of Sports.*

[61]

George had a special way with Kristy. She was his only daughter, and he was determined to give her the gentleness and understanding that usually come from a mother. He never failed to brush her hair every night before bed, telling her how beautiful she was.

"You're just like your mother, little one. And there's no greater compliment."

It was when the children were all in bed that the loneliness came. It wasn't right for a man to be alone, his friends had said. He should start over. Marry again. If not for himself, then for the children.

But for George, there would be only his Alice. Even the thought of another woman seemed to be a desecration of her memory and their love. It wouldn't be fair to her for the children to have another mother. They were hers and hers alone.

What was hardest to take during those lonely nights was the inevitability that someday the children would be gone. What would he do? What would be left?

It was when he was assailed by this fear that he would reach for the Jameson's. Just a few short drinks. Anything to bring on sleep.

But before he slept, there was always the ritual. After rising from his prayers, he would look at the picture on the nightstand. It was his favorite, taken down the shore shortly after they were married. She was posed on the stern of the *Miss Atlantic City,* her hair blown back by the ocean breeze.

"How am I doing, kid?" he would ask.

Pat gently draped the blanket over his father.

"Thank you, Patty boy," the old man mumbled. "I don't mean to be a bother."

Monsignor Patrick Carney's eyes filled with tears. "Don't worry, Daddy. I'll take care of you."

Four

MARCH 21, 1979. Though it was the first day of spring, winter was still in the air. The white-haired man walked briskly from the restaurant to the waiting Lincoln. Dinner had been relaxing, spent with his attorney, Max Gold, "the best Jew lawyer in town," and "Long John" Licata, his friend and partner of half a century.

It was only a short ride from Eleventh and Christian to his home, and he spent it talking to his driver about the old days. Johnny was new, but the white-haired man liked him. He knew how to listen.

They pulled to the curb at Ninth and Snyder, just a few steps from his home. The white-haired man remained in the car, telling of how things were during Prohibition. He was so engrossed in his story that he never saw the driver lower the power window on the passenger side.

The lone gunman walked from the shadows and placed the shotgun against the white hair. Then he pulled the trigger, causing the white hair and the head beneath it to disappear.

Fredo Annaloro, boss of the Philadelphia family, was dead. The bloodletting had begun.

"Wildcat to Lair. Our ETA is three minutes."

"We copy, Wildcat. Suggest you come in from the south."

The pilot smiled to himself. Like anyone associated with the Grosso family, he was a professional. After OCS and flight school, he had done two tours in Nam. No one had to tell him how to make his approach.

"Straight in or the scenic swing, boss?" he asked the man seated beside him.

Briefcase opened on his lap, Vince Grosso had been reviewing the transcript of a recent deposition. He had come to detest practicing law, but it was still necessary. He needed the cover, if not the money.

"Let's take the scenic swing, Major." He replaced the transcript and shut the briefcase. The traffic below on the Schuylkill Expressway was at its usual crawl. Had he driven, the trip would have taken almost an hour. By chopper it was nine minutes.

As the pilot banked gently to the left, a postcard scene unfolded. The Schuylkill River shimmered in the morning sun, gradually gathering speed as it approached the falls. Jack Kelly's river. Only in America, only in Philadelphia. Immigrant bricklayer becomes millionaire contractor, bastion of the Democratic party and first layman of the church. Snubbed by the British aristocracy and denied permission to enter the Diamond Sculls, he vows revenge. Two decades later his son, Jack, Jr., returns to London and captures the event. His daughter Grace, a product of the best Catholic schools, wins an Oscar, then becomes part of the royalty that once spurned her father. Even now, with school out of session, Jack Kelly's legacy continued as several shells pushed off from Boathouse Row.

Vince Grosso could identify with a story like that. It was all about family.

They passed over the falls. To their left was the Art Museum, an Acropolis rising from the river. It had always been a Philly landmark, but when Rocky Balboa ran up its steps, it had become a shrine. Down the parkway, the Champs-Élysées of Philadelphia. It ran from the Art Museum to the Cathedral. Two years before, every square inch had been packed with humanity, two million strong, to watch the first Polish pope say mass.

The chopper wheeled east of the City Hall Tower, topped by the statue of William Penn. By design, it remained the city's tallest structure. Like many others, Vince remembered two childhood stories about the statue. The first, told to him by his mother, was that the rim of Penn's hat was large enough to accommodate a full-size car easily. The second tale, as well as the facts of life, had been learned on the street corner—namely, that from a cer-

[64]

tain angle it appeared that Pennsylvania's founder was urinating on the city.

"We have you in sight, Wildcat," crackled the radio. "C'mon in."

When it was constructed for the Philadelphia Savings Fund Society in the late Depression, the PSFS Building had been considered an architectural wonder. Time had done nothing to diminish its reputation. It had been built with pride, which appealed to Vince. It was for that reason that he had bought it.

Five months before, his bank contacts had advised him of PSFS's decision to purchase Western Savings. It was a big venture which had to cause a cash flow problem. After meeting with his accountants to ensure that the transaction would be untraceable, Vince had moved. One of the family corporations, a conglomerate dealing in, among other things, computer time-sharing, ball bearings, meat-packing, and real estate, had made a generous offer, which was quickly accepted. The building's name was retained, as were its tenants, with one exception. The top floor was leased by the law offices of Vincent F. Grosso.

As the chopper touched down, three men emerged from the glass-enclosed control station. The glass was bulletproof; the men carried guns.

"Morning, boss," they murmured respectfully.

Vince nodded and walked briskly across the roof to the door. Two of his men entered first to scan the stairwell, followed by Vince and the third bodyguard. They descended thirteen steps to another door, where the ritual was repeated.

The door opened directly into Vince's office, which occupied the southeast corner of the floor and reflected the personality of its occupant. It could best be described as quietly elegant. The furniture had been handcrafted by Vittore de Felice, a Sicilian cabinetmaker who still held to the old ways. The only exception was Vince's desk, which paled in comparison to the other pieces. It was pine, and even a recent staining by De Felice could not hide its cheap construction. His father had sat behind it on the second floor on Fifth Street. The den was to be only temporary. It was to be a third bedroom for the other children who never came. Try as he might, the only memory Vince had of his father was sitting at that desk.

[65]

Vince pressed the button on the desk intercom.

"Good morning, Mr. Grosso," came a pleasant voice.

"Good morning, Maria. Please have Mr. Arrone join me and hold my calls."

The secretary who took the message sat in a reception room which had all the appearances of normality. Invisible was the control room directly behind her desk, bristling with electronic equipment. The office was accessible to the public only by elevator, and from the moment a visitor pushed the button in the lobby, he was under constant surveillance.

The control room operator was trained to observe five screens simultaneously: one for the lobby at the elevator entrance, one for the interior of the elevator, and three that covered the breadth of the reception room. Only one elevator ran to the top floor, programmed to make the non-stop trip in thirty-seven seconds. At the discretion of the control room operator, however, it could be stopped at any time, imprisoning its riders. The door to the elevator contained a sensitive metal detector, enabling the control room operator to know from the outset whether the visitor was armed.

The door from the reception room to the inner offices also looked ordinary, giving no clue that its walnut-grain veneer covered two inches of steel. It could be unlocked electronically only from the control rooms or from a switch under Vince's desk.

The top of the PSFS Building was more than a law office. It was a fortress, impregnable to attack. Vince Grosso had a thing about security.

Niccolo Arrone tapped twice and entered the office. He was typical of the inner corps which Vince had built around him. Thirty-four, a B.A. in economics from Fordham, an M.B.A. from Penn's Wharton School, and a Yale law degree. Most important, he was Sicilian.

"Good morning, Don Vincenzo," Arrone said. Although he was not wearing his suit jacket, his tie remained firmly knotted and his sleeves were unrolled.

"*Buon giorno, amico mio.*" With a wan smile Vince motioned him to a seat, then slid the morning *Inquirer* across the desk. "Troubles, Nick, always troubles."

"Vagnoni?"

"Yeah. What have you got?"

"Not much yet. About the same as the paper. Apparently he turned himself in to the FBI in Sacramento yesterday."

"We should have found him first."

"We tried, Vince. We were close. Our people missed him by only an hour in San Diego."

"Close only counts in horseshoes and hand grenades. Okay, how bad can he hurt us? Worst case scenario."

Arrone shifted in his chair. Vittore de Felice did not build for comfort. "I won't try to minimize, Vince. He could be another Valachi."

"Spell it out."

"As far as prosecutions, I'm not sure. It's only his word, and his testimony could be impeached by his background and by the deal the feds will be making with him. They'd need corroboration, but God only knows if he ever taped anything or kept a diary."

"Odds are he kept a diary, at least since my uncle was hit. Vagnoni was a careful man. He'd make sure he had some insurance."

"I think you're right. Depending on the quality of the corroboration he could put at least a dozen of our people at risk. But that's only part of it. Don Fredo confided in him. He had access to nearly everything. Our corporate network, our judges, police, our contacts in Congress. It's almost endless. The feds would have enough to investigate us for the next twenty years."

Vince rose and turned to the window. Out on the Delaware a bevy of tugs was easing a British frigate into Penn's Landing. He had promised the kids they would tour it. Why did life always seem simpler on the other side of the window?

"I take it there's no chance for salvage?" he asked, his eyes still fixed on the river.

"I don't see how, Vince. Even if we could get to him, there's no lever. He's a bachelor. Nothing to bargain for—except his life."

"Which is why he went to the feds." Vince returned to his seat. The options had been explored. It was time to act. "Solve the problem, Niccolo. Use Dominic's *regime* and as many of our outside people as you need. Find the soft spot and exploit it. Quickly."

"It won't be easy."

"It never is." He leaned forward, his eyes fixed firmly on Arrone. "I'm counting on you, Niccolo. Do not disappoint me."

[67]

When Arrone was gone, Vince took the *Inquirer* and read the lead story for the third time.

VAGNONI SURRENDERS TO FEDS
MOB BREAKTHROUGH SEEN

In what may be the first solid breakthrough in the two-year Philadelphia organized crime war, reputed mobster John "Scarface" Vagnoni yesterday surrendered to federal authorities in Sacramento.

Vagnoni, 73, disappeared last August amid speculation that he had been another victim of the Philadelphia mob war that was ignited by the killing of reputed Mafia chieftain Fredo Annaloro in March 1979.

According to informed sources, Vagnoni appeared at the Sacramento office of the FBI shortly before noon yesterday, requesting protective custody. "He's a very frightened man," one local police source said. "This may be just the break we need to bust the Philadelphia family wide open."

A 1978 report of the Pennsylvania Crime Commission named Vagnoni as one of Annaloro's top lieutenants, third in the line of succession behind Thomas "Chicken Man" Costa and Harry Angelucci. Costa was murdered in September 1979, when a bomb exploded on his front porch, virtually leveling his South Philadelphia house. In May 1980 the mutilated body of Angelucci was found stuffed in the trunk of his car at the Atlantic City Racetrack. He was the fourteenth victim of the mob struggle.

It is uncertain, however, that Vagnoni ever assumed control of the Philadelphia family following the Angelucci hit. "The way we see it, Vagnoni never took control," a high-ranking Philadelphia official said. "Either he didn't want the job, or more likely, somebody blocked him."

The Angelucci murder marked a dramatic change in the Philadelphia power struggle. His was the last confirmed mob killing, although four other Mafia figures have disappeared since then. The latest mobster to vanish was Angelo "Big Ox" Lucido, who was last seen on July 1 leaving a South Philadelphia restaurant.

Although opinions vary on the reason for Annaloro's murder and the ensuing war, the most widely held theory is that it involved a struggle over control of Atlantic City and its casino industry. "One way or another, the New York big boys—the Gambinos and the

[68]

Genoveses—were involved," the police source said. "If they didn't pull the trigger—and that's not certain—they fanned the flames. They wanted a weak Philadelphia family so that they could walk in and suck off the Atlantic City cream."

Who presently controls Atlantic City is not clear. Most insiders think that for the past year New York and Philadelphia have operated under some type of sharing agreement. "The truce is shaky as hell and could explode at any time," the source continued, "but so far it's held. If Vagnoni starts to sing, God knows what happens."

Born in Cinisi, Sicily, in 1908, Vagnoni came to the United States in 1927 and was naturalized in 1938. Although his arrest record, dating from 1928, contains more than 30 arrests, including murder, aggravated assault, and extortion, he was convicted only once. In 1949 he was given a suspended sentence and fined $50 for bookmaking. Since 1953 he has served as president of J-V Cheese Products. Based in South Philadelphia, the company is the largest distributor of Italian cheese in the Delaware Valley.

Although no official plans have been announced, it is believed that Vagnoni will be transported to a secure location near Philadelphia.

"A guy like Vagnoni knows where all the bodies are," a local source said. "He could sing for months. It should be one hell of a show."

Vince Grosso turned to the window again. The frigate was moored now. At that minute he only wanted to be down at the pier with his kids.

When would it end? And how did it all begin?

It was like a giant birthday party, except with big people instead of little kids.

They were dancing in the streets, hugging each other, some even crying, but in a happy way. The cars were blowing their horns; firecrackers were popping everywhere. Mr. Gennaro had stopped his gelato cart in the middle of the street and was giving away cones and Popsicles. For free!

At first Vinnie had been afraid, but Michael Agostino set him straight. Michael knew everything. After all, he was almost six.

"The war, Vinnie! It's over! We beat the Japs!"

Vinnie wasn't exactly sure what that meant. Only that it was important, something he should share with his mother. He ran to his house and bounded up the four marble steps.

He was about to call out the good news when he heard his mother scream. She knows already, he thought, no longer feeling quite so important.

He walked to the doorway of the kitchen. His mother was crying, but not in a happy way. She rocked back and forth in her chair, her head banging the kitchen table. Aunt Rose was trying to hold her, patting her like a baby. Uncle Fredo stood by the sink, staring at the floor.

"Why? Why?" his mother shrieked. "He was all I had."

Uncle Fredo shook his head without looking up. "I'm sorry, Concetta. I truly am. There was nothing I could do."

"Bastards! Filthy bastards! All of you! What's to become of me? And my son?"

His uncle looked up, and Vinnie saw his eyes. They were filled with tears. "I promise you, on the soul of our dead father, I will care for you and Vincenzo as my own."

Unseen, Vinnie crept away. Although he was very confused, his young mind understood one thing. He would never see his father again.

Fredo Annaloro was good to his word. He cared for Concetta Grosso and her son as his own. In many respects, Concetta fared far better than those women who still had their husbands. Spared the nagging financial uncertainty that afflicted so many widows, she knew, without a doubt, that the bills would be paid, food would be on the table, and, when the time came, the money for her son's education would be there. Silence was a small price to pay for such prosperity.

It was a source of considerable amazement in the neighborhood how well Concetta adjusted to life without a man. True, she sobbed throughout her husband's funeral, attempting to throw herself into the grave, but such conduct was almost obligatory at an Italian burial. Once that duty was performed, however, she settled nicely into a pleasant niche of acceptance.

Uneducated, Concetta nonetheless possessed a certain native intelligence as well as the ability to appraise herself with objectivity. She was not attractive. Her face and body carried the thick features of a peasant, and she had never cared enough to compensate for her physical deficiencies with careful grooming. A plain cotton smock and sturdy shoes designed for comfort rather than style were her uniform. There was neither the hope nor the desire that another man would come along. She knew, and most of the neighbors suspected, that Raymond Grosso had chosen her only because she was two months *incinta*. He had been convinced by Fredo Annaloro and a revolver placed to his temple that marriage was the only honorable course to pursue.

Sandy Ciccone, who never married and whom Vinnie was required to call Aunt Sandra, became Concetta's constant companion. Sometimes she even stayed overnight, something which Vinnie disliked for a reason he never fully understood. It was just a feeling, but one he was unable to shake, even as he grew older. Like Concetta, Vinnie did not seem to suffer, at least outwardly, from the loss of his father. His eight years at St. Raphael's were solid, if not exceptional. The nuns considered him an able student and extremely polite, although several remarked that it was impossible to really know him, to know what actually lay behind that placid exterior.

He had few close friends, but this was of his own choice. It wasn't that Vinnie was unfriendly or particularly shy. Instead, he seemed to be a model of self-containment, having naturally arrived at the fact that he *needed* no one except himself.

Despite the distance that he always maintained, Vinnie was accepted by his classmates for a number of reasons. He was inoffensive and even likable, he was a decent athlete, and, perhaps most important, even at a young age they realized that his Uncle Fredo was an important force in the neighborhood.

Only once during his grade school career was he directly challenged. It occurred at the beginning of seventh grade. Their nun was very young, fresh from the novitiate. Not only was she nervous, but she committed the mortal sin of trying to be nice. With a special fury unique to seventh graders, they pounced, doing their best to destroy her.

Franny Caruso was the worst. A head taller than the others, he constantly kept the young nun close to tears.

Consistent with his nature, Vinnie did not join in the assault. But although he felt sorry for his teacher, he did nothing to assist her, which was equally consistent. It simply wasn't his affair.

On a Friday afternoon, after two weeks of uninterrupted chaos, Caruso unleashed a barrage of spitballs. Naturally his victims returned the fire. Except Vinnie. He continued to read about Alexander the Great in his history textbook.

[71]

"Whatsa matter, Vinnie? Afraid?" Caruso taunted, loud enough so everyone could hear.

When he received no response, nor even an acknowledgment that he existed, Caruso's face reddened. "No guts, huh, Vinnie? I guess that's what happens when your mother's queer."

Vinnie knew that the joke had been made before, when they thought he was out of earshot. He had chosen to ignore them. It was the easiest way out for everyone. But this was different.

Calmly, with no sign of anger, Vinnie rose from his desk and walked across the room. Without a word and without changing expression, Vinnie fired a right into the bigger boy's stomach. Caruso doubled over, his right hand extended to defend himself. In one continuous motion, Vinnie flipped up the top of the nearest desk, grabbed Caruso's hand, and placed it on the desk. Then, with all his weight behind it, he brought the desktop down. Even those in the first row could hear the bones snap.

Caruso's knees sagged. Gently Vinnie lowered him into the seat. When he spoke, his voice was completely controlled. "If you ever say that again, Franny," he said almost matter-of-factly, "I'll kill you."

No one in St. Raphael's ever discussed Concetta Grosso again.

It was Fredo who decided that his nephew would attend St. Joseph's Prep rather than South Catholic. "Vinnie is special," he had told Concetta. "He should have the best education we can give him. At South, he'd be just another greaseball."

His years at the Prep were significant for two reasons. One was his exposure to the Jesuits. Vince, as he was now called, was both puzzled and motivated by the paradox of these marines of the clergy. The "pope's priests," they never hesitated to challenge Rome's authority. Stern disciplinarians, they loved poetry and good wine and classical Greek. Philosophers and theologians, they were also pragmatists who understood earthly power and grasped for it. Above all, they were proud. By their own proclamation, they were the best, just as their church proclaimed itself the one true faith.

It was perhaps the last time he would see this priest, whom he had come almost to love.

Father Joseph Scheetz smiled and slowly shook his head. "Twenty-three years of teaching, and you're my first failure."

Vince chuckled, the closest he ever came to an actual laugh. "You mean, my going to Villanova?"

"No, Vincent, though God knows I hate to lose you to the Augustinians. What you've done is destroy my confidence as an amateur psychologist. I've always prided myself on being able to read people, to know who they really were; but it's been four years, Vincent, and you're still a stranger."

Vince looked at the priest. Maybe he did love him. He wasn't sure. What he did know was that except for his uncle, he cared more for him than anyone else in the world.

"Don't be too hard on yourself, Father." The words came without any hint of self-pity, a detached assessment of the situation. "How can you expect to know me when I don't?"

"You will, Vincent. God has destined you for greatness. When you find the key, your impact on the world will be tremendous. I only pray that it will be for the greater glory of God."

The priest rose and gave his final blessing. Unaccountably his sadness was tinged with fear. "Keep part of us with you always, Vincenzo Grosso. Ad majorem Dei gloriam."

During the last part of Vince's high school career he began the relationship with his uncle that lasted until Fredo Annaloro's death. From the beginning Fredo had functioned as a father figure. It was clear that he felt a responsibility for his nephew, which Vince guessed had something to do with what had happened in the kitchen on V-J Day. Whenever a school function required the presence of a father, Fredo was there. He carefully observed Vince's progress in school, but from a distance, so as not to undermine Concetta's authority.

Sunday dinner, the multicourse Italian ritual beginning shortly after mass, was always at Fredo's, as were the holiday gatherings.

All this Vince had taken for granted, his young mind sensing that they were acts of duty, not necessarily of love, on his uncle's part. As a result, Vince's feeling toward Fredo was one of acceptance, in much the same way that he submitted to the authority of his teachers. Simply, they were there.

When Vince turned sixteen, he sensed the change. It came about gradually, as if his uncle were carefully constructing a mosaic. It wasn't so much that they were together more frequently, as that Fredo *wanted* to be with his nephew. And even though it was never discussed in his presence, Vince sensed that the major decisions concerning his future were now being made by Fredo.

Naturally, by this time Vince had heard the rumors about his uncle. The newspapers were always calling him a mobster. Actually an *alleged* mobster. They were very careful about that.

This mattered little at the Prep, since most were unaware of Vince's relationship to the man who was now being called the head of the Philadelphia crime syndicate. Even if they had known, the effect would have been minimal, since the student body was so diverse that who controlled the Philly mob was of little consequence.

Not so downtown. In South Philadelphia you knew the players. It was there that Vince sensed the change in how others treated him. Not that there was anything specific, but it was there: a certain deference; an unspoken admission that he was special.

Vince found it difficult to believe that his uncle was a Mafia chieftain. It wasn't that he weighed the morality of it. You didn't do that in South Philly. The mob was an accepted part of life, just like politics, the Eagles, or cheesesteaks. You never stopped to consider whether it was good or bad. There wasn't any point. It was there, and it would remain.

But to Vince, Fredo Annaloro was miscast for the part. He was too gentle, too loving to picture as a man who had fought his way to the top of the outfit.

Yet, as Vince slowly discovered, it was true. In a very real sense, Fredo Annaloro was an American success story, a Sicilian Jack Kelly.

Forty years before, he had left Villaba, a mountain village of squat, earthen-floored houses, with his family. All their worldly possessions were carried in two battered suitcases. Neither Fredo nor his sisters wore shoes. In fact, Fredo could still remember standing on the pier at Palermo, his mother warning him of splinters, as they waited for the launch that would take them to Naples for the steamer to America.

It is one of the larger ironies of life that the most powerful crime syndicate in the world owed its success, possibly its very existence, to the religious and moral convictions of decent Christians. Surfeited by the violence of the war to end all wars, appalled by the release of passion which followed it, they turned the nation inward. Rejecting the League of Nations and its opportunity for

[74]

world leadership, America devoted its attention to the evils of Demon Rum. Fredo Annaloro was barely ten when the Eighteenth Amendment was ratified. His life, and ultimately his death, would be controlled by this event.

While crime has existed since the beginning of time and would have continued even without Prohibition, America's going dry was the *sine qua non* of the entrenchment of the American Mafia. It provided Sicilians the opportunity to demonstrate their superiority in organization, innovation, and violence, an opportunity that was quickly seized. When repeal arrived, they had gleaned billions from the bootlegging market. With that base, they went on to construct an empire that dwarfed General Motors.

Fredo was a good soldier. He did what he was told, efficiently and without question. What distinguished him from the run-of-the-mill button man was his ability to bring people together. He had no objection to violence, but only when necessary as a last resort. Violence had a way of begetting violence, and too much violence was bad for business. Better to make friends.

By temperament, he was an ideal choice for involving the family in legitimate business—safe, solid ventures like cheese, produce, laundries, and vending companies. True to his code, he made friends, and the family made money.

Despite his successes, Fredo might have remained a capo forever had it not been for a fateful decision by the boss in the fall of 1957. Rejecting Fredo's advice, Joseph Maida chose to attend a summit meeting of Mafia chieftains at the home of Joe Barbera in upstate New York. Almost unknown before the meeting, the town of Apalachin would have remained so had it not been for a group of enterprising state police officers. Noticing the large number of out-of-state license plates, they decided to pull a raid. Dozens of mobsters were arrested, and still more, leaving their Cadillacs behind, fled on foot through the woods. Newspaper headlines trumpeted accounts of the rout from coast to coast. A half century of anonymity had been shattered in fewer than ten minutes. When Joe Valachi, breaking his oath of *omertà,* turned canary several years later, La Cosa Nostra became a household term.

Joseph Maida was one of the victims of Apalachin. It had been his fate to be answering a call of nature when the troopers struck. He took his arrest stoically, making but one request. "You guys mind if I wipe myself?" he had asked.

When that small task had been performed, Maida was turned over to federal authorities and booked for conspiracy. Three weeks later he fled to Sicily, renouncing his American citizenship.

Maida's flight created a severe vacuum in the family's leadership when underboss Sal Rugnetta died suddenly from complications following a routine appendectomy. Both Fredo Annaloro and Antonio "Jock Itch" Pollina moved to take control. Pollina, who had earned his nickname by his propensity for scratching his crotch, was the most senior *capo* in the family. Never known for his intelligence, he compensated for this shortcoming with a ruthlessness which made him feared even among his veteran compatriots. His primary delight in life was personally supervising the outfit's shylocking operation, conducting a clinic on how best to persuade a deadbeat to fulfill his obligation. First offenders were treated gently: rarely more than an oral warning—accompanied, of course, by several obligatory knees to the groin, sufficient to induce vomiting but, as a general rule, not severe enough to actually crush the testicles.

Depending on the amount owed, a second offender could expect to have a thumb, an arm, or a leg broken. When it came to someone who was behind for the third time, however, Pollina felt compelled to shed his nice guy image. At the very least an appendage had to be removed. His favorite was an ear, usually severed with surgical precision by a razor-sharp stiletto, but on occasions, when he was in a bad mood, he was known to perform the operation with his teeth.

It is not known how Pollina would have dealt with anyone foolish enough to incur his wrath a fourth time. For relatively obvious reasons, the situation never arose. The closest call involved a twenty-year-old construction worker. He was a good kid, actually. His only failing was trying to impress the ladies on a laborer's salary. He was on his lunch break at the construction site, a low-income high rise at Thirteenth and Fitzwater, when Pollina arrived. What was left of his ear had almost healed, and his hair now covered the scar. But the pain. He would never forget the pain. His stomach tightened, and all at once he knew. He used the stairway, which had been completed to the fifth floor. That would do. When he reached the edge, he looked down. Pollina was watching him, his face distorted with a savage grin. He turned away, facing south toward his home. Even now his mother would

[76]

be in the kitchen preparing dinner. He realized how much he loved her and how much he would miss never seeing her again. Then, after saying a good act of contrition just the way the nuns had taught, he jumped.

"Young kids ain't got no balls," Pollina muttered, and turned away.

Pollina reacted to the challenge for family leadership in the only fashion he knew. He put out a contract on Fredo's life, reluctantly deciding that it would be too dangerous to handle the assignment himself. Within minutes of the decision, Fredo had been warned. He gassed up his car and drove nonstop to Buffalo, fiefdom of Sylvio Pagalucci. It was just past midnight when he arrived, but he was greeted with courtesy. After the customary weapons check Fredo was ushered into Pagalucci's study, where he exercised the privilege of any family member.

"Don Sylvio, I respectfully petition the *commissione* for a hearing."

As Pagalucci listened, Fredo described the struggle in Philadelphia, the impasse over leadership, and the contract on his life. He was careful to remain completely calm since any display of fear would be seen as weakness, which in turn could be fatal. The man hearing his plea, dressed in a flannel robe, seemed the picture of gentility, but Fredo knew better. Sylvio Pagalucci was probably the most feared of all Mafia leaders. He demanded total obedience, and anyone who dared oppose him forfeited his right to survive. He was particularly ruthless on those who betrayed a family confidence, reserving for them what became a Pagalucci trademark. "Pagging," which occurred *before* the victim was killed, consisted of severing his penis and stuffing it in his mouth. Not surprisingly, it tended to discourage disloyalty.

The case which Fredo made had merit: a bloodbath in Philadelphia, on the heels of Apalachin, was bad for the organization. This was a time to maintain a low profile, to continue the move into legitimate business. Fredo could accomplish this. Pollina could not.

Impressed, Pagalucci scheduled a hearing for the following month in Wildwood, New Jersey. Until then Fredo's safety was assured. He was under the protection of the *commissione*. No one, not even Antonio Pollina, dare thwart such an edict.

A three-member *arguiamenda*, chaired by Pagalucci, heard the

[77]

case. It was an uneven contest. Pollina, a shackled giant stumbling crudely through the maze of *commissione* protocol, was no match for the brains and finesse of Fredo.

The hearing concluded with an official decision: as would quickly be known downtown, Fredo Annaloro was the new boss of the Philadelphia family and *rappresentante ufficiale* to the *commissione.*

Unspoken, but no less certain, was the fate of Antonio Pollina. He had issued a contract on the life of another member. He had been overruled by the supreme authority of La Cosa Nostra. His life was now in the hands of Fredo Annaloro.

The new boss was counseled to move swiftly. Set an example. Pollina's death would send an unmistakable message that a firm hand was in control.

Pollina was summoned to Fredo's office, the back room of the United Vending Company, which had cornered the cigarette and candy market. In the week that had passed since Wildwood, the change in Pollina had been startling. No longer was he the ruthless intimidator. He was a beaten human being, existing in a netherworld between life and death. Since childhood his only instinct had been to fight, but now even one with his limited intelligence realized the futility of resistance. If he accepted his fate, with dignity like a man, his wife and children would enjoy a comfortable life. The code required that, and he knew that Fredo would comply.

As he faced his conqueror, he groped for the words that he had memorized. Angie Lucido and Dominic Barrone were there, and this made it more difficult. A man never likes to humble himself before an audience. Still, he began, in Sicilian.

"Don Fredo, the commission has spoken, and I accept its will. By the code, my life is yours. I ask you to spare it, to permit me to return to Sicily. I swear on the life of my children that I will never trouble you again. If you deny my request, then I beg you to permit me to die with dignity. Quickly. A bullet to the heart. My body left intact so my loved ones can look at me one last time."

Only the sound of a typewriter in an adjoining office broke the silence. For what seemed like an eternity, Fredo stared at this master of torture who now was begging not to be mutilated. He glanced at Barrone and Lucido. His lieutenants betrayed no emotion, but they were ready. At Fredo's command, they would remove Pollina from the living.

Finally the new don spoke. "Both your requests are denied."

Pollina's knees sagged. Sweat from his armpits trickled down his side. Now at last he would feel the pain that he had inflicted on so many.

Fredo spoke again. "I have been chosen to lead our *borgotta*. Its success depends upon the decisions which I make. I would be a fool, a goddamn *stupido,* to begin by losing my best capo."

Only when Fredo smiled did Pollina realize the meaning of his words.

"Don Fredo," he wept, falling to his knees.

Fredo rose and walked to him. Gently he raised him to his full height, where he looked down at his leader.

"Antonio, my dear friend, what is done is done. We disagreed, but that is over. You will keep your *regime.* You will control our collection operation. Together we will make our family great."

When Pollina was gone, he turned to Lucido and Barrone. "Well, my friends?"

They remained silent.

"You think I made a mistake."

"You're the boss, Don Fredo," Barrone answered. "It is our job to obey, not to criticize."

"But you think I made a mistake," Fredo insisted.

Again, Barrone answered, "With all due respect, Don Fredo, yes."

Fredo smiled and walked to the window. Pollina was crossing the street, a giant again. "Remember these words, my friends. Anyone can kill. Only a few can give life. Even more than that, Antonio has been given back his manhood. He will follow me through hell."

Vince Grosso knew how his uncle had spared Pollina's life. Dominic Barrone had told him, just as Fredo knew he would. It was then that Vince realized how special his uncle was.

It was Fredo's idea that Vince attend Villanova. Its geography suited him: close enough to keep the ties but far enough away to develop a measure of independence. Though Vince could have commuted, Fredo insisted that he live on campus.

[79]

"Four years of college aren't much," he had said. "Get the full flavor of it."

In all likelihood, Vince would never have tasted the full flavor of college life had it not been for Kevin Murray. They met midway through their freshman year, when Kevin was engineering his first drive into campus politics. He had put together a complete slate of candidates, lacking only a Commerce and Finance resident.

The last thing in Vince's mind was involvement in a campus election, particularly as a candidate. It wasn't his style. After being exposed to Kevin's non-stop sales pitch for an hour, however, he was wavering.

"Besides," Kevin said, winding down, "if we lose, we can really use a guy like you."

"What do you mean?"

"Well, if we can't beat 'em at the polls, you can get the mob to rub 'em out for us."

Shocked, Vince was unable to speak. How did he know? How *could* he know?

If Kevin sensed that anything was wrong, he never let on. "After all," he continued matter-of-factly, "all you dagos are connected one way or the other."

Vince Grosso had a choice: he could handle this smart-assed Irishman the way he had handled Franny Caruso, or he could come aboard.

Slowly he allowed himself a slight grin and extended his hand. "Count me in, you crazy bastard."

They made an improbable pair, with personalities as different as their appearances. By the end of high school Vince had reached his full height, six feet two. Without any conscious effort, his weight remained constant at 175. His olive skin appeared to glisten, making it always seem that he had just returned from a month in Florida. The hair, a shade lighter than jet black, was kept at medium length and, as with the very well-groomed, always appeared to have been cut the week before.

He was one of the fortunate few who was born to wear clothes. Whether it was casual khakis or a three-piece suit, the cloth seemed to hang just right. Pants—uncuffed, of course—just touching the shoe without a trace of a break. Suit coat sleeves at

[80]

the precise length to display a quarter inch of shirt. Shoes highly polished without the slightest crease.

Regardless of the time of day, even after an all-night beer blast, Vince Grosso was perfection. But his most remarkable feature, the first thing one noticed about him, was his eyes.

Pale green, they seemed to slant, providing an almost Oriental effect, which, when contrasted with his bronze skin and dark hair, produced a startling result. They were eyes that pierced, not unlike the luminescent stare of a cat. Rarely was there an expression, only the same sense of mystery that had flustered the nuns of St. Raphael's and the Jesuits of St. Joe's.

There was no such air of mystery surrounding Kevin Murray. He carried his emotions on his shirt sleeve, which, like the rest of him, was generally rolled up and wrinkled. He was a half foot shorter than Vince, but his weight was about the same, depending on whether or not he was on a conditioning kick. His diet, in fact, reflected the core of his personality. Nothing in moderation. He was either gorging himself well past the point of gluttony or surviving on a Spartan regimen of fewer than five hundred calories. In either case, he was, as a reporter later described him, "short, pale, and rumpled, a door-to-door salesman who gets one foot in the door and begins his hard sell."

It was an approach that was difficult to reject, for like measles, Kevin Murray was contagious. He bounced, rather than walked, from one challenge to another, infecting those around him with his enthusiasm. When he spoke, he came at you like a machine gun, rarely pausing to reload.

He affected irritation toward anyone who called him a redhead, yet there was clearly enough of a rusty tinge to justify the label. His blue eyes were direct windows to his soul, conveying precisely his emotions. He would have failed miserably at poker, for as another reporter commented, Kevin Murray was "as spontaneous as a hiccup." ("It could have been worse," Kevin had countered. "He could have called me a fart.")

Since both Vince and Kevin were destined for lives of conflict, Villanova was the perfect training ground. Vince never expressed himself publicly on the subject, but Kevin, when he had become one of the most well-known, loved, and despised figures in Pennsylvania, put it into words. "Villanova taught me that there's al-

[81]

ways someone out there trying to kick you in the groin. The trick is to kick him first."

For almost four years it was Kevin, the general, and Vince, his chief lieutenant, slugging it out with the conservative Augustinian administration, trying to "pull this goddamn school out of the nineteenth century before the twenty-first begins."

Kevin's master strategy was simple: arouse an indifferent student body, seize its leadership, and confront the Auggies from a position of strength. The plan succeeded beyond his wildest dreams and the deepest fears of the administration. As they entered their senior year, Kevin and his troops controlled it all: student council; class offices; student newspaper and radio station. They were ready at last to joust with the Auggies.

When both sides looked back, it would all seem insignificant. In just a few years a new generation, a new way of life would emerge. Like a prairie fire out of control, fueled, if not ignited, by Vietnam, the New Left would engulf a system that almost crumbled and would never again be the same.

Right on, all power to the people! Mario Savio. You don't have to be a weatherman to see which way the wind blows. SDS. Abbie Hoffman. Venceremos. *Black Panthers. Up against the wall, motherfucker! Madison. Berkeley. Hey, hey, LBJ, how many babies did you kill today? Dr. Spock, Eldridge Cleaver. Chicago, 1968. Off the pigs! Kent State. Burn, baby, burn!*

By comparison, the war fought by Kevin and Vince seemed mundane: the installation of female cheerleaders; a used-book exchange to break the monopoly of the university bookstore; better food and service in the cafeteria; a published student evaluation of courses and profs.

They won each of those battles and a number of others, but the price in bitterness and fear was almost too high. Particularly for Kevin. ("When it comes to the Auggie shit list, only Martin Luther's ahead of me—and I'm gaining on him.")

Twice he was almost expelled, his scholarship was revoked, and his application to the law school was rejected. Worst of all, because of a course technicality, he was not permitted to graduate with his class, receiving his diploma in August after a two-credit course in library science.

Through it all, Kevin hung tough. He knew the Auggies played for keeps, and he was willing to accept the dangers. Like a rock, silent but immovable, Vince backed him. When Kevin became incensed over a particular administration outrage, cursing and kicking furniture, Vince would remain impassive, his eyes fixed on the ceiling. After the tirade had ended, he would sum things up with a brief sentence: "Now that you've finished, let's figure out a way to stick it up their ass."

Pat Carney was the voice of moderation, counseling compromise rather than confrontation. Kevin respected his opinion, although usually rejecting it, and never questioned his loyalty. Pat was a friend, a good friend. Still, Kevin couldn't shake the feeling that something was missing, something inside.

Only once, during a heated argument, did Kevin let his feelings surface. "Patrick, goddammit, I love you dearly, but you don't have any balls!"

"It's got nothing to do with balls," Pat replied. "It's a matter of perspective. There's a time and a place to fight, Kevin, but this is only college. It's not worth getting expelled and ruining your life."

Kevin shook his head sadly. "You've got it all wrong, Pat. You can't live life the way you run the mile, waiting for the gun lap to sprint. It's gotta be all the way, all the time. If you run away now, you'll spend the rest of your life running."

But if Kevin learned to fight, Vince learned even more. He learned how to live, to actually enjoy himself, and Kevin was his teacher. Spaced around winning elections and fighting Augustinians was an endless string of parties, ball games, and other assorted forms of organized mayhem. Kevin prided himself on having developed around him a hard inner corps, his Dirtballs, who could roll up their sleeves to get the job, any job, done but who could also let their hair down and raise pure hell.

It was a conscious effort on his part, designed to highlight the difference between his troops and those whom they replaced as student leaders. The Tweeds, he had labeled them, the button-down, image-conscious elite that for years had governed the student body with a mediocrity carefully calculated to appease the Augustinians. In return, a Tweed was assured of a nice spread in the yearbook, selection to *Who's Who*, and a number of cushy job referrals.

Kevin and his Dirtballs changed all that. "Beat the Tweeds!"

became their rallying cry, and they pledged themselves to crushing them at the polls and embarrassing them socially. On both counts they succeeded admirably.

Sipping a beer, a faint grin on his face, Vince would watch his leader take control of a party and turn it into a horror show. Maybe it was a beer fight or a moon contest or a few filthy verses of "Hot Nuts." Whatever approach Kevin chose, it invariably worked. He was Prince Hal, reveling in debauchery with his Falstaffs, knowing that tomorrow, he would again be Henry, leading his troops into battle.

At first Vince had been content to remain a spectator, but this was impermissible.

"C'mon, Dapper Dago!" Kevin would bellow, emptying a quart of beer on his head. "Loosen up. You may look like a Tweed, but inside you're all Dirtball."

Slowly Vince bowed to the inevitable, and to his total surprise, it was fun. He could never be like his buddy—Kevin was in a class by himself—but he began to earn his credentials as at least a quasi-Dirtball.

What he came to enjoy most were the visits to Kevin's home, the way Kevin joked with his parents and teased his little sister, the way he argued with his brother about sports and politics. It was so natural, so right. This was a home with love, and for the first time Vince Grosso had a glimpse of what he wanted from life.

They stood on the balcony, just the two of them, staring out into the darkness of the country club grounds. The band was playing "Moonlight Cocktails," and the melody drifted past them, disappearing in the pines surrounding the third hole.

They had wanted to be alone one last time, to say something special. Instead, they stood in silence.

"Hard to believe it's over," Vince finally said. "Four years."

"Four great years. A lot of things to remember."

They lapsed into silence again. The band had taken a break, and the sound of shattering glass replaced the music. The Class of '63 was going out in style.

Again, Vince spoke. "I almost punched you out that day in the Pi Shoppe, when you asked me to run."

"After what we've been through, maybe you should have."

[84]

"No way. It wouldn't have been the same without you. I'm in your debt, you crazy bastard. More than you'll ever know."

"For what?"

"For changing my life." He put his arm around Kevin. Then he summoned the courage to say the words that Kevin had used so many times but that he had found impossible. "I love you, Kevin."

Before Kevin could answer, the sliding door opened. It was Bonnie Peterson, Pat Carney's fiancée. Sobbing, she threw herself into Kevin's arms. She was Pat's now, but once, long ago, she had been Kevin's.

"Bonnie, what is it?" Kevin asked.

"It's Pat. He broke our engagement. He's entering the seminary."

Pat Carney was still running.

Five

FRESH from a stint in the FBI, Kevin Murray was prosecuting criminals in Philadelphia. Some of those criminals, the ones who could pay top dollar, were defended by Vince Grosso. The Reverend Patrick Carney, two years out of the seminary, had already begun his climb up the diocesan ladder. And Tyrone Walker, age eleven, was hawking the Philadelphia Bulletin *at the corner of Sixty-third and Market. A kid with street sense, he somehow knew that the paper he sold today carried pure dynamite.*

HIGH COURT OVERTURNS ABORTION LAWS

In a landmark decision, the United States Supreme Court today ruled that state laws prohibiting abortion violate a woman's right to privacy and must be overturned.

In a 7–2 decision, the court struck the abortion laws of Texas and Georgia, both of which made abortion a crime unless medically necessary to save the life of the mother.

The majority opinion, written by Justice Harry A. Blackmun, prohibited any state regulations of abortion during the first trimester, or three months, of pregnancy. Any restrictions imposed during the second trimester must be "reasonably related to maternal health." Only in the third trimester may a state consider the welfare of the fetus. During the final three months, abortions may still be prohibited unless "necessary . . . for the preservation of the life or health of the mother."

The Court expressly rejected the argument, held mainly by the

Catholic Church, that human life begins at conception. "We need not resolve the difficult question of when life begins," the Court wrote. "When those trained in . . . medicine, philosophy, and theology are unable to arrive at any consensus, the judiciary . . . is not in a position to speculate as to the answer."

Although several states, most notably New York, have recently enacted liberalized abortion laws, the majority still outlaw abortion. Like those in Texas and Georgia, these laws will now be void.

"I'm ecstatic," declared Cindy Berson, Assistant Director of the National Association to Repeal Abortion Laws (NARAL). "This proves that our system truly works. At long last, woman will be permitted the freedom of choice guaranteed by the Constitution."

Thomas Farrelly, Executive Director of the United States Catholic Conference, reacted differently. "The Court has granted a license to slaughter our unborn," he said. "This is one of the saddest days in our nation's history."

It was January 22, 1973. Most experts believed that the abortion battle had finally ended. Instead, it had just begun.

Kevin Murray pushed the recline button on the armrest and settled back. The next hour and a half were his.

More than anything else, it was the train that kept him in the legislature. It enabled him to commute to Harrisburg every day, mitigating, if not eliminating, the guilt about family that was an inescapable part of public life. Except when a floor debate raged late into the night, he came home every evening. He prided himself on being around for the important things: knowing what the kids were doing in school; helping them with their homework; watching their ball games. And he felt obligated to help Karen, with the dishes, getting the little ones to bed, and the hundred other things that kept her constantly in motion and threatened to turn her old before her time.

It was less a labor of love than an act of compulsion. Kevin Murray had to be as good a father and husband as he was a legislator. The demons inside permitted nothing less.

He lit a Winston and gazed out the window, trying to unwind. The Susquehanna glimmered in the late-afternoon sun, and with a stab of sadness he thought of the canoe trips he would never take again with the Sarge. It still didn't seem possible.

[87]

The river veered away from the tracks, giving center stage to the four giant cones which suddenly appeared, the most famous cooling towers in the world: Three Mile Island.

Two years before there had been panic throughout central Pennsylvania. A hastily scrolled message on the wall of the men's room in the Harrisburg train station had described it best: "Will the last person out of Harrisburg please turn out the lights?"

Now the panic was gone, and TMI had become a tourist attraction. People flocked there to have their pictures taken in the shadow of the towers, proof positive that they had visited the place where the China syndrome had almost come true.

"You must have had a busy day, Kevin."

It was an attorney from General Services who got off at Coatesville. Naturally, Kevin didn't know his name. He was terrible with names.

The lawyer was holding the latest edition of the *Bulletin.* On the front page were Kevin and Craig Harrington, beneath the four-column headline: NATION'S TOUGHEST ABORTION BILL INTRODUCED.

"Yeah," Kevin answered. "Life's no fun if it's dull."

"As long as you're around, things will never be dull."

It was starting again, the same emotional roller coaster that had torn him apart so many times before. The hate mail would pour in, together with letters from those who wanted him canonized. More than any other issue, abortion was news. The media couldn't get enough of it, and they would milk this one for all it was worth.

There would be radio and television debates, a running battle in the papers, and challenges to defend his position before hostile audiences. He would accept them all. If you were pro-life, you could never duck. You had to be willing to go into the arena and slug it out with the lions.

But why him? Why was Kevin Murray always the point man? The press had repeatedly asked that question, almost as often as he asked it of himself. He still wasn't completely sure.

Of one thing he had no doubt: Abortion was an evil that had to be fought. There had been no magical moment when, like Paul on the road to Damascus, he had arrived at this conclusion. He had felt no outrage when the Supreme Court handed down its decision eight years before. Busy adjusting to his new role as prosecutor, he hadn't even noticed. Yet when he had announced for office and the inevitable question was asked, there had been no hesitation. In the strongest possible terms he spelled out his total opposition to the "killing of unborn children."

The easiest answer, the one most often seized upon by the press precisely because it was so easy, was his Catholicism. Rome beat out the cadence, and the Kevin Murrays marched.

Kevin had pondered this point and, as objectively as anyone can be when analyzing himself, had rejected it. The longer he served in public office, the more certain he became that many of his values had been formed by sixteen years of Catholic education. The discipline, first of the nuns, then of the priests, had toughened him, had unknowingly prepared him for the challenge ahead. But in those sixteen years abortion had never been mentioned. There had been no need. Abortion was not only a sin but a crime. Had someone suggested, during a high school or college class, that in a few years abortion on demand would be legal or, for that matter, that prayer in public schools would be forbidden, he would have been laughed out of the room.

No, his religion wasn't the answer. The Church condemned abortion, and Kevin agreed. But had he been a Jew, a Protestant, or an atheist, he would have taken the same stand.

Was it ego, a craving for the recognition that comes so easily to one who embraces the pro-life standard? Kevin admitted to himself that this was at least a partial possibility. He *did* have an ego, and he *did* crave recognition. Otherwise, he would not have entered politics.

From the outset, from the beginning of his first campaign, he had a standard answer when asked why he ran.

"A man runs for office for two main reasons. First, he feels that he's the best man for the job. He feels that he can make a contribution, to change things for the better. If he didn't feel that way, he wouldn't be justified in running.

"But there's another reason, which only a few will admit. He runs because he *wants* the job, he *wants* to see his name in the paper, he *wants* to be someone. Any candidate who denies this is a damn liar.

"It's ego, pure and simple, and there's nothing wrong with it. In fact, you can't succeed without it. In anything. If I'm in the hospital for an operation, I want my doctor to be an egotist. I want him

[89]

to be the type of person who will be personally insulted if I don't completely recover. That's ego. The key is to admit you have it and to know how to keep it under control.

"And please, spare me those reluctant warriors who claim they don't really want to run, but duty calls. Whenever I hear a candidate talk like that, I'm happy to help solve his problem by voting against him. Give me the guy who *wants* the job. Once he gets it, he'll know what to do."

More than anything else, what drove Kevin into the front lines of the abortion struggle was something over which he had little or no control. Even before birth, human beings are imbued with natures, personalities that govern their conduct throughout their lives. Whether they will be compulsive or laid-back, optimistic or pessimistic, affectionate or distant is a matter that has been predetermined. Often it is a question of genes, of traits inherited from parents, but at least as frequently there is no discernible pattern that accounts for why a person is what he or she is. Otherwise, why the dramatic difference in children born of the same parents and raised in the same environment?

This is not to embrace the Calvinistic belief that each human, regardless of actions, is predestined for a particular end. As the Baltimore Catechism on which Kevin was raised had said, man possesses an intellect and free will. He is free to think and to choose and, like it or not, to be held accountable for his choices.

The road which he takes, the end at which he arrives are of his own doing. But *how* he gets there, the *style* which he uses in traveling down those roads are the result of his nature.

Kevin understood this. "You are what you are, and there's not a hell of a lot you can do about it. Try to be something you're not, and you end up fucking things up and getting an ulcer."

It was Kevin's nature to be a lightning rod, always a child of controversy. He was born to be in the middle of things, stirring up the caldron. It simply wasn't possible for him to be on the sidelines. Once he believed in something, the rest was automatic.

If the Augustinians wouldn't loosen their grip, if teachers were allowed to strike, if unborn children were being killed, then Kevin Murray would be there. Now, once again, it was time to go into battle.

At least the most tedious part had ended, the months of preparation when he and Craig had repeatedly gone over each line, each word. They had enlisted doctors and lawyers from across the country in the effort. They had to be perfect. One mistake, and like so many times in the past, the courts would strike it down. The goddamn courts.

The morning news conference had gone fairly well. Eager for the revival of the war, the media people had packed it, transforming the conference room into a maze of cables, lights, and microphones.

Kevin handled the opening statement. That was fortunate. Though most of the reporters supported abortion, they personally liked Kevin. Craig Harrington they detested, an opinion which was certainly not unique to the news media. In a shade more than two years Harrington had managed to alienate almost everyone in Harrisburg, including most of his colleagues in the House.

The legislation which Kevin described was not news to most of the reporters. For the past six months, while the bill was being prepared, they had bombarded Kevin with questions. Unlike Harrington, he always responded. He had a rule that he never gave a "no comment" to the press. That was a cop-out. And if you were pro-life, it was also dangerous. You began with the premise that the news media was against you. If you refused to respond to questions, the issue was no longer the bill but "what does he have to hide?" It wasn't fair, and it wasn't logical; but it was reality.

Actually Kevin and Harrington had begun work on the bill more than a year before, in the spring of 1980. Their intent was to draft the most restrictive abortion law in the country. The Supreme Court said they couldn't outlaw abortion, so they would try to regulate the hell out of it. The trick was to find every legal loophole and use it to their advantage.

In words that would repeatedly be hurled back at him by his opponents, Kevin had spelled it out to a *Bulletin* reporter. "Ultimate victory for the pro-life movement can come only through a human life amendment to the United States Constitution. Congress has to start that ball rolling. But in the meantime, those of us on the state level have to be as creative and aggressive as possible in coming up with laws to limit and restrict abortion. Until we get the human life amendment, we have to fight a holding action, a guerrilla war, to make abortions as difficult as possible to obtain. And if everything we do results in just one abortion not being performed, just one child being born instead of killed, then

[91]

everything we've done—indeed, my entire career—has been worthwhile."

And so, in furtherance of that guerrilla war, they had gone to work. They requested the assistance of Americans United for Life, a pro-life think tank in Chicago, for a review of all state laws as well as all the court decisions in every state and federal jurisdiction. This was to be a smorgasbord bill, selecting the very best from each of the pro-life menus. If they could pull it off, the impact would be felt far beyond the boundaries of Pennsylvania. Their bill could become a model for other state legislatures.

It had been their hope to have the bill ready for the fall of 1980. Ironically, they were postponed by the first favorable decision by the United States Supreme Court. On June 30, 1980, the High Court ruled that a prohibition against the use of federal funds for Medicaid abortions, except to save the life of the mother or in cases of rape or incest, was constitutional.

Kevin and Harrington reacted swiftly. Two days after the Court ruling they introduced a bill similarly restricting state funds.

After a struggle of almost six months it passed both houses, just before the legislature adjourned *sine die*. A reluctant governor, never known for taking tough stands, finally signed it into law a week before Christmas.

The law was still enjoined pending the court appeals that always accompanied pro-life legislation, but although the delays were frustrating, Kevin could wait. The Supreme Court had already spoken, and for once it was on their side. Sooner or later the law would go into effect and Pennsylvania's policy of tax-funded abortion on demand would end. Instead of more than thirteen thousand Medicaid abortions every year, there would be fewer than a hundred.

When the new term began in January, their batteries were recharged. Both had won reelection—Kevin in a landslide and Harrington in a squeaker—and both had taken time off during the holidays. As he always did, Kevin had spent Christmas week at home with Karen and the kids. With a bachelor's freedom, Harrington had flown to Vail, to ski during the day and divide his evening hours between reading the Bible and getting laid.

Now, eight months into the new term, they were ready. The bill

[92]

was good. Very good. Even Harrington, who considered himself a perfectionist and whom Kevin considered a "nit-picking pain in the ass," pronounced himself satisfied.

Detailed in the outline distributed at the news conference were the major provisions of the bill that would tear Pennsylvania apart for the next year:

- An informed consent section would require the doctor to inform each woman, prior to the abortion, of the physical and psychological dangers of abortion, the abortion procedure to be utilized, and available alternatives to abortion, including the location of nearby adoption agencies. Printed materials describing the characteristics of the unborn child, including color photographs of unborn children at two-week stages from fertilization to birth, must be made available to the woman.
- Except in cases of a medical emergency, there must be a twenty-four-hour waiting period from the time a woman was so advised until the abortion was performed.
- Unemancipated, minor females must receive the consent of both parents or court approval through an expedited, private court procedure before having an abortion.
- Whenever an unborn child might be viable, a second, independent doctor must be present in the operating room. That second doctor would neither assist in nor interfere with the abortion. Once the abortion was completed, he would do everything possible to save the life of the aborted child.
- Whenever an unborn child might be viable, the physician must utilize the abortion procedure most likely to produce a live birth, unless such a procedure would increase danger to maternal life or health.
- Abortion coverage in any health plan for state employees would be prohibited.
- All private health insurers must offer a plan which did not cover abortions, at a lower premium than those providing abortion coverage.
- All abortions after the first trimester must be performed in a hospital on an inpatient basis.
- The father of the unborn child must be notified before the abortion is performed.

[93]

- A death certificate must be issued for each aborted unborn child, with his remains disposed of in the same fashion as all other deceased humans.
- The remains of each aborted child must be examined by a board-certified pathologist, with a report filed in Harrisburg.
- Any referral fees for abortion services would be prohibited.
- Any fee paid for abortion services until a diagnosis of pregnancy had been made would be prohibited.
- Strict quarterly reporting for all physicians and hospitals performing abortions would be required. Although the identity of the woman receiving the abortion would not be disclosed, all other information would be included in the report. Such reports should be open for public inspection and copying.
- An infanticide section would require health care providers to provide ordinary medical care to all infants, regardless of physical or mental defects.
- There would be a statement of intent, expressing the preference of the legislature for childbirth over abortion and its belief that human life begins at conception.
- All individuals and organizations conducting in vitro fertilization (test tube conception) would be required to file in Harrisburg quarterly reports, which would be open for public inspection and copying.
- All abortifacients (drugs or devices used to produce an abortion as opposed to preventing conception) must be labeled as such and would be available only upon a written prescription from a physician. Said physician, in providing the prescription, must advise the woman that the product is an abortifacient.
- There would be strict criminal and civil penalties for violation of any provision of the bill.
- A private attorney general section would grant legal standing to any individual to seek an injunction if he had reason to believe that a section of the bill had been or was about to be violated.

When Kevin finished describing the bill's provisions, Harrington took over. Until that point the mood in the room had been good. Kevin had cracked a few jokes, and there was almost the feeling of friendship.

Lighting a cigarette, which he had felt that he had earned by a professional analysis of a complex bill, Kevin could feel the mood change perceptibly as his partner began. It was evident in the eyes of the reporters. Hostility had replaced humor. Trust had given way to skepticism.

Harrington spoke for ten minutes, rarely using a word of fewer than four syllables. He condemned the atrocity of abortion. He challenged his House colleagues to join him in the crusade for life. And worst of all, he ended by lecturing the press: "This legislation is the result of countless thousands of hours of thought and preparation, utilizing the expertise of some of this nation's most knowledgeable citizens. Admittedly, it is extremely complex, even to attorneys such as Representative Murray and myself, who are specially trained to understand such matters. Accordingly, it is incumbent upon each of you, who have assumed a sacred trust of fairness and responsibility, to fully read and completely analyze the entire bill *before* you issue your reports. Only by acting in such a manner will you be able to render an accurate accounting to those whom we both serve. Naturally, Representative Murray and I are available to assist you in this effort."

Kevin winced inwardly. How could one person be a horse's ass with such consistency? You never, ever told the media how to do their jobs. Sometimes you wanted to, but it was a no-win proposition.

Kevin returned to the podium. It was salvage time. "Well, now that you've all been properly admonished, how about some questions?"

In the question and answer period Harrington responded first. Despite his eloquence, he rarely provided a direct answer. Kevin then followed with three or four straightforward sentences, which generally seemed to satisfy the reporters.

"Representative Harrington, why won't you recognize me?" came a voice from the back row. She was the editor of Pennsylvania NOW's monthly newsletter.

"Because you're not a reporter," Harrington replied.

"But I have press credentials. I have every right to be here and have my questions answered."

"Right? You talk to me about rights when your organization denies the most precious right of all to a million and a half unborn children every year?"

"If nothing else, Representative Harrington, I expected you to be more professional. Our personal beliefs are irrelevant to this issue. The only question here is whether or not it is proper for you to refuse to answer the question of a fully accredited—"

Harrington's eyebrows arched, and he pointed his finger at the woman. "I don't care what credentials you have. There is absolutely no way—"

"My money is on Craig by a TKO in the ninth." Kevin cut in. He turned to the NOW editor. "Mary, I just can't bear to see good friends squabble. What's your question?"

She had to smile. "Thank you, Representative Murray. I'm glad that at least one of you is courteous."

"My mother loves me, too."

"What about your wife?" someone yelled.

"Got a coin?" Kevin shot back.

"My question is," Mary began, "whether you personally hold these beliefs or whether you are merely carrying out the instructions of the Roman Catholic Church."

Harrington's voice oozed contempt. "I wouldn't dignify a question like that with an answer."

"I would." Kevin smiled. "Mary, there is absolutely no truth to the rumor that I'm a flack for the Catholic Church, but before I say anything else, I have to check with the cardinal."

When the laughter subsided, Kevin continued. "Seriously, Mary, the people who say that abortion is a Catholic issue quite frankly don't know what they're talking about. The pro-life movement is comprised of people of all religions. Even atheists."

He put his arm on Harrington's shoulder. "As you may know, Mr. Sunshine here is not a Catholic. He's a Bible-spouting fundamentalist Baptist. Abortion's not a Catholic issue, Mary. It's not even a religious issue. Did the fact that the Quakers supported abolition make slavery a religious issue? Certainly not. Abortion, like slavery, is a human issue, by which we'll decide whether we continue to destroy our most precious asset—our children, indeed, our future. I take my stand because I'm a member of a very exclusive club. Not the legislature, not the Catholic Church. I'm a member of the human race, and as such, I don't have any choice but to come down on the side of life. Think about it for a minute, Mary. We live in a nation that weeps for the killing of baby seals, that pickets over the killing of porpoises by Japanese fishermen, that has enough political power to halt a multimillion-dollar dam

[96]

project down South to save the snail darter, and yet permits the killing of one and a half million innocent unborn children every year. That, I submit to you, is a masterpiece of inconsistency."

Kevin paused briefly, then smiled again. "So in conclusion, Mary, let me repeat that I'm not a toady for the Catholic Church. For your penance, say three Hail Marys and make a good act of contrition."

Kevin opened the door of the Green Pig. Since the hinge of the door had long since broken, he had exactly two seconds to throw in his briefcase and jump in before it slammed shut. It was a '71 Plymouth station wagon, a gas-guzzling pig that he'd bought when he was stationed in Detroit. The Bureau had had a contract with a Chrysler dealer, and agents had received good deals. The years, and Kevin's neglect, had taken their toll. The exterior was shabby—half a dozen rust spots and an entire length of chrome missing—and the interior was worse. But it still ran and was perfect for the short hop to and from the train station.

Kevin pulled out his last Winston, crumpling the pack and throwing it on the floor of the passenger side. He had promised that when the used packs reached the roof, he would shitcan the car. Though the pile was becoming impressive, he still had a long way to go.

He flipped on KYW, the all-news station. As he expected, the news conference was the lead story. As he also expected, Sandy Sterabin did a professional job. In ninety seconds he gave an accurate, if brief, description of the bill. You never knew where Sandy stood on the issue. That was why Kevin respected him. It was the mark of a pro.

Kevin's voice came on, responding to one of the questions, and he shook his head. Despite hundreds of interviews, he could never get used to hearing his own voice, especially the lisp. Not much of one, but enough to make him uncomfortable.

"Goddamn faggot," he muttered, switching the station in a search for music. He found what he wanted, one of his favorites.

> ... talk about God in his mercy,
> who if he really does exist
> why did he desert me?

[97]

In my hour of need,
I truly am indeed,
Alone again, naturally.

God, how that summed it up. Especially now. A wife, five children, an array of people who worshiped him, and he felt totally
alone. Whom did he *really* have? He loved the kids, loved being
with them. But he couldn't open up with them, share his fears
and his doubts. Maybe someday, but not now. And Karen? They
loved each other in their own way, but there just didn't seem to be
any time. Even on nights when he could stay home. By the time
they got dinner, did the dishes, got the little ones ready for bed,
helped the big ones with their homework, set the table for breakfast, laid out the school clothes for the next day, argued with the
big ones to go to bed, the night was shot and they were too tired to
do anything but collapse in bed with the television on, no matter
how stupid the show might be.

How did other people do it? Or did they? Did the Brady Bunch
exist in the real world—problems being solved calmly, husband
and wife having time to talk—or was it just bullshit?

And it would get worse now with Karen pregnant again. God,
where does it end?

What about his friends? Real honest-to-God friends he wanted
to be with, not the political types forced on him at the obligatory
rallies and banquets.

The answer depressed him. He didn't really have any. Part of it
was his own fault. And Karen's. Almost everything they did outside politics was family-oriented: the kids; their parents; Karen's
sisters. It seemed they were always together: holidays; christen-
ings; birthday parties; first communions; confirmations; school
plays; the kids' sports events. He wasn't knocking it—he loved a
close-knit family—but with a calendar like that there wasn't
much time to build any other relationships.

Sure, he still kept in touch with Pat Carney, but there was that
invisible line that separated priests from the rest of the flock. Besides, there had always been something about Pat, ever since Villanova, something that made Kevin keep him at a distance, at
least mentally. It was a gut feeling, intangible but insistent, that
Pat wasn't quite for real. That he never said anything that he actually meant.

[98]

It was Kevin's fault that his contacts with Vince had dwindled. Maybe his schedule really was too hectic. Maybe it was that Vince had entered another world, one that Kevin had spent most of his working life fighting. Perhaps there was self-interest as well. A friendship with a mob figure could severely taint any politician, particularly the white knight of the Pennsylvania legislature. Or, worst of all, maybe it was just jealousy. Vince had everything. Kevin possessed a dying Plymouth and a mortgage.

At least there was Brendan. His big brother would always be there, just as he had been from the beginning. But he lived a hundred miles away with five children of his own. At a certain age adults lose the freedom they wrested from their parents only a few years before. The activities of their children dictate their schedules. As a result, the brothers were lucky to see each other twice a year. Thanks to Kevin's WATS line, compliments of the Commonwealth of Pennsylvania, they talked on the phone regularly, but some things can be said only in person.

Turning onto Eagle Road, Kevin flipped his cigarette out the window. He was irritated. Why the hell had he let himself get into such a funk, especially today? They were rolling again, going back into the arena.

> I remember I cried
> when my father died,
> Never wishing to hide the tears,

Yeah, there it was. The first time he was going into battle without the Sarge.

Michael Joseph Murray. His dad. Without question, the greatest influence on Kevin's life. The standard by which he would measure all other men.

He wasn't a bank president or a famous lawyer or a successful businessman. He was a cop. For almost forty years he devoted his life to keeping Upper Darby safe. The only thing more important to him was his family. He wanted the very best for his kids, college for the boys and, when the time came for his little girl, a wedding that would make her proud.

It wasn't easy. You didn't make much on a cop's salary, not if you were honest, but Mike Murray was never afraid to work. He was always moonlighting—pallbearer at local funerals, security guard at parties and weddings, even gas pumper at the Atlantic

[99]

station. With all that he still found time to be the Scoutmaster for the church troop, usher at the nine o'clock mass, and one of the pillars of the Holy Name Society. And somehow he managed to juggle his schedule so that he was always there for the important things. He never missed the boys' football games or Melissa's recitals or even the rinky-dink class plays at St. Laurence where each kid, at best, had two lines.

It was no big deal for him. He never expected as much as a thank-you. He was the rarest of humans, a man who did things because they were right and not for any hope of recognition.

Because he was honest and because he refused to kiss the ass of any politician, he would never advance beyond sergeant, even though everyone knew that he was the best cop on the force. It bothered Kevin tremendously, but it didn't trouble the Sarge in the least. Or if it did, he kept it to himself.

"Kevin," he had said, "the one person you have to please in this world is the one you see in the mirror every morning. And if you can't look at that face, no matter how high you go, no matter what other people think of you, you're a failure."

What other people thought of Mike Murray was obvious. At Christmastime, when he took the kids shopping on Sixty-ninth Street for their mother's presents, the shop owners treated him like a god. "Don't know what we'd do without him," they would say to the children, offering them gifts or huge discounts.

The Sarge would thank them and gently refuse. "Gotta teach them early that there's no free lunch in this world."

Kevin liked his visits to the station house best of all: row after row of polished red cars, the men in their uniforms, and what seemed like a hundred telephones ringing at once. They treated him special because he was the Sarge's kid.

"You better be proud of your old man," they would say. "He's the best."

"Thank you," Kevin would reply. "But he's not my old man. He's my dad."

They would laugh, but Kevin could tell that they liked his answer.

The Sarge's first date with Maureen O'Leary was when he took her to the soph hop at West Catholic. Though they broke up at least once a month, during which time the Sarge would raise merry hell with his pals, it was taken for granted that someday they would marry. On the day he was hired onto the force he proposed. Nine months and twelve days after their wedding (you could see the people in the old neighborhood counting the months in their heads) Brendan arrived, followed by Kevin four years later and, surprise of surprises, Melissa, the week before their fifteenth anniversary.

To be sure, the Sarge and Maureen had their fights, some real dandies, but looking back on it, Kevin marveled at their love. Each was the center of the other's world. All they wanted out of life was to be together, raising the three children whose happiness they put before their own. It was a perfect love that Kevin despaired of ever equaling with Karen.

In January 1980, at the age of sixty-four, the Sarge finally packed in his badge and gun. It was time. With the kids all raised, there was no reason to break his back any longer. Besides, he was getting tired of the pressure to retire from the township commissioners.

He and Maureen had a little nest egg. They were going to take a trip across the country by car with no particular schedule. It was a chance to see all the things they had missed during the years when every penny went for the kids.

But the Sarge still had his priorities. Before the trip he had to help Kevin. His son was up for reelection, and this time he might be in trouble. For the first time in his career Kevin faced a primary challenge. His opponent was a woman, young, well educated, fairly well spoken. Most dangerous of all, she was attractive.

Normally, none of that would have constituted a threat to an incumbent endorsed by the organization, but this was different. Kevin was *the* national target of the abortion movement, his opponent but the flag carrier of an army that was out to destroy his career. They were willing to spend a fortune to remove the number one pro-life spokesman from the legislature.

And they were smart. They knew that they could never defeat him on the abortion issue per se. Everyone knew where Kevin stood on abortion. Even his opponents gave him credit for being open and honest. True, there was a small core of voters who would oppose him just because of his pro-life stand, but the vast majority of his constituents, regardless of their feelings on abortion, would not make their decision on that issue alone.

[101]

But when a legislator took a leadership role in opposing abortion, he left himself vulnerable to a charge that was difficult, maybe impossible, to refute. It wasn't that he was pro-life but that he didn't do anything besides fight abortion. A "one-issue" legislator. There was no way to avoid it, even for someone like Kevin, who was acknowledged by his peers to be the most active legislator in the state. No one was involved in more diverse issues. He was an expert on public and nonpublic education, law enforcement, health and transportation. He was a board member of four major state agencies and served as chairman of the Subcommittee on Public Utilities. And no one, absolutely no one, was ever more accessible and responsive to his constituents.

Yet, when Kevin Murray's name was mentioned, the first thing one thought of was abortion. No other issue, not capital punishment, not drugs, not even sex education, received the same glare of publicity. As a result, it was unfair but natural that when people constantly saw Kevin on television or in the papers waging the abortion war, they assumed that he had no time for anything else.

Logic dictated that this would be the focus of the opposition's attack. Kevin Murray was so busy preaching his own personal belief that he was shortchanging his constituents. It was time to elect a legislator who served all the people.

An incumbent up for reelection encounters a two-edged sword. Only he has performed in the job and established a record. Yet while he can recite his litany of accomplishments, that same record provides an inviting target to his opponent. A six-year veteran such as Kevin had cast about ten thousand roll-call votes. Some were on amendments offered on the floor, providing no time for analysis and reflection. Others were on bills containing a number of provisions, only some of which he supported. The trick in those cases was to determine whether the good features outweighed the bad. There was no easy formula, and no matter which way he came down, he was placed in a difficult position. The abortion coalition had the money and the manpower to research Kevin's voting record and isolate some of these instances.

It depressed Kevin to learn that he had a primary fight. That meant twice the work and twice the amount of money that had to be raised. Besides, he just wasn't in the mood. The first time he ran, in the special election six years before, it had been enjoyable, as most new experiences are. The adrenaline was pumping, and it

[102]

was one of the most exciting times of his life. After that it was a pain in the ass. He realized that he didn't really enjoy politics. Unlike most who plied that trade, Kevin saw reelection not as an end but only as a means. What he loved was the job itself: formulating creative ideas on how to resolve problems, then developing the best strategy to shepherd those ideas into law. To Kevin, a reelection campaign constituted an irritating but necessary interruption of that process.

He never had a doubt, at least a rational doubt, about the outcome. But winning wasn't enough. Not this time. Because the eyes of the state, and to a lesser degree the nation, would be on his campaign, his plurality would be almost as important as his victory.

The news media had locked on to the race and wouldn't let it go. Their assessment was carved in granite. If Kevin Murray failed to win by his usual two-to-one margin, it would be a defeat for the pro-life movement. Once that had been said, it was accepted as gospel.

They were locking him in just the way they had locked in Lyndon Johnson in the 1968 New Hampshire primary. Some reporter, long since forgotten, declared that anything less than a sixty percent Johnson plurality would be a devastating blow to Johnson's incumbency and a victory for Eugene McCarthy. That theory, which quickly gained general acceptance, might well have been the undoing of the president.

Forgotten by most is the fact that Lyndon Johnson, despite the problems of Vietnam and racial unrest, scored a comfortable victory in New Hampshire. But since he failed to gain sixty percent of the vote, the headlines trumpeted his demise, and for probably the first time in his life the Texan gave way. He withdrew from the race, causing a chain reaction that would directly affect America for more than a decade. Had he not withdrawn, Bobby Kennedy would not have entered the lists and would probably still be alive. There would have been no reason for a reunion of the volunteers who had worked on the Kennedy campaign, and thus Chappaquiddick would never have occurred. Richard Milhous Nixon would probably not have been elected president of the United States, and with no Nixon, there would have been no Spiro Agnew and no Watergate. Gerald Ford would have remained minority leader of the House. Without Watergate there would have been no national revulsion toward Washington that would set the stage for an outsider such as Jimmy Carter to assume the presidency.

All because of one reporter. Of such things is history made.

Now, on a smaller scale, Kevin faced the same problems encountered by Lyndon Johnson. It didn't matter that a primary had totally different characteristics from a general election, that Kevin had traditionally enjoyed heavy Democratic support in the fall campaign that would be unavailable to him in a primary, that in his district the Jewish vote was overwhelmingly Republican and could be expected to support his opponent solely because of abortion, and that, in the wealthier, Main Line sections, much of the old-money WASP vote that had supported him in the past because it would be blasphemy to vote for a Democrat would now be deserting him. To them, Kevin's abortion stand was an embarrassment. It was too Catholic an issue for their taste.

None of that mattered. The die was cast, and Kevin understood that in an election, as in most of life, perception was the only thing that counted. That which is wasn't important; only that which is perceived. It wasn't necessary that a political leader have power so long as people thought he had power. You could take any horse's ass, write a few well-placed stories labeling him a threat in the forthcoming gubernatorial election, and suddenly he was a legitimate candidate for governor.

Perception was particularly important when it came to the abortion issue in Pennsylvania. Politically, the pro-life movement was strong but not nearly so strong as most people thought. While the Pennsylvania legislature was one of the strongest antiabortion bodies in the country, *never* having defeated a pro-life bill, that record was misleading. Men like Kevin and Harrington, who had risked their careers without hesitation, were the exception. The average legislator who voted against abortion did so because he feared political retribution if he acted otherwise. Because of this, it was essential that Kevin be absolutely certain of victory before he ran a bill. The first time a bill went down, the first time pro-life reps voted the wrong way and were not immediately struck dead or turned out of office, the myth of invincibility would be shattered forever.

It was the same with his primary campaign. If the abortion co-

[104]

alition cut drastically into Kevin's margin, some of his colleagues in the House might reassess the wisdom of their antiabortion stand.

So Kevin's mission was clear. He had to win big.

He decided at the outset to run his campaign as he had all the others. In the press conference announcing his candidacy, he spelled it out in typical Kevin Murray style. "Like my other re-election efforts, this campaign will be a referendum on the job that I've done. If the people approve of my performance, they'll reelect me. If they don't, they'll throw me the hell out, which is as it should be. It's what's known as democracy."

Regardless of what his opponent might say, and he knew that the attack would be vicious, Kevin would not respond. To do so would only give her more publicity and lend credibility to her accusations. When you were the champion, you didn't stoop to the challenger's level. Let her voice be the shrill one. People quickly grew tired of mudslinging. By contrast, his campaign would be a positive one, stressing his list of legislative accomplishments and the thousands of constituent services he had performed. Most important, he would continue to be an effective and visible elected official. Business as usual, as if there were no campaign.

The Sarge assumed complete control of the campaign's mechanics, beginning with registration. His goal was to target 100 of Kevin's Democratic supporters and convince them to switch to Republican, if only for the primary. Several of the veteran pols scoffed at the idea. People who registered Democrat in a GOP stronghold like Delaware County were dyed-in-the-wool donkeys. No matter how much they might like Kevin, you could never get them to switch, and even if you could, the logistics were too difficult. Mike Murray might have been a good cop, but when it came to politics, he was an amateur. No way could he get 100 changeovers. At best, he could hope for 25.

In a way, the experts were right. The Sarge didn't get 100. He got 492. After that, the ward leaders listened to him. Even the ones who normally sat on their hands gave the Sarge whatever he asked. They respected his ability, and more important, they came to like him. When he proved them wrong about the Democrats, he hadn't tried to rub it in. He just shrugged it off and moved on to the next item, and he never told them what to do. Realizing that most political leaders were like little children, loving to be

[105]

stroked, he *asked.* He was putting into practice something that he had taught Kevin years before: "It's not *what* you do in this world that counts; it's *how* you do it."

When he wasn't in the office directing operations, the Sarge was on the street with Maureen, knocking on doors. They were always well received. People liked the personal touch. These were not politicians, drumming up support for the party's choice to save their own jobs. These were two ordinary people, just trying to help their son.

When someone would admire his loyalty, the Sarge would grin. "It's no big deal. I just figure it's cheaper to get Kevin reelected than to support him. The way his five kids like to eat, I'd go bankrupt."

Everything ran like clockwork. Handouts were delivered without a hitch. The mailings went out on schedule. Lawn signs blanketed the district. The phone banks were in place and ready. Every polling place would be well covered on election day.

And just to be on the safe side, the Sarge scheduled more than thirty coffees, sometimes two on the same evening. At first Kevin had balked at the idea. He hadn't used coffees since the special election, when he had been unknown, and he questioned if they were now necessary. He wanted to be home some nights to keep peace with Karen. But in the end he agreed. The only way to run a campaign was to go all the way all the time. You gave it your very best shot so that if, God forbid, you came up a few votes short, you could at least console yourself with the knowledge that there was nothing more you could have done to change things. It would be bad enough to lose, but it would be agony to lie awake thinking of what might have been.

The Sarge had the procedure streamlined. On the afternoon of the coffee Kevin's campaign literature was delivered to the hostess so that she could arrange it on a display table. Serving as his son's personal driver, the Sarge made sure they arrived exactly fifteen minutes late, enough time to accommodate the latecomers. Kevin personally introduced himself to each person, spoke for about twenty minutes, and answered questions for a half hour. Then it was time to go. Just short of an hour was the saturation point. If you couldn't work your show in that time, you didn't deserve to be elected.

A candidate always finds it difficult to break things off. That's why an assistant is essential. Looking at his watch, the Sarge would remind Kevin that they had another commitment, whether or not they actually did. Five minutes for thank-yous and good-byes, and they were gone. On the following morning the first order of business was a handwritten note of appreciation to the hostess.

Election day dawned clear and warm, a perfect specimen of spring. It should help the turnout. According to the book, a heavy turnout was bad for the incumbent, but Kevin was not disturbed. He had always rejected the campaign strategies to keep down the vote. That wasn't the way democracy should work. If a heavy participation by the voters would endanger his chances, he hadn't done his job.

Long ago some forgotten pol had deemed that candidates should visit the polling places. Like most election day activities, it was ineffective. If you weren't ready before election day, it was too late to try to pull it out. But it was expected, so Kevin complied. Unlike most candidates, he went it alone, without a driver. No sense wasting good campaign workers. He wanted them at the polling places, where they might get lucky and snatch a few undecided votes. The Sarge, for example, was at Brookline School, while Maureen was at Kevin's precinct. Ironically, that polling place was in the basement of the Catholic church. Even Karen got into the act, handling the senior high school. Kevin knew that she hated his being in politics, but she didn't want to see him lose. Particularly to someone who was pro-abortion.

Since Kevin's district had thirty-nine polling stations, his visits took up most of the day, thanking the poll workers, reminding them of the victory party at Cavanaugh's that night, and then, after taking off his campaign button, sticking his head into the polling place briefly to greet the judge of elections and clerks. He drank a dozen cups of coffee and smoked two packs of Winston in the process.

The car radio was tuned to KYW, which provided continuous election coverage. It surprised Kevin that his race was the lead story, even ahead of the presidential primary between Reagan and Bush. Every half hour the station focused in on the "referendum on abortion."

Here he was, driving a station wagon with two infant seats and a playpen in the back, Mr. Average Citizen, and millions of people were hearing his name. It was, at one and the same time, an exciting and unsettling experience.

They were ready. The Sarge had seen to that. Everything should be okay, but in an election you never *really* knew. Absolutely *knew*. It was a hell of a way to make a living when every two years your job—your entire career—was totally dependent upon the whims of the masses.

Surprisingly, it had been fun. A pain in the ass, a constant worry, but fun. The adrenaline had started pumping, and he had warmed to the campaign. Although he would never admit it to Karen, he was almost glad that he had been challenged.

For the first time in his life he had worked with his father, side by side. It almost fulfilled one of his dreams. He wanted to be rich, to start some type of business where he and Brendan and the Sarge, the Murray men, could be together. Maybe someday.

Most politicians, like athletes, are superstitious. Being no exception, Kevin kept to the same ritual he had maintained since the special election. Just before six, having visited all but one polling place, he drove home. After a quick sandwich, he walked to Chatham Park School, where the people of the Eighth Ward, Third Precinct voted. It was his largest precinct, heavily Jewish. Six years before, he decided to give it special attention, personally working it until the polls closed at eight.

As usual, the last hour of the longest day of the year was an eternity. Then the doors were closed and, one way or the other, his fate was sealed.

Long before he was a candidate, this was the moment that had thrilled him. The magic of America. On this special night the focus of the nation was not on the Capitol or the White House. It was on school halls, churches, synagogues, even garages, where the ballots, freely cast, were being counted. America had made up its mind, and its decision would be accepted without question. Regardless of the outcome, no troops would march, no government would be overthrown. For all the passion of a campaign, for all the back room deals and rigged votes, it was a continuing miracle, a source of pride and comfort.

But despite his infatuation with the process, Kevin would not take part in the count. Not when he was running. Instead, he walked the five blocks home, smoking two cigarettes.

He was the first one there. The rest were still gathering returns.

Young Kevin greeted him, trying to hide his concern. "Did you win, Dad?"

"Didn't I tell you? We rigged everything at ten this morning."

"C'mon. Be serious." Publicly the boy was blasé, even a little disdainful of his father's position. In truth, he idolized Kevin and would be crushed if he lost.

"Relax, big guy. We should be okay."

When he allowed himself to think about losing, and every candidate indulged in such masochism, what worried him most was the effect it would have on the kids. Children could be cruel. He feared that some of their friends might ridicule them, making them pay for their father's failure. He had tried to explain to them that anyone entering politics had to accept the possibility of defeat, but they hadn't listened. They refused to believe that their father could actually lose.

Although they would go to Cavanaugh's for the official returns, Kevin wanted his usual preview. Just to get ready. He had instructed ten committee people, five from his worst precincts, five from his best, to call him at home. That would be enough to tell.

The Sarge walked in. He wasn't frowning, but he wasn't smiling either.

"Don't just stand there, for Chrissake. Tell me."

"Not bad," his father said, breaking into a grin. "A shade over three to one."

"Hot damn!" Kevin slapped him on the shoulder. "Great job, Sarge! Get a beer. You earned it!"

The next ten minutes were chaos. The phone kept ringing while a dozen workers, including his mother and Karen, milled about. The news was the same. The bad precincts, the Jewish and WASP areas, were holding. His margin was down a little, but he was still carrying them comfortably. And the good precincts, where the Catholic vote had come out in droves, were spectacular. No doubt at all. It was going to be a rout.

After Kevin had showered and changed his shirt, they formed a triumphant procession to Cavanaugh's. The room erupted as he entered. Jim McMonigle, one of his most faithful workers, threw his arms around him. "Seventy percent!" he bellowed. "Seventy fuckin' percent! We really showed that liberal bitch!"

They all were there, the newspapers, radio, and television, forming a circle, fighting to ask the first question. Kevin tried to

[109]

pull his father into the group. Typically, the Sarge would have none of it, instead nudging Karen through the crowd to stand next to her husband.

When Kevin was finally able to break free, he sought out his father, embracing him tightly.

"What can I say, Sarge? You were fantastic. I don't know what I would have done without you."

"You would have won, Kevin. I was just along for the ride."

The November election was as anticlimactic as it was predictable. The abortion forces had shot their wad in the primary, and their heart wasn't in it the second time around. Both Kevin Murray and Ronald Reagan scored landslide victories. It did not go unnoticed, however, that Kevin outpolled the Gipper by more than two thousand votes.

Kevin had little time to savor his reelection. There were only three weeks left in the legislative term, and he still had to push the Medicaid funding bill through on final passage.

On the day of the debate the Sarge took the train to Harrisburg with him and was seated in one of the seats in the well of the House reserved for special guests. For once the session started promptly. At precisely ten minutes after ten Kevin strode to the podium. With the exception of a short lunch break, he stood there for the next sixteen hours, fending off attacks, responding to questions, and blocking more than forty amendments designed to gut the bill. Finally, shortly after two in the morning, the House voted, and Kevin Murray had won again.

When the interviews were over, when the last pro-lifer had congratulated him, Kevin went to his office. As always after an abortion battle, he wanted to be alone. Except for the Sarge, of course.

He knew that when he carried the pro-life banner, he had to keep his cool. If he became emotional, he would only play into the hands of the enemy, who would love nothing more than to paint him as a right-wing zealot. But sometimes the strain was almost unbearable. How could you really be unemotional when you were dealing with the lives of little babies?

Secure in his office with the door closed, he finally let it out. Deep sobs racked his body as the tension of the past six months ebbed out. Only when he was again composed did his father speak.

"I've always been proud of you, Kevin, but tonight was special. Watching you out there, standing for what you believe in, was the greatest thrill of my life. It makes everything worthwhile."

It was only then, at three o'clock in the morning, the last train having left six hours before, that they realized they were stranded. The Capitol was almost deserted, but they found two pro-lifers from Springfield who offered them a lift. Kevin Murray, savior of the unborn, returned home in the style befitting a conquering hero. Sitting four abreast in flagrant violation of the Pennsylvania Motor Vehicle Code, they headed down the turnpike in a pickup. Only then did Kevin realize how exhausted he was. Mumbling an apology, he began to doze. He felt the Sarge put his arm around him, steadying his head. He was little again, afraid of the dark, and his daddy was holding him, gently reassuring him that he would always be there. *And he always has,* Kevin thought as his consciousness slowly left him.

It was the last time they were together. Two days later, sitting on the sofa with Maureen, poring over travel pamphlets for their long-postponed trip, the Sarge lurched forward, grasping at his chest. Michael Joseph Murray, the finest of Upper Darby's finest, was dead. He left a wife and three children, at least one of whom would never be quite the same.

It had been a typical day for Karen Murray. The children, particularly the two oldest, had fought since the time they got up. Kevin, Jr., seemed to delight in tormenting Sean, who, suffering from the second child syndrome, refused to retaliate except for name-calling. "Faggot" was the term they most often exchanged. It was the "in" word this year. First it had been "gay." Everyone and everything were "gay." Then it was "gayhop" and, finally, just plain "faggot." It was comforting to know they had learned something at Nativity.

Megan had slept late; she would be impossible to get to bed that night. Matthew spent most of the day sulking because "someone" had misplaced part of his Star Wars set. And Peter was just Peter, an adorable two-year-old who could wreak more destruction than, as Kevin would say when the kids were out of earshot, "a dozen spades on Friday night." Today, for example, he had overturned Karen's rubber tree on the living room carpet, flushed a plastic truck down the toilet, and, although Matthew

[111]

didn't know it, scattered the Star Wars set over the entire first floor. He was also on his fifth change of clothes.

Despite everything, Karen had managed to make all the beds; clean the first and second floors; do three loads of wash; run over to Marshalls to buy school slacks on sale; pack lunch for everyone; get Megan and Matthew to the pool in time for their eleven-thirty lesson; eat lunch at the pool (arbitrating the dispute about who got the largest piece of cake); stay at the pool for another hour (since Peter was still in diapers, he was confined to the baby pool, requiring her to stand by the fence so she could watch him and the others simultaneously, her concentration interrupted by the women telling her what a wonderful job her husband was doing); get them all home for Peter's nap at two; drive young Kevin to the orthodontist, stopping at Swiss Farms on the way back for milk; drive Megan to her gymnastics class, with young Kevin bitching because he had to baby-sit ("Why didn't Sean ever complain?"); start the roast; iron a dozen shirts; get Peter up and dressed; set the table; and now, with the kitchen temperature at least a hundred because Kevin hadn't gotten around to installing the overhead fan (they had bought it only six months ago), finish dinner.

Young Kevin's band was practicing in the basement, and the noise, particularly the damn drums, had given her a headache. Naturally, her husband would ask her if she had taken anything, forgetting that she was pregnant and wanted to avoid medication. He wouldn't forget if he were the one carrying the baby. It was so easy for men. She tried not to admit it, but the colitis was coming back, and with it the terror. Please God, not the steroids again. She had agonized during her pregnancy with Peter, relaxing only when he was born healthy. But would her luck run out this time?

Her mood wasn't improved by the children running in to announce that Kevin was on the six o'clock news, followed by calls from both her mother and mother-in-law with the same information. The latter's call came just as Karen was putting the potatoes in to brown. The oven door, which Kevin had promised to fix last May, came loose and crashed to the floor, splattering her legs with grease.

"That's great, Maureen," she snapped. "I'm just thrilled he's out saving the world again!"

Matt and Megan were arguing over whose turn it was to pour

[112]

the drinks, and the band was playing "American Woman" for about the tenth time.

"Time to wrap it up, fellas," she called into the basement, taking pains to sound friendly. "Kevin, tell the children to wash up for dinner."

"Just one more song, Mom."

"Sorry, hon. We have to eat. Matt has baseball tonight."

The band members left grumbling, and Kevin, irritated because he had to stop, hit Peter for touching his guitar, setting off yet another round of crying.

Into this backdrop of harmony entered Kevin. "Daddy!" Megan yelled as she ran to him, followed closely by Matt. They insisted on the ritual, each climbing to the sixth step in the hall stairway and jumping into Kevin's arms.

Kevin hesitated before entering the kitchen. He could feel her mood even before he saw her.

"Hi, hon. How's it going?"

"Where were you?" Karen snapped without looking up.

"What do you mean?"

"You're late—as usual."

"I don't know. I took the four-twenty. I guess they're working on the track again. I dozed a little on the train."

"It's nice that at least one of us can sleep."

"Aw, c'mon, Karen. Don't—"

"Come on, yourself. Do you hear Peter screaming? That's because your oldest son is miserable!"

"What do you mean?"

"What difference does it make? You're never around to do anything about it."

He should have just let it ride, but it wasn't in his nature. "Don't start that 'never home' shit again, will you? Be specific."

How often Kevin was out remained a source of contention. To defend himself, he had started to document not only his evening schedule but the times of the trains that he took from Harrisburg. Ever the lawyer, he was always ready to destroy her on cross-examination, a tactic that served only to infuriate Karen and prolong the battle.

"You're not putting me on the stand, buddy boy! Save that for the hacks in Harrisburg." Her voice changed from anger to sarcasm. "Incidentally, dear old Mom called."

[113]

She was a master at changing the subject. Sooner or later any discussion got around to her mother-in-law.

"What the hell does that have to do with anything?"

"I just thought you'd like to know that someone appreciates you. She thought you were just wonderful on television. Sorry I couldn't watch you, but I was a little busy taking care of things like this." She pulled off the oven door and slammed it onto the floor. "It's so nice to have a man around the house!"

His self-control was ebbing rapidly. "God, it's just great to be home."

"Then why don't you stay in Harrisburg? You don't do anything around here."

"Bullshit! I help out plenty, baby, and you know it. How many husbands do you know who iron, do wash, change diapers, and all the other crap I do around here?"

Karen was ready. They'd been over it so many times. "Yeah, and how many husbands work seventy hours a week in a job that doesn't pay worth a damn? How many idiots would take a forty percent pay cut just so he could get his name in the papers? Did you see the mail today? Three overdue notices. Girard is threatening to close our account! Again."

The same old exchange. It never changed, and it was never resolved.

"Why don't you just type the speech? It's the same ration of shit over and over. That way you could save your breath and I could turn you the fuck off!"

Karen's eyes narrowed. "What kind of father talks like that in front of his children? You disgust me."

They battered each other for ten more minutes. It was Kevin who finally broke it off, telling her to stick the dinner and stomping upstairs to the bedroom.

He lay on the bed, his chest pounding. If only he could get away. But there was no escape. He was stuck with his life, and he had to live it. Matthew had a game tonight, and after that there was the meeting at St. Denis with the pro-life people. He had worried about breaking that to Karen, but now it didn't matter. To hell with her.

God, he hated her. He had never felt such rage toward anyone else, not the Augustinians, not the mobsters, not even the abortion bastards. How could you love and hate the same person so much?

[114]

And he hated himself. He knew what he was, and it repulsed him. Every day he promised himself he'd change. No more foul language, no more short fuse. His mother had her bitchy moments over the years, but never once had he heard the Sarge talk like that. And there was the other thing, the worst one of all, the one you could never erase.

Christ, what a bum he was. What a failure. Why, God? He wasn't that bad a human being, and Karen was a saint. Why did it have to be this way? Why couldn't they ever have just a little peace?

He thought of his dad, at peace in Holy Cross Cemetery, and not for the first time, he wondered if the Sarge wasn't the lucky one.

CHAPTER
Six

PAT Carney wanted a drink. He started toward the cabinet for the Jack Daniel's, then reconsidered. You never knew when the boss might pop in.

Stephen Cardinal Pulski's world was carefully compartmentalized. He wasn't a teetotaler, but drinking, like everything else, had its proper place. It was just three, a little too early. Not that the boss would say anything, but it was something that he might mentally file away in that damn computer mind for instant recall at a crucial time. Not a big deal, but maybe, just maybe, enough to slow Pat's climb to the top. When you were in the big leagues, you couldn't be too careful.

This act of self-denial served to increase Pat's irritation. It had been a bad day, one of the worst. You just couldn't predict the reaction of seemingly rational humans. Even your family.

Pat was convinced that his proposal was both sensible and compassionate. Their father needed help. He couldn't continue to live by himself.

At least the twins had been sympathetic, if not helpful. Leo's job had him on the road most of the time. It wouldn't be right to saddle his wife with the burden, particularly now that she was pregnant. Bobby and his wife had just reunited after a six-month separation. They needed breathing room to work things out and save their marriage.

But it was Kristy, his father's little princess, who had floored him.

[116]

"Can't do it, Pat," she had snapped. "I've got a husband who works sixty hours a week, three kids, and a part-time job. There just isn't any way."

"But, Kristy, he's our father."

"That's right. *Our* father."

"What the hell does that mean?"

"You know exactly what it means, Right Reverend Monsignor For once in your life, be honest with yourself. Which of us is in the best position to help *our* father?"

Pat's stomach knotted. He knew the answer because he had asked it of himself. "Be reasonable, Kristy," he said, without much conviction. "I'm a priest. How could I—"

"Cut the bullshit, Pat. You could do it in a snap. This is the modern church, remember? Plenty of priests have their own places. They wouldn't refuse you. Not when it's for your father."

"But how could I afford it?" he asked, again knowing.

"Very easily. You get an apartment near the parish. You're only in residence there anyway, and the commute to the office would be the same. You're not an order priest. You've got some money. Dad has his Social Security, and the twins and I will be happy to kick in. It's the perfect solution, and we both know it."

"Kristy," Pat whined, "I can't. I just can't."

"I know you can't, Pat. I hate to say this about my brother, but you're nothing but a goddamn phony."

The words haunted Pat as he looked out across the city. The parkway was at its best in October, its trees magnificent in their fall colors. Autumn had always been special to Pat, his favorite time of the year. He felt so alive in the crisp air, felt that life had a purpose, that there were great things to be done.

When he thought back to his childhood, the scenes that remained most vivid had occurred in the fall. Touch football in the street, trying to get in the last touchdown before darkness fell. The games generally ended when one of the mothers would call her son for dinner. (Pat always felt disappointed, not that the game had ended but that he would never hear his mother's voice calling him.) The delicious aroma of burning leaves, one of the special smells and sounds of his youth. Like the clink of tire chains in the snow, the rattle of coal tumbling down the chute, the rustle of venetian blinds in the summer breeze. Like youth itself, they had vanished forever.

[117]

The essence of fall seemed to be excitement. Getting ready for Halloween, then Thanksgiving, and, best of all, the knowledge that Christmas was on its way.

He had tried so hard to make things right for his little brothers and baby sister. His dad was great, but with no mother there were gaps to be filled, and Pat was always there. They were *his* responsibility, and no mother could have worried more. When Kristy was coughing, he would sleep on the floor beside her crib, afraid that she might vomit and choke in her sleep. When brakes would screech in the street, he would leap to the door, fear pounding in his heart. He had to protect them. They were his.

Halloween. Pat had spent two hours getting them ready. The twins were perfect as Raggedy Ann and Andy. And his little Kristy was beautiful as Cinderella. Just beautiful. Pat beamed with pride as he took them to each house. He had decided not to wear a costume. Halloween was for kids, and he was twelve.

It was past eight when they started home, their bags loaded. They were approaching Fifty-third Street when it happened. The twins were chasing each other, and Pat turned to yell at them, still tightly holding Kristy's hand. He never saw the motorcycle. Its wheels just cleared the curb as it turned. Its handlebar did not. Pat heard the sound, a sickening thud he would never forget. Kristy was torn from his hand and hurled into the street.

Then he was in the hospital waiting room, the same hospital he had visited five years before as a first holy communicant. Only this time he was alone. When would his father get here? If only he hadn't been forced to work the night shift. Pat had assured him that he could take care of them. And he had failed. They all had depended on him, and he had let them down.

Pat hadn't screamed when it happened. Not at first. He had stood there, frozen with terror. He remembered the twins standing there, Raggedy Ann and Andy, locked together in horror. And there was Cinderella, motionless in the street, one glass slipper still on the sidewalk where her big brother had held her only seconds before.

The neighbors had taken the twins, but Pat had insisted on riding in the ambulance, holding her hand. He would never let go. Never again.

Please, God. Please don't take her. You took my mommy, not my sister, too. What would he do? How could he live if she died because of him?

He looked up. His father was there, and the oldest child of the family for once was a little boy again.

"Daddy, Daddy!" he sobbed, throwing himself into his arms. "Please,

please save her. Please don't let her die. Please, Daddy."

George Carney's voice was gentle. "It's okay, Patty boy. I've just been with the doctor. Kristy is going to be just fine. Honest."

Pat felt himself falling away, slipping off the edge of the earth. The sobs convulsed his body. "I'm so sorry, Daddy. I'm so sorry. I was holding her, Daddy. Honest. I never let go. I never let go. I'll never fail you again, Daddy. Never, never. I'm the oldest. I'm supposed to—"

"Shhh, Patty boy," George said, picking him up and holding him on his shoulder, kissing the back of his head as he had so many years ago. In a different lifetime. "It wasn't your fault, Patty boy."

"Yes, it was, Daddy. Yes, it was. I should have held tighter. I should have—"

"Shhh, Patty boy. You've never failed me. You're the best son a man could ask for. I couldn't do it without you. I'm the one who's sorry, Patty. I've turned you into an old man."

Why me? Pat thought. *Why always me?* He still looked out the window, but tears blurred the view. He thought he was free when he entered the priesthood, his job completed, his dues paid. But here he was again, tortured by the same old fears. It was so unfair. So goddamn unfair.

He realized that his intercom was buzzing and absently reached for the button. "Yes?"

"Father," his secretary said, "Mr. Castagna's calling."

"Thank you, Lucille," Pat said, once again an adult, a monsignor and the director of communications of the archdiocese of Philadelphia. Eagerly he lifted the receiver.

"Hello, Phil," he said, attempting to sound casual. "How's it going?"

"Not bad, Father," the voice answered. His tone became conspiratorial. "Listen, Father, the person we discussed, the good reverend? He just made a withdrawal."

"How much?"

"All of it, Father. Two million and change. Would you like a copy of the withdrawal slip? Off the record, of course."

"I'd appreciate it. And, Phil, thank you for everything."

"Just say a prayer for me now and then, Father. Can't hurt."

Thank God for the Church's contacts, Pat thought as he replaced the phone. His father, the twins, even Kristy had vanished from his mind. It was crunch time, and he couldn't do it alone, so he

[119]

would do what he always did when he needed help: He would call Kevin and Vince.

Vince Grosso relaxed in the outside whirlpool, enjoying the contrast of the warm water on his body and the cool air on his head.

He tried not to feel guilty for coming home early. The work could wait. And he needed the time to think. Vagnoni remained a worry, a problem that had to be resolved. Quickly and finally.

Gus Toohey was doing his best to get the assignment, to be inside with the canary so that a final solution could be arranged. But so far nothing.

Therese walked down the path, wearing a terry-cloth robe. Seeing Vince, she hesitated. "I didn't know you were here, Mr. Grosso. I'll leave you alone."

"Please, Therese, come on in."

"You don't mind?"

"Not at all. I'd enjoy the company."

She unfastened her robe, dropped it to her feet, and slid into the whirlpool. Her bathing suit was white, setting off her tan, and was cut high on the hips, giving a marked accent to her long, slender legs.

They talked easily— about Villanova, past and present—but Vince felt uneasy. He never seemed to be in control when she was there. What *was* it about her? Certainly she was beautiful; but so was his wife, and so were dozens of other women whom he could have had with but a nod. Which he never did, never even considered. It had always been a matter of loyalty—and discipline.

So why did he find himself fantasizing about this woman—girl, actually—who was young enough to be his daughter? Why was he so intrigued, and frightened, by her?

Lena approached. "Nicky just called. He said that your friend received the assignment."

"Thanks, hon. That's great news."

"I'm glad. Therese, could you help the girls with their homework? When you get a chance."

"Sure, Mrs. Grosso. I was just leaving."

Alone, Vince reflected on the message. Lena had told him two things, one with her words, the other with her tone: Gus Toohey was inside. And Vince's thing with Therese had been noticed.

CHAPTER
Seven

SOME six blocks, and an entire world, away, an important strategy meeting was taking place. The participants, gathered in the conference room of Planned Parenthood, were of diverse backgrounds. They shared, however, one common goal: to stop Kevin Murray and his abortion control bill.

Of the fifteen in attendance, four were of particular significance.

Dr. Morris Abramson, director of ob-gyn at the Phillip Traynor Medical Center in New York, was one of the ranking veterans of the abortion wars. He had come aboard in the mid-sixties, long before *Roe* v. *Wade,* when the pro-abortion movement was in its embryonic stage. A prime mover in the enactment of the 1969 New York act which liberalized abortions, he was, even more important, the author of the "Catholic strategy."

"To be successful, we need a common enemy," he had argued, "someone or something with which the public can identify. The focus must be taken away from abortion and shifted to that target."

It was Dr. Abramson's studied opinion that the most suitable target was the Roman Catholic Church. Not the rank and file of the church—that would be suicidal—but its hierarchy, the archaic bureaucracy directed by Rome that had become so out of touch with even its own. That would play well, Abramson had deduced. John Kennedy's election had by no means eliminated anti-Catholism, the "anti-Semitism of the intelligentsia."

A large part of the Protestant world still adhered to the ABCs—anything but Catholic. Such fires, fueled by five hundred years of tradition, were not easily extinguished. Rome was still Rome—arrogant in its belief that it was the one true church, unbending in its refusal to compromise on issues such as mixed marriages, the religious education of children, and remarriage. Vatican II had been only window dressing. Behind the curtains still stood the pope, unchanged in his resolve to rule the world.

It was much the same with the Jews. For two thousand years they had bridled under the accusation of being Christ killers. That wasn't unique to Catholics. Christianity as a whole retained a basic distrust of the Jewish infidels. But the Catholics were the worst. Poland, one of the world's most Catholic nations, was a prime example. For a millennium, its devotion to Christ was matched only by its zeal for persecuting Jews. And then there was Pius XII, Pius the Pragmatist, who had gone to bed with the Nazis to save his church. Not once had he raised his voice against the Holocaust.

But the most promising accomplice in Morris Abramson's plan was the Catholic laity. They, more than anyone, had suffered under their church. The hope generated by Vatican II had been a mirage. Rome's ban on birth control remained, condemning millions of its faithful to alternative earthly hells. The cost of sexual safety for those who rebelled was a lifetime of torment, assaulted by the most devastating of all human emotions—guilt. Educated by the nuns and the Baltimore Catechism, they knew about mortal sin and, even worse, the "dreadful sin of sacrilege." Most of them would still go to mass, but they refrained from kneeling at the altar to receive the bread of life, a self-imposed excommunication more profound than any external edict. Worst of all, they would subconsciously look at their spouses with resentment, silently accusing them for their fall from grace.

If possible, those who obeyed suffered even more. Women endured the terror of repeated pregnancies, which occasionally cost them their lives and which frequently sentenced them and their husbands to premature old age. Their faith in God was not enough. Their children weren't like the ravens in the field. No matter how much they believed, no matter how hard they worked, the struggle continued. Bills had to be paid; children had to be fed, clothed, educated, and, most draining of all, loved.

Many of these marriages arrived at the ultimate paradox. Forbidden to practice unnatural birth control, they instead practiced abstention. But what could be more unnatural than a man and woman, deeply in love, depriving themselves of the physical expression of that love?

Predictably many of the men retreated, some to alcohol, some to other women, women who were "safe."

Yes, Dr. Abramson had calculated, *if we package our product correctly, it will sell.*

The most important part of that packaging process was language—how to convey, or hide, the truth. Toward that end, Abramson and three physician associates prepared a memo in 1966 that was circulated to certain members of the medical community. Its message contained a unique blend of candor, vision, and pragmatism.

After a nebulous opening paragraph, the doctors got right down to business.

> One point cannot be contradicted. If we permit debate to remain focused on abortion, our efforts are doomed. Human nature being what it is, a discussion of the physical essence of the act will inevitably result in overwhelming revulsion and opposition.
>
> We must, therefore, initiate a carefully orchestrated process of desensitization. To accomplish this, it is necessary for us to reject certain premises which thus far have been undisputed and which we, as experts in the science of medicine, have always acknowledged. Chief among such premises is the matter of when life precisely begins. To state it candidly, we cannot afford the luxury of a continued adherence to purely scientific data. To do so is to admit that life begins at conception, an admission that erects an impassable barrier to our course of action.
>
> Equally destructive, however, would be an attempt on our part to establish an alternative moment when life begins. First, and most important, we would be in possession of virtually no scientific data to support such a position. Secondly, we might well be limiting future options with respect to when a woman may exercise her right to choose an abortion.
>
> Accordingly, we strenuously suggest that no position be taken as to when the moment of life occurs. To state it plainly, we are advocating that the medical community throw up its collective hands in

helplessness, convinced of the impossibility of determining the commencement of life. When life begins must cease to be a medical question, capable of being answered with the preciseness that our profession demands. The answer to that question must become a uniquely personal one, based on individual morality and religious belief. Having shifted the issue to that stage, we will find our efforts have become infinitely less difficult. Of less, but still considerable, significance is the unique public goodwill which inevitably will accrue to the medical profession. Usually godlike in its infallibility, our profession for once will in essence be saying, "We don't know," a rare act of humility which will redound to our benefit.

The memo went on to detail the subsequent steps needed to establish the legality and acceptability of abortion. Once the determination of life had become a "personal judgment in an increasingly pluralistic society," the debate would be transferred to the legal and religious communities, realms which, by their very nature, were nurtured on imprecision and divergent opinions. There would no longer be black and white, only a murky gray, a color that would be embraced by the freedom of choice advocates.

While Americans traditionally revered life, their reverence for freedom was even greater. It was un-American, an unconstitutional infringement of liberty, to deny to any Americans the right to make a choice, particularly when the sole impediment to that liberty was an outdated religion that had traditionally treated women as second-class citizens.

Those who opposed such freedom were fanatics forcibly attempting to impose their personal morality on everyone, a modern Inquisition in a nation founded on the principle of separation of church and state.

Abramson and his colleagues expressed the importance of terminology, going so far as to provide a suggested glossary. One was not *pro-abortion,* but *pro-choice.* The word *abortion* was to be utilized as seldom as possible, replaced by *termination of pregnancy.* Under no circumstances would words such as *baby, child,* or *unborn child* be uttered. Instead, it was *fetus, product of conception,* or *undifferentiated mass of tissue.*

The memo concluded on a note of optimism: "Only by stu-

[124]

diously adhering to our plan can we be assured of ultimate success. Once the American public is properly desensitized, it will willingly cast aside the so-called sanctity of life ethic, realizing that when the crucial issue of life is being discussed, the quality of that life must be an integral part of that discussion."

Morris Abramson understood that more worlds were conquered by the manipulation of words than by the clash of arms. But visionary though he was, even he could not have predicted the success of his strategy or the speed with which that success was achieved. Within four years, a majority of the New York legislature had bought into this philosophy, a victory made complete by *Roe* v. *Wade*.

Abramson could take intense pride in the knowledge that largely through his efforts, all Americans now possessed freedom of choice. Certainly less important than this reaffirmation of freedom was the fact that he had acquired a substantial interest in five abortion clinics which, while ostensibly nonprofit, provided him with an annual income in excess of one million dollars.

Sheila Sendrow, formerly Sheila Bowen, formerly Sheila Cuthbert, was the president of Pennsylvania NOW. The seventh of nine children, she was raised in a middle-class neighborhood in suburban Pittsburgh. At a relatively young age she had reached two conclusions: she idolized her mother and hated her father.

On neither count could she be faulted. The story of her mother, Betsy Sendrow, was one that had been repeated countless times in middle-class America. A bright, vibrant young woman, filled with the enthusiasm of life, she had been graduated at the top of her high school class. Since it was the height of the Depression, college was out of the question. Undaunted, she took a job with a Pittsburgh manufacturing firm and quickly began her rise up the corporate ladder. Within three years she was executive secretary to the comptroller. Her performance was so outstanding that the firm enrolled her in night courses at Pitt to earn her marketing degree.

Her engagement to Howard Cuthbert was an act of acquiescence, a capitulation to the pressure from parents and friends to "settle down." A man could ignore early marriage and still be considered "normal," referred to as a "real comer" in the business world or "just looking over the field" or praised for his loyalty to

[125]

his parents. But a woman of twenty-one who was neither married nor planning to be raised eyebrows. She either couldn't land a man or was a tramp.

Howard Cuthbert was the type of man who was referred to, for want of something better to say, as "solid." Five years older than his bride, he had a steady job at the steel mill and was supremely confident that he would become one of the foremen by the time he was forty. He also had some very definite ideas about the composition of the family unit. There would be as many children as God provided, mostly boys to carry on the family name. God obviously listened, providing nine children, of which six were of the male variety.

The fact that Betsy became pregnant on her honeymoon (again, God's will) in no way affected her career since a condition of marriage had been that she resign her job and drop out of Pitt. Howard Cuthbert would not hear of his wife's working. It wasn't proper, was contrary to the very nature of things. Besides, it reflected poorly on him, a public accusation that he couldn't properly provide for his family.

It might have been easier for Sheila had she been able to convince herself that her father didn't love her. That would have clearly defined the issue, but life seldom possesses such clarity. Howard Cuthbert loved all his children and did what he thought was best for them. And what was best for his girls was that they become extensions of their mother, hardworking and soft-spoken. They should assist with the "women's work," serving as housekeepers and maids to their father and brothers.

Naturally the Cuthbert males would receive the college education that had eluded their father. It was only natural that a man wanted it better for his sons than it had been for him. That was the whole point of work: a continuing improvement, generation to generation, that had begun when men lived in caves.

It was different with the girls. College would be a waste of money, money better spent for a big wedding when the time came. High school was enough, then a temporary job until the right man came along to perpetuate the circle.

Like her mother, Sheila surrendered, marrying Keith Bowen a week before her twenty-second birthday. If possible, Sheila's husband was regarded as even more "solid" than her father. A CPA, he was beginning his third year with one of the Big Eight firms in

[126]

Philadelphia. They rented a town house in Chestnut Hill, thus providing Keith with an easy commute and an acceptable address.

Sheila, alone in a new city, was free to do as she pleased. Her husband had no qualms about her working, if that was her choice, though he felt obligated to caution her on the difficulty of the job market, particularly for someone with neither a trade nor a degree. Better yet, why not go back to school? Chestnut Hill College was nearby, a solid liberal arts college that provided a quality education, if you didn't take the religious mickey mouse too seriously. Start full-time at first, and then, when the children came, cut back to a few courses a semester. It would be stimulating for her, and it wouldn't do any harm to Keith's career either. Might come in handy at the firm's cocktail parties.

More to please her husband than anything else, Sheila enrolled, but it all seemed so pointless. Why was she there? What was the goal? It was as if the campus were a large sandbox where she was left to play, an activity that was both safe and harmless.

She became pregnant at the beginning of her sophomore year and delivered a baby boy two days after her last exam. Keith was pleased with Sheila for providing him with a male heir. He admired competence and congratulated her in much the same way he had when she received an A in economics.

He fully expected, of course, that she would return to school in the fall. There would be no difficulty in selecting a satisfactory baby-sitter, and besides, by that time the novelty would have worn off. Sheila would be ready to continue her education. To Keith's surprise, his wife, in what was her first independent decision since their marriage and, for that matter, since her birth, flatly rejected the proposal. Her place was with her baby. She would remain at home raising their son.

Sheila's life settled into a pattern which, for lack of any comparative reference, could be described as pleasant. She worshiped little Howie, deriving a heretofore unknown joy in watching him grow. Her husband she respected as a success in business and an expert in personal organization who provided her with sex that was—again she lacked a basis for comparison—not unpleasant.

Keith was a decent human being who treated her with kindness. Only occasionally was it necessary for her to reject the feeling that she was Keith's daughter rather than his wife. She even

[127]

came to erase the resentment she had felt toward her father. Like her mother, she had come to understand that a man's primary role was that of a strength figure charged with the welfare of his family.

Sheila's life might have continued in such a mode of acceptance had it not been for a summons from her mother. Betsy's unusually terse call made it clear that she wanted Sheila to spend the weekend with her *without* her husband and son, who was now three.

Upon her daughter's arrival Betsy wasted little time in getting to the point, announcing that she was suffering from liver cancer with less than a year to live.

Sheila broke into tears, reaching to embrace her mother. She was rewarded by a crisply delivered slap across her face.

"I don't want sympathy, and I don't want tears. What I want is your attention. Now sit down."

As her daughter obeyed, Betsy continued in a voice that had never before conveyed such determination. "I've been doing a lot of thinking since getting the word, and I realize that up till now my life has been a dismal failure."

Sheila began to object but again was silenced. "Please, Sheila, no protests. Just listen, and you'll realize I'm right. All my life I've played the game. I did what was expected of me. I was a good daughter, a good wife, and a good mother. Whatever those terms mean. But never, not once, did I ever do what I wanted. What's worse, what's unforgivable, is that I never even *thought* about what I wanted. I never once thought what I, Betsy Cuthbert—Betsy Sendrow—wanted to do with my life. Freedom? Free will? That's a laugh. You're not even free to think. They won't let you!"

It had all been so sudden for Sheila. Her mother was dying—and acting so strange.

"I—I don't understand, Mother," she stammered. "They?"

For the first time Betsy smiled. "Yes, 'they.' Don't worry, dear, I'm not going over the edge. The cancer is attacking my liver, not my brain. They. Parents, husbands, children. The whole damn society. Look at you. Did you really love Keith? Did you really want to marry him?"

"Mother! He's my husband! He's—"

"Totally beside the point. He's your husband, so you're ex-

[128]

pected to love him, right? Wrong! Would it shock you to know that I have never been in love with your father?"

"Mother!"

"Shocked? Don't be. I'm sure there are millions of other women who could say the same thing. They don't, of course, just as I didn't until I was handed a death sentence. Don't get me wrong, Sheila. I've come to love your father. He's a decent human being and, in his own way, a good husband and father. But I've never been *in love* with him. He's never been the man I've wanted to spend my life with. I'm not even sure I wanted to spend my life with a man."

Betsy paused and looked at her daughter. For a moment there was silence as Sheila struggled to grapple with the reality of what she just heard. That she failed was understandable. In five minutes all her values, the rocks which she had always grasped when the tides were strong, had been torn away, leaving her floating hopelessly in a sea of turmoil. Somewhere out in the fog she heard her mother continue. The voice that had been her beacon for so many years.

"It's up to you, Sheila, to give my life some meaning. You were always special, even when you were a baby. There was something extra there, some spark, that set you off from the rest. I saw so much of myself in you. I should have nurtured that spark, but I failed you the way I failed myself."

Betsy's voice became desperate. "Only for you it's not too late. I know it isn't. The spark's still there if you'll just look for it. Find it, Sheila. Live *your* life. Live it for both of us."

"But how, Mother?" Sheila asked, again a seven-year-old seeking guidance. "What should I do?"

"Only you can answer that, honey. Have the courage to be honest with yourself."

"But Keith? And the baby? What do I owe them?"

"I know what you don't owe them, and that's your life. That's too high a price for anyone to pay."

On her trip back to Chestnut Hill Sheila realized that she would never be the same. The change was not yet definable, and for the next eight months the pattern of her life retained the same outward routine. But while she functioned as wife and mother, her mind was constantly groping.

[129]

Only when she stood before her mother's casket did it all become clear. She knew what she must do.

"I'll do it, Mother," she whispered, touching Betsy's lifeless hand. "For both of us."

A month after the funeral Keith returned from work to find five suitcases stationed by the door. Sheila was dressing the baby.

"What's going on?" he asked, annoyed rather than alarmed. Probably a family problem in Pittsburgh. Normally he wouldn't mind; but the firm's spring cocktail party was tomorrow night, and her absence would be embarrassing.

"I'm leaving you, Keith," she answered calmly. After tying her son's shoe, she walked to her husband and handed him a blue-backed document. "This is a complaint in divorce. You'll probably want to see a lawyer."

"Lawyer! You've been to a lawyer?"

"Not exactly. I'm handling it myself, though I am getting some help from the Women's Law Project."

"What's that?"

"My new employer. I begin on Monday as a paralegal trainee. Twelve weeks of courses. After that I intend to go back to school at night for my bachelor's. Then, after that, I want a law degree."

"Sheila, this is crazy! Absolutely crazy!"

"Actually, Keith, it's the first sane thing I've ever done."

She kissed the cheek of the man who had been her husband and lover. "It's not your fault, Keith. It's not anyone's. I hope we can still be friends."

It would be futile for Keith to protest. He looked at the woman who had given him his son and realized that he no longer knew her. And he knew that there was no way he could care for a child.

Sheila and Howie moved into a furnished apartment at Eleventh and Spruce, one of the three-story row houses that were unique to Philadelphia. True to her word, she was amicable and more than fair to Keith. She wanted nothing for herself, only a modest support payment for Howie to defray the cost of his day care.

She loved her work and was surprised to find that she excelled at it. It was an exciting time to be part of an organization like the Women's Law Project. The pendulum of American democracy, having toppled the barriers of racial discrimination, was now swinging into the realm of women's rights, and the same excite-

[130]

ment, the same pioneer spirit that had accompanied the freedom riders in Alabama were present. The enemy was different yet the same. America, more specifically, the American consciousness with its unconscious stereotypes, must be penetrated.

It was the job of the Women's Law Project to take existing law—it was for others to lobby for new legislation—and mold it into a weapon infinitely more powerful than the matches, bricks, and guns that had ignited the race riots of the mid-sixties. The project learned how to play the game, how to tap the federal money that, since the Great Society, oozed like oil just beneath the surface for anyone who knew where to look for it and then use it to attack the system that had provided it. Rent discrimination, unequal credit ratings, employer sexual harassment, domestic abuse, abortion rights—these were the issues with which the project grappled and which became the major portion of Sheila Bowen's life. Only she was no longer Sheila Bowen. Nor was she Sheila Cuthbert. Handling it herself, as she had the divorce, Sheila successfully petitioned the court for a name change. Only when she became Sheila Sendrow did her new life really begin, the first step in keeping the promise that she had made to her dead mother. The fulfillment of that promise came in steps: her bachelor's in social studies from Widener; her law degree from Temple, her triumphs in and out of court on behalf of the movement; the feature story in *Philadelphia* magazine which labeled her one of Pennsylvania's most influential women; and, just a year before, her election as president of Pennsylvania NOW. She enjoyed her success. In fact, it could be said that she reveled in the power and recognition that she continued to acquire. But she never lost sight of the main goal. Each time she won, she would look at the dog-eared picture of Betsy in her wallet and whisper, "I'm doing it, Mother. For both of us."

Although she was the legislative director of Planned Parenthood of Pennsylvania, Bridget Kelly took greater pleasure in describing herself as the TFP—top former pape. The product of fourteen years of Catholic education, she had been valedictorian at her graduation from Regina Mundi Academy for Girls, delivering the speech with her typical eloquence as her parents and the Sisters of the Holy Child beamed with pride.

Bridget was, as one nun put it, "an exemplification of the very

[131]

best in Catholic education." Although she would have preferred a coed college, Bridget did not object to her parents' choice of St. Mary's. Its academic reputation was outstanding, it was the sister school of Notre Dame, her father's alma mater, and it was an easy weekend commute to her home in suburban Chicago.

She applied herself at St. Mary's with the same dedication that had characterized all her previous efforts. The fact that Bridget lacked natural brilliance presented no problem since she was intelligent enough to acknowledge her limitations and compensate with hard work. In addition to making the dean's list each semester, she wrote for the school paper, was a dependable sub on the field hockey team, and won a number of trophies for her debating skills.

But it was her personality that most endeared her to her classmates and teachers. Her freckled face, upon which the map of Ireland was clearly defined, seemed perpetually on the verge of laughter. Despite her heavy schedule, she never appeared pressured. There was always time for her friends, who became increasingly dependent upon her for counsel and encouragement.

The general consensus was that Bridget Kelly was a young woman who had it all together, with a future as bright as her eyes.

That is why it came as a shock when, a month before the conclusion of her sophomore year, she announced that she would not be returning in the fall. No specific reason was given, only that she had other commitments. The next seven months were spent in a small town near Seattle, where, as she said to a few close friends to whom she occasionally wrote, she was "sorting things out in my head."

That process completed, Bridget exchanged coasts, taking a third-floor flat in a Baltimore brownstone within walking distance of the job that she landed within three days of her arrival. She had seen a newspaper ad for a counseling position and, since she liked people and had always been fairly successful at helping her friends, had decided to apply. At the end of her forty-five-minute interview she was offered the job and immediately accepted it. The Coalition to Assist Females in Need (CAFIN) was a federally financed pilot project designed to assist victims of both rape and domestic violence. It was Bridget's responsibility to conduct the initial interview of the victims, blending compassion with the thoroughness necessary to obtain all the facts. Following the in-

[132]

terview, the next step, depending upon the circumstances and the wishes of the victim, was to arrange for professional counseling, a temporary "safe house" residence, or criminal prosecution. The last category brought her into frequent contact with the police and the court system, a contact which first caused her shock, then anger and finally armed her with determination that she had never before experienced.

The system treated female victims with indifference and even hostility. Those suffering from domestic violence were flatly ignored, a result of the philosophy that government should stay out of family matters. The unwritten rule with the police department was that no charges were brought if the wife could still stand.

"Christ Almighty, we're still in caves!" Bridget had blurted to a police lieutenant she had come to respect. "Beat hell out of your wife; just don't break her legs. As long as you can prop her up, even if she wobbles a bit, you're safe."

The lieutenant shook his head. "Bridget, what the hell can we do? We don't have the time, the money, or the men to act as family social workers."

"Family social workers! I'm talking about criminal prosecutions. That's your job. To arrest people who commit crimes. And when you beat someone, whether or not you're married to her, that's a crime!"

"Sure, sure. Except that when we do file charges, ninety-nine times out of a hundred the woman backs off. She and hubby make up and that's the name of that tune. We go through all the work—at taxpayer expense, I might add—and come up with nothing. Meanwhile, people are still getting mugged, murdered, and raped."

But in Bridget's mind they weren't doing really well with rape, either. It was as if the woman, not the rapist, were guilty until proved innocent. There was a feeling that they got what they deserved. It was a feeling that was not entirely unspoken. A judge even went so far as to put it on the record, dismissing a rape charge on the ground that the victim had dressed too provocatively. She had asked for the trouble she received and had no right to complain after the fact.

A considerable uproar followed the judge's decision, but within a week it had been forgotten. Except by Bridget. She remembered, and she moved. The first hurdle was causing the executive director of the coalition to take a liberal approach to how the federal funds could be spent. He was cautious, with the mind of a bureaucrat, clinging to the safety of going strictly by the book. He was also no match for Bridget.

At the same time she was building an alliance with the local chapter of Planned Parenthood and a number of service organizations. Pooling their resources, they mounted the offensive. Full-page ads were taken out in the newspapers. One showed a picture of Jackie Onassis in a bikini, under which was the caption "Does she deserve to be raped?" Concise, punchy copy followed, blasting the system's attitude toward rape victims and urging the readers to protest to their elected officials.

The ad dealing with domestic violence was particularly vivid. It showed a woman, fortyish, leaning against a wall, the obvious victim of a beating. Both eyes were swollen, her lips were puffed, and her plain smock was torn. Even without the battering she would not have been pretty, but her face could have been described as kind. Visible in the background was a man, clad in a sleeveless undershirt that accentuated his gut, drinking a can of beer while watching television. The caption read: "The loser and still standing." Several short sentences followed, explaining the plight of the beaten wife and, like the rape ad, urging citizen action.

The media pounced on it, and Bridget found herself on a series of television and radio talk shows, where she ripped apart, in quick succession, the police commissioner, a judge, two city councilmen, and a conservative state senator. Unsolicited contributions poured into the coalition, the police department issued tough new guidelines, and the state legislature enacted a spousal abuse law.

The campaign attracted national attention, even *Time* running a lengthy article that featured Bridget prominently. She enjoyed her new celebrity status but flatly rejected all questions concerning her personal life. Had she been just a bit more experienced, she would have realized that such a refusal would only whet the media's appetite, fueling the relentless search to discover who this Bridget Kelly really was.

And of course, there were the hate contacts. The letters that seemed to be written in acid. Calls in the middle of the night, forcing her to change to an unlisted number. Threatening, filthy, and venomous. She was, among other things, a "feminist cunt," a "fucking Communist," and a "perverted dyke."

These, since they were so obviously the products of sick minds, did not disturb her nearly so much as the messages from the religious fanatics. They accused her of subverting God's law, particularly in the domestic abuse area. Marriage was for better or worse, and no one, including a crusading liberal, should pull asunder what God had joined together. Included, of course, were the appropriate biblical notations. If Bridget were ever to start to pray again, it would be that God save the world from religion.

Partially to escape and partially because she was ready for a new challenge, Bridget accepted the offer of Planned Parenthood of Pennsylvania to become its legislative coordinator. Two months after Kevin Murray had been elected to the legislature, she arrived in Harrisburg, and for the past five years they had waged combat.

But dedicated as she was to the cause, Bridget could never bring herself to hate. Unlike Sheila Sendrow, whom she came to respect, if not emulate, she refused to distrust men, to consider them enemies strictly on the basis of gender. Men were people, and she liked people. Hell, she liked life. For Bridget Kelly, the Irish twinkle would always remain.

The others attending the meeting were much like Morris Abramson, Sheila Sendrow, and Bridget Kelly. Representing such groups as the National Association to Repeal Abortion Laws, the American Civil Liberties Union, and Americans for a Free Choice, they were men and women of accomplishment, dedicated to the pro-choice movement. Except for the woman who sat in the rear, constantly fondling the gold cross that hung from her neck.

Helen Osborne was an enigma to the others. She was a woman without a past, representing no one but herself. Slightly less than a year before she had appeared at the Planned Parenthood office in Philadelphia to volunteer her services. She was neither intelligent nor attractive, but her one remarkable feature was intensity, eyes burning with fervor for the cause. She never seemed to tire. No matter what the hour, no matter how menial the task, Helen was always there. The cross which she always wore was a re-

[135]

minder of the crucifixion of women. At least that's what she said. The cause was her life, her entire world, and she would gladly die for it.

The meeting was chaired by Carla Schwab, national president of Planned Parenthood. As usual, she was all business.

"In precisely fifty-five minutes we will be holding a news conference. I have been assured that it will be covered by the national media. The purpose of the conference will be to announce that Pennsylvania has become the focus of the pro-choice movement. Specifically, Planned Parenthood of America has adopted as its number one priority the defeat of the Pennsylvania abortion control bill. Toward that end we have raised in excess of five million dollars to stop this outrageous legislation. Bridget, please be kind enough to provide us with the details."

Bridget smiled, the only one in the room to do so. "Certainly, Carla. The money is being put to excellent use. We've retained the lobbying firm of Walls and Baynard, one of the best in Harrisburg. They represent the Pennsylvania Medical Society, the Pennsylvania Bankers Association, and the Pennsylvania Trial Lawyers Association, to name just a few. Their record is outstanding; their reputation, impeccable. For our media blitz, we've hired a New York PR outfit, Dirkson, Kalish, Pepper, and Smith. They just handled the anti-nuke referendum in the state of Washington. Did a hell of a job. It goes without saying, of course, that neither firm comes cheap."

Sheila Sendrow raised her hand. Her expression matched the severity of her dress: tailored blue blazer and gray slacks. A female Brooks Brothers ad. "How are they to be used?" she asked. "Specifically."

Bridget smiled again. "Certainly, Sheila. I always strive for specificity. As you know, we've had a letter campaign going since just after Labor Day, and it's been very successful. Even Kevin Murray admits that right now the mail is running five to one against the bill. The Health and Welfare Committee should be voting on it within the next several weeks, so we're now going to key on the committee members. Each of them will be visited by our lobbyist. The media ads—and we will use television, radio, and the papers—will do the same, urging people to contact the committee members for a no vote. Naturally, when the bill gets to the floor, we'll expand our efforts to the entire membership."

Sheila's eyebrows arched. "You said *when* the bill gets to the floor, but the information that I have is that it may well be defeated in committee."

"That's true," Bridget answered. "It'll be a close vote, but if I had to predict, I'd say we'll win by two votes. Don't be misled, though. That committee has always leaned toward us. If you recall, the Medicaid funding bill also went down in committee, and you know what happened. Kevin amended it into a Senate-passed bill on the House calendar. You can bet the ranch that one way or another, Kevin Murray will get his bill to the floor. Probably the same way, picking off a Senate bill. That gets around the committee process in both houses."

Bridget hesitated. *What the hell,* she finally said to herself. *Why not?*

"I might as well finish. If you want my opinion, not only will he get the bill onto the floor, but he'll get it passed. House *and* Senate. And our gutless governor will sign it into law. Which is why, as I've told Carla, I think we're making a big mistake in making this *the* national target. When you build up the level of expectation, you'd better be damn sure you can win. Look what's happening with ERA." Another smile. "End of speech."

Carla Schwab saw herself losing control, something that she did not like and would not permit. "I've discussed this with Bridget, and of course, I respect her valuable opinion. Since *Roe* versus *Wade,* we have been content to accept our losses in the legislatures—in the states and Congress—confident that the courts would come to our rescue. We no longer can enjoy the luxury of such confidence. Last year's Supreme Court decision on Medicaid funding, *Harris* versus *McRae,* must serve as a warning signal. We can no longer depend on anyone but ourselves."

Morris Abramson spoke. "Particularly with that maniac we have in the White House. God only knows what's going to happen. If he gets the chance to replace a few justices, we could have a whole new ball game."

"Precisely," Carla Schwab said. "The public opinion polls are with us. We have the money and the organization. We must move boldly. Starting right now in Pennsylvania." She looked toward Bridget. "And I know, of course, that despite her misgivings, Bridget will continue her invaluable leadership. That goes without saying."

"Then why say it?" Bridget countered, still smiling.

"Let's get back to tactics," Abramson said. "These two birds, Murray and Harrington, they're very visible. You can't turn on the tube or look at a paper without seeing them. The way I view it, stop them and you stop the bill."

"What do you mean, 'stop'?" asked Bridget. "I don't think there's any place in the budget for a hit."

"Pity," Abramson answered. "Actually I was referring to—how shall I say it?—tarnishing their images somewhat. Any possibility?"

"No chance," said Bridget. Her smile had vanished. "Not with Kevin anyway. He's probably the best legislator in the state. Even worse, he's charming. Great sense of humor, liked by his colleagues, the media, and, I'm not ashamed to admit, me. As far as his personal life, he's a Boy Scout, not one of the usual Harrisburg whoremongers. Five kids, expecting a sixth. Takes the train home every night. The only way you're going to nail him for shacking up is if you accuse him of catching a quickie on Amtrak."

"And Harrington?"

"Craig Harrington," Bridge continued, "is, for want of a better term, an ass. An intelligent but pompous ass who is detested as much as Kevin is liked. He's also bedded down half of the secretaries in Harrisburg, but since he's a bachelor, that won't play. Where we *can* make some headway is by continuing to attack him. Kevin would just ignore it or make a joke, but Harrington takes the heat. And the more he talks, the better off we are."

Carla Schwab looked at her watch. "I think we'd better wrap this up. Wouldn't do to keep the media waiting. Let me conclude by saying that while none of us doubts that this will be a tremendous struggle, there is absolutely no question in my mind that we can and will succeed. Our course is right, and I am honored to march with you to our inevitable victory."

They applauded. Particularly the woman in the rear, wearing the golden cross.

CHAPTER
Eight

HE was ready to explode, which wasn't unusual since he felt that way damn near every day. Being in the district was even worse than Harrisburg. He couldn't duck. They knew he was there, and they demanded attention. His constituents and his clients. Particularly the clients, who couldn't care less about his legislative schedule, not when they were forking out good money for his legal services.

Every day he promised himself it would be different, that things would run on a smooth schedule, that instead of juggling fifty things, he'd concentrate on ten or twelve and do them right. What a goddamn joke.

Where was he going? What did his life mean? Was this the end result of the genius brain, the bottomless energy, the unmatched drive that had made him admired since grade school?

He had it all; that's what they said. He could walk into a room, whether there were ten or ten thousand, and hold them in the palm of his hand. He could dictate for two hours without once correcting himself—legal briefs, constituent letters, bill analyses, all professional, all perfect. He could spot a problem before anyone and instinctively know how to solve it. And he knew how to deal with people; when to crack a joke, when to play hardball.

To what end? Here he was, pushing forty, not a penny in the bank, paddling like a maniac just to stay above water. He should be at a comfortable period, buying a bigger house, taking Karen on a winter cruise, socking some money away for the kids' education. That's what his friends were doing. But not him, not Kevin Murray, savior of the masses.

He had started well enough. Scholarships to high school and college. And his grades in law school weren't too shabby either, despite the fact that he never studied, sleeping between, and during, classes and driving a cab at night. They were married when he still was in law school, and ten months on the button, young Kevin arrived, two weeks after graduation and two weeks before his old man entered the FBI.

The three years with the Bureau were good ones. Milwaukee was good duty for a first office agent, small enough that you got to work a little of everything: bank robberies; check cases; interstate theft; even a kidnapping. But the fugitives were the most fun. For the last six months of his tour he and his partner, Charlie Masters, had specialized in catching them. The ultimate cops-and-robbers game. They were out there, and you had to find them.

They did it so well that they each received a special commendation from the Director as well as a feature story in the Bureau magazine.

In its own way, Detroit was just as good, even though the town was the crotch of the nation. He was assigned to the office plum, organized crime. Thus graduating from cops and robbers to cops and wops, he became an expert on La Cosa Nostra, LCN in Bu lingo.

When an agent signed up, he made a gentleman's agreement that he'd stay at least three years. As he did all others, Kevin kept this commitment, but at the end of the three it was time to go home. Not that he wanted to leave the Bureau. He might not have made it a career, but he would have given it a few more years. The problem was the Old Man. Hoover believed in moving his agents around. It took the average agent at least twenty years to get home.

It really wasn't much of a choice. For one of the few times in their married life, Kevin and Karen agreed. Life was too short for you not to be where you wanted. Both were from Philly, and all the roots were still there. They wanted their boys—Sean had arrived in Milwaukee—to know their grandparents, aunts, and uncles.

In looking back, Kevin concluded that the next step had been the most crucial. Had he joined a law firm, devoted his energies to his practice, things would have been different. Without question, he would have been a success, a brilliant trial lawyer. At a relatively young age he would have been wealthy, and Karen would have been happy with a comfortable and secure life.

But selfish bastard that he was, he opted for action, joining the staff of the district attorney of Philadelphia. It didn't take the DA long to realize that he had something special in Kevin, someone too valuable to waste on preliminary hearings and municipal court trials. Within two months Kevin had received a twenty percent pay raise and was assigned to the elite division—the special grand jury probing corruption.

Once again he was in his element, taking on the world: labor racketeering; payoffs to judges; kickbacks in the real estate tax office, and a dozen other juicy targets. He had his own technique. Before taking a witness before the grand jury, he conducted a personal interview, the preamble of which was always the same: "Before we begin, you should know a little about my background. I spent three years as a special agent of the FBI, and that should mean three things to you. First, I'm totally honest and can't be bought. Secondly, I don't give a fuck about politics. And thirdly, I learned how to investigate from the best investigators in the world. Now, shall we get started?"

The Murray approach produced results. In two years he put away more than forty public officials, including three judges, two city councilmen, and the patronage chief of the Democratic party.

And then the DA lost his bid for reelection. His successor decided to keep 139 of the 140 assistant prosecutors. The exception was, of course, Kevin, who was non-negotiable on the express orders of the Democratic chairman.

He spent the next three months in the ranks of the unemployed, in the process learning a great deal about the basic gutlessness of the average human. It quickly became obvious to him that he was a pariah. Sure, he had done an outstanding job, his praises sung in the media. But he had offended the big boys who ran the city. No law firm was willing to take the risk. He was simply too hot to handle.

It was depressing to be out of a job. The first few weeks, when he still had confidence that something would break, weren't too bad. Job interviews were sort of fun, and besides, he had extra

[141]

time to spend with the kids. But even playing Candyland had its limits. The rejections—the polite "thanks, but no thanks, we're not in a position to take on an associate at this time but will certainly keep your résumé on file"—mounted until finally Kevin had to agree that Karen should go back to work. That was one nice thing about marrying a nurse. Hospitals always needed nurses. Though she hadn't practiced in almost five years, it took only one phone call. Name your days and your hours, she was told. We'd love to have you.

Kevin tried to tell himself that it was no big deal, but it gnawed at his guts. Not that he minded his wife working. If that were what she *wanted*, if it were a release for her and a way to increase their income to buy the extras, that would be fine. But not when it was a necessity, not when she had to support *his* family.

And even though she tried to hide it, there was resentment on Karen's part. Why did it always have to be Kevin? Why him, always taking on the world? Why couldn't he just be normal, like everyone else?

What embittered her most were his last seven weeks on the job. The DA had lost, and it didn't take a genius to figure out that Kevin's head was going to roll. He should have been like the others in the office. They got their résumés out right away, lined up interviews. It was survival.

But not Kevin, not the crusader. There were two investigations unfinished. He knew damn well that if he didn't finish them, if he didn't get the indictments before the new guy came in, they would be buried.

"Goddamnit, Karen," he had said. "I'm an assistant DA. That's my job. And as long as I've got that job, I've got to give it my best shot." Left unanswered was Karen's question as to what shot he owed his family.

So while others looked after themselves, Kevin pushed harder than ever. And as usual, he succeeded, bringing in the last indictment two hours before the new DA was sworn in.

The drought appeared to be over at the two-month mark. Answering a newspaper ad, he interviewed with a professional flesh peddler to head up security for a national vending firm in Philly. The man who interviewed him was enthusiastic. A fellow Villanova grad, he thought Kevin was perfect for the position: right age; FBI background; aggressive; solid record of accomplishment.

[142]

Kevin allowed himself to hope. God, it would be perfect. The pay was excellent, the benefits were better, and it was the type of work he would love.

According to the flesh peddler, Kevin had a virtual lock on the job. There still had to be an interview with the company, but with the type of recommendation the flesh peddler would give, it was in the bag.

Kevin raced home, stopping only to buy Karen a bouquet of carnations. He couldn't wait to tell her, to let her know that he was back in overdrive.

Her expression was a little funny when he bounced in, but he figured the kids had been bugging her. "Have I got news for you," he bellowed, hugging her, then dropping the flowers into her hands. "The long siege is over, sports fans. We are about to come in out of the cold. Victory at last, a smashing—"

"Kevin—"

"Please, love, permit me my moment of triumph. I mean, the way I've been kicked around, it's only—"

"Kevin. Please."

Something in her tone made him stop. Please, God. No.

"The man from the employment agency called. The one who interviewed you. He really sounded upset, Kevin. I think he meant it."

"Meant what?" Kevin screamed. His chest felt as if it were collapsing. "For Christ's sake, get to the point!"

"I'm sorry, Kevin. They won't even interview you. They do a lot of business with the city, and they won't touch you."

He didn't eat that night, and he didn't speak, not even to the kids. Instead, he walked the streets until dawn, almost luxuriating in the bitterness that coursed through his body.

Was the whole friggin' worth it? Was any of it? You play it straight, you work your ass off, and what happens? They break your balls.

You try to do a good job in college, to be a good student body president, and they almost boot you the hell out.

You do a good job as an agent, way above and beyond the call, and what's your reward? They transfer you to some shit hole, away from the ones you love.

You do a good job as a prosecutor, run honest investigations, just following the trail wherever it leads, no politics, no deals, and they try to destroy you.

[143]

And meanwhile, all those worthless shits in the office, the ones who just went through the motions, were still there or else with some firm making money, while he, Kevin Murray, defender of truth, was playing with himself.

His brother was right. Competence scared people. Safety in mediocrity. In the end the really good ones were always crushed.

As is so often the case, the rescue came when least expected. It arrived in the form of Michael Callaghan, the majority leader of the House.

Callaghan got right to the point. "I hear you're out of work."

Kevin nodded.

"Not much fun, is it?"

"I've had better moments."

"You interested in a job?"

"Is the pope Catholic?"

Callaghan smiled. This guy might just do. With no embellishment, he outlined the offer. Myron Gordon, the incumbent governor, was running for reelection. He was a Democrat and thus the enemy. Callaghan would go to almost any extreme to knock him out of the box, and Kevin might be able to help.

The Republicans controlled the House and were about to run through a resolution establishing a select committee, with subpoena power, to probe state corruption. They needed a special counsel to run it, and Kevin came highly recommended.

Kevin tried to conceal his excitement. It was a natural. Absolutely perfect. Kicking ass again.

"You interested?" Callaghan asked casually.

"Depends."

"On what?"

"On the ground rules. I'm not gonna bullshit you. I've been out of work three months, and I'm desperate; but I'm not a whore. If I take this job, it's straight down the line, wherever it leads. If we nail Democrats, fine. But the same goes for Republicans. No whitewash, no cover-up." He smiled. It was 1974, the height of Watergate. "I should think the GOP has had it with cover-ups."

"And I'm not going to bullshit you," Callaghan replied. "I'm a politician, a hard-nosed partisan who gets a special kick out of crushing donkey balls. And I've whored out more than once in my day, too. But I'm also honest. If we go with this investigation, it'll be straight. You can put that in the bank."

Kevin looked into his face. He was convinced. If this guy gave his word, you *could* bank on it. "You haven't mentioned money," he finally said.

"Name your salary. We'll meet it. And if you're smart, you won't come cheap. This is a kamikaze mission. By the end of the year you'll probably be the most hated man in the state."

And so was born the Campbell Committee, named after its personable but weak chairman. There was no doubt that Kevin was running the show. The House leadership, pinning its hopes for the governor's office on him, gave him carte blanche.

The first job was to raise an army. He tapped as deputy counsel Mike Winters, a colleague from the DA's office. He was Kevin's type, tough, straight, and, since he had resigned from the DA's office rather than work for a "friggin' hack," out of work.

They looked over the House staff and made their selections. Research analysts, none of them had ever conducted an investigation. Kevin took care of that, giving them a three-week crash course, installing the Bureau system and training them in interview techniques, signed statements, chain of custody, and, most important, one-upmanship.

At the same time he started to build up the hype. If the committee had any shot at all, it needed media attention. Publicity gave you status. People thought you were real, and some were willing to volunteer information. Most of the time it was anonymous and off the record, but it was a start. Another factor no less important was that even then Kevin loved the spotlight.

He was able to plant an article in the *Observer,* the statewide political rag, labeling himself and Winters "hired guns" and predicting trouble for Gordon and the Democrats.

They were ready to take their show on the road, a road that would involve thirty counties and hundreds of public officials. With typical understatement, Kevin pronounced his troops the "second-best investigative unit in the state." The Bureau, of course, was first. He always had a thing about loyalty.

First stop was Westmoreland County, home base of John Tenaglio. Just beginning his rise through the Democratic caucus, Tenaglio was a minority member of the committee, outraged that his county was the first target.

Heading out the turnpike, they constituted a sizable army. Besides Kevin and Mike, there were fourteen investigators, five

[145]

secretaries, and a van crammed with typewriters, dictating equipment, and assorted office supplies. They had reserved ten rooms at the New Stanton Holiday Inn for an indefinite period.

All they lacked was confidence, and Kevin had taken steps to provide that. When they arrived in New Stanton, the *Pittsburgh Press* would be waiting, one copy in each room. The front-page headline was seven columns, the type reserved for the end of a war or an assassination: WESTMORELAND PROBE ON

But the topper, the coup that made his troops believe anything was doable, was the sight that greeted them as they turned onto the street of the hotel. The marquee of the Holiday Inn, one of the nation's more staid institutions, contained a simple greeting: WELCOME HIRED GUNS.

From that point on it was easy. And it was always fun. And when Nixon packed it in that August, they became the only ball game in town, the attention of an entire state riveted on them.

In the end they failed. Myron Gordon was reelected, control of the House was lost, and some Republicans, looking for a scapegoat, pointed to Kevin. Reality said otherwise. Forty public officials, including three cabinet members, were indicted as a result of the committee's work. Corruption was a major campaign issue, and the press and public were clamoring for a change in Pennsylvania's election laws. But not even the Campbell Committee could stem the Watergate Tide and the Nixon pardon.

Kevin figured he was on the bricks again. He had made outstanding money, permitting him and Karen to buy the house in Havertown; but now the fear was returning. Not that he had a bitch. Mike Callaghan had leveled with him at the outset. He had done his thing, made his money, and now it was time to move on—the hired gun, leaving Dodge for another town.

Callaghan had other ideas. "Where the hell you gonna go?" he asked. "Nobody would hire you, for chrissake. In case you didn't know, you're trouble—which is why I like you. I want you to stay."

"Stay?"

"By God, he's a quick study. That's right. Stay. The committee's done; but your work is just starting, and it'll be a lot easier now."

"How?"

"The campaign's over. Gordon's in again, goddammit. The

[146]

press can't knock us for being political anymore. Isn't it a bitch that you have to lose an election to gain credibility? I want you on my staff with a free rein. We won't have subpoena power, but you can still get the job done."

"What about the caucus?"

"Fuck the caucus. Sure, there's a few hotheads who want you canned, but I can handle them. You just keep pounding."

"Straight down the line?"

"Wouldn't have it any other way."

So Kevin stayed, and all in all, it was a good life. His salary was more than adequate, the work was rewarding, and, as was not the case during his tenure with the Campbell Committee, he could take the train home every night. He and Karen were happier than they had ever been. For the first time in their married life there was little tension, a Pax Murray which they both hoped would endure.

And it might have had it not been for State Representative Hope Riley Pendleton. She was reaching the height of her power, the savior of endangered elephants. The year had been a disaster for all Republicans, even the legendary Delaware County organization. For the first time in history the county—the same county that had gone seven to one for Alf Landon—went Democratic. The invincible machine had been routed, losing its congressman, five state reps, and a state senator. But what was really terrifying were the prospects for the future. Embarrassing as it was, a party could lose its state and federal people and survive. But 1975 was a different matter, an off-year election in which control of the courthouse, with all its jobs—the nuts and bolts of political power—was up for grabs.

That was where Hope came in. The pols detested her, but they had no choice. She was their top vote getter and her gender was an asset, particularly to a party that had been consistently accused of male chauvinism. And it was almost impossible to pin the label of corrupt ward heeler on a widow and mother of three.

Refusing to give up her legislative seat, she ran for County Council and pulled in the entire ticket. The courthouse was safe for another century, with Hope Riley Pendleton in full control.

She might have been content to bask in her victory and consolidate her gains were it not for Larry Singleton's propensity for falling asleep on the turnpike. The honorable state senator

[147]

cracked through the guardrail at a shade over ninety, creating both a hole in the guardrail and a vacancy in the Senate. Hope pounced, easily winning the special election. This, in turn, created a vacancy in the House and a need for another special election.

That was where Kevin Murray came in. Not that it was Kevin's idea. It was Hope's. She now regarded the county GOP as *her* party and had come to possess an almost maniacal obsession to control every aspect of its operation, firmly convinced that any misfortune suffered was a direct reflection upon her.

Her former legislative seat was a worry. The same candidate who had run her close in '74 would be the Democratic standard-bearer in the special election. He was well known and well liked, a distinct threat to shift the seat into the Democratic column for the first time in history. This in turn could cause a chain reaction, again placing the county in jeopardy.

A fresh face was needed: someone young, aggressive, with a proved record of accomplishment whose integrity was beyond reproach.

Kevin was a natural. Hope had carefully watched his performance in Harrisburg. She liked what she saw, particularly the way he handled himself under fire. No chance that he would crack during a tough campaign.

Kevin flatly rejected her. Not once but three times. He appreciated the thought, but he was happy where he was: the hired gun still hunting for heads.

But Hope was nothing if not persistent, and Kevin found himself wavering. Politics is an incurable disease, particularly for a Kevin Murray. How could someone who had grown up believing that he would be president turn his back on such an offer?

Karen, of course, was dead set against it. She was happy the way things were. Kevin would always be competitive, but the demons seemed to be gone. At long last they were at peace, and she wanted to keep it that way.

He knew that she was right. It would be brutal on her and the kids. He would be bidding farewell to law enforcement. His career, every two years, would depend upon the whims of the people. And, most practically, he would be taking a forty percent pay cut. There was no getting around it: to run for the seat would be a supreme act of selfishness.

He chose selfishness. Actually there was no choice. He had to know, rather than wonder. It was like winning the high school scholarship to Malvern. He was set to turn it down, to go to Bonner with his buddies from St. Laurence. Enter the Sarge.

"I'm not going to force you to take the scholarship, Kevin. That has to be your decision. But I want you to consider one thing very carefully. If you try Malvern and you don't like it, you can always transfer to Bonner. But if you turn it down, you'll always wonder what might have been."

As usual the Sarge had been right. Kevin had tried Malvern and loved it. And now he was accepting another scholarship. Only this time there was no transfer clause.

So he ran and won. Big. Bigger than Hope's biggest margin. His career was launched, and it wasn't long before he was being mentioned for higher office, talk which he did nothing to discourage.

Although natural talent and personality were factors in Kevin's success, the main reason was plain hard work. Particularly in his district. He understood the cardinal rule of an incumbent and frequently spelled it out to new legislators.

"It's a possibly sad, but definitely true, fact of life that the average person doesn't give a damn how his legislator votes in Harrisburg, or his congressman in Washington. What he remembers and cares about is how he's treated when he contacts your office with a problem. If you respond, show you care, do your best to help him, even if you don't succeed, that's worth five votes. If you don't get back to him, it's gonna cost you ten because people talk louder and longer when they're ticked. When you see an incumbent knocked off, it generally means he started to think of himself as a Harrisburg rep or a Washington congressman. He forgot where home was."

Kevin heeded his own words. His district office handled more than ten thousand constituent problems a year, all types and stripes. The senior citizen who needed help with his rebate application. The guy whose car registration was screwed up by Penn-DOT. People wanting recommendations for jobs or college. And on and on. Some serious. Some mundane. Except to the person with the problem. To him, it was the most important thing in the world.

One of Kevin's unbreakable rules when dealing with a constitu-

[149]

ent problem was never to make a promise. In politics, as in life, you never promised what you weren't a hundred percent sure you could deliver. All Kevin guaranteed was that he would give it his best shot. And he always did. In writing. When you were dealing with bureaucrats, you needed a record, something to pin them against the wall so they couldn't slip between the cracks. Besides, letters played better with your people. Tell a constituent you'd made a phone call on his behalf, he might not believe you. But when he received a copy of your letter, he had something in his hand, proof that his legislator was doing something.

His Harrisburg secretary maintained a tickle file, generally two weeks, so that if no response was received in that time, another letter was sent, with a copy once again going to the constituent. Two file copies of every letter were retained, one for a chronological file, broken down into month and year, in the district office and one filed by name or subject matter in Harrisburg.

Phone calls were handled in the same meticulous fashion. Each call was written down in a spiral notebook, listing date of call; name, address, and phone number of caller; nature of the problem; and, the most important column, what action was taken. Only when a problem had finally been resolved was a checkmark placed beside its listing. This system permitted Kevin, in fewer than five minutes, to scan his calls for the past month to ascertain what work remained.

Unlike congressmen, state reps have no personal staffs to handle the constituent matters. Each letter from Kevin's office—he averaged twelve thousand a year—was personally dictated by him, the reason why his portable dictating machine seemed to be a permanent appendage. And he refused to lighten his load by using the standard reply of most legislators, thanking the constituent for his views and promising to take them into consideration. To Kevin, that was a total cop-out. It didn't tell the constituent a thing. His people deserved more, and he gave it to them: detailed responses, sometimes running three or four pages, particularly when he disagreed with a point of view. In those cases, his ending was standard:

> While we happen to be in disagreement on this particular matter, I certainly respect your opinion as I am sure you do mine. Although no individual can expect to agree with his elected officials

[150]

on every issue, he has the absolute right to demand to know where they stand. That is why I have taken the time to respond to you in detail.

I very much appreciate your taking the time to advise me of your thoughts and hope that you will continue to feel free to contact me at any time concerning this or any other matter of interest to you.

It was the Kevin Murray formula for success. "You might not always agree with me, but you always know where I stand."

It worked. People had come to expect obscure rhetoric from their public officials. Kevin's candor was a breath of fresh air. Even his enemies had to respect his honesty.

He would chuckle to himself when people, marveling at his constituent service, would compliment the efficiency of his "staff." Some staff. Janet and Marlene. Janet was his Harrisburg secretary. A straight-laced Baptist, she had become accustomed to a formal working relationship, addressing the members as "Representative" or "Mr." Kevin would have none of that, insisting on a first-name basis.

"You're not working *for* me," he said. "You're working *with* me. Save your reverence for the old farts. I want your friendship."

Initially the language shocked her. But Kevin was contagious, even to a prim Baptist. Three months into their partnership he knew she had arrived. Unable to find a particular letter that Kevin needed, she allowed how her efforts would be considerably facilitated if he would occasionally "clean the shit off your desk."

She was precisely what Kevin needed: loyal, efficient, and, as a bonus, a down-the-line pro-lifer. She typed all his complicated legislative correspondence, arranged his schedule while he was in Harrisburg, and, most important, maintained all the mailing lists, constantly adding and revising.

Twice a year Kevin sent out district-wide newsletters, updating his constituents on legislative developments. The first contained a questionnaire designed so that two people from the same household could respond. The second provided the questionnaire results. Each contained some type of goody, such as a pamphlet on energy conservation, a synopsis of the Motor Vehicle Code, or a state highway map.

"People like to get things," he would say. "You can take a lump of dogshit, stick your label on it, and they'd be grateful."

[151]

To augment the two main mailings, he frequently sent packets to those on a special list: pastors, principals, senior citizens, civic associations, volunteer firemen, local officials, and the ward leaders and committee people of *both* political parties. Anyone with a constituency of his own.

The Democrats were at first shocked, then grateful that he kept them informed. And when a donkey committeeman had a constituent problem, Kevin made it a priority, never failing to credit the committeeman with the constituent. To Kevin, it was the way government ought to operate. He ran as a Republican, but he served all his people. Never once did he ask or check a political registration before responding.

It was also smart politics. The Democrats had no choice. They had to like him. Sure, every two years they would support his opponent; but their hearts weren't in it, and that was the difference.

A week never went by that Kevin didn't issue at least one press release, and these, too, reflected his unique style. They were always of substance—none of the puff that most representatives used—and always relating to something that he was personally doing. For these he relied on Bob Higgins, the staffer from House PR assigned to the delegation. He was a good one, and he enjoyed working with Kevin, one pro respecting another.

Kevin was different. The others would call Higgins down, toss out a general topic, and tell him to do a release. That was the sum total of their involvement. It was the same with the speeches they wanted prepared.

Not Kevin. For one thing, he never gave a prepared speech, choosing instead to wing it. With the releases he would sit down with Higgins and provide all the details, including exact quotes that he wanted used. Higgins would then knock out a draft for Kevin's review. Pen in hand, Kevin would examine every line, invariably making changes that, Higgins had to admit, improved the product. No reporter was ever going to call Kevin for clarification on a release and find that he had no idea what he was talking about. When that happened, credibility was forever shot to hell.

To Kevin, the releases were necessary for reasons far beyond his fondness for his name in print. "You can be the best legislator in the world," he would preach, "but it doesn't do you a damn bit of good unless you let your people know. Besides, they have a right

[152]

to know what you're doing so that they can support you, oppose you, or—and this happens quite a bit—make worthwhile suggestions. None of us has a monopoly on being right, and it's damn important to maintain a dialogue with our people."

It was just another way of stirring up the caldron. He wouldn't have been happy without an aggressive contituency.

Marlene ran his district office, doubling as his legal secretary. Like Janet, she had been with him from the beginning, arriving fresh out of high school.

Her primary job was to handle the vast majority of the constituent contacts. She, more than anyone else, would determine Kevin's future, for people often made lasting judgments on the basis of the first phone call. She was hired, first and foremost, because of her personality. Pleasant and sincere, she made people realize that she, and thus Kevin, actually cared. It also fell to her to handle the letters of congratulations. Each week she pored over the local papers, clipping out items concerning their constituents. Congratulatory notes, with clippings attached, were sent for virtually any milestone: engagements; weddings; graduations; business promotions; sports and academic achievements.

Each spring letters were sent to every grade school and high school graduate in the district. Kevin made it a point to sign each letter, and when he knew the recipient or his family, a personal note was handwritten at the bottom.

Probably more than anything else he did, these letters were appreciated. Students framed them, and parents were delighted. For once government was personal, the precise chord that Kevin tried to strike.

"When the average person ponders the concept of government, what mental picture does he get? Big buildings, long corridors, stacks and stacks of paper. Rarely, if ever, does he picture a human face. But that's all government is. Human beings, just like you and me."

He understood that nothing magic had happened at the moment of his election. He couldn't levitate, he wasn't any smarter, and he still had the same doubts and fears and weaknesses he'd always had. He was still human, and he wanted his people to know that a human being represented them.

So when a senior citizen stopped in just to talk, Kevin pushed aside his already impossible schedule and spent a few minutes with him. And when people came in with local or federal problems—most never understood the difference in the three levels of government—he never referred them to their township commissioners or their congressmen. *He* made the contacts for them.

For many, their dealings with Kevin were their first contacts with government. If he didn't respond, if he gave them the bureaucratic runaround, some would never try again. They were turned off, convinced that they didn't matter. They were the type that would refuse to vote, claiming that their votes were insignificant, and besides, "all politicians are the same."

The Kevin Murray system. It operated out of an overcrowded room in the State Capitol and a district office that *Philadelphia Magazine* described as "two dingy second-floor rooms" and that Kevin labeled "a lower middle-class urinal." It was a system that was a blend of the idealistic and the pragmatic, fueled by a genuine desire to help people and an equally genuine desire to get reelected. And it worked, rendering him invincible and providing him with a solid springboard for higher office.

Which was Congress. Specifically, the seat of Bob Allworth, Democrat, liberal, and darling of the pro-abortion lobby. Striking though it was, Allworth's '74 victory was not that great a feat. It was more backlash at Nixon and the pardon than a mandate for him. What *was* significant, and what made him a national figure, was holding the nation's most Republican seat. Three times running, he turned back the GOP challenge, each time with a larger plurality. Far more liberal than his constituency, he more than compensated by hard work, astute use of his franking privilege, and superlative staff work in serving constituents. He was perceived, accurately, as honest and dedicated and was adored by the media.

His survival was a GOP nightmare. Bad enough that a donkey was able to win in Republican country. But when he supported abortion, forced busing, and gay rights, that made the sin mortal. He had to go, and Kevin had concluded that he was the only one capable of handling the job. It would be a struggle, a classic clash between liberal and conservative. Unlike his previous campaigns, the result would not be preordained. For the first time in his career, defeat was a possibility. But so was victory.

The big question was not could he win but should he run. When he considered just Kevin Murray, the answer was always

[154]

yes. Since Allworth was a national figure, the person who defeated him would immediately achieve the same status. He would be big box office. A proven winner. Speaking invitations would flood in from across the state. And whenever higher office, such as governor or United States senator, was discussed, his name would head the list. Success begot success. Beat Allworth, and Kevin's high school and college yearbook predictions—that he would be president—might just come true.

Just as important was the cause. He would be replacing a hopeless abortionist, a net gain of two. But it was more than an extra vote. Kevin Murray, the mover and shaker who got things done, would be in Washington to kick ass and take names. The human life amendment that would insure total victory could only begin in Congress, but so far there had been frustration. One false start after another, the movement bitterly split over the form the amendment should take. He was needed there to bang heads, crack his jokes, bring the troops together, and get the job done. There wasn't the slightest doubt in his mind that he could pull it off.

But first he had to get there, so when the budget struggle was over and the abortion bill had been introduced, he let it be known that he was considering a run. Money was the most important priority. It would take a half million dollars to win, and the party, which had come to consider Allworth almost unbeatable, could be expected to kick in almost nothing. Better to save it for the off year when the real power was on the line.

For the remainder of the summer Kevin courted the business community. A new horizon was opened to him. The Catholic kid from Upper Darby was in the big leagues, lunching at the Union League, the Racquet Club, and the private dining rooms of a dozen major corporations.

It was an enlightening and enjoyable experience, but not what he expected. He had anticipated meeting with Prescotts and Biddles, Weatheralls and Wanamakers—the solid WASP backbone of Philadelphia and its Main Line. Instead, he was greeted mostly by Murphys and O'Haras, Sorgentis, and even a Jaworski. The Catholic Mafia was coming of age, its members reaching the top rungs of the corporate ladder. Kevin was one of their own. They supported his opposition to abortion and his support for aid to nonpublic schools. But first they were businessmen. They weighed

[155]

support for a potential congressman on whether he would be good for business. In Kevin they saw a candidate who, at long last, stood an excellent chance of unseating Allworth, a man whose voting record demonstrated that he understood the need for a favorable business climate. Without hesitation, they climbed aboard, pledging their own funds and their support in raising more. An early fall arrived, phase one was an unqualified success. There was now no doubt in Kevin's mind that this was a campaign he could win.

And then he bagged it. Abruptly and irrevocably. And when he did it, a weight was released from his spirit. From the start it hadn't felt right. When he first ran for the legislature, he had been able to cast aside the doubts, utilizing tunnel vision to focus on nothing but victory. Not this time. There were too many negatives.

The type of campaign that would unseat Allworth required a full year of non-stop effort. And what would he do after he won? It wasn't like Harrisburg, where he could take the train home every night. There were two equally poor alternatives. He could do what most congressmen ultimately did: uproot the family and move to Washington. To hell with roots and stability. It would be devastating, particularly to Kevin, a high school freshman, and Sean, in his last year of grade school. And it wouldn't solve the problem. Congress did most of its work at night, and for a congressman such as Kevin, the weekends would be shot. His district was close enough to Washington that constituents would demand his presence at the endless weekend picnics, parades, and dinners. He would have uprooted his family and still be a stranger to them. And in two years he could get dumped, forced to reverse the process. The other choice was to keep the family in Havertown. More stability, but at great cost. He would be reduced to the status of occasional visitor in his own home.

Kevin waged the greatest debate of his life. With himself, the one opponent he could never outtalk.

You're neded in Washington. You've got the tools to make a real contribution.

Yeah, but what about my family?

Are you saying that no one with a family can hold public office? That'd be a hell of a note.

I'm not talking about anyone else. I'm talking about me.

But you'd be doing it for your family. You'd make them proud.
Bullshit. I'd be doing it for me.
What about the cause? The slaughter of unborn children? Are you turning your back on them?
Better than turning my back on my own. I've seen some of the pro-life zealots. Saving the unborn but no time for anyone else. Sure, I care about the cause, and I love the applause. But I don't want to be one of those assholes with a messiah complex out to save the whole world except those who mean the most to me.
But if you don't do, who will?
Someone else. Nobody's indispensable. Besides, I've paid my dues. And I'll keep paying them. Only in Harrisburg, not Washington.
Does that mean you're not running?
I don't know, goddammit.

He was being forced to practice what he preached. One of the speeches he gave was about life and its essential ingredients: attitude, emotion, faith, courage, and priorities. His message was strong. You have two major priorities on earth: save your soul, and take care of your own. If you blow either one, you're a failure.

In making his point about family, he would bring in the song "Cat's in the Cradle." It told of a man who was always on the go, determined to get ahead. He wasn't there when his son was born. Instead, he was on the road, making a buck. As the son grew, he would ask his father to play with him, but the old man was always too busy getting ahead. The son understood and promised to be just like his dad. Then the son was grown. It was now that his father, who had retired, wanted to be with his boy. Only the boy was now a man and was always too busy. Sadly the father reflected that indeed, his son had turned out just like him.

Only a song, but so very true. "If you don't have time for them when they're little," Kevin would say, "they won't have time for you when they're grown."

Now it was time for Kevin to decide whether he meant the words. The decision came on a brilliant weekend in mid-September. On Saturday morning he went to young Kevin's football game. His son, an aggressive cornerback who wasn't afraid to hit, played well. After the game the boy complained that his hand ached a little. On the following morning, when the pain persisted, father and son drove to the Lankenau emergency room. The X rays were positive: a slight break just above the knuckle. Not serious but re-

[157]

quiring a cast. Since the hospital was backlogged with more serious cases, it would be three or four hours before the cast could be fitted.

Rather than wait, they drove to Manoa Field to watch Sean's soccer game, big Kevin doing his best to feign enthusiasm for a game that he never understood. There was something un-American about not being able to use your hands. Football was the sport where you could kick hell out of the guy opposite you.

When the game ended, it was back to Lankenau for the cast. Only when they were home did Kevin sort out what it all meant. *If this were a year from now, with me running for Congress, I wouldn't have been there. Not at Kevin's game, or Sean's, or at the hospital. I would have missed it all.*

And then he knew.

Fuck it. It's just not worth it. I'm not going to look back fifteen years from now, having become a "success," and realize that I didn't know my kids when they were growing up.

He spent all day Monday making phone calls to the business leaders who were committed to him. They shouldn't hear about it secondhand. Their response was uniform. They regretted losing a great candidate, but they understood and respected his decision. Then, without exception, each of them became wistful, almost morose. They envied Kevin and wished, with the clarity of hindsight, that they had made a similar choice when they were on the road to success.

The next day he summoned the media to his office and announced that he was out of the race. He refused to cite "personal reasons" as so many others did. What bullshit that was. Instead, he spelled it out, including the details of the weekend that caused his decision.

Had it been anyone but Kevin, the announcement might have been greeted with skepticism: using the family to camouflage a political decision that Allworth was too tough to tackle. But the reporters knew that Kevin Murray always spoke the truth. A number of editorials would be run in praise of a politician who was able to keep his head on straight.

When the news conference was over, he took the rest of the day off. Instead of going home, he drove to Holy Cross Cemetery, where he could be alone. Alone with the Sarge, just as he had been on that night in Harrisburg, he sobbed.

"I did the right thing, Sarge, but that doesn't make it any easier. God, how I wanted it."

But adults can't always have what they want. Maureen Murray couldn't have her husband back. And her son couldn't keep his dream. It was over. Not just the run for Congress but the whole dream. The dream that had sustained him since childhood. He had never really doubted that he could go all the way. To the White House. He had almost accepted it as his destiny. And now it was impossible. If he wanted to keep his family, state rep was as high as he could go.

But even though the White House was now a lost dream, the drive remained. He had to be the best legislator in the state.

It was his damned compulsiveness that was the problem. Sure, he wanted to get reelected. But he could reduce his work load by sixty percent and still get the same result.

More than anything, Kevin Murray hungered to satisfy not his constituents but himself. As efficient as his PR operation was, his people weren't aware of ninety percent of what he did. When there was an unemployment compensation problem or when the red tape had to be cut in the Corporation Bureau, the Chamber of Commerce came to Kevin. When a new funding formula had to be devised for special education or when the Intermediate Units were shortchanged in a budget proposal, the education people besieged him. There was a loophole in the adoption laws that endangered the confidentiality of birth parents; it fell to Kevin to close it. Bureaucrats in Education were blocking the county from being designated a district library center, which would increase funding; Kevin was the middleman who ironed out the problems. And on and on. One crisis to another. Never enough time really to study a problem to his satisfaction. Just skimming the surface, then praying to God he could pull it off on the floor.

Why did he have to be so damn intelligent? Why couldn't he be like the others? If you weren't smart enough to spot a problem, you didn't know it existed, so you didn't have to grapple with it. Blissful ignorance.

And what really frosted him, what he always complained about to Brendan, was that the assholes of the world were the ones who made it. Some of the reps couldn't wipe themselves without checking with Kevin. Yet they were rolling in it. Loaded. One

[159]

was a coal baron. Owned half of northeastern Pennsylvania. Another one, a real smacked ass who was a functional illiterate, owned a construction company, an insurance agency, and three banks.

Where was the goddamn justice? Kevin Murray: brilliant, eloquent, street-smart, and broke. Going absolutely nowhere. And getting an ulcer in the process.

It wouldn't be so bad, not half as bad, if he could just be a legislator. It was the law that was going to put him in his grave. He didn't like practicing law. Now and then an interesting case that would challenge him would pop up, but all in all, it was a colossal headache. Unfortunately it was also necessary if he was to survive and if his children were to continue to practice their favorite hobby—eating.

Not that he made all that much. His legislative schedule made that impossible. And he was such a ridiculously soft touch, as Karen often pointed out. He hardly ever got a retainer, was terrible at sending out bills and worse at collecting them. And the ones whom he cut the biggest break, reducing the fee and agreeing to installment payments—charity, really, these were the bastards who stiffed him.

And always the fear, the gnawing worry that sooner or later he was going to screw one up and get sued. When you had a general practice and were alone, you were floating in a sea of ignorance. A client came in with a problem—say, a mechanic's lien—and you had absolutely no idea what the hell he was talking about. The trick was to seem relatively knowledgeable, get the client out of the office as quickly as possible, then find out what to do. Hit the books, make a few phone calls, and become an instant expert.

Seat-of-the-pants law. Always behind. Always scrambling in the gun lap to beat a deadline. Grabbing the file and racing to the courthouse. Totally unprepared, absolutely certain that it had to end in disaster. Miraculously, it always worked out. At least so far.

Like the libel case in Bucks County. He was representing the *Suburban Sentinel,* a local newspaper that was being sued for a piece it had run as part of an ongoing series on organized crime. The piece, entitled "The Armenian Mob," named a number of Armenians in the suburbs as connected with the Philadelphia family. Actually the article was merely a restatement of a portion of the Pennsylvania Crime Commission's latest report on organized crime. The problem was that the *Sentinel* gave no credit to the Commission, making it seem that it had dug up the information on its own. The slight luster thus enjoyed by the paper was more than offset by its needless exposure to liability. Three of the Armenians sued and refused any settlement offer that wasn't in six figures. Normally Kevin was a master at pulling off settlements. Nothing good could happen if you went to court, particularly when you were unprepared and scheduled to be on the floor of the House. But not this time. He was home recovering from a hernia operation (brought about, he was convinced, by always racing for the train with a jammed briefcase in one hand and a fifty-pound document carrier in the other), enjoying the luxury of recuperation. There was something to be said for getting sick now and then. Like when you were little and had the flu and your mother brought you your meals on a tray and played games with you and your father brought home your favorite comic books and Johnny, who owned the local grocery store, sent you your own special bag of candy. If only briefly, you could escape from the world, from the tests and the homework, from the wiseass seventh grader who was always picking on you in the schoolyard. You were safe and warm, and nothing bad could happen to you.

It was like that after the operation. Sometimes when the war was being waged in Harrisburg, when the press wouldn't let up and the enemy was pounding, when the fear of failure that he always hid was tearing his guts, Kevin wanted to run. Jump into bed, pull up the covers, and stay there. Now he had an excuse.

Karen was great, of course, and the kids were relatively considerate. Propped up in bed, he alternated between reading *Hawaii* and watching television. Absolutely lovely. So lovely that he had decided to listen to the doctor and take off a second week. He might never get the chance again.

That was why he damn near came apart when he got the call. The case was listed for trial. There would be no continuance. In three days he was to appear in court, prepared to try the case.

For ten minutes after the call he just sat there, panic-stricken. He spent another ten pacing, all the while cursing the judge and chain-smoking. Then he got cracking.

He was back in the real world. *Hawaii* would have to wait. He called Marlene to bring down the file. Then he called John Templeton, a disbarred lawyer and alcoholic with the worst body odor

[161]

east of the Mississippi. It was hell to be downwind of him. His appearance and personality matched his smell, but he did have two redeeming features: he was a wizard at legal research, and he was always in need of a little extra cash.

Two days later Templeton delivered the goods—two pretrial motions and a pretty impressive brief. Kevin questioned him for as long as he could stand the smell. Then, as with his releases, he rewrote the brief, making it suit his style.

He had never practiced in Bucks County, a disadvantage made greater by nature of his opposition. The plaintiffs were represented by one of the county's most prestigious law firms. Kevin had always said that if Paul Revere had possessed his sense of direction, America would still be a colony. True to form, he got lost on the way to the courthouse, arriving a half hour late. The judge was fairly hostile, counsel for plaintiff was fairly smug, and Kevin was a basket case.

But as always, he disguised it. He presented his motions and his brief, calmly explaining that the law barred such an action. The *Sentinel* had relied in good faith on an official document. The fact that it had not identified the Crime Commission as the source was irrelevant. Since the Commission was, by statute, immune from liability, that immunity extended to any entity relying in good faith on its reports. Additionally, since the plaintiffs had been named in the Commission report, they were public figures, falling under the provisions of the landmark *New York Times* case. They could not recover unless they could prove that the article was not only false but written with malice or reckless indifference to the truth.

He sounded as if he had actually known what he was talking about. But could he bullshit the judge, who now suggested that the attorneys begin to select the jury while he reviewed Kevin's brief?

That was the next problem. Since he had never tried a case in Bucks County, he had no idea of the court's voir dire procedures. No choice but to fudge it, as he did with a minimum of embarrassment. They had selected the first two jurors when the judge summoned them to chambers.

"I have perused with considerable interest defendant's brief and thought it might be beneficial to all parties, before we be-

[162]

came inextricably involved in the proceeding, if I would apprize you of my conclusions, preliminary as they may be."

He was relatively pompous, the judge, unquestionably fond of polysyllabic pronouncements. Kind of a Craig Harrington in robes. But as Kevin listened, there was no question that this learned trustee of the law was moving inexorably toward vindication of his client.

The judge was concluding. "Accordingly it is my considered opinion that the legal issues in this case render plaintiff's position tenuous, precarious, and, quite candidly, seemingly hopeless. Were I to rule on defendant's motion for summary judgment, such a ruling would undoubtedly redound to the distinct detriment of the plaintiff."

Now the judge shifted gears. Gone was the lofty eloquence, replaced by a straightforward, down-home, good ol' boy delivery. "Boys, I don't think you need a ton of bricks to fall on you. Why don't you take a half hour or so to settle this thing? That way we all can get the hell out of here, justice having been served."

Both lawyers knew how to translate the judge's message. Kevin had won, but a shutout wouldn't be tolerated. His opposite number was a Bucks County lawyer, charging on a contingency basis, and if his clients got shut out, he got stiffed, and there was no way in hell the judge would allow that to happen to one of his own.

In precisely sixteen minutes they settled for thirty-one hundred dollars—four figures instead of six.

There has to be a God in heaven, Kevin thought as he floated to his car, *and even though I didn't get to finish* Hawaii, *I'm thanking Him.*

But even in his elation, the fear persisted. He was only holding off midnight. Sooner or later it had to come crashing down.

It was a full ten minutes before he could start the car. Until the trembling in his arms subsided.

It was early afternoon, and the office was a shambles. Even worse than Harrisburg. Each morning he vowed it would be different. Only one file at a time. No junk. A neat, orderly progression through the day.

He would take his constituent file and begin to dictate. But then a client who couldn't be ducked any longer would call, requiring Kevin to pull *his* file, followed by a call from the UPI re-

[163]

porter on his adoption bill, requiring him to rummage through the desk to locate the analysis, and Jim Wilson needed the latest subsidy stats, which Kevin had somewhere, then another reporter wanting clarification of the informed consent section of the abortion bill, which was on the other side of the room under the senior citizen flyers, and the mental health people wanted to set up a lunch, only where the hell was his calendar book, it was here a second ago, and the police chief was on hold, calling about the pension bill, and I don't give a damn if Dave Black wants to talk to me, tell him we're filing the complaint today and if he doesn't like that he can get another lawyer, and Jesus, do we have the Eagle Scout citation down yet, the ceremony's tomorrow night, and yeah, I'll meet with the insurance people, next Tuesday, but check with Janet, I think I'm meeting with the secretary of education at ten, and goddammit, tell Mrs. Rudowski that I can't print the friggin' check, they're working on it in Revenue and I'll hand carry it down as soon as it's ready, and where the hell did I put the Blue Route file, Mrs. Beatty is coming in to review it for the twentieth time, I wish to Christ her arteries would harden, and no, goddammit, I'm not giving to the FOP Children's Fund, not this year, I'm broke as shit, and call Judge Higgins's office and see if we can get a continuance for next Thursday, I've got to be in Harrisburg for a PHEAA meeting, I know it's the third continuance, but it's really important, and besides, the judges' pay raise bill is coming up and Higgins wasn't born yesterday, and Jesus, am I supposed to meet with the library people this afternoon, you'll have to cancel the woman who swears her phone is being bugged by the CIA, switch her to next week, and, Marlene, call the FOP back and tell them I'll send twenty-five dollars and Karen's on the phone? Oh, Christ, tell her I'll be right there—

"Hi," he said, trying to sound calm, even if the reporter from the *Inquirer* was on hold and the blinking light was making him feel guilty. "How you doing?"

"Fine."

This meant, of course, that there were problems. "What's wrong?"

"Nothing."

"C'mon, Karen, what's the matter?"

"Nothing, I said."

[164]

Damn, that drove him absolutely crazy. He'd been married to her for fifteen years. He might not be all-American in perceptiveness, but he knew when something was wrong. Why did it have to be dragged out, inch by inch? Why not say it? Something like "You've got bad breath, BO, and a small dork and I friggin' hate your guts." He could deal with that. But not with this maddening cat and mouse.

"C'mon, Karen. Something's wrong. Tell me." Marlene slapped a note on his desk. The township health director was here, had to see him for only five minutes (nothing was ever only five minutes). Urgent. He cupped the phone. "Tell him I'll be right there and tell the *Inquirer* I'll call back in ten minutes."

". . . want to know what's wrong? I'll tell you then, okay?"

"Fine." His finger was tapping the desk. *Karen, I love you dearly, but why today?*

". . . take it anymore, Kevin. I can't. I try. Every morning I try. But they fight from the minute they're up. At lunch today Sean was so hysterical he was twenty minutes late going back. And Peter hasn't stopped crying all day. Except when he got the bottle of syrup and poured it all over the landing. Why me, Kevin? God, why me?"

Marlene pushed the checkbook in front of him. The typewriter repairman was here to be paid; that wasn't unreasonable since he had billed them two months ago. Only there wasn't enough in the checking account. He signed it, praying that his expense money would arrive tomorrow. Otherwise the check would bounce, the repairman would be steamed, and Kevin would get hit with a twelve-dollar bank charge.

"Take it easy, hon."

"That's easy for you to say. You're not here. You don't have to put up with it. Peter!" She dropped the phone and dived. Too late. The planter crashed to the floor, shattering. "Peter, you're a bad boy," she screamed, setting off violent sobs, which in turn made her feel guilty. He *was* only two.

Marlene stuck her head in the door. The health director wanted to know how soon.

"When I'm done, goddammit!"

"What?"

"Oh, I was talking to Marlene. What happened?"

[165]

"Nothing."

He was coming apart. "Jesus H. Christ, Karen, I hear you scream, I hear a crash. I hear Peter scream, and you say, 'Nothing'!"

"Does it matter?" She was trying to cling to sanity.

So was he. "Of course, it matters, for chrissake!"

"Do you always have to curse?"

"Jesus, not again. Please. I've got a foul mouth, okay. I was born with it, maybe had it in utero. We've been married for fifteen friggin' years. Your efforts have failed, I'm still a pig, so why the hell don't you chalk it off as a lost cause? And it's totally friggin' irrelevant to what we're talking about!"

He was screaming now, the township health director undoubtedly getting an earful.

Wyoming. That was the ticket. Whenever it got bad, like now, it got back to that. Escape. By train. Only by train. There was something exciting about getting all packed on a train, ready for a long trip. Across the Great Plains, over the Rockies and into the virgin West. Clear air, clean streams, and, most of all, solitude. No constituents, no clients, no ulcers. He wasn't sure how he came up with Wyoming, maybe it was from when he had read *Centennial* a few years back, but God, did it seem inviting.

Dream as he might, though, he was still in Havertown, in his dump of an office, fighting with his wife, who had just asked him something.

"What?"

"You're not listening to me, are you?" Karen said. "You listen to everyone else, to your damn constituents and your precious pro-lifers, but never to me!"

"Yes, I do. I just didn't hear you. What did you say?"

"I said, did you call Sears about the washer?"

Silence.

"You didn't, did you? I've got five kids and a washer that's broken, and you promised you'd call first thing in the morning. Is there ever a time I come first with you? Ever?"

"I'm sorry, Karen. It's just been really hectic today. I'll call right now. I promise."

"Don't bother. I'll do it myself!" she snapped, and slammed down the receiver.

The dead phone was in his hand; the health director was waiting; two callers were on hold. He should have been moving, but he just sat there. Dreaming of Wyoming.

"Kevin, Mr. Masters is here," Marlene said, and for the first time that day Kevin felt lightened.

"Hot damn!" he said, rising from his desk. "Send the turkey in!"

"Whaddya say, McGarrett?" Masters said as he embraced his old partner. "Kickin' any doors in lately?"

"Not without you, Dano. Sit down and we'll reminisce awhile."

Ten years before they had been partners. Rookie agents chasing fugitives around Milwaukee. Two little kids having a ball. In the morning they'd flip to see who was McGarrett; then off they'd go on another adventure. It was sometimes hard to believe they were getting paid to have such fun, and if now and then it was necessary to kick in a door to get the bad guy, so much the better.

Yet as close as they had been, this was only the second time they'd been together since Charlie's transfer to Philly, more than a year and a half before. They were always going to get together, but something always seemed to come up.

As they retold war stories, like the stakeout on the roof of the German beer hall for the dude who was the dead ringer for Sonny Liston, who ran *through* a wooden fence when they were chasing him, it was easy to see why they had clicked. They complemented each other perfectly, Charlie with his laid-back Kentucky drawl and Kevin with his rapid-fire delivery. They were naturals for the nice guy–bad guy routine. It was as old as time—you saw it in movies, you read about it in books—but it always worked. They'd be interviewing a hardnose who wouldn't bend. On cue, Kevin would fly into a rage, screaming, cursing, even lunging for the guy, which required Charlie to restrain him.

"Take it easy, Kevin," he'd say. "He's trying to help."

"That's your fuckin' problem, Charlie; you're a goddamn social worker. You wanta stroke this jerkoff, fine. You got five minutes." He'd turn to the suspect. "You hear that, asshole, five minutes. You don't come across by then, I'm gonna make you wish to Christ you were never born."

Out he'd go, slamming the door. It was important always to slam the door. Charlie would shake his head, wearing a grin that gave a hint of fear.

[167]

"Sorry about that," he'd say, "but sometimes I can't control him. He's been like that ever since the murder."

They always took the bait. "What murder?"

"Couple years ago. His wife. She was out shopping. Got pulled into a back alley. Raped and stabbed to death. Never found the guy. I think that's the problem. I think he looks at every suspect as the killer. That's why I was with you in the back seat with him driving."

"What do you mean?"

"He's gonna snap sooner or later. I mean, all the way."

"Jesus."

Charlie would offer him a cigarette. "But that's not your problem. We can work this out, can't we?"

The suspect would nod. Anything to keep that madman away.

They had particular fun with the radicals. It was the heyday of the New Left, and Madison, only sixty miles away, was the national center of the movement. The Weathermen. Black Panthers. SDS. Venceremos Brigade. All violent and all with a code of silence as strict as the mob's.

After they had bagged one and were on their way to the jail, Kevin would start. "How ya gonna blow up the country if you're in jail, shithead? I thought you guys never got caught. I thought you guys never squealed on each other."

"That's enough, Kevin," Charlie would snap.

"What do you mean?" the prisoner would ask, suddenly interested.

"Solidarity. Never talk to the pigs, huh? Well, how the hell do you think we found you?"

"Knock it off, Kevin!"

"How?" The rage of betrayal showed in his eyes.

"You really want to know? Okay, pal. It was your good buddy—"

"No more, Kevin!" Charlie would say. "We promised."

"Shit," Kevin would mumble, and turn to the window, ignoring the prisoner's pleas to identify his betrayer.

There had been no one, of course. They had done it on their own, but the prisoner was now convinced that one of his own had turned. And nothing could destroy an organization like suspicion.

Then there was the telephone trick. They'd be at the house of a fugitive's relative who steadfastly denied any knowledge of his whereabouts. Only they knew he was lying. Kevin would walk to the phone, dial an imaginary number, and wait a few seconds. "Dave," he would finally say, "this is Kevin. Take down this number." He would then read off the relative's phone number. "Got it? Thanks." He would hang up, and without another word, they would leave.

Even the most intelligent individuals had no idea what was required to tap a telephone. They were totally unaware that it took months of investigation, then approval of the attorney general, and then a court order. All they knew was that this was the FBI and the FBI could do anything. Right away.

Convinced that his phone was now tapped, the relative wouldn't dream of using it. Instead, he would warn the fugitive in person. Leading Kevin and Charlie, who were staked out a block away, right to their prey.

Like Kevin, Charlie had talked about leaving after three. But partly out of fear and partly out of love, he stayed. Jacksonville, Charlotte, Boston, and now Philly, where he was a supervisor assigned to organized crime and official corruption.

"How do you think we're doing?" Charlie asked after they had finished their tiptoe down memory lane.

Kevin hesitated. "Not bad," he finally said.

"You never could lie, Kevin. Tell it straight, the way you always do."

"Okay. I'm not crazy over the way things are going. Like AB-SCAM."

"C'mon, Kevin. You're not turning liberal on me, are you? Those guys we nailed were scumbags."

"No doubt about it, and I won't shed a tear when they go to jail. It's how you did it that bothers me. I don't mind putting guys under and going along with a scam, even pushing it along a little. But Jesus, when we're the only reason why it happens, when we initiate everything, damn near force them to take the money . . . Williams refused three times, and we just kept pounding. That's not good law enforcement. It's the easy way, a shortcut. And what did it prove? Only that they were human. You could take the most faithful husband in the world, put him in a motel room and waltz in Raquel Welch nude, and all you're gonna prove is that he's human. Face it, Charlie. It was entrapment, pure and simple."

"The Court said it wasn't."

"C'mon, Charlie. You and I both know those whores float with public opinion. It's open season on politicians. Lucky Green's another example."

Charlie smiled. "State Senator Robert Faragelli. A class act all the way. I actually felt bad when we got him."

"You should have, goddammit. Not only was he a class act, but he was also innocent."

"Now wait a minute, Kevin—"

"No, you wait a minute. You didn't get him for taking money, selling his vote. You got him on the most horseshit concoction I've ever seen."

"He was padding his payroll with political hacks, for God's sake!"

"Since when is that a crime? Is government now going to score the performance of politicans and prosecute those who don't measure up? Don't we leave anything up to the people anymore?"

"Kevin, they were ghost employees."

"No, they weren't, and you know it."

"Okay, they showed up, but all they did was political work."

"And what, shit-for-brains, is political? Who's keeping score? In one sense, everything I do is political. Every constituent I help is political. I want his vote in my ongoing quest to maintain gainful employment."

"That's different."

"How? If a Republican pol comes to me for help, do I refuse? How about if he's a Democrat? Is it okay then? Where the hell do we draw the line? Look, man, don't misunderstand me. There's plenty of corrupt politicians, and when they commit a crime, nail 'em. But if you think you're cleaning up government with what you're doing, you're whistling 'Dixie.' All you're doing is driving the good ones out. Who the hell needs it? And it's all because of Nixon."

"Nixon?"

"Yeah, Nixon. The biggest tragedy of Watergate is the backlash, the overreaction against all politicians, most of whom, believe it or not, are honest. And when the good ones leave, the hacks take their place." He grinned at his old partner. "I haven't changed, Charlie. I'm still a headhunter at heart and the Bu's number one fan. Every place I go I let them know I'm a former agent. Give 'em hell and go the distance. Just do it right."

[170]

Charlie returned the smile. "You've still got the words, Mc-Garrett. I never could keep up with you. Ready for some off-the-record business?"

Kevin nodded.

"As soon as you called, I checked indices. Then I talked to a few of our people. The good Father Flaherty is quite a character. This is his fourth time in the States. During the past eight years he's popped up in Boston, New York, and Chicago, each time raising funds for an Irish shrine. To date, none has been built."

"I'm beginning to get the picture."

"You always were a quick study. Because the Church is involved, we've kept our distance, but source information leaves little doubt what he's doing."

"IRA."

"Right you are. He raises a million or two, makes a weapons contact, and presto, the heat goes up in Belfast."

"He's already withdrawn his money, so he'll be making his contact."

"I think he already has. Today. At two-fifteen." Charlie smiled, the way he had in Milwaukee after they had pulled one off. "Just between you and me, I figured I'd give you a bonus. For old times' sake. I put a car on him this morning. Unofficially, of course. Just after lunch he paid a visit to Sidney Feinstein."

"The industrial real estate guy? Eleventh and Walnut?"

"The same. He also dabbles in a number of extracurricular activities. Like being an arms broker. Through a contact in Israel. Fairly light stuff: machine guns; rocket launchers; hand grenades. Perfect for rearranging a department store in Belfast. Or London, if you prefer. Afraid that's as far as I could go."

"I owe you one, Charlie."

"No problem. But if you happen to come up with something, let me know. In the past we've kinda looked the other way when it came to the IRA. Too sensitive. But that's changing. We'd love to know who their Philly contacts are."

"I'll do what I can."

They rose, and Kevin felt a tinge of sadness. Why did it take a crisis to get old friends together? "Take care of yourself, Charlie, and give 'em hell."

When he was gone, Kevin reached for the phone. Monsignor Patrick Carney would be waiting.

[171]

HE placed the suitcase in the hallway, then turned to close the door.

"Traveling, Father Flaherty?"

He whirled. There were four of them: the one who had spoken and three goliaths standing to the rear. "I don't believe we've met."

"Then let me immediately rectify that," Pat Carney said, taking him by the arm and leading him back into the apartment. The others followed, with the suitcase. "I'm Monsignor Pat Carney, director of communications of the archdiocese of Philadelphia. I wonder if you'd indulge me for a few minutes? You can be of considerable help."

"In what?" he asked warily. Something was wrong. He could feel it. And he didn't like the way the big ones were staring at him.

"In avoiding a considerable embarrassment to the archdiocese." He nodded to the others. One remained at the door. The others began searching the suitcase.

"What's the meaning of this?" Flaherty sputtered. "Those are *my* belongings, and I'm late for a plane."

He started toward the door, but one of the giants blocked his path. Pat spoke.

"Aer Lingus Flight Six-eight-oh, to New York, thence Dublin? Forget it."

"How did you know?"

"I know a great deal. Please sit down, Father." It was a command, and Flaherty obeyed. "Now I'm going to talk to you, just briefly; then I'm going to ask you a few questions. It will be in the best interest of all parties, particularly yourself, if you answer quickly and honestly. Are you with me so far?"

Flaherty nodded.

"Fine. You arrived here on February third, aboard Aer Lingus Flight Four-five-seven. Since then you have applied yourself with dedication to the task of raising funds."

"Yes. For a shrine. Our Lady of Knock."

"Ostensibly. Yesterday you reaped the fruits of your labor. You withdrew, from the Delaware Cash Reserve"— he reached into his pocket for a slip of paper—"I've never been good with figures—yes, the sum of $2,047,359.86. This includes interest, of course. Earlier today you visited one Sidney Feinstein, a Center City real estate magnate."

"I've never heard of him. I was here all day."

"Come now, Father. We both know better. You visited Mr. Feinstein and undoubtedly transacted business with him, business having nothing to do with Our Lady of Knock. What I want to know was whether he was your only contact or whether you spread your business around with a few other arms dealers. I repeat, it is in your best interest to cooperate."

Flaherty had regained his composure. "I don't have to say a thing to you. It's in your best interest to drop the whole thing and let me be on my way to the airport. You don't hold any cards, Monsignor. You can't turn me in to the authorities. As you said, your aim is to avoid embarrassment, and my arrest would cause a massive scandal."

Convinced that he had won, he attempted to rise.

"You're right, of course," Pat answered. "Arrest is out of the question. What I had in mind is considerably more private. When this conversation is over, you will be accompanying these three gentlemen to their home, the Trappist monastery in Berwyn. Should you cooperate, you will be released as soon as this problem has been resolved, free to wing your way back to the Emerald Isle. The other option is not nearly so pleasant, at least for someone like you: to spend the rest of your life at the monastery in silent prayer and meditation, never to hear the spoken word."

"You wouldn't dare! That's kidnapping! That's a crime!"

[173]

"A crime? Possibly. But it certainly ranks behind bilking members of your own church to supply weapons to a gang of terrorists."

The older priest's eyes flared. "Not terrorists. Freedom fighters. Martyrs to the cause. Trying to free all Ireland from the yoke of British oppression that has smothered us for—"

"Save it for the pubs, Father. Now let's get down to it, shall we?"

Flaherty looked at the three monks. They had finished their search and were standing across the room from him. Staring. Silent. Ready to take him to a life worse than death.

His shoulders slumped in defeat. *He* was the one without any cards.

Joey Cariola was at peace. At last. The meatball sandwich had been delicious, best he could remember. The sky was a brilliant blue, and for maybe the first time in his forty-two years he actually noticed it. And even though he'd been a two-pack man ever since he was a kid, the kind who was halfway through before realizing that he had lit up, he was really enjoying the cigarette, savoring every drag. The things you took for granted until you were about to lose them.

When he got the word four months ago, he didn't believe it. He got a second opinion, then a third. All the same. Cancer of the marrow. Hard to say how long he had, doctors didn't like to go out on a limb, but probably less than a year.

Maybe if he had done something when he first noticed the lumps, if he had gone to a doctor right away instead of waiting a year, maybe things would be different. But who could tell? Besides, a man could drive himself crazy thinking like that.

His first reaction had been fear. Not for himself. For Stella and the kids. How would they make it? He had a little stashed away, but you never got rich pushing an eighteen-wheeler for a local oil company.

At least that worry was gone. When he kissed them good-bye this morning, he knew they'd be all right. The guys downtown had promised. And say what you wanted about them, they were good for their word.

He always liked to doze for fifteen minutes or so in the cab after

[174]

lunch. Picked him up for the rest of the day. But not this time. There would be plenty of time for sleep. An eternity.

Instead, he lit another cigarette and looked at the sky.

Special Agent Tom Ramsey stood outside the Quonset hut, shifting his weight from one foot to the other. It had been three months since he had stopped smoking, and today was sorely testing him. It didn't help when Gus Toohey lit up.

"Big day, huh?" said Toohey.

"Yeah. The day when we put it all together."

"The day when *you* put it all together."

"I know, Gus. I'm sorry. You know it's not my doing. If I had my way, you'd be with us all the way, straight through the trials."

"I know, pal. Don't sweat it."

Ramsey genuinely liked the Philadelphia detective. He was a pro. And he was honest, not like most of the locals. You could trust him with anything. But it was just like the Bureau to cut him adrift now that everything was coming together.

As a concession to "intergovernmental relations," one local had been assigned to the Bureau team that had grilled Vagnoni ever since his surrender. From here on in, however, it was strictly an FBI show.

Vagnoni had been a gold mine. He had talked almost constantly for two months: dates; businesses; organizational structure. As good as Valachi. Better. He had corroboration, a meticulously kept diary that was the real thing. Almost twenty years' worth. None of the phony stuff where you put in all the entries at the same time. The lab had tested the ink. Completely legit.

The interrogation team had lived with him at the army base, taking it all down, then separating the wheat from the chaff. Now they were ready to bring in the harvest. The grand jury was waiting. It was time to put it all on the record. Then the indictments, maybe the biggest mob haul ever.

They figured he'd testify for two weeks, maybe a little more. For that period the Federal Building would be his home. A special suite had been constructed on the same floor as the grand jury room—a fortified cage to protect the canary.

All they had to do now was get him there. And Toohey had

[175]

been right. The best way was the one least conspicuous. A procession of unmarked cars with the prize in the center. Ramsey had seen a movie once about a mob witness, just like his guy. They had dressed him up like a cop, and while everyone was looking at the double in the pin-striped suit, he rode away in the lead car. But hell, that was the movies. Sure, the outfit wanted Vagnoni. He was trouble. But they weren't dumb. To get him, they'd have to take out a half dozen feds, and that was more trouble. Much more.

On cue the car pulled in front as the door of the hut opened. "Show time, Vags," Toohey said as he opened the rear door of the third car. "And you're the star."

Vagnoni was tight, as bad as the day he'd surrendered. "This thing safe?"

"Absolutely," Ramsey said. "What looks like a run-of-the mill Chevy is more like a tank. Bulletproof glass and armor plating. Nothing can touch us."

"Not unless we meet another tank."

"Relax, Vags," Toohey said. "You'll live to piss on my grave."

Toohey turned to Ramsey. "You know, I think I'm gonna call in and take the rest of the day off."

"You've earned it, Gus."

"I've enjoyed working with you, Tom," Toohey said, extending his hand. "All the best."

As the procession moved out, Toohey casually strolled to the officers' mess and placed a dime in the wall phone.

"They just started," he said. "Third car. Blue Chevy."

The Cadillac pulled beside the cab, the driver's window down. "Get movin'. Blue Chevy, third car. No fuck-ups, understand?"

Joey Cariola nodded, turning the ignition.

"See you in hell," the driver of the Cadillac said.

Joey pulled his rig onto the highway, heading west. He had thought that when the time came, maybe his life would flash before him, the way they talked about in books. But nothing, except that he'd been given a job and he had to do it. Just as he'd had all his life.

He was almost to the bottom of the hill when he saw it. Orange Datsun, blinking its headlights. He counted back from it: brown

[176]

Ford, green Ford, blue Chevy. Right where it was supposed to be. It was going to work out fine, a steep drop at the point of contact.

Ten, nine, eight—

I love you, Stella. Have a good life.

Six, five, four—

Forgive me, Jesus, I had no choice.

Two, one—

The first two cars had cleared. The third didn't. Its driver never had a chance. The explosion came almost immediately, and the papers would report that it was heard ten miles away.

Five agents, the truck driver, and the canary died instantly, without pain. Twenty-three kindergarten students and their driver weren't so fortunate. They were singing "Inky, Dinky Spider" when their bus was enveloped. The driver was blinded, the bus overturned, and with their song unfinished, they burned to death.

Ten

THE timid little man paused at the doorway, a portrait of indecision. His feet shuffled but remained in place. Then, to his horror, he realized that he still wore his hat. Self-consciously he doffed it, holding it with both his hands in a classic pose of supplication.

Vince Grosso came to his aid. "Mr. Cusamano, how are you?" he said warmly, walking around his desk and embracing the little man. "It's been quite awhile. Mrs. Cusamano is well, I hope?"

"Except for her arthritis, Vinnie—I mean Don Vincenzo."

"It's still Vinnie, Mr. Cusamano. Just like it was when I was a little kid and you'd drive me around the block in your truck." He motioned to a chair. "Please, have a seat."

Vince's friendliness and the fact that he spoke in Sicilian relaxed the older man. For five minutes or so they exchanged pleasantries, Vince making it a point to ask about Cusamano's daughter.

Beaming with pride, the old man took out his wallet, handing Vince a dog-eared picture of his grandchildren.

"They're very good-looking," Vince said. "They look just like their mother." Part of it was true. They *did* look like Maria Cusamano: the same blank expression; the same ill-placed nose. They even seemed to have their mother's mustache, which had been the joke of the old neighborhood. Maria would have made a great "before" ad for Gillette.

"Well, Mr. Cusamano," Vince finally said, "what can I do for you?"

The old man's discomfort returned. "Maybe I shouldn't even have come, Vinnie. You're a busy man. I shouldn't bother you with my troubles."

"What are friends for if not to help each other? Please, let me hear the problem."

A side door opened, and Nick Arrone entered, carrying a notepad. "Mr. Cusamano," Vince said, "this is Nicky Arrone, from Thirteenth and Christian. He helps me try to solve problems."

Arrone greeted the old man respectfully, then sat in a chair just to the left of Vince's desk. "Go ahead," Vince said gently.

"Well, I've been retired for almost ten years. It's not easy to make it just on Social Security. By the time you pay the taxes on the house, buy medicine—my wife's prescriptions are a fortune, not that I'm complaining—and shop for food—nothing fancy, mind you—there's not much left. So a couple years back the Missus and I started to take in a boarder here and there. We gave them a clean place to live, and we made a few bucks here and there. We've got three right now. Gino Carlotti, who needs someone to care for him since his wife died. Paulie Verrica, I think you remember him. He used to work with me. Never married. His brother-in-law kicked him out awhile back. And Ernie Fusco. He's another widower. We need each other, and it works out real nice. Only yesterday a man from the city came and told me I was breaking the law. Something about running a boarding home without a license. Says I got a week to straighten things out or my friends have to leave. I didn't know what to do, Vinnie. Then I thought of you."

Vinnie smiled. "Maybe we can arrange something, Mr. Cusamano. Tell you what, you go home and sit tight and we'll see what we can do. And don't worry, I won't let you down."

"God bless you, Vinnie," the old man said, his eyes moist. "If ever I can return the favor—"

"I know, Mr. Cusamano. That's what friends are for."

When the old man was gone, Vince turned to Arrone. "Got everything?"

"Yes. How do you want me to handle it? A call to Licenses and Inspections, asking them to look the other way?"

[179]

"No. Then there's a fire and questions are asked. Let's do it right. Find out what the old man needs to be in sync with the regs. Whatever it takes, do it. And let's kill two birds with one stone."

"How?"

"Luigi Fantazzi. Twenty-second and Passyunk. General contractor who's been down on his luck, mostly from hitting the bottle. But he does good work. Give him the job and tell him to bill me. Regular price, no discount." He looked at his watch. Eight-fifteen. "That's the last one, isn't it?"

Arrone nodded.

"Good," Vince said. "I'm starved."

Like Kevin Murray, Vince understood the need for constituent work. Every Wednesday at five he left the PSFS Building, taking the private elevator to the garage, where the waiting limo would take him back to his roots. He might live on the Main Line, his family business interests might read like Fortune 500, but downtown would always be his base.

When Lucky Green was sentenced to Allenwood, Vince took over his old district office. He liked the symbolism, except for the prison part. Two hometown boys, each out to take care of his people.

Vince called it a law office, and now and then he did get a request for a will or probating a small estate. But for the most part it was a place where he held court, the all-powerful don catering to his subjects.

Arrone was always with him. It was he who would make the assignments for handling each case. And it seemed to him that his boss, for all the favors that he dispensed, received more than he gave.

When Vince was asked why he did it, why he established a weekly pattern that placed him in jeopardy to help unimportant people who could just as easily be served by any one of a dozen assistants, he simply shrugged and said, "Because that's the way it is."

What else could he say? How could he put it into words, even if he were sure? Did he say that he needed the spiritual renewal, the same way that Kevin got his batteries recharged when he spoke to a crowd of his own in a Catholic school hall? Did he say that this was part of the dream, the fantasy that he had nurtured

[180]

since he was little? Or did he just say that this is the way it was in Detroit? And Detroit, more than anything else, had shaped his destiny.

It had been Fredo Annalaro's decision that his nephew attend law school at the University of Michigan. Not that he had demanded it. Fredo never did that with Vinnie. He only suggested. That had always been enough.

Vince never regretted his decision. Michigan was one of the best, right up there with Harvard, Duke, Virginia, and Stanford. In exchange for three years of moderately hard work, he received a quality education and a prestige degree. But most important, just as his uncle Fredo had intended, he came to know the Zivellis.

Vince lived in a campus dorm during the week, but on most weekends he drove the thirty miles from Ann Arbor to Grosse Pointe Park to be with them. At first he did it as a courtesy to his uncle, but soon he did it out of love.

Though impossible to separate, there were two Zivelli families. There was the *famiglia,* the family in the traditional American sense, bonded by blood: a strong but kindly father, a devoted wife, four children, and dozens of grandchildren, siblings, aunts, uncles, and cousins.

These were the core, but only a small part, of the Zivelli *borgotta,* the last real, honest-to-God *borgotta* left in America. Only in Sicilian could the term be fully understood. It was what made La Cosa Nostra one of the most formidable powers on earth, an entity unique in the annals of crime.

Giuseppe ("Pepino") Zivelli, patriarch of his *famiglia* and his *borgotta,* understood, and Vincenzo Grosso would soon learn. "Life is a paradox, Vincenzo," the don told his charge. "If we are to keep our greatness, our techniques must change with the times. There is no standing still. But we must never change our values. If we forget our Sicilian traditions, we will become like the rest. Only by looking back can we move forward."

In Pepino Zivelli's Detroit, the old rules were kept. Only Sicilians were granted membership in the *borgotta.* Being Italian was not enough. Even at the height of his power Al Capone had been distrusted by Zivelli and his peers. The legendary czar of Chicago had come from Naples. He could never be one of them.

There was a definite pecking order within the Zivelli *borgotta,*

[181]

determined by the village in Sicily from which a member or his ancestors had come. The *favorótta*, the Zivellis and the rest of the family's upper echelon, were from Terracina. These and only these were permitted to live in Grosse Pointe Park.

Next came the *cinissati*, those whose roots were from Cinisi. Most of the family's capos fell into this category. Only they were allowed to reside in Grosse Pointe Farms. Those from Caltagirone constituted the final preferred status, their homes assigned to Grosse Pointe Woods. The rest of the family's soldiers, button men who handled the dirty jobs, were free to live anywhere else. Since most considered Detroit a city gone hopelessly black, they generally opted for St. Claire Shores or the north central suburbs.

Entry into the family was difficult and, of course, irrevocable. Before a candidate was approved, he was subjected to a background check that was almost identical to the manner in which the FBI selected its agents. Since the don regarded violence only as a last resort, the requirement that a candidate "make his bones" before acceptance had been eliminated. That had been the only concession to the times. The ancient initiation ritual was still conducted, with the candidate holding a gun in one hand and a piece of paper in the other. As the paper was lit, he recited the unbreakable oath of *omertà:* "With this oath I pledge my loyalty, before God, my country, and my family. I swear that if I ever violate this oath may I burn as this paper."

Absolute loyalty was demanded of him, to his don and his capo. Like the military, orders were obeyed without question.

Although there was no requirement that a member be married, once taken, his matrimonial vow, like his oath to the family, was for life.

"A man has to be good for his word," Zivelli instructed Vince. In Sicilian, always in Sicilian. "If he breaks his commitment once, he'll do it again."

The old man would become furious when he talked of the others who had forsaken the old ways, particularly when it came to women. "Linata in New York has a common-law wife! A Jew no less! Mother of Jesus, what is happening to us? Our greatest enemy isn't the law. It's the moral rot, the degeneration that eats away until there's nothing left. Not in Detroit! I swear on my dead mother, God rest her soul, not in my *borgotta.*"

He was the stereotype of the kindly Italian grandfather. Me-

[182]

dium height, he seemed much shorter. Since the gallbladder operation, he was always a bit stooped. His gray hair had remained
thick, cascading from under the fedora that had become his
trademark. Even when he worked in his garden or played with
the grandchildren, he wore a tie. His white shirts were the
old-fashioned type with detachable collars that had been stiffly
starched by the Chinese laundry at Jefferson and Montclair.

The family compound was on Middlesex Drive. The press
called it a compound. Actually it was a group of eight houses that
took up two blocks of the quiet treelined street. The houses were
typical of the Grosse Pointes: large, but not massive, most with
little more than a half acre of ground. Impressive, but certainly
not in a class with the estates of the Main Line of Philadelphia,
Kenilworth, or the exclusive bedroom communities of New York.

In activity as well as geography the don's house was in the center, the focal point for the entire family. He knew that he was a
lucky man. His children had grown and married yet were still
with him. And the grandchildren, especially the grandchildren, a
man's reward in life. All the pleasure and none of the responsibility. He often likened grandchildren to a creamy dessert after the
meat and potatoes of raising his own.

He and Rosalie had each other in their old age, and that was
good. But not enough. He needed the others. All of them.

Carlo lived next door. His only son and next don of the Zivelli
borgotta. That was a fact of life, accepted by all. There would be no
bloodbath when he went, no jackals clawing each other for power.
Not in Detroit. An orderly transition of power. He liked that
phrase. Just like the presidency.

Carlo was ready. If need be, he could step in tomorrow. Now in
his mid-forties, he had been groomed since his graduation from
Loyola. Content to wait his turn, he never offered an opinion
without being asked. Instead, he listened and he learned.

He was a good son, accepting without complaint the marriage
his father had arranged, providing him with five grandchildren.
Gloria was the daughter of Sal Profaci, boss of Los Angeles. The
opportunity to unite by blood two powerful families could not be
ignored.

There had never been real love, at least on Carlo's part. The
don knew that. And he knew that his son sought his passion elsewhere. That was okay. The old man had never needed it. Rosalie

[183]

had always filled his life. But he wouldn't impose that standard on others, not even his son. As long as he was discreet.

On the other side of the don's house and across the street were two of his daughters. Each had four children, and each had married well. Barbara's husband was the nephew of Louis Belardi, who had ruled the St. Louis family until his death the year before. Marita had married Thomas Boccella, youngest son of the don's underboss.

Only Clara was missing, but she visited often. Though the don admitted it only to himself, she had always been his favorite. The youngest, the surprise that had helped him keep his youth. His heart ached at her absence, but he had known the consequences when he had arranged the marriage. A woman's place was with her husband, and Clara's husband was the head of the New Orleans family. It was a valuable union, and as much as it might hurt, the welfare of the *borgotta* came first. Even before the *famiglia.*

Paolo Zivelli, younger brother and only surviving sibling of the don, lived at the end of the block. Widowed two years before, he had flatly refused to move in with one of his children. Not that he was ever really alone, at least when he didn't want to be. His sons, Gino and Thomas, lived on either side, providing Paolo with nine grandchildren for his amusement and the best of both worlds: the solitude of a bachelor and the warmth of a family. Fiercely loyal to his brother, Paolo had served as *consigliere* since Michael Zivelli's death in 1957. The remaining home was owned by Gennaro Riccobene, the don's godson, whose father and the don had been cousins and shipmates on the voyage from Sicily more than a half century ago. Gennaro and his wife had seven sons, whom the don treated as his own grandchildren. His cousin, God rest his soul, would have wanted it that way.

For most of the don's stewardship his family had enjoyed peace. There were exceptions, of course. Like when the Syrians made their move, gunning down his brother Michael as he was leaving mass. They paid. All of them.

Only once had there been trouble from within. A few of the *caltagironi,* young ones who had disdained the "mustache Petes," tried to take control. Gennaro's father had died as he sat in a barber's chair, torn apart by a machine gun. Within three days it was over. The rebels simply disappeared, snatched from the face of

[184]

the earth without a trace. Although only a few knew what had really happened to them, it was common knowledge that they would never be seen again.

The stability of the *borgotta* permitted it to prosper. By the time Vince Grosso arrived in Michigan, it was firmly entrenched as the single most powerful and well-connected family in America. In pure numbers the Gambino family was larger, but it was forced to compete with four other families in New York City, several more in North Jersey, and the Pagalucci family in Buffalo. By contrast, the Zivellis controlled all Michigan and substantial portions of Wisconsin, Indiana, Ohio, and Canada.

Their holdings were vast. They had infiltrated the unions, particularly the Teamsters and a number of UAW locals, controlling their pension and health funds. To facilitate this, the family had taken over two well-respected insurance companies. They did it without firing a shot, quietly amassing a majority of voting shares. The don was also strong on real estate, both in the inner city where they could gouge the blacks and in the burgeoning Gold Coast northern suburbs.

"Nothing changes, Vincenzo," he once told his charge. "A thousand years ago the measure of a man's success was his land. So it is today. Control the land, and you control the country."

Construction companies, a loan service, a home delivery juice company (won in a barbute game in River Rouge), the Hancock Park Racetrack, two of the city's largest hotels and a dozen of its best restaurants—all were the property of the Zivelli *borgotta.*

But the backbone of the family was still the time-honored operations: loan-sharking, bookmaking, numbers (run by the blacks but controlled by the Zivellis), and prostitution. Even narcotics, despite the misgivings of the don. Distasteful as it was, it couldn't be ignored. Not when you sat right across the river from Canada. Either you got involved or someone else would take away the action, and when that happened, you started to lose control. That could never be permitted. Not in Pepino Zivelli's Detroit. He had worked too hard, come too far to lose it now. No longer was he just off the boat with only a few words of English. He still wondered how he had survived those early times. It had seemed that he was sentenced for life to carrying pipe for the water company. Twelve hours a day for sixty-five cents, and you had to kick back

[185]

two bits to the foreman. In return, he let you keep working, but he never stopped calling you wop.

Not until he staggered out of a bar one night, bracing himself against the February wind off the river. He accepted the ride without ever seeing who offered it, then passed out in the back seat. When he awakened, he was already in the box, his hands and feet tied, his mouth gagged. Pepino smiled. "Ciao, prick," was all he said. Then he and the others began to shovel the concrete into the box. He would never forget the expression on the foreman's face, the stark terror. But he had to give him credit; the guy put up a fight, shifting his head ferociously in an attempt to keep his nose uncovered for a few last gasps of air. Even when he was completely submerged, he still fought, causing the box to rock. But soon the movement stopped, and he was gone.

Nothing was ever proved, of course, but there were whispers, just as Pepino had intended. The new foreman was considerably more pleasant.

So much had changed since those days, yet so much remained the same. The don was a loving husband, a doting grandfather, but he was still prepared to kill when necessary. He no longer laid pipe, but he still dressed like an immigrant. Though his English remained broken, he was now a big business magnate, a Fortune 500 type. His empire was vast beyond imagination. In terms of wealth and power, some compared the Zivelli family with General Motors. But not the don. He was always humble and always a realist. He settled for being equal to Ford. General Motors still had an edge, at least for now.

Vince Grosso would come to know all these things, but not at the beginning. What attracted him at first was what had always been missing in his life. For the first time, except for when he visited Kevin's home during college, he was surrounded by family and by love. Sundays were the best. All of them, even the babies, would attend ten o'clock mass. The rest of the day was spent at the don's home. The women gathered in the kitchen, which contained three stoves, to prepare the meal, chattering incessantly in Sicilian and occasionally scolding one of the children who had crept in to test the gravy with his finger. Usually, though, the children required little supervision. They were permitted to roam the house and the yard, only the don's study being off-limits. For the most part they played together happily, the older ones re-

[186]

sponsible for the others, but exercising that responsibility with kindness. Now and then a fight broke out, causing the predictable tears and requiring the intervention of one of the mothers, but such problems were quickly resolved.

The men assembled in the living room for a day of relaxation. No responsibility other than reading the paper, watching a ball game, and sipping wine. They enjoyed each other's company, swapping jokes and arguing the fate of the Lions and the Tigers. Only rarely was business discussed, and then only in the don's study. For the first year Vince knew, without being told, that he was not to be included in such meetings. Instead, he would play with the children, the younger brothers and sisters that he'd never had.

The main meal was promptly at one, the adults seated around the huge dining room table and the children in the kitchen. The don would lead his family in grace and the next two hours would be spent leisurely enjoying the nine-course fare, complete with four different wines.

While the women cleaned up, the men returned to the living room for cognac and cigars. Some would doze contentedly on the sofas. The don, exercising his privilege, retired to his bedroom for an hour nap, smiling as the sounds of the children and his women drifted up—a lullaby more soothing than music.

They reassembled at six for supper, this served buffet style: Italian cold cuts and cheese; sliced turkey; antipasto; fresh fruit. Then came the children's special treat, homemade Italian ice cream, molded in the form of a different cartoon character each week.

It generally ended around nine, farewell embraces exchanged as if they might never see each other again. Then, with the adults carrying the little ones who had fallen asleep, they would begin their journeys home, the distance of which was less than a hundred yards. Vince would take his leave then, embracing the don and kissing Rosalie. As he drove the expressway back to Ann Arbor, he never failed to have a feeling of warmth. At last he was pretty sure he knew what he wanted. It would become certain the following year, when he would meet Tony Iacobucci and a young woman named Lena.

The evening air felt good, particularly after twelve hours behind a desk.

[187]

"God, it's nice tonight," Vince said. "I think I'll walk to my mother's."

Arrone shook his head. "You can't, Vince," he said gently, almost like a parent. "You know that."

Vince nodded. There was the wistfulness of a child in his voice. "Yeah, I know. It's a bitch, isn't it? Sometimes when you have it all, you really don't have anything."

Without waiting for an answer, he walked to the limousine.

Concetta Grosso lived alone in the old house. It was the way both mother and son wanted it. Vince had never suggested that she move in with his family, and Concetta had never asked. They both had their reasons.

They visited with the regularity that arises from obligation rather than love. Each Wednesday evening, after Vince had finished in his South Philly office, he shared a late dinner with her before returning to the PSFS Building for the chopper ride home. And since Vince believed that an essential part of a child's development was knowing his grandparents, he insisted on regular visits each Saturday, one week at his house, the next at Concetta's.

As usual, she was waiting in the kitchen. "Hello, Mother," Vince said, leaning down to kiss her. The kiss was always on the top of the head. It was always Vince who delivered the kiss and the brief embrace, his mother a passive recipient. He could never remember her, even when he was little, kissing him, holding him, the way a mother was supposed to hold her child. He sometimes wondered how his father had acted toward him. But that was too long ago. All he could conjure up from those days was his father sitting at his desk upstairs.

Wednesday nights were always the same. The meals were uniformly bad, causing Vince more than once to remark, out of Concetta's earshot, that his mother was the only Italian woman in the world who couldn't cook. Even worse, she knew that she couldn't cook and she didn't care.

But the poor food could have been endured had the conversation been less stilted. They never had anything of substance to say, and since each was equally poor at small talk, there were long periods of silence, which unnerved him. How the hell could your own mother make you feel self-conscious?

Normally silence didn't bother Vince. In fact, he rather enjoyed it. There were times that he and Lena could sit together for an hour without exchanging ten words. But that was different. It was by choice. When two people were close, when they understood and loved each other, they had nothing to prove. They could enjoy each other's company without feeling obligated to talk.

When the silence came with his mother, Vince tried to tune it out, mentally shifting from the son of a distant mother to the don of his *borgotta*. There was always so much to consider. Yesterday had gone well. Vagnoni had been taken out, just as planned. The papers were speculating that it might have been a hit, but nothing could ever be proved. Not unless Joey Cariola pulled a Jesus and came back to life.

What *hadn't* been planned was the school bus. And the children. An acceptable part of the risk, he tried to tell himself. It had been more important to remove Vagnoni.

But the image refused to disappear. They could have been *his* children. Safe and happy one minute, scorched to death the next. Was anything, even the protection of his family, worth such a price?

Unable to shed the guilt, he reverted to form. He went to Pat and to confession.

"My God!" Pat had said. "Where does it end, Vince? How many times will you justify your crimes in the name of your precious family?"

"I don't know, Pat. I just don't know."

"You expect absolution?"

"That's up to you, Pat."

"In conscience, I shouldn't," Pat said. "You know that. I know that you didn't anticipate the children, and I know that you're sorry. But that's not enough. There has to be more."

"I know. A firm resolution to sin no more."

"Exactly. And do you have that? Can you honestly tell me that you'll put all this behind you?"

Vince sighed. "You know I can't."

For a moment they sat in silence. "All right," Pat finally said. "I'll grant you absolution. But this is it. I know that I've said it before, but no more."

"I understand."

After the priest had absolved his penitent, Vince rose to leave.

[189]

But even in the confessional Pat was an opportunist. Fate had given him this chance, and he couldn't let it escape. "There *is* something else, Vince. It's not related to your confession, I want you to understand that. But I need your help. The Church needs your help."

And so Vince Grosso had violated his cardinal rule, getting involved in a non-family matter. It had been impossible to refuse. Pat wasn't just his friend; he was his confessor, the one human being to whom he could bare his soul with absolute safety. And absolution, like anything else, had its price.

Sidney Feinstein had been sickening, everything that Vince despised. He was probably in his late forties, the tan no doubt the result of a recent stay in Miami. He wore a leisure suit, the top four buttons of his shirt unfastened to better display the gold chain and medallion around his neck. He must have thought he was still in Miami since even though it was October, his shoes were white patent-leather slip-ons with gold buckles.

Vince noticed two things right away. The hair wasn't his. The shithead was wearing a toupee. A pretty good one, the kind that a lot of people would accept as real. But Vince knew.

And he was soft. He wasn't really fat, but that didn't matter. You could be fat and still be hard. It depended on what was behind the fat. This shithead was soft. He'd be a piece of cake.

"Mr. Grasso," Feinstein said, extending his hand.

"Grosso."

"Right. Sit down, please. So you're a lawyer, huh? I see from your card you're in the PSFS Building. Great building. Real character. Not like the junk they put up nowadays. I've got a friend there. Fourth floor. An accountant. Murray Goldman. Do you know him?"

"No, I don't believe we've met."

"Sweet guy. Really a sweet guy. Salt-of-the-earth type, you know what I mean? Give you the shirt off his back. Well, you being a lawyer, you probably know Ike Caplan, don't you?"

"Judge Caplan?"

"Right. I knew him way back when. Real sweet guy. Down to earth as they come, even after they made him a judge."

"I've practiced before him a few times. He's very good."

"Yeah, well next time you see him, tell him Sidney Feinstein

[190]

said hello. And tell him I said to make sure you win the case."
Feinstein laughed. "But I'll bet you don't need any help like that,
do you? You look like you can take care of yourself."

"I try."

"That's the way." He motioned to the bar at the far end of the
room. "How 'bout a drink?"

"No, thank you."

"Don't drink during the day, huh? Well, I can respect that. Me,
I like to—"

"Mr. Feinstein, I'd like to get down to business."

For a split second Feinstein tensed, then quickly recovered.
"Sure. Anything I can do to help. Shoot."

"Actually this is a fairly delicate matter. I represent a client, a
large charitable organization which wishes to remain anonymous—at least for now. We have reason to believe that one of its
agents recently transacted business with you without authoriza-
tion."

Vince had to give him credit. The guy was good. No hint of recognition in his face. "Well," Feinstein said, "I keep a complete list
of all our real estate deals, so—"

"This wasn't real estate."

"That's my only business."

"I won't fence with you, Mr. Feinstein." He reached into his
pocket, removing Father Flaherty's passport. "The individual in
question undoubtedly used a false name, but this is his picture."

Feinstein shook his head, his face the picture of a man who
really wanted to help. "Sorry, Mr. Grasso—"

"Grosso."

"Right. I've never seen this gentleman."

"My client is prepared to make it worthwhile for you in the
event we can reach an agreement."

"Mr. Grosso, I'm not a religious man, but my word before God,
I've never seen the man. I like you, Mr. Grosso. You seem like a
sweet guy. I'd love to be able to help you, believe that." He
shrugged his shoulders. "It's just that I can't tell you what I don't
know."

Vince rose, extending his hand. "Thank you for your time, Mr.
Feinstein. Obviously there's been a mistake. I'll straighten things
out with my client."

"Do that. And don't forget to give Ike Caplan my best."

[191]

Vince smiled to himself. The Jew bastard had put on a pretty good performance, but he'd still be a piece of cake. He was soft.

"That was excellent, Mother," Vince said, looking at his watch, then rising.

"You hardly ate, Vincent. My food isn't good enough for you?"

"Of course, Mother. It's just that I'm trying to take off a few pounds."

"For what? You're already nothing but a stick. I should have your weight problems."

Vince leaned down and kissed her head. "*Ciao,* Mother. We'll see you Saturday."

Mercifully he was back in the limo, his duty done. As his driver swung around City Hall and east on Market, a Porsche was heading the other way. It had been a long day for Sidney Feinstein, and now it was time to unwind.

He had the world by the short hairs: more money than a man would ever need, an ex-wife who didn't make trouble as long as the check arrived on time, and a stable of gorgeous *shiksas.* All young, all ferocious in bed. They had been forbidden fruit when he was young. His mother would rather he die of cancer than mix with the goyim. But now, in his second youth, he was making up for it. Every time he stuck it to one of his beauties, he was sticking it to his mother as well.

With rush-hour traffic long since over, the ride took seven minutes. He had a thing about logistics. "Economy of movement," he often said. "If you work in Center City, you live in Center City." You had only so many minutes in your life, and Sidney was reluctant to waste any.

His condo was on the parkway, a block from the Cathedral. It had everything he wanted: location, style, and security. He turned into the driveway, nodded to the guard, and drove down the ramp to the underground garage. His reserved space was precisely nine steps from the elevator. Economy of movement.

First a hot shower, he thought, as he pushed the button of his floor. Then a drink, maybe two, before picking up Monica.

The paper was propped against the door, just as he insisted. He'd read it while he was having his drink. The lights in the living room were already on, courtesy of an electronic timer. He hated entering a dark home.

[192]

"Welcome home, Jew boy."

Feinstein started to wheel, but the arm was already around his throat. There were two of them, maybe three. He felt his toupee being ripped off and jammed into his mouth. Then the fist drove into his stomach, and he tried to scream; only his hair, or what he called his hair, gagged him. He hadn't felt pain like that since he was little, when David Gordon tackled him at the playground. He'd hated football after that.

Then the knee crashed into his testicles, and he began to vomit. Blocked by his toupee, the vomitus spurted out of his nose. Even worse than the pain was the fear that he would suffocate.

Then came the real terror. His pants were ripped off, and he was spread-eagled over a chair.

"We're gonna circumcise you again, Jew boy. Sicilian style."

Kill me, he thought as the wire was placed around his penis. *Please, God, let them kill me. Anything but this.*

The wire tightened, his penis and upper legs now smeared with blood. He lost control of his bowels, fouling the Oriental rug that was his pride.

"Disgusting bastard, aren't you?"

Then he felt the wire loosen. He was slammed to the floor, his face shoved into the excrement.

"Listen good, Jew boy. The next time we'll cut it off, not that you got much there."

Feinstein had no idea how long he lay there after they left or whether he had passed out. Then he heard the phone. It had to be Monica. Only his *shiksas* had his number. He tried to ignore it, but it kept ringing. Finally, he staggered across the room, collapsed into the recliner, and lifted the receiver. It wasn't Monica.

"Mr. Feinstein? Vince Grosso. I just wanted to tell you how much I enjoyed meeting you today. And listen, if you happen to think of that individual we discussed, I'd appreciate your getting back to me. I know you'll try, because you're a real sweet guy, Mr. Feinstein."

[193]

CHAPTER
Eleven

FRIDAY was the big night in Tunnel Hill. After a week of farm chores the young ones were ready to let off a little steam, and Charlie's Café provided that opportunity.

There was the alcohol (mostly beer), the jukebox, and, twice a month, the four-piece country and western band. But most of all, there was the tough-guy competition.

The rules were relatively basic. Two of the biggest, meanest farmhands were pitted against each other in a struggle of survival. They were permitted to use their fists, their feet, and anything else they could land their hands on except glass bottles and knives. The object was to reduce your opponent to unconsciousness or to a state where he could no longer proceed.

Usually the contest was concluded quickly, with the contestants shaking hands and returning to the bar. Only later might they drive to the hospital for the necessary stitches, splints, or casts.

The struggle of June 4, 1981, ended on a somewhat different note. Carl Tanner, age twenty-three, was more than holding his own. At six feet two inches, 218 pounds, he was a shade smaller than his opponent, but he made up for this by his quickness. A stiff left jab had successfully kept Buck Clater at bay, breaking his nose and closing his left eye in the process. In a final act of frustration, Clater charged, ignoring the blows that continued to land on his face.

Tanner would have escaped again had he not slipped on a section of the floor where someone had dropped a beer. Clater pounced, knees first. He caught his opponent, who was attempting to rise, on the top of the head. Be-

cause of the crowd noise and the jukebox, no one heard the snap. Carl Tanner never heard anything again.

It was not the type of incident that made statewide news, but it was big box office in the immediate area, the biggest story since the outbreak of hoof-and-mouth disease two years before. There was the predictable cry from civic groups to outlaw such barbarism. State Senator Mark Sawyer responded promptly, introducing legislation to prohibit henceforth all forms of tough-guy competitions.

When Senate Bill 742 was introduced, it attracted little fanfare. Soon it would become the most famous bill in the history of Pennsylvania.

There were ten of them, all crowded into Kevin's office, all hostile. They hadn't been scheduled, but when you had an open-door policy, these things happened.

"What can I do for you?" Kevin asked after personally greeting each of them.

"We're here to demand you drop your sponsorship of the adoption bill," said the leader, a woman in her mid-thirties.

Kevin refused to take the bait, instead choosing the sugar approach. "Well, I'll be happy to discuss it with you."

"There's nothing to discuss," the woman snapped. "Your bill is an affront to all adoptees. Either you remove your name from it, or we'll remove you from office at the next election."

So much for sugar. Kevin leaned forward, his eyes boring into the woman. "You come in here without an appointment, on a day that's going to be murder anyway, but that's okay. I'm happy to meet with you. Your group picketed my district office last week, but that's fine, too. You've got that right. You oppose my bill, but I've got no complaint with that. There's always room for a difference of opinion. But then you threaten, and that's a no-no. Let me give you a piece of advice on how to deal with legislators, particularly this legislator. Threats aren't necessary; in fact they're counterproductive. The fact that you've taken the time to meet with me demonstrates your concern. All you do by threatening is wave a red flag in front of a bull."

"You're a public servant. You're here to do as we command."

"A damn good public servant, lady. One who works his tail off to serve his people. But that doesn't mean I'm a slave. I still reserve the right to tell someone to go to hell when it's merited.

[195]

And with all due respect, you fall into that category right now."

The woman stood. "Does that mean you refuse to change your position?"

"Unless, in a rational discussion, with no threats, you can convince me that I'm wrong."

"Then there's no reason to continue this meeting. We'll take care of you next November, Mr. Murray."

Kevin smiled. "You know, I have a rule that I never make promises, but just this once I'm going to break it. In fact, I'm gonna make two. First, my adoption bill is going to pass—big. And secondly, next November, no matter what you do, I'm gonna win—big. Bet the ranch on it, sweetheart. And on election night, after the polls close, feel free to drop in at Cavanaugh's for our victory celebration."

Kevin arose from behind his desk. "I guess that about does it, don't you think? Regardless of what you may think, I'm a damn good legislator. And when you realize that discussion, rather than threats and insults, is the way to go, I'll be happy to meet with you again. Until then, there's the door. Have a nice day."

He had made it a point to keep his cool, but after they'd left, he exploded. "Fuckin' son of a bitch!" he bellowed, slamming his fist on the desk. Why were there so many assholes in the world? Always attacking, always jabbing at you. It just wasn't worth it.

And what really got him, what really frosted his ass, was that most of the screamers didn't know what the hell they were talking about. They were so full of the righteousness of their cause that they didn't have time to learn the facts.

Like the abortion bill. Of all the people who called to berate him, of all those who accosted him on the street, only a handful had taken the time to read it. When Kevin would ask them if they knew what the bill actually did, they would begin to stammer, their anger increasing as if they resented being called upon really to *know* about something before opposing it.

Maybe that was his whole problem, always looking for logic and consistency in the world. To him, simple self-respect dictated that before you came on like gangbusters, you made sure you were educated on the subject. Otherwise you looked like an asshole. The irony was that the ones who wrote the respectful, detailed letters of opposition, who made their points in an effective, low-key manner, were the ones who had done their homework.

He'd known the adoption bill would be volatile when he first introduced it, but always the child of controversy, he had plunged forward. Pennsylvania's adoption laws, like those of forty-seven other states, called for sealed records, providing the natural mother with complete privacy. The problem was caused by an inadvertent loophole in the Vital Statistics Law that permitted any adopted person, by merely sending four dollars to the Bureau of Vital Statistics, to obtain his original birth certificate. Such a certificate always carried the name of the natural mother, and often the name of the natural father, thus destroying the privacy guaranteed by the Adoption Code. Caused by a drafting error that went unnoticed, it was a prime example of government by mistake.

Kevin's bill closed the loophole and, for the first time, set up an involved procedure to assist adoptees in the search for their natural parents. The bill called for the establishment of a registry in the Bureau of Vital Statistics where natural parents who decided to be located could be cross-referenced with the children who were seeking them. There was also a provision permitting a court or a licensed adoption agency to search for the natural parents on behalf of any adoptee. Always, however, the natural parent had to agree before her identity or location was revealed.

When all the legal phrases were stripped away, the bill posed one central question: do adopted persons have the absolute right to know the identity of their natural parents whether or not those natural parents agree? Kevin believed that the answer was no. Not that it was an easy issue. He could empathize with the adoptees, and had those flamers who had just assaulted him given him the opportunity, he would have expressed his empathy. There was no question in Kevin's mind that were he adopted, he would want answers to the two big questions: who were they, and why did they give me away? For someone like him, who cared so much about roots, these were questions that went to the heart of what it was all about.

But the other side of the argument was even more compelling. Kevin's primary concern was for the stability of the family unit. He cited the example of the fifteen-year-old girl, unwed, who becomes pregnant, has her baby, and places it for adoption. Subsequently she picks up the pieces of her life, marries, has more children, and, for whatever reason, which is hers alone to determine, decides not to tell her husband and her children about her past. What happens to that family if, eighteen or nineteen years later, Junior shows up on the doorstep? Such an example wasn't hypothetical. It actually happened, again and again, as Kevin had been able to document. Frequently the result was the devastation of a family.

Then there was the pro-life factor. If you were pro-life, it wasn't enough merely to oppose abortion. You had to look for ways to reduce the incidences that gave rise to abortions. A pregnant woman who did not wish to raise her child had two choices: adoption or abortion. If, while pondering this, she were aware that should she choose adoption, she would not have an absolute right to privacy, she might well opt for the abortion route.

He was doing it again, searching for logic and consistency. The Supreme Court had ruled that a woman seeking an abortion had an absolute right to privacy. Didn't logic demand that the same right be extended to a woman who chose life?

Adoptees claimed a right to know their heritage, a valid claim. But they had an even greater right that the natural parents had already acknowledged: the right to life. Had that right been denied them, the identity of their natural parents would have been wholly irrelevant. They simply would not exist to demand any other rights or, for that matter, to threaten legislators.

Kevin walked to the door to greet his next appointment: the president of the Pennsylvania League of Women Voters and the League's Delaware County chairman, or chairperson, as was now in vogue. Christ, how he hated that.

Both accepted Kevin's offer of coffee, and he walked to the pot. It was outside his office, next to Janet's desk, but he absolutely refused to ask her to get it. If she were up, getting coffee for herself, he'd expect her to offer, just as he would to her, but to make it a point to have your secretary get your coffee was disgusting. Some called it male chauvinism. Kevin just called it phony. That and having your secretary dial someone's number for you, as if it were beneath your dignity to use your own finger. Nothing irritated him more than receiving a call from someone's secretary, then being placed on hold. He could understand being put on hold if he were the one making the call, but it took a hell of a lot of gall for someone to call you, then make you wait. Kevin, however, had discovered a subtle way to handle this. He promptly hung up.

They talked for almost an hour, time that Kevin couldn't afford. Not that he minded the League women. They were nice people. Genuinely committed to improving government. But like their Common Cause counterparts, their heads were in the clouds. Grossly impractical and totally unrealistic.

And they didn't do their homework. They never read farther than the label. Whenever something was labeled "good government" or "efficient," they bought in without reading the fine print.

It wasn't the least bit surprising, therefore, that the League and Kevin disagreed on virtually every issue. Today was no exception. The women had a long shopping list which Kevin, item by item, rejected.

Like merit selection of judges, which in itself was a label. The League wanted to end the practice in Pennsylvania of electing all appellate judges. Judgeships were far too important to be left to the people. Those who dispensed justice should be appointed by the governor from a list supplied by a "blue-ribbon panel of experts." In turn, so the theory went, this would lead to a far cleaner judiciary, much like the federal system where judges were appointed for life by the president.

Kevin was adamantly opposed. He rejected the philosophy that the people, the great unwashed, were unable to make the important decisions and should be protected from themselves. History proved otherwise. By and large the American people had a pretty good box score.

And since judges were no longer content merely to interpret the law, since they consistently intruded upon the legislative branch and set public policy, Kevin wanted to make damn certain that they had to run for office and state their positions on important issues such as abortion, capital punishment, and mandatory sentencing.

It was true that the federal system provided fewer scandals. It was also the system which had provided America with abortion on demand, forced quotas upon employers and universities, and banned God from the public schools. And the so-called blue-ribbon panel would be stacked with attorneys, individuals with

[199]

vested interests who would practice before the judges they selected. There would still be politics, but the people would no
longer be involved. It would be only a select group of so-called
experts.

The size of the legislature was another issue. "Good government" dictated that it be drastically reduced. This would provide
far greater efficiency since the money saved in legislators' salaries
could be utilized to hire expert, nonpartisan staff.

Kevin knew how difficult it already was for him to provide a
personal touch to the sixty thousand constituents he represented.
If the legislature were cut in half, his constituency would be doubled, thus taking government farther away from the people. And
it was an undisputed axiom that the smaller the size of the legislature, the easier it was to buy. Proof of this was frequently given by
the Pennsylvania Bankers Association, the most powerful lobbying group in Harrisburg. On an issue of importance it generally
chose to ignore the House: too big, far too cumbersome to control.
Instead, it focused on the Senate, where only twenty-six votes
were needed. And invariably money talked.

The League also supported a unicameral legislature. Having
only one legislative chamber would go a long way to clear the
logjam of bills and end the frustrating delay often encountered
before an important bill became law.

Ignored was the fact that a bicameral legislature provided a
necessary safeguard. Frequently a bill would zip through one
house before anyone really had a chance to examine it. By the
time it got to the other chamber, however, there was sufficient
time for legislators and citizens to give it a good inspection and
spot a problem that had been overlooked. The tortuous route
which a bill must take before being enacted into law was intentional, a carefully constructed obstacle to haste and steamroller
tactics.

Efficiency also dictated that the terms of House members, in
both Congress and the state capitals, be increased. A two-year
term required the member to be constantly running for office, de-
voting less time to the job than to political considerations.

Overlooked was the wisdom of the Founding Fathers, who understood the necessity of having one elected body that was
directly responsible to the people. Without the insulation of a
long term a legislator's responsiveness was assured. He knew that

[200]

the voters got a shot at him every two years. And it made the people feel that they were part of the system, a feeling that would be substantially diminished by an increase in the length of the term.

To Kevin, the League's central problem was that it viewed efficiency as the primary goal in government. Such a goal could be far better served by a dictatorship, preferably a benevolent one, since democracy was an inherently inefficient system. "Anytime you have a government of the people," Kevin told the women, "you're going to have inefficiency. It runs with the territory. But I'm not willing to trade what we have for a system that cuts out those people. When you're searching for efficiency, make damn sure you don't lose more in the apples than you gain in the oranges."

When the women had gone, Kevin realized that he was angry. Not at them. At the way things were going, at a direction that revolted and, even worse, frightened him. Every day the frustrations seemed to get a little worse. It didn't show in public, he saw to that, but it was there. He'd be watching the news with Karen or reading the paper. There was certain to be something to throw him into a rage. A report that the city had formed a Sexual Minorities Commission. ("Can you believe that! A special commission for fags! Jesus Bleedin' H. Christ, what next!")

A court order requiring furloughed female state employees to be rehired regardless of seniority. ("What absolute horseshit! That's not equal rights. That's friggin' reverse discrimination!")

The American boycott of the 1980 Olympics. ("Carter may not be the biggest asshole in the world, but he's definitely in the top three! Russia invades Afghanistan, and we retaliate by penalizing *our* athletes. Meanwhile, Khomeini still has our hostages, and all we do is send friggin' Christmas cards!")

The ACLU's suing a school district for displaying a Nativity scene. Or welfare recipients demanding a Christmas bonus. Or a court-ordered palimony award. All triggered explosions that were invariably profane, in turn triggering a fight with Karen, which in turn increased Kevin's frustration.

Was it him? *Was* he a hopeless redneck? Was he the only one out of step in a "pluralistic society?" And more important, wasn't he destroying himself? The major victim of hate was the one doing the hating. It tore you apart from inside, made you less human.

[201]

Would he end up, if he made it to the golden years, as one of those bitter senior citizens he encountered so often? Never smiling, hating all public officials, always complaining about the neighbors' kids. That didn't suddenly happen when you got old. He remembered something a priest had said: If you're bitter as a senior citizen, you've been bitter all your life. Who said that? Yeah, Father Powell. At the pro-life convention.

Father John Powell. World-famous author, lecturer, and pillar of the movement. He had spoken for an hour, and no one had moved. Great sense of humor, perfect timing, and tremendous warmth, warmth that you could almost reach out and touch. He hadn't recited the reasons to oppose abortion. That would have been preaching to the choir. His message, like that of Christ, was love. In the end that was all that counted. Love of God, love of your family, and, most important, love of your enemy

Kevin had been inspired yet deeply troubled. It was all well and good to talk about love, but how could you feel it, really feel it, when you were in a war? When you were always the point man drawing the enemy fire? When you knew that the first time that you showed weakness, the other side would cut you apart?

Sure, he still had the sense of humor. He could still be charming, crack jokes with Bridget Kelly, even remain civil to a Sheila Sendrow, but inside, he was always at battle stations, always resenting the players and the society that made him wage such a war.

Kevin had just greeted his next appointment, the lobbyist for the Pennsylvania Contractors Association, when his phone buzzed again.

"It's Ed Harvey," Janet said. "He says it's important."

Ed Harvey, House Republican counsel and probably the best legal mind in the state. Fervently loyal to the caucus and, as a bonus, a down-the-line pro-lifer.

"Got some news that might interest you, Kevin. The Judiciary Committee just reported out Senate Bill Seven-four-two."

This time Kevin *did* slam his fist on the desk, but not in rage. "Hot shit! At last we go to war. Thanks, Eddie, as usual."

He flew through the next three appointments, trying not to show that his mind was elsewhere. Then he dialed the Speaker.

"What trouble are you stirring up now, Murray?" Mike Callaghan asked.

"Michael, me boy, it strikes me that things have been too dull around here lately. I intend to give you a few more gray hairs."

"Break it to me gently. I'm not getting any younger."

"I noticed that Senate Bill Seven-four-two has just been reported out of Judiciary. It's our vehicle."

"Donning the papal robes again, huh?"

"Absofuckinlutely. What do you think about scheduling?"

"How 'bout late 'eighty-seven?"

"You cocksucker."

"Give me a break. I'm trying to quit."

"Seriously."

"Okay, let's see. We're loaded this week, and the bill needs two more readings anyway. Next week's Thanksgiving break. How's the first or second week in December?"

"Beautiful."

"You got it. But touch base with our majority leader so he doesn't pout."

"Gotcha. And, Mike, thanks."

"Go away and let me age gracefully."

Kevin replaced the phone and began to rub his hands together. It was an act of joy, of pure enthusiasm, that he had used since he was little whenever he was excited. When they were ready for vacation. When Christmas was coming. When the day of the big game had arrived.

And now another big game, maybe the biggest. A month before, the abortion control bill had gone down in the Health and Welfare Committee by the 13–11 vote that Kevin had publicly predicted. Not being members of the committee, he and Harrington had been forced to sit through the meeting, frustrated by their inability to speak, to correct the misinformation that had been served in mountainous portions. When the vote had been cast, they were surrounded by the media, eager for reaction.

"Completely expected," Kevin said, "and merely a temporary setback. As Winston Churchill once pointed out, 'Britain . . . always wins one battle—the last.' The last battle in this war has yet to be fought."

(He had liked that line. It was the type that appealed to him.

On a number of occasions he had remarked that as long as Kevin Murray was alive, the cliché would never die.)

"What's next, Representative Murray?"

"I never speak for my colleagues, but I will make one guarantee: One way or the other, the full membership of the House *will* have the opportunity to vote on this bill. Bet the ranch on it."

"How?"

"By doing whatever it takes."

The reporter persisted. "Including a discharge resolution?"

"I repeat, whatever it takes."

And that was the story, as Kevin had intended. The possibility of a discharge resolution overshadowed the committee's defeat of the bill.

No legislative procedure was used as sparingly and detested as much as the discharge resolution. It was a procedure that was, in fact, an attack upon the committee system. By rule and custom, a committee chairman had dictatorial powers over all bills assigned to his committee. If he decided that a bill should die, it died. It was never placed on the agenda, never considered by the committee members.

Similarly, when a committee did consider and defeat a bill, that was the end of the line.

A discharge resolution was an attempt to alter that reality. It required the signatures of at least twenty-five members before being introduced and placed on the calendar, where it would remain until either passed or, more likely, withdrawn by the sponsors. Its passage required a constitutional majority of the House membership. If passage was obtained, the bill was taken from the possession of the committee and placed on the House calendar for an immediate vote.

Precisely because it was an attack on the system, legislators were loath to support it. The system might not be perfect, it might reward seniority and ignore merit, it might cause good legislation to die without ever seeing the light of day, it might permit a committee chairman to play the tyrant, but it was a *system*. It provided a degree of order where otherwise there would be chaos. Most of all, there was fear. If you stuck it to a chairman or his committee for a bill that you wanted, might not you be on the receiving end the next time the shoe dropped?

For these reasons, it wasn't surprising that only two discharge resolutions were successful in the past century, both in the mid-seventies, both on the abortion issue. And both times the bitterness had remained for months.

Knowing all this, Kevin and Harrington had signed up forty cosponsors and introduced the discharge measure. For the next month it remained on the calendar, staring the members in the face every day. They faced the prospect of being forced to choose between the pro-life cause and the stability of the committee system, an unsolvable dilemma that terrified and angered them.

Kevin knew all this, too. He was banking on it. What he hadn't told anyone, not even Harrington, was that he never had the slightest intention of calling up the discharge resolution for a vote. It was the shock-and-reprieve treatment. Scare hell out of them with something drastic; then come in with something less.

Members hated to vote on abortion, it being the ultimate no-win proposition. Behind the closed doors of the caucus, Kevin and Harrington were harangued whenever an abortion vote was imminent, even by some of the cosponsors of the bills, who wanted the best of both worlds: to enjoy the support of the pro-lifers without incurring the enmity of the other side.

That was never going to change. There would always be resentment when legislators had their feet put to the fire. It was a price that had to be paid. The trick was to diminish the resentment as much as possible. And the best way to diminish the heat in this case was to pick off a Senate-passed bill and run the abortion control measure as an amendment to it.

Kevin had been successful with that strategy in the past, most notably with the abortion funding bill. Such a tactic had a double benefit. It circumvented not only the House committee procedure but that of the Senate as well. When the House amended a Senate bill, the measure went directly back to the floor of the Senate for a yes or no vote on concurrence. No further amendments were permitted.

The major obstacle was the requirement that the amendment be germane to the bill it was amending. Germaneness was an obscure term that was frequently winked at, if not completely ignored. The usual rule of thumb, however, was that the subject matter of the amendment should have *some* relationship to the subject matter of the vehicle bill. An attempt, for example, to amend a child care provision into a landlord-tenant bill would probably be ruled not germane. The problem was that there were no bills relating to abortion on the calendar, House or Senate. After huddling for two hours immediately following committee defeat of the bill, Kevin and Ed Harvey had decided that two types of bill could serve as the vehicle. The preferable one was a Crimes Code bill into which the omnibus provisions of the abortion bill would fit nicely. Failing this, a Judicial Code bill would suffice.

Two weeks before, Senate Bill 742 had unanimously passed the Senate, and Kevin held his breath. The House Judiciary Committee, to which it was referred, was as hostile to the pro-life cause as Health and Welfare. SB 742 in itself was uncontroversial. Since it was a local issue designed to help the political standing of its sponsor, it would sail through committee. If word leaked, however, that it was to be used as the abortion control vehicle, it would be forever buried.

Now it was out, on the House calendar, and nothing could stop them. The ball was finally in the pro-life court, in the forum where they had never failed: the House, the people's house.

The next two weeks would be a frenzy. An action alert to the pro-life leaders to gear up the troops across the state. Countless interviews with the media. An additional bill analysis sent to each member. Strategy sessions with Harrington and the other sponsors.

But first, protocol demanded a call to the majority leader.

"What can I do for you, Kevin?" asked Seth Harkins. Always terse, always businesslike.

"SB Seven-four-two, Seth. It's on the calendar, and we want to use it as a vehicle for the abortion bill."

"I see. You're adamant in this regard?" Harkins was far from pleased. He always voted pro-life, but the primary concern of this efficient majority leader was the orderly flow of the House calendar. An abortion fight was certain to disrupt that order.

"Yeah, Seth. God knows when we'll get another vehicle. It has to be this one."

"Very well. Timetable?"

"I talked with the Speaker. He suggested the first or second week in December. It's up to you, of course."

"I see." Kevin could hear him turning the pages of his scheduling book. "Would Tuesday, eight December, be suitable?"

Kevin almost laughed. "They won't believe it."

"What?"

"Nothing, Seth. December eighth would be fine."

Kevin replaced the receiver and shook his head, reveling in the irony. After months of waiting, of being on the receiving end of all the salvos, they were taking the offensive at last. Once again Kevin Murray was going into battle.

Everything was ready. He had the vehicle, the votes, and the date. And, if one believed in such things, a good-luck omen. The majority leader, a Methodist, had set the day of battle, though most would believe that it had been the work of Kevin Murray, professional Catholic.

Armageddon would occur on December 8, the Feast of the Immaculate Conception of the Blessed Virgin Mary.

Monsignor Patrick Carney should have been at peace with the world. As was his custom, the pastor had turned in shortly after nine, and the assistant pastor was at a meeting with the charismatics. (*Better him than me,* Pat thought. He never felt comfortable with those people.)

Pat was alone, a crackling fire, an excellent brandy, and a well-earned victory all serving to warm him. Today's press conference had gone well. The boss had been in fine form as he announced plans for the shrine of Our Lady of Knock. Flanked by a number of big hitters of the Irish laity, he praised the generosity of his flock in raising almost two million dollars to honor Mary. Construction would begin in early spring, and "God and labor unions willing," it would be dedicated on December 8, 1982. An elegantly catered reception capped the afternoon.

Flawless. And all because of Pat. A scandal, one that would have paled the Czestochowa debacle, had been averted. It had been two years since that one had broken, and the shock waves were still reverberating. All the way to Rome, to the pope himself. A group of Polish monks, the Pauline Fathers, had purchased a parcel of Bucks County farmland near Doylestown. Their intention was to erect a shrine to our Lady of Czestochowa, patroness of Poland. The monks proved to be outstanding fund-raisers, siphoning millions from the faithful, mostly poor and middle-class Poles who would gladly go without food to honor the Black Madonna.

[207]

Unfortunately most of the money disappeared amid rumors of debauchery, fraud, and even Mafia involvement. The new pope sent out a three-point directive to his fellow Pole, the archbishop of Philadelphia: salvage the effort, complete the shrine, and put the lid on all publicity. The cardinal batted two for three. Utilizing his legendary financial skills, he settled with the creditors (usually at ten cents on the dollar), pulled the project into the black, and completed the shrine. There would have been a happy ending had it not been for three reporters from the Gannett News Service. The more they dug, the more they realized what they had: a papal Watergate. Sensing a kill, they went for the jugular, straight through the Roman collar. The first of eighteen articles, a series that was to garner a Pulitzer Prize, ran on the eve of the pope's visit to Philadelphia. The lid was very definitely off.

The Church and the cardinal were durable institutions. Each was tarnished, but each had survived. Others were not so fortunate. The Church was very much like the military in many ways, particularly in the mentality that when something bad occurred, someone had to pay. Whether the individual so punished had in any way caused the misfortune in question was basically irrelevant. To put it another way, in military jargon, "shit runs downhill." In this case, it submerged a number of rising middle-management clergymen in both Philadelphia and Rome.

One of the victims was the director of communications of the archdiocese of Philadelphia, an energetic monsignor who had been considered a front-runner for the next bishop's hat. Instead, he was reassigned to a suburban mental hospital as assistant chaplain. His successor was another energetic monsignor, Patrick Gerard Carney.

The irony was not lost on Pat as he accepted the Knock assignment. Things had come full circle. If the job were botched, he, too, would be banished, all the carefully crafted plans hopelessly shattered. The fact that he would still have his priesthood was of little consolation.

He sipped the brandy slowly, a conscious effort to enjoy one of life's carnal pleasures. There would be no banishment. Quite the contrary. There would probably be a reward. He had succeeded where others had failed. A subdued Father Flaherty was back in Ireland, his American ministry completed. A suddenly enlightened Sidney Feinstein had returned the money to Vince, who turned it over to Pat, who in turn deposited the funds in a new account. Interest-bearing, of course.

As Kevin was fond of saying, the name of the game was results, and Pat had produced. Total victory, and not a word, not even a whisper, had leaked.

So why the hell wasn't he happy? Why was it that on those occasions when he had reached a summit he was never content to plant a flag and celebrate? Why did he reserve those times for the pain of self-analysis?

He had chalked it up to the solitary life. What was the point of celebrating when you had no one to share your joy? But it was more than that, at least this time.

Sure, something worthwhile had occurred. Several things, actually. A scandal had been averted, a shrine was to be built, and a large shipment of arms to international terrorists had been thwarted.

But what had *he* done? Had Pat Carney really been a part of it? Or hadn't he accomplished his goal by doing what he always did when it came to a crunch: using his friends.

Kevin was the last person in the world he should expose to a scandal. He was too valuable, too much a target already. But Kevin hadn't hesitated, as Pat had known all along. There was nothing Kevin Murray would refuse to a friend.

But it was going to Vince that had made the sin mortal. Pat didn't try to kid himself. He knew why he had made that choice. It wasn't Vince Grosso the lawyer whom he had sought. A lawyer couldn't have pulled this one off, not with someone like Sidney Feinstein. Some form of violence, or threat of violence, would have to occur before Feinstein would cooperate. Pat knew precisely what Vince was. After all, he was his confessor, the one person in the world who knew everything and could say nothing.

Pat smiled, mostly in self-disgust. It had been a very different blessed trinity that he had assembled for this task: the Roman Catholic Church, the Federal Bureau of Investigation, and La Cosa Nostra. Three of the most powerful organizations in the world. Each a model of efficiency, each ruthless in the pursuit of its goals.

Pat remembered something that Kevin had told him once, something that he had learned working organized crime in Detroit. The only organization in the world that approached the Bureau in the pains it took on screening applicants was the mob. The church ran a poor third in that category, Pat thought, particularly now with the drop in vocations. It couldn't afford to be too selective.

So here he was, with his brandy and his fire, toasting his victory and, not for the first time, loathing himself as a priest and a man. Facing another decision. There was still a way to redeem a measure of self-respect, even if it might make his victory less complete, his position less secure.

For the hundredth time he looked at the notebook, fondling its leather cover. It had been taken from Father Flaherty's suitcase during the search by the Trappists. The monks hadn't looked at it. It wasn't their place. Only Pat had studied its contents. He tried to tell himself that the names were merely those of contributors to a worthy cause, but if that was the case, why was a code name listed for each?

No, he knew better. The people listed in the book—and he recognized a number of them as leading members of the community and the laity—cared little for the veneration of Our Lady of Knock. They were in league with an Irish Jesuit for the express purpose of funneling money and weapons to the IRA. Disciples of terror, undoubtedly convinced of the righteousness of their cause. Because of their efforts, men, women, and children would be indiscriminately killed or maimed. Not on the battlefield, where one freely entered knowing the risk and taking his chances, but in places where human beings had a reasonable expectation of safety: department stores; pubs; even schools.

Pat had agonized for a month, since the day when Vince had handed him a briefcase containing two million dollars. Until that point the outcome had been uncertain. There had been no time for considerations of morality. Only when victory was certain did the internal debate begin.

It was the same confrontation he had faced so many times since entering the seminary, even before: ethics versus pragmatism. Pat Carney, priest and human, opposing Pat Carney, rising church star and efficient administrator.

He knew what was right. The truly Christian course of action would be to turn the notebook over to the FBI. Help law enforcement stem the flow of death. He could argue that the IRA were freedom fighters, just like our colonists, struggling to remove the

[210]

yoke of British oppression. But that would be bullshit. Hadn't he rejected the same argument from Father Flaherty? Nothing could justify the wanton slaughter of civilians.

But what would be the effect of this act of morality? To the Church and, even more important, to Monsignor Patrick Carney? The Bureau wanted this type of information. Kevin had told him that. It would initiate an investigation which *might* result in indictments, which *might* result in adverse publicity to the Church. An aggressive defense attorney *might* demand the source of the notebook. Pat *might* be subpoenaed, and the whole story of Knock *might* come to light. All his efforts would have been fruitless. His church and his cardinal would have another Czestochowa.

There was no point in going to the boss for advice. That would be the worst thing he could do. He would be placing the cardinal in an untenable position. Pulski would have no choice but to recommend the course of Christian morality. And although nothing would ever be said, the boss would resent Pat for trapping him in such a dilemma. The demotion might not come immediately, but it would come.

So there it was, a classic Hobson's choice. Did Pat do what was best for his soul or his career? This might well be his last chance to square things with himself, to make a clean break from the compromises that had been part of his life since Villanova.

Placing his brandy on the table, Pat rose and walked slowly to the fireplace. Succumbing to the onslaught of the flames, a log broke in two, a chorus of sparks erupting.

"Up the rebels," he finally said, tossing the notebook into the fire.

Pat Carney was still running.

CHAPTER
Twelve

AS always, Vince Grosso was in control. He sat in the back of the limousine, casually reviewing the contents of his briefcase. There was nothing in his demeanor to indicate the importance of the forthcoming meeting. He might be traveling to his mother's for another dull dinner. Instead, he was heading for a confrontation that might well determine the future of his family.

Niccolo Arrone sat beside him, tapping his knee, chain-smoking Carltons. He had switched to low tar a week ago, but it had only made matters worse. There was nothing to the goddamn things, so he ended up smoking more. Particularly at a time like this.

"Relax, *paisan,*" Vince said. "The worst that can happen is that we'll get blown away. Then our worries are over."

"You're so goddamn comforting. I really appreciate it."

"I try."

They lapsed into silence again. Vince looked out the window. The weather matched the nature of their assignment, a stiff wind driving wet snow against the panes.

Another challenge. Always a challenge. Each a test of how well he had learned his lessons in Detroit.

It was at the beginning of his second year of law school that Vince met Tony Iacobucci. Looking back, he realized that the meeting and all that followed had been carefully arranged. He had passed his first test, and the dons, both Fredo Annaloro and Giuseppe Zivelli, thought he was ready.

Tony "Iceman" Iacobucci was *cinisatti*. He would, therefore, never rise to the inner circle of the Detroit *borgotta*, never share in its decision-making process. Despite this, he was considered indispensable to the orderly operation of the family.

Iacobucci was the enforcer, the one who made things happen. It was for others to give the orders. He made certain that they were obeyed.

He was an imposing figure. Six-three, 255. Solid, not even a trace of fat. And meticulous in his appearance. Always an expensive suit, expertly tailored, the suit jacket on at all times. Monogrammed white shirts, long-sleeved and crisply starched, even in the summer.

His formal education had ended in tenth grade, when he quit school and, lying about his age, joined the marines in time to earn a Silver Star on Okinawa. Returning to Detroit after the war, he was a hero out of work with no place to go. Giuseppe Zivelli quickly resolved that. He knew potential when he saw it.

A bachelor, Iacobucci never wanted for women, but he had never found one worthy of his commitment. And in accordance with his personal code, if you weren't going to do something right, you shouldn't do it at all. As a result, the family became and remained his entire life. There was no other ideal, no other person, to siphon off any of his energies. His sole reason for being was to serve Don Zivelli and his *borgotta*. For Tony Iacobucci, that was enough.

Iacobucci's appearance at the Zivelli home in the fall of 1967 was a rarity, made at the express command of the don. Home was for *famiglia* and close friends. No one knew better than Iacobucci that he was neither. He was an employee—well respected, proficient in his work, but an employee nonetheless. It was completely without bitterness that he accepted this, in much the same way that he acknowledged the sun's rising every day, the need for relieving one's bowels, and the necessity of removing certain people from this earth. These were facts of life.

"Antonio, my good friend," the don said in Sicilian, "you honor me by your visit."

"It is I who am honored, Don Giuseppe."

Zivelli placed his arm around the giant's waist. "Come, my friend, there is someone I want you to meet." He led him into the living room and introduced him to Vince. "Vincenzo is one of us,

Antonio. *Famiglia*. His uncle Don Fredo Annaloro and I are cousins."

Iacobucci understood the message, his attitude toward Vince immediately warming. "Any friend of my don is my friend," he said, shaking hands.

"Thank you," Vince answered, trying to hide his confusion. This was more than a social visit, more than a courtesy introduction. That much, if nothing else, was certain.

"Vincenzo is studying law at Michigan," the don continued. "A fine student who makes us all very proud. But only so much can be learned from books. He must also learn of business, of life. And I can think of no better teacher than you, my good friend."

Iacobucci bowed. "It will be my honor, Don Giuseppe."

And so began another phase in the education of Vince Grosso. Classes were usually held in the office of the Detroit Linen Company, a family-owned enterprise and Iacobucci's base of operations. Like the bull that he was, the Iceman plunged right in at the first session.

"You've heard all the crap on television about the Mafia? La Cosa Nostra? Some hidden organization that controls billions? You know, the type of stories that make the Italian-American organizations go bananas?"

Vince nodded.

"It's all true," Iacobucci continued. "Most of it anyway. Now and then there's a little bullshit, but for the most part the stories are accurate." He paused, waiting for a reaction. "Surprised?" he asked when none came.

"No."

"Had it all figured out, huh?"

"I have eyes. My uncle raised me. Helped to, anyway."

"Do you respect your uncle?"

"Yes."

"Do you love him?"

"I'm not sure."

"That's honest. Well, your uncle, whom you at least respect, Don Giuseppe, whom you had better respect, myself, and all the rest—we're businessmen. Plain and simple. We're out to make money. Just like three-piece nine-to-fivers, carrying a briefcase and reading the *Wall Street Journal*, which, incidentally, some of us actually read."

[214]

"Like you?"

"As a matter of fact, yes. I learned a long time ago that you need more than just muscle to make it. I'm a high school dropout, something I deeply regret, but I've spent the last twenty years, since the war, studying. Teaching myself. No matter how long you live, there's always something to learn." He paused, suddenly somber. "Don Giuseppe made it possible for me to learn. If it hadn't been for him, I'd be breaking my back and destroying my spirit in some car factory, getting home at night too exhausted to do anything but fall asleep or maybe get drunk. I'm forever in his debt."

"I take it, then, that you respect him."

"And love him." For a moment there was silence. Then Iacobucci was charging again. "Back to business. The majority of our holdings are legitimate. We excel not because of our muscle but because of our work ethic. Our pride. Anything we do, we do right. Take this linen company. Largest in the city by far. We've got all the hotels and major restaurants locked up. Why? Because we provide an excellent product at a fair price. A maître d' calls up and says his tablecloths are soiled, there's no arguing. We pick them up, reclean them, and get them back to him the same day. No charge. And we find out who fucked up and make certain that it doesn't happen again. Our restaurants, some of the finest in the Midwest." He started to laugh. "Know who some of our best customers are? The FBI. Those bastards are always looking for a bargain. They know they'll get an outstanding meal with superb service, and it won't cost them an arm and a leg. The important thing is pride. It used to be that people took a pride in what they did, whether they were waiting on tables or making shoes or putting up a house. Most of that's gone now, and you see the result. Where can you find quality these days? We've made it a point, a conscious effort, to retain that pride. And that, more than anything else, is what makes us great."

"So that's how you'd characterize your organization? Businessmen with pride? It seems to me that a lot of Rotarians could lay claim to the same title." Vince knew that he would make a good attorney. Already he had learned the art of cross-examination.

Iacobucci grinned. As always, he enjoyed a challenge. "No, there's a lot more to it than that. Since time began, man has had his weaknesses. One way or the other those weaknesses have to be satisfied, and we see to that. If a man wants to gamble, we're only too glad to take his money. If he finds himself in a hole, we're equally happy to lend it back. At a profit, of course. If he needs a woman, no strings attached, we'll supply one. And yeah, if he wants a joint or a jolt of smack, we'll perform that service, too. If we didn't, someone else would. And like our legit operations, we're always fair. Somebody kills our bank with a long shot at Hancock Park, for example, he's paid. Right away. No excuses. It's like that in everything."

"And muscle doesn't have anything to do with our—your—success?"

"I would have thought that was so obvious it needn't be mentioned. When you strip away everything else, it's still the most important ingredient."

"I thought you said pride was."

"Hang me on every word, Counselor. Pride, muscle. You need them both. They go hand and hand. Even in our legit businesses. Take this linen company again. Assume I lose one of my best customers. Not only do I lose money, not only can it start a skid, but my pride is hurt. So I go to the customer and find out why he dropped me. I'll take every reasonable step to bring him back on board. But failing that, I utilize muscle, albeit reluctantly. Most of the time it never comes to that, of course. The mere knowledge that violence is an option is generally sufficient to induce cooperation."

"How much violence?" Vince asked.

"The minimum necessary to achieve our goal."

"Does that include killing?"

"Usually unnecessary but, in certain cases, yes."

"Have you ever killed, Tony?"

"Many times, Vincenzo. I'm not particularly proud of that, but neither am I ashamed. It was always necessary, the only available option, which is as it should be. Some men kill because they enjoy it. We quickly weed them out. They present a clear and present danger to the stability of our organization."

For the next two years the law student and the enforcer met regularly, usually once a week: Iacobucci, the articulate professor, providing an oral textbook on the operation of a vast empire;

Vince, the perfect student, usually content to listen and learn, occasionally asking a probing, on-point question.

Part of Vince's education was what could be described as mob folklore, the personalities, the violence, the history of the Zivelli *borgotta*. Stories handed down from one generation to the next. Vince Grosso, Villanova graduate and law student, heard them from the mouth of Tony Iacobucci. Several years later Kevin Murray, Villanova graduate and FBI agent assigned to the Detroit division, would be treated to the same tales. Not from anyone's mouth but from studying the transcripts of FBI wiretaps. The taps had been conducted in the early to mid-sixties, before the passage of federal wiretap legislation requiring court approval. These earlier taps were easier to obtain but less valuable, since they were inadmissible as evidence at a trial. They provided, however, a unique insight into the mentality of the Bureau's primary foe.

Sometimes Iacobucci went into his stories for no apparent reason. Like the struggle with the Syrians. He had been explaining the loan shark operation to Vince when he paused. "I ever tell you about our troubles with the Arabs?"

Vince shook his head. He knew a story was coming because Iacobucci had changed his manner of speech. Gone was the impressive vocabulary, the perfect grammar. Now he was one of the guys. "It's my guinea gangster mode," Iacobucci had once explained. "Can't have a good sidgie yarn without it."

The Iceman began. "It was back in the fifties. Lemme see. Yeah, it was 1957. November. I remember it because it was when Notre Dame beat Oklahoma to stop their streak. Forty-seven in a row. Anyway, we've always had a decent-size Syrian population in Detroit. They're okay most of the time, even though I can't stand their fuckin' food. And there's always been a Syrian mob. All the way back to Prohibition. As a matter of fact, the don worked with them running bootleg hooch over from Canada. They were all part of the Purple Gang. When we stabilized things and took control, we left a place for them. Working for us, of course, but they were doin' okay. Then along comes this wiseass. Gemaye Hassan, or somethin' like that. Full of piss and vinegar. Takes control of his crowd and starts promising them the friggin' moon. He comes to us and demands a bigger piece of the action. Fuckin' *demands*. Now, we're not lookin' for trouble. The don tells

[217]

us to settle things peacefully. Negotiate, he tells us. Bend a little if we have to. Okay, we try to sit down with this camelfucker, but forget it. No fuckin' way. Finally we tell him to kiss off. Take our offer or shove it. He storms out, but that's okay, too. We figure that once he cools off, he'll be back.

"Two days later Michael Zivelli, the don's youngest brother, is blown away as he walks out of mass. He was coming out of church with his family. His wife was wounded and never recovered. Not from the wound but from the shock. They finally had to put her away. And his daughter, she was about fourteen at the time, was there, too. Saw the whole thing."

Iacobucci paused, his teeth clenched. After more than a decade the rage was still there. As soon as he heard the news, he had gone to the don, the only time he had ever done so without being summoned. Kneeling before his leader, he had wept unashamed. They were his first tears since Okinawa, when a sixteen-year-old kid mourned the death of his sergeant.

"I swear to you, Don Giuseppe, before the day is over, you will be avenged. I will personally see to it."

Zivelli gently patted the shoulder of his enforcer. "I thank you, Antonio. For your sorrow, your loyalty, and your love. My grief and my anger are equal to yours. Even greater. After all, Michael was my brother, the little one, the one I always watched over. But we must not let our feelings blind us to our responsibility. We will have our vengeance but on our own terms. This is a challenge from outside the *borgotta*. Unless we handle it correctly, there will be other such challenges. The Greeks, the Armenians. Who knows? Maybe even the coloreds. Do nothing, Antonio, that is my order. And trust me, my friend, as you always have."

For the next three days the don remained in his study, conferring with his key lieutenants, making a number of telephone calls, and seeing to the funeral arrangements of his brother.

Two hours after Michael Zivelli had been laid to rest, the vengeance began. One of the Syrian mobsters was picked up on an unpaid traffic ticket. The judge, ignoring his offer to pay pending a hearing, placed him in a cell, where he was found hanged.

Another one was pulled over for speeding. As he reached for his wallet, the police officer opened fire, placing two bullets squarely into his brain. Reaching under his uniform jacket, he took out the throwaway revolver and placed it beside the body.

The largest Syrian restaurant in town was destroyed by fire. It might have been saved had the fire company not taken fifty-three minutes to respond. Killed in the blaze was a thirty-four-year-old construction worker. His wife immediately filed a twenty-million-dollar lawsuit. She was represented by one of the lawyers of the Zivelli *borgotta*.

Within a week, virtually all the major Syrian businesses had been padlocked for Health and Fire Code violations. Liquor licenses were revoked; surprise sales tax audits were conducted; bank mortgages were foreclosed.

The message was unmistakable. When you took on the Zivelli family, you took on the system, the entire infrastructure of government. It was a battle that could never be won.

Gemaye Hassan remained untouched. That was part of the plan. The word was put out on the street: the reprisals would continue until the Syrians cleaned their own house. Thirteen days after Michael Zivelli's murder it was over. Hassan was found dead in his bedroom, an empty bottle of sleeping pills beside him. For once he had acted wisely, choosing to end the torment and shortcut the inevitable. The Zivelli family emerged with one fewer member but with its power incalculably increased.

A different approach was required for the trouble with the *caltagironi*.

"It was five years ago," Iacobucci said. "That right? Yeah. Nineteen sixty-two. Right after the Cuban missile crisis. JFK was great in that one, wasn't he? Staring down those friggin' Russians, not to mention those worthless spics. For a change we showed some balls. First time I really felt proud to be an American since we beat the Japs. Anyway, some of the young pissants start bitching. Real horseshit. Claimed they were second-class citizens. Third, actually. Saying that the don was getting old and demanding, fuckin' *demanding*, a bigger hunk of the action.

"I'm a reasonable guy, so I try to sit down and reason with them. I tell 'em that nobody's second or third class. When you're a member of the Zivelli *borgotta*, you're first class all the way. I mean, what the fuck, here's a bunch of pissants still wet behind the ears, and they're each worth a fortune. You know, there's not a member of the family, not one, that isn't worth at least a million. Anyway, they don't want to hear it. Tell me to go fuck myself. That's exactly what they said, I shit you not. I'm not lookin' to get into a pissing contest, so I leave. I figure, let 'em bitch a little bit. Get it out of their systems. You know, freedom of speech and all that good American shit. Only the assholes weren't content to just talk."

Alfredo Riccobene was relaxing in the barber's chair, his face covered by hot towels. He never saw them enter, never saw them level their machine guns. The picture made the first page of all the papers: Riccobene's body grotesquely angled over the chair, the towels and the barber's gown soaked with blood. In the background hung a picture of Pope John XXIII.

"It was an amateur hit," Iacobucci continued. "Really fuckin' amateur. We knew right away who was involved. Four of them, two of them brothers. This time the don summoned me. I've never seen him so angry. In fact, it's the *only* time I've ever seen him angry. 'Punish them, Antonio,' was all he said. Truth is, I think that he loved Riccobene as much as his brother. Maybe more. They were cousins, you know, and they came to America together.

"Now what you got to remember about the family is that whatever we need, we got. Either we own it, or it's owned by somebody who owes us one. Say we need a deserted farm for a few days. No problem. The owners move out, no questions asked, and they don't come back until they're told. We need to make somebody disappear—permanently, that is—again no sweat. A lime factory, an incinerator. Whatever we need. This time we used the meatpacking plant in Wyandotte. We rounded up the four of them without any problem and took them there. And we had some fun. We stripped them, tied them up, and then hoisted them onto the meat hooks. The hooks went right up their ass, and the more they squirmed, the deeper the hooks dug in.

"Then we took out the cattle prods. You know, the electric ones. Christ, how they'd jump, especially when we'd give their pricks a jolt. Went at it for two days. They'd pass out, and we'd throw cold water on them. Then they'd beg for us to kill them. But I follow orders, you know what I mean? My don wanted them punished. Finally we took them down. I mean, we didn't want them to die. Not until the grand finale. One at a time we placed them on the belt leading to the meat grinder. You ever see one of those fuckers? You know, the kind big enough to take a whole side of beef. Awesome. Fuckin' awesome. Kinda reminds you of those machines the tree people use. You know, they stick the branches in one end, and it churns them to pieces. Not exactly, but you get the picture. You shoulda seen their faces when they realized what was gonna happen. Naturally, we put 'em in feet first. I mean, you put 'em in headfirst, they die right away. We took a pool to see which one would be last to pass out. I won. I bet on the third guy. The first two went out when their feet were gone, and the last fucker passed out before we even got 'em on the belt. Couldn't bring him out of it. Actually I think he probably died of fright. But my guy, good old number three, he hung right in there. The other guys say I exaggerate, but I swear to Christ he was still conscious when the machine got past his knees. Not that it mattered, seeing as how I won the three hundred bucks.

"But it doesn't end there. Now we got all this ground-up shit in the bin, and you know, it looks just like hamburg. So we pack it and freeze it. Well, within a few weeks it's pretty goddamn obvious that the four jerkoffs aren't ever coming back. As a gesture to the families of the dearly departed, the don suggests a memorial service. You know, mass, then some type of reception. Well, we're at the luncheon, and of course, you know what the meatballs were made of, don't you? As we're finishing the meal, the don rises and offers a toast. I can't remember his exact words, but something like 'We'll miss our brothers very much, but I can't help feeling that, even now, they're a part of us.' Fuckin' classic, huh?"

"Did *you* eat any of the meatballs?" Vince asked.

"Shit, yeah. Would've been rude not to. Actually they weren't bad. Little greasy, but not bad. Kinda makes you wanta give up cows."

The don's instructions regarding Vince had given Iacobucci considerable latitude: show him as much as possible without exposing him to danger. As always, the Iceman followed his orders. Vince was permitted to witness him function as the family's premier enforcer.

Iacobucci's position was unique. He was not a *capo*. He neither commanded nor was a member of any *regime*. Instead, he reported directly to the don or, more frequently, another member of the ruling *favoratta*.

He was far too valuable to waste on the run-of-the-mill collections. When an average guy got behind to his book or his loan shark, one of the soldiers made the contact. When the individual

[221]

in question was a big hitter, when the stakes were unusually high, Iacobucci got the assignment.

He would not seek out the deadbeat. That was beneath him. Instead, the debtor would be summoned, an invitation impossible to refuse.

Usually the meetings took place in Iacobucci's office, and after a few months of getting acquainted, Vince was permitted to be present. He would sit in a corner, saying nothing, never being introduced. For all the deadbeat knew, Vince could be the Iceman's personal bodyguard, a revolver stuffed under his shirt.

Michael Halloran, owner of the largest construction company in Michigan, was one such invited guest.

"Michael, my friend, what a pleasure." Iacobucci beamed, shaking hands warmly and leading him to a chair. "How's the world treating you, *paesan?* You look great. Tremendous tan. Looks like you were in Florida."

"Yes," Halloran answered nervously. "On business. Strictly business."

"I hope not, my friend. Nobody goes to Florida just on business. Life's too short. Say, would you like a drink?"

"Yeah, I sure would, Tony. Thanks."

They drank in silence, Iacobucci in no hurry to broach the subject of the meeting. Instead, he would permit the contractor to stew in his own juices awhile, withering under his gaze. It wasn't exactly a stare, rather a grinning appraisal of a quarry. Muhammad Ali sizing up his opponent before the opening bell.

"I appreciate your seeing me," Halloran finally said. "I know how busy you are."

"No problem. I mean, what are friends for?"

Neither gave any hint of the irony of the exchange, of the fact that Iacobucci had *ordered* Halloran's presence.

"I, uh, guess you know I'm a little behind?"

"Michael, my friend, I'd call three hundred thousand more than a little behind."

"Jesus, is it that much? I mean, are you sure?"

The smile vanished. "You think I'd cheat you, Michael? Is that what you're saying? 'Cause if you are, we can consider this meeting finished."

"Christ, no, Tony. Never. Never. I mean, Jesus, I'd never accuse you of that. Jesus."

[222]

"You knew the interest rates when you took our money, Michael. Nobody put a gun to your head." Again the grin. "Not yet anyway."

"Course not. Course not. Only thing is, Tony, I've really had a string of rotten luck. Shitty. Really shitty. My wife, she's sick."

"Nothing serious, I hope."

"Yeah. Cancer. She—she doesn't have much time left."

"I'm sorry, Michael. I really am."

"Thanks. She's been in and out of the hospital for months. Even with Blue Cross, the bills are incredible. And I've tried to be with her as much as I can. You know, trying to make what time she's got as nice as possible."

"That's nice, Michael."

"So, you know, with me not around as much as I should, business has kinda slipped. Then I get hit with that fuckin' strike in Flint. You know, on the condo project. Killed me. Fuckin' killed me. I don't know what's the matter with those goddamn unions anymore. I mean, I started as a laborer, worked my way up, and I wanted a decent wage. I had my union card and was damn glad to have it. But Jesus, I always put in a full day, and I never tried to break my boss's balls with nit-picking horseshit. Couple days ago I had a walkout by the carpenters. Wanta know why? One of my plumbers nailed up a couple boards to hang his tools on. You woulda thought he raped the Blessed Mother. They walked, for two days, just because using a hammer is strictly carpenter's work. I mean, what kind of horseshit is that?"

Iacobucci said nothing. He simply continued to gaze and to grin.

"I talk too much, Tony," the contractor finally said. "Look, I'm not gonna try to kid you. I'm nervous as hell. I know I owe a lot of money, I know you've really been patient, which I really appreciate, but I need a little more time. Just a little more, and I promise, Tony, I swear to God I'll make things right."

"No problem, Michael. I mean, what are friends for?"

"You mean it?" He almost yelled it, the tension draining from his face. "Christ, Tony, I appreciate it. I really do. I'll never forget it, Tony. I swear."

"You got three more days."

"What!" Halloran shrieked. "Three days! That's impossible, Tony. It's just not possible. I mean—"

[223]

"Anything is possible, Michael. Now let's cut the shit, okay? I know your wife is dying of cancer, and that's a shame. But don't give me that crap about wanting to be with her. Every chance you get you pop down to Florida—on your private jet—to shack up with that bimbo you're putting up in that penthouse apartment at two thousand a month. Plus the Mercedes, plus all the goddamn credit cards. And when you're not plugging her, you're at the track, losing your friggin' ass. You made your bed, my friend. If you wanta smell like a flower, don't dance behind the ponies. Tell your troubles to Jesus; He's a good listener. But if you don't want to beat your wife to the grave, you got three days to come across." Iacobucci stood. "Now get the fuck out of here."

"What's going to happen?" Vince asked after Halloran was gone.

"One of two things: either he'll come up with the cash or we'll have a new construction company. You see all the Household Juice Company trucks on the street? That's ours. We won it in a barbute game downriver. Turns a substantial profit. Same will hold true in this case. I've studied his books. It's a good company. We'll keep the name, tighten up financial controls, and launder some of our dirty money as well. And of course, we won't have problems with the unions. So either way we can't lose. It's what's known as a secured transaction, which you've undoubtedly studied in law school."

As he began his last year of law school, Vince found himself in an unusual position. For the first time in his life he was unsure of himself. Never before had self-assurance been a problem. He had never been afraid to walk alone, nor had he been tempted to sacrifice his independence as a price of acceptance. Those who mistook his aloofness for shyness, his calculated distance for uncertainty, seriously underestimated him.

This was most apparent at Villanova, when the comparisons between Vince and Kevin were drawn. Invariably the conclusions reached were precisely opposite to reality. It was Kevin, the outgoing leader, who was ravaged by doubt and hidden fears while Vince was absolutely sure of himself in every circumstance. Or almost every.

But the Detroit experience had been unsettling. He had been exposed first to genuine family love, then to the brutal reality of organized crime as detailed by Professor Anthony Iacobucci. He

[224]

was at a crossroads, as the dons in both Philadelphia and Detroit had anticipated. But only so much of a human's life can be planned by others. Ultimately the crucial decisions would come down to Vince. Which way would he turn? To embrace the warmth of *famiglia* was also to cast his lot with the *borgotta* and everything for which it stood.

Tony Iacobucci understood. "You're the future, you know," he once said. "Your generation will decide our destiny. If you turn away from us, if you turn your back on our traditions, we can't survive, not as a *borgotta*."

"And *famiglia?*"

"They go hand in hand, Vincenzo. They can't be separated. It's what always has made us unique."

"What if I choose to turn away?"

"Then you'll go with our blessing and our love. No questions asked, nothing expected of you except your silence."

"And if I choose the *borgotta?*"

"Then you have made a commitment for life. Choose wisely, my young friend."

The decision was made easier, and infinitely more difficult, by the arrival of Lena Zivelli. Vince had known about the don's niece, the teenager who had witnessed her father's assassination when Michael Zivelli was gunned down by the Syrians. But not until September 1967 had he ever met her. For the past three years she had been in Europe, pursuing a master's, then a doctorate in fine arts.

Lena was living at the home of the don, who had all but adopted her following her father's death and, soon after, the commitment of her mother to a sanitarium from which she never emerged. After reporting to school and purchasing his books, Vince had driven to Grosse Pointe Park to spend the weekend with what he had come to regard as his *famiglia*.

There she was, to Vince the most striking woman he had ever seen. Most of her height, almost five feet nine inches, seemed to be in long, slender legs. Her skin was the color of bronze, almost a mirror of Vince's. The jet black hair, shoulder length, was worn casually, with the assurance of one whose natural beauty required no special grooming efforts, an assurance that was confirmed when one looked into her eyes. There was always a hint of a smile in the pale blue eyes that conveyed to the object of her vision that

[225]

he was, at the same time, being trifled with and coldly appraised.

"So you're the Vincenzo I've heard so much about," she said when they met. "An excellent student, I've been told."

"I don't know about excellent. I still have to get through my last year."

"I wasn't referring to law school."

"What then?"

"It's like Louis Armstrong's statement on jazz: 'Man, if you gotta ask, you'll never know.' "

Vince decided to change the subject. "How did you enjoy Europe?"

"A welcome change."

"From Detroit?"

"From everything."

"You're a trifle cryptic, aren't you?"

"No, just cautious."

"Whatever that means."

"It means a great deal."

"I'm intrigued."

She shifted her hair with a slight, sensual turn of her head. "I'm intriguing."

It was an unusual and somewhat awkward courtship since they lived in the same home.

Protocol dictated that Vince seek the don's permission before asking Lena for a date. This was Giuseppe Zivelli's Detroit, where the old ways were honored.

"Don Giuseppe, there is something I have to ask of you," Vince had begun, hesitatingly and in Sicilian.

"Anything, Vincenzo. You know that."

"Please. If you are offended by my request, if you have even the slightest hesitation, I will understand completely and abide by your wishes. There will be no resentment, no hard feelings toward you. Only my continued respect and affection."

"What a preamble," the don joked. "This must be serious indeed."

"Only time will tell. Don Giuseppe, I ask your permission to see your niece."

"See? You see her constantly. She lives here."

Vince smiled. "I am certain that Don Giuseppe, who knows all things, understands my intentions. I wish to date—to court—

Lena if I receive your permission. And assuming, of course, that Lena agrees."

The don's eyes twinkled. "You have my blessing, Vincenzo. And I am most grateful for your respect in seeking my permission. Most young men your age would not be so considerate."

"I would never wish to offend you."

"I know. And if you'll permit an old man to express his personal opinion, you could do far worse than Lena."

"She's—how can I best say it?—she's an incredibly interesting woman."

"Yes, she is. And at the same time a very vulnerable one. She needs someone like you. For stability."

When Vince left, the don slouched contentedly in his chair. As usual, his master plan was right on schedule. To accomplish his goals, it was seldom necessary for a superior tactician to issue commands. Instead, he provided the opportunities, with an occasional nudge of encouragement, and the natural course of events provided the desired result, as he was certain it would in this case.

Giuseppe Zivelli was not disappointed. It was soon obvious that the two young people were in love. There was no question in Vince's mind that he had found the one person to whom he could freely give love, a repository for the emotions that he had kept locked within him since he was a child. For the first time he felt free to lower his defenses, to become the Vince Grosso whom no human—except, on brief occasions, Kevin Murray—had ever known.

For Lena's part, she at last felt safe, or as safe as she could ever hope to be. Unlike Vince, however, her defenses remained in place.

The wedding, which took place the day after Vince's graduation, was an *event*. It was a matter of both pride and protocol to the dons of Detroit and Philadelphia that a marriage which joined their *borgotte* by blood be an occasion to remember. More than two thousand guests attended the reception at the Grosse Pointe Country Club. Since the club's ballroom was far too small to accommodate such a throng, a special tent was designed, covering more than two acres. Hardwood flooring, cut, fitted, and shellacked just for the occasion, was laid throughout, to be donated to the new Catholic school in St. Claire Shores when the festivities had concluded. Eight mammoth compressors, the type used to cool navy ships when in dry dock, maintained the temperature at precisely sixty-eight degrees. Damage to the fairways, caused by the construction and the parking of automobiles, was slightly less than two hundred thousand dollars, an amount paid promptly and pleasantly by Don Giuseppe.

The bride and groom would never know the enforced frugality of newlyweds since their wedding gifts, invariably cash presented in plain white envelopes, totaled some fifteen million dollars.

The honeymoon was a compromise. Since it was necessary for Vince to return quickly to Philadelphia for cram school, they settled for two weeks in Hawaii, the don of Honolulu graciously placing his plantation at their disposal. Once Vince had taken the Pennsylvania bar examination, they would tour Europe for two months.

Several days before the wedding Vince had accepted Tony Iacobucci's invitation for cocktails at his home, a large Tudor in Grosse Pointe Farms.

For the most part they engaged in small talk: women; politics; sports. Business was not discussed.

"The main reason I wanted to talk with you this last time," Iacobucci said as Vince was ready to leave, "is to tell you how much I've enjoyed knowing you. You've got it all, Vincenzo: brains; class; good looks; street sense. Your future has no limits. And no matter how great your success, you'll always remain what you are right now, a very decent human being. If I ever had a son, which I never will, I'd want him to be just like you." The Iceman rose and extended his hand to his former pupil. "Good-bye, my very dear friend, and God bless."

Vince had not expected this, neither the warmth nor the sense of finality.

"This isn't good-bye, Tony. You make it sound as though we'll never meet again."

"We won't, Vincenzo. At least not in the same way."

"Tony, you've taught me everything. I'll always need your help."

"I doubt that, Vincenzo. You'll need very little help. If you ever do, and my don approves, you know I'll be there. But it will be as one who serves you, not as your teacher. You will give the commands, and I will obey."

"Friends don't command, Tony."

"You must, Vincenzo. It is your destiny."

Vince shook his head. "This is crazy talk. Three days from now you'll be at my wedding. To drink with me. To celebrate with me. As my friend."

"Certainly it will be my honor to be there, but we will hardly speak. I will take my proper place in the receiving line, to shake your hand, to pay my respect to your bride and present her with my envelope, then to move on. My table will be in its proper place, far from yours, and at the proper time I will thank the don and take my leave. That's reality, Vincenzo. We exist on different planes that can never meet."

"Don't you ever resent it, Tony?"

"Not at all. That would be a masterpiece of ingratitude. Look around you. My art collection is priceless. My library contains the finest books. I have my speedboat, my home in Florida, more money than I will ever need, and, most important, a challenging job that I enjoy. All this I owe to the *borgotta*."

"Fine. But this is 1968. There's no place for a caste system."

Iacobucci smiled. "Hasn't my prize pupil learned anything from me? Our greatness is based on the old ways. On custom, on tradition. For my sake, Vincenzo, do not begin your career by forgetting the most important rule. Have a wonderful marriage and a wonderful life, my son."

Vince received the news that he had passed the bar exam while having a gourmet lunch with Lena in Sorrento. Their tour of Europe had been perfect, both for the beauty of the Continent and the joy he derived from his bride. But for all his pleasure, he was beginning to experience the impatience of a young man embarking on his career. The news that he was now a lawyer confirmed what he had suspected for several weeks: it was time to go home.

His entry into the practice of law was not the usual one. A new lawyer was generally faced with the equally unattractive alternatives of associating with a large firm, serving as little more than a research clerk for the first five years, then being forced into a narrow specialty, or of striking out on his own, which required plunging into debt to meet the start-up expenses, then enduring the endless wait for clients to appear.

Not so with Vincent Grosso, attorney-at-law. His offices in a prestige Center City building were tastefully lavish, complete with a full secretarial staff and the latest in electronic office

[229]

equipment. Fredo Annalaro assigned to his nephew three experienced attorneys, men who would assist him during his learning process but who clearly understood that they worked *for* and not *with* the new lawyer. Cases were generated immediately, largely petty criminal matters where Fredo was picking up the tab as a constituent service and run-of-the-mill civil matters, such as wills, small estates, and an occasional divorce.

Vince learned quickly. Within several years he was the primary attorney for the Annaloro *borgotta*. He was the defense attorney against the federal strike force prosecutions that had become almost commonplace. He supervised all of the family's business transactions, becoming an expert on corporate mergers. Most important, without its ever being said, he was accepted as an essential part of the family's inner circle, a small body consisting of Fredo Annalaro and his lieutenants, that made, or attempted to make, the family's policy decisions. Vince was present as more than a lawyer, although his legal expertise was certainly valued. It was tacitly accepted that he was one of *them,* one of the chosen few who controlled the destiny of a vast criminal empire.

Emulating the leadership of the *borgotta,* and befitting his style, Vince attempted to maintain a low profile, an effort that was largely unsuccessful. The criminal cases involving family members were news events, classic confrontations between the feds and the mob. It was a struggle between good and evil, and the man who represented the forces of darkness himself became a celebrity. Vince Grosso became known as *the* lawyer for the mob, a label which did not necessarily connote disapproval. Certainly there were those who believed that anyone who represented mobsters was necessarily tainted, but even they conceded that any lawyer who was good enough for the big boys had to be a master of his craft. Maybe they disapproved, maybe they would choose not to associate with him, but should they ever find themselves at the wrong end of an indictment, it was he they would seek.

Vince had assumed that Philadelphia would be a continuation of his experience in Detroit, that the two *borgotte,* each run by a wise and powerful don, were virtually interchangeable. As he soon discovered, the truth was otherwise. Philadelphia was a weak and disorganized family; his uncle, an ineffective leader. Giuseppe Zivelli and Fredo Annalaro had much in common: an innate gentleness, a love of family, and a sincere desire to settle differences

[230]

through reason rather than violence. But there the similarities ended.

There was never any question that Zivelli controlled his *borgotta*. He invited input from his advisers, he carefully weighed his options before action, but when he spoke, his word was law. A decision by the Detroit don permitted absolutely no room for discussion. Giuseppe Zivelli understood power and how to use it.

Fredo Annalaro did not. His primary goal was to achieve a consensus, to avoid confrontation. Had he been an athlete, he would have been the type who played not to lose, instead of playing to win. As a result, the Annaloro *borgotta* never spoke with a single voice. There was no central administration through which all family operations flowed. Members freelanced regularly, so much so that more than half the family's revenue was unknown to Annaloro and his lieutenants.

To the dons of the other families, the Philadelphia *borgotta* was a joke, its don a kindly but incompetent gentleman. Fredo Annaloro retained his seat on the *commissione* more for personal affection and the size of Philadelphia than the importance of its family. In truth, the Annaloro *borgotta* was not even the most powerful family in Pennsylvania. Giacomo Turci of Pittston had spun off from Philadelphia and now controlled everything that moved in the northeastern part of the state.

Vince Grosso took it all in without comment. He never criticized, nor did he suggest to his uncle how the family's status could be improved. It was not his place. But inwardly he seethed, appalled at how a powerful organization had been permitted to degenerate. It was an affront to his Sicilian pride.

The most embarrassing moment occurred in 1977, when twelve family members were indicted on loan-sharking and mail fraud charges. Arrests, even convictions, could be tolerated as risks that one accepted when he engaged in a criminal enterprise. It was the defendants' performance at the preliminary arraignment that was unforgivable. For the purpose of setting bail, the magistrate questioned each about his employment. Ten of the twelve said that they were unemployed, one listed himself as a bartender, and the other claimed to be a cigarette salesman.

My God, Vince had thought, *what have we come to?* It was incomprehensible to him that these men, each worth millions, had never taken the trouble to establish suitable covers. His uncle should have insisted upon it. Vince knew that power was largely psychological. What mystique, what image of power could the family convey when its members painted themselves as itinerants? And on the more practical side, how could these men, who owned homes at the shore, yachts, luxury cars, and all the trappings of wealth, survive an IRS net worth investigation? It was madness, chaos created by Fredo Annaloro's permissiveness.

Vince would not interfere, but he would prepare. He knew that his time would come. It was inevitable, as inevitable as his uncle's assassination. When casino gambling in Atlantic City was legalized, Fredo's death warrant was signed. It was merely a matter of time.

The casinos presented the New York families, particularly the Gambinos and the Genoveses, an unprecedented opportunity to expand their revenue base and their power. Even if they could not crack the casinos, and they would certainly try, the spin-off industries would be a gold mine. The problem was Philadelphia, which by custom had always considered South Jersey within its fiefdom.

The recurring fear of the New York dons was of the Annaloro *borgotta,* united by the lure of the casinos, developing into a formidable competitor, an event that could not be tolerated if the master plan were to succeed. There was only one option: remove Philadelphia as a threat by destroying it from within.

It was accomplished with ridiculous ease. A family gone fat was ripe for penetration. Contacts were made, promises were given, and Fredo Annaloro was removed from the living. The civil war had begun with the strings being pulled from New York.

Vince accepted his uncle's death without emotion. It was simply another phase in his life. Certainly the old man had been good to him, had loved him like a son. And there had been a time when Vince had thought that he loved Fredo. Such love, if it had ever existed, was no longer possible. Vince Grosso demanded excellence. Intolerant of human frailty, he could never love someone whom he did not respect. Fredo was his don, and Vince was willing to accept him only on that basis. And in a certain respect he was grateful for his uncle's incompetence. When it came time for him to assume the leadership of the *borgotta,* as surely it would, there would be little opposition. They would be at rock bottom, and he would be needed.

Had Vince been a less calculating individual, he would have made his move immediately following Fredo's murder. Several of the *capos,* the old-timers who had staunchly supported Fredo through the years, urged him to do so. Vince graciously thanked them for their loyalty but declined. Others had greater seniority, he reasoned, and the family's continuity would be best served by placing someone more experienced in control. Such selfless concern for the family served only to increase the affection with which he was held, as Vince knew it would. He also knew that the year following Fredo's death would, of necessity, be a time of chaos, dooming the efforts of even the most competent leader. For the time being, he would be content to watch others fail. His moment would come.

Thomas ("Chicken Man") Costa became the don. His reign lasted exactly six months, abruptly ending when he and his house were blown apart by a bomb. He was succeeded by Harry Angelucci, who improved considerably on Costa's record. He made it to the eight-month mark. In May 1980 a parking attendant at Atlantic City Racetrack, noting that a car which had been unattended for three days was emitting a distinct odor from the trunk, summoned the police. The trunk was opened, revealing a nude Harry Angelucci, sporting thirty-three stab wounds of the chest, abdomen, and groin. Even more interesting, at least to the police and the media, was the fact that his mouth and rectum were stuffed with firecrackers, a charming piece of Sicilian symbolism which was interpreted to mean that Angelucci had been responsible for the bomb that killed Costa.

Fourteen months had elapsed since Fredo Annaloro's death, and an equal number of family members had died. It was time for Vince Grosso to move. Ever since graduating from law school, he had planned for this event. For twelve years he had carefully put together his team. Those he selected had several things in common. They were young, they were well educated, they were competent, and, most important, they were Sicilian. They were also fiercely loyal to Vince Grosso. These would be the men who would elevate the Grosso *borgotta* to greatness.

It was, of course, necessary to pay homage to the "mustache Petes." They would retain their titles and their respect, but the real power would be elsewhere. It was these men—the Antonio Pollinas, the Angie Lucidos, the Dominic Barrones—whom

[233]

Vince, with great respect, invited to his office. Carefully omitted was John Vagnoni, who was already laying claim to the title of don.

"My very good friends, my teachers, I thank you for honoring me with your presence." Vince began. "Since I was a little boy, ever since I was old enough to remember, you have been the backbone of our family. You were always loyal to my uncle, God rest his soul, and to the ideals that have made us great. When my uncle died, you paid me a great tribute by asking me to become your don. I refused, because I believed that others with greater experience were more competent than I to guide us. Unfortunately, as all of us know, the fourteen months since my uncle's death have been a disaster. An embarrassment. We have become laughing-stocks, puppets on a string pulled by the New York dons."

Vince slammed his fist on the desk. "No more! Never again! It is time for us to return to greatness, to declare that the fortunes of our family will be controlled by us and no one else!"

Vince paused and studied his audience. Everything that he had said so far, every inflection that he used, had been carefully calculated to achieve a result. The faces of the *borgotta* leaders told him that his efforts had been successful.

"The road we take will be difficult," he continued in a more subdued voice. "It will require patience and sacrifice and, above all, courage. But there is no doubt in my mind that united as brothers, we will prevail. If you will again make the offer to me that you made fourteen months ago, I will humbly accept. Not because of a desire for personal power but because I now believe that in light of the training that I have received, the advantages that I have derived from being a lawyer, and my close ties with our friends in Detroit, I am best suited to serve as don. Should you disagree, of course, I will accept your decision without question and will loyally serve whoever is chosen."

For a moment there was silence. Then Dominic Barrone stepped forward and knelt at Vince's feet. "Don Vincenzo, I will be proud to serve you."

The others began to follow suit, but Vince halted them with his raised hand. "Please, my friends, do not kneel. Brothers never kneel." He rose from his desk. "This is the proudest moment of my life. That men such as you would choose me as their don is an honor that I can never hope fully to repay. All I can do is my very best, and that I promise you. Always.

"The next six months will be the most critical for our survival. Even more than your help, I will need your trust. Difficult decisions will have to be made, decisions that may be unpopular even to you. I ask, I beg, that you trust me. But first things first. We must return to our traditions. No don can expect to lead his family until he has been made. I never have been and I ask you now to perform that honor for me."

"That's not necessary," Barrone protested. "You have always been one of us."

"It *is* necessary, Dominic. We must do things right from the beginning. There can be no shortcuts." He reached into his desk drawer and removed a gun and a sheet of paper, handing both to Barrone. "Please, Dominic, permit me this honor."

His hands trembling slightly, Barrone performed the ceremony as the new don took the solemn oath. When it was over, Vince pressed his intercom. A secretary entered and placed a bottle of wine and glasses on the coffee table. Vince poured for each man, then lifted his glass. For the first time he smiled. "It's a long way back, my friends, but we're on the way."

The first step on that road was New York. It was imperative to send a message, an unmistakable sign that Philadelphia would no longer play the fool. To accomplish this, Vince chose to violate a rule that would govern the conduct of his family as long as he was in control. He knew that occasions would arise when certain men, both within and beyond the family, would have to be removed from the living. Death was a fact of life. He also knew that what mattered was not *what* you did but how you did it.

It was Vince's belief that when termination was required, nothing should remain as a sign of the act. The individual marked for death should, quite simply, disappear forever.

Operating in that fashion had a number of advantages, not the least of which was the PR value. A bullet-riddled body was a story. It lent itself to pictures, which in turn caused the chain reaction of public indignation, posturing by public officials, and, ultimately, a police crackdown, which was never good for business.

A disappearance was infinitely more subtle. Eventually there would be a story, but there was no focus. Nothing to photo-

[235]

graph, no concrete time reference as to when, if ever, a crime had occurred. And without a body a successful prosecution was all but impossible.

But there was an even more compelling reason. There was something uniquely terrifying about someone vanishing. No greater agony exists than that of parents of a missing child or the spouse of an MIA. If a body of a child is discovered or the serviceman's death is confirmed, there is a distinct sense of relief accompanying the sorrow. Next to guilt, uncertainty is the cruelest emotion.

Hitler recognized this during World War II. His "fog and mist" tactic was designed to instill terror into Allied fliers. Downed pilots vanished without a trace, never to be heard from again.

So it would be with the Grosso *borgotta*. But not this time. Two weeks after Vince had become don, two men entered a small Italian restaurant in Greenwich Village. They ignored the customers, including the heavyset man at the table against the far wall who was dining with his mistress and another couple. Instead, they displayed city health department credentials and demanded to inspect the kitchen. It was a thorough inspection, the one man calling out deficiencies to the other, who made notes on his clipboard. He even took the time to inspect the utility closet. Their efforts proved fruitful. Behind a pile of brooms and mops were the goods: two Thompson submachine guns.

The Thompsons had been Vince's idea, their symbolism irresistible. For J. Edgar Hoover's entire reign it had been the trademark of the FBI, the gun that had killed John Dillinger, Ma Barker, and Pretty Boy Floyd. Kevin would love it, Vince had thought. Besides, he remembered his friend's commenting on the gun's accuracy and the fact that it had no kick.

Taking the guns, the "inspectors" ushered the kitchen crew into the refrigerator and walked quickly to the dining room. The heavyset man at the table against the far wall never noticed them, not until the first blast tore away his chest. More than a hundred bullets entered the body of Philip Morta, boss of the Genovese family. The others at the table, their appetites severely diminished, were otherwise unharmed. Following instructions, one of the gunmen reached into his pocket and dropped a document onto the table. It was a tourist brochure bearing a proud title: "Philadelphia—City of Brotherly Love."

The Grosso *borgotta* had sent its message. Having sufficiently attracted New York's attention, Vince quickly arranged a meeting with Michael Agostino, the all-powerful patriarch of the Gambino family. Agostino's terms were accepted without hesitation: Vince would appear alone in Agostino's office, a food distribution warehouse in the Bronx. No hostages would be required.

Having arrived by cab, Vince was forced to cool his heels for an hour in the waiting room. He had expected such a move. It was an attempt to unnerve him, a way for Agostino to assert his superiority even before the meeting began. Finally, the secretary announced that Mr. Agostino would now receive him. He was led into a dimly lit room, the center of which was taken up by a large conference table. Agostino was seated at the far end, flanked by four other men. Despite the heat, all wore dark three-piece suits.

"Please be seated, Mr. Grasso," Agostino said, ushering him to his spot at the opposite end.

"Grosso," Vince replied.

"My apology. Now that we know how to pronounce your name, maybe you can tell us why you're here."

"I should think that would be obvious, Don Michael."

"Nothing is obvious, Mr. Grasso—Grosso. Indulge me."

"Certainly. Since I have a great admiration for the efficiency of your family, including its ability to gather intelligence, I assume you know that I have been chosen to serve as the don of the Philadelphia *borgotta.*"

"Is that so? I wasn't aware of that, but then we only concern ourselves with important matters."

"Importance is in the eye of the beholder, Don Michael."

Agostino suppressed a smile. "Very true. So why does the new Philadelphia don wish to meet with Michael Agostino?"

"To learn from one more experienced. To cement our friendship. Most of all, to put an end to the insanity."

Now Agostino *did* smile. "Insanity, like importance, is in the eye of the beholder."

"Very true," Vince answered. "But in this case the madness is obvious even to those less brilliant than you."

"Are you referring to your problems in Philadelphia?"

"They are your problems as well, Don Michael."

"How so? I have made it a point never to interfere in the affairs of another family."

[237]

"With all due respect, Don Michael, we both know otherwise. As did Philip Morta, God rest his soul."

"You claim responsibility for the death of Don Philip?" Agostino asked, his eyebrows arching.

"Absolutely. To state it simply, we blew his ass away as a message that Philadelphia would no longer be New York's fucking puppet." Vince made the statement without changing expression, in the same voice that he might have commented on the weather.

"Your candor is refreshing. But if you're so convinced that I was also involved in somehow interfering in Philadelphia matters, why was I spared?"

"For practical reasons, Don Michael. The point was made with Don Morta's death. It is also true that we have a greater respect for your wisdom and your leadership. You are essential to the agreement that our families must reach so that we can jointly prosper."

"Your terms?"

"First, an agreement from the five families of New York, ratified by the *commissione,* that the territorial integrity of the Philadelphia family will henceforth be respected. Specifically, that my *borgotta* is conceded control over the entire state of Pennsylvania."

"What of our brothers in Pittston? I imagine Don Turci might not be thrilled."

"He is irrelevant. He will become a loyal member of our family. Otherwise, pending deportation proceedings against him will be accelerated, and Don Turci will find himself tending goats in Sicily."

"I admire your confidence, Mr. Grosso. Tell me, do you have anything else on your shopping list?"

"As a matter of fact, I do. Atlantic City, Playground of the World."

Agostino stiffened. "Yes?"

"Given past precedent, I could argue logically that Philadelphia and Philadelphia only has a rightful claim to Atlantic City. But I would be unreasonable, and I am, if nothing else, a reasonable man. Atlantic City is a prize large enough for us to share. I suggest, therefore, that we immediately begin to negotiate an equitable distribution of interest. Again, with ratification by the *commissione.*"

Agostino smiled, leaning forward in his chair. "I'll give you credit for having balls. A large set of balls and no brains. You come before me from a family whose dons couldn't find their way to the bathroom. You admit to killing Don Morta, then you make absolutely outrageous demands. With no cards! Nothing! I don't know what you expected, but I'll tell you what you are going to get. You're a dead man, Mr. Grosso. Your body, of course, will be found in Philadelphia, the latest victim of your family's civil war. Comments?"

While Agostino spoke, Vince had taken a notebook from his pocket and dropped it on the table. Now he spoke. "Before you carry out your decision, you might want to look at this notebook." He slid the book down the table. "On the first page is a telephone number. I suggest you call it. Assuming, of course, that you wish to see your daughter again."

Agostino reacted as if shot. The mask of indifference shattered, his eyes showing terror, his mouth open.

"You bastard!" he screamed. "You fuckin' bastard!"

"Make the call," Vince answered. "We'll talk afterwards."

Agostino lunged from his chair and staggered from the room. Several minutes later he was back. The panic was gone. The hatred remained. "You're nothing but scum, Grosso. To kidnap an innocent child breaks all the rules!"

For the first time Vince raised his voice. As usual, it was calculated. "You dare to speak of rules! You, who saw fit to assassinate Thomas Costa in the sanctity of his own home. You, who chose to gun down the innocent father of Rico Tulla as a warning to his son! You, who has allowed your family to be infiltrated by Jews, who left his wife and children to shack up with a barmaid! Don't you talk to me about rules. I regret the necessity of involving your daughter, but once we are in agreement, once you have given your word, she will be released unharmed. The choice is yours, Don Michael. Either we reach accord, in which case everyone prospers, or we do not, in which case my wife becomes a widow and you lose a daughter. Do we have an agreement?"

Agostino hesitated. "Yes," he finally said.

"I didn't hear you."

"I said yes!" Agostino screamed.

"I still didn't hear you, *Don* Michael."

[239]

Never had the New York don felt such hatred or such helplessness. It took every ounce of his self-control to respond. "We have an agreement—Don Vincenzo."

"*Grazie.*"

Vince gazed out the window again. The snow had increased, a thin layer now covering the few patches of grass that could be found in North Philadelphia.

Since becoming don, Vince had stabilized his family. With a few exceptions that were dealt with promptly, his rules were being obeyed. Even Giacomo Turci had pledged his loyalty. With the truce with New York holding, it was time to expand, but carefully, every step calculated. Ever the pragmatist, Vince knew that one wrong decision could shatter his plans—and cost him his life.

Not that anything was ever certain. There were no guarantees in life. Like tonight's meeting. Despite his assurance to Nick Arrone, Vince knew it was a gamble. There was no way to predict how a man like Julius Marzette would react.

Born in Haiti, Marzette moved to Philadelphia as a teenager. After graduating, with honors, from high school, he joined the Philadelphia Police Department. His twelve years on the force were mostly in narcotics, preparing him for his ultimate career. At the age of thirty he received a Section 32 from the force. Technically a 32 was a disability pension, but it was also used by the force to weed out undesirables. The top brass had never been able to prove anything on Marzette but had reached the conclusion that somehow he was dirty.

They were right. By the time he was thirty-five, he was the single largest drug dealer in the city, controlling everything that moved in North and West Philadelphia.

Like most successful men, he demanded and received total loyalty. It was an allegiance grounded on the most basic of all human emotions: fear. Part of the fear was based on superstition, the belief—which Marzette encouraged—that he had brought from his native land the power of voodoo. Although that could never be substantiated, his propensity for violence was a matter of record. The Marzette Treatment had become a legend. When one of his runners was suspected of withholding cash or providing information to the enemy, he was seized and bound to a horizontal

[240]

metal bar. Only his lower arms and hands could be moved. Holding a razor-sharp machete, Marzette would command the runner to place one finger on the bar. After the finger had been severed by one swipe of the machete, Marzette would begin his interrogation. The number of fingers that the runner possessed by the end of the interview depended entirely on Marzette's mood and how impressed he was by the answers that he received.

In the beginning there were a few who refused to place their finger on the bar. In that case, Marzette removed the entire forearm, then repeated his command for the other hand.

The limo stopped in front of a dry cleaner's on North Diamond, not far from the Temple campus. Vince and Arrone were met at the counter by Marzette's chief lieutenant, Shamaad Raymal. Like his boss, Raymal was coal black and huge.

"Good evening, gentlemen," Raymal said. "Please place your hands on the counter." He patted both men down, then searched Vince's briefcase. "This way, please," he said when he had finished.

They were led into a room that housed the cleaning machinery. Five or six men were seated at a table playing poker. "Mr. Arrone, you will remain here. My friends will see that you're comfortable. Mr. Grosso, you will come with me."

Vince was led up a flight of stairs. Raymal knocked twice, then opened the door at the top, nodding for Vince to enter. Marzette was seated on a small couch, his outstretched legs propped on a coffee table. His hair was close-cropped, and he was clean-shaved. Wearing a white button-down under a green crew-neck sweater, he looked more like a college athlete than the kingpin of the drug world. He remained seated, motioning Vince to take the chair opposite him, straight-backed with no arms. He obviously wanted every edge.

"How are you, Mr. Marzette?" Vince asked, opening his briefcase and taking out a file. "I've prepared an analysis of your business options, which are largely self-explanatory. Given the size of your cleaning business and the number of trucks you have on the street, I can't emphasize strongly enough the need for you to incorporate."

Utterly confused, Marzette took his legs from the table and sat upright. Before he could speak, Vince silently raised his hand, then placed his finger to his lips. "As we've discussed, the most

[241]

important feature of incorporating is limited liability. In the event of a lawsuit, only the corporate assets can be attached. Succinctly stated, it is absolute insanity for you to continue as a sole proprietorship. Assuming then that we incorporate, let's briefly explore your options."

For the next fifteen minutes, while Marzette continually shifted his legs, Vince delivered a monologue on the tax ramifications of incorporating a business. Each time Marzette tried to interrupt, Vince would raise his hand for silence.

"I'll leave the analysis for you to review fully," Vince continued. "As you'll see, it remains my opinion that a Subchapter S corporation is best suited for your purposes. Once you've completed your review, I will be available for any questions you might have. The final decision, of course, is yours. After you have made it, I will prepare the necessary paperwork to file with the Corporation Bureau."

Vince dropped the folder onto the table. His expression changed, from Vincent Grosso, expert attorney servicing a client, to Vincenzo Grosso, don of the Philadelphia *borgotta.* "And now that we've seen to the future of your cleaning business, we can get to the real purpose of the meeting—narcotics. You may now speak, Mr. Marzette."

"That's fuckin' decent of you, man. You mind telling me what the motherfuck that was all about?"

"Merely an exercise in caution. You probably take great pains in sweeping your office, Mr. Marzette, but the feds are extremely clever. One of the nice things about being a lawyer is that I can provide extra protection."

"What are you talking about, man?"

"Federal law prohibits the recording of privileged conversations, Mr. Marzette. Doctor-patient, priest-penitent, and, yes, attorney-client. That's why I make it a point to represent all my associates. Each conversation, whether by phone or in person, begins with a legal discussion similar to the one we just had."

"That was no discussion, man. You gave a fuckin' speech."

"Whatever. The point is, if our friends were recording, they would be required to stop the tape. Actually they're supposed to shut off the machine entirely, but of course, they don't. They continue to listen, but it does them no good. Anything they obtain from a privileged conversation is inadmissible as evidence, not to mention a violation of federal law. So you see, Mr. Marzette, you can relax. For once in your life you're fully protected."

"I'm always relaxed, man. And I don't need no fuckin' dago to protect me."

"As you'll soon discover, Mr. Marzette, you just might. Let's get down to business, shall we?"

"I'm listening."

"Good. Although you're undoubtedly too modest to admit it, your drug operation is the largest and most successful in the city."

"Modest, shit, man! Fuckin' A right, I'm number one. And not just the city. I'm the biggest on the whole fuckin' coast."

"There are those in New York and Miami who might dispute that, but the point has been made. You are extremely successful, and I intend to make you even more so."

"Say what?"

"My family has no desire to remain connected with narcotics in any way. My people have always been divided on this question, so up until now we've been involved, but in a half-ass way. You've heard the expression that anything worth doing is worth doing well. I believe that. So we either get in all the way, in which case you've got tremendous competition, or we get out. I chose to get out."

"Why?"

"Straight? The money is too dirty, and there're too many risks, especially now that the FBI is getting jurisdiction. We have too many other operations that would be jeopardized if we stayed in. So it's yours, Mr. Marzette. All of it."

"Don't you *ever* talk plain, man? Say what the fuck you mean."

"I mean that we want you, Julius Marzette, to take control of all narcotics in Pennsylvania. And I mean *all*. Heroin, cocaine, speed. Even marijuana. We'll provide you with our contacts and, when necessary, our political muscle. Cops, legislators, judges. Sure, you'll still have your free-lancers here and there, but they won't amount to much. When we put the word on the street that everything goes through Marzette, you'll be amazed at how your competition disappears. The whole state of Pennsylvania, Mr. Marzette. Yours for the asking."

Marzette was pacing now, clearly disturbed. "What's the catch, man? You ain't doing this out of the goodness of your heart."

[243]

"Let's say I'm advancing the cause of civil rights. Pennsylvania should be an equal opportunity employer."

"Cut the horseshit, man. What's in it for you?"

"I'm not a greedy man, Mr. Marzette. My family will be happy to receive only fifty percent of your profits."

"Motherfuck you, man!" Marzette exploded. "You expect me to do all the work, take all the chances, then let you take half? Man, you're out of your fuckin' mind."

"Not only do I expect it, Mr. Marzette, but I demand it."

Marzette slammed his fist on the table. "Who the fuck are you to demand, man? You been readin' too many comic books. The big godfather keepin' the niggers in line. Shove it, motherfucker. That Mafia shit doesn't flush with me, especially when it's a piss-ant operation like yours. Now get the fuck out of here before I blow your dago ass away."

"Certainly, Mr. Marzette," Vince answered calmly. "First, please call your assistant in. Mr. Raymal, I believe it is."

"What the fuck for?"

"Please, humor me. I think you'll find it interesting."

Marzette hesitated, then shrugged and walked to his desk. "Send Shaamad up," he said into the intercom. He turned back to Vince. "This better be worth it."

"I assure you it will be."

Raymal entered. "What's up, boss?"

"Ask the man," Marzette answered.

"Shaamad," Vince said, "do me a favor and kill Mr. Marzette."

Without a word Raymal walked to the desk. He reached into his coat for his gun, placed it against Marzette's forehead, and squeezed. Marzette was frozen. Only when he heard the click of the hammer on an empty chamber did he realize that he was still alive.

"That will be all, Shaamad," Vince said. "And thank you."

"You're welcome, Don Vincenzo."

Neither spoke for several minutes after Raymal left. Marzette remained at his desk, mouth open, eyes riveted on the wall. Smiling slightly, Vince now propped *his* feet on the coffee table. When he felt that the maximum effect had been obtained, he rose and faced Marzette.

"You look confused, Mr. Marzette, so let me explain what just

[244]

happened. We got to one of your own. Your top man, the one who's been with you from the beginning. If I had wanted, the gun would have been loaded and you would be dead. Are you beginning to see why you can never refuse me?"

Marzette turned from the wall to his conqueror. His eyes showed no hatred, no thirst for revenge. Only shock—and fear.

"How?" he asked.

"It wasn't difficult, Mr. Marzette, and he's not the only one. That could never happen with my people. I might get taken out someday, maybe by one of my own, but never on behalf of an outsider. That's why you can never win, Mr. Marzette. Because I'm Sicilian—and you're a nigger."

Vince reached for his briefcase. "In case you have any thoughts about revenge against Shaamad, I suggest you forget them. It will accomplish nothing other than assure you of an early grave. Is that understood?"

Marzette nodded.

"Good. This is the last time that we will meet. Tomorrow, you will retain the accounting firm of Spencer and Donofrio. It's ours. They will serve as intermediaries and insure that we receive the proper count. Your business will quickly expand, and with your forty percent, you will become one of Pennsylvania's wealthiest citizens."

"You said fifty!"

"That was before you refused me, Mr. Marzette. It's still a bargain, particularly since you continue to breathe."

Vince turned to leave, then stopped at the door. "Incidentally, the legal advice I provided you was thoroughly researched. I suggest you read the file and follow the instructions. In the file is a bill for services rendered, at our standard hourly rate. I insist that it be paid promptly."

"How did it go?" Arrone asked when they were back in the limousine.

Vince was looking out the window again. "We won," he answered, without turning. "Wops thirty-five, niggers zero."

Another victory, another step forward for the Grosso *borgotta*. Yet Vince was thinking none of that. His thought was the same as when he had stared down Michael Agostino: Kevin would have loved it.

Thirteen

PAT Carney scanned the press statement one last time. It was good, as good as he could manage, but it would still be tough to sell. For the fifth straight year, tuition would increase in the arch-diocesan high schools, this time to a shade less than a thousand dollars.

When would it end? How long could they continue to argue the necessity of a Catholic education while at the same time pricing it out of reach for so many? Were it any other city in America, it might have been tolerable. But this was Philadelphia, birthplace of Catholic education. It had been the legacy of St. John Neumann, the little giant, a legacy which recently had begun to tarnish.

Till the early seventies Philadelphia was unique. A free education from first till twelfth grade was offered to each Catholic student. Sure, the parents were expected to contribute in the Sunday basket, but tuition was unthinkable. West Catholic, Monsignor Bonner, Hallihan, Archbishop Prendergast—these were not considered private schools. They were public Catholic schools, open to anyone who embraced the faith.

Then it began to erode. Inflation was a factor. So was the energy crunch. But the biggest problem was the drop in vocations. Not long ago the seminaries were turning out sixty or seventy priests a year. Now they were lucky to hit fifteen. And it would get worse. A recent report predicted that by 2000 the number of American priests would be reduced by more than half. "Priestless

Sundays" would become a common term. There was a very real possibility that in many parts of the country the circle would be completed, back to where they were two centuries before, when priests rode circuit to the missions to dispense the sacraments.

It was even worse with the nuns. Pat had gone through eight years of Catholic grade school without ever seeing a lay teacher. Now a parish school that had five nuns was considered fortunate. Some of the schools were being run completely by the laity, from the principal on down. And unlike the nuns, they didn't work for free.

Even worse was the inability of the Church to keep what it had. The exodus from religious life continued to accelerate. Each week the cardinal received a half dozen or more requests for laicization.

The boss knew what had to be done and he was doing it. It was a time for belt tightening. Schools, even parishes were being closed. Others were being consolidated. Years of tradition were destroyed with the swipe of a pen. St. Thomas More. Gone. Notre Dame of Moylan. Gone. And on and on as the hit list continued to grow. St. James would be next, and after that still others. Maybe even Roman, the nation's first Catholic high school.

But why? Why was it all coming apart now? Was it just a phase, a swing of the pendulum to be balanced by a downward stroke? Another temporary crisis to be overcome by the eternal Church, like the schisms and the heresies over which it had prevailed?

Or was it deeper than that? Maybe Kevin was right. Maybe they *had* brought it on themselves. Maybe Vatican II had been a mistake, too much too soon.

"All of a sudden, after two thousand years, they yank the rocks away overnight. There's nothing left to hold on to," Kevin had said during one of their debates. Arguments actually. Kevin attacking and Pat defending. "Just like the colleges. One day they're archconservatives; the next day they're giving in to the radicals. No middle ground."

"I can't believe what I'm hearing," Pat had replied. "Kevin Murray, the world's greatest extremist, calling for moderation."

Pat smiled to himself. Kevin, God bless him. The eternal paradox. A campus radical, thorn in the side of the administration, now the leading legislative spokesman for the Church.

Kevin the archconservative. If he had his way, nothing would

[247]

change. Almost nothing. He did accept the new rules on communion, choosing to receive in his hands. As usual, he cited logic and consistency. "We're just getting back to the old ways, the way communion was received for the first few centuries. And besides, if Jesus Christ walked down the street today, wouldn't you want to touch Him?"

But in everything else he was intractable. He wanted things the old way. No meat on Fridays. Fasting after midnight for communion. Masses in Latin. The Baltimore Catechism still being taught. By the old-time nuns, the ones who beat the hell out of you when you got out of line, and when you went home and bitched to your parents, they beat the hell out of you, too, because you had to be doing something wrong for sister (s'ter) to hit you in the first place.

What Kevin failed to accept was that it was a different age. For better or worse, those days were gone, and no amount of complaining would bring them back.

Yet there was a lot of truth in what he said. "You know what the strength of the Church was, Pat? It made it hard on you. It demanded. But you know, when a lot is demanded of you, a pride develops. Like the marines. Whether it was a hundred degrees or two feet of snow, you'd see the papes fighting their way to church on Sunday, because those were the rules. Take a look around you now. It's the 'Jesus loves me the way I am' bullshit!"

One of Pat's greatest forms of entertainment was to be present when Kevin took on one of his kids. Sean would come home with a history paper, for which he had received an A.

"Great job, Sean," Kevin would say after reading it. "But you've got a bunch of misspellings."

"My teacher doesn't take off for that."

"That's not the point, buddy. You never use a word if you're not sure of the spelling. Either look it up or use another word. Take a look. You've got three punctuation mistakes in the first paragraph alone. And a slew of grammatical errors. 'Was' should be 'were.' Subjunctive mood."

Sean would turn to leave.

"I'm not done, Sean. I want to go over this with you. It's important."

"I got an A."

"That's not the point, Sean," Kevin would respond, struggling to retain his patience. "I told you, it's a good paper, but I want you to see your mistakes, particularly since your teacher didn't see fit to point them out. Look, you use *less* here. It should be *fewer*. And *it's* is a contraction for *it is,* not the possessive."

"It doesn't matter, Dad. My teacher doesn't care about those things."

That clinched it. Rational discussion was shot to hell. "But, goddammit, I do! Understand?"

"Kevin, your language!" Karen said.

"To hell with my language. Stay out of this. Look, Sean, you don't worry about spelling and grammar just in your English courses. In case you didn't know, English is a wonderful language. With the proper skill and care, you can make it sing. But you have to know the basics. Without them you're lost. And if you don't know how to communicate, you're going to screw up whatever you do."

"Aw, Dad."

"Don't give me that 'aw, Dad' crap. Now get upstairs and correct this."

"Don't take it out on Sean," Karen said. "Talk to his teacher. It's her you should be complaining to."

He couldn't resist, even though he knew the consequence. "She. And don't end a sentence with a preposition."

"Don't, Kevin! Don't you treat me like one of the kids." She turned to the priest. "Pat, he has to be the most frustrating person in the world."

"C'mon, hon," Kevin said. "I was just kidding. But just because a teacher doesn't know her ass from third base, or is too lazy to care, doesn't mean I'm going to let my kids be functional illiterates. I see too much of that outside. It's unbelievable."

"Here we go again," Karen said. "Time for 'it's not like the old days.'"

"Damn right it's not. Look at Kevin and Sean. Neither one of them knows how to diagram a sentence. And they're honor students, for God's sake."

"So what?"

"So plenty, Karen. That's absolutely essential. I still do diagrams in my head to get the right sentence structure."

"Isn't he wonderful, Pat? C'mon, Kevin, recite for us the words that take the place of linking verbs."

[249]

"Linking verbs, hell! They're copulative verbs. And since you insist, the verbs that take their place, thus requiring predicate adjectives or predicate nominatives rather than objects, are *appear, become, continue, feel, grow, look, remain, seem, smell, sound,* and *taste.* Satisfied?"

"Completely. Just like he learned in fifth grade, but then Kevin Murray always was the smartest boy in the class. If you don't believe it, ask his mother."

"You really are a shithead, you know that, Karen?" He turned to Pat, who was thoroughly enjoying the show. "Arithmetic, just as bad, Pat."

"It's called math now, caveman," Karen gibed.

"Stuff it, Karen," answered Kevin without looking at her. "They don't have the foggiest idea of the basics. And they're allowed to use calculators, even the little ones! Can you believe it?"

Pat had hoped to remain a spectator, but since the remark had been directed solely to him, he felt compelled to answer it. "In all fairness, Kevin, this is a different age. Calculators are a way of life."

"Fine. I don't quarrel with that. But only *after* you've got the basics down pat. What the hell happens someday if the batteries fail? And religion, God, you oughta see what they're peddling for religion! Pure, unadulterated horseshit!"

"Must you, Kevin?"

"I told you, Karen, stuff it." Back to Pat. "There's no such thing as catechism anymore. They have these religion workbooks that make you want to puke. Crap like 'Draw a picture of things you see on the street that show God's love.' A dog turd, maybe? A used condom?"

Karen again. "You really are disgusting!"

This time he ignored her. "Mortal sin? Forget it. It doesn't exist anymore. And before you have a chance to be a smartass again, Karen, I'll recite. A mortal sin requires a grievous matter, sufficient reflection, and full consent of the will. Okay? Sanctifying grace, actual grace, the cardinal sins. The kids never heard of them. Confession's out. Not officially, of course, but nobody goes anymore. So if you jerk it, all you have to do is tell God you're sorry and it's okay to hit the rail. You see, sacrilege is out, too. Beautiful. Friggin' beautiful."

[250]

The tirade might have gone on indefinitely had it not been for the pristine and proper Karen Scully Murray, whose remark first shocked the two men, then sent them into convulsive laughter.

"You know what your problem is, Kevin?" she had asked. "You're an old fart."

As much as he had enjoyed the answer, Pat knew that it wasn't that simple. To be sure, Kevin was set in many of his ways. Immovable. Like his adamant refusal to address priests, even the younger ones, by their first names. Pat, of course, was the exception—he was considered family—but even with him it was a limited exception. When they were in public, Kevin always addressed him by his title.

It infuriated Kevin when a priest would approach him, extend his hand, and say, "Hi, I'm Bob Jones."

"Hello, Father," he would reply.

"Please. It's Bob."

"Whatever you say, Father."

He would be happy to let it go at that, but there was always some Young Turk wanting to push the issue, explaining that the use of his first name made him more comfortable, and besides, he wasn't special. He was just the same as anyone else.

Didn't the dumb bastards realize how wrong they were? Sure, they were humans like all the rest, but they were also very different. And very special. They were taking the place of Jesus Christ on earth. Only they could change bread and wine into the body and blood of Christ. Only they could forgive sins.

And didn't they realize how special that most personal term was? The act of faith that went into addressing someone not of your flesh and blood as "Father" said it all about the Church and the legacy of its founder. Kevin thought it was sad and a bit ironic that when a priest was elevated to monsignor, or higher, he was no longer addressed in that very special way. Monsignor, Excellency, Eminence, and the ultimate, Holiness—all were impressive, but they couldn't hold a candle to Father.

But just when you thought you had Kevin pegged as a hopeless reactionary, he would surprise you. Like telling Pat that he, the man whom NOW had labeled Pennsylvania's premier woman hater, thought that women should be priests.

[251]

"Face it, Pat. The Church's stand is indefensible. Not a shred of logic to it."

Pat had taken the party line, arguing tradition. None of the apostles, the first priests, had been a woman.

"I find that argument very interesting," Kevin replied. "You justify the stand against women priests on the same ground as you do the Church's opposition to priests marrying—tradition. Well, guess what, pal. They're mutually exclusive. It's true that none of the apostles was a woman, but it's equally true that a number of those same apostles were married. You can't have it both ways. Come on, Pat, we both know the truth."

"What truth?"

"That the Church's position on both issues is based on the same factors: money and fear."

"I'm not following you."

"Because you don't want to. If priests marry, they can't live in the rectory, right? Individual housing for each priest. And children to support. I mean, it wouldn't do for a Catholic priest to practice birth control, would it? So we're talking big bucks, sports fans. Forget tradition. It's money, plain and simple. And what if the priest gets divorced or his wife starts running around? Scandal city. Much the same with the female priest issue; only in this case the scandal factor outweighs the money."

"There's the same potential for scandal with males, Kevin. It's no secret that from time to time some priests display human frailty."

" 'Display human frailty.' A cute phrase, Pat, which loosely translated means they're out dipping it. All of which is true. But the difference is that they're men and the good old dual standard applies."

"I'd ask you to explain, but I know you're going to anyway."

"Take parents, Pat. Any parents. If their nineteen-year-old son goes out and gets laid, they don't condone it, but it's accepted. Almost with a wink, a sense of pride. You know, Junior's a man now, and these things happen. If he weren't out there scoring, he wouldn't be normal. But let their daughter do the same thing, and it's the end of the world, even though the girl Junior is screwing is someone else's daughter. Weeping and wailing and gnashing of teeth over their precious flower being despoiled. Why, Pat? What's the difference?"

"There's always been a difference, Kevin. We've always put our women on pedestals."

"True. But the main reason has to do with biology. Junior, unlike the precious flower, can't get knocked up. The terrifying fear of pregnancy, the public shame of it all. And it's still there, Pat. Maybe not as much as it used to be, but still there. Sure, priests have gotten women pregnant. I'm sure you'll plead ignorance, but I know that the archdiocese has a special slush fund to support their illegitimate children. All handled very discreetly, but how do you handle it if it's a woman priest? No secret bank account can keep her belly from swelling for all the world to see her sin. Just like Hester Prynne. The only alternative is an abortion, and wouldn't that make nice headlines? So keep your philosophy and your tradition, pal. The Church may be the divine instrument of God, but it's always been immensely practical."

"When did you become such a cynic?"

"That's not cynical; it's just being realistic. Another example. What's the one Church law that will never be changed?"

"That's impossible to answer, Kevin."

"It is like hell. You'll never do away with the Sunday mass requirement. Why? Because Mother Church wants her faithful to know God? Yeah, but most of all because that's the only way the money will keep coming in. You'll never take in the same kind of cash by mail that you do in person. Nobody wants to seem like a cheapskate when the basket's passed around."

Pat shook himself from his daydreams and buzzed his secretary. "Lucille, please tell the boss that I'm ready to meet with him whenever it's convenient."

It would be a less than pleasant meeting. The boss got irritable whenever he was forced to raise tuition.

"I don't know how much longer we can hold the line," he had once said to Pat. "We're strangling our very own. If they pay us twelve years of tuition, what will be left for college? We need help, Patrick. Desperately."

It was help that was not easily given. Like abortion, the state legislature had consistently supported aid to nonpublic schools. And like abortion, the legislative efforts were largely thwarted by the courts. Indirect assistance—transportation, textbooks, auxiliary services—was permitted but the real help, the programs de-

[253]

signed to pump money directly into the schools to keep them afloat, had been uniformly stricken.

Naturally, Kevin was in the forefront of the battle. He had continually encouraged the archdiocese and the Catholic community to become more aggressive. "It's like abortion," he had said. "You can't just sit on your duff, hoping that the court will change its mind. You have to keep the issue alive."

On several occasions Pat had watched his classmate in action before a Catholic school audience, and he had marveled at Kevin's ability. Until the end there was no emotional oratory. It was a low-key, objective approach to the problem.

Kevin counseled his audience not to couch the issue in terms of public versus nonpublic. And phrases such as *fair share,* which had a whine to it and was impossible to define, should be avoided.

Kevin took the pragmatic approach. Nonpublic schools had existed for almost two centuries without asking for a penny. In the process they had saved taxpayers hundreds of billions of dollars. Now, through no fault of their own, they were in trouble and needed help. If that help were not forthcoming, they would be forced to close.

If Pennsylvania's four hundred thousand nonpublic students were funneled into the public school system, the result would be catastrophic. Since the average cost to educate one public school student was more than three thousand dollars a year, an additional one and a half billion dollars in operating revenue alone would be needed, as well as a huge increase in capital funding. The average taxpayer, regardless of his religion or whether he had children in school, would see his real estate taxes double. And that was a conservative estimate.

With the same precision, Kevin took apart the separation of church and state argument. He pointed out that no such constitutional doctrine existed and never had. What the First Amendment *did* contain was an anti-establishment clause, prohibiting the federal government from supporting a particular religion. At no time was a total separation of church and state ever envisioned. In point of fact, the United States government had on numerous occasions supported church-affiliated organizations, such as Indian missions in the West.

He also pointed out the irony that many of those opposing aid

[254]

to nonpublic schools on constitutional grounds at the same time were strong advocates of Sunday blue laws, laws which clearly violated the anti-establishment clause because they gave preference to those religions that worshiped on Sundays.

A strict adherence to a policy of separation of church and state would, of necessity, result in many programs, presently taken for granted, being declared unconstitutional: tax exemption for church properties; tax deductions for charitable contributions to religious organizations; state and federal college grants to sectarian universities.

"And yes, sports fans, a strict interpretation would make *all* nonpublic schools unconstitutional. Why? it's a state requirement that a child go to school until a certain age. In Pennsylvania the age is seventeen. Yet we permit religious schools to fulfill that state obligation. Not very consistent, is it? So let's label the constitutional challenge for what it is: a phony argument that falls under the weight of logic."

Kevin would then proceed to explore ways that government aid could be provided. His favorite was a tuition income tax credit, a method strongly supported by logic. The single largest investment made by parents, surpassing even the purchase of their home, was the education of their children. And it was an essential investment since the future of society depended upon an educated citizenry. If the two-martini lunch were deductible, if taxpayers could write off new cars and summer homes, shouldn't education be afforded at least the same status?

The particular beauty of a tax credit system was its efficiency. No bureaucracy to administer it. Absolutely no overhead. Since the money never left the taxpayers, every penny was assured of going precisely where it was intended.

Nearing his finish, Kevin would shift gears. Now the words came straight from the heart. "It's time for the Catholic Church to forget its inferiority complex. No other religion is reluctant to ask for what it wants. If we don't ask, if we don't stand up and fight for what we believe in, we can't expect to win. Life is a street fight. We can either roll up our sleeves and jump in, not certain whether we'll win or lose, or walk away, allowing a huge part of our heritage to disappear."

He lowered his voice. "I want to ask you a question. If we fail, what do we tell the ghosts? The nuns and the priests who for two centuries devoted their lives to the cause? The men and women, like our parents, who broke their backs to support their families and yet somehow found enough to support our schools? Do we tell them that it's over, that their legacy has disappeared forever? That we couldn't hold on to what they gave us? That the central stone in our Catholic heritage is a thing of the past, a victim of the times? I don't think so. And I don't want to tell my children and grandchildren that I was around when time ran out on Catholic education."

And then the climax, the way he ended many of his speeches. "I know that this is a difficult battle, but I also know that there is nothing that we cannot accomplish if we believe in ourselves and if we have it where it counts: in the heart. And to make that point, I'd like to close with a little poem. It's a poem I learned when I was a freshman in high school, trying out for the football team. Not being terribly coordinated, I wasn't doing very well and was pretty depressed. My brother at that time was a sophomore at Villanova, involved in student theater. They were putting on a play in the fieldhouse, and the actors were assigned to the lockers of the athletes. My brother was given the locker of George Raveling. Some of you have probably heard of George. He's the head basketball coach at Washington State. Back then he was captain of Villanova's basketball team. A tall black athlete from Scranton, who didn't have a whole lot of natural ability. But old George, he had a heart as big as all outdoors. He was the type of guy who would run through a brick wall to get a loose ball.

"When my brother opened the locker, he noticed a poem, an anonymous poem, taped on the inside of the door. He read it, wrote it down, and then memorized it. And when I was having my football problems, he gave it to me, and I did the same. And it's the words to that poem that always kept me going when things got tough. If you listen to the words, I think you'll agree that it says it all, both about our struggle and about life. It goes like this:

> If you think you're beaten, you are
> If you think you dare not, you don't
> If you'd like to win, but think you can't
> It's almost a cinch you won't.

[256]

If you think you'll lose, you're lost
For out in this world you find
Success begins in a person's heart
It's all in your state of mind.

If you think you're outclassed, you are
You have to aim high to rise
You have to be sure of yourself before
You ever can win the prize.

For the game doesn't always go
To the stronger or faster man
Sooner or later the victory goes
To the one who thinks he can.

"Not only do I think we can, my friends, but I'm absolutely certain that, together, we will prevail. Thanks, God bless, and keep the faith."

They went wild, of course, as they always did. It was trite, it was maudlin, and they absolutely loved it.

The intercom buzzed, and Pat sensed trouble. He had a sixth sense about things like that. Once again he was right.

"Father Wheeler, I mean, Mr. Wheeler to see you, Monsignor."

Why today? Pat thought. *And why him?*

"Send him in, Lucille," he sighed.

He tried to act natural, smiling as Wheeler entered, rising to meet him. "Good to see you, Chris. It's been too long. How's Margie? And the kids?"

"Fine. They're all fine, Pat. And you?"

"I'm hanging in there." He immediately realized it was a poor choice of words. "Sit down, Chris. So, what's new?"

"Nothing much. I was down this way on business, and I thought I'd drop in."

"Glad you did. How's the job? You're with who, now? IRS, isn't it?"

"The Federal Reserve."

"I could never keep those agencies straight. Enjoy it?"

"Yeah, all things considered. It's—well, it's a change, as you can imagine. Still seems funny sometimes."

[257]

Pat began tapping his pencil on the desk. *I know why he's here, and I can't help. Dammit, I can't. I won't.* "Two children now, right?" he asked. "Two boys?"

"Boy and a girl. Young Chris just turned eight, and Diane is three and a half."

"Rich man's family, huh?"

"Yeah, that's what they say."

"Listen, can I offer you a drink?"

"No, thanks anyway, Pat. I can stay only a minute."

Just long enough to unload on me. "You're living where now?"

"Narberth. St. Margaret's. Once a Catholic, always a Catholic."

"Great. You like it there?"

"Yeah. We love the house. It's one of those old ones. You know, three stories, all wood. Real character—and hell to maintain."

"Thank God I don't have to worry about that. It's one of the fringe benefits of the job."

Again he regretted his words. They provided an opening.

Which Wheeler seized. "That and being able to receive the sacraments. Pat, I'm desperate. I lied about being around here on business. I need help, Pat. We can't go on like this."

"That bad, Chris?"

"Yeah. Especially Margie. I'm a big boy. I realized the consequences when I left. Sure, it hurts, but I can take it. But it's destroying her, Pat. Tearing her apart inside. She's become so bitter. You wouldn't believe it's the same woman. It's gotten so bad that I don't want to go out anymore. No matter who we're with, she starts in on the Church. What really hurts her is seeing all the others being relieved with no problem. And Chris now. He's old enough to realize something's wrong, why his parents don't go to communion with him. I wanted to put him in St. Margaret's, but Margie refused. She said if we weren't good enough for the Church, the Church wasn't good enough for her son. You don't know the battle I had with her just to let him make his first communion. It's destroying us, Pat. Please. Please help me."

"How, Chris? How can *I* help?"

"Talk to the boss. He listens to you. You and I were his golden boys."

The intercom again. "The cardinal will see you now, Monsignor."

[258]

"Thanks, Lucille. I'll be right there." He turned back to Wheeler. "Okay, Chris, I'll try. I can't make you any guarantees, but I'll try."

There were tears in Wheeler's eyes as he rose. "That's all I can ask, Pat. Thank you. For all of us, thank you. I'll never forget it."

Pat gathered his papers and walked to the elevator. *Why me, God? Why the hell me? Haven't I paid enough dues for a lifetime? I don't want it! I don't want the responsibility. Enough is enough!*

He tried to collect himself. You needed a clear head when you met with the boss. Should he raise the issue with him? He had promised Wheeler that he would, and clearly the former priest was a soul in need. The desperation that had been in his voice, the pain he and Margie must be suffering.

Pat Carney and Chris Wheeler. The two hotshots of the seminary, both destined for greatness. Both handpicked by the cardinal to serve in the chancery, Pat in communications, Chris in education. The priest watchers made side bets on which would first make monsignor. No one collected. The classmates were notified of their elevation on the same day. Pat Carney accepted with pride. Chris Wheeler announced that he was leaving the priesthood. Six months later he married Margie Crawford, a former Sister of Mercy.

Technically, laicization occurred in Rome, but while the ultimate authority rested with the pope, the recommendation of the bishop was invariably honored. In the case of Chris Wheeler, Stephen Cardinal Pulski said no. No explanation was required, nor was one given. But Pat could guess at the reasons. Wheeler had been special, the protégé of a prince of the church. He had rewarded Pulski's confidence by deserting the field with a former nun.

But hasn't he paid enough? Pat thought. *Isn't it now time for Christian mercy, the mercy that Christ taught? Was Wheeler's sin, if indeed there were one, great enough to merit destroying a family? Who would benefit from that?* As a priest and as a man Pat knew that he should act.

But what would be the consequences? Would the boss be offended? After all, it was a matter that wasn't within Pat's scope of authority. And even if the boss reacted with charity, even if he let Chris Wheeler back in, would he feel challenged by one of his own, by the other golden boy who stayed? He was close, so very close to the bishop's hat. Was the risk worth it?

[259]

They spent almost an hour reviewing the statement and preparing for the news conference. As usual, Pulski was pleased with Pat's performance.

"I think that should do it for now, Pat," the cardinal said. His eyes seemed to ask a question. "Unless there's something else?"

Pat hesitated. The man never missed anything. "No, Eminence," he finally said. "I'll have the final draft typed and run off."

"You're certain there's nothing else?"

"I can't think of anything, Eminence." Pat rose. "See you tomorrow."

Another career step had been taken, and once again he despised himself.

Pat Carney was still running, with the finish line nowhere in sight.

Fourteen

SHEILA Sendrow did not enjoy foreplay. Not in sex, not in small talk before a trial, and not now, as she sipped a cup of black coffee in the greenroom of KYW-TV. Nor did she enjoy the company. Kevin Murray, as charming as he pretended to be, was the enemy. She would no more exchange pleasantries with him than she would with a convicted rapist, a simile she thought to be quite appropriate.

Although Morris Abramson was on her side in the struggle, he could never be an ally. He was a man. And no man, not her father, not her former husband, not even her son could ever assume that role.

Kevin had tried to be pleasant, rising when she entered, asking if she had finished her Christmas shopping. But he didn't need a ton of bricks to fall on him. After her terse reply that she saw no need for gifts to celebrate an artificial holiday contrived solely for commercial reasons, he turned back to the doctor. The two men had always hit it off well, Abramson talking about his getaway cabin in Sullivan County, Kevin expressing his dream to be able someday to afford a place at the shore.

Enter Marc Bowser, oily as ever. "Together again for another round, I see," he said as he shook hands with each panelist. "You've been here before, so you know the rules, the first of which is that there are no rules. Jump in whenever you please. I enjoy hostility. We're live, of course, and later on we'll be taking questions from the audience. It's packed in there, and it looks like they've come loaded for bear." He looked at his watch. "They'll be taking you over in about ten minutes, so relax for now. Any questions?"

Hearing none, he turned to Kevin. "Still at it, Kevin?"

"Always, Marc."

"When are you going to get on to something else? Leave a women's issue to the women?"

Kevin refused the bait. In all his television and radio appearances he had yet to meet a neutral moderator. They all were on the other side, and they tried to zing him not only during the show but before as well. Unlike other pro-lifers, he refused to respond when the cameras were off. There wasn't any point. Like in football, the heroes who went crazy in dummy scrimmage, then weren't worth a damn when the whistle blew. He'd save his shots for the game.

Kevin smiled. "When you make it nationally, Marc. Which insures me a long career in the pro-life movement."

"Always clever, aren't you?"

"Not always, Marc. It's just that you make it so easy."

"Ten minutes," Bowser snapped, and left.

As usual, Kevin was outnumbered. It was two to one, not counting Bowser. But that was okay. He'd rather have it that way. It gave him a greater opportunity to make his point. He knew what had to be done: seize control at every opening. Dominate the situation, just as he'd been taught in Bureau training school.

They were led across the hall to the station. Bowser had been right. It was packed and, like the composition of the panel, decidedly one-sided. Sheila's people were in the front row. If Bowser was right and they were loaded for bear, the poor bear didn't have a chance.

Kevin was following Sendrow when she stopped suddenly, her shoulders arching. She appeared to be on the verge of tears. "Get me the producer!" she snapped to a technician, her voice quivering. "I will *not* enter this studio until I see the producer."

The producer approached, his expression weary. Something always seemed to go wrong at the last minute, and he was the one who caught hell from upstairs.

"What's the problem, Ms. Sendrow?" he asked.

"Get that out of here!" she almost screamed, pointing to an

[262]

easel by the door. On it rested a blown-up picture of a recent cover of *Newsweek,* a picture of an eight-week fetus. "I am not walking through this doorway until it's removed. You promised. It was part of the ground rules. No pictures. Get rid of it!"

Kevin was powerless to resist such a unique opportunity. "Isn't this interesting?" he said, smiling. "Since when does one panelist unilaterally dictate ground rules? And why are you so terrified of the picture of a helpless baby? Kinda says something about your position, doesn't it?"

"I'm not terrified, and that's not a baby!"

"Okay, Sheila. I'll humor you. You're not terrified and that's not a baby and today's not Thursday and the earth isn't round. Happy, sweetheart?"

"Pig!"

"I love you, too."

The picture was removed, and the program began. But round one already belonged to Kevin.

Transcript of *Talk of the City* Show
Thursday, December 3, 1981
Marc Bowser, Host

BOWSER: Abortion. Is it murder, as some say, or is it a fundamental right of each woman, as others, clearly in the majority, believe? Next week the Pennsylvania House of Representatives will consider the so-called abortion control bill, labeled by its sponsor as the toughest anti-abortion law in the country. Will it pass? Should it pass? With me to discuss this controversial topic are women's rights activist Sheila Sendrow, an attorney and president of Pennsylvania NOW; Dr. Morris Abramson of New York and Pennsylvania, a nationally acclaimed medical expert on abortion and consultant to Planned Parenthood; and State Representative Kevin Murray, of Delaware County, author and prime sponsor of the abortion control bill and the acknowledged legislative leader of the anti-choice movement in Pennsylvania. Where do we begin? How about with you, Ms. Sendrow? Is Representative Murray's bill as bad as some people say?

[263]

SENDROW: Worse, Marc. Its aim is to put women back in chains by denying them fundamental rights which our courts have guaranteed.

MURRAY: Believe it or not, Sheila, in the forty-seven pages of the bill there's not one reference to chains. Unfortunately, the courts have prohibited us from halting the slaughter of unborn children. All we're trying to do is regulate it.

BOWSER: This might be a good time for a few ground rules. Definition of terms. Representative Murray, you just used the term *unborn children*. But that's just your personal opinion, isn't it? I mean—

MURRAY: Not at all, Marc. Abortion is, by anyone's definition, or I should say, by any logical person's definition, the killing of an unborn child.

ABRAMSON: I think that's a prime example of the imprecise, hysterical phraseology that Mr. Murray and his ilk engage in. That definition has absolutely no foundation in medical fact.

MURRAY: I'm disappointed in you, Doctor. I expected more from a member of the medical profession. So let—

BOWSER: Well, let's—

MURRAY: Excuse me, Marc. Let's take one point at a time. We're on the definition of abortion, and I've stated that abortion is the killing of an unborn child. Let's examine that. There are two major parts to that definition: killing and unborn child. Notice I didn't say murder since murder connotes knowledge and premeditation; as, I'm sure we'll discuss later, most women undergoing abortions have virtually no knowledge of the facts. Regardless of what you may hear, it's commonly agreed that life begins at conception. Dr. Abramson, for example, will agree to that, as will virtually every opponent I've ever debated on the issue. Life occurs when the sperm is united with the egg, creating a living, growing

[264]

thing. Some, of course, will argue whether it's human life, but since dogs have dogs and horses have horses, it's a relatively safe bet that humans have humans. Whenever something is living, be it a plant or an animal, and you want to make that something stop living, there is only one way you can do it: kill it. Thus the first part of the definition. Now the second part. The other side does everything it can to use phrases that obscure the truth: *product of conception, undifferentiated mass of tissue, termination of pregnancy,* and, yes, *fetus,* although I've never heard a pregnant woman who wants her child refer to it as her fetus. She says, "My baby." But even using the other side's language, it is interesting to note that the word *fetus* comes from the Latin meaning "little person" or "unborn child." I therefore repeat: abortion is, by definition, the killing of an unborn child.

SENDROW: I think we're wasting our time playing with words. The point is that a woman has a constitutional right to terminate her pregnancy, a right that Mr. Murray and his followers seek to revoke illegally. Abortions are legal, safe, and inexpensive, and they must remain so.

MURRAY: Legal, safe, and inexpensive. You know, Sheila, that has a catchy ring. Like a commercial. Like the billboards we see advertising abortion. Which isn't surprising when you consider that, above all, abortion is big business. A half billion dollars a year.

ABRAMSON: I take exception to that. Representative Murray is—

MURRAY: Really, Doctor. I would have thought you would be the last person to dispute that claim. Perhaps you'd like to tell our viewers how much money you've personally made from the killing of unborn children, how much revenue your so-called nonprofit clinics have pumped into your bank accounts. You don't exactly qualify as a disinterested person.

BOWSER: I don't think we have to get personal, Mr. Murray.

[265]

MURRAY: Really, Marc? I think it's safe to say that unborn children just might take their deaths personally. Death is a uniquely personal matter. But since Sheila is so eager to announce the availability of abortions at a bargain rate, perhaps she'd be kind enough to describe for the audience, in precise detail, the procedures used.

SENDROW: I hardly think that's necessary.

MURRAY: On the contrary, Sheila, it's essential. Logic dictates that if you're promoting a commodity, you take the time to explain its properties. Isn't it true, Sheila, that there are three commonly used abortion procedures?

SENDROW: Yes.

MURRAY: Then, come on now, Sheila, describe them for us.

SENDROW: Very well. Suction abortion, dilation and evacuation, and saline injection. Satisfied, Representative Murray?

MURRAY: Not at all, Sheila. That didn't tell us anything. And since you're obviously reluctant to go into detail—a reluctance wholly justified, I might add—let me do it for you. Suction abortion. Used in early-term pregnancies. A tube is inserted into the uterus and the amniotic fluid is sucked out. All goes well until the fluid is drained. Then there is a slight jolt as the unborn child is sucked into the tube, torn apart, and spit into a bucket.

BOWSER: I don't really think that this is necessary. In fairness to our viewers.

MURRAY: Given the fact, Marc, that your three previous programs this week dealt with male strippers, sex changes, and lesbianism, very few would consider *Talk of the City* a family show. I strongly doubt the kiddies have switched from *Sesame Street* to watch us. Let's get back to the issue. The second procedure is D and E. Usually the doctor crushes the baby's skull with forceps. Then a knife is inserted, and the baby is cut apart and removed, piece by piece. Now if the

[266]

doctor is doing his job correctly, he then has to reassemble the baby outside the mother to make certain that no pieces are left in her that might cause infection or hemorrhage. In late-term abortions (and it's legal to perform abortions throughout the full nine months. If you kill the child a second before delivery, it's a legally permissible abortion; a second after, it's child abuse and murder) a saline solution is injected into the amniotic fluid, causing premature contractions. It also causes babies to go into convulsions and frequently scalds them to death. These procedures not only are deadly, which is their purpose, but cause excruciating pain to the baby, who can feel pain at an extremely early age.

ABRAMSON: I wasn't aware that you were a physician, Representative Murray.

MURRAY: I'm not, Doctor. I don't play golf.

ABRAMSON: Be that as it may, it has never been medically proved that a fetus experiences pain.

MURRAY: I respectfully suggest, Doctor, that you go back to your medical books for a refresher course. It is a medically accepted fact that at nine weeks, possibly earlier, the baby will respond to a touch on the side of his foot or will bend his hips and knees to move away from the touching object.

BOWSER: But hasn't all this been settled, Representative Murray? Abortion is the law of the land. Aren't you beating a dead horse?

MURRAY: Good choice of words, Marc. I'd rather beat a dead horse than kill a live baby. And abortion is the law of the land not by the will of the people through their elected legislators but by the edict, nine years ago, of seven nonelected officials, the Supreme Court of the United States. Until then, as I have said time and again, in almost every state in the Union, the people, through their elected legislators, had laws which prohibited—not limited or regulated—prohibited abortions. I respectfully submit that the Supreme Court

[267]

has never had a monopoly on being right, and in this instance they blew it. As a matter of fact, even those legal scholars who support abortion admit that the opinion in *Roe* versus *Wade* was a pathetic one, historically incorrect, incredibly vague, and poorly drafted. The results, however, are very specific. As a direct result of the Court decision, one and a half million unborn children are killed every year. Think about that number. One and a half million children. One in every three pregnancies ends in abortion. The number of unborn children killed each year is almost double the number of all Americans killed in all our wars. Three babies are aborted each minute, every day of the year. This is a one-hour show, and while we're debating, a hundred and eighty unborn children will die. In a society, mind you, that weeps for the killing of the baby seals—

SENDROW: Not the seals again. How many times do we have to listen to that, Representative Murray?

MURRAY: Until it sinks in, Sheila. A society that pickets over the killing of porpoises by Japanese fishermen, that has enough muscle to shelve a multimillion-dollar dam project down South to save the snail darter. There are thousands of species of animals protected by state and federal laws. It's even illegal to ship a pregnant lobster. And yet we permit the slaughter, the annual holocaust, of one and a half million innocent unborn human beings. As I've said many times, that is a classic masterpiece of inconsistency.

BOWSER: All right, let's say you prevail somehow and abortions are once again illegal. Won't they still continue? And in the back alleys, instead of clinics, threatening the lives of women?

MURRAY: Certainly there will still be abortions, Marc, but not nearly as many.

ABRAMSON: That statement has absolutely no basis in fact. There were just as many abortions before abortion was legalized as there are now.

[268]

MURRAY: I'd be interested to know how you came up with that little gem, Doctor, since no statistics were kept. I do know that in states that have cut off public funding, abortions have decreased by more than twenty-five percent. When we win, the availability won't be there. There won't be the same Madison Avenue hype to get rid of the baby. Half the time the first question an obstetrician asks a woman when he discovers that she's pregnant is: "Do you want the baby?" Can you believe that? A problem develops early in the pregnancy, and the doctor tells the woman that "we might have to take the baby." Nice phrase, isn't it? "Take the baby." Sounds like you're going out for a walk in the park or a trip to the zoo. Why don't they say what they mean: "We might decide to kill your baby." It's for these reasons that our bill contains an informed consent section, requiring the doctor to inform the woman of all the facts. The subtle hype that's being used on them, the pressure to do the fashionable thing never give her the chance to reflect on the essence of the act. So, Marc, absolutely yes, there will be many fewer abortions if they are once again outlawed. But sure, they'll still continue. We have laws against rape, murder, and robbery, but they still occur. What's the answer? Repeal the laws? And yes, some women may go to the back-alley butchers, although not many since a whole generation of doctors, skilled in the art of killing unborn children, will be loath to give up such a profitable occupation. But you know, people right now get sick or die from bad batches of heroin and other drugs. Again, should we legalize drug use? I think not.

BOWSER: So women will be prosecuted for making a personal decision, is that it?

MURRAY: Once again, Marc, you failed to do your homework. Would it surprise you to know that for the century that abortion was illegal in this country, not one mother was prosecuted? The prosecutions were against the individuals performing the abortions.

[269]

BOWSER: That's hypocritical.

MURRAY: Not at all. It is an accurate assessment of the fact that in every abortion there are two victims: the baby *and* the mother. We know, of course, what abortion does to the baby. It kills him or her. But it is also devastating, physically and psychologically, to the mother. Just an example. The University of Ohio recently published a study indicating that a large percentage of women who had abortions attempted suicide on the day their children would have been born. It is a medically established fact that a woman who undergoes an abortion has a tremendously increased chance of becoming sterile, and how would you like that for your epitaph: "I killed the only baby that I'll ever have"?

SENDROW: I have to jump in here. I can't believe that Representative Murray, who has done more than anyone else to deny women their reproductive rights, is now posturing that he is concerned about women. He says that women are victims, and that's true. They've always been victimized, but not by abortion. They've been victimized by a hypocritical dual standard that deprives them of their freedom. They've been forced to endure pregnancies that they didn't want, that were harmful to them—sometimes fatal—both physically and psychologically. Women whose careers, whose very lives were destroyed by pregnancies. Like the woman I counseled before abortion was legalized. She had been illegitimate; she had been on welfare; she had been degraded all her life. But she rose above it. She went to school, received her bachelor's degree and was a year away from her master's. Her future was promising. Then she got pregnant, and no one was there to help. Certainly not the father of her child, but isn't that always the case? She didn't have the connections or the money for an illegal abortion, so she tried to do it herself. She almost died, spent three months in the hospital, and is now back on welfare. Yes, the child survived, and she's raising

[270]

him; but her dream is over. One life, probably two ruined. It's easy for Representative Murray to pontificate about his concern. He's a man. He'll never face that situation.

BOWSER: That's a powerful story, don't you agree, Representative Murray?

MURRAY: Sure. Of course, if we're going to tell horror stories, I could tell a few myself. Like the seventeen thousand aborted babies discovered in California. Like the experiments performed on aborted children. Like the fact that collagen from aborted babies is used in many cosmetic products. Like the Washington hospital that made sixty-eight thousand dollars selling aborted babies, money used to purchase a television and cookies and soda for the staff. Sheila's story may be powerful, but a master's degree isn't worth the life of a baby.

BOWSER: Well, it's time for a station break. When we return, we'll take questions from the audience. At this point, at least, we can agree on one thing: we're dealing with a very complicated and complex matter.

MURRAY: It's not complex, Marc. Emotional? Yes. Divisive? Yes. But not complex. The issue is very basic: can anything justify the killing of an unborn child?

BOWSER: We'll be right back.

[Commercial]

BOWSER: We're back again. I'm Marc Bowser, your host for *Talk of the City*. The topic today is abortion, and with me are Dr. Morris Abramson, a consultant for Planned Parenthood; Sheila Sendrow, president of Pennsylvania NOW; and State Representative Kevin Murray, of Delaware County. Well, so far it's certainly been lively. Now we're going to liven it up even more with questions from our audience. You first, madam. The woman in the second row.

WOMAN: Yes. I have a question for Representative Murray. Don't you believe that a woman has a right to control

[271]

her own body? And how can you, as a man, justify involving yourself in a matter that affects only women?

MURRAY: Actually you have two questions. Your first, dealing with a woman's right to control her own body, is based on a false premise—namely, that any of us, male or female, have an absolute right to control our bodies. We don't and never have. None of us, male or female, can sell our bodies in prostitution. That's against the law. We can't take certain drugs. That's against the law. As a matter of fact, we can't even take our own lives, since suicide is against the law, although I admit that it's a little difficult to prosecute the successful perpetrator. There is no absolute right. Sheila mentioned reproductive rights a few minutes ago. Hell, we're not trying to limit anyone's right to reproduce. Have as many or as few children as you wish. Just don't kill unborn babies. As far as my right to involve myself in this issue, it's because of my membership in a very exclusive club, and I'm not referring to the Pennsylvania legislature. I am a member of the human race, and any individual, male or female, who sits idly by and watches its self-destruction is remiss in his or her duties. Abortion isn't a woman's issue; it's a human issue, even though, by mathematical certainty, half of the one and a half million unborn children killed every year are women. I should point out that the vast majority of our female legislators vote pro-life and always have, but I'm not about to disqualify myself from voting because of my sex. Every day I'm called upon to vote on diverse issues—bills, for example, dealing with physicians, engineers, senior citizens, you name it. I'm not a doctor. I'm not an engineer. I'm not even a senior citizen, although someday I hope to be, considering that the alternative is ever so bleak, so should I refuse to vote on all these matters? Under that rationale the only member of Congress who could vote on the space program would be John Glenn.

[272]

BOWSER: Another question. The woman over on the left, wearing the rose. We have to be fair.

WOMAN: I have a question for either Dr. Abramson or Mrs. Sendrow.

SENDROW: Ms.

WOMAN: Sorry about that. Anyway, one of the sections of Representative Murray's bill deals with a minor receiving the consent of her parent before getting an abortion. Do you oppose that? And if so, why?

SENDROW: Yes, I oppose that provision. Obviously the ideal situation is for a girl to discuss the matter with her parents or at least one of them. Family involvement is essential, and all the counseling groups advocate it. But sometimes this is impossible, such as in the case where the parents might force the daughter to carry to term or, even worse, might do physical violence to her. Family involvement should always be encouraged but never mandated.

ABRAMSON: I have to agree. Ultimately the decision has to rest with the person whose body is affected, the pregnant woman. I've seen too many tragic situations occur where parents react irrationally. How many parents are willing to discuss sex with their children, to be the ones to teach them the facts of life? Not many, so can you reasonably expect a supportive atmosphere when the daughter becomes pregnant? Sheila hit it right on the head. Certainly encourage parental involvement, but never require it.

BOWSER: Okay. How about you in the—

MURRAY: Not so fast, Marc. No way I let that one slide by. Let's again talk facts. For every surgical-medical procedure under the sun, including getting her ears pierced, a minor needs written parental approval with one exception. That's right, sports fans, abortion. A twelve-year-old girl can receive an abortion not only without her parents' consent but without them ever even knowing about it. There are abortion clinics which

[273]

specialize in the twelve- or thirteen-year-old girl who kisses her parents good-bye under the guise of going to school, meets an employee of the clinic, is driven to the clinic, has the abortion, and is returned in time that she can walk home with the rest of her class. Isn't that beautiful? That goes way beyond abortion. It goes right to the heart of family responsibility. It rots away the fabric of the family unit. Mom and Dad, denied even input into the welfare of their daughter. It's also illogical. By law, a parent is responsible for the physical care and health of his child. Yet here he is denied even knowledge of the situation that might jeopardize the health of that child. No law can require straight parental consent. The courts have ruled that unconstitutional. What we can do, and what our bill does, is require either parental consent or court approval through an expedited, private court procedure.

ABRAMSON: Meanwhile, the poor girl bleeds to death.

MURRAY: Read the bill, Doctor. You'll see that there is a specific exception for medical emergencies.

BOWSER: We'll take another question. The gentleman back there, who's been waving his hand since we began. Go ahead.

MAN: The papers are full of stories about child abuse, usually committed by the parents. Atrocities, unspeakable. Children that were never wanted, never loved. Representative Murray, since you're so big on insisting upon birth rather than abortion, how can you guarantee that these children will be spared such a fate?

MURRAY: Guarantee? I can't. There are no guarantees in life except death. Your argument, sir, is the old "It's better to have an abortion than have an unwanted child" tune. The first problem with it is that it flies in the face of the facts. It's a fact, not an opinion by Kevin Murray but a statistic agreed upon by the ex-

[274]

perts, that the vast majority of victims of child abuse—some say as high as ninety percent—are not unwanted children, but planned, wanted children.

SENDROW: I refuse to accept that. You would have to show me documentation before I would ever accept such an obvious fantasy.

MURRAY: I'll be happy to provide you with all the data, Sheila. Actually, though, if you think about it, the premise is not difficult to accept. One of the greatest evils of child abuse is that it's cyclical, passed on from generation to generation. An abused child becomes an adult and decides to have children so that she can provide to the children all the love that she was denied. Reliving her childhood through her children; only this time it will be perfect. Except, as we all know, there is no perfection on earth. If you want perfection, you have to wait until you die and go to heaven. So when problems develop with the children, the dream of the parent is shattered, and he or she lashes out, the same way his or her parents did. But let's get back to the gentleman's question. Let's assume that statistic I just cited doesn't exist, that unwanted children may not be treated properly. The argument is that because a child might not have a perfect life, might in fact be abused, we'll do the child a favor and kill him or her. Somehow that doesn't strike me as being very logical. The ultimate form of child abuse is killing. You know, probably no one alive has enlightened and entertained as many people as James Michener. *Hawaii, Centennial, The Source, Chesapeake,* and many others. Well, guess what? James Michener's real name isn't Michener. He doesn't know what his real name is. He was an unwanted, abandoned child. But isn't it fortunate for him and for all of us whom he's entertained that his mother gave him one thing—life? And then there's the story of the little black boy about twenty-five years ago who was found wandering on the streets of North Philadelphia, unwanted and abandoned. He

[275]

was about four years old, and he had a severe speech impediment; but it sounded like he was saying Matthew, so they named him Matthew. And since this was Philadelphia, the city of Ben Franklin, they gave him the last name of Franklin. Matt Franklin, now Matthew Saad Muhammad, the former light heavyweight champion of the world.

BOWSER: Let me jump in here for a minute. After all, it's my show. What about the other children, the ones diagnosed before birth as having severe problems? The ones who, if born, will suffer all their lives with severe handicaps, often grotesque and painful. The ones whose families will agonize with them, placing a burden on them that is frequently impossible to bear? Isn't abortion, at least in those cases, the more humane approach for all concerned, including the child?

ABRAMSON: I wish you could see, Marc, some of the horrors that I've witnessed. No, actually I don't. I wouldn't wish that on anyone. Children born without a brain. Tay-Sachs victims doomed to a short and agonizing life. Children so severely retarded they will never walk, never talk, never even be able to control their bladders. Beings, poor little creatures, bearing no resemblance to life as we know it. What quality of life can they expect? Where is the humaneness, the justice, in forcing them to be brought into this world? Isn't the more compassionate course—that is, if it is the wish of the parents—to let them go? To let them be at peace? The Kevin Murrays of the world, steeped in self-righteousness, proclaiming themselves judge and jury, indeed, even God, would say no. They would demand birth, then walk away, letting others bear the suffering.

MURRAY: Interesting speech by the good doctor. Boiled down, what he is saying is that it is better to have an abortion than have a child who isn't normal. And whenever I hear that, the first questions I ask are what's

[276]

normal and who's keeping score. What disqualifies a child from life? Tay-Sachs? Down's syndrome? What about a clubfoot or a cleft palate? What about freckles or red hair or a lisp? In other times, in other societies, similar attempts have been made to clean things up, and the results have been devastating. Did you notice the buzzwords the doctor used? He used two phrases that are clues to where someone is coming from: *Life as we know it* and *quality of life*. The good old quality-of-life ethic which holds that life is reserved for only the planned, the privileged, and the perfect. That we should be able to determine who lives or who dies on the basis of what so-called quality of life someone may or may not enjoy.

SENDROW: No one is saying that we should decide that. What we are saying is that it should be a decision reserved for the parents, not the state. I should think that a conservative such as you would embrace that concept, Representative Murray.

MURRAY: Why should any human, including parents, have that right? Sure, parents are responsible for their children, but they don't own them. They can't abuse them; they can't refuse to send them to school. In most cases they can't deny them medical care. They can't abandon them. All they can do is kill them. And at best, medical predictions of abnormality, whatever that term means, are only calculated guesses. As advanced as medical technology has become, prenatal tests are by no means foolproof. There are countless examples of such predictions being groundless, of totally healthy children being born.

ABRAMSON: Those examples are becoming fewer and fewer, Dr. Murray. We are rapidly approaching the point where there will be complete certainty as to whether or not a fetus is defective.

MURRAY: "Defective." God, don't you love it? It sounds like we're talking about an appliance or a car. Is that what we've come to? Let me tell you a little story.

[277]

SENDROW: Not another story, please.

MURRAY: Sorry, Sheila, but I'm a regular Uncle Remus. There's a doctor in a medical school in California who gives each new class the following hypothetical: A mother has tuberculosis; the father, syphilis. They've had four children. One was blind, one was stillborn, one was deaf and mute, and one had tuberculosis. The mother is pregnant again and is seeking advice. Class, what do you recommend? Invariably the vast majority of the med students recommend abortion, to which the doctor replies, "Congratulations. You've just killed Beethoven." True story.

ABRAMSON: I've heard that story, and yes, it's true. But it is in no way reflective of the majority of cases. Most children born with horrible physical problems never write symphonies or novels or anything else. They suffer, Mr. Murray. They suffer a fate that no one should be forced to bear.

MURRAY: You know what it comes down to? Love. Where's the love? If our mother undergoes a mastectomy, if our father has a limb amputated, if our spouse is disfigured in an automobile accident, do we reject them? Do we tell them that we no longer love them because they're not perfect, not normal? Of course not. Should it be any different with our babies? Let's say our baby is born with no arms. Shouldn't we say to him, "Welcome, little baby. We love you just the same. In this age of technology artificial arms can be provided. And if that is impossible, we'll be your arms?" Isn't that what love is all about? And let's get something straight: the killing doesn't end with abortion. Right now, in hospitals all over the country, we're killing children *after* they're born. Look at what happened in Indiana. Infant Doe, the little boy who was never even given a name, was killed, starved to death on the instructions of his parents, because he wasn't "normal." Fourteen couples offered to adopt him, but the parents refused. They didn't want to

[278]

give him up; they just wanted to kill him. And they did, with the blessing of the Indiana Supreme Court. That's not just killing. By anyone's definition, that is flat-out murder of a born human being. My God, how can any society hope to prosper, even to survive, when it continues to destroy its precious asset—its children, indeed, its future.

ABRAMSON: What future? What future do the children have? I'll tell you. A future of incalculable pain and suffering, to them and their families. And incredible medical expenses of a magnitude that would financially destroy the average person.

MURRAY: So that's what it comes down to, huh? The dollar sign. We decide who lives and who dies by the good old balance sheet. Is that it, Doctor?

ABRAMSON: To a large extent, yes, and that's not nearly as callous as it sounds. We live in an increasingly complex world where the advances of science are making it possible for people to live indefinitely, regardless of their conditions or state in life. We are going to have to face up to some very difficult decisions. We must face the fact that we have finite resources, and, in fact, a finite amount of room on this planet. The goal of civilization must always be to advance the quality of life—and no, Mr. Murray, I'm not ashamed to use that term—of its citizens. Quality, not a purposeless worship of quantity. And yes, we're going to have to weigh, given all the circumstances, where we should utilize our life-sustaining resources—medical and other—and where we should not. That may not be pleasant, but it is reality.

MURRAY: I want to thank you, Doctor, from the bottom of my heart. In the last sixty seconds you have done more to advance the pro-life cause than I could have hoped to accomplish in a lifetime. You've taken the mask off, Doctor, and shown all of us what can happen when the sanctity, not the quality, but the sanctity of life is not preserved. It doesn't stop with abortion, does it?

[279]

Once the killing starts, it's impossible to end. First, the unborn, then "defective" infants, then senior citizens.

SENDROW: Aren't you overdramatizing just a bit? There is no comparison between a senior citizen and a fetus, an entity that cannot sustain itself, which must depend on its mother for existence.

MURRAY: Is that the yardstick, being able to live on your own? Great. Then we can save the taxpayers a whole lot of money. Go to any nursing home and see all the elderly who cannot live on their own, who, left on their own, will die. Why don't we just cut all of them adrift? Are they fair game? Dr. Abramson talks about the advance of civilization while expounding the only-the-strong-survive doctrine, thus taking us back to the status of cavemen. You either respect all human life or respect none. There's no middle ground. And if we don't revere life, all life, we're on the road to disaster. You know, if someone fifty years ago were to predict what would shortly occur in a very civilized nation, a nation that gave us engineers and playwrights and philosophers of unparalleled excellence, he would have been labeled a common crank and laughed off the streets of Berlin. And yet it did happen; the Holocaust did occur. And for all the books that have been written, no one has yet been adequately able to explain how a civilized nation could systematically eliminate six million Jews and altogether eleven million human beings. And don't think that that was a onetime aberration. The Holocaust can occur whenever human life, in any form, becomes cheap.

ABRAMSON: As a Jew I find that comparison particularly offensive.

MURRAY: And as a human I find it right on point.

ABRAMSON: If you wish to have your religious beliefs, that's fine, but don't offend mine. For you to attempt to—

MURRAY: Hold it right there, Doctor. First, don't wave the flag of anti-Semitism at me. I'm not about to run. And secondly, who's talking about religious belief?

BOWSER: But isn't that what this is really all about? Different philosophies, different religious beliefs? And is it right for any of us to try to force those beliefs on others. You are Catholic, Representative Murray, so I'd expect you to oppose abortion. But should Dr. Abramson, as a Jew, or anyone else for that matter, be forced to march to your church's tune?

MURRAY: You know, that really cracks me up, Marc. So typical. If you can't hold your own on the issues, shift the focus by bringing up religion. Who are we kidding? Abortion isn't a Catholic issue. It's not a religious issue. It's a human issue. Sure, the Catholic Church opposes abortion, as do a number of other churches, but it also opposes welfare cuts and nuclear escalation. Does that make them religious issues? Was slavery a religious issue because the Quakers, at least originally, were the driving force behind abolition? And what really gets me is the dual standard used. I've appeared on a number of shows with Bishop Landy, the Episcopal bishop who fashions himself as the Reverend Coffin of the eighties. He sits there, in religious garb, mind you, and supports abortion, while at the same time saying that pro-lifers shouldn't impose their religious beliefs on others. How come it's a religious issue only if you're pro-life? I've heard the good doctor here play that game. He'll try to tell you that a tenet of the Jewish religion is to provide abortion rights. Isn't that religious? And incidentally, it's also dead wrong.

ABRAMSON: Now you're not only a medical expert but a Judaic scholar.

MURRAY: I've done my homework, Doctor. In all Judeo-Christian history, until very recently, abortion was considered not only immoral but a crime. And this never hinged on when human life began. The philosophy

[281]

was: he is a man who will be a man. The Book of the Covenant outlawed abortion at any time. Like Aristotle, the early Jews believed that human life began at formation, which was considered forty days. Abortion before this point was penalized by confiscation of property, imprisonment, or banishment. After formation, the penalty was death. Do you dispute any of that, Doctor?

ABRAMSON: I wouldn't know. I'm not religious.

MURRAY: How convenient.

BOWSER: Let me ask you this, Representative Murray. You see abortion as this horror, this incredible evil. And yet, at least if the polls are to be believed, the vast majority supports it. Who are these people? Are they all evil? Are they murderers?

MURRAY: First off, let me dispute one of your points. To this day, in all the debates that I have participated in, I haven't found one person—not Sheila Sendrow, not Dr. Abramson, not Bishop Landy, not any elected official—who supports abortion. The answer invariably is: "I'm personally opposed to abortion, but I believe people should have the right to choose." Isn't that great? That's so phony it makes me nauseated, particularly when it's said by an elected official because his personal opinion on any issue is irrelevant. People are concerned with how he's going to vote. Just once I'd like to hear someone say, "Yeah, I support abortion. It's a good way to control the population." I'd disagree with him, of course, but I'd respect him for his honesty. But let's examine that answer a little bit. The question I ask anyone who uses that line is why does he personally oppose abortion. No one has yet responded, because if he's honest, he has to admit that the essence of the act is horrendous. It's a perversion of the natural process of birth, the only process which assures the continuation of the human race. The other side knows this. They know they can't win if they stay on the specific issue, so they obscure things. Bringing in religion, for example, but most of all with the choice argument. At least we're honest. Pro-lifers never object to being called anti-abortion. But the other side seethes if they're labeled pro-abortion. They're strictly pro-choice. And where did this absolute right of choice come from? You know, if I said that I personally opposed rape or murder, but I believed everyone should have the right to choose, or if I said that I personally opposed denying a segment of our population its civil rights on the basis of race, but I believed that everyone should have the right to choose, I'd either be laughed out or stoned out of the room. Yet here we are swallowing the right-to-choose line when it comes to the killing of unborn children.

BOWSER: But you still haven't answered my question, Representative Murray. Who are all these people who oppose you? And are they evil? Are they murderers?

MURRAY: Fine. I put them in three categories, Marc. First—and these are the ones for which I have absolutely no time—are those who realize that abortion is big business and are in it strictly for the money. The profiteers, the doctors, the abortion entrepreneurs, who make their livings from the blood of unborn children. Believe me, they exist. And, Dr. Abramson, you may object, but all I can say is, if the shoe fits, slip it on and run like hell. The second category is comprised mostly of women—for the most part, decent, honest people who would never dream of having an abortion, but who see the issue as an integral part of the women's movement. They see pregnancy as the yoke that has enslaved so many women, while permitting men complete freedom. Regardless of what anyone may say, I empathize and support the drive for women's equality. For far too long they have been denied equality in career opportunities, legal protections, and dozens of other areas. But for the reasons that we've discussed, abortion is not and cannot be part of that movement, and to include it as such jeopardizes that entire movement. An authority far

[283]

greater than Kevin Murray made the decision that it would be the female sex that would carry and bear children. Some people would like to blame me for that, too, but I have to plead not guilty. And finally, there is by far the largest group: the ones who simply don't know the facts and who accept the choice argument because it seems like the fashionable thing to do. Believe it or not, the average person has no idea of what the characteristics of an unborn child are and what abortion does to that unborn child. It is this group that will ultimately provide us our victory. When I first got involved in the abortion issue, I believed that no amount of debate or rhetoric would change anyone's mind. You were where you were. That was wrong. The name of the game is education, which, incidentally, is the major thrust of our bill, a bill which we have barely discussed during this program. In fact, I think the only part we've talked about was the parental consent section. Since we don't have too much time left, why don't we get on to the bill?

BOWSER: Fine with me. But first, let's take one more question. The lady on the left over there. Wearing the button. What's it say?

WOMAN: "I'm pro-choice and I'm proud." I want to ask Representative Murray a question. Mr. Murray, you prolifers seem to care about people only until they're born. The ones who vote against abortion rights are the ones who refuse to support the vital human service programs. If you get your way and abortions are stopped, who's going to support all of the extra children, many of whom will be born into poor families?

SENDROW: Not many. Most. Probably the worst part of Representative Murray's position is that it discriminates against the poor. Like his law to cut off Medicaid funds for abortions. And if abortions are made illegal, the rich will still be able to obtain them, just as they did before *Roe* versus *Wade*.

[284]

MURRAY: I could have sworn that question was for me. To answer you first, ma'am, I refuse to put a dollar sign on a human life. I've consistently stated that if we succeed, the cost is irrelevant and that I'll be only too happy to support whatever appropriation is required. This does not mean that I support cradle-to-grave assistance for anyone. People try to portray fiscal conservatives as being cruel. That just isn't so. I consider myself a fiscal conservative, yet I'm willing to help those who cannot help themselves. The day you begin to weigh human life by its cost in dollars is the day when your society begins to deteriorate. Sheila talked about discrimination. Yes, our bill cut off state funding of abortions. But even if her polls, the ones Marc here pointed to, are used, the vast majority of Americans oppose such funding. It's one thing to permit unborn children to be killed; it's quite another to be forced to pay for it. The argument goes that since abortion is legal, everyone should have access to it. That argument can be taken to absurdity. It's legal to take a month's vacation or to own a Cadillac or to have a face-lift. Are we saying that because some people can afford these items, everyone should be entitled to them—at taxpayers' expense? Cigarettes are legal. Harmful, but legal. Should we have state funding for those who can't afford them? But Sheila's right on one point. It is discriminatory, but not the way she means. Because of the Supreme Court, we're discriminating against the unborn of the rich and the middle class. We can't stop them from being killed, but we can save at least some of the babies of the poor. You know I hear all this talk about rights, but aren't we forgetting our history lessons? The first statute of this country, on which the United States was formed, was a document called the Declaration of Independence. Let me quote from it. "We hold these Truths to be self-evident, that all Men are created equal, that they are endowed by their Creator with certain unalienable Rights, that among these are Life, Liberty, and the Pursuit of Happiness." Please

[285]

note that the first right, the first unalienable right, is life. Which, of course, is only logical. You can't have liberty or happiness or any quality of life if you don't first have life itself. Now, Marc, can we get on to the bill?

BOWSER: Fine. Go ahead, but please try to keep it brief. We don't have much time.

SENDROW: Why don't I begin? After all, Representative Murray has once again succeeded in monopolizing the show.

BOWSER: Okay, Sheila. You've got the floor.

SENDROW: Thank you. Representative Murray's bill, by his own admission, is designed to restrict abortions as much as possible and to harass women seeking to exercise their constitutional abortion rights. The twenty-four-hour waiting period, for example, requiring a woman seeking an abortion to wait at least one day after consulting with a doctor before the operation is performed. No purpose other than harassment. In many parts of the state gynecological services are not available. If the waiting period becomes law, a woman would have to travel to the doctor, often a great distance, then either rent a room for the night or drive home and back again. Many women don't have the money or the ability to do this. And I should also point out that the courts have consistently stricken waiting requirements. Then there is the so-called informed consent section, which would have the state legislature practice medicine. Doctors are told what they are permitted to say to the patients, a classic intrusion into the confidential doctor-patient privilege. Reporting requirements. I can't see how Representative Murray can call himself a conservative after spinning this bureaucratic nightmare. Doctors in hospitals are required to file so many reports that the only winners will be those who own stock in paper companies. There's a requirement that any abortions after the first trimester be performed in a hospital on

[286]

an inpatient basis. Again, no other purpose than harassment. Abortions are just as safe in clinics, where a patient is treated promptly and professionally, as in a hospital, frequently more so. How about the requirement that pathology examinations be performed on all aborted fetuses? Just one more requirement to increase the expense, to make the cost so prohibitive that women will become discouraged and continue their unwanted and frequently dangerous pregnancies. Take the insurance provision. How can a self-proclaimed conservative support a provision that dictates to insurance companies—private companies, mind you—what coverage they're permitted to offer? And Mr. Murray isn't content to stick to abortion, not by a long shot. Despite what he says, he wants to restrict a woman's right to exercise birth control. There's an entire section in the bill dealing with this, requiring doctors and pharmacists to limit a woman's freedom to choose the contraceptive measure of her choice. A classic example of putting government directly into the bedroom. Added together, the provisions of this bill, by design, constitute an indefensible chilling effect on women and the free exercise of their rights. It is government at its very worst. The Health and Welfare Committee was correct and courageous in rejecting this legislation, and I sincerely hope that the entire House will follow suit. But regardless of the outcome of the vote, one thing is certain. This outrageous and repressive piece of legislation will be stricken by the courts and relegated to its proper niche in our society—the trash can.

BOWSER: Well, Ms. Sendrow, if Representative Murray did monopolize the early part of the show, you certainly made up for lost time. Representative, would you care to respond?

MURRAY: I sure would, Marc. Point by point. Let's take the second physician requirement. The *Philadelphia Inquirer,* certainly no ally of the pro-life movement, recently published an exposé titled "Abortion—The Dreaded

[287]

Complication." It dealt with those instances, which frequently occur, where an abortion is performed but the baby refuses to cooperate. He has the bad taste to survive—and is left to die. In a bedpan, a drawer, a utility closet. That's not just killing, Marc. By anyone's definition, that is murder, the murder of a born human being who is outside the mother. Keep in mind that the Supreme Court ruled that a woman had the right to an abortion, meaning a termination of her pregnancy. It never said that she had a right to a dead baby. All our bill says is that in late-term pregnancies, when the baby might be viable, the operating physician choose the abortion procedure most likely to give rise to a live birth, *provided* that such a procedure does not increase the risk to maternal life or health. And in those cases, a second, independent physician, who will neither take part in nor interfere with the abortion, must be present in the operating room. Once the abortion has been completed, that second doctor will take control of the now-born child and do everything in his power to save him or her life. How any human being can oppose such a provision is beyond me.

BOWSER: Okay. But Ms. Sendrow mentioned birth control, and that intrigues me. Aren't you and all the other pro-lifers opposed to birth control? I mean, the Catholic Church has made that pretty clear, hasn't it?

MURRAY: First, Marc, I never use the term *birth control.* Far too broad a term. In one of its publications, under the heading of "Birth Control," Planned Parenthood lists eleven methods. And guess what number eleven is? That's right, sports fans, abortion. And who can argue? Abortion does have a tendency to control births. What you are referring to is contraception. True, the Catholic Church opposes artificial contraception, as is its right. It has never, however, attempted to have that position embodied in law. The pro-life movement neither supports nor opposes contraception, believing it to be a personal matter that has no place in public policy. The other side attempts to lump contraception and abortion together to confuse the issue, but clearly they are separate and distinct. Contraception is the prevention of life. Abortion is the taking of it.

BOWSER: Then why does your bill get into birth control? Contraception, if you will.

MURRAY: It doesn't. What it does do is require the labeling of abortifacients.

BOWSER: What are they?

MURRAY: Drugs or devices, ostensibly used as contraceptives but which in reality cause abortions. The IUD, for example. It doesn't prevent conception. It causes an irritation which destroys the fertilized egg. All our bill says in this regard is that abortifacients be labeled as such and that physicians advise their patients as to the specific facts. A woman has an absolute right to know the facts before she chooses to use such a measure. And in this day and age, with a concerted drive ongoing for truth in labeling in virtually every area, I fail to see any grounds for opposing such a truth-in-labeling provision.

BOWSER: I hate to interrupt, Representative Murray, but we're at the five-minute mark. Please try to wrap up, so each of you will have time for a brief closing statement.

MURRAY: Fine. Let me jump to the waiting period section. Is that so unusual? There's a waiting period for almost all of the important things in our lives. A marriage license, driver's license, Social Security number, and so forth. What we're saying is that except in the case of a medical emergency, a woman be given the opportunity to reflect for twenty-four hours on a decision which one way or the other will stay with her for the rest of her life. Same rationale with the informed consent section, which is the most important provi-

[289]

sion of the bill. We require a doctor to do what he should do in the first place: advise the patient of all the facts and all the options. And that simply isn't happening now. The average woman receives no counseling or consultation at all before having the abortion. Generally, the first time she sees the doctor is when she's on the operating table. Under our bill the doctor would have to advise his patient, in detail, of the procedure to be used and of the risk of *both* childbirth and abortion. Printed materials, listing the addresses of local adoption agencies, would be made available to her. These materials would also contain information on the characteristics of an unborn child, including photographs of an unborn child at two-week stages from conception to birth. And this, more than anything else, is the provision which terrifies the other side. It's the one aspect of the bill they cannot tolerate. They know they can't win if the facts are known. They know that their greatest enemy isn't Craig Harrington or Kevin Murray. It's the truth. Once the truth is known, their cause is doomed. And pictures tell the truth. That's why no pro-abortionist will ever take part in a debate when pictures of unborn children are shown. That's why Sheila Sendrow here, a seasoned lawyer, a veteran of many a courtroom battle, became almost hysterical this morning and refused to enter this room until a picture was removed. A picture just like this. [*Takes picture out of coat and displays it.*] Look at it, friends. It's the cover of *Newsweek* several months ago.

SENDROW: That's outrageous! I strenuously object! [*Unsuccessfully grabs for picture.*) The worst type of sensationalism!

MURRAY: Sensationalism, Sheila? Not at all. Just the truth. This picture which terrifies you so is of an eight-week unborn child. And I don't blame you for being terrified. Because when you look at a picture like this, one, truth becomes very evident. That's not a fetus; that's not a product of conception; that's not an undifferen-

[290]

tiated mass of tissue. That's a baby. And once you make that concession, it's all over. Game, set, and match. Because who the hell can kill a baby?

SENDROW: [*Rising*] If I ever attempted a cheap trick like that in a courtroom, I'd be held in contempt. And that's all you deserve, Murray, contempt. I refuse to remain here and dignify your disgusting exhibition. [*Exits.*]

ABRAMSON: [*Rising*] A very good lawyer just walked out in disgust. A very good doctor is doing likewise. [*Exits.*]

MURRAY: Well, Marc, here we are. I could always crack my knuckles to "Home on the Range" if it would help kill time.

BOWSER: Kevin, what gives you that rare and special ability to incense people?

MURRAY: Some people resent the truth, Marc. That's not my problem. It's theirs.

BOWSER: Well, we have a minute left. Since you're the only one remaining, would you like to wrap things up?

MURRAY: Love to. We've heard a lot of talk today, and it's up to each of us to decide what is truth and what is fiction. And while you're deciding, do a little bit of historical research. Because if you study history, you'll realize that the more things change, the more they remain the same. You'll find that the same arguments, word for word, used to defend abortion were used almost a hundred fifty years ago on a different issue: slavery. Phrases like "We don't know whether it's a human" or "Don't impose your personal beliefs on me." And the same Supreme Court that nine years ago ruled that it was permissible to kill unborn children ruled almost a hundred fifty years ago that not only was slavery legal, not only was it uncertain whether a slave was a human, but if you killed a slave, it wasn't murder but a property offense against the slaveowner. Fortunately, though, there was a group of people back then who understood one cen-

[291]

tral truth: that no matter how much society changes, there are certain values which can never change. There are certain things which are inherently wrong. And if something is inherently wrong, it's wrong not just for you and me but for all of us. Those people believed that owning any human was inherently wrong. They were called abolitionists, and they were vilified, labeled do-gooders, zealots, misguided moralists, much as the pro-lifers are criticized today. But they didn't give up, and in the end, even though it took the Civil War, the Emancipation Proclamation, and the Thirteenth and Fourteenth Amendments, they won. They won because they were right. And now today we have another group that believes, with the same conviction as the abolitionists, that the killing of unborn children is wrong. It's the honor of my life to be a member of that group, and there is absolutely no doubt in my mind that in the end we will prevail.

BOWSER: Well, time is up. It's been, to say the least, interesting. Only time will tell if Representative Murray is right. I thank him for his participation, as I do our audience and our other panelists, Dr. Morris Abramson and Ms. Sheila Sendrow, who made a somewhat early departure. Tomorrow's topic will be "Parents of Gays—Agony or Acceptance?" Until then this is Marc Bowser, wishing you a pleasant day.

CHAPTER
Fifteen

IT was a typical night for Kevin Murray. Peter's bath went smoothly until the shampoo was applied, setting off a cacophony of screams and Megan's advice, entirely unsolicited, that "Mommy doesn't do it that way."

"You believe in God, Murgatroyd?" Kevin asked his daughter. "Sure."

"Open your mouth once more, and you're gonna meet Him."

It was Megan's turn after Peter. She required a completely dark bedroom while Kevin told her a ghost story. Matthew came next, riding his father's shoulders into the bedroom, a wounded B-29 limping home to England after a bombing raid on Berlin. They almost made it, but halfway over the Channel, they were set upon by Messerschmitts and tumbled toward the icy water and into Matthew's bed.

The final item for the children's agenda was the standard argument with his two oldest sons to turn off the television and get to their homework. As usual, Sean obeyed, but it took a ten-minute battle with Kevin, Jr. Of the five, his eldest was unquestionably the biggest challenge. Sean, with his lack of self-assurance, his willingness to live in the shadow of his older brother, was worrisome, but young Kevin tried him to the breaking point. He always had something to say, always had to get in the last word.

A born leader and natural competitor, he carried with him a massive resentment of authority. Parents, teachers, coaches—none of them had the right to tell Kevin Murray, Jr., what to do.

In short, he was just like his father. Which was the most troubling point. Wasn't Sean better off? Wasn't it preferable just to be a nice person, content to receive what life gave you? Wasn't Sean, with all his shyness and insecurity, infinitely more fortunate than his brother? Through no fault of his own, young Kevin had inherited the curse of his father, doomed to a life of torment, of struggling with the demons, of always grasping for the unattainable. Yes, the potential for greatness was there, but for most men greatness is not a gift. It is a sentence.

How should Kevin handle his firstborn? There was a delicate line that had to be straddled. He had to teach his son that there were rules, there were authority figures that, like it or not, had to be obeyed. But he had to accomplish this without extinguishing the spark. Channeled properly, the rebelliousness could be a virtue. How many times had Kevin seen the result of unquestioning submission to authority? How many times did his House colleagues whore out on a crucial vote because of pressure from the caucus leadership? Wasn't that what Watergate had been all about? And My Lai? And Nuremberg? It took the rare and special person to stand in the face of authority and say, "Bullshit! This is wrong, and I won't do it!"

Young Kevin could be one of those people. Just by being in it, Sean would make the world a better place. His older brother could change it.

During the past year Kevin had hit upon an effective way to communicate with his eldest. Rather than endure a running debate, he would often write young Kevin a note. No interruptions, no point-counterpoint, and young Kevin had the advantage of reading it in privacy without feeling compelled to respond.

Take early September, just before the beginning of football season. The boy's dejection was obvious. He was starting on defense, but the coach had him running as second-string tailback. This was his eighth-grade year, the season he had pointed to, when everything would come together. And young Kevin felt in his gut that he was better than the number one tailback. Only every time he had a good play the coach seemed to be looking the other way. He was down, so depressed that he was even treating Sean with civility. His father, trying to comfort him, received only hostility for his efforts. So he wrote a note, propping it on his son's pillow.

Dear Kevin,

I know what you're going through, how frustrated you feel over not starting on offense. And I know how important it is to you. I won't try to b.s. you and tell you that it's just a game, because I remember how important it was to me when I was in grade school. (St. Laurence—powerhouse of the suburbs, not some faggot school like Nativity.)

The important thing is that you've hung in there. You could've quit, you could've taken an I-don't-care attitude, but you didn't—and I'm really proud of you. Proud to have you as my son.

I'm not certain what's going to happen, but if you keep hanging tough, I have the feeling things will work out.

Let me tell you a little story. It's about a quarterback. Pretty good college ballplayer, good enough to get drafted by the pros. But when he got to the NFL, all he did was ride the bench, watching the veteran George Shaw run the team. It was tearing him up, particularly because he knew he could do the job. But he hung in there, and one day Shaw got hurt, so the bench warmer went in. And he never came out. His name was Johnny Unitas.

Hang in there, pal.

Love,
Dad

P.S. This letter will confirm something you've already suspected. As long as I'm alive, the cliché will never die.

Karen was in the attic, wrapping Christmas presents.

"The kitchen's done, and the kids are in bed, hon. I'm going out for a while."

"Where?"

"No place special. Just to be alone."

Karen nodded. Normally she would have asked him to help. Eighteen days till Christmas and still so much to be done. But not tonight.

He got in the car and, without thinking about it, headed for the only conceivable destination: home, back to his roots.

He was nervous, even though logic told him that he was ready. He had spent the entire day in Harrisburg with Craig Harrington, reviewing every amendment that would be thrown at them. They had prepared a defense for each: concise, logical, buttressed by facts. There would be no surprises, nothing that they couldn't handle.

Yet the fear persisted. The stakes were so high. What if they had missed something? What if they had miscounted the votes? What if it all came crashing down, destroying the pro-life movement in Pennsylvania?

He turned off the pike onto Pennock, then to Parkview. *His* street.

It was cold, well below freezing, and no one was out. Better that way. He loved the old neighbors—they had been part of his youth—but tonight he didn't want the necessity of explaining why he was there.

He parked and walked to the front of the house. *His* house. The only home he had known for the first twenty-four years of his life. The light was on in the living room. Maybe someone was in there lying on the floor, watching television, just the way he and Brendan and Melissa used to do. There had been no den, no playroom. This was Upper Darby, blue-collar, middle-class Upper Darby, where a living room was for just that. It and the kitchen, where they ate all their meals except Sunday and holiday dinners, had been the focal points of their lives. Maureen sitting in the easy chair, darning socks. The Sarge lying on the sofa, falling asleep but, when challenged, claiming that he had just been resting his eyes.

There were no Christmas lights this year. They had always gone up on the first Saturday of December, framing the front window and the door, which also would feature white shoe polish snowflakes and a wreath, made by Maureen from the backyard yew tree. In later years the Sarge had strung the dogwood tree with the miniature lights, and always there had been the Nativity scene on the porch. Handmade, three feet high, with fresh straw for the Baby's manger.

So many memories. Maureen making tollhouse cookies and lining the mantel and stairway with holly. The Bing Crosby Christmas album that seemed to play continuously. Going to Sixty-ninth Street with the Sarge to pick out his mother's presents.

The tree never went up until Christmas Eve and, when they

[296]

were little, not until they had gone to bed. Then his parents would go nonstop. Trimming the tree, placing the presents in the piles (Kevin's was closest to the tree, right beside the easy chair), assembling the toys, and setting up the trains. Sleep was out of the question. They would finish in just enough time to wake the children for the five o'clock high mass.

"Did he come yet?" Kevin would ask.

"Yes, sweetheart. Santa came, and he left you lots of toys," Maureen would answer. "But first we have to get ready for mass."

Given the choice, Kevin would have rather gone straight for the presents, but he knew that was impossible. First things first. It was the birthday of the Baby Jesus. When he was ready, he had to stand at the top of the steps. Then, one at a time with a hand over their eyes, Brendan, Melissa, and he were led down, to the living room and onto the front porch. He could have peeked, of course, but he never did. That would have spoiled it.

It was still dark as they waited for Maureen and the Sarge on the open porch, and there always seemed to be something electric about the air. It crackled, as if it, too, were impatient to celebrate Christmas. Even now, after all these years, whenever Kevin was up before dawn in the winter, he thought of Christmas on Parkview Road.

Once inside church, Kevin was usually able to take his mind from what was waiting for him in the living room. There was so much to see. The altar, awash with evergreens and poinsettias, and off to the side, the Nativity scene. Huge, three times the size of the one on the porch. The procession of altar boys, first the cross bearer and the acolytes, then the thurifers gently swinging the incense pots that filled the church with an ethereal aroma, then all the others, a sea of white surplices and cassocks, processing up the center aisle. And the choir in the loft, the best in the suburbs, bringing tears to the eyes of the parishioners with their hymns of Christmas. In Latin, the way they were meant to be sung. Angels once again descending upon the shepherds to bring the glad tidings of the birth of Jesus.

Magic. Pure magic. The type that could be produced only by the Roman Catholic Church.

Then home again and another wait on the porch as his parents turned on all the lights and lit the candles. Only then were they permitted to enter and run to their piles.

[297]

God, he thought, Maureen and the Sarge really did it nice. Little touches that meant so much. Like the year that Brendan got his bike. They had finished going through the presents, and Brendan's pile was noticeably smaller than the others. He didn't say anything, though, didn't act as if he'd even noticed. Had it been Kevin, he would have undoubtedly bitched, but not Brendan. Maybe it was that he had too much class. Or love. Or maybe he really just didn't care. He was like that. Then the Sarge brought out the string, and Brendan had to follow it. Through the living room, around the dining room table, into the kitchen, and down the stairs to the cellar. And there, with a huge bow attached, was a shiny new Schwinn.

Kevin sighed. He was oblivious of his surroundings, unaware that a passerby might find it strange that he just stood there, staring at the house. He walked to the side and looked up at his bedroom. His and Brendan's. Where they had played basketball with a rolled-up pair of socks. They were brutal contests, one trying to score by throwing the socks into the hole made by the chair pressed against the corner, the other doing his damnedest to stop him. One point was deducted if an errant shot knocked one of the hand-carved ducks off the wall, two points if the duck was broken. Freckles invariably refereed, barking and snapping at their heels.

Kevin's bed had been closest to the window, protected by his big brother from anything that might come through the door. He loved the view out back, the yard, then the P&W tracks, then the woods of the golf course. Particularly in the fall, when, as Maureen always said, God took out his paintbrush.

Sometimes it seemed that he had never lived there, that he could remember nothing from his childhood. Yet at other times, it all was so vivid. Lying in bed, listening to the P&W clack by on its run between Sixty-ninth Street and Norristown. Playing stickball in the common driveway (Mrs. Clark never seemed to mind when they rooted in her ivy for the cut-up pieces of rubber hose they used. There still had to be dozens in there, hidden forever). Building the forts in the back, each able to withstand the Indians or the Germans or, later, the Koreans and the Chinese.

He wanted to go in, to walk up the steps and into the house. Only it wasn't his house anymore and never would be again.

It had been almost a year since Maureen had moved to the apartment, and still, he couldn't accept it. The house was too big, she had said, and there were too many memories. She had thanked him for his offer to move in with them—an offer in which Karen, aware of the problems it might cause, had nonetheless sincerely joined—but had firmly rejected it. She wanted to be on her own, to be dependent on no one.

He turned away, walking up the alley between Oakley and Pennock, the alley he and Brendan had gone down so many times. Wagons in the summer, sleds in the winter. Then onto Lennox, pausing at Johnny's. Only it wasn't Johnny's anymore. A Vietnamese woman had opened a tailor shop. But looking through the darkened windows, he could still visualize every detail of the way it had been.

When he was young, the supermarkets were still a thing of the future. People shopped at the corner stores, and Johnny's was theirs. Twice a day, coming home for lunch and after school, Kevin would stop in to see if his mother had ordered anything. If she had, it would be bagged, waiting for him. He never paid, of course. It was put on a tab, and Maureen would settle up at the end of the month.

It was more than a store. It was *the* local gathering place. Adults were always there, sitting around, drinking sodas, exchanging gossip. And it was a magnet for the children, too, as they pondered which treasure to invest their dimes on.

The front display window was for the kids: yo-yos (an eternal clash between Duncan and Cheerie), Yankee and Confederate hats (there was always a time of year, usually lasting four or five weeks, when, by some unspoken edict, they appeared, everyone in the schoolyard wearing one), cap and water pistols, punks, rubber balls, and jacks. Then there was the candy rack. Buckets of penny candy and an endless variety of candy bars (all a nickel except Klien's, which went for three cents). Beside the counter was a huge pickle barrel, tongs tied to the handle. The meat counter, the produce bin, and, over on the left, in a little cubicle, the cereal. (When you wanted one from the top shelf, Johnny had to get it down with a giant tweezer on the end of a wooden handle.)

Johnny and Annie lived in the back, and despite their fights, which they never attempted to conceal from the customers, they were devoted to each other. And they did okay. Well enough to set up their only son in his dentist office, where Brendan Murray was his first patient.

[299]

Kevin continued up Lennox to Carol, past the house where his first den mother had lived. His first meeting had been traumatic. He had announced that he would walk home. It was only three blocks, he was eight years old, and besides, all the other kids did. Only it was October and dark, and the kids all told him there were bats and he looked up and saw something flying and it had to be a bat.

He ran, lungs bursting, all the way, into the house and Maureen's arms.

"It's okay, Kevin. You're home. Listen to your heart. Do you know what it's saying?"

Kevin shook his head.

"It's saying, 'I love you, Mommy. I need you, Mommy.' "

He turned up the alley by the field. The "rockpile" where the St. Laurence Tigers had done battle. Was anything more exciting to a boy than football in the fall? The sound of cleats pounding the turf, the smell of chewing gum, the delightful feeling of well-earned exhaustion when you had finished a scrimmage?

Across St. Laurence Road to the school. He walked past the rectory to the front schoolyard which had been for the girls and the first- and second-grade boys. It was also where they had the May processions, girls in white dresses, boys in best suits, singing "Bring flowers of the rarest" in honor of Mary. The length of the school building separated the yards, so that the girls and the youngest boys were not forced to witness the mayhem that occurred on the other side. Yet no matter what violence was occurring, everyone froze when the first bell rang. With the second bell they would walk to their line, forming up in twos. Only the papes.

There was a light on in the school basement, so he tried the door to the vestibule. It was open. To the right was the church; to the left, the school. In the center was the statue of St. Laurence, who, while being martyred on a gridiron, was reported to have said, "You can turn me over now. I'm done on this side." That had always struck Kevin as being a tremendous line, given under considerable pressure.

He walked into the school, to the first room on the right, where it had all began. He had been terrified that first day, terrified of those big ladies in black and white. All he wanted to do was stay home with his mother, but they wouldn't let him. So he had run away from school. Not once, but five times. After the fourth escape the nun had placed him in the middle seat of the middle row, figuring she could nail him before he made it to the door. But Kevin, displaying ingenuity at even an early age, had crawled down the aisle and made a clean getaway.

Maureen and the nun had been concerned, a concern that was short-lived. Within a month he had become leader of the class gang, a position he held for all eight years. He was brilliant in his studies and public enemy number one in his conduct. That was perfectly consistent for Kevin Murray: always the extreme, nothing in moderation.

He drew upon the old days when he spoke to Catholic groups. "One of the things I enjoy most are the letters I receive from my old nuns, praising me for my stand on abortion and aid to non-public schools. But you have to remember that these are the same nuns who called me a 'bold piece,' a 'brazen article,' and the 'instigator of all bad things,' predicting a life of crime for me. Actually they weren't too far wrong. I ended up in the Pennsylvania legislature."

He squeezed into one of the desks. Every day at the beginning of class they would stand for prayers and the pledge of allegiance. Then they would bow to the nun. "Good morning, Sister. God bless you, Sister," and to each other, "Good morning, classmate. God bless you, classmate." And whenever another nun, or any adult for that matter, would come into the room, they would leap to their feet and give that greeting.

Yeah, that was what it was all about. Now it was fashionable for people his age to say how they had been warped by Catholic education, but that was pure bullshit. Cocktail party bullshit. It was here that he had been given his values, and he had no apologies. He bought it all. The Roman Catholic Church, its teachings, its disciplines—all of it. Sure he might criticize now and then, but he was on board for the duration. He had never, not even in college to be fashionable, gone through a period of doubt, of questioning. He had always been content to have the faith of a child, accepting without question the sacred mysteries. As always with his nature, there was more than a touch of logic, of pragmatism. The way he saw it, there were too many earthly issues to grapple with to have time to worry about the big ones, over which he had no control.

Sure, the nuns had been tough. Brutal, in fact. They were the

IHMs. The Green Bay Packers of the sisterhood. But they were also the finest teaching order in the world. He wished to God that his kids were getting the same teaching.

He was conscious of someone in the doorway. Monsignor Hennessy, his old pastor, now pastor emeritus. He had come to St. Laurence in 1956, and Kevin had served his first mass. He was close to eighty now, but he still had the twinkle.

"One of the sodality ladies said that someone was in the classroom. I figured it might be a troublemaker, and I was right."

Kevin rose. "Hello, Monsignor, how are you?"

"Fine, Kevin. I'd ask what you're doing here, but I think I know. Tomorrow, huh?"

Kevin nodded. "Yeah." He hesitated. "I'm scared, Monsignor."

"Of course you are. That's only natural."

"I don't know. It's just that I feel—so alone. I'll be up at that podium, and no matter how many others are with me, I'll be alone."

"You're wrong there, Kevin. You'll never be alone. There are so many of us who are with you, who are so proud of what you stand for. We must have done something very right at St. Laurence to produce a Kevin Murray."

Kevin knelt. "Monsignor—Father, could I have your blessing?"

"Certainly, my son." He made the sign of the cross in the air. "May the blessing of Almighty God, Father, Son, and Holy Spirit, descend upon you and remain with you forever. Go in peace, Kevin, and give them hell tomorrow."

As he drove home, he felt much better. It had been exactly what he had needed. He was ready now. For sure.

Karen might never understand. She might always consider him a hopeless romantic, living in the past. But to Kevin, it was very basic: You have to know where you come from before you know where you're going.

CHAPTER

Sixteen

KEVIN's office resembled a Manhattan subway at rush hour, legislators, pro-life leaders, priests, ministers, and nuns crammed together, spilling into the hallway. The gathering wasn't really necessary, at least not for strategic reasons. If they weren't ready by now, they never would be. But it had seemed only natural to assemble for these last few minutes, the human desire to be with others when something important was about to happen. And where else but in the office of their leader?

For the most part they had laughed, Kevin trying to keep them and himself loose. He hurled a few insults at Craig Harrington, did his impersonation of Sheila Sendrow bolting the debate, and cracked the few jokes he knew that were clean enough for the audience. He capped it off by leading a rendition of "V for Villanova," followed by the Notre Dame "Victory March."

Not a bad performance, even though his mind was elsewhere. He still couldn't believe that it was finally here, that the months of waiting were over. Sometimes it had seemed so distant, almost unreachable, like Christmas to a six-year-old in October: the interminable time required for drafting the bill; the defeat in committee; then the frustrating wait for a vehicle to appear on the calendar. During that time hardly a night went by that Kevin hadn't dreamed about it. Even when he was completely removed, like when he was playing with the kids, his mind would drift back to it and his stomach would knot.

Now, when they were about to go into battle, it seemed to

Kevin that there should be more. When John Wayne and his troops hit the beach, there was always music, the kind that made you want to jump up and enlist or buy bonds. But this was reality, not a movie. There was no fleet, no music. Just Kevin, alone in a crowd, accompanied by his fears.

He looked at the clock and sighed. "Well, sports fans, I guess this is it."

Heads were bowed as one of the ministers led the prayer. The fundamentalist Protestants were growing stronger every day. Down-the-line pro-life, and unlike the Catholics, they felt no hesitation to lay it on the line, no inferiority complexes to retard the drive. They lobbied straight from the pulpit, naming names, demanding action from their flocks. But, God bless them, they were incredibly long-winded when it came to prayer. Kevin would have settled for a quick Hail Mary.

Finally it was over, and they all looked to Kevin for a final word. Once again, he was back at St. Laurence, right before the kickoff, huddled around the coach.

"Our Lady of Victory," he said.

"Pray for us," they responded.

He rubbed his hands together and headed for the door. "Okay, gang, let's go kick some ass."

As he neared the entrance to the House, he was met by Brian O'Connell, a Democrat and one of his own.

"Good luck, old buddy," O'Connell said. *"Et introibo ad altare Dei."*

Kevin grinned. *"Ad Deum qui laetificat, juvem tutem meum."*

The chamber exploded when he entered. Boos and cheers. Hard to tell which were louder. He had never seen the chamber so packed, even on swearing-in day. To accommodate the overflow, temporary seats had been set up along the side aisles and in the rear. Over in the press box reporters fought for space, the Harrisburg regulars jostling with the national media people who were on hand for the show.

Kevin looked up to the gallery. An invisible but very real line separated the opponents. He smiled. It was fitting that the pro-lifers were on the right. Philadelphia. Scranton. Altoona. Pittsburgh. They all were there. And on the extreme right, equally fitting, was Henry Lassiter with a few members of his Army of

Life. The hardest of the hard core, they were not supporting Kevin's bill. Some were actually opposing it. It didn't go far enough. Nothing short of total victory was acceptable, regardless of what the court said.

Kevin's eyes turned to the left, to the pro-abortion forces. He felt the stares of hatred upon him. All except one. Seated beside Sheila Sendrow, Bridget Kelly waved to him. Kevin waved back, then scanned the rest of the gallery. Right in the middle of the pro-abortion troops was a woman wearing a golden cross. Were things getting so bad that a nun would publicly join up with the enemy?

He turned his attention back to the floor and saw Sean taking a cup of coffee to one of the members. Because of the holy day, there was no school, and Sean was serving as a page. It was a chance to earn a few bucks in tips and, most of all, to be with his dad.

Kevin walked to the podium and set up camp, placing his files on it, then looking around. Ed Harvey was seated a few feet away with a portable locker full of backup materials. Beside him was Phil Marlowe, attorney for the Pennsylvania Catholic Conference and, like Harvey, a brilliant legal talent. In the row behind them was Dr. Dennis Doyle, a gynecologist and president of the Pro-Life Physicians Guild.

Kevin gave them the thumbs-up and turned back to the rostrum. He doffed his jacket, rolled up his sleeves, placed two packs of Winston on the podium, then turned to Harrington. "Say anything about my smoking today, and I'll kick you right in the nuts."

"No problem, cowboy. I've bestowed a dispensation on you for the entire day."

"I'm touched. Ready?"

"Yep."

Kevin nodded to the Speaker, who banged the gavel. "The chair calls up Senate Bill Seven-four-two and recognizes the gentleman from Delaware, Mr. Murray, who offers the following amendment. Amendment A-four-two-six-seven."

Several dozen cameramen clustered around, taking shots, which was fine with Kevin. He never tired of seeing his picture in the paper or his name in the headlines. "Thank you, Mr.

[305]

Speaker," he said. "Before discussing the merits of this amendment, I have a sneaking suspicion that there will be several procedural challenges. I yield the floor for that purpose."

The challenges, to both the constitutionality and the germaneness of the amendment, presented the greatest danger. It was here that members who lacked the courage to vote pro-abortion straight up could jump ship, claiming that they supported the concept of the amendment but not its form.

Brad Kauffman led the attack from the other side. A skilled lawyer, he was a board member of Planned Parenthood and the ACLU. When he had concluded, Kevin provided a point-by-point rebuttal, followed by almost twenty speeches on both sides. The order of pro-life debate was dictated by Kevin. Well in advance he had designated twelve legislators, half of them females, to help him carry the banner. On a nod from Kevin, or a message carried by Harrington, one of them would rise to be recognized. Kevin had thoroughly prepped them. But what they said didn't matter very much. The important thing was to keep it from becoming the Kevin Murray Show, to display a broad base of support, particularly from the women.

Constitutionality was handled in just less than an hour, the challenge being rejected 112–87. Germaneness took fifteen minutes and went down 116–83. Not a blowout, but comfortable enough. It would get better from here on in.

The Speaker banged the gavel. "It's eleven forty-five. If we keep going, I get excommunicated, so the chair will now declare a recess until one-thirty."

The cathedral, two blocks from the Capitol, was packed. It was a holy day of obligation, and most of the faithful still marched to the cadence of the Church. The bishop said the mass, praying for the passage of the abortion bill. Yet when the collection was taken, there was Pete Waters, state rep from Dauphin County, pillar of the Church and a consistent pro-abortion vote, taking up the collection. *God deliver us from our friends,* Kevin thought. *We can take care of our enemies.*

The afternoon session began with another procedural motion, this time Kevin moving to suspend the rules. House rules prohibited amendments to an amendment. Because of this, Kevin could have forced the issue, a straight yes or no vote on the entire amendment. Unquestionably he would have won. The votes were there. They would have boxed the House membership in through parliamentary tactics, effectively stifling debate. The whole show could be over in a few hours.

It was tempting, but Kevin rejected it. They had to be above that, had to be completely open. The passage of the bill was incredibly important, but only one battle in a protracted war. You always had to be looking to your next battle, and the next four or five steps down the road. If they railroaded the amendment through, they would have created a side issue. The media, looking for just such an opening, would scream. Even more critical would be the effect on the members. They already resented being forced to vote on the issue. A no-amendment power play would make them seethe. Most would go along, but sometime in the future, when they were desperately needed, they might exact their vengeance. Better to play it straight.

It was for these reasons that Kevin moved, without opposition, to suspend the rules to permit amendments. Forty-seven such amendments had already been prepared, each seeking to weaken the bill. Most were subtle, little sniping movements rather than a frontal assault, requiring a minor to receive the consent of only one parent before having an abortion; including the health as well as the life of the mother as an exception to the prohibition against state funding; reducing the waiting period from twenty-four hours to four; permitting counselors as well as physicians to obtain the woman's informed consent.

It took almost five hours to defeat the first ten amendments, each by a comfortable margin, during which time a pattern developed. The maker of each amendment would take the floor to explain it. Kevin was next, listing four or five reasons why it should be defeated, followed by general debate. During this period Kevin would alternate between responding to interrogations from opposing members and huddling with his team to plot strategy on the next amendment.

The interrogations were never for the purpose of eliciting information. The questions were offensive weapons, designed to embarrass, to obscure, to weaken the position of the bill's sponsors. Kevin made it a point, whenever the question pemitted, to begin each answer with a simple "yes," "no" or "I don't know," followed by his explanation. They had almost lost the Medicaid funding bill two years before, when Harrington refused to give

[307]

straightforward answers. When you waffled on an answer, even your own people began to think that you were hiding something. There would be no repeat of that mistake. Harrington had reluctantly agreed to let Kevin handle all the interrogations.

When everyone had been recognized, some twice (House rules prohibited a member from speaking more than twice on any one amendment or bill), Kevin would give a brief wrap-up, and a vote would be taken.

With ten convincing votes under their belts, the pro-lifers were on a roll. The other side had hoped for at least one or two minor victories. Now they were demoralized, their appetite for battle gone. All but Kauffman. Kevin had to give him credit. He might disagree with him, but the son of a bitch had balls. No way was he going to retreat. Quite the opposite. He decided to shoot the whole wad. The ripper amendment, the one that gutted virtually the entire bill. If it passed, there would be no abortion control act.

Kevin's wrap-up speech was longer this time. Sensing a possible knockout, he decided to pull out all the stops. He drew the comparison with the seals, the porpoises, and the snail darter; he talked about truth being the enemy of the pro-abortion movement; he even brought in the similarities to the slavery issue. When he finished, the gallery and a good portion of the House membership erupted in applause, requiring the Speaker to bang the gavel repeatedly before taking the vote. This time it *was* a blowout: 147–52. Had they been able to continue for just an hour, it would have been all over. It was an hour they didn't have. There was an eight o'clock Democratic fund-raiser in Philadelphia, and by custom and courtesy, the Speaker was obliged to adjourn at six.

Tomorrow would just be a mop-up, Kevin tried to tell himself. The pro-lifers surrounded him in the aisle, ecstatic over certain victory. Reporters scurried to file their stories, all proclaiming the inevitable passage of the bill. The jury was in; the evidence, tangible. Thirteen challenges had been successfully repelled, the victory margin increasing with each vote.

But in his gut Kevin knew better. For reasons beyond his control, the cardinal sin of a warrior had been committed. When you had your opponent down, you buried him. Instead, a dangerous enemy, after taking a brutal beating, had been let off the hook. He had been given a second life, which made him even more dangerous. The other side would be up all night, plotting strategy and drafting new amendments. Could it come up with anything new, something that would light the spark to blow the bill apart? Probably not, but you never knew. The thought tortured Kevin as he tried to sleep on the train. How often it was that history turned upon an unrelated whim, a quirk of fate. Lincoln deciding to attend the theater. Bobby Kennedy taking the back way out of the hotel, through the kitchen. The Japanese scout plane, the one that would have spotted the American fleet at Midway, developing engine trouble. The Immaculate Reception of Franco Harris. Kevin had seen it in his own life. Like in the DA's office, when three city officials almost escaped indictment because the duplicating machine broke. The grand jury term was about to expire, and without copies of the presentment it was powerless to act. A year of work, and the fate of three human beings rested upon the proficiency of the repairman.

It had been the same with the Medicaid funding bill in 1980. Four days before the House adjourned *sine die,* the voting board malfunctioned. The experts from California were summoned, but the West Coast was socked in by fog. They were bussed to Denver, then flown by charter jet, which developed engine trouble and was forced to land in Pittsburgh, where a state police car raced them to the capital. There were eight hours left in the term when the board was finally ready. Just enough time.

Now it was a Democratic dinner, scheduled routinely with no thought that it might directly affect the outcome of the most controversial bill in the history of Pennsylvania.

They began the following morning at ten, and nothing seemed to have changed. New amendments had been drafted, but by the lunch break the first twelve had been turned back easily. The afternoon pace was considerably slower. Black legislators began to drag out the debate, causing a marked increase in the hostility level of the chamber.

Joe Criswell stormed down the aisle. "What the fuck are we gonna do about those cocksuckers?" he bellowed. "This is fuckin' ridiculous!"

"Am I to infer that you are not wholly satisfied with the manner in which our black brethren are proceeding to articulate their positions?" Harrington asked.

"Fuck you, Harrington! I don't need your shit." He turned to Kevin. "We've gotta do something, Kevin."

"Not much we can do, Joe."

"Move to limit debate to three minutes a speech."

"Come on, Joe. You know that isn't the answer. We'd spend more time debating the motion than if we let the bastards talk."

"Yeah, I guess you're right." He started to walk away, then turned back. "You know, if it wasn't for Lincoln, we'd be bidding on those bastards instead of listening to them."

It was shortly after eight when the Speaker banged the gavel. "Any of you who checked out of your hotels today might want to reconsider. We still have a number of amendments to take up, and it is the intention of the chair to remain in session until we have disposed of the bill one way or the other. There will be no dinner break. Sandwiches and soda are being brought to the floor. To make you even happier, I've been told that it's snowing in the western part of the state. How long we remain here depends entirely on your performance."

The announcement produced a chain of boos. Anger was spilling over into the aisles, and Kevin sensed danger. The members were looking for someone to blame, and that someone was Kevin. Sure, the blacks had prolonged the agony, but if it hadn't been for Murray and his goddamn crusading, they wouldn't be there in the first place. He and that pompous asshole Harrington.

But despite the bitterness, the votes were holding, and by midnight it looked as if they might be home. Then it came.

"Take a look at this," Harrington said. "I think we're in trouble."

It was a new amendment, one they hadn't seen, and it was definitely trouble, the spark that might blow them away: "The provisions of this act shall not take effect unless approved by the electorate at the next general election following its passage."

"Jesus," Kevin whispered after reading it. "Who dreamed this up?"

"Bender," answered Harrington.

"Bender! What the fuck's going on? He's one of ours, for chrissake. He's a goddamn cosponsor of the bill!"

"What can I say, Kevin? Why don't we ask one of the other guys from Erie?"

"Hell no. We'll ask Bender. Watch the mike for a minute."

Kevin left the podium and walked to the rear of the chamber. Chad Bender was sipping a cup of coffee. When he saw Kevin, his face reddened.

"Out of curiosity, Chad, would you mind telling me what the fuck is going on?"

"I'm sorry, Kevin. I had to."

"What do you mean, you had to?" How many times had he heard that phrase, the standard cop-out when a member whored out on a vote?

"I'm pro-life, Kevin, you know that. But I'm getting too much heat. Planned Parenthood has been hounding me, which I can survive, but now the Protestant churches are attacking me, too. I had to do something, Kevin."

"Don't you realize your amendment can destroy us, undo everything we've worked for?"

"I'm sorry, Kevin, honest to Christ, I am. But I won by only eight hundred votes last time. I can't take the chance."

Kevin looked at him. Christ, how he hated gutlessness. He wanted to take his fist and smash it into the coward's face. Instead, he smiled. "You know, Chad," he finally said, "you've got all the instincts of a dog except loyalty."

He walked back to the podium, making it a point to stop a few times to crack jokes with some of his colleagues. He couldn't show concern. That could cause a stampede. Like an airline stewardess during a storm, the eyes of the passengers fixed on her.

Cool at all times, not a worry in the world.

They began debate on the Bender amendment. Bender's speech had a compelling logic. "Look, I'm pro-life. I support the bill. I'm even a cosponsor. But I'm not infallible. All my amendment does is put the final decision in the hands of the people, where it belongs. That's called democracy, and I don't know how anyone can oppose that."

The perfect opportunity to back out. Support the bill, oppose all the attempts to weaken it, then vote for the Bender amendment. You could be pro-life, but with a sense of fair play.

Kevin did his best, but it wasn't enough. After almost an hour the amendment passed 107–92. Applause filled the gallery, the first time in two days the abortion forces had reason to cheer.

The tide had turned. If Kevin didn't move quickly, the whole thing could turn into a rout. He was surrounded at the podium, his troops bordering on panic, cameramen swept into a new frenzy of activity.

"Okay, sports fans, we've got work to do. We have to get our people back on board. Spell it the fuck out to them. The Bender amendment is an abortion vote, plain and simple. No dancing. They're either with us or against us. Feed any switches you get to Craig. He'll coordinate the vote count. But keep an ear to the debate. Sure as hell they're going to reconsider some of the amendments that went down. We've come a long way, gang. Let's not piss it away."

He signaled for Phil Marlowe. "Phil, get our people out of the gallery and onto the phones. They know what they have to do."

Kevin turned back to the podium as the first reconsideration motion was introduced. He was like a naval commander whose ship had just taken a hit, dividing his time between damage control and fending off the next attack.

Three more salvos landed. The amendment requiring the consent of only one parent for a minor's abortion passed. So did the amendment removing the private attorney general action. Then the requirement that a death certificate be issued for an aborted child was repealed.

He felt it starting to slip away, and for a minute he wanted to bail out. To flee the sneers coming from the other side, to run from the helplessness etched on the faces of his own. Right to the train station and home. Better yet, to Wyoming.

Instead, he sucked it in and went back to war. The next amendment was to remove the requirement for an independent doctor when an unborn child was viable and might survive the abortion. Kevin was recognized.

"Mr. Speaker, I'm aware that some of my colleagues have enjoyed the opportunity to thank me and the other sponsors of this bill personally in a manner which they deem appropriate. Fine. I accept that. But I can't believe that even though it's late, even though it's snowing in the West, even though the debate has been interminable, we're willing to throw away everything we've accomplished in the last two days. This is a good bill, a damn good bill, and I'm proud to be a sponsor.

"Our opponents say that they oppose abortion, that they want only freedom of choice, but take a look at this amendment. If it

[312]

passes, one of the most important provisions of the bill will be stripped. It doesn't deal with choice, with whether or not a woman should have an abortion. It deals with children who survive abortions, who are outside the mother and by anyone's standards are human beings. All we say is that you can't let that baby—that's right, my friends, *baby*—die. You can't place her in a bedpan or in a trash can or in a utility closet to die from malign neglect. Question: How the hell can any human being oppose that? We've had our fun, my friends; we've extracted our pound of flesh; now let's get back to the business of passing a damn good bill. And we can begin by rejecting this atrocious amendment."

The amendment went down, as did the next three. Kevin gave a sign of relief. Maybe the worst was over.

Meanwhile, the pro-life leaders were engaging in one of the most unusual lobbying campaigns ever witnessed in Harrisburg. Armed with copies of the roll-call vote of the Bender amendment, they commandeered the offices of pro-life legislators and began to call throughout the state: pastors; community leaders; key ward leaders—anyone with clout. In turn these individuals called back to Harrisburg, to the phones at the rear of the House chamber. Member after member was summoned from his seat to take a call, then another, then another.

Still listening to the debate, Kevin turned to Harrington. "How we doing?"

"We're getting there, cowboy. The calls are working. Right now I have us up by two."

"Too close. Let me know when we're up by five."

"Right. Hey, have you eaten anything?"

"No. I'm not hungry."

"You have to eat something. Try this."

"Thanks." Kevin took the candy bar, biting off the end just as the Speaker recognized him.

"Thank you, Mr. Speaker," he said. He grimaced, spitting out the candy and turning back to Harrington. "What the hell is this? It tastes like shit!"

Before Harrington could respond, the floor erupted with laughter.

Trying to control himself, the Speaker hit the gavel. "The chair would suggest to the gentleman from Delaware that should he

[313]

wish to continue his assessment of Representative Harrington's taste in food—an assessment with which the chair wholeheartedly agrees—he first cut off his microphone."

It hadn't been intended, but it had helped. The mood of the chamber lightened.

Seeing its momentum fade, the other side adopted a new strategy. It withdrew all reconsideration motions and called for an immediate vote on the bill, which still contained the Bender amendment.

"No choice," Kevin said to Harrington. "We have to go for it now." Objecting to a vote on final passage, he moved to reconsider the Bender amendment. There was a hush as Kevin was recognized. Everyone knew that this was the big one.

"Mr. Speaker, I urge my colleagues to reject the Bender amendment for a number of reasons. First, regardless of your position on abortion or this bill, the Bender amendment sets a dangerous precedent. In his speech Mr. Bender cited democracy, but he seems to be unaware of how a democratic system works and how it was always intended to work. The people elect their representatives, charging *them* with the responsibility for making policy decisions. That's our job! To be placed squarely on the dime and take a stand. Not to duck, not to run, not to dump it back to the people who elected us. To do so would be to betray their trust. And if we pass this amendment, where do we stop? Do we take a referendum before we ever vote a tax increase, before we ever increase welfare benefits, before we ever vote ourselves a raise? Are we even necessary anymore? Why not take an electronic poll on every issue and plug it into the vote board?

"And does approval by any electorate automatically make an issue right? If Hitler had taken a poll of the German people before he began his program of systematic slaughter, would an affirmative vote have made the Holocaust less barbaric? The vast majority of southerners supported slavery. Did that make it right?

"Let's not kid ourselves. This is *our* decision, *our* responsibility to decide how we feel about the slaughter of innocent, unborn children.

"Do I want this bill to pass? Absolutely. More than I've wanted anything in my life. Because there's no doubt in my mind that it's the right thing to do.

[314]

"You know, Mark Twain once said that when he was eighteen, his parents didn't know anything, but when he was twenty-one, he was amazed at how much they had learned in the last three years. So true. I can remember something my father, my best friend, said to me when I was little. He said that the only person you have to please in this world is the one you see in the mirror every morning. And if you can't look at that face, then no matter what else you've accomplished, no matter what anyone else thinks of you, you're a failure. My good friends, let's look at ourselves tomorrow and smile. Please, reject the Bender amendment and then pass the bill."

He was exhausted. He had shot it all. Now all he could do was wait. But his speech had an unforeseen effect. Legislators who had always voted pro-life but had never spoken were taking the floor. Like Gavin Caufield, a Democrat from Scranton. A big, beefy guy, he was probably the most well-liked member of the House. He always had a joke or a new impersonation. This time he didn't even smile. "Mr. Speaker, I'm good at cracking jokes, but I'm not much of a speaker, so I hardly ever take the mike. But by God, I refuse to stay in my seat and make Kevin Murray, who has more guts than anyone I have ever seen, do all the work. I'm pro-life. I'm against abortion. It's murder. Pure and simple. And I don't give a good goddamn what it does to my political future. If it costs me my election, that's okay, because you gotta stand for something. The Bender admendment stinks. Let's bury it!"

Shortly before three the Speaker called for the vote, and Kevin Murray said two silent prayers. One to his father: *I need you, Sarge, more than ever.* And one to the Mother of God: *Please, Mary, not now. Not when we've come this far.*

The Bender amendment failed, 94–105.

"We've got them running," Harrington said. "It's critical that we move to reconsider the amendments we lost."

"No fuckin' way," Kevin answered. "We're getting out while we can."

"I disagree!"

"Tough shit! We move to reconsider anything now, they lynch us. It's still the best bill in the country."

He signaled the Speaker, twirling his finger in the air to roll the vote on final passage. Callaghan took the cue, called for the vote, and locked the board within thirty seconds. It was 146–53. The abortion control bill was halfway down the road.

Circled by well-wishers and the media, Kevin lit a Winston, inhaling the first drag deeply. Trying to appear casual, he grasped the rostrum for support. The man who had just pushed through the nation's toughest abortion bill now found it an effort just to stand. With the exception of the short lunch break, he had been at the podium for seventeen hours. He hadn't eaten in fourteen. His clothes were wrinkled beyond redemption, the fingers were nicotine-stained, and he was in desperate need of a shave. Standing beside him, Craig Harrington looked precisely as he had when the day began.

After the interviews had concluded, Kevin would seek the sanctuary of his office, where he could come apart privately. Then he would compose himself and look for a ride home. Only this time it would be different. There would be no pickup truck. And no Sarge.

CHAPTER

Seventeen

GROSSE Pointe Park glistened under four inches of fresh snow, insuring a perfect Christmas for Vince.

Just perfect. The house bustled with activity, the happy voices of the children mingling with those of the women as they prepared the traditional Christmas Eve dinner. It would be a marathon affair, twelve courses, with the little ones being permitted to leave the table after finishing each course. By custom, one adult would accompany them, each time reading them a Christmas story before the fire, then permitting them each to open one present, not one of the major gifts but a little bauble selected just for the occasion, the kind which usually delights children more than the expensive items do. Squealing with pleasure, they would run back to the dining room to show off their new treasures.

After the meal there would be songs, with Lena at the piano. It was an edict of Don Giuseppe, now eighty-six and still in moderately good health, that everyone join in, and songbooks were handed out to accomplish this.

Standing there with the tree and the fire and the holly, sharing the joy and love of Christmas with his family, Vince would be at peace. This was what it was all about. Precisely. It was what he'd never had as a child and what he needed now as much as air to breathe or bread to eat. It was what had guided all his decisions, why he had chosen the path he was following.

It wasn't for money or even power. It was to belong, to become part of something, to build a tradition that could be passed from generation to generation. And no single event crystallized this concept as did Christmas with his own.

It was right to be in Michigan, and so long as Don Giuseppe lived, they would continue to do so. But when the old man was gone and Vince's children were older, it would be time to begin a new tradition and celebrate Christmas at home. Later there would be marriages and grandchildren, and Vince would preside over the gathering of *his famiglia.*

Concetta came running in. "Daddy, can you help us build a snowman, can you, please?"

"What's in it for me, woman?"

"A kiss." She reached over and hugged him.

"Sold," Vince said. "Come on."

They had finished the snowman and were sitting in the kitchen, sipping hot chocolate, when Michael and Anthony, who had gone to the playground, came in. Without a word Michael stormed through the kitchen, slammed the door, and stomped upstairs.

"What's with him?" Vince asked his second eldest.

"He was in a fight," Anthony said. "And lost."

"You seem happy, Anthony."

"He had it coming, Dad. He started it. He always starts fights."

"What did you do?"

"Nothing. I just watched."

"I see. Get your brother and go up to my room. I'll be right there."

When he entered, the boys stood, Anthony shifting uneasily, eyes to the floor, Michael defiant as ever, staring straight into Vince's eyes.

Without a word Vince slapped each boy across the face, just once, with an open hand but with enough force to make it sting.

"Do you know what that was for?" he asked. "Michael?"

"For fighting, I guess."

"No, not for fighting. For starting a fight. That's never the answer, Michael. Stop looking for trouble. There's enough trouble in life without asking for more. And if you have to fight, if it's absolutely necessary, make goddamn sure you don't lose."

He turned to Anthony. "Your turn. Why did I hit you?"

"I don't know. I didn't do anything."

"Exactly. You stood by and watched your brother get beaten up."

"It was one against one, Dad! It wouldn't have been fair for me to help."

"Listen closely to me, Anthony. Normally I'd say you were right, but not when family's involved. I know you and Michael fight, but he's your brother, your own flesh and blood. And family comes first, above all the other rules. Afterward, if you wanted to punch Michael in the mouth for getting you involved, fine. But first you help him against outsiders. *Famiglia* always comes first. Understood?"

The boy nodded.

"Okay, guys, come here." He put his arms around them. "You each deserved that belt, so I don't apologize for it. But I wanted to do it here, alone, because it's nobody else's business. It's over now, right? Let's enjoy Christmas."

"When's Mom getting back?" Anthony asked as they were leaving the room.

Vince looked at his watch. "She should be home soon. An hour or so."

"Why does she go there? She always seems sad when she comes back."

"Because she wants to."

"To be sad?"

"No. To go there."

"Why does she always go alone?"

Vince sighed. "Because that's the way she wants it."

The gray-haired woman sat in the chair, her eyes vacant. She barely moved. She never spoke.

Lena made up for that. For the past half hour she had conducted a monologue as she brushed the woman's hair.

"Michael's almost fourteen, can you believe it? Where does the time go? He'll be in high school next year. Vince wants him to go to the prep. St. Joe's, just like he did, but I don't know. It's a bad neighborhood. I know you can't shield them forever, but it seems to me sending a son into Seventeenth and Stiles four years in a row is asking for trouble. You know, playing with the odds. I thought about Devon, it has a great academic reputation, but Vince refuses. He says he'll never send a son to any high school that doesn't have football. Says it's un-American. I'd be just as happy if they never went near a football. The head injuries terrify

[319]

me. They can play soccer. Maybe Malvern Prep. One of Vince's friends—Kevin Murray, I told you about him—went there and can't say enough about it. We'll see. We still have a month or two to decide."

A white-uniformed matron appeared in the door. "It's almost time, ma'am. Five more minutes."

"Thank you." Lena returned to brushing the lady's hair. The strokes were more rapid as desperation set in once again. "Please, please, just look at me. Say something to me. Hold my hand. Anything. Just let me know you're aware I'm here."

For a moment she thought there was a glimmer, but no, still nothing. Just as it had been for twenty-seven years, ever since Uncle Giuseppe had taken her away. He had promised it would be for only a few weeks, but Lena had known.

It was for her own good, they had said, and obedient Lena had acquiesced. But not inside. Never. They had been thinking of themselves. This gray-haired woman had once terrified them. They could never be sure what she would say, or to whom. The rage over her husband's murder couldn't be controlled, and that was dangerous.

They didn't let Lena see her for the first year, when the damage was done. All very neat, very legal. With complete kindness they took away her mind, so that she was never a threat again.

After putting down the brush, Lena embraced her. "I love you so," she sobbed. "If I could just make you understand."

The gray-haired woman didn't move. Reluctantly Lena rose, wiping her eyes. Then she bent down for a final kiss. "Merry Christmas."

Then, as she always did just before leaving, she made the same solemn oath: "I'll avenge you, Mother. I promise."

CHAPTER
Eighteen

PAT Carney stared out at the lights on the Philadelphia Electric Building. PEACE ON EARTH, they read. He wondered if that was ever possible. At least for him.

The office party had been a duty, one that he couldn't refuse, but he had slipped out as quickly as he could with any measure of grace. He just wasn't in the mood. Not for Christmas. Not for anything. Christmas was an unwelcome time to examine his life, to measure the magnitude of his failure.

He was alone, so unalterably alone. In a few hours he would conduct midnight mass, surrounded by people. But they weren't *his* people. He didn't have any people. Not anymore, not really.

He would dutifully go to Kristy's for dinner tomorrow. It would have been rude to refuse her dutiful invitation. They all would be there: Kristy, the twins, the children, even George Carney, a shell of a man, still living alone in his shell of a house. But none of them belonged to him anymore. His duty to them had ended years before, and he had nothing left.

"Am I intruding?" a voice said. It was the boss.

"Eminence," Pat stammered, half rising. "Of course not. Please, come in."

Stephen Cardinal Pulski carried a bottle and two glasses. "The most astute administrator in the American Church, that's what *Newsweek* called me. I'm not certain I'd go that far, but I'm astute enough to know when something is bothering one of my own." He poured a drink for each, then raised his glass. *"Ad multos annos."*

Pat raised his glass to his lips. He wasn't in the mood for Irish Mist, but to refuse would be rude. And unwise. "*Ad multos annos,*" he replied.

"Would you like to talk about it, Patrick, my son?"

Pat hesitated. There was possible danger here. The boss might be genuinely concerned for "one of his own," but he still was the boss. Better to be cautious.

"It's nothing really," Pat answered. "I just get a little melancholy around Christmas, that's all."

"And you're dreading the four days that the office will be closed. Right?"

Pat was bewildered. "Yes. How did you know?"

"Do you think I'm any different? We share the same curse. Loneliness, a disease to which even princes of the Church are susceptible. What is there besides our work? And that's the paradox. We immerse ourselves in our work because we're lonely, but it makes us less, not more, effective."

"I'm not sure I follow you, Eminence."

"Sure you do, Patrick. Take the average man in the outside world. He works hard, but then he goes home because he has one. And a wife and kids and a car and two weeks' vacation. If he succeeds, he gets a bigger house, a second car, four weeks' vacation, and maybe that swimming pool he's always wanted. And most important, he can share his success with others. His own. But what about us? Where are the incentives? No matter how well we perform, we still go back to that empty room. To nothing. So our work becomes our entire world, which in turn gives birth to the kingdom syndrome. We guard our little niches of responsibility. They're our fiefdoms, into which no man dare enter. Any suggestion, any change, and we immediately take to the ramparts. It's not just our job that transgressor is jeopardizing; it's our very existence. Which, of course, dooms us to waddle along in mediocrity. You see it, Pat; you're just too judicious to admit it. Our hospitals, our schools, right here. How many times have you been frustrated in trying to get our supposedly well-oiled machine, our unstoppable monolith to function?"

Pat shifted in his chair. Did he dare agree? Could it be a ploy? Could the most conservative voice in the American Church mean what he was saying? "You've confused me, Eminence. I had no

[322]

idea, never an inkling, that you opposed the celibacy requirement."

Pulski smiled, pouring himself another. "You're putting words
in my mouth, Patrick, the cardinal sin of a PR professional. I
support Church law, whatever it may be. I was merely pointing
out an indisputable reality."

He walked to the window. Like Pat, he fixed his eyes on the
Philadelphia Electric Building. When he spoke again, it was in a
voice that Pat had never heard: distant, melancholy. "Stephen
Cardinal Pulski. Achievement beyond the wildest dreams of most
men. The head of a massive archdiocese. A member of the College
of Cardinals, the most exclusive club in the world. Trusted confi-
dant of the pope. By anyone's standard a national celebrity. Most
important, a man who has devoted his life to the Church of
Christ. That should be enough, but God forgive me, it isn't. It
doesn't make up for that empty room. Somehow there ought to be
more. I'm still a man, and a man needs someone of his own.
Someone to love. Someone to leave behind to carry on his name.
Someone who will know and care that Stephen Pulski ever
walked this earth."

There was silence, adding to Pat's confusion. This was a side of
the man that he had never seen. This was not the administrative
genius, the financial wizard, the steel-edged giant who could hold
his own with presidents. This was a human, lonely and maybe a
little afraid. A man to whom Pat, at long last, could talk, a receptacle for the flood which for so many years had remained
dammed. He discarded caution, knowing that this opportunity
might never be repeated.

"May I speak, Eminence, of something very personal?"

Pulski turned, his reverie over. "Since when does an Irishman
ever need permission to speak?"

"My vocation, from the day I entered the seminary, has been a
lie. A sacrilege."

The cardinal reached for the Irish Mist. Pat had always marveled at how much the man could drink with no noticeable effect.
"Come now, Patrick. Aren't you being a trifle dramatic?"

"Not at all. Not one bit. For the first time since I can remember
I'm being honest. I didn't enter the priesthood to serve God. That
was the farthest thing from my mind. I wasn't even sure I believed

[323]

in Him. I'm still not. I joined to escape. From responsibility. Not like this, handling our PR or directing a department or running a school. I can handle that. But I didn't want to be responsible for any human being. You probably don't know it, but I was engaged my senior year at Villanova, to a wonderful girl. I loved her. I'm sure of it. But I ran from her, straight into the seminary. That's why I was so delighted when you appointed me to the North American College after ordination. I'll be honest. I politicked for it, the same way I politicked to get back here. Anything to avoid parish work. I've dreaded becoming involved in counseling, in becoming a part of the problems of others. Even now I avoid hearing confessions when I can. You've been deceived too long. I've made a mockery of the priesthood and its mission of service. I know you're shocked. I know you'll have to act, and whatever decision you make, I'll accept and understand it. I just hope I haven't caused you too much pain."

The cardinal reached into his pocket, taking out two cigars. "My doctor would have a fit, but it's Christmas. Care for one?"

Pat shook his head.

"They're Cuban."

"No, thank you, Eminence."

"Suit yourself." Deliberately he wet the end, bit off the tip, and lit it. "Ah," he said after the first puff, "such pleasure is undoubtedly sinful."

He settled back in his chair, a picture of total contentment.

Pat shifted uneasily. Was the boss finally showing his age? Had he lost track of the conversation, forgetting the revelation Pat had just made? The answer came quickly.

"You're wrong on all three counts, Patrick. I'm not the slightest bit shocked, you've caused me no pain, and my plans for you remain unchanged."

"I don't understand."

"What's to understand? Do you think that your little—what should we call it?—stream of consciousness surprises me? Of course you entered the priesthood to escape. Perfectly understandable. Seven years old when his mother died, on his first communion day, suddenly saddled with responsibilities that would stagger the most mature adult. Serving as a mother and a father to your sister and two brothers while your father worked a double shift. Acting as his companion when he was home. Agonizing

[324]

with the guilt of your sister's almost dying while she was in your charge. So you ran. From your family. And from Bonnie. I don't find such conduct all that mystifying."

Pat struggled for control. The room seemed to be moving, and for all his efforts he could not get his mouth to close. "How?" he finally stammered. "How?"

"Please, Patrick, give me a little credit. Read *Newsweek*, if you must. No young man whom I haven't thoroughly researched enters St. Charles."

"But if you knew from the beginning, why—"

"Why did I permit you to study for the priesthood, then assume positions of responsibility? Why not? God sent you, and I readily accepted His will."

"How can you accept me? I used you and the Church."

"And we, you. It's been an equal partnership. Do you honestly believe that every priest enters because he feels called by God? Of course not. The permutations are endless, as endless as the human spirit. In many respects, the sacrament of holy orders is identical to that of matrimony. How many men and women marry solely for love? For some, like you, the compelling force is escape. For others it is financial security or a desire for permanence or a sense of obligation or just to have a companion. Are all these marriages doomed? I think not. I suspect many of these survive the test of time far better than the unions formed by ardor. Can I interest you in another drink?"

"Please."

"You have served the Church well," Pulski said as he poured. "How you serve yourself is another question. I'm happy to help if I can, but the ultimate decision is yours."

Pat sighed. "I am grateful, Eminence, but I'm so confused. What should I do?"

"Well, at the risk of being told to mind my own business, I'll make one suggestion. If my father were still alive and living alone when he shouldn't be, I'd resolve the problem—whether or not he had an acute fondness for the bottle. Just my personal opinion, worth nothing more than that, but I thought you might like to hear it."

Pat rose, walked to his boss, and knelt to kiss his ring. His eyes were moist. "You have no idea how grateful I am. Thank you, Father."

[325]

"You're welcome, my son."

Pulski rose and walked to the door, then turned. "Merry Christmas, Pat. *Ad multos annos.*"

Tapping his fingers on the dashboard, Pat waited for the light to change. He was the impatient little boy again, anxious to celebrate Christmas. For the first time in years it really *was* Christmas again. He wanted to sing, to lose himself in the joy of life.

When midnight mass had ended, he had run to his car. He was in a hurry. To set things straight, to make up for the years he had wasted. To go home again.

He looked at his watch. Almost two. So what? If his father were asleep, he'd wake him the hell up. They'd have a drink together and talk. Just the two of them, the way it used to be on those Friday nights. He'd spend the night there. Then they would go to Kristy's to celebrate, *really* celebrate, Christmas. On the following day he would get to work, finding an apartment for the two of them. Sure, there would be problems, but none that he couldn't handle. The boss was on his side.

He would always be grateful to the boss. In a fifteen-minute conversation he had changed Pat's life. He was more than a cardinal, more than an efficient administrator. He was a priest in the finest sense of the word. And one hell of a human being.

It wasn't all sorted out for Pat, not yet. Even now, in his ecstasy, he felt guilt, shame that he had needed encouragement—a guarantee, really—from the boss before he became a son again. But there would be time for soul-searching later. The first order of business was George Carney. Thomas Wolfe had been dead wrong. You *can* go home again.

As he turned onto his block, he saw the flashing lights: two fire engines and an ambulance. They were in front of his house.

Gripped by panic, he sprinted from his car, a little boy again at the hospital, clutching a rose. *Please, God,* he said to himself. *Not now. Not before I've made things right.*

They were carrying out a stretcher, its cargo covered by a blanket.

"Afraid you're too late, padre," one of the paramedics said. "Damn shame."

"What—what happened?"

"The usual. Smoking in bed. Probably never knew what hit

[326]

him. Passed out. You know, from the booze. It's not the first time. This guy was an accident waiting to happen."

Pat knelt by the stretcher and gently pulled down the blanket. George Carney looked as if he were asleep. The flames hadn't gotten him. Just the smoke.

When he thought about it later, Pat would realize that he never gave the last rites, but then a little boy rarely thinks of such things. Instead, he buried his head on his father's chest.

"I failed you, Daddy," he sobbed. "I didn't take care of you."

Nineteen

BING Crosby was on the record player, and the tree was being trimmed, accompanied by the usual sounds of Christmas.

"You're bunching the balls up, Megan!" Matthew said. "Let me do it!"

"I am not, am I, Daddy?"

"It's just fine, Murgatroyd," Kevin answered.

"C'mon, Dad." Sean chimed in. "She's got six balls on one branch. It looks ridiculous!"

"Does not!" wailed Megan.

Kevin leaned over and kissed her. "Don't listen to them, toots. You're doing great."

"You always side with her." Matthew pouted. "Because she's a girl."

"Right. She's my favorite, the only one I love. Does that make you feel better?"

It was par for the course. Christmas Eve was a time for family holiday joy and the traditional arguments. The first invariably occurred when Kevin strung the tree lights. Ever the perfectionist, Karen would insist that none of the wires be seen, a task that Kevin found impossible.

"It looks good," he would say. "Once you get the balls and the garland on, you'll never notice the wires."

"It looks horrible," Karen would counter. She would still be smarting from her husband's selection of a tree, always the largest one on the lot, taking up half the living room. The shape didn't matter so long as it was big. Karen preferred the smaller, more symmetrical ones. "It looks like a power station."

Thereupon they would negotiate, with Kevin making as many adjustments as he could without restringing the whole tree.

Except for the highest ones, the balls and other decorations were the responsibility of the children. Kevin served largely as a referee. After the smaller ones were in bed, he would make a few adjustments, subtly enough to avoid a formal protest.

Then came the real confrontation. Until the last few years they had used tinsel. Kevin's idea of applying it was to stand back several feet and throw. Karen insisted that each strand be hung perfectly. She also had rejected Kevin's plea for multicolored tinsel—green, red, and gold to go along with the standard silver. "You should have been Italian," he had said. "Flamingos on the lawn and polka-dot tinsel on the tree."

To avoid such a conflict, they had decided a few years before to replace the tinsel with a garland, but even that was not without its perils. Karen had rules for everything, including the garland. It had to circle the tree gracefully, its dips and rises perfectly coordinated. Kevin would begin the task and become exasperated with the coaching, requiring his wife to enter from the bullpen.

When the tree was finally complete and feelings were relatively soothed, each child would be permitted to open one present. Usually it was something that could be used that evening or the following morning: a robe; pajamas; slippers; a camera.

The kids would then be lined up in front of the fireplace with their stockings for the annual picture. It was a certainty that at least one would be crying, wearing a scowl, or refusing outright to pose. Before going to bed, Megan, Matthew, and Peter would bring out the food to be placed on the hearth: cookies and milk for Santa; lettuce and carrots for the reindeer. Once he was certain they were asleep, Kevin would replace the food, making certain to leave a few crumbs and a ring of milk in the glass.

With the house relatively peaceful, Karen would begin to stack the presents while Kevin attacked the job he hated most: setting up the trains. He had absolutely no talent for it: not for laying the track (it was always the same unimaginative oval), not for setting up the goddamn plastic villages, which would collapse when the first child approached and which Kevin vowed to glue each year; not for hooking up the transformers to the right wires. If the Sarge had been around, the damn things would have been running in fifteen minutes, but he wasn't the Sarge.

Finally, at around three, if all went well, Kevin and Karen would share a miniature split of champagne and open their presents to each other. That way the morning would be strictly for the children.

In short, it was complete chaos, total frustration, and unique joy. It was Christmas, and this year was the same as all others yet very different.

He had sat in his office the whole afternoon, waiting. Following House passage of the abortion control bill, the Senate had moved swiftly. On December 14, without debate, it approved the measure, 28–22. The governor had ten days to act. He took the maximum, issuing his decision in the early evening of Christmas Eve, the slowest press day of the year.

Kevin received the advance call just before five. It was Joe Kellogg, executive director of the Pennsylvania Catholic Conference and a close friend.

"I have bad news, Kevin. The governor's office just called me. He's going to veto the bill."

For a moment Kevin said nothing. He felt as if he had been kicked in the stomach, as he had when he'd fallen in the St. Laurence schoolyard and been unable to catch his breath.

"Are you there, Kevin?"

"That cocksucker!"

"I'm sorry, Kevin. We're all disappointed, but I know how you must feel. But remember this, nothing can diminish your accomplishment. I'll be forever grateful."

Kevin tried to think clearly, to shake off the anger and the hurt and stay on the issue. "Did you see the veto message?"

"I just got it. It's seven pages, so I've had a chance only to scan it. He claims he opposes abortion but then cites a number of problems he has with the bill. There is one hopeful note, though. He ends up by expressing his willingness to work on a new bill which accomplishes our goals while resolving his objections. I guess we have to assume that he's a man of honor and take him at his word."

Kevin was far less of a gentleman. "Dan Talbot is a motherfuckin' political whore! He never had an honest conviction in his entire goddamn life. I'll get that prick, Joe. So help me Christ, I will."

"Please, Kevin, don't let it spoil your Christmas. Nothing is worth that. You've earned a week of peace and happiness with your family. We'll have plenty of time after the New Year."

"Yeah, right. God, I can't believe I failed."

"You didn't fail. And even if you did, it's not important. When we stand before our Creator on the final day, He won't ask if we succeeded but if we tried. And no one has tried harder than Kevin Murray."

"Thanks, pal."

"Thank *you*. And Merry Christmas."

Ten minutes later the phones began to ring and continued without letup for two hours. Every paper, every wire service, every radio station wanted his response. The networks wanted film. Two came to his office, two more to his home after dinner, disrupting the Murrays' Christmas routine but thrilling the children. Even Karen was a bit impressed. The last was Arnie Katz, of Channel 6. His station was the top-rated one in Philadelphia, largely because of Katz's no-nonsense machine-gun style.

Two chairs were pulled in front of the fireplace, the camera lights went on, and Katz began. "Representative Murray, your reaction to the governor's veto."

"Disappointment, frustration, anger, but increased determination to win this struggle."

"Were you surprised?"

"Not really. You never know where Dan Talbot is coming from."

"What do you think caused him to veto the bill?"

"That's difficult to assess. But if I had to guess, I'd say it was the lobbying of the Pennsylvania Medical Society. You know, that virtuous group devoted to saving lives."

"You sound bitter."

"I can't stand hypocrisy, Arnie. PMS says it takes no position on abortion, then attempts to sabotage every bill we introduce under the guise that it opposes any effort to restrict the practice of medicine."

"Isn't that a valid concern?"

"Only to a degree. Some of the doctors, not all of them, but the

[331]

ones who run the society, want a blank check. They want to be judge, jury, and executioner, deciding who lives and who dies. Apparently they haven't recently read the Hippocratic oath, which contains a specific admonition against abortion."

"Is money a factor?"

"You tell me, Arnie, with sixty-five thousand abortions in Pennsylvania every year."

"What do you think of the veto message?"

"I haven't received it yet, but parts have been read to me. It's vintage Talbot. Trying to be all things to all people. It's not a message; it's a waltz."

"What's the bottom line, Representative Murray?"

"The issue is whether or not we wish to continue our present policy of unrestricted, unregulated killing of unborn children. By his veto, Dan Talbot has answered yes."

"What now?"

"Back to the trenches. One way or the other, with or without Dan Talbot, the abortion control bill will become law."

"How?"

"By doing whatever is required."

"Including going to war with a Republican governor, who runs for reelection next year?"

"If that's what it takes."

"Will you win?"

"Yes. Because we're right. Nothing justifies the killing of unborn children. We'll win this battle, and ultimately we'll win the war. If you're a homeowner, Arnie, bet the house on it."

Katz nodded to the cameraman, and the lights went off. He was always professional, but Kevin assumed the obvious. He was a member of the media, and he was a Jew, so he must support abortion.

To Kevin's surprise, the anchorman was in no hurry to leave. He talked to each child, then chatted amicably with Karen, complimenting her on the house.

Kevin walked him to the door.

"Nice family, Kevin. You're a lucky man."

"Thanks, Arnie."

"For what it's worth, I'm with you all the way. Abortion is repulsive. When I was in New York, we filmed the first abortion ever shown on television. Butchery. And the women were treated

[332]

like cattle. No guidance, no counseling. Just an assembly line."
He paused. "You look surprised."

"A little."

"Made the obvious assumptions, huh?"

"Guilty. Sorry."

"No problem. Just keep up the fight." Katz extended his hand.
"Shalom, Kevin. And God bless."

Smiling, Kevin returned to his family. He *was* lucky, and nothing was going to spoil their Christmas. For the next week it would
be peace on earth, goodwill to men.

Until January 2. Then it was war with that bastard of a
governor.

And so 1981 came to an end for Vince Grosso, Pat Carney, and
Kevin Murray. For each of them 1982 would be a year of challenge.

For one of them it would be his last.

BOOK
TWO

1982

CHAPTER
Twenty

KEVIN stood motionless at the window. He could just make out the tiny figure in the rear. It didn't seem possible that anything that small could actually be alive, could survive the tubes and the wires attached to him.

Hang in there, Andrew. Please. Your mommy and I want you so much. Please, God, please save him. Please don't do this to us.

The door opened, and one of the intensive care nurses approached.

"How is he, Nurse?" His own voice sounded so foreign. So desperate.

"There's no change, Mr. Murray. It's still touch and go. Why don't you try to get a little rest? I promise, we'll call you the minute there's any change."

"Thank you." He walked down the hall to the solarium, lighting up as soon as he entered. Rest. How the hell could he rest? When one of your own was holding on by a thread, you didn't rest. You stayed with him, even if you couldn't help. Even if you couldn't hold him and make things right. Even if the only thing you could do was stand and stare. And pray.

How many times had he been there before, in a hospital welcoming one of his own into the world? They had been times of joy and excitement and wonder. It had always started at night, somehow adding to the excitement. Timing Karen's contractions. The call to the doctor, then the ride to the hospital, his heart pounding with anticipation and fear. At the emergency room entrance Karen, clutching a little bag, which—so much like Karen—had

[337]

been packed for a month, was taken to maternity by the nurse while Kevin went to admissions for the paperwork. When Karen was being prepped, he paced in the waiting room, chain-smoking. Then would he put on the gown and join his wife, feeling powerless during her labor but wanting her to know that her Kevin was there. Finally they were in the delivery room, Kevin standing by Karen's head, both of them looking in the mirror as the miracle began. Little Kevin, the first, the wonder, the one who made them realize how much a human could love. How could they ever love another the way they loved him? But then came Sean, their Bureau baby, born in Milwaukee during the first fall snow flurry, and they realized how easily such love could be shared. Matthew, the moose, weighing in at ten pounds, his blond curls the envy of the nurses. Megan, their long-awaited daughter, exercising a woman's prerogative to be late, requiring Karen to be induced. Then Peter, the surprise, the wonderful mistake, who had made them all a little younger.

Each time it had been special. Different yet the same. A healthy baby (the first thing Kevin did was count the fingers and the toes), tears of joy in the delivery room, the parents holding their child for the first time. Then, as Karen was taken to recovery, Kevin accompanied his newborn to the nursery, where the baby was weighed, cleaned up, and placed on display.

Kevin stared through the window at the little bundle, mesmerized. That was *his* baby. Something that he and Karen had created. How could anything that wonderful occur? And how could anyone who witnessed it not believe in God?

Before he rejoined Karen, there were phone calls to be made. But first things first. A stop at the chapel, where he knelt at the altar rail and sobbed without shame. *Thank you, God. Thank you for taking care of my own.*

Only this time it was different. The day had started out well. They had New Year's dinner with Karen's family and returned home just after eight. The two Kevins had stayed up for the Orange Bowl, watching Clemson prove that it was for real.

At two-thirty Karen had awakened him. "I think I'm going into labor."

"What? How? It's not for another two months."

"Something's wrong, Kevin. I'm scared."

They just made it to the hospital. A team of nurses was waiting to whisk Karen to delivery, this time without her husband. Kevin protested, but the doctor was firm. So he waited, pacing and smoking, gripped by terror. Dawn was just breaking when the doctor entered. He was grim.

"Where do I begin, Kevin? You have a baby boy. Karen's lost a lot of blood, but with rest she'll be fine in a few days."

"Thank God." He hesitated, afraid to ask. "And the baby? My son? *Our* son?"

"It's not good, Kevin. He's two months premature, and there are problems."

"Problems? Like what?"

"The specialists are examining him now, but I'm certain there are problems. With his heart."

"Can it be fixed? Can you operate? Something can be done, can't it?"

"I don't know, Kevin. Not yet. The pediatricians will be in as soon as they're done. We'll know more then."

"Thanks," he said numbly. The room seemed to be turning, his wife, his baby, his world, all revolving in space. "Can I see Karen?"

"Sure, but just for a minute. She's been through a lot, Kevin."

He started to leave, then turned back to the doctor. "Has he, has Andrew"—the words almost choked him—"been baptized?"

"Yes. Sister Mary Daniel baptized him."

Karen was asleep. She looked so pale, so vulnerable. Gently he stroked her arm. "I love you, my princess," he whispered.

Her eyes opened, and she took his hand. "How is he, Kevin? Our baby?"

"He's gonna make it, honey. Don't you worry."

Then she was asleep again. Kevin walked to the intensive care unit, to peer through the window at the people in white uniforms hovering over his baby.

Please, little guy, cry. Let me hear you. Tell me you're okay.

Dr. Charles Sullivan headed the team. A close friend and a pillar of the movement.

"It's not good, Kevin."

Was that all they could say? I know it's not good, for Christ's sake! If it were good, Karen and I would be holding our baby now.

Sullivan continued. "The heart is underdeveloped. It just can't get the job done."

"What can you do?"

"Right now we've done everything we can. Surgery at this point is out of the question. If he stabilizes, then maybe—"

"Will he?"

The pediatrician hesitated. "I don't think so, Kevin. We have to pray for a miracle."

Okay, goddammit, that's what we'll do! We'll pray for a miracle. I'll demand it. God owes me! I've been fighting his battles; now it's time for Him to pay up.

"Charlie, can I be with him for a minute? Can I—" He checked a sob. "Can I hold him? Just once?"

Again Sullivan hesitated. "Sure. Come on," he finally said. "You'll have to put on a gown, and it can be for only a second."

His skin was so soft, just like the others. And he was awake, his little fists clenched, struggling to hold on to life.

"I love you, Andrew. Your mommy and I love you so much. And Megan and your brothers are waiting for you. Please stay with us."

He snubbed out the cigarette and returned to the window. No change. Then he looked at his watch. Andrew Murray was six hours old.

It had finally happened, what he had feared, what had terrified him from the moment of young Kevin's birth. How many nights had he lain awake, thinking of all the things that could happen to the kids? Leukemia. Hit by a car. Drowning at the beach. Or the worst, snatched away. Disappeared, never to be heard from again.

How many times had he begged God to spare him that. *Anything: lose my job, get beat for reelection, become crippled, or even die. All that's okay. Just don't let anything happen to my kids.*

It was usually at night that the fear would assail him. Watching them sleep, he would be overwhelmed by the responsibility. They were *his. His* responsibility. It was up to *him* to protect them, to shield them from harm. To be like Holden Caulfield, standing in the rye, waiting to catch them if they neared the cliff. Now his Andrew was on the edge, and there was nothing he could do.

He fought the exhaustion that was closing in. He had to stay awake. Nothing bad could happen while he was awake, while he was standing guard.

As a slight concession to his body he sat in a chair across the corridor. From there he could still see everything, could be ready if he were needed.

His eyelids closed, and he was at the shore, in the bay near his uncle's home. The raft was still twenty feet away, but he couldn't move. They were waving to him, urging him on, but some weight seemed to be dragging him down. Everything seemed to be in slow motion. Their faces grew dimmer, and he knew that he would never see them again. Then he felt the hand on his arm. It was the Sarge, calm as ever. "I got you, buddy. You're fine."

The pressure on his arm increased.

"Kevin. Kevin."

He opened his eyes. The face was familiar.

"Sorry to disturb you, Kevin. I'm Stephen Pulski."

"Yeah," Kevin said groggily. "Hello, Stephen. Cardinal. Your Eminence."

Pulski was smiling. "It's hard to believe we've never met. I'm certain there are those who believe we're never apart."

"Yes. That's true."

"It's my fault, Kevin. I should have made it a point long before this. To tell you how much I deeply appreciate everything you've done for us. I know all about you. Malvern, Villanova, the FBI, your unmatched work in Harrisburg, and your wonderful family. God bless you."

"Thank you, Eminence." He glanced at the ICU window, then at his watch. He had been asleep almost an hour. How could he? "Excuse me, Your Eminence. I have to check." He tried to rise. "My baby, our baby—"

The hand which had never left his arm tightened. "Kevin, my son, little Andrew went to God a few minutes ago. I gave him the last rites, not that he needed it."

For a moment Kevin remained frozen. Then he collapsed into the arms of the archbishop of Philadelphia.

"Oh God, oh God, I failed him," he sobbed. "I failed him."

"You've never failed anyone, Kevin."

"I fell asleep. I couldn't even stay awake for the little time he was with us."

"He'll always be with you, Kevin."

But no words could console Kevin Murray. He had failed to catch his son.

* * *

Even at Christmas midnight mass the Church of the Nativity had never been so jammed: the governor, both United States senators, state legislators, community leaders, pro-lifers, neighbors, friends, including Vince and Lena Grosso, and those who were just curious. And Bridget Kelly, entering a Catholic church for the first time in twelve years.

Twenty-seven priests, including the cardinal, were on the altar. Monsignor Patrick Carney celebrated the mass of the angels. In his homily he did his very best, fighting for composure the entire time.

"I know that nothing can take away the pain that Kevin and Karen and their children and relatives are experiencing. It's my pain, too, because—because little Andrew Murray was one of my own.

"But in our sorrow we have to remember why we're here. In the face of eternity our lives, no matter how long we live, are just a speck. From the moment we're born, we begin our journey back to God. That is the sole reason for our existence. Life is only a trial run, to determine whether we will merit eternal happiness with God.

"Unlike any of us, Andrew Murray, in his short time on this earth, has obtained that happiness. At this moment he is with God. That is without question, for the Lord has a special love for the very young and the totally innocent. So I say to the Murray family, don't pray for your little baby. Pray to him, for you have your own St. Andrew in heaven."

There was only one pallbearer at the cemetery: Andrew Murray's father. Gently he lowered the tiny white casket to the ground. Then he and Karen, followed by each of the children, placed a single rose on top of it.

It was over, and they returned to their cars; but Kevin lingered. He took one last look at the casket, then turned to the headstone beside it.

Michael Joseph Murray
1916 to 1980

"Take care of my baby, Sarge," he said. "The way you took care of me."

[342]

CHAPTER
Twenty-one

FEBRUARY in Philadelphia is depressing. It is an interim month. The thrill of oncoming winter has long since dissipated, and no hint of spring has yet arrived. December has Christmas; January, the rebirth of resolution and the Super Bowl; March, the changing of the seasons. February has nothing. Football has been concluded, leaving the addicts in an agony of withdrawal. Baseball is still a mirage. Hockey and basketball have entered that nether period of filling time before the play-offs.

And the weather is atrocious. Just enough snow to keep things dirty and dangerous, the type that melts during the day and freezes at night.

The average citizen living in the Philadelphia area was required to assume an air of dreary acceptance. Vince Grosso, not being an average citizen, was seldom required to accept anything. Philadelphia Februaries were not to be endured. Instead, the month was spent in St. Thomas, at Vince's villa. It had been constructed to his specifications amid a grove of mangoes with a front veranda that controlled an unobstructed view of Megan's Bay.

Tutors were provided for the children, bodyguards surrounded the villa, and, although Therese was unable to accompany them because of classes, which Vince regretted and which seemed to cause Lena inordinate sorrow, a full housekeeping staff was lodged on the premises.

For Vince, it was a month of being with his family while attending to business in a manner not possible in Philadelphia. And business was good, the *borgotta's* progress actually ahead of Vince's schedule. A medium-size oil company had been the latest acquisition. It had come aboard in a bloodless, legal, and wholly unnoticed takeover. By the end of the month a computer firm, an Oregon fish cannery, and a health insurance company would be added to the *borgotta's* growing list of legitimate enterprises.

A fiscal conservative, Vince was wary of overextending his venture capital. At the same time he was committed to expanding and diversifying his family's holdings. To solve this dilemma, he had on several occasions looked west, to Detroit and Don Giuseppe, who had agreed without hesitation to such joint ventures. Vincenzo Grosso was a wise and forceful leader. More important, he was the aging don's nephew by marriage. Detroit and Philadelphia were separate and distinct *borgotte,* but they were one *famiglia.*

Illegal activities were also flourishing. Julius Marzette was proving to be a faithful employee, expanding his narcotics operations throughout the state and across its borders. He could, of course, never be completely trusted. Any man whose authority, whose manhood, had been stripped away would always constitute a potential threat. But so far the books had been relatively clean.

The truce with New York was holding, permitting both families to enjoy the fruits of Atlantic City. Despite the protestations of New Jersey politicians, a number of the casinos themselves had been successfully infiltrated. Even more lucrative, however, were the spin-off industries—linen, glassware, bus companies—and the unions representing bellhops, cocktail waitresses, dealers, and construction and transport workers.

Added to this, of course, was the corollary crime—narcotics, prostitution, and loan-sharking—which invariably accompanied casino gambling.

The division of booty between the Agostino and Grosso *borgotte* had been orderly, the result of discussion, negotiation, and, at Vince's insistence, *commissione* approval. On the few occasions when the dons had met, Michael Agostino had been gracious, but even his Sicilian self-discipline could not hide the hatred in his eyes. He would bide his time, forced for the present to coexist with Vincenzo Grosso. But there would be a day of reckoning. Nothing but vengeance could erase the affront to his pride. No man who had kidnapped his daughter, who had humiliated him in front of his lieutenants could be permitted to survive.

Vince knew this, accepting it as a fact of life. It was an absolute certainty that at an unknown time in the future Michael Agostino would seek his revenge. The survival of Vince Grosso depended upon his constant vigilance.

But nothing—not the specter of Julius Marzette or Michael Agostino, not even the increased attention being paid to him by the feds—could diminish his optimism. His family was on the move. The grand design was actually coming true. Now it was time to grasp for two treasures—both in his own backyard. The two gems bore a number of similarities. Each would be incredibly lucrative. Each catered to human weakness. And each required the blessing of the Pennsylvania legislature.

There are no private liquor stores in Pennsylvania. It is a control state, the largest in the nation. Whiskey and wine may be purchased only in state stores, owned and operated by the Pennsylvania Liquor Control Board.

The LCB began its reign on January 2, 1934, when, America's flirtation with Prohibition having ended, Demon Rum made its triumphant return. If a successful political compromise occurs when everyone is equally unhappy, the birth of the board was the epitome of success. To the wets, it was government intrusion, into both the personal lives of its citizens and a commercial area best left to private enterprise. Ignoring the fact that Pennsylvania had been the thirty-fourth state to ratify the Twenty-first Amendment, the drys labeled it a capitulation to the forces of evil, an irreversible step on the road to national ruin.

As if in tribute to its estranged parents, the LCB was given two goals which happened to be mutually exclusive: the control of alcohol and the generation of revenue from its sale. In the ensuing fifty years it performed neither job very well. Prices soared, far outstripping those of neighboring states. To begin with, there was a huge markup. Next came an eighteen percent "temporary" tax, levied in the late thirties to help western Pennsylvania recover from a flood. The waters had long since receded, but the tax remained. The crowning touch was a six percent sales tax, levied on the retail prices *and* flood tax.

[345]

All that could have been tolerated if the operation had been even marginally marketable. It wasn't. Customers at a state store had no opportunity to browse and inspect the merchandise. Instead, they were forced to stand in line, sometimes for half an hour, until it was their turn at the counter to order. A clerk, frequently rude and prohibited by law from making recommendations, would take the customer's order and then depart into the abyss of the stock shelves. All too often he would return to announce that the requested purchase was out of stock, requiring the customer to make another choice while those in line behind him became increasingly hostile.

The central warehouses, where the booze was shipped from the manufacturers, were cesspools of waste and corruption. Millions of dollars of stock disappeared each year. In a throwback to Prohibition, the state was awash in bootleg whiskey, purchased in other states at a fraction of the local prices.

The state liquor operation was directed by a three-man board, appointed by the governor with the advice and consent of the State Senate for staggered ten-year terms. By legislative design, these members, once appointed and confirmed, were responsible to no one. The goal had been praiseworthy: to insulate them from political pressure. But it was a two-edged sword, insulating them from accountability as well. There was no reward for efficiency, no penalty for incompetence. They could do whatever they damned well pleased. Even the ten-year term was deceptive. A member whose term had expired continued to sit until the Senate could agree on a replacement, which invariably became a political football and often took years.

It was not surprising, then, that there were numerous clarion calls for the abolition of the LCB and a return to private enterprise. Such crusades were always supported by the press, since private ownership of liquor stores would provide a huge increase in advertising revenue. And for once the media and the people were in agreement. Every opinion poll demonstrated overwhelming public support for a changeover.

Despite the outcries, the system remained. There were a number of reasons. Most important, the LCB was a bureaucracy, manned by bureaucrats, who, if nothing else, were survivors. In Washington and in the state capitals the scenario was the same. Presidents, governors, legislators, reformers—they all would come

[346]

and go, but the bureaucrats would remain. Their roots firmly anchored in civil service protection, they would ride out each storm, bending when necessary but never letting go.

The state's heritage was also a factor. With the exception of the Pittsburgh and Philadelphia areas, Pennsylvania is basically a Bible Belt state. The Protestant churches wield enormous power, and woe be to any legislator who opposes them. There were also the unions. AFSCME, the largest public employee union in the nation, and the Retail Clerks Union represented most of the LCB employees. Since a switch to private enterprise would jeopardize their jobs, virtually all unions, in the spirit of solidarity, were vehemently opposed.

Now another battle was about to be waged. Governor Dan Talbot, incensed by his inability to replace the board chairman, whose term had actually expired five years before, had come out publicly for the abolition of the system. Since part of his proposal was for the sale of beer and wine in grocery stores, he had enlisted the support—and the bankrolls—of the major food chains. Most political observers felt that this time the result might be different.

No one was more interested in the outcome than Vince Grosso. He had long known that he was sitting on a potential gold mine. It was why he had challenged Michael Agostino, why he had insisted on *commissione* ratification of the agreement that he had reached with the New York don. Everyone had assumed that his goal was a share of the spoils of Atlantic City. Certainly that was significant, but it paled in comparison to the importance of the other part of the agreement, which had been approved without objection or discussion. The entire state of Pennsylvania was now the undisputed territory of the Grosso *borgotta*. When the changeover to private liquor occurred—and Vince was determined that it would—there would be no one else to claim a share of the prize.

It was a prize of incalculable dimensions. The governor's plan called for the state to award a thousand private liquor licenses. Vince estimated—conservatively, as he always did—that he could control at least a quarter at the outset. Straw parties with unblemished records would be selected, money would be exchanged, and his family would instantly become liquor entrepreneurs. Within five years, ten at the most, he would have a monopoly. Little or no violence would be necessary, although that always remained an option. With an unlimited bankroll his stores

[347]

could sell at prices that defied competition. And when a rival store folded, he would be there to pick up the pieces. Naturally, once the competition had been eliminated, he would readjust the price, but never to the point of gouging his customers. It would be Sicilian business as usual, outstanding service at a fair price.

The stores would also provide a unique opportunity to launder the family's dirty money, thus diminishing the ever-present threat of the IRS. Finally, his people would be able to commingle bootleg and hijacked booze with the legitimate stock with almost complete impunity.

Most definitely a gold mine. And when the claim had been staked out properly, Vince would reach for the second mother lode. He would look to the northeast, to the Poconos.

Pennsylvania's travel brochures proudly proclaimed the Pocono Mountains as the nation's premiere resort area, surpassing even Niagara Falls in the number of honeymooners it entertained. Its appeal was year-round: skiing in the winter; water sports and camping in the summer. Only the recalcitrance of the state legislature—responding to the same opposition that had blocked private liquor—had deprived it of the activity for which it, more than any spot in America, was uniquely suited: casino gambling.

Las Vegas was a desert. Except for the casinos, there was nothing to recommend it. Atlantic City had the ocean, but that was good for only a few months. And once past the boardwalk it was a slum, a Camden by the sea. Casinos in the Poconos would make both towns irrelevant. It was a destiny waiting to be fulfilled, and when that fulfillment occurred, only Vince would be there to embrace it. As usual he was prepared. He already owned more than twenty thousand acres, including *the* prime location for the airport that was both necessary and inevitable, and a dozen resorts.

Private liquor and casino gambling: their birth would raise Vincenzo Grosso from a powerful don to an emperor. Giuseppe Zivelli had taught him well, but even the Detroit don's vision was limited. He was content to be Ford. Vince would be General Motors.

Michael Grosso's arms throbbed. He had been at it for almost an hour and he wanted it ended.

"I can't hold it, Dad!"

"Sure you can," Vince said calmly. "You're almost there."

"I can't! Please, take the rod. Just for a few minutes."

"Can't do it, Michael. It's your marlin."

"I don't care! I don't want the damn fish!"

"Sure you do. You'll hate yourself if you quit now."

The boy gritted his teeth and turned the reel.

"Not too fast, Michael."

Suddenly the tension was gone, and the boy reeled in an empty line. For a moment he was silent, fighting back the tears. "If you'd helped me," he finally said through clenched teeth, "I would have had him."

"No, son," Vince answered gently. "If I'd helped you, you would have had nothing. It's better to lose than to quit." He patted the boy's head. "You'll get the next. Stay with it. I'll be back in a little while."

"Where are you going?"

"Business."

"Always business. Even in the middle of the Caribbean."

Vince smiled. "Can you think of a better setting?" He nodded to the men who had been lounging on the forward deck, then walked into the salon. It *was* a perfect setting for business. A sixty-five-foot Bertram, alone on the Caribbean on a clear February morning. Perfect. And safe. International waters. If somehow the boat was bugged, as was unlikely, there was no jurisdiction for a conspiracy charge.

Three men filed in after Vince and took seats: Niccolo Arrone; Peter DellaCroce, head of Pennsylvania's largest Teamsters local; and Joseph Pagano, senior partner in a Harrisburg lobbying firm.

"Would you care for drinks, Mr. Grosso?" asked the first mate.

"No, thank you, Kirk. We'll be fine." When the mate left, Vince turned to the trio. "I know you'd prefer to stay on the foredeck, darkening your tans, but we have business. Political business. If our *borgotta* is to continue its growth, two things must happen in Pennsylvania: private liquor stores and casinos in the Poconos. We take liquor first. Beginning today, it is our top priority. And we *will* succeed. Is that clear?"

Pagano shook his head. "It will be difficult, boss. Very difficult."

"Life is difficult, Joseph, but we manage to live."

"Yeah, but this is different. I'm in Harrisburg. I know. This is a

[349]

tough state when it comes to things like booze and gambling. Enormous problems."

Vince smiled, but his eyes were cold. "I'm not the slightest bit interested in problems, Joseph. Only solutions. That's what you're paid for, quite handsomely. That's why you were sent to Princeton, why you have a Yale law degree, and why the family bankrolled your firm."

His face flushed, Pagano rose, arms spread in supplication. "Vince—Don Vincenzo—you know I'm grateful! No one is more loyal to you. I have always—"

"I've never questioned your loyalty or your gratitude. What I'm looking for now is your determination." He turned to the others. "Joseph is correct that this won't be easy, but we have a number of things going for us: media, public opinion, and now, the governor." He grinned. "I know that our WASP blue-blood governor would be shocked, but it's our job to lend him assistance. Peter, we particularly need union support."

"I know, boss," DellaCroce answered. "We'll do okay. AFSCME will never come aboard, of course. They can't. But we control enough locals to keep this from being a solidarity thing again."

"Be specific," Vince said.

"Okay. The Teamsters will stay neutral statewide. So will the AFL-CIO. First time ever."

"Is that certain?"

"Nothing is certain, boss. You taught me that. But it's a damn good bet."

"What about the teachers?"

DellaCroce shrugged. "Hard to say. They usually stand with AFSCME."

"I've been giving that some thought," Vince said. "If the bill passes, the state will be granting private licenses—at an undoubtedly substantial fee. What if the bill requires a portion of each license fee, and the annual renewal fees, to be earmarked for education?"

Pagano spoke, eager to show his enthusiasm. "Great idea! PSEA's first concern is the buck. They'd sell out their mothers for money."

"Yeah, that might do it, boss." DellaCroce agreed. "At the very least, it'd probably keep them neutral."

[350]

"Then let's explore it. Joseph, make contact with the bill's sponsors, PSEA, the School Boards Association, and any other education groups you can. Start a ground swell."

"Okay. But what's my cover? I don't represent anyone directly affected by the issue."

"Yes, you do," said Niccolo Arrone. "Eastland, Inc. Owns a string of convenience stores. Not as big as Seven-Eleven, but growing. It also happens to be ours—since last Tuesday. The governor's proposal permits beer and wine in grocery stores, so that logically brings you in."

"Down the road, of course, we'll drop that provision," Vince said.

"Why?" DellaCroce asked.

"Because it'll kill the whole bill. A state which just passed one of the toughest drunk driving laws in the country can't turn around and put booze in grocery stores."

"That's absolutely right," Pagano said. "Mothers Against Drunk Drivers would raise all kinds of hell."

"Okay," said Vince. "That's the overall strategy. Now we get down to the specifics. We need a hundred two votes in the House and twenty-six in the Senate. As of today, Niccolo is my designated keeper of the list."

"That's news to me," Arrone said. "What list?"

"The master list of where we stand on the vote." Vince smiled. "A long time ago, when I was at Villanova, I learned from the master. He was running for student body president, which was a very complicated process. The students didn't vote. Only the incoming and outgoing members of the student council. To make it even more complex, some members—the ones who were elected, like class president and council reps—had full votes. The rest were appointed to represent organizations, like the school paper, radio station, fraternities, and they had half votes. So this political genius drew up a master list with the name of each member. He made a lot of copies, too, which were marked up and changed frequently. But a 'yes' or 'no' was *never* placed on the master list until the vote was certain, one way or the other. He even had index cards made up for each member containing everything about him. Where he was from. Whom he was dating. His favorite drink. Everything."

"Did it work?" Pagano asked.

[351]

Vince was clearly enjoying the memory. "To use one of his favorite phrases, fuckin' well told, it worked. The night of the election he handed me an envelope and told me to open it after the vote. He had the count on the head. Right on the goddamn head. Any questions?"

"I'll indulge you," Arrone said. "Who was this great man, as if I didn't know?"

"I thought you'd never ask. Kevin Murray. Now State Representative Kevin Murray. And you can be absolutely certain that even now, when he runs a vote, he keeps a list. Like to know who kept the list back then?"

"Sure," Arrone answered.

"I did. And now I'm giving it to you, Niccolo. I expect the same results." He turned to Pagano. "All right, Joseph, let's get started. First the House, then the Senate."

"What do you want, Vince?"

"The fruits of your labor. A rundown on each member."

"Now?"

"Right."

"Jesus, Vince. There's two hundred fifty-three of them. It'll take hours!"

"You were going somewhere?"

"No. It's just that—"

"Good. Then let's get started."

Pagano sighed. "Okay. We'll begin with the speaker. Mike Callaghan. Republican from Delaware County. Fifty-four years old. Divorced. Four kids. Youngest is a junior in college. Holy Cross. The rest are out of school and married. In his eleventh term. Very effective floor leader. Tough, hard-nosed partisan. Generally sides with the governor when he's a Republican, but this won't be a caucus position. In the past he's been lukewarm in opposing private stores. In his spare time he has a place at the shore and likes to fly his private plane. Despite his years in Harrisburg, he seems to have stayed clean. He's a lawyer with a fairly successful practice. Six figures."

"What type of law?" Vince asked.

"Varied. Corporate, domestic relations, some criminal. But mostly estates."

"Estates, huh?" Vince said. "If a lawyer's going to get dirty, it's usually with estates. Check it out. Thoroughly. Next."

[352]

Each House member was similarly dissected. No one was taken for granted, not even the ones who had publicly committed for private stores. They were looking for any lever, any area of vulnerability that would make a threat, a bribe, or maybe just a favor worthwhile. The rep from the northwest who was a closet homosexual. The devout Catholic from Pittsburgh who had knocked up his Harrisburg secretary, then arranged for her abortion. The member of the Professional Licensure Committee who had taken cash on a recent optometrist bill. The rep from Allegheny who needed labor support and untraceable cash to run for Congress. The lawyer from Montgomery County who could use the legal work from one of the family's insurance companies. The guy from Lackawanna who had furnished his Harrisburg apartment with hijacked goods. The rep from the northern tier with the cocaine habit. The woman from the southwest who had managed to squelch her daughter's solicitation arrest. It was most definitely hardball, and no one was spared.

It was about four hours before Pagano reached the last member. "I've left the most important one till last, Vince. Your classmate. Kevin Murray. You know all about him, so I won't bore you. The most effective and the most respected legislator in the House. And absolutely no lever. Disgustingly clean. He's always opposed private stores. Says it would be an open invitation to the mob."

"What cynicism," Vince mocked.

"Yeah, well, you can laugh, boss, but without him we're in deep trouble. On the moral issues half the members check his vote before they pull their switch. Even if the church groups, including the Catholic Conference, come out against us, Murray's support would probably outweigh them. The Church may not like his vote, but it'd never attack him. So any other member who went along could say that Kevin Murray voted the same way. Suddenly the action is no longer immoral. But if he opposes it, if he gets up and debates the issue, we're probably dead. I hope you don't get pissed at me again, Vince. I don't like having my don angry. But that's a fact. We need Kevin Murray, and we have no lever. None at all."

Vince rose and slowly walked to the salon door. Michael was still in the cockpit, eagerly awaiting the next strike. The boy was a natural fighter, always coming back for another challenge. Just like his godfather, the man Vince desperately needed if his plans were to succeed. He knew what had to be done, but he hated the thought.

Finally he turned back to the men. Once again his head was clear and his eyes were hard. "You worry about the others," he said. "Leave Kevin Murray to me."

CHAPTER
Twenty-two

PAT Carney discreetly looked at his watch and sighed. Over an hour already. The boss had known what he was doing when he ducked this one, dumping it instead on Pat. Actually, Monsignor Jimmy Farrell was doing most of the work. Theology and social justice came under his bailiwick. On the boss's instructions Pat was there mainly as an observer but also as an ally if Farrell needed one. And wimp that he was, Farrell badly needed help. The adversaries were a group of nuns, although that fact would have been impossible to ascertain from their manner of dress. Not a habit was visible. Mostly skirts and sweaters, with a few wearing slacks. There were about twenty of them, mainly in the thirty- to fifty-five-year-old range.

The wave of the future, Pat thought, as he tapped his fingers on the table. Members of CDC, Catholics for Democracy in the Church. Outspoken opponents of the pope's authoritarian rule.

What are we coming to? Pat wondered. *Where are the old days, when you could tell a nun a mile away? When they had gone about their duties—whether it was teaching the young or healing the sick—asking no questions, making no waves. When Rome had been the law without hesitation, without dissent. Had that been so terrible? Hadn't the educational product of our schools been better, the spiritual well-being of the flock more secure?*

The only consolation was the fact that nowhere in the group could be found a Sister of the Immaculate Heart of Mary or a Sister of St. Joseph. The Notre Dames, the Mercys, the Holy

Childs—they were there. But not a Mac and not a St. Joe's. Thank God some things didn't change.

Sister Patricia ("call me Trish") Ann Langan had been holding forth for fifteen minutes. "All of us share a love for the Church. That goes without saying."

Then why say it? Pat thought.

The nun continued. "If the church is to remain a viable institution in an increasingly pluralistic society, however, it must be broad enough to encompass and respect a healthy diversity of opinion. To do otherwise is to expose it to ridicule and turn away millions who believe—quite validly, in my opinion—that a faith unquestioned is a faith unfounded. Regrettably our pontiff seems unwilling or unable to grasp this reality. His approach, which I describe as cafeteria-style Catholicism—the spoon-fed, take-it-or-leave-it approach—invites disaster."

"Thank you, Trish," Monsignor Farrell said. "Your points are well taken. Certainly the Church, as the mystical body of Christ, must take advantage of the physical, spiritual, and mental resources of all its members in precisely the same manner that a human body derives strength from all its parts. Appropriate diversity is both necessary and welcome. There will always be a need for us to dialogue with each other. But—and this is essential—it must be conducted within proper parameters."

Jesus, Pat thought. *Pluralistic society, dialogue (as a verb, not a noun), parameters—they're rolling out all the buzzwords.*

"I don't want you to misunderstand me, Jimmy," Sister Trish said. "I appreciate your time and patience. We all do. But whenever we meet, it is never with the cardinal. We set forth specific grievances, and all we receive is the standard general response. A patronizing pat on the head to keep us at bay. Appease the children, then back to the real world." She turned to Pat. "Monsignor, you haven't spoken since we began."

"It's just that I've been so very enthralled by the dialogue, Sister."

"Please, it's Trish. And may I call you Patrick?"

"A few of my close friends call me Pat, *Sister.* But for now let's just make it Monsignor."

The nun blushed, but only slightly. "Very well, Monsignor. At any rate, I think we'd all appreciate the benefit of your thoughts."

[356]

"Very well, Sister." A few months ago he would have handled this diplomatically. But since Christmas Eve he was a different man. "To be perfectly candid, I think we've just wasted over an hour." He looked at his watch. "Sixty-eight minutes, to be exact."

"You're inferring, then, that the issue of a democratic Church is not worth discussion?"

Pat suppressed a chuckle. When you were a friend of Kevin Murray, it was impossible to be unaware of diction. "I'm not *implying*, nor should you *infer*, anything. I'm merely stating a fact. Talk of democracy in the context of the Church borders on the ludicrous."

"Ludicrous, Monsignor? I think not. Particularly with reference to the American Church. In a nation whose very roots are enmeshed in democracy, any organization which fails to provide a healthy atmosphere of freedom is bent on self-destruction."

"Sister, by definition, the Church cannot and must not ever become a democratic institution. God was never elected, nor am I aware of Christ's ever taking a poll among his apostles before acting. The pope, that Polish peasant whom you seem to hold in such disdain, takes the place of Christ here on earth. He orders and we obey. That simple."

"There's no room for discussion? The windows opened by Vatican Two are to be closed forever?"

"Certainly there is room for discussion. There always has been, but internally. Publicly we speak with one voice because we are the Church, founded by Jesus Christ. I've listened to some of your specific complaints, and you're sadly mistaken if you think that they're founded in Vatican Two. Let's take your allegedly maligned sister in Christ from Michigan. She accepted the governor's appointment as secretary of health and welfare, a position in which she must administer the public funding of abortion. And not only do we have the abortion problem, which in itself is conclusive, but her acceptance of the appointment violated the pope's ban on religious holding public office. Totally unacceptable. The Church took the only action possible under the situation. She was offered a choice, and regrettably, she chose to forsake her vocation in favor of her public position."

"She was forced from her vocation, Monsignor. The Church

[357]

talks of family, yet her religious community was her family, and she was driven from it."

"Not at all. The choice was hers. To be honest, I think that the Church was lenient."

"Lenient?" The nun was almost shouting. "What more could they have done to her?"

"In a word, excommunication. Physical or moral involvement in an abortion remains grounds for excommunication. And it strikes me that funding abortions clearly constitutes such involvement. Which, of course, brings us to your organization. More specifically, the full-page ad in the *New York Times* that a number of your members, including several from this archdiocese, signed."

"That has been blown entirely out of proportion."

"I think not. It stated, and I quote, 'There is a diversity of opinion within the Church on the question of abortion.' Not true. The teaching of the Church on abortion is monolithic. There is no room for individual interpretation. It's forbidden, and that's the name of that tune. Rome, quite properly, has ordered each religious who signed the ad to issue a retraction or face expulsion. Again, the only proper course of action."

"And one designed, once again, to drive women away."

"The Church cannot concern itself with popularity. Only with what is right. You may disagree with this position, just as you may disagree on contraception, celibacy, and the female priesthood. These are Church rules which someday may be altered, but for now they are binding. But when we move into dogma, that is an entirely different matter. In those situations the pope has spoken *ex cathedra*. Accordingly public questioning of articles of faith such as the Virgin Birth is heresy, pure and simple."

"Some feel that a reversal of this doctrine would make the Church more relevant for women. Mary, as a woman in the fullest sense of the term, is far more relevant than a vestal virgin enshrined on an isolated pedestal."

"Doubtful and, far more important, *irrelevant*. It is an issue of faith and morals, on which the pope speaks with infallibility. That's it."

"I can see we're not getting very far."

"Probably not, Sister. What it really gets down to is rules. If you want to join a club, you have to go by the rules. In this case the club is the Church. If you don't go by its rules, you're not in

[358]

the club. You're not a Catholic. You may think you are, you may call yourself one, but you're not. That's not being judgmental, to use another word that seems to be in vogue these days. It doesn't mean that you're not a good Christian or a good person. It just means that you are not a Catholic. The choice is left to each of us, and I pray God that we make the correct one."

Pat looked at his watch a final time. "It's been enlightening, Sisters, if not enjoyable, but I really must go. I'm certain, however, that Monsignor Farrell—Jimmy to you—will be happy to dialogue further on the relevance of the Church in a pluralistic society."

Pat's secretary was nearly hysterical when he returned. "You're supposed to be at the *Standard* staff meeting in five minutes. UPI has been trying to get you for the last hour, and you haven't prepared your speech for the college leaders' meeting this afternoon."

"Relax, Lucille. It'll all work out. Have trust in God."

"Tell me about it. Oh, yes, and Chris Wheeler called again. It's the third time this week, Monsignor. He sounds, I don't know, almost desperate."

"I haven't been ducking him," Pat answered defensively. "Things have just been so hectic."

He went into his office to gather his notes for the meeting. He *hadn't* been ducking Chris. Not anymore. Later today he'd meet with the boss and raise the issue of laicization. And if the cardinal was offended, screw him. It was nice to be immune, the only good thing that came out of Christmas Eve.

Without notice, the cardinal materialized at the doorway. "Word travels fast, Patrick. I hear you weren't overly sympathetic with our sisters in Christ."

"I probably *was* a bit harsh, Eminence. In grade school I got straight Cs in self-control."

"Not to mention tact. Sorry, Pat, but we can't have that type of conduct from one of our top staffers. I'm afraid a change is in order."

A few months ago such news would have been shattering. Now it didn't matter. "Whatever you say, boss," Pat answered. "I'm your obedient servant."

"It might prove difficult for you, Pat. I know you're not fond of headwear, but you'll have to get used to wearing a hat."

Pat was thunderstruck. "Are you saying—"

[359]

"Yes, I am. Actually I made the decision several months ago, but it was confirmed by Rome only this morning. You're now the newest, and youngest, auxiliary bishop of Philadelphia. Congratulations."

Pulski turned to leave, then paused. "Incidentally, we're making the announcement at a four o'clock news conference. It might be nice if you attended."

It was with mixed emotions that Pat inched home along the Schuylkill Expressway. He had dreamed about a hat for years. Indeed, most of his actions since entering the seminary had been channeled toward that goal. There could now be no doubt that he was a success, one of a tiny handful of priests to ascend to episcopal rank. And suddenly his future was without limit.

The only benefit of the rush-hour crunch was that he was able to hear KYW's coverage four times, each time more extensive. It always amazed him how quickly the media could move. They had his entire background: the early death of his mother, his care for his younger siblings, the years at West Catholic and Villanova, his peformance in the seminary—all the way through to his father's tragic death. Past and present associates were interviewed: the cardinal, of course; one of his seminary instructors; the pastor of his residence parish; several of his colleagues at the chancery; and his college classmate State Representative Kevin Murray.

All very soothing to the ego. It was nice to be recognized. Even nicer to be rewarded. And the rewards might grow larger. Who could tell? The cardinal wasn't getting any younger. Perhaps someday he might be wearing both a bishop's hat and a cardinal's ring. And after that, maybe, just maybe, the ultimate. If the College of Cardinals could break four centuries of tradition to elect a Polish pope, wasn't it inevitable that an American would one day occupy the throne of Peter?

It was all possible now for the kid from MBS. But there would be pitfalls along the way, requiring him to be very careful.

That was the problem. And the paradox. The hat was a blessing and a curse. It had rekindled the spark, once again giving him an appetite for power. But to continue his advance as a leader of the Church, he would have to retreat, as a priest and as a man.

His father's death had devastated him, for it came at a time when he had finally, with the help of the cardinal, sorted out his life. George Carney had been his last chance, the final opportunity to tear down the walls which Pat had carefully constructed and to experience once again the joys and pains of humanity.

The initial shock had given way to self-bitterness. No longer did he care what others thought. Not his colleagues, not the public, not even the boss. Screw all of them. As Kevin would say, screw the world except six, and save them for pallbearers. Ironically, Pat became more effective, in his work and his dealings with others. No longer were his actions calculated, weighed on a scale of career opportunity. He said what he felt; he did what he thought was right. And even though he could never grant self-forgiveness, he began, ever so slowly, to like himself. He realized that he was becoming something that he had unconsciously envied for years but could never attain. He was becoming like Kevin Murray.

Now, fight it though he might, it had to change. He lacked the strength to do otherwise. He wasn't Kevin Murray, who could turn his back on higher office. He was Pat Carney, a future member of the College of Cardinals, willing to pay any price for admission. He would no longer be able to like himself, but that was part of the price.

The KYW beeper interrupted the program. It was used sparingly, reserved for a late-breaking crisis. Pat listened, curious to learn what event could upstage the selection of a new bishop.

"This is a KYW news bulletin. This just in. Narberth police officials have reported an apparent murder-suicide in that suburban community. Although details are sketchy, the dead have been identified as Christopher Wheeler and his wife, Margaret. Sources on the scene indicate that Wheeler apparently shot his wife, then took his own life. Wheeler is a former priest, his wife a former nun. More details as soon as they are available."

Pat pulled the car to the expressway shoulder and staggered out, gasping for air. Using the car for support, the new auxiliary bishop walked several steps, then began to retch.

Twenty-three

COLLEEN Campion had a great deal to celebrate. She had just received a promotion, purchased a new Corvette, and scheduled an April vacation in Barbados. Most important, it was the first day of spring. The party had been fun. Excellent conversation, good scotch, and a few sniffs of coke. The love-making hadn't been bad, either, even if she couldn't remember his name.

She had just pulled onto Roosevelt Boulevard, ignoring the yield sign. The driver of the truck did his best, jamming on the brakes and swerving to his left. He succeeded in avoiding a full collision, just grazing the side of the Corvette. That was enough. Colleen lost control, and her car, after jumping the curb, slammed into a tree. Twenty minutes later a comatose Colleen Campion was in the emergency room of College Hospital. The report of her examination painted a somber picture: shattered hip, broken ankle, broken arm, broken jaw, broken nose, and substantial neurological damage. The examination revealed one other troublesome factor: Colleen Campion was pregnant.

It was like being in the FBI again, working the good guy–bad guy routine with Charlie Masters. Only this time Kevin was the good guy. It hadn't been planned. Instead, it was merely a natural outgrowth of having Craig Harrington as his partner.

Harrington shook his head. "Absolutely unsatisfactory. The governor's position on this section indicates a willful deficiency in either logic or courage. And I would think that you'd be too embarrassed, Frank, even to consent to convey it."

Frank Nugent's jaw hardened. The governor's legislative liaison was a professional who prided himself on his loyalty to Dan Talbot and his ability to handle even the most difficult meetings with poise. In Nugent's three years with the governor only Craig Harrington had been able to threaten that poise.

"I've never been embarrassed to work for Dan Talbot," Nugent answered. "And as I've told you before, Craig, personal attacks will solve nothing. We both have a job to do. Let's accomplish it as pleasantly as possible."

"Pleasantness, when unaccompanied by common sense—and courage—constitutes the paradise of a fool."

"By Christ, I like that!" Kevin Murray said. "Mellifluous as catshit. You have to admit, Frank, the boy has a way with words."

Nugent grinned. Kevin he could deal with, even when they disagreed.

Harrington ignored the remark. "Okay, Frank, nothing personal. Let's stay on the facts. Now, while personally opposed to abortion, our governor believes in freedom of choice for women. Isn't that correct?"

Nugent nodded. "Yes."

"Fine. He bases that opinion on the court decisions which legalized abortion, right?"

"Correct."

"Accordingly, he accepts the legality of abortion. True?"

"Yes."

"He also supports the section of our bill which provides for the reporting of all abortions performed. I believe the exact phrase in his veto message was 'such information is valuable in collecting and collating information crucial to an enlightened discussion of this wrenching social issue.' Ring a bell?"

"Certainly, Craig. With a few minor exceptions, the governor supports the reporting, storing, and publication of this data."

Harrington leaned forward, his finger pointed at Nugent. "And yet he insists that the data to be published protect the anonymity of not only the woman—who was already protected in the bill—but the abortionist as well. I humbly implore you to show me even the slightest thread of logic in that position."

"The governor believes that the identity of the physician—"

"Abortionist."

"—physician should not be publicly disclosed. He doesn't

believe that such information is either vital or necessary."

"Freedom of choice, Frank! The same right to choose that our leader—and I use that term with considerable reservation—purports to embrace. Women have the right to know whether or not the doctor who is touching them uses those same hands to slaughter infants."

"The governor believes that the publication of physicians' names would needlessly single them out for abuse and even violence."

"But if abortion is so very innocuous, so very socially acceptable, what rational man can foresee a backlash against those who perform such a service to women?"

"Come on, Craig, we both—"

"No, you come on, Frank. Let's put an end to this exercise in self-delusion. The only reason we're even in these negotiation sessions is that *your* governor, who would never qualify for a chapter in *Profiles in Courage,* is concerned about the political fallout from his veto, particularly since he's running for reelection this year. So he's willing to throw us a bone as long as it's acceptable to the Pennsylvania Medical Society. And that august body will never consent to the names of abortionists' being published. Another classic example of Dan Talbot wetting his finger to see which way the wind is blowing."

Harrington rose and walked to Nugent's desk, where he jabbed his finger again, this time into the staffer's chest. "Remind that fearless statesman that sometimes a wind becomes a hurricane, blowing everything before it away. Including incumbent governors!"

The veins in Nugent's face bulged. Slamming his fist on the desk, he began to respond. "I've taken just about all—"

"Time out, sports fans," Kevin said, standing and taking Harrington by the arm. "We've reached the saturation point for today. Let's reflect on what we've discussed and get together again early next week." He tugged at Harrington's arm. "Let's go, partner. You've spread enough charm around for one day."

Outside, Harrington was furious. "Thanks for all your help."

"You were doing just fine by yourself, partner."

"We're supposed to be a team."

"We are. You've got a rare and special ability that's invaluable to me. As long as you're around, I look good in comparison."

"I'm glad you can be so goddamn nonchalant about this. You seem to have forgotten what's at stake."

"*Au contraire,* shitbrain. We did okay today. A couple of hours from now Frank Nugent will call me, totally bent out of shape over your performance. I'll crack a few jokes, stroke him a little, and we'll end the day with a net gain."

"I hate it, Kevin. All of it. It's so goddamn demeaning."

"No argument there, pal. It's the most frustrating thing I've ever gone through, but what's the choice?" He looked at his watch. "I gotta get back to the office. Keep smiling."

Harrington was right, Kevin thought on the way back. It *was* demeaning. But it was the only route available if the abortion bill was to become law. Talbot's veto had given them no alternative. An override was out of the question. It took a two-thirds majority, and they were at least three votes short in the Senate.

They were forced to accept the invitation the governor had made in his veto message. The first meeting, in late January, at the governor's mansion, was strictly a media event. Newspeople jammed the outside gates when Kevin and Harrington arrived, anxious for details that didn't exist. Dan Talbot was charming, of course. He always was. There was nothing he desired more than to be liked. He had never been overly concerned about respect.

It was agreed that Kevin and Craig would begin to meet regularly with Talbot's staff, headed by Frank Nugent. No guarantees were made, and Kevin was in no position to demand one. The governor was holding all the cards—and the pen.

It would have been easier if the governor had been a man who strongly believed in something. Anything. His predecessor, for example, had been down-the-line pro-abortion and made no bones about it. You could deal with that. You either had the two-thirds to override the veto or didn't run the bill. It was different with Talbot. He had signed the abortion funding cutoff, vetoed the abortion control bill, and you still didn't know where he was.

A point in Kevin's favor was timing. Talbot was up for re-election in November, and after a slow start the pro-life rank and file were pounding him with letters and phone calls. By contrast, the pro-abortion contingent, while ecstatic over the veto, didn't completely trust him. They were still smarting over the funding cutoff. Most experts predicted a close race for Talbot, whose opponent was squarely in the abortion camp. Kevin let it be known,

[365]

through the right contacts, that the pro-lifers would sit this one out if no abortion bill were signed. And in a tight election that could spell the difference.

So they negotiated, Kevin using every ounce of self-control to refrain from exploding and calling them the phony whore-mongers that they were. He was hoping to resolve the matter by June, before the summer recess, but in no event could the battle drag on any later than early October, far enough before the election so that his colleagues might not draw and quarter him.

All and all, an extremely frustrating, but totally necessary, process.

The office was even worse than usual. Janet was armed with a dozen messages, each one urgent.

"KYW wants an interview on the city wage tax. They're on deadline. The printing office wants to know when you'll have the newsletter proofed. Catholic Conference wants to know if you can meet with them this afternoon on the textbook appropriations. The Speaker would like you to brief him on the curriculum bill before it runs tomorrow. Jane Glass from the *Daily Times* wants you to call her on the adoption bill, and the UPI wants an update on the abortion negotiations. And Marlene called. Mr. Donaher is complaining that you haven't handled his aunt's estate."

"Jesus. Any more good news?"

"Yes. You've had a number of pro-life calls. There's this pregnant woman in a coma in Philadelphia. Her mother is demanding an abortion."

The room seemed to be closing in on him. "Goddamn, doesn't it ever let up?"

"It's your monster, Kevin. You created it."

"Just what I need right now, a goddamn lecture."

"I try to please. What do you want to handle first?"

"The train reservation."

"What train reservation?"

"The one to Wyoming."

"Seriously."

The problems wouldn't go away. There was nothing to do but attack. First, though, he wanted to call the one person left in the world to whom he could talk. Really talk. "Give me ten minutes. I'm going to call my brother."

Although five years apart, Brendan and Kevin Murray had always been close. Always. Even when they were kids, when it wasn't cool for Brendan to have his little brother around.

As with any two humans, there were distinctions. Brendan, for example, had been far more pragmatic in his choice of a career. After graduating from Villanova, he had plunged into the business world, landing a position with IBM. His move up the corporate ladder, if not spectacular, was more than satisfactory. It provided him with a six-figure income, an elegant house in a North Jersey lake community, and a summer place in Margate.

When Maureen Murray was asked about her sons, her answer was a model of accuracy. "They're both doing fine. Brendan makes the money, and Kevin gets the headlines."

Brendan was in a staff conference when the phone rang. "Brendan Murray."

"This is *Newsweek* calling. We're taking a random survey of the benefits of grace before cunnilingus."

His face was instantly transformed from the businessman to the little kid. "How are you!" he said, beaming, then turned to his colleagues. "Ten-minute break, gang. It's my brother." Then back to the phone. "So how the hell are you?"

"Can't complain. Doesn't do a damn bit of good."

"I know, shithead. You checked the obituary page this morning, and you weren't on it, thereby disappointing thousands of people."

"Fuckin' well told. Busy?"

"Up to my ass," Brendan answered. "As usual. You?"

"Don't ask. It's always a zoo. Did you ever wonder if it's worth it, Brendan? You know, the whole thing."

"I don't know, buddy."

"Oh, well."

"Yeah. How are the kids?"

"Good. Fine. We have to get them all together soon. It's been too long."

"I know. It's just with all their activities—"

"I know. It's a bitch, isn't it? How's Sally?"

"Good. And Karen?"

Kevin sighed. "Okay, I guess. She's going back to work."

"No kidding?"

"At the hospital. Just a couple days a week. Middle shift. She needs it, you know, just to get away a little. It's been rough."

"Yeah."

His voice started to crack. "We think of him all the time, Bren. We talk about him with the kids. Andrew. It's like—it's like we have to. That if we don't, we're being disloyal. You know, when I meet people and they ask me how many kids I have, I can't just answer five and be done with it. I can't. I have to say six, but one is dead. I can't help it. I'm not trying to get sympathy or anything like that. I just can't turn my back on him." He fought to hold back the tears. "Why the fuck couldn't it have been me instead of him?"

"Come on, pal."

"No, I mean it. I swear to God. I'm better off dead—to everyone. At least they'd get the insurance money, which is one fuck of a lot more than I make."

"Cut it out, Kevin!"

"I'm serious. Honest to Jesus. I don't make shit; I can't support my family right; Karen and I are always at each other's throat." His voice broke. When he spoke again, it was with hatred. "I couldn't even stay awake for the little time my son was alive."

"Knock it the fuck off, Kevin!"

"You know it's true, Bren. You even said it. You told me I was crazy to be doing this. You were smart. You work your ass off, but you're making money."

Brendan spoke through clenched teeth. "You listen to me, god-damn you!"

"Look, I—"

"Shut the fuck up and listen to me. Sure, you fight with Karen. So what? I fight with Sally. What else is new? When you have a lot of kids, there's a lot of pressure. It doesn't mean you don't love each other. Sally and I fight like bastards sometimes. Every bit as much as you and Karen."

"Yeah, but at least you never—"

"Don't bring that up again, Kevin, for Christ's sake. That was years ago. You've done enough penance."

"Have I?"

"You're damn right. You're a damn good husband—and a damn good father."

"Horseshit."

"I mean it! Maybe you're too dumb to see it, but your kids idolize you. They're really proud of you, Kevin, and what you've done. Even little Kevin, even though at his age it's not cool to show it. And as far as your being in politics, sure, I told you to get out. But that was Kevin Murray's brother talking. Selfish. Looking out only for someone he loves. Sure, I was smart. I made money, but I envy you, you son of a bitch!"

"Envy me? What crap!"

"Is it? You know what your problem is? For all that cocky image you put on, you've always sold yourself short. Yeah, pal, I *envy* you. Unlike me, you've had the guts to get involved. Look at all the people you've helped. Look what you've been able to accomplish. Things that nobody else could make happen. You've given a whole lot of people new faith in government because for once they see a guy who's totally honest and has the guts to take a stand. You're special, Kevin. You always were. Do you realize that there are children out there right now, probably thousands, who wouldn't be alive if it weren't for you? How many people can say that? And as far as falling asleep with Andrew, you were exhausted. Physically and mentally. If your idol, St. Peter, could fall asleep on Christ *three times,* who the hell are you to condemn yourself? Do you understand?"

"Yeah. Good speech. I'll give it a ninety."

"Don't get sarcastic with me, you little bastard. I'm worried about you, Kevin. Are you gonna be okay?"

"Sure. Really."

"I mean it. Look, do you want me to come down? I'll cancel everything and jump on the train. We can talk."

"No. Thanks, but I'm okay. Honest."

"Stop hating yourself, Kevin. You *are* special. There're only two people in this world I've really admired. One was the Sarge. The other is my brother. I love you, Kevin."

"I love you, too, pal. Keep the faith."

After replacing the phone, Kevin leaned back. He had needed that, and only Brendan could give it to him. And his brother had been right, at least about a lot of it. He *did* sell himself short, torn apart by doubts and guilt

God, he thought, *a shrink would have a field day with me.*

The phone rang, and he was back in reality. The first order of business was a pregnant young woman in a coma. Wyoming would have to wait.

CHAPTER
Twenty-four

"YOU'RE a thousand miles away, Vincent. Aren't you the one who brags about leaving his work at the office?"

Vince sighed. "Sorry. It's been a bear of a day. Want another drink?" He rose and walked to the bar at the far end of the den.

"No, thanks," Lena answered. "Want to talk about it?"

He sighed again. "No, not really. I don't even want to think about it."

"It isn't easy to ignore, Vincent. Not when it's on television and all over the papers."

"I know, I know." He walked back to the sofa. "I never intended it to be this way."

"What did you expect? Did you actually think it could be any other way?"

Her voice was carefully measured, wholly without reproach, which made the reproach even worse. Vince hesitated. They were approaching dangerous grounds. He never discussed what he *really* did, never admitted to her what he *really* was. It was a charade, but one which he felt compelled to play.

"I guess it runs with the territory," he finally said. "When you're a lawyer, you get tainted with the people you represent."

His wife leaned over and kissed him. "Sure, Vincent."

Vince held her and kissed her neck. She had always been able to arouse him quickly, with a touch, a brief kiss, even just a look. He had never taken her beauty for granted, particularly now, when she still retained most of her St. Thomas tan. The top two buttons of her blouse were undone, displaying the contrast between her bronze body and the whiteness of her breasts.

"Listen," he said, "I've got a great idea."

"Not now. The children are still awake."

"I thought they were in bed."

"The girls are, but Michael and Anthony are still doing their homework."

"Maybe you haven't heard, but there's been a great new invention, called a door. Like the one on our bedroom."

"I know, but I just don't feel comfortable, knowing they're not asleep. Later."

"Is that a promise?"

"A Sicilian vow. Satisfied?"

Vince smiled. "It's an offer I can't refuse."

"You could have chosen a better phrase, Vincent, given existing circumstances."

"Yeah, you're right," he hesitated. "Any reaction from the kids? You know, about today?"

"Not from the girls, of course. They're too young to grasp anything."

"And the boys?"

"Nothing will affect Michael. He won't allow it. Long ago he made up his mind to be just like his father. Anything you do is right. He has your strength, Vincent, and the same ability to frighten people. None of his classmates would dare make any comment."

"And Anthony?"

"My poor, vulnerable Anthony. He's the one I worry about. He'll never tell me if there are problems, but I could sense something when he came home from school. Children can be so cruel."

"Adults can't?"

"Certainly, but not like children. To be completely cruel, you must be completely honest, and adults aren't. We learn to be subtle, to avoid saying exactly what we think."

"What can I do, Lena? How can I make it easier for Anthony? For all of them?"

Again, a casual reproach. "I don't know. You're the one who's made the decisions. It can be only you who answers that." She rose. "I'm going to check homework. Be back in a few minutes."

"Okay. Remember our deal."

"I'm Sicilian. I never forget."

Vince stretched out on the couch. He was exhausted but still wound too tight for sleep. *Nothing's ever easy,* he thought. *For each thing you want out of life, there's a price.*

Like today. He had been the guest of the Pennsylvania Crime Commission, subpoenaed to testify before it. He had no time for the organization. Strictly bush-league. The feds he could respect. They were professionals. Prosecutors. When they came after you, you worried. The commission was a joke. It had no law enforcement powers, unable either to indict or to prosecute. All it could do was investigate. That usually consisted of reading a few books on organized crime, reviewing surveillance reports from local law enforcement, randomly subpoenaing targets, then publishing a public report which invariably was a masterpiece of unsubstantiated character assassination. When you weren't stuck with a case, when you weren't responsible for taking it into court and winning on the merits, and when you were exempt from libel actions by statute, it was easy to say whatever you pleased.

Not surprisingly, Vince's appearance had been leaked to the media. They all were there when he arrived, cameras shoved into his face, reporters jogging beside him, firing one salvo after another.

The commission attorney was young, obviously relishing his first media exposure, his first chance to confront an actual Mafia figure.

"Mr. Grosso, I am Keith Barnaby. Thank you for coming."

"I wouldn't have missed it for the world, Mr. Barnaby."

"Yes. Will your attorney be here soon?"

"No one else is coming, Mr. Barnaby. I didn't feel it necessary to bring counsel."

Barnaby was taken off guard. "Why is that?"

"It's not my style. I've never been afraid to walk alone. How about you?"

"I'm not the issue today, Mr. Grosso. You are. Please come with me."

"Certainly, Mr. Barnaby."

He was led into the conference room. The members of the commission were seated behind a raised conference table. For once they all were there, reluctant to miss such an opportunity.

Off to one side was a court stenographer, ready to take down every word.

Vince was seated in the lone chair placed in the middle of the room. It was straight-backed with no arms, reflecting a desire by the commission to get every possible edge. Vince was familiar with the strategy, identical to that used by Michael Agostino when he had confronted the New York don.

After swearing in his witness, Barnaby began. "Mr. Grosso, before we begin and for the record, I note that you are not accompanied by counsel. You are aware that you have a right to counsel of your choice?"

"Yes, I am, Mr. Barnaby. So that the record is clear, I have voluntarily chosen to come alone."

"That, of course, is your right. In view of this, however, I would, again for the record, like to spell out the additional rights you have."

"That won't be necessary, Mr. Barnaby. I am an attorney, 1968 graduate of the University of Michigan Law School—Law Review—and am fully cognizant of my rights. Specifically, I am aware of my Miranda rights, as well as my right to invoke the protection of the Fifth Amendment of the United States Constitution as well as Article One, Section Nine of the Pennsylvania Constitution. I am also aware of the elements of the crime of perjury and the penalties for commission of such a crime. I freely waive these rights and am prepared to execute the written waiver."

"Written waiver? Uh, we have none."

"Oh? Most professional law enforcement agencies do. Be that as it may, I am at your disposal."

Barnaby hesitated, shuffling his notes. Vince's confidence had unnerved him. "Very well," he finally said. "Please state your occupation."

"I'm an attorney engaged in the private practice of law with offices in Center City and South Philadelphia."

Barnaby decided to hit him quickly, shake some of the confidence. "And isn't it true that you were set up in that practice by your uncle Fredo Annaloro, former head of the Philadelphia organized crime family?"

"Actually you've asked several questions," Vince responded calmly. "It's true that Fredo Annaloro was my uncle, and it's

[373]

equally true that he assisted me in the establishment of my practice. As to his being involved in some type of organized crime family, as you put it, I have absolutely no knowledge of that."

"You're not aware that your uncle was listed as being in charge of organized crime in Philadelphia?"

"Listed? By whom?"

"Well, there have been numerous published reports. This commission, federal grand jury presentments, congressional hearings, news media accounts—"

"Ah. Well if the news media said so, it must be true. After all, we know that the news is always accurate."

"You're saying that these accounts are incorrect?"

"I've read a number of stories about my uncle's alleged ties to organized crime. All I can say is that I have no personal knowledge of any such link."

"What, then, did he do for a living?"

"He was a businessman. I wasn't privy to most of his business dealings, but I know that he had a vending company and at least part of an importing business."

"You were close to him?"

"Yes, I would say so. He was a devoted uncle, particularly since my father died when I was quite young."

"All right. Let's touch on another area. Do you know one Julius Marzette?"

"I do."

"And isn't it true that you have met with him on several occasions?"

"One, if my memory serves correctly."

"And what was the substance of your conversation? In detail, please."

"I regret that I must decline to provide specifics of my conversation with Mr. Marzette."

Barnaby's eyes brightened. "You're invoking the Fifth Amendment?" he asked eagerly. Here was the chance to earn his spurs, to put away a Mafia leader as had been done in New Jersey. If Vincent Grosso took the Fifth, Barnaby would immediately adjourn and petition the court for immunity. Once cloaked with immunity, a witness could no longer invoke the Fifth. If he persisted in refusing to answer questions, he could be jailed for contempt of court. It was a powerful prosecutorial tool, particularly when you

[374]

were faking and had nothing on the witness. The New Jersey Commission on Investigations had jailed three high-ranking mafiosi in this fashion, a success it never could have scored on a substantive offense.

Barnaby's excitement was short-lived. "Not at all," Vince answered. "I met with Mr. Marzette in my capacity as an attorney. Accordingly, everything which we discussed is subject to the attorney-client privilege which, by the canons of ethics, I am not permitted to waive. Only the client can provide such a waiver. If Mr. Mazette is willing to do so, I would be more than happy to respond in detail."

Barnaby hesitated. "All right," he finally said. "Then let's talk about your meeting with Michael Agostino. You know him?"

Vince smiled. "A businessman in New York, whom my firm has represented on several occasions."

"I sense that you will also invoke the attorney-client privilege concerning your conversation with Mr. Agostino."

"I have no choice, Mr. Barnaby."

Barnaby saw it all unraveling. There would be no knockout, no dramatic development. His opponent was too quick, too polished. There was nothing to do but question him for another half hour or so to save face, then get him the hell out so that he could lick his wounds.

The media were waiting for Vince when he left.

"Did you take the Fifth, Mr. Grosso?" one reporter asked.

"Certainly not. Isn't it our civic duty to assist the government whenever possible?"

"What did you discuss?"

"Sorry. I've been admonished by the commission attorney not to discuss any of my testimony. Their rule, not mine."

"Do you consider yourself harassed?"

Vince smiled. "I consider myself harassed when I have two days to prepare for a case when I need a month. I consider myself harassed when I try to reason with two teenage sons. I *really* consider myself harassed when I try to find a parking space in South Philly. Life is harassment, so what's a little more?"

Vince knew that he'd carried it off well. All of it. They hadn't come close to laying a glove on him, and for that he should be pleased. He wasn't. Even though it had been expected, he became incensed when he saw Barnaby standing before the cameras, stat-

[375]

ing to the world that the information obtained from Vincenzo Grosso had been "significant" and that the investigation into organized crime was "continuing." *God,* Vince thought, *what they can do with innuendo.*

He picked up the remote control and switched to PRISM. Oiling up for the play-offs, the 76ers were sticking it to the Cavaliers. Not that Vince cared all that much. He found it difficult to get worked up over pro ball. Too mechanical, too perfect. And with the shot clock and no zone defense, where was the strategy? Where were the coaching decisions? He'd take college ball any day in the week. Particularly Villanova. Nothing compared with Big East ball. Great athletes, superb coaching, tight zones, scores in the mid-fifties. And incredible hustle, bodies all over the floor. Unfortunately the college season had ended, Villanova going down in the regional finals to North Carolina, which went on to beat Georgetown in one of the all-time great national championship games. So Vince was stuck with the pros, and it wasn't enough to take his mind off the problems at hand.

The crime commission didn't worry him. It was candy. But his appearance before it increased the danger. Every time he was singled out in the media, every time the television lights were on him, he became a bigger target. By now everyone knew that he was the don, a man whose power was increasing daily. He was a prize to be bagged, a trophy for some prosecutor's case. The strike force had made him its top priority, and when the feds were involved, there was cause to worry. Their resources were unlimited, and sooner or later they would find a way to get him. And if they couldn't get him on substance, they'd look for a back-door approach. The don of New Orleans had gone to prison for swinging at a Coast Guard officer who was inspecting his boat. Santino Galente, underboss of Cleveland, was doing time for drunken driving. Miami's *consigliere,* Vito Cerese, was under indictment for statutory rape. All chickenshit, but with devastating consequences.

Vince Grosso was under glass. His taxes, his payroll deductions, his driver's license, and all the other regulations imposed on modern man had to be perfect. The first time he faltered the hounds would have him at bay.

These were the ones who wanted to prosecute him, to put him in jail, but at least they played by some rules. There were others

[376]

who wanted to kill him, who were waiting for their opportunity to blow up his car or take his head off with a shotgun, and they followed no rules except a law of survival.

He stretched out on the couch and closed his eyes. Was it worth it? Did the dream compensate for the pain? Could anything replace the things that he had taken for granted, things that could never be his again? Like walking to the corner store or being alone with your kids on the beach. Just once he'd like to be able to do something on his own, without being followed by bodyguards who treated him as if he were cut glass. To walk into a room without wondering if it was bugged. To pick up a phone without fear of a tap. To wake up just one morning without wondering whether today would be the day "they" would get him, the day when they would take away his freedom—or his life.

Vince Grosso, empire builder. Intelligent, rich, powerful—and a prisoner. Sentenced to play a lifetime of defense.

"You're a bundle of fun," Lena said. "I leave you for ten minutes, and you fall asleep."

Therese was with her, and once again Vince was struck by how much the two women resembled each other. And he was aware of Lena's tenseness, a tenseness which seemed always to exist when Vince and Therese were in each other's company. A fear on Lena's part that was groundless. Sure, Therese *did* turn him on in a unique way which he had never been able to analyze. But nothing would ever come of it. He wouldn't let it. He kept his promises. Besides, if Lena was so apprehensive, why didn't she solve the problem? Why didn't she send Therese back to the dorm, removing the source of temptation?

"Taking a break from the books?" he asked.

"Yes. Mrs. Grosso says I work too hard."

"She does," Lena said. "She's up till one or two every morning."

"I have to. Exams are less than a month away, and I want to make dean's list again."

"That's good," Vince said. "Hard work never hurt anyone."

"Listen to the old man," Lena replied. "If what I heard is true, you didn't exactly kill yourself at Villanova."

Vince smiled. "I tried, but Kevin wouldn't let me. Every time I got into the books, he'd be pulling me away. Always some party or something. Claimed he was broadening my education."

"Kevin? Is that your friend Kevin Murray? The state representative?" Therese asked.

"Yeah. We go back a long way."

"I saw him on television last week, talking about his adoption bill. He's very good. Still, I think adoptees should have the right to know. That's why I'm going to send away."

"Send away for what?" Lena snapped.

"My birth certificate. The original one. If Mr. Murray's bill passes, I won't be able to get it. So I'm sending for it. I just got the application. I may not be able to find my mother, but at least I'll know her name."

"Good for you," Vince said.

"Yes, that's wonderful," Lena said. She looked at her watch. "It's late. I think I'll go up."

"How come?" asked Vince.

"At my age, I need my beauty rest."

"Can I get you anything, Mrs. Grosso?"

"No. Thank you, Therese, good night."

When she reached her room, Lena sat on the edge of her bed. Her chest was pounding, and she found it difficult to breathe.

"Not yet, darling," she whispered. "Not yet."

Twenty-five

THE man knew that he shouldn't be there, but he tried to convince himself that it was legitimate research. A person with his profession had to know everything, including the seamier side of life.

The books amazed him. He couldn't believe that they were actually legal. Particularly the pictures of the children. Where did they find them? Was it possible that the parents knew?

He entered one of the booths and placed a quarter in the machine. Unbelievable. Fascinating. And, as much as he hated to admit it, exciting.

"Mind if I join you?" It was a man, about his age.

"Suit yourself," he answered, trying to sound casual.

The man's hand was on his thigh. He knew that he should push it away, but he didn't. He couldn't. He did nothing, except close his eyes. Waiting.

Only when his arms were yanked behind him and the handcuffs put on did he realize that the man was a cop. The surprise was returned an hour later, at the station during the paperwork. It was then the police officer discovered that his quarry was a priest.

"Have a seat, Father," Pat said, trying to sound casual. He had tried to duck this one, but the boss wouldn't let him off the hook.

"Thank you, Excellency."

"Not yet. Not until the ceremony. For now, it's still Monsignor. Pat, if you like."

They hesitated, each wanting the other to begin. Finally Pat took the ball. "It's an unfortunate situation, Father. Particularly the publicity. I did my best to keep the lid on, but the press loves something like this."

"Yes. I know."

"Well, our job now is damage control. For you and the Church."

"I understand."

"It appears that we can resolve this with a minimum degree of embarrassment."

"I'd hardly call what has already occurred minimal, Monsignor."

"I understand. At any rate, I have spoken with the district attorney. Directly. He wants to help."

"That's kind of him."

"Kindness is not his motivation, Father. He intends to run for governor next time around. Since he's Jewish and the wrong way on the abortion issue, he'd like to do something at least to neutralize the Church."

"I see."

The priest's calm, his dignity, unnerved Pat. It would have been far easier had he been a screamer, pounding his fists on the desk and demanding his rights. "Because of the publicity, it's impossible to have the charges dropped."

"I assumed that."

"However, the next best thing can be arranged. The DA has agreed to allow you to enter a special program. It's called ARD. It's a probationary period, without a trial. There is no admission of guilt on your part. Six months' probation, with limited counseling, and the entire matter is expunged."

"Would I be permitted to teach while on probation?"

Pat sighed. Now it really got rough. "There won't be any teaching, Father. One way or the other. I'm sorry."

At last the calm, if not the dignity, was shattered. "My God! No teaching! I've taught high school students all my life. It's my vocation."

"And I've been told that you are very good at what you do, Father. But it's out of the question. At least for now. You'll be transferred to the diocese of Kansas City and assigned to parish work. The DA has agreed that your probation can be served there."

"You've touched all the bases, haven't you, Monsignor? But did it ever occur to you, to anyone, to ask my side of the story?

Would it interest you to know that I am innocent? That I did absolutely nothing?"

"Frankly, no. I don't want this to sound callous, Father, but the image of the Church is more important than any individual. Your guilt or innocence does nothing to resolve this scandal. You *were* in a porn shop. You *were* arrested. You *were* charged with sex crimes."

"So your damage control has nothing to do with me after all. Isn't that right?"

"Not exactly. But the Church must take precedence over any of us."

The priest's tone became desperate. "Please, Monsignor, I'm begging. All I have in this world are my students. I'm good for them. I care about them. I'm not sure I can survive if I'm not permitted to teach."

"We all must bear crosses," answered Pat, immediately despising himself for such a pompous phrase.

"And if I refuse? You seem to forget that I'm a human being, a citizen of this country. I have rights. Constitutional rights. And I can win this case."

It was time for Vatican hardball. "Unquestionably, Father, you have rights as a citizen. But as a priest you have certain duties, which sometimes are in conflict with those rights. One of these duties is obedience to the Church. Should you refuse our request—our order—I have been instructed to advise you that you will be immediately stripped of your priestly powers and excommunicated from the Roman Catholic Church."

The priest stared at his superior. "Can it really be possible that we serve the same God?"

Pat rose. The priest's last words had found their mark, but the bishop designate was a pro. And when you were a pro, you never acknowledged the wounds. You just played the game. "I must insist upon your answer by noon tomorrow. Good day, Father."

When the priest was gone, Pat sat back in his chair. He had performed well, as was expected. And no one ever said that a pro had to like himself.

Twenty-six

SHEILA Sendrow's day could best be described as uneven. It had begun well enough. She had appeared in distict court representing the plaintiff under the Spousal Abuse Act. It was a continuing fulfillment of a private vow made when she accepted the presidency of the Pennsylvania NOW. Despite the administrative demands of her position, she was first and foremost an attorney, a skilled advocate who excelled in defending the rights of women before a judge or jury. Unlike riding a bike, courtroom competence was not something which one always retained. You either continued to sharpen your skills or you regressed.

There would be no such regression for Sheila. At least twice a month, and more often whenever possible, she would enter a courtroom on behalf of a client. By doing so, she was able to remember a central truth that all too frequently was overlooked. The totality of her cause was comprised of individual human beings, individual women, with very real needs. Philosophy and principle had their place, but never could they be permitted to overshadow the individual.

As was generally the case, her efforts that morning had been successful. The abusing husband was ordered from the home and required to submit to counseling. Certainly not an earth-shattering result, but satisfying nonetheless.

Lunch had been decidedly less satisfactory. She enjoyed Mark Herbert's company, but his lack of sensitivity was maddening.

She forgot exactly what started it this time. Maybe it was his assumption that Sheila could schedule her vacation around his.

"You're too goddamn sensitive!" Herbert finally exploded. "Why in the hell do you have to look at every man as an opponent?"

"I don't. I just want men, particularly the ones I care about, to regard me as an equal."

"Why don't you get off the soapbox, Sheila? Someday maybe you'll realize that it gets pretty lonely up there." He rose, throwing the tip onto the table. "At the risk of offending you even more, I'll pay the goddamn bill!"

Maybe Mark was right, Sheila thought as she stepped off the elevator. At least partially. She had to strike more of a balance, in her private life anyway, a middle ground between the helpless female, whom she despised, and the ardent crusader, who intimidated her peers. Easy to assess, difficult to attain.

"Hello, Sheila. How was court?" her secretary asked, handing her the mail and phone messages.

"Fine, Lorraine. We were successful."

"Again."

Sheila smiled. "Again."

She was halfway through the mail when her secretary buzzed. "Bridget Kelly is on the line from Harrisburg, Sheila. She says it's important."

"Thank you." She pressed the button. "Bridget."

"Hello, Sheila. How are you?"

"Fine, thank you. What can I do for you?"

"Well, I just received a call from one of our counselors in the Harrisburg clinic. She just interviewed an eighteen-year-old girl. Woman. Freshman at Carlisle. She's pregnant. Her boyfriend wants her to carry to term. Says he's willing to marry her, but she's very confused."

"The same litany I've heard so many times. But why are you calling me? This certainly isn't anything new to Planned Parenthood."

There was a pause before Bridget spoke. "The boyfriend, Sheila. The baby's—the fetus's—father."

"Yes?"

"It's your son."

[383]

Kevin was content to allow Joe Kellogg to handle the initial pleasantries. That way he could study his two adversaries, for there was no doubt in his mind that by the end of the meeting they *would* be his adversaries. That pained him. It wasn't that he minded conflict, but these were two of his own. Or should be anyway. Products of the system from grade school through college. Even now they carried the banner, at least outwardly. Each still attended Sunday mass; each was an usher at his church.

Where have we failed? Kevin thought. *How has the Church let so many slip away?*

It was a slippage that continued to escalate. Kevin had to laugh when his opponents labeled abortion a Catholic issue. Would that it were. The truth was that Catholics—sometimes even the Church hierarchy—were frequently more a hindrance than help. Like his own alma mater. In the past several years Villanova had blown it—publicly—on at least four occasions. It had invited Father Drinan, the Jesuit congressman who had consistently supported abortion funding, to speak at its commencement and receive an honorary degree. This had been followed by the presentation of an alumni award to one of the men who now sat across the table.

But what hurt him even worse was the school newspaper, the paper which Kevin had served as a student reporter and later its sports editor. Last fall it had editorialized against the abortion control bill. *Kevin's bill.* The editorial had stated that abortion was a matter exclusively between a woman and her doctor. It even mentioned Kevin by name, chiding him for his insensitivity. The same paper had recently provided a free ad for the enemy: Planned Parenthood.

Kevin was confused. What the hell was happening? How could things change so much so quickly? It hadn't been all that long ago that he was a student there, at a school that was several shades to the right of Attila the Hun. The paper had been censored to the point of absurdity, the classic example being the front-page picture of the female lead in the play. She was seated in a chair, her skirt hiked, displaying a minute amount of slip. Gene Boylan, moderator of the paper and perpetual toady to the Augustinians, could not permit such a lascivious display. With a black felt pen he inked in a border for the skirt, an adjustment that was abundantly obvious to even the most casual observer. For this flash of artistic brilliance Boylan earned himself the enduring title of "No Beaver Boylan."

No one had fought the Augustinian stranglehold more vigorously than Kevin, and he had no desire to see a return to the old days. But God, there had to be a balance. The paper shouldn't be censored, but there should at least be supervision. It was mailed to thousands of alumni across the country as well as virtually every major college and university. Right or wrong, it was perceived to be the official voice of Villanova University, a Catholic institution.

Which really got to the issue. Was Villanova *really* a Catholic university anymore? Was it possible for any college to remain Catholic in a "pluralistic society"? It wasn't just that there were fewer priests and thus a corresponding decline in the amount of Catholic atmosphere on a campus. It was a change in attitude, a seeming desire to keep pace with the times, a belief that religion, by definition, made a university less academic.

The Villanovas, the Georgetowns, the Notre Dames—they seemed to be crying out for the world to notice that they had shed the monolithic garments that had been woven in Rome. And so Villanova University, rather than have a Gene Boylan penciling in hemlines, had assigned an atheist to serve as moderator of the paper. Georgetown considered recognizing a gay rights club as an official campus entity. Dayton, another Jesuit institution, permitted the students to vote on whether cyanide tablets should be stockpiled on campus for distribution in the event of nuclear attack. A considerable number of theology profs at Notre Dame were either atheists or agnostics.

And it wasn't only the colleges. The high schools were just as bad. Archbishop Prendergast had invited Congressman Bob Allworth to speak on ERA, the same Bob Allworth who sported an unblemished pro-abortion voting record. Some of the nuns even wore Allworth buttons. Regina Mundi Academy had hosted as a career day speaker the woman who had carried the abortion banner into the 1980 primary against Kevin.

Then there were the parishes. In the Catholic Church the pastor of a parish was much like the captain of a ship. Total control. The chancery, like the admiralty, might issue general directions. But once at sea, the pastor called all the shots.

[385]

Some of them were dynamite, marching in lockstep with Kevin, time and again raising the abortion issue. But others, the majority, while nominally pro-life, simply chose not to get involved. The issue was too emotional, too divisive. It distracted from the more important considerations, like raising funds and keeping the ship on an even keel. Try, for example, to show a pro-life film at a home and school association meeting, and there was always an excuse: not enough time; an already filled agenda; more appropriate for a later date.

It was much the same on the national level. A month before, the *Inquirer* had announcd that Bob Allworth would travel to Ireland to discuss the problems of Latin America. In addition to being confused over the somewhat convoluted geography of the process, Kevin was incensed that the trip had been organized by the National Catholic Conference. Naturally he raised hell, writing to the executive director of the Conference, with a copy to Cardinal Pulski. The initial response was far from satisfactory. The executive director indicated that the Conference's sponsorship of the trip should in no way be construed as supportive of Allworth's position on abortion. Although Kevin detested protracted wars of correspondence—paper pissing contests he called them—there was no way that he could accept such an answer. His second letter informed the executive director that the intention of the conference was wholly irrelevant. What mattered was the public perception.

When the National Catholic Conference, representing all of America's Catholics, sponsors a trip for a congressman, it is only reasonable to infer that the Conference, and thus the Church, supports the overall performance of that public official. I would have thought that such a truth would be evident to even the most inexperienced novice.

Such a perception is devastating not only to the goals of the Church but to the efforts of those of us on the battle lines, pitted against a formidable foe. These enemies love nothing more than to grasp at a blunder such as that perpetrated by your Conference and throw it back into our collective faces.

Simply stated, Monsignor, you blew it. None of us, of course, is perfect, and nothing can be done about the trip of Congressman Allworth, who, as I dictate this letter, is winging his way to the Emerald Isle. I hope, however, that you desist from your pathetically weak attempts to justify a decision that can have no justification.

To Kevin's surprise, he received yet another response. The executive director's tack this time was to acknowledge and accept all the points raised by Kevin. He agreed that the trip should never have been arranged. Unfortunately, the individual in charge of the matter had been unaware of Allworth's voting record.

Kevin could only shake his head. There would be no more letters. How could you respond? What more could you say to an organization, based in Washington, that pleaded ignorance of the voting record of an eight-year incumbent?

And on and on and on. The nun in Michigan overseeing abortions. Catholics for Democracy in the Church. Catholics for a Free Choice. The ads in the newspapers. The dissident priests on the Phil Donahue show.

Where would it end? What was the logical conclusion of such madness? Was it any wonder that the laity was off the reservation? Didn't every public opinion poll show a majority of Catholics supporting the right to choose?

Maybe the best answer had been given to Kevin last summer, at the pool several days after one of his television appearances. He was playing with the kids when Sally Moran approached. She was a neighbor, living right up the street. Born in Ireland, she had emigrated years ago. By the power of her will, no trace of the brogue remained. The sense of humor was still there, though, together with a manner of speaking that left no doubt where she stood.

"I've been following you on television, Kevin. You've caused me to lose a lot of sleep."

"How's that?"

"Because you're right, goddammit. But you know what my problem's been? I want to be fashionable. And the fashionable thing to say is 'I personally oppose abortion, but I believe in the right to choose.' It's bullshit, of course, but when I say that at a cocktail party, I'm showing everyone that I'm not a mick off the boat. I'm not a typical narrow-minded Catholic doing what the bishop says."

Kevin smiled. "Go on."

"Nothing, except from here on I'm on board. Anything I can

[387]

do to help. Stuffing envelopes, making phone calls, whatever. I'd rather be right than fashionable."

For Kevin it had been a special moment. It was always special when one of your own came home. But not all of them did. Like the two men sitting across the table. Kellogg had succeeded in creating a friendly atmosphere. Kevin would quickly shatter it.

"Dr. Devlin, Mr. Tunstall, I appreciate your taking the time to meet with us," Kevin began. "You've probably guessed why we're here. Four days ago a twenty-three-year-old woman was involved in a serious automobile accident on Roosevelt Boulevard. She's presently in a coma in your hospital. She's also seven weeks pregnant, and her mother is demanding an abortion."

Devlin attempted to answer. "Actually, the—"

"Excuse me, Doctor," his colleague said, turning to Kevin. "As the attorney for College Hospital I must advise you that we are not at liberty to discuss the specifics of any patient. It is our ethical and legal responsibility to maintain complete confidentiality."

Kevin smiled and lit a Winston. The lawyer was young, no more than thirty, a junior associate of a major center city law firm which represented the hospital. A piece of cake. "I understand. Just so you know, however, I am aware of all the facts surrounding Colleen Campion."

He had thrown out the name to get a reaction, and it did.

"I don't see how that's possible," Tunstall said. "And as far as the identity—"

"Not only is it possible," Kevin countered, "but it's absolutely true. To make you happy, however, we'll couch our conversation in a mode of supposition. Now, Doctor, suppose the scenario that I just set forth were true? What would be the hospital's position? What would be your recommendation, as chief of ob-gyn?"

"That's hard to say, Kevin. You don't mind if I call you Kevin, do you?"

"Not at all. I've been called a hell of a lot worse."

"Fine. To answer your question, a great deal would depend upon the facts. The specific medical facts relating to the patient."

"Okay. Let's say that the initial diagnosis was that the pregnancy presented absolutely no significant danger to the life, indeed, to the health, of the mother, which, as we both know, is the precise diagnosis, with specific reference being made to the report of a member of your staff, one Dr. Bruce Walters."

The lawyer leaned forward in his chair. "How do you know that? That's confidential information."

Kevin was enjoying himself. "I notice you don't deny it, Counselor. To answer your question, pro-life legislators have a special pipeline to the Holy Spirit."

Tunstall's face reddened. "Nothing will be gained by sarcasm."

"Come on, Bobby—you don't mind if I call you Bobby, do you?—you have to protect your confidentiality, and I have to protect mine. Now let's cut the bullshit, shall we? We all know the facts. So does the press. I hate to spoil your day, but it's gonna be all over the *Inquirer* tomorrow. They'll protect Colleen's identity, but everything else is open season."

"How do you know?" Devlin asked.

"Because one of the reporters spent a half hour inteviewing me today. He's probably trying to get you right now. So let's get to the bottom line. We all have a problem. What are College Hospital, and Dr. Michael Gerard Devlin, going to do about it?"

"What would you do, Kevin?" asked Devlin.

"Deny the mother's request. No need, no abortion."

"It's not that simple," Tunstall said. "The courts have ruled that a woman has a right to an abortion for any reason. A strong argument can be made that the patient's mother, as her legal guardian, has the right—"

Kevin jumped in. "Hold it right there, Bobby. Mrs. Campion is *not* Colleen's legal guardian. In case you've forgotten, Colleen is an adult. Twenty-three years old. Since she's unmarried, her mother is next of kin, but that in no way makes her the legal guardian. That can be accomplished only by a petition, hearing, and court order."

"Technically you might have a point."

"Technically, hell! I'm giving you the law. Now if Mrs. Campion wants to file such a petition, so be it, in which case I can assume that a number of organizations will petition to intervene on behalf of the baby."

Devlin spoke. "Kevin, I'm not certain such a course of action will benefit anyone. The patient was involved in a very serious accident, suffering significant trauma. There might be considerable damage to the fetus—from both the accident *and* the X rays."

Kevin wasn't about to make it easy on him. "Spell it out, Doctor."

"Well, it's just that—it might be in the best interest of everyone involved simply to terminate the pregnancy."

"The baby might be damaged goods, so kill him, right?"

"No. Of course not. It's just—"

"Look, Doctor, I'm not going to fence with you. I just want to know what you're going to do."

There was a pause. Finally Tunstall spoke. "After consulting with members of my firm, I have recommended that the hospital protect itself by petitioning the court for an adjudication."

"Do you agree, Doctor?" Kevin asked.

"Yes. Yes, I do."

"And what position will the hospital take at this hearing?"

"No position," Devlin answered.

Kevin's voice was bitter. "Pontius Pilate with the good old basin, huh?"

"Kevin, that's not fair," Devlin said.

"Let's not talk about fair, Doctor. Let me ask you this: you'll permit Dr. Walters to testify and express his medical opinion?"

Devlin hesitated. "Dr. Walters is no longer the attending physician."

"Who is?"

"Dr. Forer."

"Louis Forer?"

"Yes."

"Oh, Christ, that's classic. And you have the balls to say that you're not taking a position? You yank a doctor who says an abortion is unjustified and replace him with the most prolific abortionist in the city. The goddamn pinup boy for Planned Parenthood."

Devlin leaned forward, arms spread in the pose of a supplicant. "Kevin, please. I support you, you have to believe that. I'm on your side. But it's complex. Incredibly complex. In my position I can do a lot of good for us, but there are compromises that have to be made. We have powerful enemies, you know that. If I don't straddle the line, I'll lose my effectiveness."

"Not to mention your position."

"That, too. You don't know how hard it was for a Catholic to become chief of ob-gyn. It's important that I remain there. For all of us."

Kevin shook his head. When he spoke, he made no attempt to

[390]

conceal his disgust. "Who the hell are you kidding? You think that I don't know all about you? Michael Gerard Devlin. Transfiguration. West Catholic. Villanova. Jefferson Medical School. A bright, rising young doctor and pillar of the lay community. Devoted his time to Catholic Social Services and served on the archdiocesan school board. But then something happened, didn't it? You wanted to gain the acceptance of your peers, the big hitters of the medical community. So in 1970 you appeared before the governor's rigged panel on abortion rights. Shall I quote your testimony? 'Although a wrenching social issue with dire consequences for all of society, abortion is, and must remain, a uniquely private matter, within the exclusive domain of a woman and her physician.' I love it, I really do. And it helped. Suddenly you were big box office among the right people. I mean, here at last was an Irish Catholic saying all right things. Three years later you became the chief of ob-gyn at this wonderful institution, and since that time you have presided over the operation of one of the largest abortion mills in the state, specializing in late-term abortions. In fact, wasn't it only a few months ago that one of the nurses, who couldn't take it anymore, placed on your desk a package wrapped in towels? An eight-month unborn child, scalded and killed through the good old saline method. True, you've never personally performed abortions. You just hold the coats for the goddamn butchers who do, which makes you just as bad. Maybe worse."

Kevin rose and turned to Kellogg. "Joe, I haven't let you get a word in. Do you want to add anything?"

Kellogg shook his head sadly. "Not really. I might not have phrased it the same way, but I agree with everything Kevin has said. We're terribly disappointed in you, Michael."

They walked to the door. Then Kevin turned. "You've got it all, don't you? Fat salary, a big Cadillac, a house in Cape May, on all the right invitation lists. Enjoy it, *Doctor*, because you've paid a hell of a price."

He started to leave once more but couldn't resist. Reaching into his pocket, he took out a dime. "Here, pissant," he said, flipping the coin onto the desk in front of Tunstall. "Call your mother and tell her you met a real lawyer."

CHAPTER
Twenty-seven

MIKE Callaghan was not enjoying his lunch. He preferred to dine alone or with friends. Not with lobbyists. It wasn't that lobbyists offended him. As much as anyone, he understood the necessity for them. He was always willing to meet with them, to weigh their proposals, and to provide them with straight answers. He just didn't like doing it over a meal.

Joseph Pagano, however, had been insistent. When Mike pleaded an overloaded Harrisburg schedule, Pagano was only too happy to travel to Delaware County on a non-session day. Given such eagerness, Mike had expected a hard sell from the outset. Instead, Pagano discussed sports, family and general political gossip. Not until dessert did he touch upon the reason for the engagement.

"As you might know, Mike, I'm representing a grocery chain interested in the liquor bill."

"Join the crowd. Everybody's interested in the liquor bill one way or the other."

"How do you feel about it, Mike?"

"To be honest with you, I haven't made up my mind. The governor's big on it, and I generally try to help him; but this one's definitely not a caucus issue. Everyone does his own thing."

"I understand. Well, I'd just appreciate your consideration."

"No problem. You always have that."

"Thanks. Well, enough business. How's your law practice?"

"Not bad. It's hectic. You know, juggling Harrisburg with the practice, but I can't complain."

"I know what you mean about juggling. Whenever the legislature's in session, I have to be on the Hill, but I still can't ignore my other clients. It's a bitch, particularly the estates. You handle a lot of estates, don't you?"

"Yeah. About half my practice."

"Hell of a responsibility, I'll tell you. You can't screw up with somebody else's money. And I'll admit it, there's always the temptation, particularly when your cash flow is low. You know, just a temporary transfer. It's poison, though, real poison."

Pagano paused, as if waiting for a response. When he received none, he looked at his watch. "Mr. Speaker," he said, rising and extending his hand, "I appreciate your time. And thanks for any consideration you might give to the liquor bill."

"No problem," Mike said. When the lobbyist was gone, he remained, sipping his coffee. Outwardly he was as calm as ever.

It's probably nothing, he thought. *Just a meaningless, casual piece of conversation.* Bullshit. Pagano was sending him a message. He hadn't driven from Harrisburg just to chat.

He looked at his calendar watch. April 1, but this was no joke. Mike Callaghan was a realist, faced with a terrifying reality. At long last the nightmare might be coming true.

Gus Toohey was a bitter man. Thirty-three years on the force and for what? A broken marriage, two kids who couldn't "relate" to him, and a row house in Kensington. But he could have taken all that if it weren't for the other crap. Time was a cop could be a cop. There was good and there was bad and it was a cop's job to stamp out the bad. Whatever it took. You thought someone was peddling smack, you went to his house. None of this search warrant shit. And if you found any stuff, you didn't read the son of a bitch his rights. You hauled his ass away, in cuffs. Then you grilled him at the station. Just you and your partner. No lawyer to screw things up. And if the son of a bitch didn't cooperate, you persuaded him. Interview tools. Like a nightstick in the groin. Then he went to trial. Just like that. None of this pretrial suppression garbage. And then you put the son of a bitch where he belonged—in jail. Real honest-to-God law enforcement. Making the streets safe for the decent people.

[393]

No more. It had all gone to hell. Now the decent people were prisoners in their homes while the criminals walked the streets. Progress. What bullshit.

So Gus Toohey had made a choice and never looked back. He got transferred from vice to organized crime and made his contacts. At least those guys understood some rules. And they never hurt any of the decent people. The innocent ones. Except the kids on the school bus, and that was an accident.

It was a mutually beneficial situation. He supplied information that the guys downtown could use, for which they paid handsomely. Not money. He'd die first. He had never taken a note, not even a clean one. What he received for his services was far more valuable. He got results.

Gus sat on the park bench, finishing his hot dog, then took out the newspaper. The article he wanted was on the third page.

ACCUSED KILLER SET FREE
JUDGE CITES POLICE ERRORS

Charges against the man accused of slaying a West Philadelphia florist last November were dismissed today by Common Pleas Court Judge Paul V. Robinson. Tyrone Sadler, twenty-three, of the 4300 block of Baltimore Avenue, was set free when Robinson ruled in favor of defense motions that Sadler's confession and a subsequent search of his house be suppressed. The court accepted the argument of Defense Attorney Bruce Silver that Sadler's confession was inadmissible since police failed to readvise the accused of his rights before commencing an interrogation at police headquarters an hour after his arrest.

A search of Sadler's home following the interview produced a .38 caliber revolver, said to be the murder weapon. That evidence was also suppressed since "coming as the direct result of an illegal interview, it constitutes fruit of the poisoned tree."

Sadler, unemployed, had previously been arrested on charges of armed robbery, rape, and aggravated assault. He received probation on the robbery charge and served six months in Graterford Prison for the rape. The aggravated assault count was dropped when the victim refused to testify.

In the present case Sadler was arrested in December for the November 9 slaying of Richard T. Kelly, owner of Kelly's Flower

Shop, at 5318 Chester Avenue. Kelly, sixty-four, was gunned down in his store during a robbery which netted $24.97. He had operated the store for forty-two years.

The family of the deceased was outraged when the decision was announced. "Where in the hell is the justice?" asked Larry Kelly, thirty-six, one of the victim's sons. "For more than forty years my father served the community. His store was a legend. Thousands of people knew and loved him. The weddings, the proms, the funerals—he was always there doing his best to help. We told him to get out when the neighborhood got bad, but he wouldn't. It was his neighborhood and he'd never leave."

Toohey reached into his pocket for a red felt pencil, carefully circling the article. Then he rose, folded the newspaper, and placed it in the nearest trash can. Several minutes after he had gone, a man rose from a nearby bench. He walked to the trash can, carefully removed the paper, and, without looking at it, placed it under his arm. Then, after lighting a cigarette, Dominic Barrone walked away.

Sheila Sendrow was nervous. The harmless-looking woman—girl, actually—sitting across from her presented a threat. A threat to her son, a threat to her grandchild, and, most important, a threat to the thing which she cherished most, her integrity.

She had agonized following the call from Bridget Kelly. Wasn't it better to ignore the entire matter, to treat the situation as just one more trauma to be endured by a woman? She hadn't counseled in years, so why begin now? Why not leave it to the professionals, the ones who worked at it day in, day out and who, despite what the pro-life fanatics might say, genuinely cared about their clients?

Despite her misgivings, Sheila had taken the early train to Harrisburg the morning following Bridget's call. She knew that it was probably a mistake, that her action, one way or the other, would have far-reaching implications. And she wasn't at all certain why she was doing it. What disturbed her was the possibility that perhaps subconsciously she was testing herself, attempting to determine whether her training and years in the trenches permitted her to make an objective judgment even when someone whom she dearly loved was involved.

[395]

"Laurie, I want our talk to be as open and honest as possible, so at the outset it's vitally important that you know who I am."

"I do, Mrs. Sendrow—I'm sorry, Ms. Sendrow."

Sheila's smile was warm and genuine. "How about Sheila?"

"Thank you—Sheila. I know that you're Howie's mother. He's spoken of you often. He loves you a great deal. He doesn't always agree with you, but he loves you."

"And I love him, Laurie. A great deal. But I want you to know that any advice that I might give you will be based solely on what I consider best for you, and you only. That may be difficult for you to accept, but I sincerely mean it."

"Thank you."

"Why don't you begin, Laurie, by telling me about yourself? Anything you feel is important."

"Well, I'm eighteen years old. I'm a freshman at Dickinson, majoring in journalism."

"Do you want to be a writer?"

"Someday. I think I'd like to be an investigative reporter with a newspaper. A good newspaper, like the *New York Times* or *Washington Post*. But there are other things I want to do first."

"Such as?"

"I'm an athlete, Mrs.—Sheila. A runner. Half miler. I'm—I'm good. Last year I was state champion. In fact, my coach feels that if I continue to improve, I might have a shot at Los Angeles."

"Los Angeles?"

"Yes. The Olympics. In 1984."

"That's marvelous!"

"Well, it's still a long shot."

"It must be difficult, going to school and training at the same time."

"It's almost impossible, at least for me. I had planned on dropping out of school at the end of the year. Just temporarily. My coach had arranged for me to move to California, near San Jose State, to train under Keith Dolan. He's the best. Devote two years, full-time, to going for it. If I make it, great. If not, I can say that I gave it my best. Either way I'll go back to school and get my degree."

"You seem to know what you want, Laurie."

The girl hesitated. "I thought I did, but now—I just don't know. Everything is so complicated."

"Well, let's try to sort things out. Step by step. Have you talked to your parents?"

"God, no! I mean, I love them and all that, but they'd never understand. They'd die, especially Daddy. I'm the only girl, and—I just couldn't tell him. I couldn't. I know I should, but—"

Her voice was cracking. Tears filled her eyes.

"It's all right, Laurie. I understand. Really. How about Howie?"

"He knows. I wasn't going to tell him, but I thought I owed him that. I mean, it's his baby, too. He wants me to have it. He says he wants to marry me."

"Do you love him?"

"I enjoy being with him more than anyone I've ever known. He's kind and considerate and intelligent. When he's with me, I feel safe—and warm. Is that love? I'm not sure. I'm not even sure I know what love is. That kind anyway."

"Have you ever thought of spending your life with him?"

"Not until I found out I was pregnant. Before that the only thing I thought about—really thought about—in the future was the Olympics."

"And now?"

"I don't know. It's weird. You know, the thought of spending your life with any man. I always figured that I'd get married and have children—I always wanted children—but down the road." She gave a half smile. "You know, when I grow up."

"Are you grown up now?"

"I guess I have to be, don't I?"

"How much does your career mean to you, Laurie? Running, the Olympics?"

"How much?" She paused. "It's everything, Sheila. It's the only thing I've ever really wanted, ever since I can remember. I knew when I was little that I had special talents. I'm a natural athlete. I'm not bragging. I mean, I was born that way. I could always plays sports, as good as the boys. Baseball, basketball, even football. But running was special. The happiest times of my life have been when I'm running. I felt so free, so alive, even when I was just jogging through my neighborhood. And then I started competing, and it was so, I don't know, so special. There's something special about knowing you're at your peak, pushing yourself to the limit. You hurt, but it's a good kind of hurt, do you know what I mean? And when you know, *when you really know,* that you're the best, that nobody can beat you, that's really special."

Her eyes were burning now. It was as if Sheila didn't exist, as if this young runner were speaking only to herself, to something within her that drove her to excellence.

"And when you feel that way, there's only one goal, only one climax that makes it all perfect. The Olympics. There hasn't been a day in years that I haven't pictured it. It's so real I can almost touch it. Coming out of the pack in the last turn, feeling it all come together. Reaching out for everything you have and knowing that it'll be there. They're all on their feet now, waving American flags and screaming, 'USA, USA,' and when I hit the tape, I keep right on going, around the track one more time, drinking it all in. Then I step onto the stand, and they place the gold around my neck. They raise the American flag and play 'The Star-Spangled Banner.' Sometimes I can even feel the tears running down my cheeks as I realize that I did it, that I went all the way. God, how I want it." The sparkle left her face, and she looked at Sheila, as if for the first time. "But I want the baby, too," she finally said.

"Is it possible to do both, Laurie? Can you have the baby and still return to training in time?"

The girl shook her head. "No. It's impossible. I'd lose almost a full year. When you're going up against the best, you can't afford to give away that kind of time. I wouldn't have a shot at the trials. I thought some about 'eighty-eight but that's a joke. When you're at your peak, you're at your peak. Oh, a few have been able to stay around, like Mary Decker, but they're unusual. Besides, they're generally at the longer events. No, it's either 'eighty-four or never."

Tears rolled down her cheeks; only there was no band and no gold medal. "What should I do, Sheila? It's tearing me apart!"

How many times had Sheila witnessed the same tragedy? How could anyone say that women took it lightly? Maybe if the Kevin Murrays of the world were there to witness firsthand the agony that a woman suffered, they wouldn't be so quick to pass judgment.

The girl sitting across from Sheila was a survivor. Her fate would not be like some of the others. There would be no lifetime on welfare, nor would there be a news story of an anguished young woman abusing her child or taking her own life. Instead,

Laurie's sentence would be the destruction of a dream. The spark that radiated in her eyes as she spoke of her quest would be extinguished forever. Indeed, there would be survival, but no longer would she be one of those humans who truly lived her life. She would merely exist, in a world of what might have been.

Sheila reached across the table and tenderly grasped the girl's hand. She might be the mother of Sheila's grandchild—perhaps the only grandchild she would ever know—but far more important, she was her sister.

"There's no easy answer, Laurie. There never is. No matter what decision you make, it might stay with you the rest of your life. It would be so easy for me to tell you to have your baby— yours and my son's. That your sacrifice would be a noble act, one that would bring you peace and contentment. But I don't think it would. I see a very real potential for the destruction of three lives: yours, Howie's, and the child, who, no matter how much you loved it, would always remind you of the dream you surrendered. Sometimes, Laurie, the kindest thing for everyone involved is simply to let go." She leaned over and kissed the girl who would probably never be her daughter-in-law. "Good luck in Los Angeles, Laurie. And God bless you."

Sheila felt pain on the train ride back, but it was mixed with pride. She had passed her self-imposed test. Most definitely she had been a professional, providing a soul in need with objective advice. In doing so, she probably salvaged the life of a fine young woman.

But there was the fear that in the process she might have lost a son.

[399]

Twenty-eight

VINCE Grosso rose from his desk and walked to the window. He looked north. Over the trees he could just make out the dome of the basilica. It would be starting just about now, he thought, but here he remained, a prisoner in his office. He had wanted to go. Badly. Lena was there. And Kevin and Karen.

Not that he hadn't been invited. Pat had been gracious, but they both knew that the offer had been perfunctory, one that had to be declined. Sure, they would still get together. Pat was his confessor. But not in public, particularly not at an event that was being covered by the news. Neither he nor Pat could afford it. It was just one more example of the way things were, of the price that had to be paid.

The door opened, and Nick Arrone entered. "Niccolo, my friend. You have them?"

"Yes," answered Arrone, handing over a manila folder.

Vince studied the documents briefly, then looked up. "Good. Very good. No one else was involved?"

"Absolutely no one, Vince. Just the way you said."

"And our friends?"

"No problem. Our friend at the bank owes us money, much more than he can pay. The other one—the one at the clinic—has a very heavy cocaine habit, one that we can cut off tomorrow should we choose."

Vince nodded. "Good job, Niccolo. As usual. Anything else?"

"Just this." He handed Vince a newspaper, with an article circled in red. "Our friend again."

"How long has it been since we've assisted him?" Vince asked after scanning the article.

"Two months. Almost three."

"He continues to be helpful?"

"Very."

Vince handed back the newspaper. "Handle it," he said.

Kevin could feel the chills begin. Just like when Notre Dame's band broke into the Victory March or when they played Kate Smith's "God Bless America" at the Spectrum before a Flyers game.

The Cathedral was jammed. It wasn't every day that a bishop was consecrated. At the sound of the organ that seemed to fill every niche of the church, the congregation rose and faced the rear as the procession filed through the massive doors. The dazzling array of clerical vestments seemed without end. First the priests, scores of them, followed by the monsignors. Next came the bishops, the four from Philadelphia and several dozen from across the country. But the last two were the special ones: Stephen Cardinal Pulski, archbishop of Philadelphia, and the object of the exercise, Patrick Gerard Carney.

It was all that Kevin could do to hold back the tears as the scene unfolded. These were *his* priests, *his* church. No matter how frustrated he sometimes became with it, no matter how exasperated he was with some of its leaders, he knew that it was the cornerstone of his life, of everything that he valued. And as he watched the procession slowly make its way up the center aisle, he was struck by the thought that it extended infinitely farther than the eye could see, back over two thousand years to Christ and a fisherman named Peter.

Walking beside his leader, with the eyes of the congregation and the media upon him, Pat caught Kevin's eye and flashed him a wink. He was surprisingly calm. On a number of previous occasions he had participated in similar ceremonies, when the emotion had been almost overwhelming, but never had he been *the* celebrity, and like so many long-awaited dreams that finally came to fruition, he was finding it difficult to grasp the reality of the event.

[401]

The cardinal said the mass, which was concelebrated by the four auxiliary bishops. His sermon was concise but warm, imploring God to grant His newest bishop the strength and wisdom to fulfill his responsibilities. Pat heard all this, yet none of it really penetrated. It was at the consecration that he first felt the pangs of emotion. At Pat's request the cardinal chose Eucharistic Prayer IV, the least used but most beautiful.

> He always loved those who were his
>   own in the world
> When the time came for him to be
>   glorified by you, his heavenly
>   Father,
> He showed the depth of his love.
> While they were at supper,
> He took bread, said the blessing,
>   broke the bread
> and gave it to his disciples, saying:
> Take this, all of you, and eat it:
> this is my body which will be
>   given up for you.

His own. Who were *his own?* Pat thought. Did he really have anyone whom he could call his own? He looked at the first pew. Kristy was there, and the twins, with their families, but were they his anymore? Hadn't he, by design, erected the wall? Hadn't he made the decision that career, not family, took precedence? *Where has it all gone? What have the years done to us—to me?*

How many times had he shielded the twins from harm, tucked them in their beds, and read to them, just the way George Carney did when he wasn't working a double shift.

He looked at Kristy, the fruit of his mother's last act. His baby sister. Little Cinderella. How he wanted to hold her again, to grasp her hand and protect her from the motorcycle. Only now she didn't require his protection. It was he who needed help, but found it impossible to ask for.

And then his mother was there in front of him, every detail as vivid as if it were yesterday. She wore her smile, her special smile, the one that said, without words, how much she loved him. She

[402]

was comforting him now, giving him strength as she led him up the steps of MBS.

For his symbol the new bishop has chosen the rose, which, according to the missalette specially prepared for the occasion, was "Symbolic of strength, renewal, and respect for life." All correct, yet woefully incomplete, for more than anything, it reminded the new bishop of a little boy in a hospital on his first communion day. She had left him that day without ever saying good-bye. Left him standing there, clutching the rose that he had brought for her. Yet despite his sorrow, despite the ache that had never completely dissolved, there was no guilt. He had been innocent, a soul without blemish. There was no action he could have taken to save her. Strictly the will of God. If only he could plead the same innocence with respect to his other parent, but it was a case that he would never take to trial. There was no way he could get around the fact that George Carney was in his grave because of the inaction, willful and premeditated, of his son.

As they rose for the Our Father, Pat shook himself from his reverie. There was nothing to be gained from self-reproach. The past could not be changed, nor, in his case, could the future. There was nothing to be done except enjoy the show.

When the mass ended, the mood changed abruptly as the church exhibited its versatility. Expert at orchestrating a religious pageant, it was equally adept at throwing a party. And it was some party. Taking place at the Franklin Plaza, across the street from the cathedral, it was a study in Roman hedonism. Open bar, hors d'oeuvres, and a sit-down, six-course dinner for five hundred, featuring three wines, filet mignon, and, as the *coup de grace,* flaming baked Alaska served in a darkened banquet hall.

When the crowd had been loosened by drink and sated with food, the real entertainment began. Each incumbent auxiliary bishop took the dais, each with but one goal: to zing their boss and their new colleague. It was no holds barred, a rare opportunity to attack a prince of the church with complete immunity. Pulski enjoyed it immensely, and when it was his turn to rise, he gave as much as he took. Then Pat strode to the mike, and the crowd hushed noticeably, anxious to see how the new kid on the block would perform. They were not disappointed. He combined just the right blend of humor, sincerity, and humility. Even Kevin, the most stringent of speech critics, was impressed.

The speeches were over, but one tradition remained, a tradition unique to the archdiocese of Philadelphia. On an unspoken cue, the priests rose and sang a tribute to their leader:

Domine, salvum fac patrem nostrum, Stephanum,
Et exaudi in die,
Qua invocaverimus te.

The second stanza was rendered in honor of the newest shepherd, Patricium. It was a tradition first instilled in each of them while seminarians. Whenever the bishop was present, they joined voices in ecclesiastical salute. No one listening could fail to be moved by the warmth and sincerity which they gave to the effort. When the dinner was concluded, they would break up into cliques, criticizing the hierarchy, backbiting their peers, and speculating on who was on the cardinal's hit list by failing to receive an invitation. But for one brief moment, in the glory of an ancient language, they were united.

"We haven't spoken to Pat yet," Karen said as they were planning to leave. "Do you want to go over to see him?"

Kevin glanced across the room at his friend, who was surrounded by well-wishers. "Nah. He's got his hands full. I'll call him tomorrow."

He steadfastly refused to stand and wait to speak to anyone. It wasn't a matter of pride but consideration born from personal experience. Nothing was more uncomfortable to him than to be at an affair where he was an attraction, talking to someone but knowing that there were others waiting. Should he cut the conversation short? Should he ignore those waiting? Should he bring the second person into the discussion, thereby necessitating an introduction that he might blow? It drove him crazy, and he had no desire to put someone else, particularly a friend, through it.

Out of the corner of his eye, Pat saw them leaving. "Excuse me for a minute," he said, rushing past those who had surrounded him. "Kevin! Kevin!" he yelled, almost running across the room.

Karen greeted him first, throwing her arms around him. "Congratulations, Pat, we're so proud of you."

"Thanks, baby. I'm so glad you were able to come."

"You know we wouldn't miss it. You're family."

"Thanks, Karen," he said.

[404]

Kevin had been standing back, almost shyly. It was as if he were unsure of how to approach this new leader of the church. "Congratulations, Your Excellency," he said, smiling, stepping forward to take his ring and kiss it.

Pat would have none of it. He embraced Kevin, and his words seemed to carry a tone of desperation. "Nothing's changed, Kevin. Nothing. Please stay with me. I need you more than ever."

"No sweat, Patrick. I'll always be there. Count on it."

It was three in the morning, but Darryl's Den, in flagrant violation of the Pennsylvania Liquor Code, was still going strong. Inside, Tyrone Sadler was holding court. He had become something of a celebrity in West Philadelphia, a man who had beaten the system. And when you beat the system, you spit in whitey's face, which was what it was all about.

By popular demand, Sadler was once again recounting the details of his court triumph. "And I'm tellin' you, bros, when the man comes down with his decision, I thought the good old district attorney, who was black, of course—they always try to use an Oreo against his own—I thought the motherfucker was gonna turn white, no shit. The family of the dearly departed, they're goin' fuckin' nuts, screamin' and cryin' and raisin' all kinds of hell. And me, I'm just standin' there with this shit-eatin' grin, starin' 'em down, sayin' 'fuck you' without usin' words. Then we're out in the hallway and all the cameras are around and they're askin' me how I felt and my lawyer gives some bullshit about the vindication of our judicial system. Ain't that fuckin' great? Nice ring, huh? Nice white man phrase, bein' used on behalf of Tyrone Sadler."

"Tell 'em what you said to the son, Tyrone. This is unfuckinreal."

Sadler laughed. "Yeah. I really gotta kick outa this. The son comes up to me. They gotta hold him back, he's so pissed. I mean, he looked like a fuckin' Indian or somethin', his face was so fuckin' red. He said somethin' to me, I don't know, about gettin' even or somethin', and I just smiles and says, 'Hey, man, you dudes still sellin' flowers? I wanna send some to my old lady to celebrate.' "

He threw his head back and roared. "He went nuts, absolutely fuckin' nuts. The cops hadda take him away. And there I am, in my three-piece suit, just like my lawyer said, totally composed. They thought they were gonna fry my ass, and I walked."

The door opened, and three cops entered. White. Big. One carrying a shotgun.

The bartender scurried to meet them. He was concerned. These guys were new. Maybe they didn't know about his arrangement.

"Look, Officers, I know it's past closin', but I haven't been servin'. I swear to God. Last call was at two o'clock. They just been sittin' around. Honest."

They ignored him, walking over to Sadler. "Tyrone Sadler?" one asked.

"You got it, man."

"Come with us."

"Aw, come on, man. I ain't lookin' for no hassles tonight."

"I said come with us."

"What's the charge, man?" one of the bystanders asked.

The cop with the shotgun turned, tilting it ever so slightly in his direction. "You got a problem, pal?"

"Hey, it's cool. It's cool," Sadler said. "Let's nobody get uptight." He swung off the stool and turned to his friends. "No sweat, bros. They got nothin' on me. They just want to hassle me a little. See you tomorrow."

They led Sadler into the rear of the police van waiting outside. Without a word two of them climbed in beside him.

"Well," Sadler finally said, "ain't you gonna play the game? Read me my constitutional rights and all that good shit?"

There was no response as the van pulled away. Ten minutes later it turned into the alley, stopping at the rear of Kelly's Flower Shop. Since the slaying of its owner, it had been vacant, but in anticipation of the event about to unfold, the rear door lock had been neatly picked.

"Inside," one of the cops said, pushing Sadler through the door.

Suddenly he realized where he was, and his stomach started to knot. Something was wrong. Real bad wrong.

"Hey, man, what the fuck's goin' on? What am I doin' here? I beat that rap, remember? You know, man, double jeopardy? There's not shit you can do. I'm clean."

"Wrong, nigger," one of them said, pulling out a silencer-equipped pistol. "You're dead. You just lost your last appeal."

He fired just once, but that was enough. The bullet entered

[406]

through Sadler's left eye and went out through the back of his head, together with tissue, bone, and most of Sadler's brain. The ropes had already been installed, and they hung him quickly, right in front of the main window so that when the sun rose, West Philadelphia could witness the spectacle. When the deceased was discovered, it would be no coincidence that his pockets would contain exactly $24.97.

In another twenty minutes the van, the uniforms, and the murder weapon were locked in the jaws of the same machine that had disposed of Angie Lucido nine months before.

Once again Gus Toohey had been paid in full.

CHAPTER
Twenty-nine

IT was a garbage legislative day, as most Mondays were. Rarely did anything important happen on Monday. The session started late—one o'clock—to give members time to trek in from their districts. A few housekeeping bills would be run, just enough show to justify the per diem; then the rest of the day was devoted to caucus.

But even slow Mondays had their moments. Clete Homer was at the mike, begging for an appropriation for a bridge across a small river in his district.

"Hell, it ain't much of a stream, Mr. Speaker," Homer said. "I can pee halfway across it."

The chamber exploded in laughter. Finally the Speaker attempted to return at least a modicum of order. "The gentleman is out of order," he said.

"Damn right," Homer shot back. "If I wasn't, I could pee *all* the way across it."

Before breaking, there was a condolence resolution. Whenever a former member died, a resolution was prepared, recounting the significant facts in the life of the deceased: education, military service, civic achievements, family, and anything else that seemed important. It was something like a posthumous *This Is Your Life* and the writers in Legislative Reference were creative enough to make even the biggest bozo sound like a candidate for *Who's Who.*

When the citation had been read, the entire House membership would rise and stand in silence until the Speaker dropped the gavel. This time it was for a three-term Democrat from Erie whose career had ended in the Nixon landslide. As he stood in the silence of the usually tumultuous House, Kevin reflected upon the significance of it all. Here was a guy who had no doubt been well known in the community, an elected public official, Silver Star winner, and president of his Rotary. And who remembered him? Who really cared that he was gone? All that he got was a lousy piece of parchment sent to his wife and a minute of silence. That quickly life was gone.

The gavel banged, and Kevin gathered his files. "You know, Lorenzo, someday they'll be reading one of those for us. Just my fuckin' luck they'll debate mine."

"And defeat it."

"Probably. Let me know if anything important happens in caucus, will you?"

Kevin stopped in the cafeteria for a sandwich. He never ate there, instead returning to his office, where he closed the door for fifteen minutes to eat and read. Like the train, this was his own time which no man dare invade.

As usual, Kevin walked back to his office by way of the rotunda. A demonstration in support of the handicapped had just ended. At least a dozen of them remained, all in battery-operated wheelchairs. Their heads hung to one side, their mouths were open, and several had spittle dribbling down their chins. But what got to Kevin most was the sound of the wheelchairs. Most needed oil and gave off a squeak, a sound which seemed to portray perfectly the condition of their occupants. His blood running cold and his stomach turning nauseated, Kevin fled. Only when he was safe in his office did he reflect upon his action.

You worthless shit, he said to himself. *You goddamn phony. The leader of the pro-life movement, the one who rejects the quality of life argument, and you can't even look at people who aren't perfect. You talk about Christ in your speeches. Sure, He said, "Suffer the little children to come unto me." But He also loved the lepers. You'd better practice what you preach, shithead, or pack it the hell in.*

His buzzer sounded. "I know you're eating lunch," Janet said, "but Joe Kellogg is here. Can he see you for a minute?"

Kevin sighed. "Shit. Yeah, okay. Send him in."

"I'm sorry to bother you during your lunch, Kevin," Kellogg said. "I'll take only a minute."

[409]

"No problem, pal. I've always got time for you. I want to be able to receive communion on Sunday."

"Did you hear about the Campion court decision?"

"Yeah."

"Pretty bad, huh?"

"Goddamn atrocious. I've got a call in to the attorney general."

"Well, keep me posted. But that's not the reason I dropped by. I wanted to tell you a little story."

"Suddenly you're Uncle Remus. Go ahead."

"I've been involved in the pro-life movement a long time. Considerably before *Roe* versus *Wade*. In the late sixties we saw the handwriting on the wall in places like New York and California, and we knew that a problem was developing. So we held our first national conference. I think it was 1968. At Barrett College in Illinois. There weren't too many of us, nothing like today, but the Church was well represented. We all agreed that we had to organize to combat the anti-life forces. We agreed on something else: that the only organization that was willing and able to coordinate our movement was the Church. Do you remember, when we went to Washington last spring, our visit to the National Catholic Conference?"

"Sure."

"Do you remember visiting Monsignor Bright?"

"Yeah. Good man. Real good man."

"You remember his office? Not much bigger than yours and just as poorly furnished. Well, that's where it all began. In that tiny office the Church directed her educational and political operation. She stood alone then, receiving the slings and arrows from the media and the pro-abortion side. But she never wavered. Instead, she got stronger and stronger. She kept her finger in the dike to hold back the flood that would have drowned us all. She bought us time and, little by little, she awakened the conscience of many others—Jews, Protestants, even atheists. You see the results. Today our members are counted in the millions. It goes far beyond the Catholic Church. But none of that would have been possible if it hadn't been for a little office in Washington."

Kellogg rose. "I know that you're frequently frustrated by the Church, Kevin. By the Dr. Devlins, the Father Drinans, the pastors who don't seem to care. And you're justified. The Church isn't perfect, Kevin. It can't be. It's composed of humans. But

[410]

whenever it's crunch time, it's always there, willing to stand up and be counted."

Kevin also rose and clasped Kellogg's hand. "You know, you're a good man, Joe Kellogg. One of the best. And like they say in the Mennen commercials, thanks, I needed that."

He was just starting his platter when Janet buzzed again. "Looks like you're not meant to eat today. The attorney general's office is returning your call."

He hit the lit button. "Hello."

"Kevin. Mike Trammel."

"Oh. Hello, Mike." Trammel was a shit, and Kevin made no attempt to disguise his feelings.

"I'm returning your call for the general."

"Actually, Mike, I had hoped to speak to him personally."

"His schedule is incredible, Kevin. But I'm certain that I can be of assistance."

"Just like last year, right?"

"Come now, Kevin. Bygones are bygones."

"Whatever you say."

The year before they had clashed bitterly over a funding bill which contained a half-million-dollar appropriation for payment of legal fees incurred by Planned Parenthood during its successful federal attack on Pennsylvania's 1974 Abortion Act. The judge, citing a provision of the Civil Rights Act, had ordered the commonwealth to make full payment of the attorneys' fees. Incensed, Kevin had drafted an amendment which deleted the appropriation. Trammel had called before the ink was dry.

"I hear you're drafting an amendment to House Bill Nine-two-two, Kevin."

"Correct."

"Deleting the legal fee appropriation?"

"Right again, Mike. You're on a hot streak."

"Kevin, you can't do that."

"Now you're two for three. Can and will, Mike."

"I don't think you understand, Kevin. We didn't request that appropriation because we wanted to. We're under a federal court order."

"I know."

"Then you must know that we can't defy the court. The general, to whom the order is directed, could be held in contempt."

"I'll visit him in jail, Mike. Tell him to brush up on his pinochle."

"This is serious, Kevin. For you even to attempt to delete that appropriation is an act of utter irresponsibility."

"Listen very carefully to what I have to say, Mike. It's *exactly* what I am going to say on the floor of the House when I introduce the amendment, which will pass. Until recently, we helped fund Planned Parenthood through our family planning appropriation. That august body, in a classic example of biting the hand that feeds it, sues us. Unfortunately, it's successful, and a number of sections of the 'seventy-four act are stricken. That's bad enough, but to make the sin mortal, it turns around and gets a court to order us, the state, to pay its expenses in suing us. What you have, therefore, is a state-funded entity suing its benefactor and then seeking reimbursement. Seeking it from a legislature that, time and again, has stated that it considers abortion anathema. Mrs. Murray's son may not be very bright, but it doesn't take a genius to figure out that this appropriation can't be approved. Sure, a federal judge has ordered it. So what? No judge can force a group of sovereign elected officials to vote a certain way. My amendment is a unique opportunity to suggest to Planned Parenthood and the federal courts, respectfully but firmly, that without either passing go or collecting two hundred dollars, they go straight to hell."

True to his words, Kevin repeated this speech a week later on the floor of the House. The Murray amendment passed 163–30. Planned Parenthood was never paid, and Mike Trammel never forgot. He saw the present conversation as a chance to even the score.

"How can we help you?" Trammel asked. "Specifically."

"Collen Campion. The pregnant woman in the coma in Philly. Are you familiar with the situation?"

"Somewhat."

"The court ruled against us this morning."

"Us? Who is us?"

"You know goddamn well what I mean. I want your office to appeal. Immediately."

Trammel chuckled. "Is that all? Sorry, Kevin. Not a chance. For any number of reasons, I have personally counseled the general against intervention. Nothing personal, of course."

"Of course. But, Mike, there are any number of compelling reasons, some of which even you might understand, why the general must get involved. I've no intention of detailing them for you. You're a subordinate. Actually, a flunky and not a very good one. I want the general's answer directly from his lips."

"That's impossible. I told you, his schedule—"

"Listen to me carefully, Mike, since it could affect your future. The news media and thousands of pro-lifers—who, incidentally, strongly supported the general when he ran—will be clamoring for an answer. From me. Considering that the general is up for re-election this year, I don't see how it can help his future—and yours—when I am forced to admit that not only did he refuse to get involved, but he didn't even have the courtesy to discuss the issue with me. I expect to hear from the general in half an hour, and fuck his busy schedule. That's thirty minutes, Mike, in case the math is beyond your grasp."

Kevin slammed down the receiver. Christ, why wasn't it ever easy? Why couldn't, just once, something go smoothly without the goddamn ass-kicking confrontations?

His hands were trembling. He wanted this one. Badly. More than he had wanted anything else, even the abortion control act. This one was different. He wasn't just fighting for a principle, for the millions of unborn who were slaughtered. This one was personal. One *baby*. One specific little one who was trying to hold on to life. It was a boy. Kevin had no doubt of that. A little boy to make up for Andrew, in some small way to take his place. A chance to lessen—it could never erase—the pain Kevin felt over the death of his son. He knew that he was making a mistake, allowing it to become personal, but he couldn't help it. One way or the other that little boy was going to be born.

There was a backlog of work that needed to be handled: constituent letters; phone calls to be returned; a half dozen bills to be drafted. Instead, Kevin paced. And smoked. Waiting for a call. It was only a ten-minute wait. Trammel had obviously delivered the message.

"How are you, Kevin?" the attorney general asked.

"Can't complain, Dick. Doesn't do a damn bit of good, and nobody listens to you."

"Know what you mean. I hear you had an interesting conversation with Mike."

[413]

"I could describe it a number of ways, Dick, but interesting isn't one of them."

"He means well, Kevin. Anyway, what's up?"

As if you didn't know, Kevin thought. "A pregnant woman in a coma in Philly. Her mother is demanding an abortion."

"I'm aware of it."

"You're also aware of today's court decision?"

"Vaguely. Fill me in."

"The judge ruled in favor of the mother. He ordered the abortion. The old quality-of-life argument. He questioned what type of life, physically and psychologically, the child could expect. Pure shit, totally unaccompanied, I might add, by any medical facts. But then he made a mistake, which is where you come in."

"How?"

"He stated that the existing law was deficient in that it had no provision for a situation where the woman can't give consent and there's no legal guardian. He's questioning the constitutionality of the statute, Dick, and you know the law as well as I do. Anytime the constitutionality of an existing statute is challenged, the attorney general has automatic standing to intervene."

"Jesus, Kevin, that's tenuous. I really don't have any scope."

"Balls, buddy. Scope is something you wash your mouth out with. You ran as a pro-life candidate, Dick. And you were supported by us for precisely a situation like this, where the law is hazy and you can go either way. Let me lay it on the line. You're either with us or against us on this one. I'll tell you what I tell all those people who claim to be against abortion but sit on their ass: if you're not part of the solution, you're part of the problem. There's a lot of people right now waiting to see exactly where Dick Kiley stands."

"I need time, Kevin."

"You don't have any. For all we know, they could be pushing her into the operating room right now. You have to move right away. Petition for an immediate injunction."

"Let's say I do. What do we gain?"

"Time, baby. Another hearing will be required. She's about seven or eight weeks pregnant right now. We can stall long enough to get her into the second trimester, where the burden on the other side is a lot more difficult. The clock's running, Dick. Yes or no?"

[414]

"You're a bastard, Kevin."

"Absolutely. Yes or no?"

"Yes, goddammit!"

"Thanks, pal. I owe you one."

After hanging up, Kevin broke into a grin and began to rub his hands together. There was still a long way to go, but at least little Andrew Campion now had a fighting chance.

The student nurse was frantic. "The gallbladder in six-five-four is out of bed again. And he's nude!"

"He has a name, Julie," Karen Murray said. "It's Mr. Halliday, and he's just a little disoriented. I'll handle it."

Karen caught him near the elevator. "Mr. Halliday, I think you should be in your room. Let me help you."

"No! I'm going home!"

"Soon, Mr. Halliday, but not right now."

"Please, I want to go home. Just for tonight. I'll come back tomorrow."

"I don't think that's a good idea. Besides, you didn't finish telling me about your grandson. The one who just graduated from Annapolis."

The man's face softened. "Didn't I? He's a fine boy. Michael. Named after me. He's going to fly. Jets."

"That's wonderful. I have a son who wants to be a navy pilot."

"What's his name?"

"Sean."

"That's a nice name. I have a grandson named Sean. He works for the railroad. Good job."

"You must be very proud of all of your grandchildren."

"Yeah. Well, most of them, anyway. One of them's having problems. You know, drugs."

"That's a shame."

"It's terrible. Terrible. When is my operation?"

"It's over, Mr. Halliday. Two days ago."

"Over?"

"That's right. You did fine. All you need now is a little rest. Let's get you into bed."

All the while Karen had been gently leading him back down the hall. Now they were back at his room.

[415]

"You're very nice, Nurse," the old man said, allowing Karen to put him into bed.

"Thank you. So are you, Mr. Halliday. Now get some sleep, okay?"

"I'm afraid."

"Of what?"

"Of going to sleep. I'm afraid I won't wake up again."

Karen gently touched his hand. "Mr. Halliday, do you trust me?"

"Yeah. Sure."

"*Really* trust me?"

"Yes."

"Then listen to me. I promise you that you'll wake up. You'll wake up, in a few days you'll leave the hospital, and you'll see all your grandchildren again."

"Do you mean it?"

Karen smiled. "You said you trusted me. Do we have a deal?"

"Yes. Thank you, Nurse."

"You're welcome. Good night, Mr. Halliday."

It's a full moon, Karen thought as she walked back to her station. They always came off the walls when there was a full moon.

"How's the best-looking nurse on Six West?"

Karen blushed. "Hello, Dr. Richter."

"Karen, how long are you going to be so formal? I've told you before, it's John."

"Okay."

"How's it going?"

"It's been a madhouse."

"Maybe, but I see you have it under control. As usual. You're the best thing that's happened to this hospital since I've been here."

She blushed again. "Thank you."

"I mean it. And you look great. God, it's refreshing to see a nurse in a uniform. Everything's become so casual."

"I guess I'm just old-fashioned."

"I'd never call you old-fashioned. Not the way you look. I can't believe you're the mother of—what is it, five?"

She hesitated. "Six, but one died."

"I'm sorry. I'm a bachelor, but I imagine that must be very, very difficult."

"It is."

"Are you going on break?" Richter asked.

"Yes."

"Mind if I join you?"

Karen hesitated. "No. That would be fine."

They walked to the snack bar, where Richter ordered Cokes, and sat at a table at the far end of the room.

"Do you mind if I ask you something personal?" asked Richter.

Karen's eyes became wary. "No," she finally said. "Go ahead."

"I told you how great you look, but you never seem to smile. Why is it that you always seem to be carrying the weight of the world on your shoulders?"

Karen sighed. "A lot of reasons, reasons you wouldn't want to hear."

"Try me. I've always been a good listener."

"Maybe someday I will."

"But not now, right?"

"Right," Karen answered.

"Fine. I'll respect your privacy, but I want you to know that if you ever need someone to talk to, a friend, all you have to do is yell."

"Thank you. I'm very grateful."

"You're welcome. And what's my name?"

She smiled. "John."

"You're getting there."

Karen thought about the conversation when she returned to her shift. There was no question that Richter found her attractive—and useful, a thought that did not displease her. It was nice to be appreciated. No one else did. Kevin was too busy saving the world. And the kids—they were kids. The more you did for them, the more they took it for granted.

How could she have answered Richter's question, explained the doubts that gnawed at her constantly? Was this what it was all about, the sum and substance of a woman's existence? To care for her home and family and expect nothing more? What about Karen Murray? Shouldn't there be something for her, too? Shouldn't she have her own identity? She was more than a wife and a mother. She was a person, a distinct and unique human being.

Why was she thinking such thoughts? Why did it all seem to be crumbling? This wasn't the way it was supposed to be. The script called for her to be just like her mother. Self-sacrificing perfection. Hadn't she tried? Wasn't her home always as immaculate as her mother's? Didn't the children always glisten, no matter how many times a day she had to change their clothes? And hadn't she—until now—stayed home, just so she'd be there when they needed her?

But if she had achieved all her goals, why did she feel like such a dismal failure? Why did she feel resentment, rather than pride, over her husband's accomplishments? And why, no matter how much she loved them, was it such a burden sometimes to care for the children?

Kevin was right. She didn't know what she wanted. Maybe it was a clash between duty and desire, between what she wanted and what was expected of her.

How many times did they have the same conversation? Kevin would ask her what she wanted, what *she* really *wanted*—forgetting duty, money, obligation, and any other practical considerations. The tragedy was that she could never answer. Her response was always in the negative—what she didn't want. She didn't want to feel so regimented. She didn't want to nickel-dime it constantly. She didn't want the feeling of helplessness that, try as she might to combat it, assailed her every morning as she climbed out of bed.

Kevin was the lucky one. He always knew what he wanted, impossible as it might be. Always dreaming, never practical.

Her problem was the reverse. She was *too* practical. She could never let go, never loosen the strings that had bound her since she was a child. Would it have been different if she had married someone else, had never married? Probably not. You were what you were. It would have been all right if there had been occasional triumphs. But what accomplishment was it to clean a room, particularly when, five minutes after you were done, the kids had it destroyed?

She found herself questioning granitelike truths. Had her mother really been happy? Or was it all part of the act, a phony façade called for by the script? And just who in the hell wrote the script? Where was it carved in stone that a woman always gave without any hope of receiving?

And then there was Andrew, the ultimate hurt, the ultimate

[418]

failure. She had failed the son she had never held. It was a woman's job to carry her babies, to make sure they entered the world healthy—and she had failed. It was a failure that had driven her back to work, where, despite a small measure of self-satisfaction, the guilt was even greater for deserting her own. It didn't matter that it was only two days a week, that the children were probably better off for the change of pace. What mattered was that she wasn't strong enough to follow the script.

What was left? Where did she go now? Did Karen Murray—Karen Scully—even exist anymore?

It was all so confusing. How could she expect anyone, even a kind, considerate man like John Richter, to understand?

She thought of Richter again and admitted to herself that there was something special about him. When she had mentioned that one of her children had died, he could easily have changed the subject, but he hadn't. Instead, he had been sincere, willing to share her pain.

Maybe she would accept his offer. Merely to listen, of course.

CHAPTER
Thirty

AS he crossed Chestnut Street, Charlie Masters spotted the subject. He was walking slowly, just to the rear of Independence Hall, a seemingly aimless tourist attempting to soak up some history through osmosis. Masters knew otherwise.

He used a group of schoolchildren, being hustled through the courtyard by their teacher, as a shield, bringing him to within twenty feet of the subject. Now came the most difficult part. If the subject turned, there would be no surprise, no prisoner. Instead, there would be confrontation, which only one would survive.

Masters's luck held. He traveled the twenty feet without detection and grasped the subject by his left arm. "Freeze motherfucker. FBI."

"You haven't changed a bit, shithead," Kevin said without turning. "I saw you when you crossed Chestnut Street."

"Nobody's perfect," Masters said, shaking his old partner's hand. "So how the hell are you?"

"Happier than a faggot in Boys Town, Charlie."

It was partially true. April had ended well. Legislatively, Kevin was on a roll. His adoption bill was out of committee in the Senate, his corporate reporting bill had been signed by the governor, and in his greatest coup, he had pushed through the House legislation reducing the Philadelphia wage tax paid by suburbanites who worked in the city. It would probably fall a vote or two short in the Senate, but at least there was now momentum. Not to mention tremendous ink in the suburban press.

Negotiations on the abortion bill with the governor's staff were progressing. It was still a tough road, but there was now light at the end of the tunnel: if not by summer recess, at least by early fall. Dan Talbot wanted the issue resolved before Pennsylvania's voters went to the polls.

Kevin's law practice was faring better than usual. A few checks had even come in. He was still broke, his checking account was still in a deficit status, but it felt nice to get paid for work performed.

Most important, he had struck pay dirt on the Colleen Campion issue. When the attorney general intervened and was granted a stay, the publicity intensified, creating pressure that the mother of the comatose woman was unable to withstand. In withdrawing her demand for an abortion, she publicly attacked Kevin for insensitivity and willfully endangering her daughter's life. That was fine with Kevin. The name of the game was results.

All and all he had experienced worse months.

"How's Karen?" Charlie asked. "You know, with everything."

"Pretty good, Charlie. It's not easy, but we're getting there. She went back to work."

"Oh, yeah? Where?"

"Lankenau. Two evenings a week. Three to eleven shift. My mother baby-sits until I get home."

"That's great!"

"Yeah. It's good for her, after all she's been through."

"So. Where do you want to eat?" Masters asked.

"It's too nice to be inside. Let's have a Philly special."

"Gotcha."

They stopped at one of the vendors that dotted the city's corners to order hot dogs smothered in mustard and sauerkraut.

"You're having only one?" Charlie asked.

"That's right."

"Oh, Christ, let me guess. You're on another one of your diets, which never do a damn bit of good."

"Fuck you."

"That's my Kevin. Christ, I'm glad you haven't changed."

[421]

They picked a bench at Independence Mall, strategically located to observe the lunch-hour scenery.

"Christ, don't you love it, Kevin?"

"Absolutely, pal. You know, they didn't make them like this when we were young."

"Ain't that the truth. God, I can't believe the ones I see going to high school. Grade school even. Some poor son of a bitch thinks he's tapping someone nineteen or twenty, and he ends up facing a statutory rape charge. They all screw now."

Kevin shook his head. "Why couldn't it have been that way when we were growing up? My timing was always shit. When I got them, they either hadn't started yet or used to bang like a bunny but had reformed."

Charlie said, "Well, now that we've established that we're dirty old men, to what do I owe the honor of Kevin Murray's coming into the city from his suburban kingdom? I know it wasn't just to have lunch with me."

"Believe it or not, I'm actually practicing law. A deposition in the office of my old classmate, an individual who I believe is known to you."

"Who's that?"

"Vince Grosso."

"You kiddin'?"

"No."

"Must be a big case to have Grosso involved."

"Just the opposite. It's a nickel-dime slip-and-fall case."

"Doesn't add up."

"I know. I can't figure it out."

"Do you know him well?" asked Charlie.

"Yeah. I mean, I haven't seen him much lately, but we were very close. I was best man at his wedding; he was an usher at mine. I'm godfather to his oldest son; he's Sean's godfather."

"You know what he is, don't you?"

"Well, I know he represented a lot of mobsters, and I've seen in the news lately that he's supposed to be more than that."

"Cut the bullshit, Kevin. He's the fuckin' don of the family, and you know it."

"You sure?"

"Come on, Kevin. You know we don't make mistakes like that. We've still got our sources inside. He's it. One tough son of a bitch. Smart, cool, and absolutely ruthless. You're aware he went to law school in Michigan?"

"Sure."

"That's where he got his training. In Detroit. From Tony Iacobucci."

"The Iceman," Kevin said.

"Right. Now there's a real mean bastard. The ultimate enforcer. He's the one who did Hoffa in."

"I heard that."

"It's true. Met him at the restaurant, took him to an apartment, where he blew his brains out, then dumped him in an incinerator in Hamtramck."

Kevin laughed. "Hamtramck. Good old Polish paradise. I was on a raid there once."

"That's right! I forgot. After Milwaukee you went to Detroit."

"Yep. Worked the mob. Iacobucci was one of my cases. The cause of one of my greatest temptations."

"He offered to blow you?" Masters cracked.

"I'm serious. I'm walking downtown one morning—I forget where I was going—and I pass the barbershop. I look in, and sure as hell, there's Iacobucci getting his hair cut. So I figured I'd bust his balls a little. You know, I was always great for that."

"I never would have guessed."

"Anyway, I walk in, sit down, and stare at him. He makes like he doesn't notice me, but he does. He leaves, and I follow him. I'm not talking about any discreet surveillance, mind you. I'm a foot or two behind him the whole way. He goes into a tobacco shop, I go in with him. He stops for a cup of coffee, so do I. I sit right beside him. I mean, *right* beside him. I mean, I can reach out and touch him if I want to. Finally, after almost an hour, he walks into the parking garage to get his car. We get on the same elevator. His car's on the third or fourth level, and we're all alone up there. Just he and I. Then I get this thought. If I called to him and he turns, I can blow him the fuck away. No witnesses. I can say that he was coming at me or going for his gun. Who'd investigate? Not even the friggin' ACLU would mourn his passing. And good old J. Edgar would've probably given me a letter of commendation—and a transfer home. I hate to admit it, Charlie, but I was really tempted."

[423]

"You should have done it, pal. Squeezed off two or three into his head."

"Come on."

"I'm serious, Kevin. The man's no goddamn good. He's a killer, a fuckin' animal. You try like hell to get these guys through the system, but they're too slick. Plus the fact they've got the law stacked in their favor. You would have performed a service by blowing him away."

Kevin lit a cigarette. For a moment he was silent, staring across the mall at the nation's birthplace. "You're wrong, Charlie. Sure, Iacobucci's a bastard. They all are. But if we take things into our own hands, they win because we become as bad as they are. Kind of like Vietnam. 'We had to destroy that village to save it.' " He rose. "Thus far the words of today's Holy Gospel."

"Jesus," Charlie said. "Kevin Murray turning liberal. Who would believe it?"

"No chance of that, pal. Always the caveman." He extended his hand. "Gotta go practice law. Let's do it again soon."

"Right. And give my regards to Don Vincenzo."

There were two occasions when Vince Grosso permitted himself to drop the icy veneer of a Mafia don. One was when he was with his immediate family. The other was with Kevin.

Vince had his reasons for the meeting, but he was genuinely happy to see his old classmate. "Whaddya say, dirtball!" he bellowed, leaping up from his desk and embracing him.

"Hello, Vince." For once the roles were reversed. It was Kevin who was reserved. But despite his misgivings, there was still an affection for the man with whom he had shared so much.

"It's been too long, Kevin. Which isn't my fault." Vince said it casually, but the indictment was clear.

"Yeah, I know. Christ, with the job and the kids there isn't any time."

"I know what you mean. Come on, sit down." He led Kevin to a conference table by a window. You didn't sit behind a desk when you were with a friend. "I'm just about to have a little lunch. Interested?"

Kevin shook his head. "Thanks anyway. I already had a hot dog."

[424]

"One hot dog? Let me guess. Another one of the famous Kevin Murray diets, none of which does a damn bit of good."

"I didn't have to travel to Center City to get insulted. I can get that at home."

"How *is* everybody, Kevin? The kids?"

"Doing good. Getting big. I can't believe Kevin starts high school in September."

"So does Michael. Your godson. He's always asking for you." A pause. "Where's Kevin going?"

"My old alma mater."

"Malvern! No shit! So's Michael. God, Grosso and Murray together again."

"I don't think the Augustinians are ready for an encore."

The door opened, and a secretary entered and placed a tray on the table. Without looking, Kevin knew what it was. Only one thing smelled that good.

"Hoagie, huh?" Kevin said as Vince prepared to eat.

"Yeah. But of course, since you're on a diet, I know you're not interested."

"Right." He reached toward the plate. "Maybe just a little piece."

Vince swatted at Kevin's hand. "My firstborn, my wife, my home, take them all. But not my hoagie." He reached for the phone and pushed a button. "Now, please."

Again the door opened, and another platter was delivered, this time to Kevin. He eyed the hoagie briefly, then surrendered. "You really are a bastard, you know that, don't you?"

"Absolutely. I knew you'd fold."

As they devoured the hoagies, they talked about their Villanova days, and Kevin felt himself begin to relax. It was just like old times, and Kevin realized how much he had missed his friend. And he was touched by Vince's going to so much trouble—somehow getting a case that wouldn't cover his tips for a week—just to get them together.

"How's Karen?" Vince finally asked. "You know what I mean. How's she coming along?"

"Okay. It's no picnic. But we're getting there."

"You okay, Kev?"

"Yeah. Sure."

[425]

"Really?"

"You know the kid. Nothing keeps him on the canvas."

"Still full of it, huh?"

"What can I say?"

"Lena and I think of Karen all the time. You, too. We'd like to see more of you."

"Yeah. It's like I said, though, things are so hectic—"

"Come on, Kevin. It's Vince, remember? Your old buddy. You've never tried to bullshit me before, so don't start now. It's been almost *two years*. And we live fifteen minutes apart. You've turned down every invitation we've sent. Not only that, you sent back my last two campaign contributions. Kevin, we're family. Level with me."

"Okay, you got me. It's jealousy. You live in a castle, you're rich as shit, and I don't have a pot to piss in."

"Bullshit. You're gonna have to do better than that."

Kevin grinned. "I figured I would. Okay, pal, I'll lay it on the line. We live in different worlds. It was one thing when you were the mob lawyer. Now you're the don. The enemy. Christ, I fought against you guys when I was in the bureau."

"Come on, Kevin. You don't believe all that stuff you see in the papers, do you?"

"*You* come on, Vince. It's Kevin, remember? Your old buddy. You've never tried to bullshit me before, so don't start now. You're the don, the boss of the Philadelphia *borgotta*. That's a fact. You've had people killed. Fact. You're involved in goddamn near every crime under the sun. Fact. How do you expect me to feel?"

Vince leaned back in his chair. "Let's assume, just for argument's sake, that you're right. Mind you, I'm admitting nothing, even though I know you're not wearing a wire. Even if that's true, how's that change us? How does that come between two friends, almost brothers?"

"Christ, Vince, we're not talking about some slight philosophical dispute. You're the mob, for Christ's sake."

"Is that so terrible?"

"Fuckin' well told it is."

"Why? Is my way of life so different from yours?"

"In a word, yes."

[426]

"Not really. You say that we kill. You don't? What about the CIA? Or more subtle, Washington decides to withhold funds from a certain nation, which signs the death warrant of the leader. Or it sends arms to a particular group, like the rebels in Nicaragua, knowing well that death will occur. My way or yours, the result is the same."

"That's Washington, pal. Not Harrisburg."

"Same thing. It's still government. Official, duly constituted government, peddling death."

"You're stretching it, Vince. Sounds like a lot of rationalizing bullshit to me."

"Okay, let's take you. You're Republican, and you want to make sure your party keeps control of the House. Right?"

"Sure."

"So you plot to defeat the enemy. To knock off Democratic incumbents. It doesn't matter that you're talking about a guy's career, his livelihood. The name of the game is control. Just like us."

"The last time I checked, I didn't have a damn thing to do with drugs, gambling, or shylocking."

"No? Drugs? Look at the FDA. A real cesspool. Some of the shit they allow on the market is instant death, but that's okay as long as the right people have been stroked. Gambling? What a joke. You have a goddamn state-run lottery, but because government is doing it, that makes it harmless. Off-track betting is illegal, but every night on TV and radio we hear the results of the day's races. The ones who are at the track betting legally already know, so who is the media, licensed by the FCC—government—catering to? Loan-sharking? Just take a look at the way banks are ripping people off. Look at the extortion you have to accept to get a mortgage. All legal, with the blessing of government. The truth is, you're jealous."

"I said that a few minutes ago, and you wouldn't believe me."

"Not of me personally, Kevin, or of my wealth. You're jealous because we do the very things that you'd like to do."

"Like what?"

"How many times have you gotten screwed by some son of a bitch who's out there for no other reason than to stick it to you? Take the abortion people. They're no goddamn good; there's no

[427]

way you can be reasonable with them. Haven't you ever had the urge to smash their face in? To settle the issue in the most basic of all ways, by stomping them into the ground? Tell the truth."

"Of course."

"And wouldn't it make you feel good to do it?"

"Yeah."

"Then why don't you?"

"Because you can't."

"Why not?"

"Because there are rules."

"Whose rules?"

"Come on, Vince. Society's."

"Whose society?"

"Ours. All of ours."

"Not mine, buddy. Your rules don't work, and you know it. Kevin, I'm really proud of the way you fight, especially on abortion. It's goddamn murder and has to stop. But you keep getting screwed by your own society. By the courts. My way is a hell of a lot more effective."

"Jesus, Vince, I don't believe this conversation. You just said that abortion is murder. How is it different from what you do?"

"All the difference in the world, Kev. Those babies are completely innocent. I can issure you that the people we're forced to deal with are far from that."

"What makes you a judge?"

"What makes those assholes on the Supreme Court judges?"

Kevin sighed. "It's a great hoagie, Vince, but this is going nowhere."

Vince smiled. "I agree. Enough philosophy. Let's get down to practical matters. I need your help."

"On what?"

"A bill. The liquor bill, to be precise. Several of my clients are supporting it."

"Clients, shit."

"What's in a name? The point is, Kev, I really need that bill."

"Vince, no matter what, I still love you dearly, but there's no fuckin' way I support that bill. For most of my adult life I've fought you guys. There's no way I'm gonna be a part of handing you a multimillion-dollar industry."

"We'd do a damn good job, at a fair price."

[428]

"The price would always be too high, Vince, even if you were giving it away."

"Still a stubborn bastard, aren't you?"

"You'd be disappointed if I weren't."

"Yeah, you're right." Vince laughed. "At least keep an open mind, will you?"

"I always do, but I wouldn't hold out too much hope on this one. Anyway, when do we start the deposition?"

For a second Vince seemed puzzled. "Deposition? Oh, that. No deposition. You don't know what I went through to get this case. I figured it was the only way I had of meeting with you. As we both know, your case is a piece of shit. Agreed?"

"I might have phrased it a trifle differently, but you're relatively accurate."

"Damn right. For openers, there's no liability. Your client admits that he wasn't looking where he was going. He also admits he had been drinking."

"You always were a picky bastard."

"And the specials are complete horseshit. There's only about a hundred dollars of legitimate medical expenses, and that's being generous."

"Great speech. What's the bottom line?"

"Three thousand. Approximately ten times what the case is worth. Besides, three divides nicely into that number. This isn't one of your goddamn charity cases, is it? You *are* getting a third?"

"Yeah."

"Good. Deal?"

"Is a pig's ass pork? Sold."

"Good. I'll get you the file. Just get your client—if he's sober enough—to sign the waiver, then file the praecipe."

Once again Vince buzzed his secretary. Once again the door opened. Only this time it was a different woman.

Kevin couldn't believe his eyes. "Bonnie!" For a moment he sat motionless. Then slowly he rose. "How the hell are you?" he stammered.

"Fine, Representative Murray," she said coldly, then turned to Vince. "Here's the file, Mr. Grosso."

"Thank you. That will be all."

Kevin was stunned. "Vince, what the hell is going on?" he finally sputtered after she left.

[429]

"Long story. I'll tell you about it someday." He handed Kevin the file. "This is just routine, mind you, but make it a point to read it when you get a chance. Let me know if you have any questions."

"Right."

Vince extended his hand. "Great seeing you, Kevin. I mean it. Keep up the good work."

"Yeah. I'll try."

"Let's get together soon. And give my best to Karen and the kids."

"Right. Same here."

When he was alone, Vince went back to his desk. But instead of returning to work, he opened his drawer and took out a photograph. It was of the two of them, giving the V sign on the night Kevin was elected student body president.

After a minute he replaced the photo. The rest of the day would be depressing. He was a powerful man, a Mafia don capable of almost anything. But not even Vince Grosso could turn back the clock.

It was crowded on the el, but Kevin was able to get a seat, just beating out a middle-aged woman, who gave him a nasty look. Too bad. He needed to sit. For a few minutes he stared at his briefcase, afraid to act. Vince may have missed him, but this had been no social call. Bonnie's appearance and Vince's insistence that he read the file added up to more than a coincidence.

Finally he took out the file. His chest pounding, he read it quickly, then read it again. He was wrong. It wasn't as bad as he expected.

It was worse.

CHAPTER
Thirty-one

"WOULD you care for dessert, Your Excellency?" She was one of the countless young Irishwomen whom the Church employed for rectory duty. Grateful to be in America, they were willing to work for a price that was most reasonable. They generally lasted for a year or so, at which point the Americanization process had been completed and they moved on to greener pastures. "What is it to-night, Deidre?"

"German chocolate cake."

"Tempting, but I think I'll pass. Just coffee, please."

Not a bad way to live, Pat thought as he lingered over his coffee, subconsciously delaying the meeting that would immediately follow. Easy to take for granted. Excellent meals, served in a handsome dining room. Sure, the pastor and curates of his residence parish were about as stimulating as watching grass grow. But the service more than compensated. You never had to wait for dinner. Never had to help in preparing or serving it. And when the meal was over, it was over. Cleaning up was for others. Not bad.

He looked at his watch. His penitent would already be waiting. Excusing himself, he walked across the lawn to the church, where he stopped at the door marked "Reconciliation Room."

In the old days confession was known as the sacrament of penance, administered by the priest behind a darkened screen. The forward thinkers of the Church had considered that too intimidating, so the name had been changed. Now it was the sacrament of reconciliation, and at the option of the penitent, sins could be confessed face-to-face with the priest.

Progress. Except in the old days people flocked to the confessional. Most went once a week. Now there was only a trickle. For many, including the most devout of Catholics, more than a year elapsed between confessions. Score one more for the "refreshing winds of Vatican II."

Not that Pat minded. Given the choice, he would never hear a confession. Leave that to others. The ones who didn't fear becoming personally involved in the life of a fellow human. But tonight's penitent was one he couldn't avoid.

"Sorry I'm late, Vince," he said as he entered.

"No problem, Patrick. How's it going?"

Pat shrugged. "About the same. You?"

"I've had better days."

What now? Pat thought. *What else are you going to saddle me with?* He hadn't wanted to be Vince's confessor, to know in detail the workings of a mob leader. But Vince was a friend, and friends helped each other. Besides, it never hurt to have someone with Vince's power in your debt. And maybe there was something more. Something juvenile but nonetheless real. Deep down he had always resented the closeness which Vince and Kevin had with each other. Sure, it had been the three of them at Villanova, but he always felt that when push came to shove, he was only along for the ride. As Vince's confessor he was privy to things which Kevin could never know. Like what Lena Grosso had told him yesterday.

"Before we begin, Vince, there's something I want to discuss with you. Under the seal of confession, of course."

"Go ahead."

"Let me put this as delicately as possible. I know you love Lena deeply, but have you been experiencing desire for another woman?"

"C'mon, Pat." Vince laughed, a little too quickly. "When you stop looking, you're ready for the grave."

"I'm serious, Vince. Is there someone in particular for whom you have a special feeling?"

Vince hesitated. "Yes," he finally said.

"Who is she?"

"Therese, the girl who lives with us."

[432]

"How serious is it?"

"I don't know, Pat. Honest to God I don't. This is very difficult for me. I'm ashamed of myself. Don't get me wrong. Nothing's happened, and nothing ever will. I promise you that."

Pat's voice had a special urgency. "Please listen to me, Vince, and don't ask any questions, because I can't answer them. But for God's sake, stay away from that woman. You can't imagine the destruction that it would cause."

"You're being cryptic, Patrick."

"Because I have to. Don't try to figure it out. Just do as I ask, as I beg."

"I've already told you, nothing will happen. You have my word."

"Good." Pat sighed. "Now it's your turn."

"Bless me, Father, for I have sinned. It has been one month since my last confession."

"How can I help you, Vince?"

"I saw Kevin today. He was in my office."

"Great! How's he doing?"

"Probably not so good right now. I'm blackmailing him. My best friend, and I'm blackmailing him."

Pat was shocked. "You're what? Why?"

"Because I have to. He has something that I need. Desperately."

"What could he possibly have done that justifies blackmailing him? I've listened to a lot of what you've done, Vince, and I've been horrified. But nothing matches this. In God's name, why?"

"I need his vote. On the liquor bill. It could make or break my family."

"Kevin's your family, too! Remember? You've been closer to him than to any of your relatives."

"You're not telling me anything I don't know, Pat. I didn't come here to argue."

"No. Just to dump your guilt on to me. Take the absolution and walk away, right? Just like it's always been. You cause someone to be killed, that's okay. Twenty-three children burn to death in a school bus, no problem. You've got a friend in the business. Just go to good old Father Carney and have the slate wiped clean. Well, not this time, pal."

"I understand your anger."

[433]

"That's very good of you, Vince." He paused. "Do you want to tell me how you're doing this?"

"It involves Bonnie."

"*Our* Bonnie?"

"Yeah. Kevin had an affair with her."

The hammerblows were pounding Pat's skull. "Kevin? And Bonnie? When?"

"Long time ago."

"When?" Pat was struggling against hysteria.

"When he was still in the DA's office."

"When, dammit?"

"Nineteen seventy-three. September. Just a few weeks. She had an abortion. I can show that Kevin paid for it."

"Never! Not Kevin. The affair, maybe. He's human. But not the abortion."

"You're right. But what's true and what you can prove are two different things."

"What *is* true?"

"He had the affair. Bonnie had the abortion. But Kevin didn't pay for it, not knowingly. It wasn't even his baby. We both know that, don't we, Pat?"

Pat buried his head in his hands. As usual, Vince was right. It wasn't Kevin's baby. It was his.

Sheila Sendrow was exhausted. Each day seemed to get longer. In the office by seven, then nonstop for the day. As she turned the key in the door of her Head House Square town house, it was almost eight. All she wanted was a light dinner, a warm bath, and then a good book in bed.

But she realized that tonight this would be impossible. Howie had been terse on the phone, saying only that he had to meet with her.

It had been the first time in more than a month that she had spoken to her son, since shortly before her Harrisburg meeting with Laurie. She had wanted to call him, to find out what decision had been made about the baby—her grandchild—but she couldn't. As always, professionalism had controlled her emotions. Howie might not even know about the counseling session, and it wasn't her place to tell him. That decision was Laurie's.

She wasn't involved, she had tried to tell herself, but for once

[434]

Sheila Sendrow was unpersuasive. Of course, she was involved. It was her son and her grandchild. And despite her advice to Laurie, she still hoped that it would work out, that they could be family together, the four of them.

Her son was seated on the sofa when she entered, absently thumbing through an issue of *Time*.

"Hello, Mother," he said, rising but making no move to approach her.

"Hello, Howie." She walked to him and kissed him on the cheek. He neither turned away nor responded.

"Sit down, sit down," Sheila said nervously. "How's school?"

"Fine. At least the grades. But there's more than that, isn't there?"

"Yes."

"You did your job well, Mother. Laurie had the abortion She didn't tell me until it was over."

"I'm sorry, Howie."

His voice carried no hatred, only pain. "Sorry? How can you say that you're sorry? It's what you told her to do."

"That's not exactly true."

"You're not in court now, Mom. We both know the truth. You had a job to do, and you did it. Successfully, as always."

"I don't know what to say, Howie."

"How could you, Mom? How could you do it? It was your grandchild. Your own flesh and blood. Didn't you wonder whether it would be a boy or a girl? What he'd be like? What he'd become? I did. I always will, and I'll always wonder."

For a moment there was silence. "How are you and Laurie?" Sheila finally asked.

"It's over. What did you expect? There can't be anything left after what we've lost. Every time I looked at her, I'd remember. The same way I do when I look at you."

"Howie, I know right now you can't understand this, but I did what I thought was right. For Laurie *and* for you."

"Me? Since when have you ever cared about me?"

"That's not fair."

"No? Be honest, Mother. Haven't you always resented me? All my life I knew there was one thing wrong with me. I was a male, and no matter how you tried to hide it, that made me the enemy. You have your causes, and I've always respected you for that. The

[435]

problem is, they always came before your own son. And now your grandchild."

He rose and walked to the hallway, where two packed suitcases stood. "I guess you know that this is good-bye, Mother. When I'm home from school, I'll be staying with Dad."

"I see."

"Don't blame him. He tried to talk me out of it."

"I understand."

"I don't think you do, Mother. That's the tragedy."

He was gone, and she was alone, numb, unable to cry, to focus on the reality of what had occurred.

She walked into the den and stared at the photographs on the desk. A chronicle of her son, her only son: Howie in his christening gown, on his first day of kindergarten, in his Little League uniform, at his high school graduation.

She *did* love him, no matter what he thought. For so long he had been all she had, and in a vague way it struck her that now she had nothing. She had done what was right, and it had cost her everything.

Her eyes shifted to another picture, her thoughts to the promise of so long ago.

"I'm trying," she said to the picture. "Honest to God, I am."

But for the first time Sheila Sendrow, keeper of the promise, wondered if her mother was asking too much.

Kevin Murray was not the only legislator to receive a file. Mike Callaghan's was delivered to his law office.

"What's this?" he asked his secretary.

"I don't know. Some man dropped it off just now. Said you'd know what it was."

"Who was he?"

"I don't know. I never saw him before. I asked his name, but he just turned around and left. You don't think it's a bomb or anything like that, do you?"

"No. Just some more constituent crap. Routine. Thanks."

As he broke the seal, he knew it wasn't from a constituent and he knew it wasn't routine. It was all there. As a professional Mike had to admire the documentation.

The phone call was right on schedule, just as he expected.

"Mike? Joe Pagano. Listen, I never got around to sending you a thank-you note for our lunch, and I just wanted you to know how much I enjoyed it."

"That's very thoughtful of you, Joe."

"And listen, about the liquor bill, I don't expect a commitment. I'd just appreciate your consideration."

"Sure, Joe. Take care."

The Speaker leaned back in his chair. Oddly he felt almost relieved. The uncertainty had ended. There could no longer be any doubt.

The nightmare had come true.

As usual Lena Grosso's day would be a full one. Shopping with the girls, a meeting of the Performing Arts Forum at Villanova, an hour of tennis at the club, then over to St. Aloysius for a meeting of the Graduation Committee. After dinner there was a meeting of the parish Home and School Association. The new officers would be installed, with Lena serving as treasurer.

"Get in the car now," she said to her girls after brushing their hair.

"Can we stop at Farrell's after we shop, Mommy?" asked Concetta. "Please say yes."

"We'll see."

"Does that mean maybe?" chimed in Lucia.

"Yes. That means maybe."

"Goody. Thank you, Mommy."

They each kissed her, then ran to the car. "Don't forget the mail," Lucia called back.

She almost had. She walked to the desk and picked up the envelopes. Standard. Bills, responses to several invitations, Michael's health history for Malvern. And one more, the one that she had been dreading. It was in Therese's handwriting, addressed to the Pennsylvania Bureau of Vital Statistics.

Frozen, Lena stared at the envelope. It looked so harmless, yet it held the key to so much. To Therese's heritage—and Lena's secret, a secret which only Pat Carney shared.

Lena did not attempt to delude herself. Therese had the right. Anyone did. It was a basic human desire to know your roots, to know from where you came. The question was when. Now? When Lena's secret would be laid bare before she was ready, ruining the plans she had painstakenly constructed? Or later? When the

[437]

promises Lena made so long ago had been kept, as only a Sicilian can keep a promise?

Would Therese suspect? Probably not. She had been told that because of Kevin Murray's bill, there was a large backlog at Vital Statistics. And in two weeks exams would be over, with Therese gone for the summer, a summer that would provide any nineteen-year-old—particularly one as good-looking as Therese—with more than enough distractions to make her forget the quest for her roots. Temporarily, anyway, and that was all that Lena sought. Just a little more time.

The car horn honked. "Come on, Mommy! We're waiting for you!"

"I'm coming, darlings," Lena answered. She swept the letters into her handbag. Except one, which was placed in the garbage disposal. Then Lena flipped the switch, knowing all too well that it would be her last chance to hold back midnight.

CHAPTER

Thirty-two

SEAN had been eagerly awaiting his father. "Come on, Dad," he yelled from the basement, where he had been glued in front of the television for almost a month.

"What's the latest?" Kevin asked.

"We got six more planes. Lost one Harrier, maybe two. And the whole island's blockaded."

"God, I love it!" Kevin said, rubbing his hands together. "Rule, Britannia. Kicking ass and taking names."

Karen came out of the washroom carrying a basket of clothes. "Are you two at it again? All you've done for the last month is watch that stupid war."

"Stupid? Bite your tongue, woman. How can you call such a masterpiece stupid?"

"Because that's exactly what it is. People killing each other over a pile of rocks that aren't worth anything."

"Pride, my girl. The pride of the British lion."

"Well, I hope that someday one of our sons doesn't have to die for pride."

Kevin's face turned to a scowl. "How did you develop that rare and special ability to put a damper on everything? We've been through this before, but let me spell it out for you one more time. Maybe the Falklands are worthless, and maybe they're not. It doesn't matter. What *does* matter is the fact that Argentina invaded. Illegally. It seized what belongs to England. The Brits had no choice. If you knuckle under to aggression or terrorism once, all you insure is that it'll happen again. Just like the bully in third grade."

"Please. Not the third-grade bully again."

"Okay, fourth grade. But as long as the SOB thinks you won't fight back, he'll keep stealing your lunch money. It's a shame people have to die, but that's unavoidable." He smiled, his good mood returning. "Now will you kindly let my son and me enjoy it? It happens to be a classic, a throwback to the halcyon days of empire, which may never return."

"Wonderful. Dinner's in fifteen minutes."

"Dinner? What a mundane consideration at a time when Britannia is poised to seize eternal glory. My God, woman, where is your sense of romance?"

"In the kitchen. Fifteen minutes."

Kevin turned back to the tube. It *was* a classic. Right out of a Hornblower novel. A small nation that had once ruled the seas— indeed, the world—returning, if only temporarily, to its former glory. A nation united, rallying around the Union Jack and behind a woman of steel named Thatcher. Just like the old days, when Elizabeth sent Drake and his sea dogs out to take on the Armada.

And it was a clean war, a pure naval conflict that brought back memories of World War II. The type about which movies were made and books were written. Nothing complicated. No nuclear threat. No goddamn jungles. No slogging day after day without any appreciable change. Quick action. Immediate results. Ships sunk, planes downed, and, all the while, the British tide moving inexorably forward.

It had been the same with the Six-Day War in 1967. That one had also carried with it WW II nostalgia. Israeli tanks racing through the desert conjured up memories of the classic duels between Rommel and Montgomery.

All this in marked contrast with the Vietnam morass, when every night the wonders of television reminded you of a nation seething at home and bogged down abroad. That had been a different war, the first to be brought into the homes of America on a daily basis. The first war America fought without first setting objectives, without defining beforehand what would constitute victory. Shortly after America's entry into the Second World War the Casablanca Conference decided that victory for the Allies would occur only when the Axis had unconditionally surrendered. It was a simplicity easy to grasp, easier to support.

Israel's goal in 1967 had been equally basic: it wanted to survive. And now in 1982 Britain approached its task with the same singleness of purpose: to wrest back what belonged to it.

There had been so many differences with Vietnam. A war where the objective was *not* to capture territory. A commuter war, where the troops were choppered to the front each day, craftsmen of death punching in at nine and out at five.

And then there were the body bags, probably the most poignant symbol of America's longest war. Prior to Vietnam, the slain were buried where they fell. Much neater. There is something both romantic and patriotic about neat rows of white crosses covering a Flanders field or a knoll on Iwo Jima. Death is less real, more glamorous in such a setting. The horror of humans killing each other gets driven home far more convincingly by a stack of bags on an airport tarmac, each containing the whole, or parts, of what was once a human being. How many planes made how many flights bringing home those bundles of lifeless flesh?

War could never be enjoyable, but if you had to have one, the Brits and Israelis knew how to do it right.

The Falklands continued to be the topic of conversation during dinner, which drew Karen's ire.

"You're unbelievable," Kevin said. "You get ticked when Kevin and I talk sports; now you're bent out of shape because Sean and I want to discuss the Falklands. I mean, if you can't talk sports or war, what's left?"

"You could ask your children about school, or wouldn't that occur to you?"

"Fine. Kevin, how was school today?"

"It sucked."

"Great. Sean, how about you?"

"It sucked."

"Progress. For once, Kevin and Sean agree on something. Matthew?"

"It was okay. We had a great fight in the schoolyard."

"God bless Catholic education. Megs?"

"Fine. I got a hundred on my spelling test."

"Great! Way to go. Peter, how was school?"

"I don't go to 'cool." He was never able to pronounce an *s*.

[441]

"Oh. You have a job?"

"No."

"Let me get this straight, young man. You neither go to school nor have a job. How come?"

" 'Cause I'm too little." Peter laughed. He loved the game.

"That's right! How could I forget? Okay, that takes care of school. Now can we get back to blowing away the Argentines?"

Karen sighed. "I don't know why I try."

"Neither do I, but I love you anyway."

Since the days were getting longer, the children were allowed a half hour outside between dinner and homework, the only time in the evening that Kevin and Karen were certain of being alone.

"I have to talk to you," Kevin said after the coffee was poured. "I've been meaning to for a few days, but there never seems to be the right time."

"What about?"

"Remember I met with Vince last week?"

"Yes. On a law case."

"Well, there's one thing I didn't mention. He's blackmailing me."

"Vince? *Blackmailing you?*"

"He knows about Bonnie and me. She works for him."

Only her trembling hands gave away her emotions. She reached for a cigarette. "Why? What does he want?"

"He wants me to support the liquor bill. You know, the state stores going private."

"Are you? Will that end it?"

"No. To both. The bill stinks. It'll make millions for the mob. And the first time you give in to blackmail, you're just guaranteeing that it'll happen again."

"Like your speech on the Falklands."

"It's a pretty good comparison."

"Do you think he means it? You're his best friend."

"I don't think that matters, Karen. He's the head of the mob, and it plays for keeps. Even with friends." Kevin shook his head. "I know all that, and I still can't believe it. I can't believe that Vince is doing this to me, after all we've been through. What we've meant to each other."

They sat in silence, Kevin staring out the window, Karen gazing into her cup. "How much does he know?" she finally asked.

[442]

"Everything. More, actually."

"More? How can there be more?"

"He can show that Bonnie had an abortion and that I paid for it."

"No. Not that. Not you."

"I didn't. I told you I never made love to her. I swear to God. She obviously was pregnant from someone else."

"Then how are you involved?"

"There *is* one thing I didn't tell you. About a week after I ended it, she called me. She was desperate. Said she was broke and her landlord was going to evict her. She sounded horrible. I mean, really terrible. I wrote her a check for three hundred dollars. Somehow Vince got a copy of the canceled check. Bonnie just endorsed it over to the abortion clinic."

"Why?" Karen asked.

"Why what?"

"Why did you give her the money?"

"I don't know. Like I said, she was desperate. And I guess I figured I owed her something."

"I see," Karen said quietly. "You owed *her* something."

"I'm sorry, Karen. Honest to God I am."

"Is there anything else that you haven't told me? Please, Kevin, I have to know."

"Nothing. I swear."

"Okay. I believe you." She stubbed out her cigarette and rose. "We'll just have to face whatever comes along."

Kevin stared at his wife. He was almost irritated by her strength, which only added to his guilt. In some ways it would have been easier had she screamed and cried. "You amaze me, Karen, honest to God. You bitch and yell about little things, and then a crisis comes along and you're a rock. I don't deserve you."

"I have to go out to the children."

"Why does it have to come back now? After all these years? It was behind us. Forgotten."

"I haven't forgotten, Kevin. I never will."

Kevin sat alone in the kitchen. The sounds of the children drifted in. Happy. Carefree. Totally innocent. Saddled with neither the guilt nor the fear of their father.

So here he was again. Ravaged by the same agony that had almost destroyed both of them nine years before. How could

[443]

he have let it happen? How could he have risked everything he had?

September 1973. They had just returned from the shore, two weeks in Ocean City, the same Ocean City that had captivated him as a boy. When he had been young and alive, exhilarated by life. When he had prowled the boardwalk and the beaches, looking for conquests. Lying about his age, of course. If you were a high school junior, you automatically became a college freshman. It was expected, part of the game. She knew you were lying, but that didn't matter. What mattered was the game.

It had been a good vacation. It always was. He never tired of the shore. When he crossed the bridge into town, everything else was forgotten. The DA's office could burn to the ground, and he wouldn't have been the slightest bit upset. It was then, in the early days of his career, that Kevin had adopted a practice that he never violated. When on vacation he *never* called the office. It always amazed him how many of his colleagues checked in by phone every day. No way. Nothing good could happen when you called the office. Even now, as a legislative leader and an attorney, he refused to have a phone in any shore apartment they rented. If a crisis developed and your secretary couldn't reach you, something interesting happened. *She* solved it, for there was no alternative. Kevin Murray understood a truth that far wiser men consistently failed to grasp: no one was indispensable. In his lifetime a popular president had been assassinated, and despite the genuine grief felt by almost everyone, the country didn't miss a beat in moving forward.

"Lemme tell you," Kevin would say, "I'm a pretty popular legislator, but if I dropped dead today, the people of my district would somehow survive, and in two weeks it would be 'Kevin who?' "

It was one of the great frustrations of Karen Murray's life that her husband's attitude applied only when he was at the shore. Once home, he was again the indispensable workaholic.

As much as he had enjoyed the '73 vacation, Kevin had for the first time experienced an unsettling feeling. They just had the two boys then, and Karen was pregnant with Matthew. Their days consisted of going to the beach with the little ones, their nights at the boardwalk amusements. That was fine with both of them since they loved being with the children. But now and then Kevin would look at a group of teenagers on the beach. They were so young, and it seemed so long ago that he was one of them. He had just turned thirty-two and was beginning to have doubts. Maybe he wasn't the eternal kid after all.

It wasn't that Kevin allowed himself to brood over the matter. He would quickly shake off the mood and return to building a sand castle with Sean or playing horseshoes with Kevin. Still, a gnawing uneasiness remained, tucked far away, but still there.

When they got back to Philly, Kevin's work load was monstrous. The DA was up for reelection in two months, and he wanted Kevin's investigations completed. It never hurt to indict some big hitters just before an election. It meant long hours, well into the night.

For dinner Kevin had found a small café just off Market Street. It made great cheesesteaks and, as a bonus, sported a jukebox that specialized in fifties songs—tailor-made for the king of nostalgia. Kevin thoroughly enjoyed eating there, sitting alone in a rear booth with his book. It began one evening, just as he was getting into *The Drifters*.

"Mind if I join you, dirtball?"

Bonnie. He hadn't seen her since college, when Pat had traded their engagement for the seminary.

But long before she had been Pat's, she had been Kevin's. His first girl. His St. Laurence sweetheart. All through seventh and eighth grades they were *the* couple: Bonnie the captain of the cheerleaders, Kevin the school's leader.

The beginning had been almost a disaster. Their first date was to the Tower Theater, Kevin meeting her on West Chester Pike, where they took a trolley to Sixty-ninth Street. Before leaving for his rendezvous, Kevin had been so nervous that he threw up, rallying, of course, to be Mr. Suave when he greeted her. Bonnie had handled her nervousness more maturely, controlling it until they were seated. Five minutes into the movie she excused herself for the ladies' room, where she mirrored Kevin's earlier performance. Unlike Kevin, however, her stomach rejected a rally. She told her date that she would have to leave, insisting that he remain for the show. Gallant at even a young age, Kevin would have none of it.

She fought back tears on the trolley ride home. "I'm sorry. I know I spoiled your day."

[445]

God, she was pretty when she cried. "Can I tell you a secret? We must be meant for each other. I got sick ten minutes before I met you."

"Honest?"

"If you don't believe me, I'll take you home and show you the shirt I had to change. Can we do it again?"

"If you want to."

"I do. Next Saturday?"

"Okay."

There were many Saturdays for them. To Kevin, Bonnie was special, even after they had stopped dating. As the beer ad says, you never forget your first girl. There was a feeling he had when he was with her that he could never capture again, not even with his most ardent loves. A uniqueness that only could come from the first. Actually to be with a girl. To touch her, smell her, listen to her talk.

When Kevin started at Malvern, they began to drift apart. There was no crisis, no clear-cut breaking point. Just a gradual loosening of the ties that often happens when high school begins and the parish is no longer the whole of a youth's universe.

After high school Bonnie was hired as a secretary with an insurance agent. But their paths were meant to cross again. In his sophomore year at Villanova Pat Carney began to date her. Since Pat, Kevin, and Vince were inseparable, the old lovers were together constantly for two years. There wasn't any doubt that Bonnie loved Pat. You could see it in her eyes. That was fine with Kevin, or at least he told himself so. But try as he might, even though he knew that they could never be an item again, even when he began to date Karen, Kevin couldn't shake a little tinge of jealousy. Irrational as it was, in a certain way she would always be *his* Bonnie.

The engagement announcement came as no surprise. Kevin's congratulations were sincere, and he was touched that Pat asked him to be his best man. The wedding was set for just after graduation, plans that were shattered on prom night, when Pat chose his God over his girl.

Despite the ten-year separation, there was nothing stilted during their first meeting in the café. It all seemed like yesterday, and Kevin felt younger than he had in years. They reminisced, they laughed, and they fed quarters into the jukebox. "Twilight Time," "Only You," "All in the Game," "Silhouettes," "Why Do

Fools Fall in Love?" When they said good-bye, more than an hour later than Kevin had planned, they knew that they would meet again.

They did. Almost every night for the next two weeks. Kevin found himself working late even when it wasn't necessary. And like a little kid looking forward to the Saturday night dance, he found himself counting the hours until he met her at the café. It was inevitable, of course, that things would not remain confined to dinner.

"Do you have to go back to the office?" she asked one night. *That* night. Until then Kevin had been clean. Nothing to confess, except maybe impure intentions.

"Why?"

"I thought you might like to come back to my apartment."

This was it. He knew what it meant. There was definitely sufficient reflection to make the sin mortal.

"Why not?" he answered, with full consent of the will.

Her apartment was at Nineteenth and Walnut, so they walked, holding hands like teenagers on the way to the malt shop.

Then, with the Platters' record spinning, they were in each other's arms again. The same touch, the same smell, the same excitement that he only had for his first girl.

Quickly, almost brusquely, he removed her clothes, then his.

> Heavenly shades of night are falling
> It's twilight time.
> Deep in the dark your kiss will thrill me
> It's twilight time.

"Oh, Kevin, I've missed you so."

The years melted away. They were back in Margie Quinlan's basement, playing post office. Except that it was rigged. Bonnie had given him her number.

"God, I love to kiss you, Bonnie. Do you like it as much as I do?"
"You're not supposed to ask me that."

> When purple colored curtains
> Mark the end of day
> I'll hear you, my dear
> At twilight time.

[447]

"Do you?"

She buried her head in his shoulder. "Yes."

"You'll always be my girl, Bonnie. Always."

The others were banging on the door, angry that they were taking so long. It was time to call another number, but they just sat there, holding each other. Finally the door opened.

"C'mon, Kevin. Let's go." It was Kevin Quinn and Jackie Hamilton and Janet Cappe and the rest.

Only now the faces were changing. Now it was Karen. And the children. And it was over before it really began. He rolled to the side of the bed, turning away from his first girl.

"I can't, Bonnie. I'm sorry."

She put her hand on his back. "Sorry? For what? For being in love with your wife?"

He dressed quickly, then paused at the door. "Nothing stays the same, does it?"

"No. We all change. That's life, I guess. I enjoyed seeing you again, Kevin. I really did."

"So did I. See you later, Bon."

"No, you won't, Kev. We both know that. Good-bye."

That was it. Except for a brief phone call from her a week later. She had lost her job, and the landlord was threatening to evict her. As much as she hated to ask, could he possibly lend her some money? She would repay it as soon as possible.

Without hesitating, Kevin mailed a check, payable to cash, for three hundred dollars. After all, she was still a friend.

But even though it had ended, for Kevin it had just begun. It almost seemed that he took pleasure in torturing himself. He had failed, failed in the most important task a man had: to be true to his own. All his life he had looked up to the Sarge. There wasn't any question in his mind that his father had never even looked at another woman.

The world of the Sarge was a basic one. You kept your commitments. No exceptions. His son was not as strong. He had cheated on his wife, betrayed his children, and confirmed something which he had always suspected. Kevin would never be the man that his father was.

He tried to tell himself that it had never happened, that it all had been part of a dream, that he could shake himself awake and it would be all right again, the way he did with the other dreams, the ones where he had been part of a crime, generally an armed robbery. After he fled the scene, he realized what he had done. He had crossed the line, and there could be no return. Nothing he could do would make amends. He was no longer part of society. He was one of the hunted, and sooner or later he would have to pay. But even in the deepest of sleeps something in the corner of his mind told him that it wasn't real, that it was just a dream. And by a conscious effort he could force himself awake and give flight to the demons. *Thank God,* Kevin said to himself on such occasions. His wife was still sleeping beside him, his children were in their rooms, and he was still part of them, still on the right side of the line.

Not this time. No, there had been no armed robbery. There would be no arrest. His only prosecutor would be himself, but no one could have fought harder for a conviction. No matter what he was doing, Harrisburg or Havertown, helping a client or playing with the kids, it was always with him, an anvil weight that ultimately would crush him.

There was only one escape. Confession. Not to a priest, though he did that, too, but to his wife. Far from a noble act, it was the epitome of selfishness, trading his guilt for Karen's pain. They survived, because that was the way they were. And even though the slate could never be clean, in time the memory dimmed. They made love, created three more children, and went on with their lives. Now and then it would be resuscitated during a fight, but less and less frequently as the years passed.

Until now. Until Vince Grosso handed his best friend a folder containing copies of a canceled check and the report of an abortion performed on Bonnie Peterson on the same day that the check was cashed.

He heard Karen in the backyard, gathering the children. Nothing could keep her from meeting her commitments. Not even an unfaithful husband who threatened to destroy them all.

CHAPTER
Thirty-three

HIS Excellency Patrick Carney was working his show. When it came time for the homily, he disdained the pulpit. You didn't use the pulpit when you were dealing with a confirmation class of fourth graders. Instead, he worked the center aisle, walking back and forth, talking not to the parents but to the students.

"Big day for all of you, right?"

"Yes, Your Excellency!" they chanted in unison.

"Sister tells me that each of you is ready to become a soldier of Jesus. Is she right?"

"Yes, Your Excellency!"

"Ready to answer any question I ask, right?"

"Yes, Your Excellency!"

"Okay, I'll bet none of you can get my very first question. What's my middle name?"

The church echoed with laughter, but one little boy was taking it seriously, confidently raising his hand.

"There's a brave soul in the second row with his hand raised. Do you know the answer?"

"Yes, Your Excellency. Gerard."

"What's your name, son?"

"Paul Crosby, Your Excellency."

"Paul, I predict great things for you. You're either going to be a cardinal or president of the United States."

He went on like that for fifteen minutes, just long enough. Asking a question here, making a point there. It was an approach geared to the mind of a ten-year-old, making the sacrament that each child was about to receive meaningful and easy to understand.

When mass was over, he led the procession down the aisle. Staff in hand, he emulated his pope, stopping to bless each little child. That task performed, he remained at the rear of the church, greeting all who approached him and posing for pictures. All in all, a masterful performance.

"You'll join us in the rectory, won't you, Excellency?" asked the pastor.

"It's still Pat, John. Thanks, but I have to pass. I'm up to my neck in paperwork."

It was a lie, designed to refuse with grace an invitation that he normally would have accepted with pleasure. Confirmations constituted one of the premier social events of the clergy, each pastor attempting to outdo his colleagues in hospitality. There was always a huge spread and a rectory awash in booze. Even more enjoyable was the conversation: the jokes; the barbs; the speculation on who was in and who was out at the chancery. Naturally, the presence of Pat, since he had received the hat, would have an intimidating effect on the other priests, but only temporarily. When the alcohol had loosened their tongues and eroded away their deference, they would once again consider him one of the boys.

But in his present state of mind there was no way Pat could attend. Despite outward appearances, it was all he could do to struggle through the confirmation ceremony, looking at those innocent young faces, any one of whom could have been his child. Could have been but wasn't.

Ever since Vince Grosso's last confession Pat had suffered the tortures of the damned, which he most definitely considered himself to be. Despite his vow of celibacy, he had sired a child, had helped create another human. One of his own. But that son or daughter would never walk the earth, would never call him "Daddy," would never be baptized or confirmed, would never play with other children, would never be a comfort to him in his old age. That baby's voice had been silenced.

Pat had thought that the greatest sorrow of his life would be the knowledge that through his own cowardice, his father had died, alone and unwanted. But this was worse, far worse. At least

[451]

he had known George Carney. Had touched him and loved him and been a part of his life, even if only when convenient.

He had never known his baby and never would, so the questions continued to assault him. Was it a boy or girl? What would he have looked like? What would he have done? What would he have accomplished? Would he have published a novel or composed a symphony that gave pleasure to millions? Would he have been the one who discovered the cure for cancer? Would he have sired, or would she have borne, other children, continuing a line of humans that stemmed directly from Pat Carney? Wasn't it possible, even likely, that the abortion of his only child would have an endless impact, that thousands, even millions of human beings would not be born into the community of man?

What kind of father would he have been? At that point the questions became particularly unsettling because they raised more questions. Not about Pat's baby but about himself. Would he have acknowledged the baby? Would he have risked the almost certain destruction of his career to step forward and say to the world, "This is my child"? How would he have supported him? Would he have left the priesthood? Would he have married Bonnie, the mother of his child? Would he, at the very least, have pleaded with her to permit their baby to be born? Or would he, once again, have reached for the basin of Pilate? Most painful of all, hadn't he already done that nine years ago?

Bonnie had told him that she might be pregnant, but he had chosen to dismiss such a possibility. After all, she had never been regular. This was just another false alarm. But was it merely a coincidence that Pat had chosen then to sever finally their relationship? Why was it that it was at that precise time that his conscience was finally awakened, that he had chosen to return to his vow of celibacy?

Pat Carney may have broken his engagement on the night of the senior prom, but he had never stopped loving, or needing, Bonnie Peterson. During his first year in the seminary he had been able to reject the temptation. Actually it was less a matter of will than of circumstance. Since new seminarians had less freedom than a prison inmate, there had been no opportunity. During his first summer vacation, however, Pat had sought her out. She needed little coaxing, convinced that she would be able to wrest her man away from the sterility of the seminary. And so

[452]

they began. Always discreet, always careful, Bonnie intelligent enough to make no demands, Pat wary enough to make no promises.

Their liaison continued for seven years. There were interruptions, of course, some for considerable periods of time. Experiencing either guilt or fear of discovery, Pat would flee the field, leaving Bonnie alone to pick up the pieces. On several occasions she almost succeeded. Once she had even been engaged. He was an electrical engineer with Westinghouse, ten years her senior. Kind and considerate, he would have given her a life of security and moderate happiness, if not passion. But then Pat returned, never considering the possibility that she might not be there. She had never disappointed him. Fully aware that she was sowing the seeds of her own destruction, she exchanged common sense for false hope and accepted him back each time.

Until the last time, in the summer of 1973, when she told Pat that she might be pregnant. She saw the look on his face and knew that finally, without any hope of a reprieve, she had lost him.

Looking back on it, as he did so many times, Pat realized how poorly he had performed. Speechless at first, he finally stammered out a few questions. When Bonnie told him that she had not yet been to a doctor, his response was that it was probably a false alarm but that she should let him know. Clumsily, he then laid the foundation for his escape.

"I've been meaning to talk with you for some time now. About us. I've given it a lot of thought. You know how I feel about you. I love you, and I always will. But I think it's better for all parties concerned if we stop seeing each other. Once and for all."

"What does that mean, Pat? What does 'all parties concerned' mean? I thought this involved just you and me."

"It's more complicated than that, Bonnie. You know that. I'm a priest."

"You're also the man I love. Why all of a sudden does your priesthood disturb you? I've never made any demands."

"I know you haven't. You've been great. Better than I deserve. But the Church—there're so many people involved, so many people who would be hurt by a scandal."

"Scandal? Do you think that I'd ever expose you?"

[453]

"Of course not, but you know how things get out. It's just a matter of time."

"Time? We've managed to keep our secret for seven years."

"All the more reason for us not to press our luck. Besides, I've been unfair to you. Incredibly selfish. You're young, attractive, a wonderful, warm human being who should be getting on with her life."

"You *are* my life, Pat. The only thing in the world I care about." She was about to say more but checked herself. It would be unfair to beg. And it wouldn't do any good.

So Pat Carney left, to immerse himself in his career and, as an inescapable adjunct to that career, his God. By design, his schedule was staggering, usually eighteen hours a day. No time to think of what might have been. His energy did not go unnoticed by his superiors in the chancery. If love were denied him, he would settle for power, and nothing would stand in his way.

Bonnie was not so fortunate. There was no career to fill the void, no breakneck schedule to use as a shield. She was shattered and alone, save for the unborn child within her who would never know its father. Although she later visited a doctor who made it official, there had never been any doubt that she was pregnant.

Her brief encounter with Kevin was purely coincidental. She had planned on going to a movie, alone, and on a whim stopped for a quick sandwich at a café that she had never previously patronized. And there he was, sitting in a booth, reading a book. Her Kevin, her youth. For those brief weeks he had been a harbor, a place where she could escape the winds of reality. It was an opportunity to slip into the safety of a port, to defer the decision that loomed ahead.

But then Kevin, like Pat, was gone, and once again it was just Bonnie and her baby. What should she do? Was it fair to bring a child into the world under such circumstances? What would she tell him when he was old enough to understand? That he was a bastard, that his father was a priest who would never acknowledge him?

And what about her? What would her life be? It was 1973, and even though values had changed considerably, an unwed mother was still a leper. Datable, of course, someone with whom a man could attempt to score with relative safety, but not the type of person with whom he would wish to build a relationship.

[454]

If only she could start fresh, begin again with a clean slate. Pat would never return. She would have to get him out of her system. Difficult but not impossible. But there could be no new beginning, no unsullied blackboard, so long as the child was there as a reminder of her hopeless love for one of God's chosen.

She had been raised a Catholic, and even though she hadn't practiced in years, a vestige of the guilt remained. The step that she was considering was a sin, an affront to God and His church, sentencing her to everlasting damnation.

Quite a choice, she had bitterly reflected. A life of hell or an eternity of it. In the end, the doctor made it easy.

"Congratulations, Mrs. Peterson. You're pregnant."

"I know."

"Your first?"

Why didn't doctors ever read their charts? "Yes."

"I'm sure your husband will be very excited. I'd like to have him accompany you for your next visit. It helps if he's part of things from the beginning."

"I'm not married."

"Oh. I see. Uh, do you want to keep the baby? What I mean to say is, do you want to continue your pregnancy?"

"No," she heard herself saying.

"I see. Very well. I can arrange for a termination. That's certainly your right. Once the decision is made, the sooner the matter is resolved, the better. There's very little risk at your stage. Would this afternoon be suitable?"

"How much is it?"

"Three hundred dollars."

She hesitated. "I'll need a few days."

"All right." He handed her a card. "Here's the clinic's address. I'll telephone, so they'll be expecting you. Whenever you're ready. It'll be over before you know it."

He was right. The people at the clinic were extremely friendly.

"Nothing to worry about," the receptionist said smiling. "It's routine."

When Bonnie looked back on it, it was always obscured by a haze, as if she were watching a movie in slow motion and the audio had been turned off. She vaguely remembered reading *Cosmopolitan* in the waiting room. Then she was taken back, prepped, and placed in the stirrups. She had been given anesthesia, and

[455]

even though it was local, she was groggy. She wasn't certain if she was even aware of the sound of the suction machine. It was over quickly, and after a half-hour recovery period she was on the way back to her apartment. With a clean slate.

Without thinking about it, the first thing she did was take a shower. Toweling dry, she knew that she should begin planning her new life. What was that saying? "Today is the first day of the rest of your life." She was reborn, she told herself. Pat, Kevin, the baby—all that was in the past. Only the future counted now. She was no longer a kid, but she wasn't old either. After all, thirty wasn't exactly ancient. Plenty of time for accomplishment, to make her life a full one. But all she could do that evening was collapse into bed. Plenty of time, she had said to herself before drifting off. Tomorrow.

With the morning the haze began to lift, replaced by the starkness of reality. The film speed returned to normal, the sound was increased, and she began to grasp the enormity of her act. Try as she might to elude them, she was assailed by recriminations, the same agony, over the same lost child, that Pat Carney was to suffer nine years later, when Vince Grosso exposed him to the inescapable truth.

If it was true that each day was the first day of the rest of Bonnie's life, it was equally true that each day was worse than the one before. For seven years she drifted aimlessly, unable to hold a job or a man for more than a month or two. It was inevitable that she would grasp for salvation, first in the form of a bottle, then a syringe. There were a hundred fresh starts and a hundred failures, one of which was almost fatal. She could never be certain whether or not the overdose had been intentional. Only a busybody landlady, who subsequently canceled her lease, and a crack paramedic squad kept her alive, kept her from moving from one hell to another.

Then, because of an improbable coincidence, her life changed. Had she not been arrested for possession of a controlled substance on the same day that mob figure Benito Fortiliano was busted for loan-sharking, she would not have been booked at the Roundhouse at the precise time that defense attorney Vincent Grosso was obtaining bail for his client.

At first Vince didn't recognize her. He walked past, then turned. "Bonnie? Bonnie Peterson?"

"Hello, Vince."

"Bonnie, what are you doing here?"

"Possession."

"You? Why? How?"

"It's a long story, not worth telling."

"It's one I want to hear. Who's representing you?"

"I don't know. I guess I'm getting one of those, you know—"

"Public defenders? No way." He turned to an assistant. "Inform the PD that Bonnie Peterson is now my case."

From that moment on things began to move. Within an hour she had been processed and released on her own recognizance. Within a day she had been examined by a team of physicians and transported to a plush rehabilitation home in Montgomery County. And within a month she had found herself becoming whole again.

The home was excellent, its staff as kind as it was professional. But perhaps Bonnie's best therapy was the almost daily visits from Vince. He never probed, never attempted to extract anything from her. Instead, he listened, permitting her to choose the pace. In time she told him everything: her relationship with Pat, her pregnancy, her brief affair with Kevin, her abortion, and her disintegration. Not surprisingly, the more she talked, the more she bared her soul, the better she felt.

When she left the home, a tastefully furnished apartment in Society Hill Towers was waiting. She balked at such generosity, but Vince was ready with an answer. "It's an investment, Bonnie."

"What do you mean?"

"Beginning today, provided you agree, you're a part of the law firm of Vincent J. Grosso."

"Me? That's crazy. I'm not a lawyer. I'm not even a good secretary."

"Maybe not. But I've got an eye for talent, and there's no doubt in my mind that you have the ability to be an excellent paralegal, something I desperately need. What do you say?"

She smiled and shook her head. "I owe you everything."

"You owe me nothing. That's what friends are for."

Upon graduating, with honors, from paralegal school, she began work in Vince's office. As usual, he was right. Bonnie proved to be an outstanding addition to the firm. Thorough yet

[457]

quick, she had a natural talent for both research and procedure.

But as her self-worth was gradually restored, there was an accompanying increase in bitterness. Funny, but when she had been at her lowest, when she had aborted her child, become addicted to drugs, and attempted to take her life, she blamed no one but herself. Now, realizing that she was neither weak nor worthless, she also realized how much of her life had been needlessly wasted, years that could never be retrieved. She seethed with a rage which, unless released, posed a greater threat to her survival than the needle which had almost destroyed her.

Whom to blame? Whom to select as the outlet, the target for her venom? Logically, it should have been Pat, but she was not ready for that. He may have been weak, he may have manipulated her for his own pleasure, then discarded her at the first sign of danger, but he was still the man she loved. And certainly not Kevin. He had been innocent, led on by her at a time when, like herself, he was most vulnerable. Besides, to hate him would be to hate her youth, to hate the good memories, to hate the boy who had comforted her on the trolley ride home from the movies.

So she chose the Church. Hadn't it been the Church that had taken away the man she would always love? So typical of an institution which preached love, then forbade its priests to practice it. And it had been the Church, a body which in its every action displayed its indifference, even contempt, for women, that had labeled her a sinner because she had made the only choice available to her. Eunuchs in white collars dictating to women a course of action which they would never have to face.

Holy Mother Church had stolen fifteen of the best years of her life. It was a sin that could never be forgiven, and someday, somehow she would wreak her revenge.

Although Bonnie never gave voice to these emotions, Vince understood them. He also understood that someday they might be used to his advantage. There had been no ulterior motive, no hidden calculation, in throwing a life preserver to Bonnie. She was a friend, one who needed help. But as he listened to her and became aware of the personal sins of a fast-rising cleric and a high-ranking public official, he was unwittingly handed a weapon which he found impossible to refuse. It was a rifle that would never be fired, he told himself. Nothing could cause him to betray his two closest friends. But then the liquor bill came along and Vince was forced

[458]

to choose between his friendship and his *borgotta*. Since he was Sicilian, he chose the *borgotta,* finalizing his decision in the salon of a cabin cruiser. He knew that Bonnie would not choose to hurt Pat or Kevin. But he also knew the depth of her hatred. If destruction of either were necessary to exact vengeance upon the Church, she could be convinced.

There was nothing Vince desired more than to be able to refrain from pulling the trigger. He had made certain that each step taken so far was one that could be erased should Kevin pull a green switch on the liquor bill. And once that had been accomplished, there would be no encore, not even for the Poconos gambling legislation. The records of both the bank and the abortion clinic would disappear, thus assuring that Kevin's sin, as well as Pat's, would remain forever hidden.

Wasn't that being fair? Who in his position would behave so honorably? The standard rule with the mob was once you got a public official on the hook, you never let him off.

One lousy vote, that's all he was asking. Was that too much to expect from a friend? It wasn't as if he were asking Kevin to do something that was wrong or might jeopardize his career. The overwhelming majority of his constituents wanted a yes vote, and in the end the big winner wouldn't be Vince Grosso or his family. It would be the public. But without Kevin and his moral leadership, the bill was certain to go down, and all of them would lose.

Dammit, Kevin, don't be a hardhead. For once, just once, in your life, compromise. Take all of us off the hook.

Maybe Pat would be able to help. Vince hadn't confessed his blackmail to him just to receive absolution. More than anything, Pat was a survivor. As devastated as he might be by the revelation that Bonnie had been pregnant, and his child aborted, he was equally concerned about the threat that this fact posed to his career. Kevin, not he, was the target, but things like this had a way of coming home to roost. Unless Vince were mistaken—and he prided himself on having a feel for people—the new auxiliary bishop would somehow counsel Kevin to opt for discretion. Maintain a low profile, cast a yes vote on the bill, and put the matter behind him—behind all of them—once and for all.

Pat found it difficult to make his way to the car. Parents of the *confirmandi* sought him out, bestowing compliments and requesting pictures with their children. He should have been honored, but each accolade served only to increase his self-revulsion. The final tribute, as he was preparing to unlock his car, was the worst.

"The ceremony was beautiful, Your Excellency," a beaming mother said. "I've had four other children confirmed, but this was by far the most impressive. All because of you."

"You're very kind."

"The way you were able to relate to them, to talk to them on their own level. I wish I had that talent."

"I'm sure you do."

"No. Not the way you have. It's almost a shame."

"About what?"

The woman hesitated. "Actually I shouldn't have said that. All I mean is, well, you're a wonderful priest, and someday you're going to be a cardinal. Why do some people have all the talent? You would have made such a wonderful parent."

Thirty-four

"IS that it?" asked Vince Grosso.

"Yep," answered Nick Arrone. "Another light night. Thank God for summer, huh?"

"Yeah. Half of South Philly must be in Wildwood right now. Is the car ready?"

"They're just bringing it around, boss."

They walked from the office into the humid South Philadelphia evening. Down the street the inevitable stickball war was still being waged. Once it had been concluded, a fire hydrant would be opened for some postgame relaxation.

Vince paused on the steps. "I still love it, Nicky. I've got a palace on the Main Line, but this will always be home."

"Don Vincenzo!" A figure was hurriedly approaching, holding a brown paper bag. The bodyguards tensed briefly, then relaxed. It was Mr. Cusamano. Even since Vince had resolved his boarding home problems, the old man had expressed his gratitude on a weekly basis, bringing fruits and vegetables that he had grown in his rooftop greenhouse.

"Hello, Mr. Cusamano. How are you this evening?"

"Fine, Don Vincenzo. I was afraid I'd miss you. Here. Fresh tomatoes, the kind you'll never find in a supermarket."

"*Grazie*. My wife will be delighted."

"Please give her my respect."

Vince hadn't noticed the car that knifed from the alley. Arrone had. He dived past Cusamano, tackled his boss, and rolled with

[461]

him down the steps. Almost simultaneously the machine guns opened up. Bullets cascaded against the steps where Vince had been standing, splintering the door behind. It ended as abruptly as it began, the car screeching away before any of the bodyguards had a chance to draw their weapons.

Looking back on it, Vince couldn't be sure how long he lay there, his body entwined with Arrone's. There was total silence, and Vince, his eyes still shut, wondered whether he was dead. Then he became conscious of the ache in his knee and the smell of cordite and burned rubber. He rose slowly, then grasped Arrone's hand and helped him up.

"You okay, Nicky?"

"Yeah. You?"

"No," Vince answered, shaking his head, then pointing to his knee. The fall had torn his pants, opening a small cut on his kneecap. "This was a new suit."

Vince surveyed the scene. Mr. Cusamano had not been as fortunate. His body was twisted at a grotesque angle halfway down the stairs. He had caught two bullets, one in the chest and one in the head. There would be no open-casket viewing. The bag of tomatoes was untouched.

With a motion of his hand Vince summoned his bodyguards. None of them had been hit.

"Did any of you see anything?"

"It was a late-model Lincoln, boss," one of them answered. "Green. And they were niggers."

"License plate?"

They all shook their heads. "Fine," Vince continued. "Sal, please call the police. Tell them there's been a shooting. Nothing more. They'll want to interview each of you."

"What'll we tell them, boss?"

"Exactly what you saw, which is very little. And call your wives. Tell them that you're all right and that it will probably be a late night."

Vince turned to Arrone. "Come with me, Nicky." They went back into the office. Vince took off his suit jacket and carefully draped it over a chair. "Interesting way to make a living, huh?"

"How the hell can you be so calm? Somebody just tried to blow us the hell away."

"And failed, Nicky. Which is what counts." He sat behind his desk. "All right, let's get down to it. The police interviews should be no problem. We know nothing, we saw nothing, and there's nothing they can do. Oh, they might take us down the station just to bust our stones a little and keep the photographers happy, but that's okay. The important thing is to find out, with absolute certainty, who ordered this. I have my suspicions, but I want it confirmed. Use everything we have, Niccolo. Our police, press, street people. Everything. I want to know within twenty-four hours. I insist upon it."

"I'll get right on it, Vince."

"But first things first. After you call your wife, attend to Mrs. Cusamano. I don't want her to hear about it from the police. Contact one of her relatives. Her sister lives on Christian. Thirteen hundred block. I think her name's Pelosi. Should be in the file. Have the funeral bill sent to us. Once the funeral is over, arrange something for her. Tactfully, of course. I want her taken care of as long as she lives."

Arrone nodded. Vince waited until he had reached the door. "You saved my life, Nicky. I'm grateful."

"No sweat, Vince."

"Nice balance, isn't it?"

"What's that?"

Vince smiled. "I owe you my life, and you owe me a new suit."

"You're unbelievable, boss."

Alone, Vince slumped back in his chair, no longer careful to control his breathing, which now came in long, struggling gasps, as if each might be his last. He had just put on a vintage performance. Pure steel in the face of death. But he was terrified, even more now as the full impact sank in.

He had known the risks when he became a don. The possibility of instant death ran with the territory. But that had been in the abstract, something that he *knew* but had never *felt*. Now, after he had pulled himself up off a South Philadelphia pavement and seen what remained of an innocent old man whose only crime had been gratitude, the point had been driven home. For once he was assaulted by doubt.

Were it possible right now, would he bag it all? Resign his leadership of the *borgotta* and devote his time to practicing law? Better yet, retire and spend all his time with his family? Not that it mattered. Some things would never be possible. Kevin Murray could retire from politics. Pat Carney could leave the priesthood. But for Vince Grosso the only escape from the life he had chosen was through death.

His hands still trembling, he lifted the phone and dialed home. Michael answered.

"How are you doing, pal?"

"Hi, Dad. How's it going?"

"Okay. Sorry I couldn't make your game this evening. How did you do?"

"Good. We won, eight to three."

"How did *you* do?"

"Good. One-for-two. Double."

"Only two at-bats? How come?"

Michael hesitated. "Well, I played only three innings."

"Why? Coach bench you?"

"No. Not exactly."

"Come on, Michael. What does 'not exactly' mean?"

"Well, uh, the double I got, I tried to stretch it to three. I made it, too, Dad. I really did! I went in headfirst. He never made the tag, honest!"

"What you're trying to say is that you got thrown out of another game, right?"

Michael sighed. "Yeah."

"When are you going to learn, Mike? How many times have we talked about this? That temper of yours is going to get you in trouble."

"But I was safe, Dad! The ump was a retard!"

"Michael, the ump may not always be right, but he's always the ump. He's got the last word. Never fight a battle you can't win."

"Yeah, you're right."

"That's what you always say, Mike. Then you go out and do it again. You keep it up, and the coach is going to bench you. Permanently. He doesn't want somebody he can't depend on. Do you understand that, thickhead?"

"Yeah. I do. Honest."

"I hope so, Mike, for your sake. Now let me speak to your mom."

"What's wrong, Vincent?" Lena said when she came to the phone. "I thought you'd be on the way home by now."

[464]

"Something came up. I'm going to be tied up for a while. Hours, probably."

"What is it?"

"A little complication. Nothing serious."

Lena's voice turned hard. "What *is* it, Vincent?"

"There's been a shooting. In front of the office. You remember Mr. Cusamano? He was killed. The police should be here any minute."

"Someone tried to kill you."

Vince hesitated. "Yes."

"Are you all right?"

"Yeah. I swear. I wasn't hit. I wanted you to know before you heard it. You know, on the news."

"Yes."

"I have to go now, Lena. I love you."

As she placed down the receiver, Lena Grosso was assailed by conflicting emotions. Fear: someone had tried to kill her husband. Relief: he was unhurt. And irony: she had almost been spared her most difficult decision.

Karen Murray absently sipped her Coke, her eyes fixed on the far wall. It had been a slow night, which was the worst. More time to think about what lay ahead.

Since receiving the news of Vince's blackmail, she had been obsessed by the consequences. How would they survive? How would the children survive? Particularly young Kevin and Sean. They were old enough to understand and grasp fully the disgrace.

Would they have to move? Say good-bye to their roots and their relatives in their flight for anonymity? Could there ever be peace again?

"A penny for your thoughts. In fact, with inflation, I'll go up to a dollar."

Karen looked up. "Hello, Dr. Richter—John."

"Karen, you look like you have the weight of the world on your shoulders."

"Something like that."

"Want to talk about it?"

Karen sighed. " I don't know. I just don't know."

"Well, my offer still stands. I have late rounds tonight, so if you

[465]

need a shoulder to lean on, just yell. A drink, maybe. I'm not pushing, Karen. You be the judge."

"Thank you, John."

She gave out medications to half a dozen patients, then brought her chart up-to-date. But her mind was elsewhere.

She looked at the phone, then lifted the receiver as if it were a bomb, tentatively dialing the number.

"Havertown Zoo," Kevin answered.

"Hi. How's everything?"

"Not bad. Dinner was a qualified success, no one's broken any bones, and we had a relatively spirited game of Candyland."

"Are they in bed?"

"Yeah. The little ones. Kevin and Sean are just finishing their homework. How's work?"

"Okay. Busy. Listen, I'll probably be a couple of hours late tonight. We're shorthanded, and they need me."

"Okay. Get that overtime."

"I love you, Kevin."

"I don't blame you. I love you, too."

She carefully replaced the receiver. Kevin should be proud of her. For once she wasn't being practical.

Like her husband nine years before, Karen Murray was about to cross the line.

CHAPTER
Thirty-five

THE taxpayers of Pennsylvania were about to engage in a collective sigh of relief. Since it was an election year, there had been no tax increase, the budget had been passed on time, and now, after handling a number of housekeeping chores, the legislature was recessing for the summer.

The press, of course, would label it a "vacation," something that never failed to irritate Kevin. Vacation, hell. He was always busier when the legislature was out of session. The constituents knew he was in the district, and they swarmed, each with a problem that couldn't wait. Still, it was nice to know that for the next two months he could control his own schedule. He would still have to go to Harrisburg a day or two a week to keep up with routine office work; but the days could be of his own choosing, and he could take the early train home. There might even be time to practice a little law.

After banging the gavel for the final time, the Speaker motioned to Kevin.

"What's up, boss?"

"You taking the train home?"

"Beats walking."

"Listen, the next train doesn't leave for two hours. I'm shoving off in fifteen minutes. Want a ride? I feel like some company, even you."

"I'd love to, boss, but I'm snowed under." He hesitated. "Unless there's a problem, in which case I'll bag everything."

"No problem."

"You sure?" Kevin asked. The Speaker didn't seem quite himself.

"Kevin, how can there be a problem when we're done for the summer? In a few hours I'll be in Ocean City, and all will be right with the world. Have a great summer. You and the family."

"You, too, Mike."

Bridget Kelly was waiting in his office. "The Kelly girl," he said as he entered. "To what do I owe this pleasure?"

"Just thought I'd brighten your day, Kevin."

"You always do, although I have to admit that right now I'm in a pretty good mood even without you. No more of this bullshit for two months."

"Makes me just as happy. When you guys aren't here, I don't have to be either."

"Now that we've exchanged pleasantries, let me guess. You're here to check the status of the abortion bill."

"That, and any other goodies you might be cooking up for September."

Whenever Kevin decided upon a pro-life legislative agenda, Bridget was one of the first to know. Even before the bills were introduced, he provided her with drafts. It wasn't just that he liked her. To Kevin, it was the only way to operate. If you had to rely on a Pearl Harbor to get things done, you weren't very good. He believed in the Vince Lombardi approach. Everyone knew when the sweep was coming. People just couldn't stop it.

"Okay," Kevin said. "We're pretty close to wrapping up negotiations with the governor's people. Things have moved pretty well in the last few weeks. I think they're getting tired of Craig."

"I don't blame them."

"Be charitable. Anyway, unless something unforeseen happens, we should have everything put together by August. We come back mid-September. By early October it all should be finished. Both houses and the governor's signature."

"You're cutting it pretty close to the election, aren't you? I imagine some of your colleagues aren't real thrilled."

"True. Any number of them will be pissed beyond words, but there's no alternative."

"Why not wait until after the election?"

"No way. We're in for only two weeks, maybe less, before *sine die.* Too risky. The abortion bill will become law *this* term, not next."

"What's it going to look like?"

"I can't give you any details, Bridget. We made a commitment to the governor that no specifics would be discussed until just before we ran it. What I *can* tell you is that it will still be the toughest abortion bill in the country."

"Thanks for making my day."

"I always try to please." Kevin paused. "Can I ask you something?"

"Sure."

"I just heard that you are not only Catholic but the product of sixteen years of Catholic education. Is that true?"

"Not quite. Fourteen. And I *was* Catholic."

"Why, Bridget?"

"You really want to know? Just between us?"

"Yeah, I do."

"All right. In that case, only because I love you, I shall tell you the heartrending saga of Bridget Marie Kelly, good Catholic girl. Catholic grade school, Catholic high school, and two years of Catholic college. St. Mary's in good old South Bend. Notre Dame wasn't coed in those days, of course. Anyway, our heroine was a pretty good student, a pretty good athlete, and a very good girl. The type nuns love. But even good girls can get pregnant, as our heroine did in her sophomore year. By a good Catholic boy, I might add. One of Notre Dame's finest."

Her smile faded as the memories returned, and with them, the bitterness. "He was the first boy I ever slept with. I loved him. I really did. And I thought that he loved me. Wrong. When I told him I was pregnant, he acted like I had the plague. I'll say this for him, though. He was honest. Told me flat out that marriage was out of the question. His parents would kill him. He had to finish college, then med school. Which, incidentally, he did. He's a doctor now, in St. Louis. Oh, yeah, how could I forget? He offered to pay, if I wanted, and this is a quote, 'to take care of things.' Classic, huh?"

"Did you tell your parents?"

"Oh, yes. We were always close. I could tell them anything. At least I thought I could. To put it mildly, they were horrified that their gold star girl had been deflowered. And absolutely terrified

[469]

of the scandal. My mother was beautiful. Asked me if I wanted the baby. I told her that I wasn't sure, that I'd wait until after it was born to decide whether to go the adoption route. 'What I mean, dear,' she said, 'is do you *want* the baby?' Don't you love it? Keep several things in mind, Kevin, just for flavor. We're talking about 1970, when abortion was not only a sin against the church but a crime. My mother was president of the parish sodality; my father, the head usher at the ten-fifteen. How's that for practicing what you preach? But it gets better, if you're still interested."

"I am, Bridget."

"Okay, then let me bum one of your cigarettes."

"I didn't think you smoked," Kevin said, handing her a Winston, then lighting it.

"Only when I'm enthralling an audience with a class D soap opera." She was smiling again, but Kevin noticed that her hand was shaking.

Bridget continued. "My parents even brought in the heavy artillery. Our pastor. Good old Monsignor Fowler, a friend of the family for as long as I can remember. My father's golf partner every Saturday. He nodded his head as my parents explained my predicament—that's what my mother kept calling it, 'Bridget's predicament'—took a long sigh, then said, and this is verbatim, 'As a priest I'm obligated to counsel you to have the baby. But speaking as a friend, I say do what you think is best for Bridget.' How's that for the monolithic voice of the Catholic Church? Incidentally, he never once looked at me. His comments were directed to my parents."

"What did you do?"

"Representative Murray, you may control the flow of debate on the floor of the House, but I determine the pace of my stories."

"I stand corrected, Ms. Kelly."

"And forgiven. Well, no matter what my parents or the goddamn priest said, there was no way I was going to have an abortion. I couldn't. I just couldn't. So I set up an appointment with Catholic Social Services. Just to get some information on the adoption procedure. You might have thought I was the town slut. They treated me like dirt. It was like they were doing some huge favor for a sinner, but only out of duty. You know, Kevin, the Church has to decide which way it wants it. If it's going to oppose abortion, it can't treat a pregnant girl like Hester Prynne. Like

[470]

the Catholic high schools. Do you know that most of them still have a policy that if a girl gets pregnant, she has to leave school? To paraphrase a great statesman, one Kevin Murray, where in the hell is the consistency in that?"

"What can I say, Bridget? You're right."

"Anyway, when my parents saw that I was adamant about having the baby, they arranged for me to stay with relatives in Seattle. Actually it wasn't in Seattle. It was some hick town about fifty miles away. I didn't want to go. I wanted to stay, to be with my family. I'll be honest, I was scared. But my parents made it clear that it would be better 'for all parties concerned'—that's another of my mother's quaint phrases—if I blossomed in anonymity. They were hoping, of course, that I wouldn't do something idiotic like keep the baby and bring him home."

She stubbed out the cigarette, then stared at the floor. "I'm not sure *what* I would have done. I never got the chance to find out. The baby was stillborn. He strangled on the cord during delivery. It was a boy. I held him. I even had him baptized. I was finished with the Church, but I wasn't taking any chances. You know, to this day I wonder if things would have been different if I had stayed home. Gone to a better hospital than the hick one in Washington."

"I'm sorry, Bridget. I really am."

"Thanks." She sighed, then went on. "I sent my parents a letter. It was very short, so I remember every word. 'Your worries are over. The baby's dead.' I have never spoken to them since, and I've never set foot in a Catholic church. Until—" She glanced at Kevin and hesitated.

"Until Andrew's funeral."

"I'm sorry, Kevin. I didn't mean to—"

"That's okay, kid. I really appreciated your being there."

"Anyway, I packed my things, went to Baltimore, and started over, determined to have some good come out of my experience. When I needed help, there was no one there. I made up my mind that I was going to help other girls. No one should have to go through something like that alone. And I made up my mind to fight the hypocrisy that I had seen firsthand. I know how much you detest those who say they're personally opposed to abortion but believe in the right to choose. Well, that's me, Kevin. I still am personally opposed. I could never do it. Screw the Church. I

[471]

don't need it telling me what abortion is. I know. I made a decision, which I've never regretted. But it was *my* choice, which is what every woman deserves. And that, my friend, is the end of the story. What do you think?"

"I think you're a hell of a woman who's been through a hell of a lot. I also think you've chosen a course for all the wrong reasons. You're retaliating, Bridget. Against your parents and, even more, against the Church. *Your* church. So a priest of that church acted outrageously. So what? Does that justify your supporting something that you know, by your own admission, is wrong?"

"You're oversimplifying things, Kevin."

"The hell I am. And let me tell you something else. You're fighting a losing battle."

"On abortion?"

"No. Against the Church. When someone constantly bad-mouths the Church, it's a pretty safe bet that he's a fallen-away Catholic. The fact that he takes the time to do the bad-mouthing shows that he's not secure. The classic love-hate relationship of the Roman Catholic Church. You might leave the Church, Bridget, but the Church will never leave you. And someday you'll come back."

"Never."

"Never say never. You know the story of St. Monica and St. Augustine, don't you?"

"Sure."

"Well, I'm going to be your St. Monica. And sooner or later we're going to get you back."

Bridget rose. "I wouldn't hold my breath, Kevin."

"You're worth waiting for." He leaned over and kissed her. "Have a good summer, Bridget."

Exactly four hours from the time he left Harrisburg, Mike Callaghan was approaching the Ninth Street Bridge into Ocean City. Traffic had been light, in sharp contrast with next week, when the hordes would elbow their way in for the Fourth of July weekend, the real beginning of the summer shore season.

Anxious to get to his home, then the airport, he lost five minutes because of a bridge opening. But that was okay. Even welcome. There was something special about a place where no matter how important or busy you might be, your schedule came second to a boat going through a bridge.

Callaghan pulled into the carport beside his home, a two-story ocean front at Twenty-seventh and Wesley.

"Finished for the summer, Mike?" one of his neighbors called.

"You got it. You can sleep safely until mid-September."

He walked into the kitchen, placed a roast he had just purchased in the oven, then set the table for one. It seemed that now he always set the table for one, but that was okay. Even welcome. As long as he had a good book to read during the meal, as he always did. He was into another Alistair McLean novel, which he placed beside his plate.

Callaghan mixed a whiskey and water, took two sips, then carried it upstairs, where he changed into cutoffs and a T-shirt. Then he unlocked his bike and, as always, pedaled the five blocks to the airport.

The controller greeted him warmly. He was a big fan of Mike's. "Hi, Mr. Speaker. I heard on the radio you guys finished up. Congratulations."

"Thanks, Kenny. It's nice to be done."

"I'll bet. Going up for a little while?"

"Yeah. An hour or so. Nothing special. Up the coast and back. Just to unwind before dinner."

"Know what you mean. Well, enjoy. You earned it."

Since the divorce and the kids' growing up, flying had been Callaghan's chief source of pleasure. It was a great combination. Unique. You had the challenge of operating a complex machine, and at the same time you were at peace. Alone, above it all, where you could think things out.

He flew just north of Long Beach Island, then banked into an easy turn. The sunsets were always breathtaking, but this time it was special, the best he ever remembered. For which he was grateful. It was a good way to end.

On the drive from Harrisburg, Callaghan had wondered if he'd have second thoughts when he was up. But no. From his vantage point two thousand feet above the sea, he saw even more clearly that this was the only way to go, the only way out. There would be no shame, no scandal for him or his family. He couldn't take a scandal, not after so many years. In thirty years he had never

[473]

taken a dime for his services as a public official. He was a partisan, he would cut your throat to keep his party in power, but he was honest.

But seven years before, he had also been financially strapped. Three of the kids were in college, and he had just completed an expensive property settlement with his ex-wife. He hadn't sought the estate, hadn't asked to be named executor, but there it was, an opportunity that he couldn't ignore. The deceased, a former client, had been extremely well heeled, leaving an estate that was both large and complex, the type that took years to settle. It had been easy to transfer the funds. And as soon as he was back on his feet, he had paid it back. Professionally handled, impossible to detect. But then why had he agonized, every day for seven years, that someone, somehow, would find him out?

Someone had, and now was trying to blackmail him. They had him, and when they had you, they kept you on the hook.

That was no way to live, always wondering what was next, always despising yourself for being owned. Better this way. Clean and quick. No disgrace in a plane crash. These things happen sometimes. Without question, the insurance policies would be paid. His legacy to his children would be security, not shame.

After a final look at the sunset, Callaghan increased his airspeed and began his final dive to the patient Atlantic.

For Michael Joseph Callaghan, Speaker of the Pennsylvania House of Representatives, the nightmare was over at last.

Thirty-six

VINCE Grosso shifted in his chair, his fingers lightly tapping the desk. The arguments were persuasive. For once his financial experts were in agreement. For fifty-five million dollars he could buy out the nation's third-largest video games company. A steal, considering that it had grossed six hundred million in 1981. Fortunately for Vince the owner had an affinity for the roulette tables in Atlantic City. He needed quick cash.

"It's a once-in-a-lifetime opportunity, Mr. Grosso," one of the experts said in closing. It had been a high-powered presentation, complete with charts and slides. "The growth potential in the market is literally without limit."

Vince adjusted his chair again. They all were watching him, anxious for a reaction. "Excellent presentation," he said. "Obviously well researched, for which I'm very grateful. But I think I'm going to pass."

No one spoke, but the surprise was almost audible. This one had seemed to be a lock. The boss had always been aggressive when it came to acquisitions.

Vince continued. "I can't hope to match your expertise in explaining why I'm against this venture. It's a gut feeling, and gut feelings are hard to put into words. What we're dealing with is a market controlled almost exclusively by young people. Children. So far they can't get enough of it. Kids are cutting classes, giving up sports and blowing their allowances just to play these games. But kids are funny. They crave discipline; they want regulation.

And if no one regulates them, they'll do it themselves. I have a feeling—a gut feeling—that not too far down the road the kids are going to say, 'Enough is enough.' And when that happens, the industry goes down the toilet. We have enough tax shelters already. We don't need another white elephant."

He rose from the desk, the meeting obviously over. "Thank you, gentlemen, and good day."

Alone, Vince rotated his neck from shoulder to shoulder. It was stiff. It seemed that whenever he had a tough decision to make, his neck got stiff. At least he could do something about it. He lifted the phone and pressed the buzzer. "Put everything on hold for an hour. I'm going down the hall."

Shortly after buying the PSFS Building, Vince had indulged in one of his few luxuries. The east wing of the top floor had been turned into a gym. Small but more than functional. Nautilus, sauna, and a hot tub. The hot tub was his favorite, situated beside the window so that Vince could gaze out at the Delaware while the bubbling water worked its soothing effect.

He had just started to doze when the door opened. "Sorry, boss. I know you don't like to be bothered in here," said Niccolo Arrone, "but I didn't think this could wait."

"No problem, Nicky. What is it?"

"We have the information you want." There was pride in his voice. "Less than two days after the incident, and we have a definite confirmation. It was New York. Agostino. The gunmen were from Bedford-Stuyvesant. Part of his drug operation."

"You said 'definite,' Nicky. Is there any margin for error? Any at all?"

"None. We triple-checked our sources. It was Agostino. We retaliate, don't we?"

"Absolutely." Vince sighed. "Julius Marzette. Take him out. Quickly."

"Marzette? Boss, I just told you. It was Agostino. Marzette had nothing to do with it. He's been fine. Oh, he plays a few games with our percentages, but by and large, he's been an asset."

"I know, Nicky. But he has to die."

"I hate to admit it, Vince, but I'm totally confused."

"I'm not the slightest bit surprised that it was Agostino who ordered the hit. I knew it when I was still on the sidewalk. And down the road he'll have to be dealt with. But not now. We need

[476]

him. Business is good in Atlantic City. Remove Agostino, and we have chaos, which is bad for business. We'll have to let Don Michael know, of course, that we know. But for now he lives."

"But why Marzette?"

"Somebody has to die, Nicky. Let an attempted hit go unpunished, and it gets habit-forming. Marzette's expendable. We can move Raymal right into his place. And let's face it, sooner or later Marzette was going to come after me, at which point he would have to go. We're just expediting the inevitable."

"Okay. Normal procedure?"

"No. Not this time. I want it public, Nicky. And symbolic."

Julius Marzette enjoyed his life. He enjoyed telling people what to do and having them obey without question. He enjoyed the respect that he was always given, whether it was in the North Philadelphia ghetto or the most exclusive Center City restaurant. He enjoyed his wealth and what it provided: his Rolls-Royce; his cabin cruiser in Atlantic City; his villa in the Bahamas. And all the women a man could want.

Most of all, he enjoyed the game, the challenge of staying on top. You always had to be one step ahead of the other guy and a defense lawyer ahead of the cops—the ones you couldn't buy. True, things weren't as good now that the wops were involved. He was making even more money than before, but the operation wasn't his own. But what the hell, only a few people knew the real story. There had been no loss of respect. And the problem was only a temporary one. When the time was right, he would deal with the wops.

But first things first. Tonight he had a job to do, and he was looking forward to it. It was never good for more than a few months to elapse without utilizing the Marzette Treatment. And tonight he had a reason. One of his street men had been playing fast and loose with the cash, Marzette's cash. It was one of Marzette's best men. Dependable, street-smart, balls of cast iron. And the amount that he was pocketing wasn't all that great. A piss in the bucket really. Less than a thousand a week, not enough for Marzette even to feel.

But the amount wasn't important. A dollar, a thousand, it didn't matteer. It was a matter of respect. If someone could steal from you and get away with it, you lost respect. And when you

[477]

lost respect, you became a target. Others would try to steal from you, take away your operation and, ultimately, your life.

Marzette understood reality. Like a teacher in the classroom, he had to have discipline. Except his tool wasn't a yardstick. It was a machete.

His driver pulled into the parking lot of the warehouse. Two of Marzette's men were guarding the door, nodding politely to the boss as he entered.

Shamaad Raymal had seen to the preparations and was waiting inside. So was the object of the exercise, who, probably in anticipation of what was to come, was sweating profusely while puffing on a joint of marijuana. Two of Marzette's men loosely flanked him, but there was actually no need. He was no threat to flee. After receiving the summons, he had come of his own accord. What was the alternative? Where could he run? Sooner or later Marzette would find him, and then it would be his life instead of tonight's temporary pain. He knew the routine. Marzette was nothing if not consistent. His greed would cost him a finger, maybe two. That was it. Sure, the pain would be intense for a while. The trick was to wrap the stump right away, then have someone drive him to the nearest hospital. In two or three days he'd be back on the street, still one of Julius Marzette's most trusted men. He would also be a living advertisement for his boss's sense of justice.

"Hello, Darrell," Marzette said, almost kindly, as he approached his victim.

"Boss."

"I regret this, Darrell, I really do, but you know the rules."

The victim nodded. Nothing was to be gained by pleading or arguing. From past experience he knew that Marzette was immovable.

"You're a good man, Darrell, one of my best, so I'm gonna cut you a break. Only one finger. Your choice."

Darrell hesitated briefly, then extended the little finger of his left hand, the one he didn't use to hold a knife.

"Excellent choice," Marzette said, as if his victim had just ordered a vintage wine. "This way, please."

They walked to the far end of the warehouse, where Raymal had arranged the accoutrements of the ceremony. The metal bar

[478]

had been erected according to specifications. Beside it, on a small table, lay the machete, its blade painstakingly honed to a fine edge.

"Rope, Darrell?"

"No," answered the victim. He had the option of having the hand tied to the bar, but there had been no choice. Accepting the rope signified weakness, which wouldn't do him any good when he was back on the street. There was, however, a danger in rejecting the offer. If he moved, causing Marzette to miss the anointed digit, the entire hand went.

Marzette took the machete. "All right, Darrell, let's do it."

It was over in an instant. Almost simultaneously with the victim's placing his finger on the rail, Marzette's hand flashed, slicing the finger off just above the knuckle. As the sound of the blade on the rail rang in his ear, the victim felt his knees sag. Only after he looked at the stump, saw the blood, did he feel the pain. Choking in a scream, he staggered to the wall. One of Marzette's men handed him a towel and led him to the parking lot for the ride to the hospital.

Marzette tightened his tie, then turned to Raymal. "Got a date tonight with a very foxy lady in Atlantic City. Hostess at one of the casinos. I'll probably be back tomorrow evening."

"Before you leave, boss, we have company upstairs."

"Company? Who?"

"Our Sicilian friends."

"What the fuck do they want?"

"I'm not sure, but I think they want to talk about the books."

"Fuck them! I deal through their accountant."

"Are you refusing, then, to meet with them?"

Marzette paused. He'd love nothing more than to tell those wop bastards to shove it, but he wasn't ready. Not yet. "No. I'll talk to them. How many are there?"

"Three."

"Okay. I want you and four of my men inside. Send the others home."

"You're the boss, but I think it's a mistake."

"Why?"

"I'm the only one of our people who know about your, uh, Sicilian arrangement. It's to your benefit to keep it like that."

[479]

"Yeah, you're right. But what if the suckers try something?"

"Not likely. Business has been too good."

"Okay." Marzette turned to his driver. "Wait for me in the car. The rest of you can go home."

Raymal went upstairs and returned with three men. Marzette recognized one of them. He had been with Grosso at the cleaner's the night they had cut off his balls.

Niccolo Arrone spoke. "Mr. Marzette, you may not remember me. I'm Nick Arrone. I represent Don Vincenzo Grosso."

"I remember."

Arrone smiled. "I'm flattered. At any rate, to the point, which is a relatively unpleasant one. We have reason to believe—to know actually—that for the past several months the information our accountants have been receiving is—how shall I put it?—incomplete."

"What the fuck you talkin' about, man?"

"What I'm talking about, Mr. Marzette, is your failure to give us accurate collection amounts on a number of your—our—operations. Erie and Scranton, for example."

He was bluffing, Marzette decided. True, he *had* played games with the numbers, but only a little. A piss in the bucket. Less than a hundred thousand a week, not enough for the wops even to feel. "Bullshit."

"Not bullshit, Mr. Marzette. Fact. And now it's time for a settlement."

Marzette breathed more easily. So they were just asking for money. That was one thing he could afford. "How much?"

Arrone smiled. "I was watching your performance from upstairs. Stellar, truly stellar. And just. So we'll settle for the same payment."

Marzette could feel the sweat under his arms. His stomach knotted. "Whaddya mean, man?"

"You're a good man, Mr. Marzette, one of our best, so we're going to cut you a break. One finger. Your choice."

"Wait a minute—"

"Nonnegotiable, Mr. Marzette." Arrone turned to the metal rail. "Shall we?"

Marzette nodded. So it had come full circle. The master of the Marzette Treatment was to become a victim of it. Okay, he would

[480]

handle it. He hadn't risen to the top by being weak. The pain would be intense but temporary. He would wrap his stump immediately and have his driver take him to the hospital. In two or three days he'd be back on the street, the victim of an accident while he was working on his boat engine. Still the boss, still the object of respect.

"No rope," Marzette said, without being asked, as they approached the rail. And no screaming, he said to himself. He'd grit his teeth, take the pain, then walk out like a man.

"Very well," Arrone answered. He handed the machete to an assistant, a six-five Sicilian who had been over for less than a year. "Sergio is a professional," Arrone said, as if to reassure Marzette.

"That's fuckin' great."

The blade flashed in the Sicilian's hand, and Marzette closed his eyes, but the blow never came, the sound of steel on steel was unheard. Instead, the Sicilian redirected his aim in midair, burying the blade in the side of Marzette's neck.

During many periods of history, decapitation by sword was the preferred method of execution. It was quite popular, for example, within the Roman Empire. But historical accounts of such executions are invariably neat. The head is always obliging, being lopped off with one stroke. A descendant of those ancient Romans, Sergio failed to imitate their success. Clearly the first blow was fatal, severing an artery and Marzette's windpipe. But the head stayed on, even though it was hanging at a weird angle. It took three more whacks to finish the job, and by that time Sergio and the remains of Julius Marzette were bathed in blood.

Marzette's trunk was left in the warehouse. His head was wrapped in a cloth, driven to 400 North Broad Street, and deposited on the steps of the *Philadelphia Inquirer*.

Refusing to depend upon the expertise of the Philadelphia Police Department, Vince Grosso had made certain that a *borgotta* contact on the *Inquirer* staff was alerted in advance, thus providing a mutual benefit. The reporter got an exclusive, and Vince had his message publicly delivered. Were there any doubts that Marzette's death was in retaliation for the assassination attempt, they were dispelled by the enterprising reporter. In a masterpiece of investigative reporting, the article was able to state with certainty that the head of Julius Marzette had been wrapped in a flag. Not

[481]

an ordinary flag, but a special and significant one, containing the coat of arms of the Grosso *famiglia.*

As he did every night before retiring, Michael Agostino walked onto the bedroom balcony of his mansion. It was a clear night, and it seemed that he need only raise his hand to touch a cluster of stars. There was a gentle breeze off the Sound, briefly tempting him to sleep on the balcony chaise. But even though his mansion was impregnable, a fortress befitting a king, there was no sense pressing his luck. Inside, with the curtains drawn, he was completely safe—safer than the president. Much safer.

He retreated into the bedroom, changed into his silk pajamas, and, after kneeling for his prayers, climbed into bed. For reassurance, he reached under his pillow to touch the revolver. Better than any sleeping pill.

Only this time it wasn't there. In its place was an envelope. Curious and fearful at the same time, Agostino flipped on the light. The note was typed.

> Dear Don Michael:
>
> Despite what you may have read in the papers, we both know the truth.
>
> I have chosen to overlook your foolishness and to send you this note rather than a more drastic response.
>
> Our relationship has been mutually beneficial, and since we continue to need each other, I will not play the amateur. As always, my personal feelings remain secondary to business considerations and the welfare of those for whom I am responsible. Should you ever again display a similar lack of judgment, however, my response will be swift, appropriate, and final.
>
> Have a good night's sleep.
>
> Your friend from Philadelphia

Agostino's hands were trembling as he placed the note on the nightstand. This was the second time he had underestimated Vincenzo Grosso. On the first occasion it had almost cost him his daughter. Now, within his impregnable fortress, it had almost cost him his life.

The message had been received.

[482]

CHAPTER
Thirty-seven

KYW beeped eight o'clock on the car radio. Late again. As usual. It seemed to Kevin that he spent his life running. Always behind, never able to catch up. And never, ever reaching the finish line.

The last thing in the world he wanted to do tonight was give a goddamn speech to a pro-life group. He had completely forgotten about it until the night before, when he checked his calendar.

The light had just turned red, but he ran it.

"That was a red light, asshole!" someone bellowed.

"Fuck you!" countered the legislative spokesman of the Catholic Church, not knowing or caring if it was a constituent. Years before, however, he had taken one precaution, refusing to purchase the special legislative license plates that most of his colleagues cherished. "No friggin' way," he had explained at the time. As usual he had been logical. "If I wanta gross out some son of a bitch who's trying to run me off the road or if I'm parked in front of a whorehouse, I don't see any point in advertising my state in life."

His fingers tapped the steering wheel as he stopped at an intersection. It seemed that every time he had to give a speech or participate in a debate, he went into it torn up inside. He could take anything else if only he and Karen were able to hit it off, but it seemed that never happened. Especially now, when the sword of Vince Grosso hung over their heads. After the blowups he would hate himself, particularly for his language in front of the kids. God, what a terrible example he set for

[483]

them. How would it affect them down the road in their adult lives?

In a few minutes he was going to walk into a crowd that adored him. They were proud to be led by him, completely unaware that he was a miserable failure. As he pulled into the parking lot of the Knights of Columbus, he asked himself the usual question. How was he going to get through the speech, not to mention inspire his people? For a brief second, while the engine was still running, he considered leaving. But when you had a commitment, you kept it.

They rose as he entered, and once again Kevin Murray was on. The most important thing about performing was sizing up your audience. These were committed pro-lifers. No point in trying to convert them. That would be preaching to the choir. All they wanted—and needed—was to get their juices flowing.

He opened up with a few jokes. One was about the Notre Dame football player in confession being berated for the dirty game he played—until the priest discovered that his opponent had been Southern Methodist. The other dealt with the Gospel story when Christ encountered the adulterous woman who was about to be stoned. Kevin played it straight until the part where Christ challenged anyone without sin to throw the first stone. At that point a woman came from the back of the crowd with a huge rock and proceeded to splatter the sinner all over the ground. Christ shook his head and said, "You know, Mom, sometimes you really tick me off."

Then, after reporting on the status of the abortion control bill, Kevin got into the meat of his message.

He told about the price that each pro-lifer paid for his involvement in the struggle: the heartache, the emotion, having his guts torn out over the slaughter.

> "I can tell you very honestly that since the abortion bill was introduced, there hasn't been one night that I haven't dreamed about it. And as cool and calculating as I try to be when I'm debating the issue, there is yet to be a time when I've left the floor of the House after winning an abortion vote that I haven't gone into my office, closed the door, and cried. How can you not be emotional over little babies?"

Kevin spoke of the roller-coaster ride that was the pro-life movement: scoring great victories and suffering tremendous frus-

[484]

trations; passing important legislation, only to see it vetoed or dismantled by the court.

"But we must never, ever give up. We must display the virtue of relentlessness, coming back time and again and again until we have won. And we *will* win. As a matter of fact, although I don't make many promises, I'm going to make one right now. I promise you that, with or without Dan Talbot, the Pennsylvania abortion control bill will become law."

They were on their feet now, cheering as if at a pep rally. Gone were Kevin's frustrations, his feelings of failure. He was on a roll, and nothing else mattered. Holding up his hands for silence, he continued. He listed the attributes needed to win the war: courage; perseverance; intelligence; street sense; a sense of humor. But most important, faith.

"Faith. The knowledge, with absolute certainty, that there is a God in heaven who knows and loves us very much. Each of us is certain to suffer setbacks in our lives, sometimes severe ones. The death of a loved one, the destruction of a marriage, or perhaps failure in business. When such difficulties arise, we have two choices. We can drop back ten and punt, or we can come back. And no matter what the trial, no matter how badly we have failed, faith will permit us to make that comeback."

He told the story of a man who lived many years ago and wasted much of his life in dissipation. He drank, ran with fast women, and traveled all over the land, carousing and living only for today. All his friends and loved ones gave up on him, wrote him off as a lost cause. All except one: his mother. She followed her wayward son across the land, begging him to change his ways. And praying. And in the end, her prayers were answered.

"The mother? St. Monica. Her son? St. Augustine. One of the greatest minds and brightest lights in the history of the Roman Catholic Church, without whom there would be no Augustinian order and thus no Malvern Prep, no Villanova University."

He talked about a man who had a dream that he was walking on the beach with the Lord. While they walked, the important events in the man's life flashed by. And for each such event there was a corresponding set of footprints in the sand. When they had finished walking, the man looked back at the beach and was disturbed. He noticed that for those times during his life when he had been the most troubled, there was only one set of footprints.

"And he turned to the Lord and said, 'Lord, during those times of my life when I was at my lowest and needed you most, why did you leave me?' And the Lord replied, 'Oh, my precious one, I would never leave you. During those times when you needed me most, that is when I carried you.' "

Kevin paused. He had them. Every one of them. Most of all, he had himself.

"And you know, when you stop to think about it, in all of recorded history only one person has ever been guaranteed salvation. Not the Blessed Mother, not any of the apostles or saints. It was a criminal, a thief, who was being executed for his crimes by means of crucifixion. He was being crucified beside a radical, a rebel leader, who was paying the ultimate price for preaching a new and dangerous order of things. And right before he died, that criminal, that thief, turned to the rebel leader and said, in the most perfect act of faith of all times, 'Lord, remember me when you come into your kingdom.' And that radical, that rebel leader, Jesus Christ, in the most beautiful words of all time, replied, 'This day you shall be with me in paradise.'

"Faith, my friends. Without it, we cannot survive. With it, we cannot fail."

Kevin told them that in their struggle for the unborn they should pattern themselves after St. Peter. Peter, the paradox. Perfect? Certainly not. You could fill a book with his faults: impetuous, brash, emotional, a man who frequently thought with his heart rather than his mind.

"When Christ walked on the water, it was Peter who leaped out of the boat to greet him. But then he lost his faith and would have drowned if the Lord hadn't saved him. And remember the scene at the Last Supper, when Christ began to wash the feet of the apos-

[486]

tles? Only Peter objected, saying that he was unworthy. But when Christ told him that unless he permitted Him to wash his feet, they could no longer be together, good ol' Peter, the master of overkill, replied, 'Then not only my feet, but my hands and my face as well.'

It was Peter who pledged undying loyalty to the Lord, who unsheathed his sword in the garden to protect him, only to deny his Savior, not once, but three times.

"But he always came back. And when it was time for Christ to hand over the keys to his Church, it was the fisherman he chose. 'Thou art Peter, and upon this rock I will build my church; and the gates of hell shall not prevail against it.'

"You know, it is no coincidence that one of our sons is named Peter. Not because we particularly liked the name, but for what it symbolized. If Peter were alive today and were a professional fighter, he'd be the type of guy who'd get knocked down about eight times within the first five rounds. But nobody would ever be able to count ten over him. And about the twelfth round he'd come back to win by a TKO.

"Is our road difficult? Absolutely. Is there pain? No question about it. But would we exchange places with anyone else? To answer that question, we need only ask three more. If not us, who? If not now, when? If not for this, then for what?"

Kevin told them that despite the pain, they were very fortunate. They had been given a chance to be on the cutting edge of history, involved in the central struggle in the history of the human race, precisely because it would determine what would happen to that human race. And he expressed to them his absolute certainty that they were going to win.

"Last January 22 I took my first trip to Washington. I was on the bus on the way down, and I looked out, and it gave me chills. Hundreds and hundred of buses bringing seventy thousand people to Washington, in the dead of winter, to protest *Roe* versus *Wade*. I saw people from Missouri, who spent twenty-six straight hours on the bus. They got off, marched for three hours, then got right back on for another twenty-six-hour ride. I saw people from Alaska and California and Hawaii who used their vacation days to come. Sev-

[487]

enty thousand people and not one of them had anything personal to gain except the triumph of right. How are you going to beat that?"

They were waiting for the poem, and he gave it to them, explaining how his brother had copied it from George Raveling's locker and what it meant to him. When he finished reciting it, he extended his hand to the audience. "Not only do I think, but I know that together, for life, we can and will prevail."

It seemed that they would never stop cheering. Internal demons notwithstanding, Kevin Murray had accomplished his mission.

Kevin looked at his watch as he crossed the City Line Bridge. Almost midnight. He should have ended the evening on a note of triumph, returning home with the applause still ringing in his ears. Instead, he had agreed to attend the meeting at the home of Henry Lassiter, local chairman of Army of Life.

Nothing better exemplified the split within the pro-life movement than Lassiter's organization. Its members despised the rest of the pro-lifers almost as much as they did the abortionists. They were the hardest of the hard line. You could hear the hate in their voices, see the venom in their eyes. Their rallying cry was "No compromise." Nothing short of the paramount amendment, an amendment to the federal Constitution which would define life as beginning at conception and outlaw abortion, was acceptable.

Kevin had tried to reason with them on a number of occasions, including tonight, stressing the need for unity. He shared their goals, he opposed abortion just as vigorously as they, and sure, he'd love the paramount amendment. But the votes—two-thirds in both the House and the Senate—weren't there, might never be. So you took what you could get, like the Hatch Amendment. In essence, Hatch would declare that abortion was not a constitutional issue, giving each state legislature the right to regulate, restrict or outlaw abortions. It would put the issue precisely where it had been before *Roe* v. *Wade,* which was fine with Kevin. As soon as the amendment was ratified, Kevin would introduce a bill to outlaw all abortions in Pennsylvania, this time without any fear that a court would strike it. Pennsylvania would be the first, the magnet. Kevin figured that within a year of the bill's passage, at least half the states would have followed suit. Then they would

[488]

prioritize the rest of the states and pick them off one by one, leaving the tough ones—such as New York and California—until last.

Lassiter and his flock wouldn't hear of it. They actually lobbied *against* the Hatch approach. The principle was the important thing, and they were willing to wait thirty years, if necessary, to win a no-compromise victory.

Kevin had shaken his head. "You know, Henry, principle is wonderful, but sometimes we get so hung up on it, we get our egos so involved, that we lose sight of what we're fighting for. We're not talking about some abstract concept. We're taking about real, honest-to-God babies. One and a half million of them slaughtered every year. You say you are willing to wait thirty years. You don't have to be a math genius to figure that that means forty-five million more babies. That's a hell of a price to pay for principle."

It had fallen on deaf ears, Lassiter shifting the conversation to the abortion control bill. From the outset the Army of Life had been lukewarm in its support of what it considered a halfway measure. But now that Kevin was negotiating with the governor, Lassiter and his followers were incensed.

"No compromise, Kevin. Don't give an inch."

"I don't have a hell of a lot of choice, Henry. We don't have the votes to override."

"Then we'll get them. We'll picket the homes of the ones who're against us, just like we did to Allworth."

Kevin exploded. "That may not be the dumbest goddamn thing I've ever heard, Henry, but it's definitely in the top three! How friggin' stupid can you get? You never, ever picket the homes! All you'll do is gain them sympathy. I'd love, absolutely love the other side to picket my home. With my wife there and my five children. Christ, it'd be perfect. And the truth is, Henry, you assholes have gotten more votes for Allworth than he could ever get on his own. Your stupid goddamn bumper stickers, 'Stop Abortion—Stop Allworth.' And your flyers calling him a baby killer. Nothing personal, Henry, but when I look at flamers like you, I'm still convinced that we're going to win. Not because of you but in spite of you."

Christ, Kevin thought, as he crossed Belmont Avenue, *what an army we've got. Church officials who are afraid of their own shadows and a bunch of crazies who could piss off the pope. Don't they understand that the only shot we have at winning is to stay together?* The recurring night-

[489]

mare that Kevin had was of self-destruction. When the final battle was fought, if the other side won because, flat out, it had too many guns, Kevin would be disappointed, of course, but consoled by the fact that his people had given it their best shot. But if they lost because they did it to themselves, because they couldn't stick together, then only God could forgive them.

He sighed. In the space of four hours he had gone from irritation to exultation to frustration. The pro-life roller-coaster ride.

After Kevin Murray had left, the Army of Life returned to business. Harry Lassiter turned to the half dozen members who remained in his living room.

"A complete waste of time," one of them said.

"Not at all," responded Lassiter. "It demonstrates, clearly and unequivocally, that Representative Murray is also the enemy."

"Another wimp for life."

Lassiter nodded. "Precisely, but far more dangerous than most. He carries with him the imprimatur of the movement, more than anyone in Pennsylvania. As such, he can be devastating to our goals. A Neville Chamberlain, without the umbrella."

There was silence as Lassiter paced the room. They were content to let him think, then to obey any edict he might issue. Each member had made a commitment: to do whatever was necessary to thwart abortion. It wasn't enough to picket or counsel or to support pro-life legislation. It was time for direct—and dramatic—action. If abortion clinics could not be closed by demonstrations or lawsuits, they would be destroyed by fire. If God, for whatever reason, were unwilling to call the right Supreme Court justices from this earth, they would expedite the process, permitting their pro-life president to appoint new justices who revered the sanctity of life. But first, their own backyard needed attention.

Lassiter stood in the middle of the room. "Sometimes those things which must be done are distasteful. The unpleasantness of it, however, makes it no less necessary. If there is a threat to our cause, it must be removed, much like a cancerous growth is excised. In this case there is a double benefit. In addition to the surgery, we will have gained that which is necessary for the success of any cause. A martyr." He looked across the room. "Are we in agreement?" They all nodded. "Are you ready, Helen?"

"Behold, I am the handmaid of the Lord," answered the

woman. As her eyes glistened with fervor, her fingers gently caressed the golden cross around her neck.

The phone was ringing when Kevin got home. It was Norm Wallace, a reporter for the *Daily Times*.

"I'm calling you as a friend, Kevin, not as a reporter," Wallace said. "This isn't easy for me, and I want you to know that I didn't go looking for it. One of your enemies fed it to me, thinking that we'd run with it. But believe it or not, even the press has its standards."

The reporter's message was short but very much to the point. Having replaced the receiver, Kevin walked into the living room and sat on the sofa, staring.

He was still there an hour later, when Karen entered. She looked at her husband, and she knew.

"I got a call about an hour ago from a reporter," Kevin said, "one who's usually accurate. He seems to think that your late hours recently haven't been spent at the hospital."

Karen had never been able to lie, especially to her husband. And she didn't want to. She wanted it over. "I'm sorry, Kevin. Honest to God, I am."

"Who is he?"

"A doctor. John Richter."

"What is he like?"

She hesitated. "He's kind."

"Just kind? How is he in bed?"

"Please, Kevin."

"Where? In a motel?"

"No. In his apartment. I'd never go to a motel."

"Well it's comforting to know that you still have taste. How many times?"

"Three, not counting tonight."

Kevin gave a pained grin. "What, tonight doesn't count? What was it, nonleague competition?"

"Nothing happened tonight, Kevin. I ended it."

"Swell."

"Don't you want to know why?"

"Why what?"

"Why I ended it?"

He was screaming inside. He wanted to lash out at her, at her

[491]

lover, at his miserable goddamn life. He wanted to beat her into unconsciousness, then kill the son of a bitch who had seduced her. Instead, he remained on the sofa. "It's not really very important, is it, Karen?"

"Yes, it's important. It was his apartment. A bachelor's apartment. Everything very expensive and everything in its place. I looked around it tonight and realized that it wasn't my life. My life is here, Kevin, with the house torn apart by the kids. With your horrible job, which I'll always hate. And with my frustrations. I love you, Kevin."

"Why doesn't that comfort me right now?" He rose and walked to the stairs, then turned. "I have to give you credit, Karen. You sure do know how to even the score."

CHAPTER
Thirty-eight

KEVIN Murray sat behind his desk, staring at the mountain of paperwork that invariably accompanies a return from vacation but making no attempt to attack it. He wasn't in the mood. If anything was more depressing than being in Harrisburg in mid-September when you'd still rather be at the shore, it was being in Harrisburg in mid-September when you'd still rather be at the shore, when you had hardly spoken to your wife in the two months following your discovery of her affair, and when in less than an hour you would be called upon to cast a vote which might destroy your political career and expose you and your family to public ridicule. Never, absolutely never, had Wyoming seemed so inviting.

Kevin hadn't left his wife, had never even considered it, just as Karen, nine years before, had never considered leaving because of her husband's infidelity. Despite their relative youth, they were from the old school, the school that taught the value of commitment. Once you made a promise, no matter how tough things might become, you kept it.

Kevin knew that he sounded like an old man when he talked about it, but that was the one thing that was missing today, the single biggest problem with modern society. No commitment. The marriage isn't perfect—and there never was one made in heaven—get a divorce. You don't like the job, quit. You don't want the baby, have an abortion.

Not so with either Kevin or Karen Murray. The code wouldn't

permit it. When things got tough, you hung in there and worked them out. And you didn't leave your spouse.

But for Kevin it was more than just the code. What about the kids? What effect would a split have on them? And on him? He couldn't be without them, he knew that. He could never be one of those Sunday afternoon fathers, picking up the kids and taking them to a ball game or to the zoo. He was their father, not a goddamn Big Brother doing his charitable bit once a week. And what if Karen started dating and the boyfriend were in *his* home, with *his* kids, taking *his* place? He couldn't deal with that. It was bad enough picturing his wife with another man, but to lose the kids, even partially, to someone else would make him crazy. That was the stuff of which headlines were made, the estranged husband taking a gun and blowing away the boyfriend, or the wife, or even the kids. Then himself. No, they were his, on a permanent basis, and nothing could change that.

And there was something else, something that, no matter how much he and Karen might have fought over the years, he always knew. He loved her, pure and simple, and he couldn't envision his life without her. Sure, she had her faults, but she was a wonderful human being, far better than the man she married. He marveled at how she was with the kids. How could there ever be a better mother? It wasn't just the care; it was the love. Every morning, when they got up, you could see her eyes brighten. She greeted her family as if she hadn't seen them in years. Each one special, each unique.

And maybe she wasn't as demonstrative as Kevin would have liked, but she loved him just as much. Always there, always putting herself last. Like the washing machine. Kevin had noticed a small can on top of the washer, half filled with coins.

"What's this?" he asked.

"All the money that comes out during the wash. I tell everyone to check pockets, but no one listens. So it's mine. When I get enough, I'm going to buy dinner for the family at the pool."

Not a new blouse or a new bathing suit for *her*. Dinner for her family at the pool.

And her smile. It always got to Kevin. There was something so innocent yet so devilish. It was the first thing he had noticed about her so many years before. He wished he had known her growing up, as a student at St. Francis de Sales and West Catholic

Girls, the freckled blonde in her crisp blue starched uniform, jitterbugging at the dances or cheering on the Burrs at Fifty-eighth and Elmwood.

Why don't you smile anymore, my West Philly princess? Don't you know how much I love you? I know I haven't given you much of a life, baby. I only hope that someday I'll be able to make it up to you.

So Kevin stayed. But commitment is one thing, forgiveness another. They might remain in the same home, they might occupy the same bed, but as far as Kevin was concerned, they were strangers. At least for now. Try as he might, he was unable to erase Karen's affair from his mind.

How many times had he gone over it in his mind, picturing in detail his wife in bed with another man? He tried to imagine it turning out differently, being tipped off in advance. He watched them enter the apartment, but ever the lawyer looking for hard evidence, he waited, giving them time so that he would catch them in the act. Then, just as in his Bureau days, he kicked in the door, tossed out a great line like "I really hate to bother you, Karen, but I can't find the toothpaste," then proceeded to pound John Richter, M.D., into unconsciousness. He had acted, drawn blood, rather than merely sat on the sofa in his living room.

And even though he knew it was both juvenile and unworthy, he found himself becoming angry with his performance with Bonnie nine years before. To hell with conscience and nobility of nature. He should have nailed her when he had the chance.

But as angry as he was, he still tried to be honest. Was he really trying to forget, let alone forgive? Wasn't the bitterness that coursed through his body a catharsis for so many of his other frustrations? And wasn't there a sick satisfaction to be gained from knowing that for once *he* was the offended party? Hadn't Karen done him a favor by, if not removing, at least mitigating the guilt that had been part of his baggage ever since his encounter with Bonnie?

And there was the other question, the one which, thank God, he would not be called upon to answer. What if Karen had become pregnant by John Richter? Could the leader of the pro-life movement practice what he preached? Might not he, at the very least, consider the unthinkable? And if the baby were born, how would he react? Would he be able to enter the delivery room with Karen, just as he had with the others, to welcome a new life into

[495]

the world? And could he ever accept the child as one of his own, rather than John Richter's son or daughter, a constant reminder of his wife's infidelity?

Screw it, he thought. There was nothing to be gained by psychoanalyzing himself. Not when the roof was about to fall in. Actually Karen's affair made things easier. When Vince blew the whistle on him, he wouldn't have to feel guilty. At least not to his wife. Instead of apologizing, he could say, "Tough, bitch, you had it coming."

The lobbying war that had been waged all summer on the liquor bill was coming to a head today, one way or the other. Both sides had agreed that now was the time to run it. Like the abortion bill, scheduled for a vote next week, it was better to get it out of the way at least a month before the election. Much like his colleagues, Kevin had been bombarded: church groups; food chains; tavern owners; senior citizens. But only he had been lobbied by a bishop.

Pat had stopped at the house a few days before, tan from a recent trip to St. Croix. Ostensibly it was just a social visit, but Kevin sensed that there was something more, particularly when Pat volunteered to drive with him to Malvern. Once again young Kevin had missed the bus.

"Is everything okay with you, Kevin?" he had asked when they were in the car.

Kevin hesitated. "Sure. Great." What the hell was he driving at? Did he know about Karen and him? No. How could he?

"What I mean is, is anything bothering you?"

Maybe he *did* know. Well, no way Kevin was going to bare his soul. It was none of his goddamn business. "Well, now that you mention it, Pat, there is something." He paused. "It's gonna be a disaster if the NFL goes on strike."

"You never could lie, Kevin. I have to be very careful in phrasing this, since the sanctity of confession is involved, but are you being blackmailed? On the liquor bill?"

So that was it. Kevin had forgotten that Pat was Vince's confessor. "Yeah, as a matter of fact, I am. But then you know that, don't you?"

"I don't *know* anything. Really."

"None of the gory details?"

"No," Pat lied.

[496]

"Pity. It's powerful stuff. Involves sodomy with a cocker spaniel. Ain't that a bitch?"

Pat didn't smile. There was too much at stake. "Have you decided what you're going to do?"

"I'm voting against the bill. Fuck Vince and his threats. If the mob takes over Pennsylvania, it'll be without my help."

"Aren't you exaggerating?"

"A little, maybe, but I'm allowed. I'm a politician."

"There could be a scandal."

"True."

"Doesn't that concern you?"

Kevin snapped. "What the fuck do you mean, 'Doesn't that concern you?' Of course, it concerns me, for Christ's sake. You think I'm some kind of fuckin' masochist?"

"Of course not. I just hope you've carefully weighed everything."

"I've done nothing else for the last four months. The answer's still no. Why the hell do you care anyway? You a closet alky?"

"Like father, like son?"

"I'm sorry. You know I didn't mean that," Kevin said. He realized that he was taking his bitterness out on Pat when actually it was directed at his best friend, the man who was blackmailing him and threatening his family and his career.

"I know. I'm just concerned about you, Kevin. You're my friend. More. And I'm selfish."

"What do you mean?"

"You're the best thing going for us. The Church, I mean. On things a whole lot more important than where booze is sold. Is it worth throwing all that away, Kevin?"

"I love you dearly, Pat, but you haven't changed a bit since Villanova. Always looking for the easy way out, the safe way. Moderation, right? Compromise, right? But any way you cut it, pal, I'm still being blackmailed, and what they're asking me to do is wrong. If the Church is embarrassed, I'll be sorry. But I can't cave in."

They left it at that, Pat convinced that he could do no more, Kevin grateful for the concern of his friend.

Now, as Kevin prepared to go onto the floor and cast a red vote, he considered the specifics. It was going to be close. Very close. Each side claimed about seventy-five hard votes. That left fifty or so uncommitted, fifty who would listen to the debate and scan the vote board before deciding which way to go.

From a personal standpoint Kevin was praying that despite his no vote, the bill would pass. He'd be off the hook, without question. Above all, Vince Grosso was a pragmatist. All he was looking for was private liquor in Pennsylvania. Friendship aside, if the bill passed, there was nothing to be gained by retribution.

Kevin was equally certain that if the legislation went down, Vince would be required to make good on his threat. The question was when. Not on the day of the bill's defeat. Too sloppy, too direct. The ax was more likely to fall the following week, when the abortion bill was considered and Kevin Murray was once again in the media spotlight. Probably right after the vote, not before. Vince was pro-life. He wanted the bill passed. Besides, the ideal timing for maximum coverage was the post-debate interviews.

Although Kevin had refused to break, he had tried to cut his losses. He had steered clear of interviews dealing with the liquor bill, citing his involvement with his adoption bill, which the Senate was now poised to pass, the abortion bill, and the Philadelphia city wage tax.

He had also made up his mind to stay in his seat when debate began. Strictly along for the ride. Dictating constituent letters until it was time to throw his switch.

The debate lasted three hours with telling points made on both sides. Kevin was dictating a response to a woman demanding that the steel jaw trap be outlawed when Lorenzo nudged him. "They want you, Kevin."

Kevin looked up. Fat Boy Tenaglia was at the mike, smiling. "I repeat," Tenaglia said, "will the gentleman from Delaware, Mr. Murray, stand for interrogation?"

Confused, Kevin rose and walked to the majority leader's podium. "Yes, Mr. Speaker."

"Thank you," Tenaglia said. "Mr. Speaker, isn't it a fact that you are a former special agent of the FBI?"

"Yes, Mr. Speaker."

"And isn't it true that when you were stationed in Detroit, you specialized in investigating organized crime?"

"Yes, Mr. Speaker," answered Kevin. "That was my assignment."

"And isn't it also true that as an assistant DA in Philadelphia you conducted grand jury investigations into city and state corruption, including one dealing with liquor?"

"That's correct, Mr. Speaker."

"And isn't it also true that you were special counsel to the so-called Campbell Committee, again probing corruption on a statewide basis?"

"Right again, Mr. Speaker. Unlikely as it may be, you're extremely accurate today."

"I thank you. Given your background, then, wouldn't you say that of all two hundred and three members of this august body, you possess the greatest expertise with respect to the investigation of corruption and organized crime?"

Kevin had a sick feeling in his stomach, but as usual he hid it. "You flatter me, Mr. Speaker, which is also unlikely. To answer your question, it's not for me to characterize my expertise in comparison to any of my colleagues. That would be presumptuous."

Tenaglia refused to be put off. "Then let me do it for you, Mr. Speaker. Since your expertise is clearly without parallel within this body, I would like your opinion as to what effect the passage of this legislation would have on Pennsylvania with respect to organized crime and corruption."

Kevin hesitated. Even when he wanted to, he could never be a spectator. St. Laurence, Villanova, the DA's office—nothing had changed. Always the goddamn lightning bolt just over his shoulder. He could take the easy way out, the Pat Carney approach, stating that anything he might say would be pure conjecture, impossible to document. He was tempted, but then he thought of the Sarge and about looking at yourself in the mirror.

"Mr. Speaker, to borrow the vernacular used by our youth, including my children, this bill sucks. It's fit to be used only as toilet paper and then only in a dire emergency. If we pass it, we will be rolling out the red carpet for the mob. Let me explain."

And he did, for fifteen minutes, after which they took the vote: 83 for, 112 against. The private liquor bill was dead, and so was Kevin Murray's career.

CHAPTER
Thirty-nine

LENA answered on the fifth ring. She had been cleaning out Michael's closet, something her son had been promising to do for more than a year.

"Hi, hon."

"What's wrong, Vincent?" He never called in the afternoon.

"Nothing. Honest." Nothing except that he was still depressed over the defeat of the liquor bill. Vince Grosso never liked to lose.

"So why are you calling?" asked Lena.

"The office. It's getting to me. I don't think I'll come home tonight. I'll stay at my mother's and leave in the morning for some fishing. I just want to be alone for a while."

"Okay. I think that's a good idea. You need some time off."

"It'll just be for the day. I'll be home tomorrow evening. Don't wait dinner. I love you."

"I love you, too."

Slowly Lena replaced the receiver. So here it was. There would never be a better opportunity. Therese was back, and convinced that her birth certificate had been lost in the mail, she had applied for it again. It was no longer possible to hold back midnight.

She began to pace. Why was she hesitating? Isn't this what she had planned for all these years? Wasn't she justified? Who had more of a right to exact revenge, to keep the promise that she had made before God?

Both her parents snatched away, her father in the grave, her mother nothing more than a vegetable in a Michigan clinic. But she could have survived that. She had been well on her way to overcoming it, the bitterness gradually draining from her soul.

Because of Jimmy. Jimmy Verrechia. Even now she could picture him perfectly: the brown hair always in need of a comb; the eyes that convinced her that she was special; the mouth that always seemed on the verge of a smile and that spoke such words of kindness.

She had loved him from the first time they met, during her senior year at the University of Detroit. There was never a doubt that he was the one with whom she would share her life. But while Lena had no doubts, her uncle did. Sitting behind his desk in the study, Giuseppe Zivelli tried, as gently as possible, to explain to his niece that the relationship must end.

"But why, Uncle Giuseppe?"

"Lena, my lamb, you are young, and there are many things you don't understand. Trust me, like your cousins have always trusted me. Later on you will thank me, I promise."

"That doesn't answer my question!"

"Some things are difficult to put into words, Lena. You are special. Jimmy is a nice boy, I don't deny that. But he's not for you. He comes from nothing." The don paused. "And he is not Sicilian."

"What does that matter, Uncle? This is America!"

"It matters a great deal, my lamb. Someday you will understand that."

"I know what it is," Lena exploded. "A marriage to Jimmy won't help *you*. Just like your own children. They weren't marriages; they were mergers. To benefit *you*!"

Zivelli's hands gripped the desk, his knuckles white. No one had ever shown such disrespect. But she was the daughter of his brother, God rest his soul. "Not to benefit me, Lena," he said softly, "to benefit the family. The family must always come first. That, too, you will come to understand."

But Lena didn't. Willing to risk the wrath of the don for the man she loved, she announced that she would marry Jimmy Verrechia, and to hell with the family. She didn't need their approval, and she could live without their money.

One week later Jimmy Verrechia was dead, his mangled body found in his car at the bottom of a steep ravine. It was listed as an accident, of course, but Lena knew and confronted the don.

[501]

"Uncle, I have a favor to ask."

"Anything, my lamb."

"If I ask you a question, will you answer me honestly?"

Zivelli looked at his niece. She should have been a man. Pure steel. "Yes," he finally said.

"How did Jimmy really die?"

"I beg you, Lena, let it alone. It won't do any good."

"Please, Uncle."

"Very well. After you refused to listen to reason, Anthony Iacobucci was sent to talk to your friend."

"He had a name," Lena said through clenched teeth. "His name was Jimmy."

"Jimmy. At any rate, and this I swear to you, no harm was to come to him. Anthony's instructions were simply to speak with him, convince him that he must stop seeing you."

"He's dead, Uncle!"

"I know, my lamb. Your friend—Jimmy—was even more determined than you. They argued, and he attacked Anthony, who only defended himself. During the struggle he hit his head. Freakish. There was no choice but to make it appear to be an accident. I'm sorry, Lena."

She looked into his eyes. He was telling the truth; at least she thought he was. But it didn't matter. Jimmy was still dead.

But not completely. There was something left, something with which her uncle would have to deal.

"What happens to me, Uncle?"

"You're young, my lamb. With your whole life in front of you. This will pass, I promise you."

Despite her grief, Lena smiled. Even the greatest don didn't know everything. "There's only one problem, Uncle. I'm pregnant."

Giuseppe Zivelli dealt with the pregnancy as he would any other problem confronting his *borgotta:* analytically and decisively. There were three options, two of which were unacceptable. Abortion was out of the question; they were Catholics. And Lena could not be permitted to keep the baby. It could not become a part of the *famiglia.* It was not Sicilian. Besides, no one except a chosen few must know about Lena's pregnancy. He still had plans for her, plans which involved undamaged goods.

That left option three, and for that Zivelli reached out to his

[502]

old friend Fredo Annaloro. Lena was dispatched to Pennsylvania, where Annaloro arranged her stay with a good Sicilian family in Allentown. Her delivery was uncomplicated, even though despite her protest, she was placed under general anesthesia. She never saw her baby, and only by overhearing a nurse did she know that it was a girl. Three weeks later she was in Paris, where she studied fine arts. When she returned to Detroit, Vincenzo Grosso was in his second year of law school, having been all but adopted into the Zivelli *famiglia.*

Giuseppe Zivelli was gratified at Lena's acceptance and at the respect and affection she lavished on him. Once again the wise don had been right. His niece had grown, had matured into a young woman of wisdom who now understood that, just as her uncle had said, everything had been for the best. He was even more gratified as he watched the chemistry develop between his niece and Vincenzo. Perfect. A marriage and, yes, a merger.

But even an omnipotent don could not penetrate Lena's soul. Rather than disappear, the bitterness increased each day. And the resolve. She had but two goals in her life: to find her daughter and exact her revenge. Giuseppe Zivelli had indeed been right. She was pure steel.

The first task took her eighteen years, eighteen years of agony. Not a day passed that she didn't think of her daughter. Wondering. What was she like? What was she doing now? Did she look like Lena? Or Jimmy? Were her guardians—she could never bring herself to call them parents—taking good care of her?

She would read a story of child abuse and panic. What if that were happening to her? Abused and alone, with Lena powerless to help. She must find her. It was all that kept her alive.

Terror. What if something had happened to her? What if, even now, Lena's search were doomed? Children died. It happened every day. A drunk driver, leukemia, drowning. There were so many things that could happen to a little one, particularly one without her mother. Her real mother. *Please, God, please don't let it happen. You've taken everything away from me. Please leave me this one thing.*

How many times had she tensed on the street, in a store, at school, when she saw a little girl about her age? Could that be her daughter? How would she know? She could pass her baby on the street—maybe had already—and not even know.

[503]

There were no leads, of course, nothing to trace. Her uncle and Fredo Annaloro had seen to that. And all the official records were sealed. Was it possible, would God permit it, that Lena would spend her whole life on earth without ever seeing her daughter, the human being created by the love which she and Jimmy shared?

And then Lena found her. Two years ago. Absently she glanced at the calendar on the door of Michael's closet. September 21. My God, *exactly* two years ago! That had to be an omen.

Lena was at Villanova. She was a board member of the Community Arts Forum, which was just gearing up for the new school year. After the meeting she and several others stopped in the Pi Shoppe for a Coke. It was fun to watch the students after they returned from the summer, bringing back memories of youth. And there she was, sitting at the third table from the door with two other girls.

Lena knew. A mother knows her own daughter, even one whom she had never seen. She wanted to run to her right then, to embrace her, to sob to her how much she loved her and how she had never forgotten. Instead, just to make certain, she turned to the priest beside her. "Father," she said offhandedly, "you know all the students. Who's the girl over there, in the yellow blouse?"

The priest looked over, then turned back to Lena. "That's Therese Leary. One of our freshmen. From up near Allentown."

Stay calm, Lena told herself, relieved that no one could hear the pounding of her chest. "Leary." she laughed. "With that skin? Must be one of the Black Irish."

"Actually, she's adopted. The oldest of three adopted children. Very nice family—and she's a very nice girl. And patient, thank God."

"What do you mean?"

"We've been having problems. It seems that in our concerted drive to become coed, we overbooked dorm space for the girls. Some of the freshmen, like Therese, are doubling up, sleeping on cots, until we can find off-campus housing. Sticky, to say the least."

Lena measured her words carefully. "What a coincidence. I think I may be able to help."

It was arranged within a week. In return for minimal duties in supervising the children, Therese was provided her room, meals,

[504]

and a modest stipend. From the start they got along well. It seemed that Therese looked to Lena as the older sister she never had.

Lena lined the last of Michael's shelves with Con-tact paper. She looked around the room for something else to do. Anything to delay the decision. As she stripped off sheets that had been washed only the day before, she began the litany once again. One last time. Hadn't Vince been a good husband? Always kind, always considerate. And always faithful, she'd bet her life on that. And how could he be a better father? He always had time for the children, and they worshiped him. And wasn't he innocent? He had nothing to do with any of it—not her parents, not Jimmy, not the daughter who had been stolen from her for eighteen years.

But then more questions. Hadn't she vowed that there would be only Jimmy, that everything she did would be to honor—and avenge—him and the rest of her own? And wasn't Vince a part of it, part of the system that killed and cheated, that put everything—wives, friends, even little children on a school bus—second to their *borgotta*? Hadn't he willfully enlisted, accepting the training of Anthony Iacobucci, the man who had killed her Jimmy? And by destroying Vince, wouldn't she also be destroying, partially at least, the main villain? The Detroit and Philadelphia families were connected because of Vince. Remove him, and Giuseppe Zivelli's influence was lost, along with the millions that he had poured into Vince's enterprises.

And another point. She had noticed how Vince was around Therese. That was something that couldn't be risked, the ultimate sacrilege, her husband entwined in an affair with her daughter.

Lena put the sheets back on and remade the bed. The answers were still the same. She reached into Michael's change jar, taking out a handful of quarters. Then she walked to her desk and removed a slip of paper from the bottom drawer. After all these years she didn't need a gun or a knife. Just some quarters and a slip of paper.

Michael entered as she was about to leave. "Hi, Mom."

"Hello, Michael," she said, kissing him. "I just cleaned your closet. You know, the one you were going to take care of?"

"Aw, thanks, Mom. Where you going?"

"To the store for some bread and milk."

"Want me to go on my bike?"

[505]

"No, that's okay."

Five minutes later she was at a phone booth. Her hands trembled as she put in the coins, then dialed.

"Yeah," a husky voice answered.

"I must speak to Michael Agostino. Please tell him it concerns Vincenzo Grosso."

Like their men, Sicilian women kept their vows.

Pat Carney listened intently to the briefing. As usual, Corey Suter was very good. There were any number of corporations that would give their eyeteeth, and a huge salary, to have him as their legislative liaison.

"It's set for tomorow," Suter said. "The governor has signed on. He hasn't said it publicly, of course, but he's in."

"No problem with passing it, is there?" Pat asked.

"No. It's running first in the Senate this time. Kevin found a House bill that just came out of Senate Judiciary."

"He always manages, doesn't he?"

"He sure does. Anyway, the Senate runs it in the morning. First thing. They won't even debate it. They never do. Then over to the House right away for concurrence. Since it's a concurrence vote, there's no amendments. No two-day marathon like last December. Just a straight-up yes-no vote."

"How badly was it cut up by the governor?"

"Not bad. Kevin handled that very well at this morning's press conference. Craig Harrington tried to say that it was stronger than before, which raised some eyebrows, but Kevin cut him off. He admitted that it wasn't quite as strong. The doctors don't have to be identified, and the fetus pictures don't have to be made available during informed consent. On the other hand, the definition of infanticide is tighter, and the pathology reporting requirement is back in. As Kevin said, it's still the toughest bill in the country."

"What's the effective date? Sixty days?"

Suter grinned. "Not exactly."

"What does 'not exactly' mean?"

"By design, rather than coincidence, the effective date of the Pennsylvania Abortion Control Act is none other than December eighth, 1982."

[506]

"Good old Kevin," Pat laughed.

"He's the best, Excellency. What would we do without him?"

The briefing was over, but Suter's questions still gnawed at Pat. What *would* we do without Kevin? It appeared that they were about to find out because of Pat.

He sighed. Another notch in his gun. Would the carnage caused by him ever end? His father, choking to death on smoke, alone? Chris Wheeler and his wife, their torment over, their children orphans. Bonnie, cast away like a piece of driftwood. And his baby, slaughtered in its mother's womb. He could have changed each ending. Could have but hadn't.

And now Kevin, his closest friend, the best and the brightest.

Pat looked up. Like last Christmas Eve, Pulski was standing in the doorway. "Corey brief you?" he asked.

"Yes. It's go."

"At last, thank God. Are you going up tomorrow?"

"Harrisburg?"

"Yes."

"No, I'd like to, but I'm snowed under." Pat paused. "Do you have a minute, Eminence?"

"At my age I'm never sure. Problem?"

"No. Not with the job anyway. I wanted to ask you, to whom do we owe our responsibility?"

"Are we back in theology class?"

"Please, boss. Indulge me."

"All right. We owe responsibility to God, His church, our fellow man, and ourselves."

"In that order?"

"Not necessarily. God's always first, of course, but circumstances dictate the order of the others."

"Are we more responsible as individuals or priests?"

"You've lost me there, Patrick."

"What I mean is, in a particular situation should we as priests do what is right or what is best for the Church?"

Pulski grinned. "I was under the impression that the two always coincided."

"Not necessarily. What if there's something—something you should do—that you *know* is right but would embarrass the Church?"

[507]

The cardinal looked at his young bishop for whom he had such a deep regard. Affection actually. Almost like a son. Something was bothering Pat, but he wouldn't pry. He'd just try to help.

"Pat, we must never lose sight of the fact that our first responsibility is to God. That responsibility is *always* fulfilled by doing what is right, regardless of temporal consequences. And by serving God, we save our own souls, which is why we're here. The Church, sacred as it is, is only corporal. Nothing more than a mechanism to execute the will of God. In the end, on the final day, it will be dissolved, its mission accomplished. Helpful?"

"Very. Thank you, Eminence."

Pulski turned as he reached the door. "And I wouldn't worry too much about scandals. The Church has seen more than its share and survived. It would have even survived the Knock thing if it had blown open. Which it didn't, thanks to Patrick Carney." He broke into a knowing grin. "With a little help from his friends."

Pat continued to stare at the doorway after his boss had gone. Was there anything the man didn't know? And once again the cardinal had shown him the way. The question was, Would he follow it?

Finally he rose and walked to the door. "Lucille, do me a favor, will you? Cancel everything I have for tomorrow. I'm going to Harrisburg."

As he drove home from the train station, Kevin Murray felt relieved. It was almost over. Tomorrow the abortion struggle would end, at least this chapter. The votes were there, and the governor would sign it.

And one way or the other, the thing with Vince should be resolved. There wasn't any doubt in his mind that it would be a disaster, but it would beat the hell out of the waiting. For almost five months it had gnawed at him, every day, no matter now much he had tried to dismiss it. God, how could some of his colleagues take bribes? Forget the morality of it. How could you wake up every morning wondering if this would be the day when you'd get caught? It was like being in a bar when you were underage, always looking at the door, always expecting a cop or an LCB agent to come walking through it.

Screw it, he thought. It was beyond his control. Anyway, it

[508]

wouldn't be all that bad. After he had been publicly exposed as a lecher and closet abortionist, he could always sign on as a ranch hand in Wyoming.

Karen was waiting when he arrived. "The *Inquirer* called," she said. "Dave Brennan. Colleen Campion has gone into labor."

Kevin felt a chill. "I have to go there."

"I know. I hope it works out."

"Thanks."

Word had traveled quickly. By the time Kevin arrived, the hospital lobby was jammed with media. He sought out Brennan. "Thanks for the call, Dave. Any details?"

"She went into labor a little over an hour ago. Almost a month premature. They've promised to brief us when it's over."

So once again it was waiting, Kevin pacing the lobby, chain-smoking Winstons. This was it, what it was all about. This was Andrew, and he had to make it.

Three hours later Robert Tunstall appeared, obviously enjoying his importance. "Preliminarily, simply a caveat that the same rules apply. Anonymity is to be maintained. Are we all agreed?"

They nodded, and the young attorney continued. "Approximately a half hour ago, at nine-oh-two eastern daylight time, the comatose woman gave birth to a girl, four pounds thirteen ounces. Because of her size, and merely as a precaution, she has been placed in the hospital's infant intensive care unit. Preliminary examinations, however, have indicated that she is normal in all respects with an excellent prognosis. The condition of the mother is unchanged. No questions at this point. We hope that within the hour the attending physician will conduct a news conference to provide greater details and answer any questions you might have. Thank you."

The cameras shifted to Kevin for a reaction. He did his best to answer the questions, even though tears were rolling down his cheeks. A girl! He had been so certain that it would be a boy. Not that it mattered. Not one bit. What mattered was that a baby had been born, someone to make up for his Andrew.

When it was over, Tunstall, who had watched patiently on the fringe, approached him. "Representative Murray, would you come with me, please?"

They rode the elevator in silence to the eighth floor. As the doors opened, Tunstall turned to him. "For what it's worth, Kevin, I'm glad you won."

"We all won, Bobby."

"Yes."

Tunstall led him to the window of the infant ICU, where a tall gray-haired woman was waiting.

"Representative Murray, this is Mrs. Campion, Colleen's mother. I'll leave you two now."

The woman turned to the window, pointing to a tiny bundle under a pink blanket. She took Kevin's hand. "My granddaughter. I hated you, Kevin. For interfering in something I thought was best for my daughter. And, I'll admit it, best for me." She tightened her grip on Kevin's hand. "How could I ever have not wanted her? She's here because of you, Kevin, and I'll never be able to thank you."

He was barely able to talk. "You already have, ma'am."

"It's true, isn't it?" the woman said, pointing to a picture on the wall. It was of a newborn and under it was written: *"Each baby comes with the message that God is not yet discouraged with man."*

"Yes." Kevin choked.

"Had it been a boy, I would have named him Kevin. What do you think?"

He could hardly see through his tears. "Thank you. I had—we had—a little baby about her age who didn't make it. His name was Andrew and—"

He couldn't finish. The woman took her hand and wiped away his tears, as a mother would do to her little boy. "How about Andrea?" she said. "Andrea Campion. It has a nice ring, don't you think?"

"Yes, ma'am, it does."

She turned back to the window. "She survived an auto accident, a comatose mother, a grandmother who wanted to destroy her, and a premature delivery. She was meant to be born, Kevin. One of God's children.

Vince Grosso took a final bite, trying not to grimace.

"Dessert?" his mother asked.

"No," he said. "It's time for truth, Mother, not dessert. The meal was terrible, as usual, but that's okay. I want you as a mother, not a cook."

[510]

"What does that mean?"

"It means I want us to talk, Mother. Finally *talk*. About you and me—and my father."

"What's to say?" she said casually. Too casually, Vince thought. He thought he saw something in her eyes.

"The desk, Mother. The one in my office, that used to be upstairs in the study."

"A desk? Why are we talking about a desk?"

Vince looked into her eyes again. There *was* something there. He had been right all along. "I remember him, Mother. At least I think I do. It's hard to tell how much you remember and how much others tell you. But I know he was a collector and I know he got drunk a lot and I know he was short with the money. The family's money, and that cost him his life. One thing I *do* remember. It wasn't long after he died. I was up in the study playing. I used to play tank commander and crawl under the desk. There was a lever on the bottom. I had never seen it before. I pulled it, and it opened, and you know what was inside, don't you, Mother? Money. A lot of it. I was frightened. I thought you'd be angry, so I put it all back and closed the little door. But I never forgot about it. It was the collection money, wasn't it? You put it there, probably when he was drunk, because you knew what would happen sooner or later. You killed him, Mother. You killed my father. Why?"

Concetta Grosso grasped the table. She thought it all had been buried with the man she despised, but a lifetime later she was being haunted by another world.

"Why?" Vince repeated. "He was my father!"

"He was an animal!" Concetta snapped, fear giving away to a lifetime of rage. "I never wanted him. It wasn't my idea. But they insisted. Your dear uncle Fredo and the others. So I went out with him, and he forced himself on me. And once I was pregnant, there wasn't any choice. I had to marry him, to preserve my honor. And the family's. Always the family. Why couldn't they have let me alone? Why was it such a sin for a woman to be without a man? Oh, I heard the snickers. I knew the gossip. I knew what you did to that boy in grade school."

"You knew?" Vince said, astounded.

"Of course I did. And I know why you did it. It wasn't what that boy said; it was that you believed it. I know what

[511]

you thought. Aunt Sandra and me. It wasn't true. Never. She was just a friend. I enjoyed her company. Some people just aren't meant to marry."

Her face hardened. "What gives men the right to dictate to women? And our men are the worst. I hope you're not like that, Vincent. I pray you're not. I could have been happy. I just wanted to be left alone. Maybe open a little shop. You know, sewing. Something of my own. But they wouldn't let me."

"You never wanted me, did you?"

Her voice became gentle. "Oh, yes. You were the only good thing to come out of all of it. And I'd go through it all again just to have you."

"But you never seemed to care."

"I cared, but I couldn't show it. Your uncle may have seemed kind and gentle, but he was determined. You were his responsibility, not mine. He had plans for you. I was an outsider, a stranger to my own son."

"Do you know you've never kissed me? Never."

"Oh, how wrong you are, Vincenzo. Every night, after you were asleep, I came into your room. I'd sit on the bed beside you, sometimes for hours, stroking your hair, kissing you and telling you how much I loved you."

They both were in tears now. "I never knew," Vince said. He walked to her and embraced her. "I'm awake now, Mama."

"I love you, my little boy," she said, kissing him. "I always have."

CHAPTER
Forty

IT was just past seven when the limo crossed the Walt Whitman Bridge. Vince reached for the telephone and dialed Ocean City.

"Vince Grosso, skipper. I'd like to do a little fishing today. ETA in just about an hour."

"Yes, sir, Mr. Grosso," came the crisp reply. "I'll be ready."

Vince smiled as he replaced the phone. The skipper was always ready. Not that he shouldn't be. For a fat salary, all he had to do was keep the boat ready. And if Vince didn't call by nine, the rest of the day was his, as it was sometimes for months on end.

The key was the hour's notice, not enough time for any enemy to plan. Even his office never knew when he would head for the shore. You could never afford to set a pattern.

When they arrived at the marina, the *Lena* had already been gassed, its engines running. Below, breakfast would be waiting.

"Need me, boss?" asked the driver.

"No. I'll be fine." Vince liked to be alone when he fished. Just he and the skipper. No bodyguards. It was the only time he was ever really free. "After you call the office, you've got the day to yourself. Be back at four."

"Right."

"Morning, skipper," Vince said as he jumped to the deck. "How's it going?"

"Fine, Mr. Grosso. Breakfast is waiting below."

"You're a good man. How they biting?"

"Not bad, sir. I figure we might get some blues out near Twenty-eight Mile Wreck."

[513]

"Fine." The aroma of coffee was tantalizing, and Vince went below. The table was set for one, but there were two guests, wholly uninvited, each holding a gun.

"Good morning, Don Vincenzo," one of them said. "Breakfast is served."

It was like Christmas Eve, Pat thought as he drove up the turnpike. Yet different. Then he had been like a little boy, alive and carefree, on his way to give his father a new life. Until he saw the fire engines—and George Carney's corpse.

It was a different feeling now. There was dread. No one relished the prospect of self-destruction. But there was freedom, too. His self-imposed chains were off. No more compromise, no more calculation, no more of the Pat Carney two-step.

He was going to Harrisburg, and if they tried to drop a bomb on Kevin, he'd be there to deflect it. The affair with Bonnie, however brief it might have been, Kevin would have to handle, but that shouldn't be any great problem. There wasn't any proof. But the abortion was Pat's ball game. He would explain that the check was typical of Kevin Murray, trying to help a friend who was out of work. It certainly wasn't for an abortion. Where was the motive? The baby wasn't Kevin's. It was his. And if it really got sticky, to hell with the seal of confession. He'd expose Vince for the blackmailing bastard that he was, make Kevin a hero.

Not a pleasant prospect, but what was the choice? He was giving up his career, but maybe he was saving his soul.

"Big day, huh, Kevin?" the conductor said, taking the ticket.
"Yeah, Steve. At last."
"Any problems?"
"No, there shouldn't be."
"Good man, Kevin. Keep it up. Keep sticking it to the bastards."
"I'll try, pal."

Kevin smiled as he opened the paper. It seemed that all the conductors had three things in common: They were Irish, they were Catholic, and they were down-the-line pro-life. It made for a more pleasant ride.

He was exhausted. Between thinking of the baby—Andrea Campion—and what lay ahead, he hadn't slept much. Now it

[514]

was a struggle to keep his eyes open. He finished his coffee and the sports page by Coatesville, then drifted off, resigned to let the chips fall where they may.

In the rear car, fondling her gold cross, another passenger was on the way to the capital. This was the day. Salvation at last. And vindication. She could still see the nun's face, so superior, so condescending, telling her that she was unacceptable for the convent. "Emotionally unstable," the nun had said. Well, she would show them. She would prove that she was worthy to give her life for Jesus and His babies.

Once more, for reassurance, she reached into her purse and felt the steel of the revolver. "Soon, Jesus," she whispered to herself, one hand on her cross, the other on the gun. "Soon."

"You look terrible, Mom," Anthony Grosso said, reaching for another piece of toast. "What's the matter?"

"Nothing. Really. I just didn't sleep very well last night. Hurry up, now, or you'll miss your bus. You, too, Michael."

"Right," Michael sighed.

"What's the matter?" Lena asked.

"Nothing."

"Come on, Michael, something's bothering you. What is it?"

"Nothing. It's about football and the coach. You wouldn't understand."

"Try me."

"No. Thanks anyway. I'll talk to Dad tonight. No offense, Mom, but you know, he understands those kinds of things, you know what I mean? He makes things seem so clear. You're not mad, are you? Or hurt?"

"No, honey. Honest. I'm glad you think so much of your dad."

She sat in the kitchen, her four children in school. Five, she corrected herself. Could she let go, after all these years? Was the promise so important? Who would benefit? She loved Therese dearly, but there were four other children. And a husband she loved very much.

She looked at the clock, then at the phone.

Charlie Masters was almost at the door when his secretary called. "There's a woman on the phone who wants to speak to an agent. Says it's urgent."

"Shit!" Charlie muttered. He had been on his way to breakfast. "Why do I get all the nuts? Okay." He picked up the phone. "Agent Masters."

"Please listen to me. This isn't a crank call. Vincent Grosso is about to be murdered. In Ocean City. On his boat. The *Lena.* Please hurry. There isn't much time."

"Could I have your name, ma'am, please?"

"I can't."

"I'm sorry, ma'am, but if you don't give your name—"

"Please. I'm telling the truth."

The line went dead in Masters's hand.

"Anything?" the secretary asked.

"No. She hung up. Just like I said, another nut."

It probably *was* a nut, he said to himself as he walked to the car. And if it wasn't, so what? Let the bastards kill each other off. The world would be better for it.

He was almost out of the parking lot when he thought of his lunch with Kevin. *If we take things into our own hands, they win because we become as bad as they are.*

"God damn you, Kevin," he said, shifting into reverse.

"Back so soon?" the secretary asked.

"Get the Atlantic City office on the phone! It's an emergency!"

"I'm sorry, Mr. Grosso. I didn't have any choice. They've got my wife and kids."

"I understand, skipper. Don't worry about it."

"What do you think they'll do?"

"You don't have to worry," Vince lied. "It's me they want."

Tied to the bunk, Vince couldn't see out the porthole. They had been steaming due east for almost three hours, so he figured they were about fifty miles offshore. It would be soon.

He was right. In a few minutes he heard the engines of another boat. And one of the gunmen came below, carrying a box, which he placed on the floor near Vince's head. Then he drew his gun and turned to the skipper. "Sorry, pal. We got no bitch with you, but you're a witness."

He fired two shots into the skipper's head, casually replaced his gun, then turned to Vince. "We didn't want him to suffer. Like I said, he's an innocent victim. But you, Don Vincenzo, are special." He pointed to the box. "In case you haven't guessed, this is

[516]

a bomb. A very powerful bomb. It's set to go off in thirty minutes, time enough for us to be long gone and time enough for you, Don Vincenzo, to think. For the last thirty minutes of your life, Don Michael wants you to think, about respect and how no pissant from Philadelphia can survive after insulting him. Nothing personal, Don Vincenzo. Those are Don Michael's words, not mine."

"I understand."

"Good. Well, that's it then. *Ciao,* Don Vincenzo."

Kevin heard the gavel over the squawk box, then Seth Harkins calling the session to order. He still expected to hear Mike Callaghan's voice, even though he never would again. Seth was okay in a straitlaced sort of way, but he wasn't Mike. Nobody was.

Janet buzzed. "They've just called from the floor. They're going to run the bill after the master roll."

"Thanks, Janet. I'll be there."

He opened his briefcase for the abortion file. There was an envelope addressed to him. From Karen. He opened it.

Dear Kevin,

No matter what happens today, I'm right beside you. Now and always.

I love you.

Karen

He threw the note on the desk and walked toward the door. Then he stopped and turned. "Fuck it," he mumbled, then reached for the phone.

"Mrs. Murray," he said when she answered, "this is your state representative. Receipt of your correspondence is acknowledged." His tone softened, almost a whisper. "I love you, Karen. I always have, and I always will."

Without waiting for a response, he replaced the phone and walked to the floor. Like nine months before, it was mobbed, even though there was a sense of anticlimax. He went over to the special guest section, where Pat was sitting with Joe Kellogg. "Your Excellency, to what do we owe this honor?"

"I wanted to see if you still lisp."

"If we were in private, Excellency, I'd have several words for you."

[517]

"Two, I believe."

"Something like that."

Pat extended his hand. "Good luck, Kevin. And God bless."

"Thanks, Pat."

It was just as expected. A brief explanation by Kevin, several dispirited speeches by the other side. Then the vote—and victory.

"Congratulations, pal," Pat said as the chaos started to subside. "Another victory for our side, compliments of Kevin Murray."

"I'm just glad it's over."

"News conference now?"

"Yeah. They're all waiting in the back."

"I'll go with you, if you don't mind."

"Be my guest. We'll confirm their darkest suspicions."

Together they walked up the aisle to where the media—and a woman with a cross—were waiting.

When he was young, Vince Grosso had often thought of dying. Even dreamed of it, shaking himself awake, his pajamas sweat-soaked, to discover that he was still among the living. Gradually the fear had receded until the assassination attempt two months before, when it had returned with increased intensity.

But now death was here, and it wasn't that bad. Certainty has a way of dissolving most fear. It wasn't that he wanted to die. Far from it. But it was inevitable, so he spent his last half hour in reflection rather than panic.

He thought of Lena, the only woman he had ever loved. Had he given her a good life? What was lacking in him that he had been unable to bridge the distance that, no matter how close they were, she always kept?

Until today the thought of her with another man would have driven him insane. Now he hoped she would find someone else. She was still young, with a full life to lead.

He thought of the boys, his big, strong boys. They would be all right. Anthony would find himself, and with maturity Michael would learn to control his temper. But the girls distressed him. Not for themselves but for him. They were so young. Would they remember him? How much did he remember about his own father? He wanted them at least to know that they had a daddy who was real and who had loved them very much.

He also thought of Therese. She was special. She always

[518]

had been. Yet he realized that whenever he had thought of Therese, had fantasized about her, it had been about Lena as well.

And he thought of Kevin. Good old Kevin. More than anyone, even Lena, Kevin had showed him how to drop his barrier, at least in private. He had watched how Kevin was with his kids, and subconsciously he had imitated him. If the Grosso children felt loved, if they felt wanted and secure with the way their father had treated them, came down to their level, they owed it to Kevin Murray. And in return, Vince had blackmailed him. *Forgive me, Kevin,* he thought. *I never meant to harm you.*

He was so immersed in his thoughts that he was oblivious of time, oblivious even of the sound which grew until it could no longer be ignored.

A helicopter! Jesus, a helicopter! Please be looking for me. With the certainty of death diminished, the fear returned with a flood. He struggled against his ropes, to no avail. *Please, God, there's not much time.*

He heard something on the deck. Then a man, wearing a life jacket, carrying another, appeared in the cabin. He looked at the skipper's body.

"He's dead," Vince said.

"No shit!" He looked at the ropes binding Vince. "You got a knife?"

"Over there, in the locker."

"There isn't much time," Vince said after he was free. He pointed to the box. "Do you know how to defuse it?"

"Fuck you, pal! I'm a diver, not a demo expert." He handed Vince the life jacket. "Put this on. We're getting the hell out of here."

They raced into the pilothouse, where the diver slammed the throttles into full forward. Then they leaped onto the transom and into the sea. In seconds first Vince, then the diver, were being hoisted into the hovering chopper. In silence they all stared below at the *Lena.* There was a flash, then a deafening roar that buffeted the chopper as the pilot fought for control. When they looked down again, all that remained were scattered pieces of fiberglass bobbing in the swell.

"That could have been you, Mr. Grosso. Ted Ketner, FBI."

"Thanks."

[519]

"Don't mention it. We save mob leaders from getting blown apart every day. It's in the job description."

"I'm grateful."

"But not grateful enough to help us, are you? You wouldn't have any idea who did this, would you?"

"No, really. No idea."

"And you wouldn't be able to identify them even if you saw them again, would you?"

"I'm afraid not. They wore masks."

"*Omertà* wins again, right?"

Vince shrugged.

"You guys are really something," Ketner said.

They flew in silence for a few minutes. "How did you find out?" Vince asked.

"Why the hell should I tell you?" Ketner shook his head and sighed. "Oh, what the hell. It was a call to Newtown Square. A woman. Wouldn't give her name, but quite obviously, she was telling the truth. Okay?"

"Thanks." A woman. Lena flashed before his eyes. Then Therese. And he began to understand.

As they walked through the lounge onto the rotunda balcony, Kevin looked around. He wasn't sure what he expected. Who would be wielding the ax? Bonnie Peterson? The head of a women's group? Then he was surrounded by the press, his attention diverted to answering their questions.

Pat noticed the strange woman in the crowd, the one wearing the cross. He watched her edge her way through until she was directly opposite Kevin. Her hand went into her purse. It was a gun. Pat leaped—too late. She fired four shots, then placed the gun in her mouth. "I'm coming, Jesus," she said, and pulled the trigger.

Even before the sound Kevin was aware of a burning in his chest, then one in his leg. Then there was chaos, and he was suffocating. He struggled to get free, to get air. There seemed to be a thousand bodies about. Then he felt himself falling.

He rolled down the marble steps, coming to rest on the landing—beside the body of the youngest auxiliary bishop of the archdiocese of Philadelphia.

Pat Carney had finally stopped running.

[520]

Forty-one

IT was after midnight when Vince Grosso returned home. Lena was waiting.

"Bad day for Villanova," Vince said.

"You've heard."

"Bits and pieces. I can't believe Pat's dead."

"They say he jumped in front of the gun. He saved Kevin."

"Funny, I always thought it would be the other way around. What's the latest on Kevin?"

"He should be okay. They removed the bullets, and they think he'll make it."

"Karen?"

"I finally got through to her a half hour ago," Lena said. "She's holding up."

There was silence. "I did a lot of thinking on the ride home," Vince finally said. "A lot of things came together. There was only one person who knew that I was going to the shore. Only one person who could have set me up."

Lena felt no fear. Only a deep sorrow. "Yes" was all that she was able to say.

"Why, Lena? You're my wife."

"There were so many reasons, Vincent. My father, my mother, a boy that I loved very much—and Therese. She's my daughter."

Vince nodded.

"You knew?" asked Lena.

"Like I said, I sorted out a lot of things on the ride home."

Lena told him everything, about Jimmy, the search for the daughter she had never known, and the vows which she had made at the grave of her father and to a mother who no longer had a mind.

"But you called the FBI," Vince said. "You saved me."

"I'm not as strong as I thought I was, Vincent. I loved you too much to keep my promises."

"Where do we go from here, Lena?"

"After all this, can there be anything left?"

Vince put his arms around her. "We can try. That's all any of us can do. I know what I am, Lena. Maybe I chose this life; maybe I was thrown into it. I don't know. But I'm in it, and I can't get out. I need you with me. I can't make it without you."

"Where do we begin?"

He smiled. "First things first. Let's go check the kids. All five of them."

At almost precisely the same time that Vince Grosso returned home, Sheila Sendrow was entering her town house. And like Vince Grosso, someone was waiting.

"Keith!"

"I used Howie's key. Thought you might need a friend," said her former husband.

"I do. Oh, I do."

"Rough day, huh?"

"The worst. The phone never stopped. It's terrible. I knew that Helen Osborne was a little strange, but I never thought—" She glanced at Keith. "You don't think I'd ever—"

"Of course not, Sheila."

"It's devastating to us, to the movement. Sets us back years. But you know, all day I was more concerned about Kevin Murray and his family. I despise what he stands for, but he's a human being, Keith. Do we get so taken up in our causes that we forget that we're all humans?"

"Including Sheila Sendrow?"

"Yes, including Sheila Sendrow."

"You need a friend, Sheila. A lot has happened between us, most of it my fault. I'm not saying it can ever be the way it was, but I'd at least like to be that friend. Not a male opponent, not an ex-husband, just a friend."

"I think I'd like that, Keith." She paused. "And Howie?"

"He's doing fine."

"Does he ever—"

"Not yet, but give him time. Time mellows everything."

"Even me?"

"I think so." He pointed to the picture of Sheila's mother on the desk. "I know you loved her, Sheila, but I think all your debts have been paid in full."

"Maybe they have," she said.

Gently stroking her hair, Vince gazed at the face of his wife. There was a glow of contentment that he had never seen. And never before had their lovemaking been so intense. Without waking her, Vince slid out of bed and walked to the phone in his den. Dominic Barrone answered groggily.

"I'm sorry to wake you, Dominic, but I must see you first thing in the morning."

"An assignment, boss?"

"Yes. The most difficult one you've ever had. It involves *famiglia*, not just *borgotta*."

"Whatever you say, Don Vincenzo."

Pat Carney was buried from the Basilica of Sts. Peter and Paul. It was the largest ceremony in memory, attended by thousands and televised nationally. A notable absentee was the man whom he had saved, who was still in intensive care.

Three days after the funeral Kristy Broderick went to the rectory of her brother's residence parish. They were expecting her, providing both sympathy and a small suitcase containing Pat's personal belongings.

Not much for a life of service to Christ. A few books, some clothing, a rosary. And a treasure, something Pat's little Cinderella would always cherish. It was his first holy communion booklet, precisely the same age as Kristy. Tucked inside was the present that he still saved for his mother—a withered rose.

[523]

CHAPTER
Forty-two

KEVIN Murray spent three weeks in the hospital, during which time he had any number of visitors. One was Governor Dan Talbot, who, always with an eye for big box office, insisted on signing the Pennsylvania Abortion Control Act of 1982 into law in Kevin's presence—as well as the media's.

They clustered around Kevin for a comment, and weak as he was, he still loved it. He gave the pro-life pitch, bantered with the reporters, then became somber. "I found a very important thing about myself during this ordeal," he said as the reporters wrote feverishly. He allowed himself a dramatic pause. "I can't stand bedpans."

A day after the bill became law, Bridget Kelly entered his room. "Greetings, wounded warrior. I guess congratulations are in order."

"And condolences for you, right?"

"Hell, no. We'll beat you in court."

"I didn't mean the bill. I meant my surviving."

"You don't know how grateful I am for that, Kevin. I prayed for you, in church. I asked God to save you." The impish smile returned. "I don't know what it is about Kevin Murray. I've been in church twice in the last twelve years, and both times it's because of you."

"I told you, kid, I'm your St. Monica. And we *will* get you back."

[524]

Another visitor was Vince Grosso. "Some guys will do anything for a headline," he said.

"It seems to me that on the day in question you were also prominently mentioned in the newspapers."

"Yeah. Damn boating accidents. Terrible."

"Absolutely. Incidentally, I saw where Michael Agostino just met with an untimely death."

"Yeah, it's a bitch, isn't it?"

"Absolutely."

"How are you, Kevin?"

"I don't know, Vince. How *am* I?"

"What do you mean?"

"I mean, when do I get castrated? I assume my little misfortune only postponed the inevitable."

"The liquor thing? That's over."

"What do you mean, over?"

"Just what I said. Everything's been destroyed. The only documents in existence are your copies."

There was a time that Kevin would have believed him without question. Now he wasn't so sure. "And Bonnie?" he asked.

"She never wanted to hurt you. She wasn't even involved. Besides, she's got nothing. No proof."

"I can't believe this. You betray me, you put me—and Karen—through hell. Then you just snap your fingers and say, 'Forget it.' "

"Kevin, I was never going to follow through. Sure, I tried to get your vote. I wanted the liquor bill, which sooner or later we'll get. But I'd never hurt you. You're family. I may be a bastard, but I'm not a prick."

"You're unbelievable."

"I'm a lot of things Kevin, most of them bad. But if it's any consolation, of all the things I've done, I hate myself most for what I did to you. I'm sorry. I truly am."

They stared at each other. Then they embraced, and for a brief moment they were back on the country club balcony.

"I said it once before, Kevin. I love you."

"I love you, too, you dago hoodlum bastard."

"I'm proud of you, pal. I mean that. You've done a lot of good."

[525]

"Yeah, and look at the rewards. An overdrawn bank account and two bullet holes."

"There's a reward. The big guy has a special place waiting for you. Me, I've burned my bridges."

"I wouldn't be so sure, Vincenzo. We're all God's children, even dirtball legislators and mob leaders."

"Get well, Kevin. *Ciao.*"

"Good-bye, Vince."

As he watched his friend leave, Kevin knew two things: He *did* love him, and he would never see him again.

Epilogue

SHEILA Sendrow remained a force in the women's movement, but there was a difference. Although always aggressive in court and formidable in a debate, she began to live for herself. Keith had been right. Her dues had been paid in full.

And her former husband had been right about something else: time did mellow everything. Their son eventually married and had three children, whom Sheila adored. And even though there would always be something there, a resentment on Howie's part impossible to eradicate completely, they did become, at least, friends.

Bridget Kelly never married. She never had the chance. A month after her hospital visit to Kevin she was killed on the Pennsylvania Turnpike. But Kevin's prediction, at least partially, came true. Her last request was for a priest.

Vince and Lena Grosso remained together—for exactly one month. Walking across Lancaster Pike after a meeting at Villanova, Lena was killed instantly in a hit-and-run accident. The driver was never identified. Unlike their women, Sicilian men *always* kept their vows.

Twelve years after his narrow escape from death Vince was not so fortunate. His luck ran out in a hail of bullets on a street corner in South Philadelphia. Succeeding him as don was the man who had arranged the murder—Niccolo Arrone. Arrone's reign, however, was extremely brief. He was killed by his successor, Michael Grosso, thus honoring his father and continuing the cycle.

Kevin Murray remained in the legislature until his death, continuing the pro-life struggle. And when a newly constituted Supreme Court reversed *Roe* v. *Wade*, he kept his promise. Pennsylvania was the first state in America to outlaw abortions.

He was the last survivor of the Villanova three, but not by all that much. What bullets did to Pat and Vince, the cigarettes did to him. He was little more than a shadow at Megan's wedding, but he was there. He willed himself to stay alive until he walked her down the aisle and danced with her to "Daddy's Little Girl." A week later he joined his Andrew and the Sarge.

And on a bright May day in the Year of Our Lord 2004, Villanova University completed its 161st year of education. When the commencement ceremony had concluded, the graduates streamed from the stadium, seeking their loved ones.

An attractive lady stood in the crowd, searching for her graduate. Only a slight limp gave witness to her ordeal. Finally they found each other, and after an embrace the graduate handed her the diploma.

"Congratulations, honey. I love you," said the proud mother.

"I love you, too, Mom," answered Andrea Campion.